Acclaim for *The Time of Our Singing*

"A heady, panoramic novel, scored, like so much of Powers's work, for full orchestra. . . . Passage after passage carries us to what feels like the innermost sanctum of the singer's art. . . . Powers is one of our most lavishly gifted writers. The arc of his career is rising steadily and honestly, and his intelligence is humane and nourishing. . . . *The Time of Our Singing* rewards on many levels—musical, structural, intellectual."

—*rker*

"*The Time of Our Singing* is a fierce a⸤̶⸥ ⸤̶⸥d."

—*⸤̶⸥be*

"There is a great deal to admire in ⸤̶⸥ ⸤̶⸥rs makes. . . . Remarkable . . . a fas⸤̶⸥ ⸤̶⸥, and moving artistic imagining of a harmony that continues to elude us in life."

—*The New York Times Book Review*

"*The Time of Our Singing* is an astonishment but not a surprise. . . . Richard Powers has been astounding us almost every other year since 1985. . . . We can no longer be surprised about whatever he dares to think in ink about."

—*Harper's Magazine*

"An expansive, haunting novel full of grace and beauty."

—*Esquire*

"A rich, compelling account. . . . Out of the troubled zeitgeist of the past half-century, he has fashioned a major cantata in a minor key."

—*Chicago Tribune*

"Keenly observant . . . superb and persuasive."

—*The Washington Post*

"Richard Powers is a wonder . . . [*The Time of Our Singing*] is beautifully, meticulously crafted."

—*The New York Observer*

"One of the most accomplished, most powerful novels of American life in the twentieth century to come along in recent years . . . *The Time of Our Singing* is a high point that recalls some of the masterful sagas of American families produced by our best contemporary novelists in recent years."

—*The Post-Dispatch* (St. Louis)

remarkable novel sings from its tortured soul as much as from its polyphonic mind."

"Massive and dazzling. . . . Each chapter of this marvelous saga is a set piece of remarkable clarity, rhythm, and drama. One imagines all other novels lining up behind it for the big awards."

—*Memphis Commercial Appeal*

"Opens up a universe of thought and makes you hear the legendary music of the spheres."

—*Salon.com*

Richard Powers

THE TIME
OF OUR SINGING

Richard Powers is the *New York Times* bestselling author of
Bewilderment, *The Echo Maker*, *The Time of Our Singing*, and
many other novels. In 2019, his novel *The Overstory* won
the Pulitzer Prize in Fiction. He is a MacArthur Fellow
and has received a National Book Award. He lives in the
Great Smoky Mountains.

ALSO BY RICHARD POWERS

Bewilderment

The Overstory

Orfeo

Generosity: An Enhancement

The Echo Maker

Plowing the Dark

Gain

Galatea 2.2

Operation Wandering Soul

The Gold Bug Variations

Prisoner's Dilemma

Three Farmers on Their Way to a Dance

THE

TIME

OF OUR

SINGING

RICHARD POWERS

PICADOR

FARRAR, STRAUS AND GIROUX

NEW YORK

Picador
120 Broadway, New York 10271

Copyright © 2003 by Richard Powers
All rights reserved
Printed in the United States of America
Originally published in 2003 by Farrar, Straus and Giroux
First paperback edition, 2004
Picador reissue edition, 2022

The Library of Congress has cataloged the
Farrar, Straus and Giroux hardcover edition as follows:
Powers, Richard, 1957–
    The time of our singing / Richard Powers.
      p.   cm.
    ISBN 0-374-27782-6
    1. African American women singers—Fiction.   2. Parent and adult
child—Fiction.   3. Racially mixed people—Fiction.   4. Interracial
marriage—Fiction.   5. Interfaith marriage—Fiction.   6. Immigrants—
Fiction.   7. Jewish men—Fiction.   8. Scientists—Fiction.   9. Singers—
Fiction.   I. Title.

PS3566.O92 T55 2002
813'.54—dc21

                                                        2002022397

Paperback ISBN: 978-1-250-82967-2

Designed by Jonathan D. Lippincott

Our books may be purchased in bulk for promotional, educational, or
business use. Please contact your local bookseller or the Macmillan Corporate
and Premium Sales Department at 1-800-221-7945, extension 5442, or
by email at MacmillanSpecialMarkets@macmillan.com.

Picador® is a U.S. registered trademark and is used by Macmillan Publishing
Group, LLC, under license from Pan Books Limited.

For book club information, please visit facebook.com/picadorbookclub
or email marketing@picadorusa.com.

picadorusa.com • instagram.com/picador
twitter.com/picadorusa • facebook.com/picadorusa

1   3   5   7   9   10   8   6   4   2

THE
TIME
OF OUR
SINGING

In some empty hall, my brother is still singing. His voice hasn't dampened yet. Not altogether. The rooms where he sang still hold an impression, their walls dimpled with his sound, awaiting some future phonograph capable of replaying them.

My brother Jonah stands fixed, leaning against a piano. He's just twenty. The sixties have only begun. The country still dozes in its last pretended innocence. No one has heard of Jonah Strom but our family, what's left of it. We've come to Durham, North Carolina, the old music building at Duke. He has made it to the finals of a national vocal competition he'll later deny ever having entered. Jonah stands alone, just right of center stage. My brother towers in place, listing a little, backing up into the crook of the grand piano, his only safety. He curls forward, the scroll on a reticent cello. Left hand steadies him against the piano edge, while right hand cups in front of him, holding some letter, now oddly lost. He grins at the odds against being here, breathes in, and sings.

One moment, the Erl-King is hunched on my brother's shoulder, whispering a blessed death. In the next, a trapdoor opens up in the air and my brother is elsewhere, teasing out Dowland of all things, a bit of ravishing sass for this stunned lieder crowd, who can't grasp the web that slips over them:

Time stands still with gazing on her face,
Stand still and gaze for minutes, hours, and years to her give place.
All other things shall change, but she remains the same,
Till heavens changed have their course and time hath lost his name.

3

Two stanzas, and his tune is done. Silence hangs over the hall. It drifts above the seats like a balloon across the horizon. For two downbeats, even breathing is a crime. Then there's no surviving this surprise except by applauding it away. The noisy gratitude of hands starts time up again, sending the dart to its target and my brother on to the things that will finish him.

This is how I see him, although he'll live another third of a century. This is the moment when the world first finds him out, the night I hear where his voice is headed. I'm up onstage, too, at the battered Steinway with its caramel action. I accompany him, trying to keep up, trying not to listen to that siren voice that says, *Stop your fingers, crash your boat on the reef of keys, and die in peace.*

Though I make no fatal fumbles, that night is not my proudest as a musician. After the concert, I'll ask my brother again to let me go, to find an accompanist who can do him justice. And again he'll refuse. "I already have one, Joey."

I'm there, up onstage with him. But at the same time, I'm down in the hall, in the place I always sit at concerts: eight rows back, just inside the left aisle. I sit where I can see my own fingers moving, where I can study my brother's face—close enough to see everything, but far enough to survive seeing.

Stage fright ought to paralyze us. Backstage is a single bleeding ulcer. Performers who've spent their whole youth training for this moment now prepare to spend their old age explaining why it didn't go as planned. The hall fills with venom and envy, families who've traveled hundreds of miles to see their lives' pride reduced to runner-up. My brother alone is fearless. He has already paid. This public contest has nothing to do with music. Music means those years of harmonizing together, still in the shell of our family, before that shell broke open and burned. Jonah glides through the backstage fright, the dressing rooms full of well-bred nausea, on a cloud, as though through a dress rehearsal for a performance already canceled. Onstage, against this sea of panic, his calm electrifies. The drape of his hand on the piano's black enamel ravishes his listeners, the essence of his sound before he even makes one.

I see him on this night of his first open triumph, from four decades on. He still has that softness around his eyes that later life will crack and line. His jaw quakes a little on Dowland's quarter notes, but the notes do not. He drops his head toward his right shoulder as he lifts to the high C, shrinking from his entranced listeners. The face shudders, a look only I can see, from my perch behind the piano. The broken-ridged bridge of his nose, his bruised brown lips, the two bumps of bone riding his eyes: almost my own face, but keener, a year older, a shade lighter. That break-away shade: the public record of our family's private crime.

My brother sings to save the good and make the wicked take their own lives. At twenty, he's already intimate with both. This is the source of his resonance, the sound that holds his audience stilled for a few stopped seconds before they can bring themselves to clap. In the soar of that voice, they hear the rift it floats over.

The year is a snowy black-and-white signal coming in on rabbit ears. The world of our childhood—the A-rationing, radio-fed world pitched in that final war against evil—falls away into a Kodak tableau. A man has flown in space. Astronomers pick up pulses from starlike objects. Across the globe, the United States draws to an inside straight. Berlin's tinder-box is ready to flash at any moment. Southeast Asia smolders, nothing but a curl of smoke coming from the banana leaves. At home, a rash of babies piles up behind the viewing glass of maternity hospitals from Bar Harbor to San Diego. Our hatless boy president plays touch football on the White House lawn. The continent is awash in spies, beatniks, and major appli-ances. Montgomery hits the fifth year of an impasse that won't occur to me until five more have passed. And seven hundred unsuspecting people in Durham, North Carolina, disappear, lulled into the granite mountain-side opened by Jonah's sound.

Until this night, no one has heard my brother sing but us. Now the word is out. In the applause, I watch that rust red face waver behind his smile's hasty barricade. He looks around for an offstage shadow to duck back into, but it's too late. He breaks into leaky grins and, with one prac-ticed bow, accepts his doom.

They bring us back twice; Jonah has to drag me out the second time. Then the judges call out the winners in each range—three, two, one—as if Duke were Cape Canaveral, this music contest another *Mercury* launch, and America's Next Voice another Shepard or Grissom. We stand in the wings, the other tenors forming a ring around Jonah, already hating him and heaping him with praise. I fight the urge to work this group, to assure them my brother is not special, that each performer has sung as well as anyone. The others sneak glances at Jonah, studying his unstudied pos-ture. They go over the strategy, for next time: the panache of Schubert.

Then the left hook of Dowland, striving for that floating sustain above the high A. The thing they can never stand far back enough to see has already swallowed my brother whole.

My brother hangs back against the fly ropes in his concert black, appraising the choicer sopranos. *Stands still and gazes.* He sings to them, private encores in his mind. Everyone knows he's won, and Jonah struggles to make it mean nothing. The judges call his name. Invisible people cheer and whistle. He is their victory for democracy, and worse. Jonah turns to me, drawing out the moment. "Joey. Brother. There's got to be a more honest way to make a living." He breaks another rule by dragging me onstage with him to collect the trophy. And his first public conquest rushes to join the past.

Afterward, we move through a sea of small delights and epic disappointments. Congratulating lines form up around the winners. In ours, a woman hunched with age touches Jonah's shoulder, her eyes damp. My brother amazes me, extending his performance, as if he's really the ethereal creature she mistakes him for. "Sing forever," she says, until her caretaker whisks her off. A few well-wishers behind her, a ramrod retired colonel twitches. His face is a hostile muddle, duped in a way he can't dope out. I feel the man's righteousness, well before he reaches us, the rage we repeatedly provoke in his people simply by appearing in public. He waits out his moment in the queue, his anger's fuse shortening with this line. Reaching the front, he charges. I know what he'll say before he gets it out. He studies my brother's face like a thwarted anthropologist. "What exactly *are* you boys?"

The question we grew up on. The question no Strom ever figured out how to read, let alone answer. As often as I've heard it, I still seize up. Jonah and I don't even bother to exchange looks. We're old hands at annihilation. I make some motions, ready to smooth over the misunderstanding. But the man backs me off with a look that chases me from adolescence for good.

Jonah has his answer; I have mine. But he's the one in the spotlight. My brother inhales, as if we're still onstage, the smallest grace note of breath that would lead me into the downbeat. For a semiquaver, he's about to launch into *"Fremd bin ich eingezogen."* Instead, he pitches his reply, buffo-style, up into comic head tones:

> "I am my mammy's ae bairn,
> Wi' unco folk I weary, Sir . . ."

His first full night of adulthood, but still a child, giddy with just being named America's Next Voice. His unaccompanied encore turns heads all around us. Jonah ignores them all. It's 1961. We're in a major university town. You can't string a guy up for high spirits. They haven't strung up anyone for high spirits in these parts for at least half a dozen years. My brother laughs through the Burns couplet, thinking to leave the colonel sheepish with eight bars of good-natured cheek. The man goes livid. He tenses and puckers, ready to wrestle Jonah to the ground. But the eager line of admirers moves him along, out the stage door, toward what the prophetic look spreading across my brother's face already knows will be a paralyzing stroke.

At the end of the conga line, our father and sister wait. This is how I see them, too, from the far side of a life. Still ours, still a family. Da grins like the lost immigrant he is. A quarter century in this country, and he still walks around like he's expecting to be detained. "You pronounciate German like a Polack. Who the hell taught you your vowels? A disgrace. *Eine Schande!*"

Jonah caps a hand over our father's mouth. "Shh. Da. For Christ's sake. Remind me never to take you out in public. 'Polack' is an ethnic slur."

" 'Polack'? You're crazy. That's what they're called, bub."

"Yeah, bub." Ruth, our mimic, nails him. Even at sixteen, she's passed for the man more than once, over the phone. "What the hell else you going to call people from Polackia?"

The crowd flinches again, that look that pretends not to. We're a moving violation of everything in their creed. But out here in classically trained public, they keep that major-key smile. They push on to the other winners, leaving us, for a last moment, once again our own safe nation. Father and eldest son reel about on the remnants of Schubert still banging about the emptied hall. They lean on each other's shoulders. "Trust me," the older one tells the younger. "I've known a few Polacks in my day. I almost married one."

"I could have been a Polack?"

"A near Polack. A counterfactual Polack."

"A Polack in one of many alternate universes?"

They babble to each other, the shorthand jokes of his profession. Clowning for the one none of us will name this night, the one to whom we offer every note of our contest prize. Ruth stands in the stage footlights, almost auburn, but otherwise the sole keeper of our mother's fea-

7

tures in this world. My mother, the woman my father almost didn't marry, a woman more and longer American than anyone in this hall tonight.

"You did good, too, Joey," my little sister makes sure to tell me. "You know. Perfect and all." I hug her for her lie, and she glows under my grasp, a ready jewel. We wander back to Da and Jonah. Assembled again: the surviving four-fifths of the Strom family chorale.

But Da and Jonah don't need either of us accompanists. Da has hold of the Erl-King motif, and Jonah thumps along, his three-and-a-half-octave voice dropping into bass to whack at his imitation piano's left hand. He hums the way he wanted me to play it. The way it ought to be played, in heaven's headliner series. Ruth and I draw near, despite ourselves, to add the inner lines. People smile as they pass, in pity or shame, some imagined difference. But Jonah is the evening's rising star, momentarily beyond scorn.

The audience this night will claim they heard him. They'll tell their children how that chasm opened up, how the floor dropped out of the old Duke concert hall and left them hanging in the vacuum they thought it was music's job to fill. But the person they'll recall won't be my brother. They'll tell of sitting up in their seats at the first sound of that transmuting voice. But the voice they'll remember won't be his.

His growing band of listeners will chase Jonah's performances, prize his tickets, follow his career even into those last, decoupled years. Connoisseurs will search down his records, mistaking the voice on the disk for his. My brother's sound could never be recorded. He had a thing against the permanent, a hatred of being fixed that's audible in every note he ever laid down. He was Orpheus in reverse: Look *forward*, and all that you love will disappear.

It's 1961. Jonah Strom, America's Next Voice, is twenty. This is how I see him, forty years on, eight years older now than my older brother will ever be. The hall has emptied; my brother still sings. He sings through to the double bar, the tempo falling to nothing as it passes through the fermata's blackness, a boy singing to a mother who can no longer hear him.

That voice was so pure, it could make heads of state repent. But it sang knowing just what shape rode along behind it. And if any voice could have sent a message back to warn the past and correct the unmade future, it would have been my brother's.

8

But no one ever really knew that voice except his family, singing together on those postwar winter nights, with music their last line of defense against the outside and the encroaching cold. They lived in half of a three-story Jersey freestone house that had weathered over half a century to a chocolate brown, tucked up in the northwest corner of Manhattan, a neglected enclave of mixed, mottled blocks where Hamilton Heights shaded off into Washington Heights. They rented, the immigrant David Strom never trusting the future enough to own anything that wouldn't fit into a waiting suitcase. Even his appointment in the Physics Department at Columbia seemed a thing so fine, it would certainly be taken away by anti-Semitism, anti-intellectualism, rising randomness, or the inevitable return of the Nazis. That he could afford to rent half a house at all, even in this tidal-pool neighborhood, struck David as beyond luck, given the life he'd already owned.

To Delia, his Philadelphian wife, renting seemed as perennially strange as her husband's pallid theories. She'd never lived anywhere but the home her parents owned. Yet Delia Daley Strom, too, knew that the world's relentless purifiers would come after their happiness through any open chink. So she propped up her refugee husband and turned their rented half of the freestone into a fortress. And for pure safety, nothing beat music. Each of the three children shared the same first memory: their parents, singing. Music was their lease, their deed, their eminent domain. Let each voice defeat silence through its own vocation. And the Stroms defeated silence after their own fashion, each evening, together, in great gulps of free-playing chords.

Rambling scraps of song started even before the children were awake. Strains of Barber from the bathroom collided with *Carmen* coming out of the kitchen. Breakfast found them all humming against one another in polytonal rowdiness. Even once the day's home schooling started—Delia teaching the reading and writing, David doing the arithmetic before heading down to Morningside to lecture on General Relativity—song drove the lessons. Meter markings taught fractions. Every poem had its tune.

In the afternoon, when Jonah and Joey raced home from forced excursions to that strip of playground adjoining St. Luke's, they'd find their mother at the spinet with baby Ruth, turning the cramped drawing room into a campsite on the shores of Jordan. Half an hour of trios dissolved into bouts of ritual bickering between the boys over who got first dibs with their mother, alone. The winner set to an hour of glorious piano duets, while the moment's loser took little Root upstairs for read-alouds or card games without real rules.

Lessons with Delia passed in minutes for the praise-heaped student, while stretching out forever for the one waiting in line. When the excluded boy started calling out finger faults from upstairs, Delia turned those catcalls, too, into a game. She'd have the boys name chords or sustain intervals from the top of the stairs. She'd get them singing rounds—"By the Waters of Babylon"—from opposite ends of the house, each boy weaving his own line around the distant other. When they hit the limits of their boy's patience, she'd bring them together, one singing, the other playing, with little Root inventing spectral toddler harmonies that strove to join this family's secret language.

The sounds her boys made pleased Delia so much, it scared them. "Oh, my JoJo! What voices! I want you to sing at my wedding."

"But you're already married," Joey, the younger boy, cried. "To Da!"

"I know, honey. Can't I still want you to sing at my wedding?"

They loved it too well, music. The boys shrugged off sandlot sports, radio dummies and detectives, tentacled creatures from the tenth dimension, and neighborhood reenactments of the slaughter at Okinawa and Bastogne, preferring to flank their mother at the spinet. Even in those narrow hours before their father returned, when Delia stopped their private lessons to prepare dinner, she had to force-march the boys out of the house to take another dose of torture at the hands of boys more cruelly competent in boyhood, boys who rained down on the two Stroms the full brutality of collective bafflement.

Both sides in the neighborhood's standing war went after these stragglers, with words, fists, stones—even, once, a softball bat square in the back. When the neighborhood children weren't using the boys for horseshoe stakes or home plate, they made an example of the freakish Stroms. They sneered at Joey's softness, covered Jonah's offending face in caked mud. The Strom boys had little taste for these daily refresher courses in difference. Often, they never made it to the playground at all, but hid themselves in the alley half a block away, calming each other by humming in thirds and fifths until enough time had passed and they could race back home.

Dinners were a chaos of talk and tease, the nightly extension of the years-long Strom-Daley courtship. Delia banned her husband from the stove when she worked. She found the man's pot-dipping an outrage against God and nature. She kept him at bay until her latest inspired offering—chicken casserole with candied carrots, or a roast with yams, small miracles prepared in those moments between her other full-time jobs—was ready for the stage. David's task was to accompany the meal with the latest bizarre developments from the imaginary job he held down. Professor of phantom mechanics, Delia teased. Da, more excitable than all his children, laid into the wildest of details: his acquaintance Kurt Gödel's discovery of loopy timelike lines hiding in Einstein's field equations. Or Hoyle, Bondi, and Gold's hunch that new galaxies poured through the gaps between old ones, like weeds splitting the universe's crumbling concrete. To the listening boys, the world was ripe with German-speaking refugees, safely abroad in their various democracies, busy overthrowing space and time.

Delia shook her head at the nonsense that passed for conversation in her home. Little Ruth mimicked her giggle. But the preteen boys outdid each other with questions. Did the universe care which way time flowed? Did hours fall like water? Was there only one kind of time? Did it ever change speeds? If time made loops, could the future curl into the past? Their father was better than a science-crazed comic book, *Astounding Stories*, *Forbidden Tales*. He came from a stranger place, and the pictures he drew were even more fantastic.

After dinner, they came together in tunes. Rossini while washing the dishes, W. C. Handy while drying. They crawled through loopy timelike holes in the evening, five lines braiding in space, each one curling back on the other, spinning in place. They'd do workhorse Bach chorales, taking their pitches from Jonah, the boy with the magic ear. Or they'd crowd around the spinet, tackling madrigals, poking the keyboard now and then to check an interval. Once, they divvied up parts and made it through a whole Gilbert and Sullivan in one evening. Evenings would never be so long again.

On such nights, the children seemed almost designed for their parents' express entertainment. Delia's soprano lit across the upper register like lightning on a western sky. David's bass made up with German musicality what it lacked in beauty. Husband anchored wife for any flight she cared to make. But each knew what the marriage needed, and together they used the boys shamelessly to hold down the inner lines. All the while, baby Ruth crawled among them, hitching melodic rides, standing on her toes to peek at the pages her family studied. In this way, a third child came to read music without anyone teaching her.

Delia sang with her whole body. That's how she'd learned, even in Philadelphia, from generations on generations of Carolina churchgoing mothers. Her chest swelled when she let loose, like the bellows of a glory-filled pump organ. A deaf man might have held his hands to her shoulders and felt each pitch resonating, singed into his fingers as if by a tuning fork. In the years since their marriage in 1940, David Strom had learned this freedom from his American wife. The secular German Jew bobbed to inner rhythms, davening as freely as his great-grandfather cantors once had.

Song held the children enthralled, as tied to these musical evenings as their neighbors were to radios. Singing was their team sport, their Tiddlywinks, their Chutes and Ladders. To see their parents *dance*—driven by hidden forces like creatures in a folk ballad—was the first awful mystery of childhood. The Strom children joined in, swaying back and forth to Mozart's "Ave verum corpus" the way they did to "Zip-a-Dee-Doo-Dah."

Surely the parents heard what was happening to music at that hour. They must have felt the manic pulse—half the world's GNP, looking for its ruder theme song. Swing had long since played Carnegie, that brash razz already housebroken. Down in the blistering bebop clubs, Gillespie and Parker were nightly warping the space-time continuum. A cracker kid in a designated white house in a black neighborhood off in fly-bitten Mississippi was about to let loose the secret beat of race music, forever blowing away the enriched-flour, box-stepping public. No one alive then could have missed the changes, not even two people as willfully against the grain as that refugee physicist and the Philadelphian doctor's daughter, his trained-voice wife. They raided the present, too. He had his accented Ella and she her deep-palette Ellington. They never missed a Saturday Metropolitan broadcast. But every Sunday morning, the radio trawled for jazz while David made foot-wide mushroom and tomato omelettes. In the Strom's singing school, upstart tunes took their place in a thousand-year parade of harmony and invention. Cut-time, finger-snapping euphoria gave those nights of Palestrina all the more drive. For Palestrina, too, once overthrew the unsuspecting world.

Every time the Stroms filled their lungs, they continued that long conversation of pitches in time. In old music, they made sense. Singing, they were no one's outcasts. Each night that they made that full-voiced sound—the sound that drove David Strom and Delia Daley together in this life—they headed upriver into a sooner saner place.

Delia and David never let a month go by without a round of their favorite public flirtation: Crazed Quotations. The wife settled on the piano bench, a child pressed against each thigh. She'd sit, telegraphing nothing, her wavy black hair a perfect cowl. Her long russet fingers pressed down on several keys at once, freeing a simple melody—say Dvořák's slow, reedy spiritual "From the New World." The husband then had two repeats to find a response. The children watched in suspense as Delia's tune unfolded, to see if Da could beat the clock and add a countersubject before their mother reached the double bar. If he failed, his children got to taunt him in mock German and his wife named the forfeit of her choice.

He rarely failed. By the time Dvořák's stolen folk song looped back around, the fellow found a way to make Schubert's *Trout* swim upstream against it. The ball bounced back to Delia's court. She had one stanza to come up with another quote to fit the now-changed frame. It took her only a little meandering to get "Swanee River" flowing down around the *Trout*.

The game allowed liberties. Themes could slow to a near standstill, their modulations delayed until the right moment. Or tunes could blast by so fast, their changes collapsed to passing tones. The lines might split into long chorale preludes, sprinkled with accidentals, or the phrase come home to a different cadence, just so long as the change preserved the sense of the melody. As for the words, they could be the originals, madrigal *fa-las*, or scraps of advertising doggerel, so long as each singer, at some point in the evening's game, threaded in their traditional nonsense question, "But where will they build their nest?"

The game produced the wildest mixed marriages, love matches that even the heaven of half-breeds looked sidelong at. Her Brahms *Alto Rhapsody* bickered with his growled Dixieland. Cherubini crashed into Cole Porter. Debussy, Tallis, and Mendelssohn shacked up in unholy ménages à trois. After a few rounds, the game got out of hand and the clotted chords collapsed under their own weight. Call and response ended in hilarious spinouts, with the one who flew off the carousel accusing the other of unfair harmonic tampering.

1 3

During such a game of Crazed Quotations, on a cold December night in 1950, David and Delia Strom got their first look at just what they'd brought into this world. The soprano started with a fat, slow pitch: Haydn's German Dance no. 1 in D. On top of that, the bass cobbled up a precarious Verdi "La donna è mobile." The effect was so joyfully deranged that the two, on nothing more than a shared grin, let the monstrosity air for another go-round. But during the reprise, something rose up out of the tangle, a phrase that neither parent owned. The first pitch shone so clear and centered, it took a moment for the adults to hear it wasn't some phantom sympathetic resonance. They looked at each other in alarm, then down at the oldest child, Jonah, who launched into a pitch-perfect rendition of Josquin's *Absalon, fili mi*.

The Stroms had sight-read the piece months before and put it away as too hard for the children. That the boy remembered it was already a wonder. When Jonah engineered the melody to fit the two already in motion, David Strom felt as he had on first hearing that boys' choir soar above the double chorus opening Bach's *Saint Matthew Passion*. Both parents stopped in midphrase, staring at the boy. The child, mortified, stared back.

"What's wrong? Did I do something bad?" The child was not yet ten. This was when David and Delia Strom first knew that their firstborn would soon be taken from them.

Jonah shared the trick with his little brother. Joseph began adding his own crazed quotes a month later. The family took to ad-libbing hybrid quartets. Little Ruth wailed, wanting to play. "Oh, sweet!" her mother said. "Don't cry. You'll get airborne faster than anyone. Fly across the sky before too long." She gave Ruth simple trinkets—the Texaco radio jingle or "You Are My Sunshine"—while the rest made Joplin rags and bits of Puccini arias lie down together around them in peaceable kingdoms.

They sang together almost every night, over the muffled traffic of distant Amsterdam Avenue. It was all either parent had with which to remind them of the homes each had lost. No one heard them except their landlady, Verna Washington, a stately, childless widow who lived in the brownstone's other half and who liked to press her ear to their shared wall, eavesdropping on that high-wire joy.

The Stroms sang with a skill built into the body, a fixed trait, the soul's eye color. Husband and wife each supplied musical genes: his mathematician's feel for ratio and rhythm, her vocal artist's pitch like a homing pigeon and shading like a hummingbird's wings. Neither boy suspected it was at all odd for a nine-year-old to sight-sing as easily as he breathed. They helped the strands of sound unfold as easily as their lost first cousins might climb a tree. All a voice had to do was open and release, take its tones out for a spin down to Riverside Park, the way their father walked them sometimes on sunny weekends: up, down, sharp, flat, long, short, East Side, West Side, all around the town. Jonah and Joseph had only to look at printed chords, their note heads stacked up like tiny totem poles, to hear the intervals.

Visitors did come by the house, but always to make music. The quintet became a chamber choir every other month, padded with Delia's private singing students or her fellow soloists from the local church circuit. Moonlighting string players from the Physics Departments at Columbia and City College turned the Strom home into a little Vienna. One noisy night, a white-maned old New Jersey violinist in a moth-eaten sweater, who spoke German with David and frightened Ruth with incomprehensible jokes, heard Jonah sing. Afterward, he scolded Delia Strom until she cried. "This child has a gift. You don't hear how big. You are too close. It's unforgivable that you do nothing for him." The old physicist insisted they give the boy the strongest musical education available. Not just a good private teacher but an immersion that would challenge this eerie talent to become everything it was. The great man threatened to take up a collection, if money was the problem.

The problem wasn't money. David objected: No musical education could beat the one Jonah was already receiving from his mother. Delia refused to surrender the boy to a teacher who might fail to understand his special circumstance. The Strom family chorale had its private reasons for protecting its angelic high voice. Yet they didn't dare oppose a man who'd rooted out the bizarre secret of time, buried since time's beginning. Einstein was Einstein, however Gypsy-like his violin playing. His words shamed the Stroms into accepting the inevitable. As the new decade opened onto the long-promised world of tomorrow, Jonah's parents began searching for a music school that could bring that frightening talent into its own.

Meanwhile, days of instruction that the children swallowed whole went on segueing into evenings of part-songs and improvised games of musical tag. Delia bought a sewing machine–sized phonograph for the boys' bedroom. The brothers fell asleep each night to state-of-the-art long-playing 33⅓ rpm records of Caruso, Gigli, and Gobbi. Tiny, tinny, chalk-colored voices stole into the boys' room through that electric portal, coaxing, *Further, wider, clearer—like this.*

And while he drifted off to sleep one night on this chorus of coaxing ghosts, Jonah told his brother what would happen. He knew what their parents were doing. He predicted exactly what would become of him. He'd be sent away for doing, beautifully, what his family had most wanted him to do. Cast out forever, just for singing.

MY BROTHER'S FACE

My brother's face was a school of fishes. His grin was not one thing, but a hundred darting ones. I have a photograph—one of the few from my childhood that escaped incineration. In it, the two of us open Christmas presents on the nubby floral-print sofa that sat in our front room. His eyes look everywhere at once: at his own present, a three-segment expanding telescope; at mine, a metronome; at Rootie, who clutches his knee, wanting to see for herself; at our photographing father deep in his act of stopping time; at Mama, just past the picture's frame; at a future audience, looking, from a century on, at this sheltered Christmas crèche, long after all of us are dead.

My brother's afraid he's missing something. Afraid Santa switched the gifts' name tags. Afraid my present might be sweeter than his. His one hand reaches out to Ruth, who threatens to fall and crack her head on the walnut coffee table. His other hand flies upward to comb down his front curl—the hair our mother forever loved to brush—so the camera won't capture it sticking up for all eternity like a homemade fishing lure. His smile assures our father that he's doing his best to make this an excellent picture. His eyes dart off in pity for our mother, forever excluded from this scene.

The photo is one of the first Polaroids. Our father loved ingenious inventions, and our mother loved anything that could fix memory. The black-and-white tones have gone grainy, the look the late forties now have. I can't trust the shades of my brother's photographed skin to see just how others might have read him then. My mother was light for her family, and my father, the palest Eurosemitic. Jonah fell right between them. His hair is already more wavy than curly, and just too dark for carrot. His eyes are hazel; that much never changed. His nose is narrow, his cheeks the width of a paperback book. What my brother most resembles is a blood-drained, luminous Arab.

His face is the key of E, the key for *beautiful*, the face most known to me in the whole world. It looks like one of my father's scientific sketches, built of an open oval, with trusting half almonds inlaid for eyes: a face that forever says *face* to me, flashing its seduction of pleasure, mildly surprised, its skin pulled smooth on the rounded bone. I loved that face. It seemed ever to me like mine, released.

Already he shows the wary distrust, the testing of innocence. The features will narrow as the months move on. The lips draw and the eyebrows batten down. The half-pear nose thins at the bridge; the puffs of cheekbone deflate. But even in middle age, his forehead still sometimes cleared like this and the lips rose up, ready to joke even with his killers. I got an expandable telescope for Christmas. How about you?

One night after prayers he asked our mother, "Where do we come from?" He couldn't have been ten yet, and was troubled by Ruth, scared by how different she looked from the two of us. Even I already worried him. Maybe the nurses at the maternity hospital had been as careless as Santa. He'd reached the age when the tonal gap between Mama and Da grew too wide for him to call it chance. He gathered the weight of the evidence, and it bent him double. I lay in my bed, flush against his, cramming in a few more panels of *Science Comics*, starring Cosmic Carson, before lights-out. But I stopped to hear Mama's answer to the question I'd never thought to ask.

"Where did you come from? You kids?" Whenever a question caught her on the chin, Mama repeated it. It bought her ten seconds. When things turned serious, her voice grew piano, and settled into that caramel, mezzo register. She shifted on the edge of his mattress, where she sat caressing him. "Why, I'm glad you asked me that. You were all three brought to us by the Brother of Wonder."

My brother's face twisted, dubious. "Who's that?"

"Who . . . ? How did you get so curious? You get that from me or from your father? The Brother of Wonder is named Hap. Mr. Hap E. Ness."

"What does the *E* stand for?" Jonah demanded, trying to catch her out.

"What does the *E* stand for? Why, don't you know that? Ebenezer."

Presto: "What's Wonder's middle name?"

"Schmuel," my father said, a tempo, from the doorway.

"Wonder *Schmuel* Ness?"

"Yes, sure. Why not? This Ness family has many secrets in the cabinet."

"Da. Come on. Where did we come from?"

"Your mother and I found you in the freezer case at the A & P. Who knows how long you were in there. This Mr. Ness claimed to own, but he never produced the ownership papers."

"Please, Da. Truth."

Not a word our father ever violated. "You were born out of your mother's belly."

This inanity reduced the two of us to helpless laughter. My mother lifted her arms in the air. I can see her muscles tighten, even now, twice as old as she was then. Arms up, she said, "Here we go."

My father sat down. "We must go there, soon or late."

But we didn't go anywhere. Jonah lost interest. His laugh staled and he stared off into space, grimacing. He accepted the deranged idea—whatever they wanted to tell him. He put his arm on Mama's forearm. "That's okay. I don't care where we came from. Just so long as we all came from the same place."

The first music school to hear my brother loved him. I knew this would happen before it did, no matter what my father said about predicting the future. The school, one of the city's two top conservatory prep programs, was down in midtown, on the East Side. I remember Jonah, in a burgundy blazer too large for him, asking Mama, "How come you don't want to come?"

"Oh, Jo! Of course I want to go with you. But who's going to stay home and take care of Baby Ruth?"

"She can come with us," Jonah said, already knowing who couldn't go where.

Mama didn't answer. She hugged us in the foyer. "Bye, JoJo." Her one name for the two of us. "Do good things for me."

We three men bundled into the first cab that would take us, then headed down to the school. There, my brother disappeared into a crowd of kids, coming back to find us in the auditorium just before he sang. "Joey, you're not going to believe this." His face all eager horror. "There's a bunch of kids back there, and they look like Ming the Merciless is chewing their butts." He tried to laugh. "This big guy, an eighth grader at least, is spitting his guts out in the washbasin." His eyes wandered out beyond the orbit of newly discovered Pluto. No one had ever told him music was worth getting sick over.

Twenty bars into my brother's a cappella rendition of "Down by the Salley Gardens," the judges were sold. Afterward, in the stale green hallway, two of them even approached my father to talk up the program. While the adults went over details, Jonah dragged me backstage to the warm-up room where the older kid had puked. We could still smell it, lining the drain, sweet and acrid, halfway between food and feces.

Official word came two weeks later. Our parents gave the long typed envelope to Jonah, for the thrill of opening it himself. But when my brother foundered on the first two sentences, Da took the letter. "'We regret to say, despite the merits of this voice, we cannot offer a place this fall. The program is overenrolled, and the strains on the faculty make it impossible . . .' "

Da let out a little bark of dismay and glanced at Mama. I'd seen them shoot the look between them, out together in public. By ten, I knew what it meant, but I kept that fact secret from them. Our parents stared at each other, each working to deflect the other's dismay.

"A singer does not get every part," Da told Jonah. Mama just looked down, her half of the oldest music lesson there was.

Da made inquiries, through a colleague in the Music Department at Columbia. He came home in a mix of weariness and amazement. He tried to tell Mama. Mama listened, but never stopped working on the lamb stew she was making for dinner. My brother and I crouched down, hiding on either side of the kitchen doorway, listening in like foreign spies. Grown men had been electrocuted for less.

"They have a new director," Da said.

Mama snorted. "New director, pushing through some old policies." She shook her head, knowing everything the world had to teach. She sounded different. Poorer, somehow. Older. Rural.

"It is not what you are thinking."

"Not—"

"Not your contribution. Mine!" He almost laughed, but his throat wouldn't let him.

Da sat at the kitchen table. A sound came out of him, horrid with wear, one he'd never have let go of had he known we were listening. It cracked into something almost a giggle. "A music program without Jews! Madman! How can you have classical music without Jews?"

"Easy. Same way you had baseball without coloreds."

Something had happened to my father's voice, too. Some ancient thickening. "Madness. They might as well refuse a child for being able to read notes."

Mama set the knife down. One wrist worked to hold the hair back out of her eyes. The other held her elbow in a fist. "We fought that war for nothing. Worse than nothing. We should never have bothered."

"What is left for such a place?" A shout came out of Da. Jonah and I both flinched, as if he'd hit us. "What kind of chorus do they think they put together?"

That night my father, who'd never checked "Jewish" on any form in his life, whose life was devoted to proving the universe needed no religion but math, made us sing all the Phrygian folk tunes he could remember from a life of dedicated forgetting. He took over the keyboard from my mother, his fingers finding that plaintive modal sorrow hidden in the chords. We sang in that secret language Da dropped into sometimes, in streets north of ours, English's near cousin from a far village, those slant words I could almost recognize. Even in quickstep, those scales, glancing with flat seconds and sixths, turned love songs to a pretty face into shoulder shrugs at blind history. My father became a lithe, nasal clarinet, and the rest of us followed. Even Ruth picked up the chant, with her eerie instant mimicry.

Our parents resumed the search for a proper school. Mama was militant now. She only wanted to keep her firstborn nearby, in or around New York, as close to home as possible. And only music and this newfound urgency could have let him go that far. Da, the empiricist, steeled himself against all considerations but the school's worth. Between them, they made the awful compromise: a boarding preconservatory up in Boston, Boylston Academy.

The school was growing famous on the strengths of its director, the great Hungarian baritone János Reményi. My parents read about the place in the *Times*, where the man had declared this country's early voice training to be a travesty. This was exactly what a nation struggling under the mantle of postwar cultural leadership most feared hearing about itself, and it rewarded its accuser with generous support. Da and Mama must have thought a Hungarian wouldn't care where we'd come from. The choice seemed almost safe.

Visit the Cafe!

Now through 8/31/2023

Buy 1
Fresh Baked Cookie
Get 50% OFF a
2nd Cookie

Mix or Match any flavor!!!

See Cafe for details.

BARNES & NOBLE
BOOKSELLERS

PAPER✻SOURCE

B.DALTON

BOOKSTAR

B.DALTON

BOOKSTAR

PAPER✻SOURCE

BARNES & NOBLE
BOOKSELLERS

B.DALTON

BOOKSTAR

B.DALTON

BARNES & NOBLE
BOOKSELLERS

PAPER✻SOURCE

B.DALTON

BOOKSTAR

B.DALTON

PAPER✻SOURCE

BARNES & NOBLE
BOOKSELLERS

B.DALTON

BOOKSTAR

B.DALTON

PAPER✻SOURCE

This time, we traveled together to the tryout, our whole family. We drove up in a beautiful rented Hudson with the fender worked right into the body. My mother rode in the backseat with me and Ruth. She always rode in the back whenever we traveled together, and Da always drove. They told us it had to do with Ruthie's safety. Jonah told me it was so that the police wouldn't stop us.

For his trial, Jonah prepared Mahler's "Wer hat dies Liedlein erdacht?" from *Des Knaben Wunderhorn*. Mama accompanied him, working up the piano reduction for weeks in advance, until it glistened. She wore a pleated black silk dress with draped shoulders, which made her look even taller and thinner than she was. She was the most beautiful woman the judges could ever hope to look upon. János Reményi himself was one of the three auditioners. My father pointed him out as we entered the hall.

"Him?" Jonah said. "He doesn't look Hungarian!"

"What do Hungarians look like?"

Jonah shrugged. "Balder, maybe?"

Only a handful of singers tried out that day, those who'd made it through the rigorous screening. Mr. Reményi called the name Strom from a checklist. Mama and Jonah walked down the aisle to the stage. A woman intercepted them before they could reach the steps. She asked Mama where the accompanist was. My mother sucked in her breath and smiled. "I'm accompanying." She sounded tired, but trained.

The exchange must have flustered her. Up onstage, she set out of the gate at a tempo faster than they'd ever taken the piece in their thousand run-throughs at home. I'd heard the piece so many times, I could have sung it in reverse. But at the tempo Mama set, I'd have missed the entrance. Jonah, of course, came in perfectly. He'd only been waiting for the thrill of that moment to take the song aloft.

I saw the judges share a look when Jonah hit his first rising figure. But they let him finish. The song vanished into history in under two minutes. In my brother's mouth, the tune turned into impish myth. It spoke of a world without weight or effort. *The Boy's Magic Horn*, sung at last by a boy still under the spell.

One of the judges started to clap, but a look from Reményi froze her in midtwitch. The director scribbled some notes, took off his glasses, lifted his eyebrows, and gazed at my brother. "Mr. Strom." I looked at my father, confused. His eyes fixed on Reményi. "Can you tell me what this song means?"

Da leaned forward and began thumping his head against the seat in front of him. Mama, onstage, folded her hands across her beautiful black dress and studied her lap. In Jonah's singing voice, my parents felt utter confidence. But spoken words were not their son's forte.

Jonah stood ready to help this Hungarian out with any troubles he was having. He looked up at the stage lights, cribbing the answer there. "Uh . . . Who thought up this little song?" He gave an embarrassed sigh, passing the buck to the poet.

"Yes, yes. That's the *title*. Now what do the words mean?"

My brother brightened. "Oh! Okay. Let's see." My father's head banging accelerated. Six-year-old Ruthie, on his other side, squirmed and started to hum. Da shushed her, something he never did. "There's this house up in the mountains," Jonah explained. "And a girl at the window."

"What kind of girl?"

"German?"

All three judges cleared their throats.

"A sweet girl," Reményi said. "A *darling* girl. Go on."

"She doesn't live there. She has this mouth? And it's magic? It brings dead people back to life." The idea played in his eyes: ghouls, soul-suckers, zombies. "And then there are these three geese, who carry this song around in their beaks . . ."

"That's enough." Reményi turned to my mother. "You see? Not a song for young boys."

"But it *is*," my father blurted from back in the hall.

Reményi turned around, but his look, in the dark room, went right through us. He turned back to Mama. "This is a song for a mature voice. He should not be singing this. He can't do it well, and it might even do his vocal cords harm."

My mother hunched over the piano bench, under the weight of her compounded mistakes. She'd thought to delight the great man with her son's brightness, and the great man had snuffed out her little lamp. She wanted to crawl into the piano and slice herself to ribbons on the thinnest, highest strings.

"Maybe in twenty years, we will learn Mahler properly. The child and I. If we're both still alive."

My father coughed in relief. Mama, onstage, straightened up again and decided to live. Root started chattering, and I couldn't hush her. My brother picked at his elbow onstage, seeming to have missed the whole drama.

Out in the corridor, Jonah bounded up to me. "Maybe the guy just doesn't like music." A tide of sympathy rose in his eyes. He wanted to work with the man, to show him the pleasures of sound.

We wandered around the school's compound, its mock-Italian palazzo wedged between the Back Bay and the Fens. Da talked to a couple of the students, including one German-speaking son of a diplomat. All swore devotion to the academy and its vocal program. Some of the better older voices were already placing in competitions here and in Europe.

Jonah dragged me around the building, poking into the crannies, oblivious to the head-turning we all caused. Our mother walked about the grounds in lead shoes, as if to her own funeral. Every new proof that this was the right next step in her son's life added a decade to hers.

Da and Mama conferred with the school officials while Jonah and I entertained Ruth, letting her throw bread crumbs at the sparrows and pebbles at the marauding squirrels. Our parents returned, flustered by something Jonah and I didn't ask about. Together, the five of us headed toward the rented Hudson for the long drive home. But a voice called to us as we made our way down the front walk.

"Excuse me, please." Maestro Reményi stood in the academy's entrance. "May I have a moment?" He looked right past Da, as he had at the auditions. "You are the boy's mother?" He studied Mama's face and then Jonah's, searching for the key to a mystery larger than Mahler. Mama nodded, holding the great man's stare. János Reményi shook his head, a slow processing of the evidence. "Brava, madame."

Those two words were the great musical reward of my mother's life. For fifteen seconds, she tasted the triumph she had sacrificed by marrying my father and raising us. All the way home, in the gathering dark, with Jonah up in the front, humming to himself, she predicted, "You're going to learn whole worlds from this man."

Jonah got into the Boylston Academy of Music with a full scholarship. But back in the shelter of Hamilton Heights, he began to balk. "There's so much more you can still teach me," he told Mama, going for the kill. "I can concentrate better here, without all the other children."

Mama chanted to him in her history teacher's voice. "JoJo honey. You have a skill. A special gift. Maybe only one out of thousands of boys—"

"Fewer," Da said, doing the calculation.

"Only one in a million can even dream of doing what you'll do."

"Who cares?" Jonah said.

He knew he'd crossed a line. Mama held him in place, lifting his chin. She could have killed him with a word. "Every living soul."

"You have a duty," Da explained, his consonants crisping. "You must grow that gift and give it back to creation."

"What about Joey? He plays piano better than I do. He's a faster sight-singer." Tattletale-style: *He hit me first*. "You can't send me without Joey. I don't want to go to any school he's not gonna go to."

"Don't say 'gonna,' " Mama said. She must have known the real terror. "You go blaze a trail. Before you know it, he'll follow you."

Too late, our parents saw they'd let us spend too much time indoors. Home school was their controlled experiment, and it had produced two hothouse flowers. They spoke to each other at night, in low voices, undressing for the night behind their bedroom door, thinking we couldn't hear.

"Maybe we too much protected them?" Da's voice couldn't find the path it wanted.

"You can't leave a child like that loose in a place like this." The old agreement, the thing that bound them together, the endless work of raising an endangered soul.

"But even so. Maybe we should have . . . They don't have one real friend for the two of them."

My mother's voice lifted a register. "They know other boys. They like the likable ones." But I could hear it in her, wishing things otherwise. Somehow, we'd failed to make their plan work. I wanted to go tell them about the hurled brick shards, the words we'd learned, the threats against us, all the things we'd sheltered our parents from. Yellow boy. Half-breed. I heard Mama, at her vanity, drop her tortoise brushes and stifle a sob.

And I heard Da shelter her, apologizing. "They have each other. They will meet others, like them. They will make friends, when they find them."

An oboist acquaintance of Da's in the Columbia Math Department had long pestered Da to let us sing for the campus Lutherans. And for just as long, our parents had turned the man down. Mama took us to neighborhood churches, where our voices joined hers in the general roof raising. But beyond that, they'd kept us safe from the compromised world of public performance. "My boys are singers," she said, "not trained seals." This always made Jonah bark and clap the backs of his paws.

Now our parents thought the Lutherans might prepare Jonah for his bigger step that fall. Church recitals could inoculate us against the more virulent outside. Our first forays down into Morningside Heights for choir rehearsal felt like overland expeditions. Da, Jonah, and I headed down on Thursday nights on the Seventh Avenue local, coming back up in a cab, my brother and I fighting to ride in the front with the cabbie and practice our fake Italian. At the first rehearsals, everyone stared. But Jonah was a sensation. The choir director held up practice, manufacturing excuses just to listen to my brother sing a passage alone.

The choir contained several talented amateurs, cultivated academics who lived for the twice-a-week chance to immerse themselves in lost chords. A few powerful voices and even a couple of pros, there as a public service, also kicked back into the kitty. For two weeks, we sang innocuous anthems in the northern Protestant tradition. But even that young, Jonah and I scorned the cheesy, predictable modulations. Back in Hamilton Heights, we'd torture the lyrics—"My redeemer Lumpy; yes, my Jesus Lumpy." But on Sundays, we were stalwart, singing even the most banal melody as if salvation demanded it.

One of the group's real altos, a pro named Lois Helmer, had designs on my brother from the moment his voice cut through that musty choir loft. She treated him like the child she'd sacrificed to pursue her modest concert career. She heard in Jonah's bell tones a way to grab the prize her career had so far denied her.

Miss Helmer had a set of pipes more piercing than that church's organ. But she must have been of an age—101, by Jonah's dead reckoning—when the pipes would soon start rusting. Before her sound leaked out and silence took over, she meant to nail a favorite piece that, to her ears, had never received a decent hearing in this world. In Jonah's sonar soprano, she found at last the instrument of her delivery.

I couldn't know it then, but Miss Helmer was a good two decades ahead of her time. Long before the explosion of recording gave birth to Early Music, she and a few other narrow voices in a wide-vibrato sea began insisting that, for music before 1750, precision came before "warmth." At that time, big was the vogue in everything. Bethlehem, Pennsylvania, still mounted its annual zeppelin-sized, cast-of-thousands performances of the Bach Passions, devotional music in the atomic age, where mass released a lumbering spiritual energy. Miss Helmer, in contrast, felt that, with complex polyphony, God might actually like to hear the pitches. The sparer the line, the greater the lift. For energy was also proportionate to lightness squared.

All her life, she'd wanted to take that brilliant duet from Cantata 78 out for a test spin, proof that small was beautiful and light was all. But she'd never found a woman soprano whose vibrato warbled less than a quarter tone. Then she heard the ethereal boy, maybe the first since Bach's Thomasschule in Leipzig able to do justice to the euphoria. She approached Mr. Peirson, the choir director, a bloodless respecter of andante who thought he could reach the calmer patches of Lutheran purgatory if he only respected all the dynamics and offended no listener. Mr. Peirson balked, capitulating only when Lois Helmer threatened to remove her assets to the Episcopalians. Mr. Peirson surrendered the podium for the occasion, and Lois Helmer lost no time hunting up a skilled cellist to hold down the springing *Violone* line.

Miss Helmer had another wild idea: music and its words ought to agree. Schweitzer had been onto this for decades, pushing for word painting in Bach as early as the year that Einstein—the violinist who bent my brother's life—dismantled universal time. But in practice, Bach's music, no matter the text, stood coated in that same caramel glow that masked old master paintings, the golden dusk that museumgoers took for spirituality but which was, in fact, just grime.

Miss Helmer's Bach would do what its words said. If the duet began *"Wir eilen mit schwachen, doch emsigen Schritten"*—"We rush with faint but earnest footsteps"—then the damn thing would rush. She harassed the continuo players until they brought the song up to her mental tempo, a third faster than the piece had ever been performed. She swore at the bewildered players during rehearsal, and Jonah relished every curse.

He, of course, stood ready to blast through the piece at the speed of delight. When Jonah sang, even in rehearsal, making his noise for people who weren't like us, I felt ashamed, like we were betraying the family secret. He matched this woman phrase for phrase, a mynah latching onto his trainer's every trick, their free-play imitation finally converging in perfect synchrony, as if both had found a way to catch up to their own eerie echoes and rejoin.

On the Sunday of their performance, Jonah and I clung to the choir loft's rail, each in a black blazer and a red bow tie that had taken all Da's knowledge of low-degree topology to tie. We stood on high and watched the congregation mill about the pews like iridescent bugs under a lifted garden stone. Da, Mom, and Ruth came late and sat way in the back, where they couldn't bother anyone else by being seen.

The anthem followed the Gospel. Most weeks, the moment passed, a sample swatch of spiritual wallpaper that the customers of grace fingered and set down. But that week, the bobbing cello obbligato launched such spring that even those already dozing sat up in their pews, alarmed by pleasure.

Out of the eight jaunty bars, the soprano lifts, an overnight crocus, homesteading the winter-beaten lawn. The tune is propelled by the simplest trick: Stable *do* comes in on an unstable upbeat, while the downbeat squids away on the scale's unstable *re*. With this slight push, the song stumbles forward until it climbs up into itself from below, tag-team wrestling with its own alto double. Then, in scripted improvisation, the two sprung lines duck down the same inevitable, surprise path, mottled with minor patches and sudden bright light. The entwined lines outgrow their bounds, spilling over into their successors, joy on the loose, ingenuity reaching anywhere it needs to go.

Eight bars of cello, and Jonah's voice sailed out from the back of the church. He sang as easily as the rest of the world chatted. His voice cut through the Cold War gloom and fell without warning on the morning service. Then Lois entered, spurred on to match the boy's pinpoint clarity, singing with a brilliance she hadn't owned since her own confirmation. We rush with faint but earnest footsteps. *Ach, höre.* Ah, hear!

But where were we rushing? That mystery, at age nine, lay beyond my ability to solve. Rushing to aid this Jesu. But then we lifted our voices to ask for his help. As far as I could hear, the song reversed itself, as split as my brother, unable to say who helped whom. Someone must have botched the English translation, and I couldn't follow the original. Mama spoke only voice-student German, and Da, who'd escaped just before the war, never bothered to teach us more of his language than we sang together around the piano.

But the German was lost in that beam of light that hung above the congregation. My brother's voice washed over the well-heeled pews, and years of pale, northern cultivation dissolved in the sound. People turned to look, despite Jesus' order to believe without seeing. Lois and my brother sailed along in lockstep, their finely lathed ornaments taken up into the heart of the twisting tune. They leapfrogged and doubled each other, a melancholy mention of the *sick* and *wayward* before brightening toward home, while all the while moving the idea of home three more modulations deeper into unspinning space. *Zu dir. Zu dir. Zu dir.* Even Mr.

Peirson fought to keep his lower lip from quivering. After the first stanza, he stopped trying.

When the cello did its final da capo and the high-voiced tandem toboggan took its last banked turn, the song wound up where all songs do: perfected in silence. A few stricken listeners even committed that worst of Lutheran sins and clapped in church. Communion, that day, was an anticlimax.

In the chaos after the service, I searched out my brother. Lois Helmer was kissing him. He stared me down, cutting off even a snicker. He abided Miss Helmer, who hugged him to her, then let him go. She seemed completed. Already dead.

Our family scooted out to the street, doing its traditional disappearing act. But the crowd found my brother. Strangers came up and pressed him to them. One old man—out for his last Sunday on God's earth—fixed Jonah with a knowing stare and held on to his hand for dear life. "That was the most beautiful Handel I ever heard."

We escaped and cackled as we ran. Two ladies snagged us in midflight. They had something momentous to say, some secret they weren't supposed to tell, but, like girls our age, they couldn't help themselves. "Young man," the taller one said. "We just want you to know what an honor it is for us to have . . . . a voice like yours in the service of our church." *Like yours.* Some sinful Easter egg we were supposed to discover. "And I just can't tell you . . ." The words caught in her throat. Her friend put a white-gloved hand on her arm to encourage her. "I just can't tell you how much it means to me, personally, to have a little Negro boy singing like that. In our church. For us."

Her voice broke with pride, and her eyes watered. My brother and I traded smirks. Jonah smiled at the ladies, forgiving their ignorance. "Oh, ma'am, we're not real Negroes. But our mother is!"

Now the adults passed a look between them. The gloved one patted Jonah's amber-colored head. They stepped away and faced each other, brows up, clutching each other's elbows, searching for the right way to break the news to us. But at that moment, our father, fed up with crowds and Christians, even academic ones, came back into the nave to fish us out.

"Come on, you two. Your old man is dying of hunger." He'd picked up the line from "Baby Snooks" or "The Aldrich Family," those radio serials about assimilated life that held him in such interplanetary awe. "You have to get your old Da back uptown, to his dinner, before anything happens."

The ladies fell back from this ghost. Their known world crumpled faster than they could rebuild it. I looked away, taking on their shame. Da waved apology to Jonah's admirers. Their hard-won campaign of liberal tolerance crashed down around them in one impertinent flip of the physicist's wrist.

On Broadway, the first three cabs we flagged wouldn't take us. In the cab, Mama couldn't stop humming Bach's exultant little tune. We boys sat on either side of her, with Ruth on her lap and Da up front. She wore a black silk dress printed with little lambs so small, they might have been polka dots. Cocked on her head was a cupped potsherd hat—"your mother's yarmulke," Da called it—with a piece of black net she pulled down like a half veil in front of her face. She looked more beautiful than any movie star, with all the beauty Joan Fontaine never quite pulled off. Singing in a cab on Broadway, surrounded by her triumphant family, she was black, still young, and, for five minutes, free.

But my brother was elsewhere. "Mama," he asked. "You are a Negro, right? And Da's . . . some kind of Jewish guy. What exactly does that make me, Joey, and Root?"

My mother stopped singing. I wanted to slug my brother and didn't know why. Mama looked off into whatever place lay beyond sound. Da, too, shifted. They'd been waiting for the question, and every other one that would follow, down the years to come. "You must run your own race," our father pronounced. I felt he was casting us out into coldest space.

Ruth, on our mother's lap, laughed in the face of the glorious day. "Joey's a Nee-gro. And Jonah's a Gro-nee."

Mama looked at her little girl with a crooked little smile. She lifted her veil and held Ruthie to her. She rubbed her nose into her daughter's belly, humming the Bach. With two great bear arms, she drew our heads into the embrace. "You're whatever you are, inside. Whatever you need to be. Let every boy serve God in his own fashion."

She wasn't telling us everything. Jonah heard it, too. "But what *are* we? For real, I mean. We got to be something, right?"

"Have." She sighed. "We *have* to be something."

"Well?" My brother fiddled to free his shoulders. "What something?"

She released us. "You two boys." The words came out of the side of her mouth, slower than that morning's glacial sermon. "You two boys are one of a kind."

The cabbie must have been black. He took us all the way home.

This was all our parents said about the matter, until the end of summer. We went back to the local church circuit with our mother, where ours were just a part of the deep, concerted voice. August trickled out, and Jonah readied to leave home. Our evenings of song tapered off. The chords we made were no longer crisp, and no one had the heart for counterpoint.

Sometimes at night, through our parents' door, we heard Mama weeping at her mirror, and Da trying for all the world to answer. Jonah did his best to comfort them both. He told them Boston would be good for him. He'd come back singing so well, they'd be glad they'd sent him away. He said he'd be happy. He told them everything they wanted to hear, in a voice that must have destroyed them.

EASTER, 1939

This day, a nation turns out for its own wake. The air is raw, but scrubbed by last night's rain. Sunday rises, red and protestant, over the Potomac. Light's paler synonyms scratch at the capital's monuments, edging the blocks of the Federal Triangle, turning sandstone to marble, marble to granite, granite to slate, settling down on the Tidal Basin like water seeking its level. The palette of this dawn is pure Ashcan School. Early morning coats every cornice with magentas that deepen as the hours unfold. But memory will forever replay this day in black and white, the slow voice-over pan of Movietone.

Laborers drift across a Mall littered with scraps of funny papers scattering on the April wind. Sawhorses and police cones corral the lawless expanse of public space. Federal work teams—split by race—finish ratcheting together a grandstand on the steps of the Lincoln Memorial. A handful of organizers gazes over the reflecting pool, swapping bets about the size of the crowd that will turn out for this funeral turned jubilee. The crowds about to descend on them in three hours will swamp their most outrageous guesses.

Knots of the curious gather to witness these last-minute preparations. Accounts have been flying for some time now—word of this forbidden concert. American Dream and American Reality square off, their long trajectories arcing toward midair collision. The ancient ship of state, gone too long without a hull scrape, groaned at anchor last night in the

Washington Navy Yard, upriver on the Anacostia, and now entire neighborhoods of the city, this Easter morning, 1939—in crowds already assembling to the east of Scott Circle and north of Q Street, all the way up into the Maryland suburbs; whole communities still in church, calling out their response to this year's recounting of the ancient Resurrection fable—begin to wonder whether today might witness the leaky old brig's mercy scuttling, a full-fledged burial at sea.

"How long?" the church songs ask. "How long until that Day?" As late as last Friday, no tune dared more than *soon*, no singer thought sooner than *never*. Yet this morning, by some overlooked miracle, the stone has rolled away, Rome's imperial elite lie sprawled about the tomb, and the messenger angel floats front and center, beating its wings over the Jefferson Memorial, saying *now*, singing release in the key of C.

Over on Pennsylvania Avenue, pink children in vests and pinafores hunt for Easter eggs on the White House lawn. Inside the Oval Office, the silver-tongued president and his speechwriters conspire on the next fireside chat to a country still hoping to evade the flames. Each new paternal radio address stores up more strained reassurances. "Brutality," the old man tells his fireside family, "is a nightmare that must waken to democracy." A loving-enough lie, perhaps even believable, to those who've never strolled northward up Fourteenth Street. But Roosevelt's address on the widening crisis goes hunting, this Easter, for an audience. Today, the nation's radios tune to a different performance, a wider frequency. Today, Radio America broadcasts a new song.

Democracy is not on the program this afternoon. Freedom will not ring from Constitution Hall. The Daughters of the American Revolution have seen to that. The DAR have shut their house to Marian Anderson, the country's greatest contralto, recently returned from a triumphal tour of Europe, the sensation of Austria and the toast of the Norwegian king. Sibelius embraced her, declaring, "My roof is too low for you!" Even Berlin booked her for multiple engagements, until her European manager confessed to the authorities that no, Miss Anderson was not 100 percent Aryan. The great Sol Hurok has taken her into his fold of international stars, sure he can replicate, at home, the wonder of the jaded Old World. Last year, he booked Miss Anderson on a seventy-concert U.S. tour, the most grueling ever performed by a recital singer. This same alto has just been barred from the capital's best stage.

Who can say what revolution the DAR staves off, sandbagged behind its blinding-white Roman portico? "Booked through the end of winter," the programming director tells Hurok. "Spring, as well." The agency's associates call in another booking, for a different artist, this one 100 percent Aryan. They get a choice of half a dozen slots.

Hurok tells the newspapers, though this story is hardly news. It's the country's longest-running serial feature. The press asks the Daughters for comment. Is this permanent policy, or some vague stopgap? The DAR answers that, by tradition, certain of the city's concert halls are reserved for performances by Miss Anderson's people. Constitution Hall is not one. It's not DAR policy to defy community standards. Should sentiment change, Miss Anderson might sing there. Sometime in the future. Or shortly thereafter.

The *Daily Worker* has a field day. Artists vent their outrage—Heifetz, Flagstad, Farrar, Stokowski. But America ignores these foreign interventions. Thousands of petition signatures produce nothing. Then the real bombshell falls. Eleanor Roosevelt, First Mother of all First Daughters, resigns her DAR membership. The president's wife rejects her roots overnight, declaring that no ancestor of hers ever fought to found *this* republic. The story makes headlines here and in capitals abroad. Miss Anderson plunges, attacca, from lieder into high opera. But her alto remains the sole calm in the middle of a national outcry. She tells the press she knows less about the situation than any of them. Her poise is a gentle puff, yet breath enough to fan old cinders into flame.

On segregation, the presidency has held silent since Reconstruction. Now a classical vocal recital becomes the battlefield for this administration's public stand. High culture signs on to battle not just another affront to the downtrodden Negro but a slander against Schubert and Brahms. The First Lady, former social worker, is furious. Long an Anderson fan, she had the alto sing a command performance three years earlier. Now the woman who sang at the White House can't use the rented stage. Eleanor's ad hoc Protest Committee looks for an alternate venue, but the Board of Education denies them Central High School. Central High, unavailable to *Variety*'s third-biggest performer of the year. "If a precedent of this sort is established, the board will lose the respect and confidence of the people and bring about its destruction."

Walter White, NAACP president, heads to the Capitol with the only possible solution, one large enough to turn catastrophe to work. Harold Ickes, secretary of the interior, agrees to the idea in a heartbeat. The secretary has at his command the perfect venue. Its acoustics are awful and the seating worse. But oh, the capacity! Miss Anderson will sing outdoors, from the foot of the Emancipator. There's no hiding place down here.

Word of the plan goes out, and hate mail pours in. Makeshift crosses of Japanese cherry pop up like daffodils in the White House lawn. Still, there's no weighing the human soul except singly. The Texas chapter of the Daughters wires in an order for two hundred seats. But Ickes and Eleanor have saved their trump card. The tickets for this cobbled-up Sunday concert will go for free. Free is an admission price the nation understands, one that guarantees a house to make the DAR blanch. Even those who don't know a meno from a molto, who couldn't pick *Aida* from *Otello* out of a chorus line, plan to spend this Easter on the Mall.

Tens of thousands make the pilgrimage, each one for private motives. Lovers of free-flying danger. Those who'd have paid fortunes to witness this Europe-stealing phenomenon. Devotees who worshiped this woman's throat before the force of destiny slipped into it. People who simply want to see a face like theirs up there on the marble steps, standing up to the worst the white world can throw at it and giving it all back in glory.

Over in Philadelphia, at Union Baptist, that temple towering over Fitzwater and Martin, this is the hour of deliverance, a congregation's payback, though they've never sought the slightest reward. On this great gettin'-up morning, the pastor works Miss Anderson into his Easter sermon for the special early service. He speaks of the sound of a life that keeps on rising, breaking out of the grave, no matter how hard the far-flung empire might want it dead and buried. The great crescent banks of polished pews lean in to the message and ring it with amens. The children's choir lets loose a noise more joyful than any it's made since little Marian's heyday, and the sound rises up to roost in the arcing carved rafters.

The gospel is good, and the church empties its worshipers like the contents of that old tomb. In Sunday finest, the great flock mills on the church porch, waiting for the busses, trading excitement, remembering the student recitals and the benefit concerts, the dimes pooled: Educate Our Marian, the pure voice of her people's future.

The busses fill with song rolling across all registers, rich suspensions bridging the wilderness and Canaan. They sing searing anthems, tear off gospel hand-clappers, and lay into stolid four-part hymns. They sing a field full of spirituals, including their Marian's favorite: "Trampin'." "I'm trampin', I'm trampin', trying to make heaven my home." The more pragmatic sing, "trying to make a heaven of my home." Only this once, among the endless earthly schisms, the two inimical persuasions lie down alongside each other, separate parts in the same chorus.

Delia Daley's adopted parish heads for the promised land without her. In her agony of one, Delia feels them leaving, abandoning her on the wrong side of those parting waters. She's even had to miss the special sunrise service, saddled with her morning shift at the hospital, which she cannot slip. She stands at the nurses' station, still begging for a charitable crumb, just an hour, half an hour's mercy. The brick-complexioned Feena Sundstrom doesn't even blink at her. "Everyone, Miss Daley, would like Easter Sunday off, our patients included."

She considers leaving early anyway, but the Swedish Storm Trooper is already set to fire her just for looking sideways. Without the money coming in from her hospital hours, Delia can wave the last year of her voice training good-bye. She'd have to beg from her father again, just to have enough to graduate, something the man would no doubt almost love. She's had to listen to the speech every semester for the last four years. "Allow me to remind you of a little matter of economic reality. You've heard about this party the high and mighty have dreamed up, a little thing called the Depression? Half our people, workless. It's wiped out almost every Negro this country hasn't already wiped out. You want to learn to sing? Take a look at what we folk have to sing about."

When she told her father she wouldn't be heading to Washington with Union Baptist, the doctor all but beamed. When she added that she'd be going later, by train, at extra expense, he turned back into Old Testament patriarch. "How is this indulgent excursion supposed to contribute to your making a living? Is that more of your magic of high art?"

No good telling him *she* makes ends meet. Miss Anderson makes a better living than ninety-nine hundredths of *we folk*, not to mention almost every white man alive. Her father would only repeat what he's said endlessly since she entered school: The world of classical music makes professional boxing look like an ice-cream social. Gladiator combat unto death. Only the ruthless survive.

Yet Delia Daley has survived—her own brand of ruthless. Ruthless toward herself, toward her bodily strength, her available hours. A four-year, around-the-clock marathon, through every wall, and she's ready to keep running, as long as she has to. Full-time at the hospital, twice that at school. Let her father see the power of high art.

But today art's power falters, threatens to fall. The predawn shift is worse than murder, with nowhere to appeal. The feeble and infirm—always with us, as Jesus says, but somehow more numerous than usual, this Easter—lie waiting in their own waste for her to come clean them. She twice needs help in moving patients to get to the soiled linen. Then the Brick Nightingale makes her do second floor west's bathrooms, just because the woman knows what today is. Feena the Fascist stands over her the whole while, sighing about colored people's time. "You people are so slow getting in and so damn fast getting out."

To augment the agony, three separate patients yell at her for clearing their breakfasts away before they've finish pecking at their vulcanized eggs. So Delia is almost a full, unpaid hour late getting out, counting the ten minutes of Feena's reprimand. She runs home to wash and throw on a decent dress before rushing to the train, whose fare will set her back a week's worth of hospital-subsidized lunches.

At home, her worst nightmare settles in for a double feature. Her mother insists she sit down for Easter dinner. "You have a bite of my holiday ham and get something green and filling in you. Specially if you're taking a trip."

"Mama. Please. Just this once. I'm going to miss her. I have to make the early train, or she'll be done singing before I even—"

"Nonsense." Her father dismisses her. "You won't be late for anything. What time is she supposed to start? When has a singer of our race ever started a concert at the advertised hour?" He repeats the same litany each week when he takes her to Union Baptist for choir. His mirth is a running testament to how bitterly she has dashed his hopes.

Black's not even half the battle. She, William Daley's firstborn—*cleverest baby ever birthed, either side of the line*—has been his dream for achievement beyond even the unlikely heights he's scaled in this life. She should go to medical school. He did. Pediatrician, internist, maybe. Do anything, if she weren't so headstrong. Pass him up. Go to law school, first black woman ever. Force them to take her, on pure skill. Run for Congress, Lord help him.

Congress, Daddy?

Why not? Look at our neighbor, Crystal Bird Faucet. Rewriting all the rules—

and she makes you look like Ivory soap. Washington's next. Has to happen some-day. Who's going to move it down the line, if not the best? And the best, he insisted, was her. Somebody's got to be the first. Why not his little girl? *Make history. What's history, anyway, except uncanting the can't?*

This is the measureless confidence that has led her astray. His fault, her singing. Stroked too much while growing up. Be anything. Do anything. Dare them to stop you. When she found her voice: *You sound like the angels raised from the dead, if they still bothered with the likes of us down here. A sound like that could fix the broken world.* How could she help but be misled?

But when he learned she meant to make singing her life, his tune changed keys. *Singing's just a consolation prize. Just a pretty trinket, to be put away for the day when we have some decent clothes. No one's ever freed anybody with a song.*

In her father's house, standing over her mother's linen table, Delia feels the creases in her shoulders. She gazes at her little brother and sisters spreading the holiday plates. Poor souls will have the fight of their lives just making it to adulthood. Just as much pressure from inside as from out.

Her mother catches her looking. "It's Easter," Nettie Ellen says. "Where else you going to eat, if not with your family? You're supposed to set some example for these young ones. They're growing up lawless, Dee. They think they can run around and do it all, no rules, just like you."

"I have rules, Mother. Nothing but rules." She doesn't push. She knows her mother's real terror. The doctor's boundlessness will do his offspring in. There's a lesson outside this house, a truth too long and large to do much about. He should be readying his children, tempering their illusions, not setting them up for the kill.

Lawless Delia sits to dinner. She almost chokes, wolfing down a hunk of sugar-glazed ham. "It's good, Mama. Delicious. The greens, the beets: Everything's perfect. Best year ever. I have to go."

"Hush. It's Easter. You don't have to leave for a while yet. It's a whole concert. You don't need to hear every song. There's your favorite mince pie, still coming."

"My favorite train to Washington's coming before that."

"Long gone," brother Charles sings, twelve-bar, in a good tenor wail, new as of last year. "Long gone. That train that's gonna save ya? Long gone." Michael joins in the taunts, warbling his parody of a classical diva. Lucille starts to cry, sure, despite all reassurances, that Delia's putting herself in danger, traveling to Washington all by herself. Lorene follows suit, because she always finishes anything her twin starts.

The doctor gets that look, the glare of domestic tranquillity. "Who is this woman to you, that you have to curtail Easter dinner with your family in order to—"

"Daddy, you hypocrite." She wipes her mouth on her napkin and stares him down. He knows who this woman is better than anyone. He knows what Philadelphia's daughter has single-handedly accomplished. He's the one who told Delia, years ago, opened her eyes: *The woman's our vanguard. Our last, best hope of getting the white world's attention. You want to go to singing school? There's your first, best teacher.*

"Hypocrite?" Her father stops in midforkful. She's overstepped, one shade of will too deep. The doctor will rise up, a pillar of righteousness, and forbid her to go. But she holds his eyes; no other way out. Then the side of his mouth skews into a smirk. "Who taught you those big two-dollar words, baby? Don't you ever forget who taught you them!"

Delia walks to the head of the table and pecks him high up on his balding crown. Through puckered lips, she hums "Lift Every Voice and Sing," just loudly enough for him to hear. She hugs her scowling mother and then she's gone, off to the station on another musical pilgrimage. She has made them for years, ever since the chance broadcast that changed her life. Made the trips to Colorado Street, Miss Anderson's girlhood home, and to her second house on Martin Street. Walked around the halls of South Philly High, conjuring up the girl who walked them. Passed for Baptist, to her agnostic father's dismay and her A.M.E. mother's horror, just to attend, each week, the church of her idol, the woman who taught her what she might do with her life.

A framed magazine photo of that regal face has stared down from Delia's desk these last two years, a silent reminder of all that sound can do. She heard it in that deep river of song flowing from her radio's speaker, five years ago, and again in that shaft of light she basked in during Miss Anderson's too-brief Philadelphia recital last year. She has shaped her own mezzo around that voice, fixed in her memory. Today she'll see again, in the flesh, the owner of those sounds. Marian Anderson doesn't even need to perform, for this trip to D.C. to pay off. All she needs to do is *be.*

Delia Daley subvocalizes on the train, shaping the lines in her mind. "The sound doesn't start in the throat," Lugati chides her every week. "The sound starts in the thought." She thinks the notes of Schubert's "Ave Maria," that Anderson standard, promised on the program for this day. They say the archbishop of Salzburg made her sing the Schubert twice. They say when she sang for a room of Europe's best musicians a spiritual no one in the room could hope to have grasped, they grasped her anyway. And not a person dared applaud when her last note faded.

How must it feel, tone riding free on a column of breath, banking on the spirit's slightest whim? Open throat, placement—all the techniques Lugati, her patient teacher, has harped upon these last years—will not teach her as much as this one train trip. Miss Anderson is her freedom. Anything her race cares to do, it will.

She steps off the train into a capital huddling under blustery April. She half-expects the cherry trees to greet her right inside Union Station. The coffered barrel vault arches over her, a fading neoclassical cathedral to transportation that she steps through, making herself small, invisible. She moves through the crowd with tight, effacing steps, waiting for someone to challenge her right to be here.

Washington: every fortunate Philadelphia schoolgirl's field trip, but it has taken Delia until twenty to see the point of visiting. She heads out of the station and bears southwest. She nods toward Howard, her father's school, where he suggested she go make something of herself. The Capitol rises up on her left, more unreal in life than in the thousands of silver images she grew up suspecting. The building that now stands open to her color again, after a generation, bends the very air around it. She can't stop looking. She walks into the waking spring, the river of moving bodies, giggling even as she hushes herself up.

The whole city is a postcard panorama. Like being inside a white hand-me-down grade school civics text. Today, at least, the monument-flanked boulevards flow with people of all races. The group from Union Baptist told her to look for them up front on the left, near the steps of the Lincoln Memorial. She has only to hook right, on Constitution Avenue, to see how naïve those plans were. There'll be no rendezvous today. To the west, a crowd gathers, too dense and ecstatic to penetrate.

Delia Daley looks out over the carpet of people, more people than she knew existed. Her father is right: The world is vicious, too huge to care about even its own survival. Her steps slow as she slips in behind the mile-long crowd. All in front of her, the decades-long Great Migration comes home. She feels the danger, right down her spine. A crowd this size could trample her without anyone noticing. But the prize lies at the other end of this gliding crush. She breathes in, forcing her diaphragm down—*support, appoggio!*—and plunges in.

She expected something else, a lieder-loving concert crowd, only a little larger. The program today is hardly the Cotton Club. It isn't even Rudy Vallee. Since when have Italian art songs pulled in such armies? She drifts across a barricaded Fourteenth Street at the crowd's stately pace, falling under the outline of the Washington Monument, the world's largest sundial, a shadow too long to read. Then she's inside the whale's belly, and all she can hear is the huge beating heart of the beached creature.

Something here, a thing more than music, is kicking in the womb. Something no one could have named two months ago now rises up, sucking in its first stunned breaths. Just past Delia in the press of bodies, a girl the color of her brother Charles—a high schooler, though from the look of her, high school is a vanished dream—spins around, flashing, to catch the eye of anyone who'll look at her, a look of delivery that has waited lifetimes.

Delia pushes deeper into the sea, her throat, like a pennant, unfurling. Her larynx drops, the release Lugati has been hounding her these last ten months to find. The lock opens and a feeling descends on her—confirmation of her chosen life. Fear falls away, old leg chains she didn't even know she was wearing. She's on her appointed track, she and her people. Each will find her only way forward. She wants to kick back and call out, as so many around her are already doing, white people within earshot or no. This is not a concert. It's a revival meeting, a national baptism, the riverbanks flooded with waves of expectation.

Inside this crowd, she feels the best kind of invisible. The slate-colored combed-silk dress that serves so well for Philadelphia concerts is all wrong here, too sleek by half, her hemline missing low by a full two inches. But no one marks her except with pleasure. She passes people fresh off mule-drawn tobacco-farm carts, others whose portfolios are padded with blocks of General Motors. To her right, a convention of overalls gathers together, huddled against the public. A stooped couple in black formal wear fresh from its Armistice Day outing brush past her, eager to push up close enough to catch a glimpse of the dais. Delia takes in the topcoats, capes, raglans, pelerines, the whole gamut from ratty to elegant, the necklines cowled, draped, squared, and bateaued, all rubbing eager shoulders.

Her lips form the words, and her windpipe mimes the pitches: Every valley, exalted. A balding man about ten feet away from her, ghost white, with the Cumberland Gap between his two front teeth, perching inside a thin gray suit, starched blue shirt, and tie printed with Washington landmarks, hears her sing aloud what she has only imagined. "Bless you, sister!" the ghost man says. She just bows her head and lets herself be blessed.

The crowd condenses. It's standing room only, flowing the length of the reflecting pool and down West Potomac Park. The floor of this church is grass. The columns of this nave are budding trees. The vault above, an Easter sky. The deeper Delia wades in toward the speck of grand piano, the stickpin corsage of microphones where her idol will stand, the thicker this celebration. The press of massed desire lifts and deposits her, helpless, a hundred yards upstream, facing the Tidal Basin. Schoolbook cherry trees swim up to fill her eyes, their blossoms mad. They wave the dazzle of their pollen bait and, in this snowstorm of petals, fuse with every Easter when they ever unfolded their promissory color.

And what color is this flocking people? She's forgotten even to gauge. She never steps out in a public place without carefully averaging the color around her, the measure of her relative safety. But this crowd wavers like a horizon-long bolt of crushed velvet. Its tone changes with every turn of light and tilt of her head. A mixed crowd, the first she's ever walked in, American, larger than her country can hope to survive, out to celebrate the centuries-overdue death of *reserved seating*, of *nigger heaven*. Both people are here in abundance, each using the other, each waiting for the sounds that will fill their own patent lack. No one can be barred from this endless ground floor.

Far to the northwest, a mile toward Foggy Bottom, a man walks toward her. Twenty-eight, but his fleshy face looks ten years older. His neck is a pivot, his eyes behind their black horn-rims steadily measuring the life all around him. Just his being alive to measure this unlikeliness defies all odds.

He walks from Georgetown, where two old friends from his Berlin days put him up, sparing him from looking for a room, an act of practical politics that would have defeated him. He has come down by train last

night from New York, where he has lived this past year, sheltered by Columbia. Yesterday, David Strom was out in Flushing Meadows, getting an
advance peek at the World of Tomorrow. Today, he woke up in Georgetown's parade of yesterday. But now there is only and ever *now*, every in-
finitesimal in the delta of his step a subtended, theoretical forever.

He's here by George Gamow's invitation, to talk at George Washington University on possible interpretations of Milne and Dirac's dual time
scales: probably imaginary, he concludes, but as staggeringly beautiful as
truth. He was down three months before, for the Conference on Theoretical Physics, where Bohr told the assembled luminaries about the existence of fission. Now David Strom returns, to add his private notes to the
growing stockpile of infinitely strange things.

But he makes the trip for a more pressing reason: to hear again the
only American singer who can rival the greatest Europeans in tearing
open the fabric of space-time. Everything else—the visit with his
Georgetown friends, the talk at George Washington, the tour of the Library of Congress—is excuse. His thoughts tunnel backward. His each
step toward the Mall peels back the four last years, exhuming the day
when he first heard this phenomenon. That sound still hangs in his mind,
as if he were reading it off the conductor's score: 1935, the Wiener
Konzerthaus, the concert where Toscanini proclaimed that a voice like
this woman's came around only once every hundred years. Strom doesn't
know the maestro's timescale, but Toscanini's "hundred years" is short
by any measure. The alto sang Bach—"Komm, süsser Tod." "Come,
Sweet Death." By the time she reached the second strophe, Strom was
ready.

Today is Easter, the day Christians say death died. To date, Strom has
seen little evidence supporting the theory. Death, he feels reasonably
confident, is poised to make an impressive comeback. For reasons Strom
cannot grasp, the angel has passed over him three times already. Even the
most confirmed determinist must call it caprice. First, following his
mentor, Hanscher, down to Vienna after the Civil Service Restoration
Act, escaping Berlin just before the Reichstag erupted in flames. Then
getting the habilitation. Making a splash at the Basel conference on quantum interpretations, and winning an invitation to visit Bohr in Copenhagen just months before Vienna dismissed its Jews—practicing or
otherwise—from the faculty. Escaping with the letter of recommenda-
tion from Hanscher, the shortest, most effusive that man ever wrote:

"David Strom is a physicist." At last securing asylum in the States, a mere year ago, on the strength of a single theoretical paper, whose confirmation came a decade before it might have, hastened by a cosmological confluence that happens once every other lifetime. Three times, according to David's own count, saved by a luck even blinder than theory.

It all seems proof of a temporal rift no theory can mend. Four years ago, he was happily attending European concerts, as if Europe still heard some fixed key. Nothing sounds the same on this repeat listen, old music in a newfound land. In between that theme and its recapitulation, only a harrowing development section, jagged, atonal, unlistenable. His parents in hiding near Rotterdam. His sister, Hannah, and her husband, Vihar, trying to reach his country's capital, Sofia. And David himself, a resident alien in the land of milk and honey.

Time may turn out to be quantized, as discontinuous as the notes in a melody. It may be passed back and forth, carried along by subatomic chronons as discreet as the fabric of matter. Tachyons, restricted to speeds faster than light—fantasies allowed by Einstein's most rigorous prohibitions—may bombard this life with word of everything that awaits it, but life below the speed of light can't see them to read them. David Strom shouldn't be here, free, alive. But he is. Is here, walking across Washington, to hear a goddess sing, live, in the open air.

Strom turns onto Virginia and sees the throng. He has never been so close to such numbers. He has seen them back in Europe only on newsreels—the crazed World Cup finals, the mobs that turned out three years ago to watch Hitler refuse to give out gold medals to the non-Aryan *Übermensch*. This crowd is more sweeping, more blissfully anarchic. Music alone cannot account for this. Such a movement can only come from some vaster libretto. Until this instant, Strom has no idea what concert he walks into. He fails to grasp the issue until he corners and looks on it.

This eye-level wall of flesh knocks the wind from him. The shimmer of tens of thousands of bodies, humanity broken down to atoms, an electrostatic n-body problem beyond any mathematics' ability to solve, panics him with its groundless physics, and he turns to run. He heads back up Virginia toward the safety of Georgetown. But he can't erase more than a few dozen meters of his path when he hears that voice up inside his ears. *Komm, süsser Tod.* He stops on the sidewalk and listens. What's the worst that oblivion might do to him? What better sound to bring on the end?

He turns back toward this roiling crowd, using the terror in his chest the way a seasoned performer would. Breathing through his mouth, he slips into the churning surf. The fist in his chest relaxes into eddies of pleasure. No one stops him or asks for identification. No one knows he is foreign, German, Jewish. No one cares that he's here at all. *Ein Fremder unter lauter Fremden.*

Sunlight breaks free for a minute, to shine on earth's most mutable country. David Strom wanders lost inside a social realist drawing, hemmed in by a crusade he can't identify, waiting again, this year, for the myth to turn real. Where else in the world have so many for so long believed that so much good is so close to happening? But today, these New Worlders may be right. He shakes his head, working his way toward the makeshift stage. Prophecy may yet come true, if there's anyone left to receive it. Already, Europe has slid back into the flames. Already, the smokestacks are hard at work. But that is tomorrow's fire. Today has another glow altogether, and its heat and light draw Strom forward.

He bobs in sync with the bodies around him, searching for a good sight line. Monuments hem this huge hall in—State Department, Federal Reserve—white lintels and pillars, the hallmarks of indifferent power. He is not the only one staring at them. It strikes Strom, in America only a year, that he might come to say *my country* more easily than half of those he passes, people who arrived here twelve generations ago, on someone else's travel plan.

A hundred thousand drifting feet batter the April ground into a cattle trail. He passes a preacher waving a pigskin-bound Bible, three small children standing on an orange crate, a squad of blue and brass police as dazed as the swarm they patrol, and three dark-suited, broad-shouldered men in felt hats, menacing gangsters compromised only by the beaten-up bicycles they push alongside them.

A shout comes from the forward ranks. Strom's head jerks up. But the crisis has passed by the time its wake reaches him. Sound travels so slowly, it might as well be stopped, compared to the *now* of light. Miss Anderson is on the platform, her Finnish accompanist beside her. The dignitaries packing the cobbled-up bleachers rise for her entrance. Half a dozen senators, scores of congressmen including one solitary Negro, three or four cabinet members, and a justice of the Supreme Court each applaud her, all for private reasons.

The secretary of the interior addresses the brace of microphones. The crowd near Strom stirs with pride and impatience. "There are those"—

the statesman's voice bangs around the vast amphitheater, launching three or four copies of itself before dying—"too timid or too indifferent"—only the echo shows how immense a cathedral they stand in—"to lift up the light . . . that Jefferson and Lincoln carried aloft . . ."

God in Heaven, let the woman sing. In the burst of idiom he heard on the train coming down, *Clam up and take it on the lam.* Where Strom comes from, the whole point of singing is to render human chatter irrelevant. But the secretary politicks on. Strom inches toward the Memorial, the wall of people in front of him solid yet somehow always leaving a little space to fill.

Then Miss Anderson stands, a modest queen, her long fur coat protecting her against the April air. Her hair is a marvelous scallop shell, open against both cheeks. She's more otherworldly than Strom remembers. She stands serene, already beyond life's pull. Yet her serenity shivers. Strom makes it out, over the heads of these thousands. He has seen that wavering before, up near the pit of the Vienna Staatsoper, or through opera glasses, from the student leaning posts in the halls of Hamburg and Berlin. But so unlikely is the tremor in such a monument that Strom can't at first give it a name.

He turns and looks out across the crowd, following her glance. Humanity spreads so far over the Mall that her sound will take whole heartbeats to reach the farthest ranks. The numbers undo him, an audience as boundless as the ways that led it here. Strom looks back to the singer, alone up on her Calvary of steps, and names it, the ripple that envelops her. The voice of the century is *afraid.*

The fear coming over her isn't stage fright. She has drilled too long over the course of her life to doubt her skill. Her throat will carry her flawlessly, even through this ordeal. The music will be perfect. But how will it be heard? Bodies stretch in front of her, spirit armies, rolling out of sight. They bend along the length of the reflecting pool, thick as far back as the Washington Monument. And from this hopeful host there pours a need so great, it will bury her. She's trapped at the bottom of an ocean of hope, gasping for air.

From the day it took shape, she resisted this grandstand performance. But history leaves her no choice. Once the world made her an emblem, she lost the luxury of standing for herself. She has never been a champion of the cause, except through the life she daily lives. The cause has sought her out, transposing all her keys.

44

The one conservatory she long ago applied to turned her away without audition. Their sole artistic judgment: "We don't take colored." Not a week passes when she doesn't shock listeners by taking ownership of Strauss or Saint-Saëns. She has trained since the age of six to build a voice that can withstand the description "colored contralto." Now all America turns out to hear her, by virtue of this ban. Now color will forever be the theme of her peak moment, the reason she'll be remembered when her sound is gone. She has no counter to this fate but her sound itself. Her throat drops, her trembling lips open, and she readies a voice that is steeped in color, the only thing worth singing.

But in the time it takes her mouth to form that first pitch, her eyes scan this audience, unable to find its end. She sees it the way the newsreels will: 75,000 concertgoers, the largest crowd to hit Washington since Lindbergh, the largest audience ever to hear a solo recital. Millions will listen over radio. Tens of millions more will hear, through recordings and film. Former daughters and stepdaughters of the republic. Those born another's property, and those who owned them. Every clan, each flying their homemade flags, all who have ears will hear.

NATION LEARNS LESSON IN TOLERANCE, the newsreels will say. But nations can't learn lessons. Whatever tolerance graces this day will not survive the spring.

In the eternity that launches her first note, she feels this army of lives push toward her. Everyone who ever drew her on to sing is here attending. Roland Hayes is in this crowd somewhere. Harry Burleigh, Sissieretta Jones, Elizabeth Taylor-Greenfield—all the ghosts of her go-befores come back to walk the Mall again, this brisk Easter. Blind Tom is here, the sightless slave who earned a fortune for his owners, playing by ear, for staggered audiences, the piano's hardest repertoire. Joplin is here, the Fisk and Hampton jubilees, Waller, Rainey, King Oliver and Empress Bessie, whole holy choirs of gospel evangelists, jug banders and gutbucketers, hollerers and field callers—all the nameless geniuses her ancestors have birthed.

Her family is there, up close, where she can see them. Her mother stares up at Lincoln, the threatening, mute titan, appalled by the weight her daughter must carry for the collected country, now and forever. Her father sits even closer, inside her, in the shape of her vocal cords, which still hold that man's mellow bass, silenced before she really knew him. She hears him singing "Asleep in the Deep" while dressing for work, always the first line, endlessly caressing, never managing to get all the way to the phrase's end.

The size of the crowd, its gravity, splinters her measure's first beat. Common time goes cut, allegro to andante to largo. Her racing brain subdivides the notes in her first number's introduction, eighth note turns into quarter, quarter becomes half, half whole, and whole expands without limit. She hears herself inhale and the pickup spreads into standstill. As she forms the note's forward envelope, time stops and pins her, motionless.

The tune that the minuscule grand piano strikes up opens a hole in front of her. She can look through and see the coming years as if scanning a railroad timetable. Down this narrow strip of federal land she witnesses the long tour ahead. This day changes nothing. She'll sit outside the Birmingham, Alabama, train station four years from now, waiting for her German refugee accompanist to bring her a sandwich, while German prisoners from North Africa occupy the waiting room she can't enter. She'll be given the keys to Atlantic City, where she'll perform to sold-out houses but won't be able to book a room in town. She'll sing at the opening of *Young Mr. Lincoln*, in Springfield, Illinois, barred from the Lincoln Hotel. All coming humiliations are hers to know, now and always, hovering above this adoring, immeasurable crowd as the piano homes in on her cue.

The Daughters will repent their error, but repentance will come too late. No later justice can erase this day. She must live through it for all time, standing out here in the open, singing in a coat, for free. Her voice will be linked to this monument. She'll be forever an emblem, despite herself, and not for the music she has made her own.

These faces—four score thousand of them—tilt up to seek hers out, Easter's forgetting bulbs seeking the feeble sun. Those who until this afternoon were sunk in hopeless hope: too many of them, swarming the shores of Jordan, to get over in one go. Their ranks carry on swelling, even as she traces their farthest edge. In the convex mirror of 75,000 pairs of eyes she sees herself, dwarfed under monstrous columns, a small dark suppliant between the knees of a white stone giant. The frame is familiar, a destiny she remembers from before she lived it. A quarter century on, she'll stand here again, singing her part in a gathering three times this size. And still the same hopeless hope will flood up to meet her, still the same wound that will not heal.

Down one world line she sees herself crushed to death, twenty minutes from now, when the audience surges forward, 75,000 awakened lives trying to get a few steps closer to salvation. Those who've spent a life condemned to the balcony will push toward a stage that is now all theirs, release driving them toward themselves, toward a voice wholly free, until they trample her. She sees the concert veer toward catastrophe, the mass accident of need. Then, down another of this day's branching paths, she watches Walter White stand and come forward to the microphones, where he pleads with the crowd for calm. His voice turns the mass back into its parts, until they are all just one plus one plus one, able to do no worse to her than love.

Oceans past this crowd, larger ones gather. Six hours ahead, six zones east of her, night already falls. In the town squares, vegetable markets, and old theater quarters where she has performed, inside the *Schauplätze* that wouldn't engage her, voices build. She looks on the world's only available future, and the coming certainty swallows her. She will not sing. She cannot. She'll hang on the opening of this first pitch, undone. Her choices close down, one after the other, until the only path left is to turn and run. She casts a panicked look back, toward the Potomac bridge, across the river into Virginia, the only escape. But there's no hiding place. No hiding place down here.

A girl's spinto soprano inside her strikes up its best warding-off tune. *When you see the world on fire, fare ye well, fare ye well.* She uses the time-honored performer's cure. She need only focus on one face, shrink the mass down to one person, one soul who is with her. The song will follow.

Deep in the crowd, a quarter of a mile forward, she finds her mark, the one she'll sing to. A girl, an earlier her, Marian on the day that she left Philadelphia. That soul looks back, herself already singing, sotto voce. The girl calms her. In the frozen fermata before her downbeat, she reviews the program she must complete. "Gospel Train," and "Trampin'," and "My Soul Is Anchored in the Lord." But before that, Schubert's "Ave Maria." And before the Schubert, "O mio Fernando." Of this whole grab bag of tunes, she'll remember singing exactly none. It will be as if some ghost placeholder walks away with the experience and she comes away with nothing. She'll read of her delivery much later, learning through the clippings how each song went, long after the fact, after the deed is done and gone.

But even before the coming amnesia, she must make it through "America." Time thaws. The piano starts up again, unrolling the last of those simple block chords, a sequence under the skin of anyone born in these parts, a perfect cadence, as familiar as breathing. All she can hear as the brief lead-in starts up again a tempo is the sound of her own lungs. For one brief beat that stretches out as far as the filled horizon, she forgets the words. Their overlearned familiarity blocks them from coming. Like forgetting your name. Forgetting the numbers from one to ten. Too known to remember.

Again, the crowd surges forward, a great wave needing only to sweep over and drown her. This time, she lets them. She may forget. But time reorders all. A lightness rises, a way point in this gathering sea of dark, the darkness that belonging itself has made. For a moment, here, now, stretching down the length of the reflecting pool, bending along an arc from the shaft of the Washington Monument to the base of the Lincoln Memorial, curling down the banks to the Potomac behind her, a state takes shape, ad hoc, improvised, revolutionary, free—a notion, a nation that, for a few measures, in song at least, is everything it claims to be. This is the place her voice creates. The one in the words that come back to her at last. That sweet, elusive *thee*. Of *thee* I sing.

MY BROTHER AS THE STUDENT PRINCE

Jonah moved up to the Boylston Academy of Music in the fall of 1952. Before he left, he entrusted me with our family's happiness. I stayed home that year, the harder posting, washing all the dinner dishes to spare my mother, playing with Ruth, faking happy understanding of my father's scribbled dinner-table Minkowski diagrams. Mama took on more private students and talked of going back to school herself. We still sang together, but not as often. When we did, we stayed away from new repertoire. It didn't seem right. Mama, especially, didn't want to learn anything Jonah couldn't learn with us.

Jonah returned to Hamilton Heights three times that year, starting with Christmas vacation. To our parents, he must have seemed much the same boy, as if he'd never left. Mama wanted to swallow him whole, even as he came up the front steps. She grabbed him in the doorway and smothered him in hugs, and Jonah suffered them. "Tell us everything," she said when she let him up for air. "What's life *like* up there?" Even I, standing behind her in the foyer, heard her guarded tone, the bracing.

But Jonah knew what she needed. "It's okay, I guess. They teach you a hunk of things. Not as much as here, though."

Mama breathed again, and swept him into a room steeped in ginger cookie smells. "Give them time, child. They'll get better." She and my father exchanged *all clears*, a secret look Jonah and I both saw.

His few days at home were our happiest all year. Mama made him seared potatoes with ham, and Ruth showered him with weeks' worth of crayon-scribbled portraits from memory. He was the returning hero. We had all our old repertoire to catch up with. When we sang, it was hard for the rest of us not to stop and listen for changes in his voice.

Over Christmas, we read through the first part of the *Messiah*. At his spring break, we did part two. I saw Jonah studying Da while he wandered through the text. Even Da noticed him stealing glances. "What? Do you think I can't be a Christian, too, for the length of this piece? Did you know stutterers never stutter when they sing? Did they not teach you that, away at your school?"

Jonah insisted I join him at Boylston. Mama said the choice was mine; no one wanted anything from me that I didn't. At age ten, choosing felt like death. With Jonah gone, I had Mama's lessons almost to myself, sharing her only with Ruthie. My piano skills were exploding. The record player and the collection of Italian tenors were all mine. In trios, I got to sing the top line. I was the rising star in our evenings of Crazed Quotations. Besides, I was sure I wouldn't pass the Boylston auditions. Mama laughed at my doubts. "How will you know unless you try?" Failing, at least, would take things out of my hands and remove the constant sense—so many times my own body weight—that whatever I chose to do, I'd let *someone* down.

I sang above myself at the trials. Also, the judges probably listened very generously, wanting to keep my brother with the school. Maybe they thought I'd grow to resemble him, given a few years of training. Whatever the reasons, I got in. They even offered my parents some scholarship money, not as much as they'd offered for Jonah, of course.

I broke the news of my decision to Mama and Da as gently as I could. They seemed delighted. When they cheered me, I burst into tears. Mama swept me up into her. "Oh, honey. I'm just happy my JoJo is going to be together. You two can protect each other, when you're three hundred miles away." An honest-enough hope, I guess. But she should have known.

They must have thought that home schooling would be our best, first fortress and preparation. But already, in New York, even before Jonah left, we'd begun to see the cracks in their curriculum. Six blocks from our house in Hamilton Heights, every neighborhood supplementary exercise made a lie of our home lessons. The world was not a madrigal. The world was a howl. But from the earliest age, Jonah and I hid our bruises from our parents, glossed over our extracurricular tests, and sang as if music were all the armor we'd ever need.

"It's better up at Boylston," Jonah promised me, at night, behind the closed bedroom door, where we imagined our parents couldn't hear. "Up there, they beat the shit out of the kids who *can't* sing." To hear him talk, we'd stumbled onto the lower slopes of paradise, and perfect pitch was the key to the kingdom. "A hundred kids who love complicated, moving parts." Some part of me knew it was a bait and switch, that he wouldn't need me with him if the place were as he said. But my parents seemed to need me less, and here was my brother, chanting, *Come away.*

"You two boys," Mama said, trying to smile good-bye. "You two boys are one of a kind."

Nothing he told me prepared me for the place. Boylston was a last bastion of European culture, the culture that had just burned itself alive again, ten years before. It modeled itself on a cathedral choir school, with ties to the conservatory across the Fens. The children lived in a five-story building around a central courtyard that, like Mrs. Gardner's private fantasy just down the curving Fenway, wanted to be an Italian palazzo when it grew up.

Everything about Boylston was white. The minute my trunk was installed in the younger boys' dormitory, I saw how I looked to those who stood gawking at my arrival. My new roommates didn't flinch; most had just spent a year around my brother. But my brother's honey-wheat color did not prepare them for my muddy milk. They stood sharing a knowledge of me, the whole gleaming limestone wall of them, as I walked into the long hospital-style dormer under the arm of my father. I didn't know what whiteness was—how concentrated, how stolid and self-assuming—until I unpacked in that room, a dozen boys watching to see what fetishes would come out of my luggage. Only when Da said farewell to us and headed for South Station did I see where my brother had been living.

And only when I scrambled from the dormitory to rejoin Jonah did I see what his year away, in this mythical place, had really done to him. For a year, alone and unprotected, he had thrown the entire student body into the panic of infection. As he walked down those halls, sheepish now, in my seeing how it was, I could make out the limp from those first twelve months that I hadn't seen at home. He never talked to me about those months by himself, not even years later. But then, I never brought myself to ask. He wanted me to see only this: The others meant nothing to us, and never would. He had found his voice. He needed nothing else.

My brother took me on a tour of the building's mysteries—the walnut-stained hallways with their moldering lockers, the dumbwaiter shafts, the choral rehearsal rooms with their ghostly echoes, the loose electrical faceplate through which one could peer into a pitch-darkness he swore was the seventh grade girls' dormitory. He saved his coup for last. In solemn caution, we ascended to a secret entrance he'd discovered in hours of solo play. We came out on a rooftop overlooking the Victory Garden plots, those home-front mobilizations that outlived the war that spawned them. My brother drew himself up into his best Sarastro. "Joseph Strom, because of your skill and blameless actions, we elect you an Equal and allow you to join us at all our meetings in the Sanctuary. You may enter!"

I crushed him by asking, "Where?" The castle of fair welcome turned out to be a drywalled janitor's closet. We piled in, two boys too many, and huddled in an urgent meeting that at once ran out of agenda. There we sat, Equals in the Sanctuary, until we had to emerge again and join the uninitiated masses.

In the dining hall that first week, a sunny-headed new boy blurted out, "You two have black blood? I'm not supposed to eat with anyone with black blood."

Jonah pressed a pickle fork into his finger. He held out the bleeding tip, giving it a twist suggesting rituals that Sunny-Head didn't want to know about. "Eat with that," he said, spreading the stain across the poor boy's napkin. It caused a sensation. When the proctor came, the whole awed table swore it was an accident.

I couldn't make sense of this place. Not these boys' exchangeable names, not their slack-jawed distaste or their limp flax looks, not the labyrinth of this child-filled building, not the bizarre, chief fact of my new existence: My brother—the most solitary, self-sufficient boy alive—had learned to survive the company of others.

I'd gone up to Boston thinking I was rescuing Jonah. He'd led our parents to believe he was thrilled up here, and our parents needed to believe him. I knew otherwise, and sacrificed myself to keep him from solitary misery. It took me only days before I saw the truth: My brother had spent this last year planning to rescue me.

I went to bed those nights as guilty as I'd ever felt. It didn't matter that I hadn't planned this act of betrayal; I'd still committed it. Yet after a few weeks, I began to suspect that there were worse places than Boylston to be in exile. I roamed the building and the Fens, took my place at emergency meetings of Sanctuary Equals, and in time came to feel myself more exempted from society than excluded. In the passage of those final childhood days, I learned where I stood in the world.

Da and Mama had raised us to trust tones more than we trusted words. I had grown up imagining part-songs to be my family's private ritual. But here, in this five-story Parnassus in the crook of the Charles, Jonah and I found ourselves, for the first time, in the company of other classically trained children. I had to struggle to keep up with my classmates, racing to acquire all the phrases they already knew how to say in our common secret tongue.

The Boylston students had better reasons than racial contamination to hate my brother. They'd come from all over the country, singled out for a musical skill that set them apart and gave them identity. Then Jonah came and made their wildest flights fall to earth and thump about, wounded. Most of them probably wanted to hold a pillow over his soprano mouth, up in that long choirboy's ward where the middle boys slept. Stop his lungs until his freakish capacity for breath ran out. But my brother had a way of lifting off, surprised at his own sound, that made even his enemies feel they ought to be his accomplices.

They feared what they thought was his fearlessness. No one else was so indifferent to consequence, so unable to distinguish between resentment and esteem. He masterminded a rooftop scat sing of Haydn's *Creation* that drew a sidewalk crowd and would have resulted in his reprimand had the impromptu concert not been joyously written up in the *Globe*. During breaks in choral rehearsal, he'd strike up a minor-modal "Star-Spangled Banner" or organize a demented "Row, Row, Row Your Boat," with each new staggered voice entering a half step above the last. Mad dissonance was his favorite stunt, training his ear to hold its pitch in harder intervals to come.

He and the boys who could keep up with him argued for hours over the merits of various tenors. Jonah championed Caruso over all living challengers. As far as my brother was concerned, vocal skill had been deteriorating since the golden age, just before we were born. The other boys argued until they gave up on him, calling him perverse, insane, or worse.

János Reményi, Boylston's director, imagined that he disguised his favoritism. But not a child was fooled. Jonah was the only student Reményi ever called by first name. Jonah came to dominate the school's monthly public recitals. Reményi always passed the plump solos around democratically in rehearsal, but for performances, he usually contrived some artistic reason why the piece had to be done by a voice of exactly Jonah's color.

Any number of these children might have taken my brother out to the playground and held him upside down from the monkey bars until his lungs slipped out his throat. And if Jonah's voice had been merely extraordinary, they might have. But finally, the sunlight's blaze doesn't threaten the yellow of a flower. We only resent what we can still hope to be. His sound put him beyond his classmates' hatred, and they listened, frozen in the presence of this outlandish thing, holding still as this firebird came foraging at their backyard feeder.

When Jonah sang, a sadness colonized János Reményi's face. Grief filled the man as if he was eager for it. In Jonah, Reményi heard everything his younger self had almost been. At the sound of my brother's voice, the room filled with possibility, each of his listeners remembering all those places their paths would never reach.

In time, the other students accepted me as Jonah's brother. But they never lost that look of disbelief. I don't know what bothered them more: my darker tone, my curlier, more ambiguous features, or my stubbornly earthbound voice. I did manage to make small stirs of my own. I could sight-read rings around any student up to the eighth grade. And I had a feel for harmony, learned from long afternoons at the keyboard with Mama, which won me a kind of grudging sanctuary.

Although accredited, the school gave little attention to subjects other than the performing arts. Most of what I took that year I'd already learned, in greater depth, from my parents. But I had to sit through the old material all over again. The clock in the room where I suffered through sentence diagramming tortured me. Only when its second hand swept through a whole circumference would the recalcitrant minute hand, with a granular thud, snap ahead a single tick mark toward salvation. In that interval before the lurch, motion froze and all change died away. Boredom fossilized time in amber. The minute hand hung on the edge of its stagger, refusing to move, despite all the mental force I pushed with. The hour of English grammar spread to paper thinness and worldwide width, until I had lived out the next sixty years of my life in detail and memorized the faces of my grandchildren, all in the instance before Miss Bitner could get to the end of her sentence's ever-dividing diagram.

Without our father to turn the world into a puzzle, Jonah and I fell away from all mental playgrounds but music. After a few months, we were struggling to solve the teasers that used to be our routine dinner-time fare. Our science teacher, Mr. Wiggins, knew about our father's work, and he treated us with scary and undeserved respect. I had to work for two, keeping Jonah on top of his assignments while completing my own, just to protect the family name.

The Boylston students would have crowned my brother king had he looked just slightly more like them. The elite members of the junior division tried to interest Jonah in Sinatra. They played up that crooner's illicit pleasure, huddled up together, listening in secret, out of earshot of the faculty. Jonah, after flashing one quick smile at the insouciant bobby-soxer anthems, clucked in disgust. "Who on earth would get something from such a song? You call that a chord progression? I can tell you what this melody's going to be before it even starts!"

"But what about that voice? Top-drawer, huh?"

"The man must gargle with cough syrup."

The transgressing suburban choirboys stopped in mid finger snap. One of the older kids snarled. "What's your problem, buddy? I like the way this makes me feel."

"The harmonies are cheap and silly."

"But the band. The arrangements. The *rhythm* . . ."

"The arrangements sound like they were written in a fireworks factory. The rhythm? Well, it's jumpy. I'll give you that much."

Thus spake the twelve-year-old, as certain as death. The older boys tried Jonah on Eartha Kitt. "Isn't she a Negro?" I asked.

"Get out of here. What's your problem?" They all glared me down, Jonah among them. "You think everyone's a Negro."

They tried him on singers even hipper than Sinatra. They tried him on rhythm and blues, hillbilly, wailing ballads. But every crowd-pleaser suffered verdicts just as swift and expedient. Jonah covered his ears in pain. "The drum sets hurt my ears. It's worse than the cannons that the Pops fires off for the *1812 Overture*."

For someone with miraculous throat muscles, he was a clumsy child. He never felt comfortable piloting a bike, even on wide boulevards. When school forced us onto a softball diamond, I'd stand helplessly in left field, trying to pin grounders without risking my fingers, while Jonah drifted in deep right, watching fly balls plop back to earth around his ankles. He did like to listen to games on the radio; his classmates managed to hook him on that much anyway. He often had a game going while he vocalized. "Helps me hold my line in chorus, when everyone else is bouncing all over the place." When the National Anthem played, he added crazy, Stravinsky-style harmonies.

Those easy heirs of culture, charmed boys who'd never even *spoken* to another race, were willing to reach out to us, so long as the terms of exchange were theirs. We offered our classmates the desperate mainstream hope that everything they most feared—the armies of not-them just down the Orange Line, the separate civilization that sneered at every word out of their mouths—might turn out to be just like them after all, ready to be converted to willing Vienna choirboys, given a good education and half a happy chance. We were singing prodigies, color-blind cultural ambassadors. Heirs of a long past, carriers of the eternal future. Not even teenagers. What could we know?

He refused to glance at football. "Gladiators and lions. Why do people like watching other people get killed?" But he was the biggest killer of all. He loved board games and cards, any chance to vanquish someone. During marathon sessions of Monopoly, he thumbscrewed with a zeal that would have made Carnegie blush. He wouldn't finish us off, but kept lending us more money, at interest, just for the pleasure of taking more away. He got so good at checkers, no one would play with him. I could always find him in the basement practice rooms, voweling up and down endless chromatic scales while dealing himself hands of Klondike on the top of an upright piano.

There was a girl. The week I arrived, he pointed out Kimberly Monera. "What do you think?" he asked with a scorn so audible that it begged me to add my contempt. She was an anemic girl, frighteningly pale. I'd never seen her like, except for pink-eyed pet mice. "She looks like cake frosting," I said. I made the crack just cruel enough to please him.

Kimberly Monera dressed like the sickly child of Belle Epoch nobility. She favored crème de menthe and terra-cotta. Anything darker made her hair turn into cotton wool. She walked with a stack of invisible dictionaries perched on her head. She seemed to feel naked going out in public without a wide-brimmed hat. I remember tiny buttons on a pair of gloves, but surely I must have made those up.

Her father was Frederico Monera, the vigorous opera conductor and even more vigorous composer. He was always shuttling about from Milan to Berlin to the eastern United States. Her mother, Maria Cerri, had been one of the Continent's better Butterflies before Monera captured her for breeding purposes. The girl's enrollment at Boylston lent the school a luster that benefited everyone. But Kimberly Monera suffered for her status. She could not even be considered as a pariah. The normal, threatened midsection of the student body found her too bizarre even to laugh at. Kimberly walked the school's halls effacing herself, getting out of everyone's way before they had even come within six yards of her. I loved her for that perpetual flinch of hers alone. My brother must have had very different reasons.

She sang with a rare sense of what music meant. But her voice was spoiled by too much premature cultivation. She did this fake coloratura thing that, in a girl her size and age, sounded simply freakish. Everything about her was the opposite of that easy joy our parents bred in us. For the longest time, I was afraid that her voice alone might drive Jonah away.

One Sunday afternoon, I came across the two of them on the front stoop of the main entrance. My brother and a pale girl sitting on the steps: a picture as faded as any other fifties color photo. Kimberly Monera seemed a scoop of Neapolitan ice cream. I wanted to slip a piece of cardboard underneath her, so her taffeta wouldn't melt on the concrete.

I watched, appalled, as this outcast girl sat naming the Verdi operas for Jonah, all twenty-seven, from *Oberto* to *Falstaff*. She even knew their dates of composition. In her mouth, the list seemed the purpose of all civilization. Her accent, as she rolled the syllables across her tongue, sounded more Italian to me than anything we'd ever heard on recordings. I thought at first that she must have been showing off. But my brother had put her up to it. In fact, she had at first denied knowing anything about Verdi at all, letting my brother expound, smiling at his botched details, until it became clear to her that, with Jonah, her knowledge might not be the liability it was with the rest of the student world. Then she let loose with both barrels.

As Kimberly Monera went into her recitation, Jonah craned around and shot me a look: We two were backwoods amateurs. We knew nothing. Our tame home schooling had left us hopelessly unprepared for the world of international power artistry. I hadn't seen him so awed by a discovery since our parents gave us the record player. Kimberly's mastery of the repertoire put Jonah on highest alert. He grilled the poor girl all afternoon, yanking her down by her bleached hand whenever she tried to get up to go. Saddest of all, Kimberly Monera sat still for his worst treatment. Here was the best boy soprano in the school, the boy whom Boylston's director called by first name. What it must have meant to her, just this one little scrap of selfish kindness.

I sat two steps above them, looking down on their exchange of hostages. They both wanted me there, looking out, ready to bark a warning if any well-adjusted kid approached. When her feats of verbal erudition trickled out, the three of us played Name That Tune. For the first time, somebody our age beat us. Jonah and I had to dig deep into the recesses of our family evenings to come up with something the pastel Monera couldn't peg within two measures. Even when she hadn't heard a piece, she could almost always zone in on its origin and figure out its maker.

The skill broke my heart and maddened my brother. "No fair just guessing if you don't know for sure."

"It's not just guessing," she said. But ready to give the skill up for his sake.

He slapped his hand down on the stoop, somewhere between outrage and delight. "I could do that, too, if my parents were world-famous musicians."

I stared at him, aghast. He couldn't know what he was saying. I reached down to touch his shoulder, stop him before he said worse. His words violated nature—like trees growing downward or fires underwater. Something terrible would happen to us, some hell released by his disloyalty. A Studebaker would roll up over the sidewalk and wipe us out where we sat playing.

But his punishment was limited to Kimberly Monera's lower lip. It trembled in place, blanched, bloodless, an earthworm on ice. I wanted to reach down and hold it still. Jonah, oblivious, pressed her. He would not stop short of the secret to her sorcery. "How can you tell who wrote a piece if you've never even heard it?"

Her face rallied. I saw her thinking that she might still be of use to him. "Well, first, you let the style tell you *when* it was written."

Her words were like a ship breaching the horizon. The idea had never really occurred to Jonah. Etched into the flow of notes, stacked up in the banks of harmony, every composer left a cornerstone date. My brother traced his hand along the iron balustrade that flanked the concrete steps.

The scattering of his naïveté staggered him. Music itself, like its own rhythms, played out in time. A piece was what it was only because of all the pieces written before and after it. Every song sang the moment that brought it into being. Music talked endlessly to itself.

We'd never have learned this fact from our parents, even after a lifetime of harmonizing. Our father knew more than any living person about the secret of time, except how to live in it. His time did not travel; it was a block of persisting nows. To him, the thousand years of Western music might as well all have been written that morning. Mama shared the belief; maybe it was why they'd ended up together. Our parents' Crazed Quotations game played on the notion that every moment's tune had all history's music box for its counterpoint. On any evening in Hamilton Heights, we could jump from organum to atonality without any hint of all the centuries that had died fiery deaths between them. Our parents brought us up to love pulse without beginning or end. But now, this pastel, melting ice-cream girl threw a switch and started sound moving.

Jonah was nothing if not a quick study. That one afternoon, sitting on the concrete steps of the Boylston Academy in chinos and a red flannel shirt alongside the pale Kimberly in her pressed taffeta elegance taught him as much about music as had his whole first year at school. In an instant, he learned the meaning of those time signatures that we already knew by ear. Jonah grabbed all the girl's offerings, and still he made her trot out more. She kept it up for him as long as she could. Kimberly's grasp of theory would have been impressive in someone years older. She had names for things, names my brother needed and which Boylston dribbled out too slowly. He wanted to wring the girl's every scrap of music out of her.

When she sang tunes for us to guess, my brother was merciless. "Sing naturally. How are we supposed to tell what you're singing, when your vibrato's a whole step wide? It's like you swallowed an outboard motor."

Her jaw did its terrifying tremolo. "I *am* singing naturally. You're not *listening* naturally!"

I struggled to my feet, ready to bolt back into the building. Already, I loved this antique girl, but my brother owned me. I saw nothing in this trade for me but an early death. I had no stomach for waiting around until disaster bloomed. But one glance from my brother cut my legs out from under me. He grabbed Kimberly by both shoulders and launched his best Caruso, as Canio in *I Pagliacci*, right down to the crazed stage laugh. She couldn't help but sniffle back a smile.

"Ah, Chimera! We were just kidding, weren't we, Joey?" My head hummed with nodding so fast.

Kimberly brightened at the spontaneous nickname. Her face cleared as fast as a Beethoven storm breaking on a single-chord modulation. She would forgive him everything, always. Already, he knew it.

"Chimera. You like that?"

She smiled so slighty, it could yield easily to denial. I didn't know what a chimera was. Neither did Jonah or Kimberly.

"Fine. That's what everyone will call you from now on."

"No!" She panicked. "Not everyone."

"Just Joey and me?"

She nodded again, smaller. I never called her that name. Not once. My brother was its sole proprietor.

Kimberly Monera turned and squinted at us, a little drunk on her new title. "Are the two of you Moors?" One mythic creature to another.

Jonah checked with me. I held up my weaponless palms. "Depends," he said, "on what the hell that is."

"I'm not sure. I think they lived in Spain and moved to Venice."

Jonah pinched his face and looked at me. His index finger drew rapid little circles around his ear, that year's sign for those strange geometries of thought our fellow classmates called "mental."

"They're a darker people," she explained. "Like Otello."

"It's almost dinnertime," I said.

Jonah bent inward. "Chimera? I've wanted to ask you something forever. Are you an albino?"

She turned a ghastly shade of salmon.

"You know what they are?" my brother went on. "They're a lighter people."

Kimberly drained of what little color Italy had granted her. "My mother was like this, too. But she got darker!" Her voice, repeating the line her parents had fed her from birth, already knew the lie would never come true. Her body returned to spooky convulsions, and once more, my brother fished her out from the fires he'd lit under her.

When at last we stood to return to the building, Kimberly Monera paused in midstep, her hand in the air. "Someday, you'll know everything I know about music, and more." The prophecy made her infinitely sad, as if she were already there, at the end of their lives' intersection, sacrificed to Jonah's voracious growth, the first of many women who'd go to their graves hollowed out by love for my brother.

"Nah," he said. "By the time Joey and I catch up, you'll be way down the line."

They became strange comrades, on nothing but understanding. Our city of children hated even the tacit bond between them. Boyhood, by law, didn't fraternize with the otherworldly camp of girls, except for hasty, unavoidable negotiations with a sister or singing partner. The school's best voice, whatever his suspect blood, was not allowed to consort with the princess of furtive oddity. Jonah's classmates were sure he was secretly mocking her, setting her up for the public kill. When the expected ritual humiliation failed to materialize, the middle form boys tried to shame him back to decency. "You working for the SPCA?"

My brother just smiled. His own isolation ran too deep for him to understand what he risked. Total indifference accounted for half his boy soprano's spectacular soar. When there was no audience anywhere worth pleasing except music itself, a voice could go anywhere.

We were Kimberly's Moors, a standing offense to everyone at Boylston. He got a scribbled note: "Find a darkie girl." We laughed at the scrap of paper together, and threw it away.

When our parents picked us up at Christmas in another shiny rental—my mother, as always, riding in the back to prevent arrest or worse—Jackie Lartz came up to fetch us in the thinned-out Junior Common Room. "Your father and your maid and her little kid are here to pick you up." His voice had that edge of childhood: half challenge, half bashful *correct me*. I've spent a lifetime trying to figure out why I didn't. Why I said nothing. My brother's reasons went with him to the grave. Whatever safety we were after, whatever confusions we avoided, we left for vacation far more thoroughly schooled than we'd arrived.

Mama fussed over us all vacation. Rootie crawled all over us, talking, trying, before we left again, to tell us her last four months of adventures. She copied me, the way I walked, the foolish new learning in my voice. Da wanted to know everything Boylston had taught me, everything I'd done while away. I tried to mention everything, and still it felt like lying by omission.

When we returned to Boston, we knew at least what country we returned to. But if we two were tinged with Moorish contamination, the famous conductor's daughter was infected with something almost as bad. She represented everything wrong with albinohood the world over. She was the Empire gone hemophiliac and feeble-minded. She disgusted even

60

her precocious schoolmates. All the operas of Verdi, in chronological order, at thirteen: Even music's fiercest student had to call it freakish.

My brother loved that freak in her. Kimberly Monera confirmed his suspicion: Life was stranger than any libretto about it. That winter after we returned, she showed him how to read a full orchestral score, how to keep separate each threading cross section of sound. On Valentine's Day, she gave him his first pocket edition, a shy, secret offering wrapped in gold foil: Brahms's *German Requiem*. He kept it on the nightstand beside his bed. At night, after lights-out, he'd run his fingers over the printed staves, trying to read their strains of raised ink.

"It's all decided," Jonah told me on a cold March evening, three-quarters of the way through my first year at Boylston. Our parents had just stopped János Reményi from letting Menotti audition Jonah for Amahl in the opera's NBC television broadcast, thinking they could still preserve a halfway normal life for their wholly abnormal child. "We have it all worked out." He pulled from his wallet a picture Kimberly had given him: a tiny pinafored girl in front of La Scala. Proof irreversible of a lifetime pact. "Chimera and I are getting married. Just as soon as she's old enough not to need her father's permission."

After that, I never looked at Kimberly Monera without shame. I tried not to look at her at all. When I did, she always looked away. I couldn't love her anymore, or hope hopelessly that the world or any of us might be other than we were. But I felt a trickle of pride at our new, secret affinity. She now belonged to our little nation. One day, she'd sing with our family. We'd take her home to Mama and Da, where we'd show her, by easy example, how to relax into a tune.

Jonah and Kimberly performed their engagement with that deadly permanence available only to first-time adolescents. Their pact implicated us all in espionage. No one could know but we three, and the secret lent us a giddy gravity. But after Jonah informed me of their engagement, he and Kimberly had even less contact than the little they'd had before. He returned to our rooftop fort, Kimberly to her solitary study of scores. The school did its best to erase them both. Their great secret engagement went underground. She was his betrothed, and that was that. For once two just-teens declare their undying love, what else is left for them to do?

Did the boy soprano think he, too, was white? He didn't have that name yet, nor the notion. Belonging, membership: What need had Jonah Strom for things that had no need of him? His self required no larger sea to drain into, no wider basin. He was the boy with the magic voice, free to climb and sail, changing as light, always imagining that the glow of his gift offered him full diplomatic rights of passage. Race was no place he could recognize, no useful index, no compass point. His people were his family, his caste, himself. Shining, ambiguous Jonah Strom, the first of all the coming world's would-be nations of one.

"Geh weg von mir, geh weg von mir. Ich bin der stolze Hans!" He alone can't· see the figure he cuts, out there onstage, in the Dacron Alpine costume—permanent-press lederhosen and long socks, topped by a green felt elf's cap—some Radcliffe costume designer's fantasy of pre-Holocaust Grimm. A honey-amber southern Egyptian kid, a just-disembarking Puerto Rican plunked down into this Rhenish masterpiece of arrested childhood. Black Jewish Gypsy child with russet coiled hair, upstage left in a plywood hut as picture-perfect as it's supposed to be poverty-stricken, singing, *"Arbeiten? Brr. Wo denkst du hin?"* But when he sings: when clever Hänsel sings! Then no one sees any seams, so lost are they in the seamless sound.

He can see his own arms and legs sticking out of the Schwarzwald fantasy costume. But he can't glimpse the full-dress discord the audience must sort out. The costume feels good; the suspenders pull his shorts up into his crotch. The rub of the fabric as he dances fuses with the pull of his Gretel, alongside him, patiently teaching him the steps. His opposite these performance nights is Kimberly Monera, my brother's first concentrate of desire. *"Mit den Füsschen tapp tapp tapp."* The pull of her blondness draws him on. *"Mit den Händchen klapp klapp klapp. Einmal hin, einmal her, rund herum, es ist nicht schwer!"*

His sister-partner's hold on him, the warmth that fuels his air supply courses through him in all three acts, a breadth underpinning his breath. *Blinder Eifer*: blind thrill in doses so large, they carry him through all the chance catastrophes of performance. He feeds off his sister's instruction, the seed that will form his lifelong taste for the small and light. When his Gretel, sweet dancing teacher, stammers in a moment of stray stage bewilderment, he's there to feed her back the courage she has lent him.

Any blondness might have done. But it's with the Chimera that he lies down in this night forest, the warded circle where the spell first takes hold. She is his *Waldkönigin*, the queen of his woods, whose pale hand he holds, the one who comforts him on the dark stage of self-blinding childhood.

There is an evil in the woods. This is what the oblivious parents must discover with each new performance, after they send their unwitting children into the cursed place to make their own sighting. *Eine Knusperhexe*, baker of children, operator of her own child-ready ovens, hides in the copse, awaiting discovery. This is the doom the pair's stage parents send them to, night after night, pretending to knowledge only after the fact.

Children, children? the forest asks. *Are you not afraid?* Some nights, when the cuckoo teases them with echoes from infinite space, clever Hänsel can feel the alarm pulsing from his Gretel's flanks. The down on her arms dampens with fear, a fear more delicious than the rest of his life will ever succeed in recovering. The boy takes her fright through his fingertips, just touching her moistened arm hair. Her terror draws him inward, like a lens. How close they must huddle against each other, lost under these trees, their basket of berries eaten, darkness falling in their childish neglect, and no way on but under. She looks away from him, eyes forward, into the hall's blackness, breathing hard, straining in her dirndl skirt and flower-embroidered white top, waiting again this evening for the wondrous pain, each new shape these accidental brushings take.

In that charm of darkness—a blue gel slipped over the megawatt spot—the little Arab child in his lederhosen grows more plausible. The amber boy and his blond, anemic sister grow to resemble each other in performance's enchantment, splitting their difference in the falling dusk. They kneel in the dark, resorting to prayer, that version of magic already crusted with ancient protocols long before any word of the Semitic Savior reached these northern woods. Trembling Gretel folds her palms in front of her, cupped against her breasts' slight buds. Her brother, kneeling alongside, plants his hand in the ravine running down the small of her back. Blocked from the eyes of the gazing audience, he lets it trickle south some nights, over the drumlin that tips up to meet it. *Now I lay me down to sleep, fourteen angels watch do keep.* This is how my brother closes out his childhood, in a series of repeat performances. Asleep in the woods, wrapped against blondness, surrounded by protecting angels. *Two stand here above me. Two stand there below me.* What color are the angels? No one can say, here in the half-light. Years later, in an Antwerp art museum, killing time before a recital, he'll glimpse the creatures that protected him, their wings all the hues in beating existence, bent out of the colorless air.

Only in opera do angels need skin. Only in opera and imagination. Among the fourteen singers in that angel umbrella is Hänsel's brother, helping to weave a halo of safety around those twinned innocents. I am the darkest, nuisance angel, as wrong in my flowing white robes as my brother in his lederhosen. I can't see my own face, yet I know how it must play. I can see its wrongness in the eyes of the seraph host: burlesque intruder, guardian of a forsaken tribe.

The boy we angels circle to protect curls up under this shield as if it is a universal grant of childhood: a walk in the woods, guarded by a chorus that takes up this wayward duet and propagates it, with rich, full harmonies, even while he and his Gretel lie in the thrilled simulation of sleep. The forest and its stolen berries are his; he and this girl can lose themselves in darkness, every night, with impunity. But there is hell to pay, in the final act. The mother from act one, the harsh mezzo, scarred by poverty and driven to punish her dancing children by turning them out of the cottage, comes back, in double casting, as the child-eating witch.

Clever Hans does all he can to keep our own blood parents from coming to see our operatic debut. He means to protect them from the twists of this production. Maybe he's ashamed of his look, his role. "It's not that great," he tells them. "More for children, really." But our parents wouldn't miss this premiere for the world. Of course they must come see what their offspring have gotten themselves into. Da brings the foldout camera. Mama dresses up majestically in cobalt dress and her favorite feathered hat with veil. She does something to her face, almost like her own stage makeup. She smells like babies.

The edible cottage, the night they come, gleams as it has rarely done: a profusion of sugared offerings, a child's glimpse of heaven. But with his parents in the house tonight, little Hans loses his appetite. He sees their silhouettes even over the glare of the footlights, this couple who can't touch each other in public. He sees his real sister, nappy-headed, shocked by this candy beauty, wide-eyed under the forest's curse, reaching out her hand in appetite or self-defense.

Hänsel's real-life mother must sit still and watch the story transform all mothers into witches. His father must hold still and watch this German-singing *Hexe* try to trap his dusky child and force him into the order-making oven. The boy looks for comfort to his Gretel, but her dirndl-wrapped waist seems tonight a circlet of public shame. Yet he must stay by her, his stage sister, his albino woods mate, however much his agitation throws poor Kimberly off. When his distress at last overwhelms the girl and she comes in a major third below her note, clever Hans is there to hum her back to pitch.

When all the enchanted gingerbread children are freed again from their fixed, repeating nightmare, when the witch fries in her own device and the now-pious family reunites over her cremains, the curse of the role lifts from him. For the first time, he takes his bows capless, his curly russet hair bared for all to see. Something darkens in his face, his eyes. But he bows to fair enthusiasm, accepting the weight of this liberal love.

I look for my brother afterward. He is a pillar of indignation, racing through the boys' dressing room. He tears away from the backstage admirers. He doesn't wait for me to catch up. My brother Hänsel explodes out of the lobby, into the cove of our parents, his arms waving apologies, full of corrections, explanations: take-backs, do-overs. But our mother, crouched over, takes us both in her arms. "Oh my boys. My JoJo!" My father's compensating smiles assure the passersby there's no need to intervene. "Oh my talents! I want you to sing at my wedding. You're going to sing at my wedding." She can't stop hugging us. This is her concert triumph, though not the one she trained for. "Oh my boys, my JoJo! You were both so beautiful!"

IN TRUTINA

At the next summer recess, Jonah told Da they didn't need to come up to Boston to take us back to New York. He said we wanted to take the train home. We were old enough; it would be easier and cheaper, he claimed. God only knows how the request played with our parents, or what they heard in it. All I remember is how thrilled Mama was when we stepped out onto the platform at Grand Central. She kept spinning me around in the waiting room, sizing me up, like something had happened to me that I couldn't see.

Rootie wanted up on my shoulders. But she was growing faster than I was, too big to carry more than a few steps. "How come you're getting weaker, Joey? The world is beating on you?" I laughed at her, and she got angry. "Serious! That's what Mama says. She wants to know how many ways the world is going to beat on you."

I searched my parents for an explanation, but they were fussing over Jonah, consoling him over the *World's Best Opera Plots* clothbound edition he'd forgotten on the train.

"Don't laugh at me." Rootie pouted. "Or I'll fire you as my brother."

We sang together that summer, for the first time in half a year. We'd all gotten better, Ruth most dramatically. She held down moving lines, following along on the staff, getting rhythms and pitches together on only a couple of tries. She had succeeded in cracking the musical hieroglyphics earlier than any of us. She seemed different to me now, a kind of charmed creature. She rolled about, cackling at her luck in having her brothers around again. But she no longer needed us, nor thought to tell me the million discoveries she'd made in my absence. I felt shy around her. A year apart had made us forget how to be siblings. She performed for me, miming anyone I could name, from Da's craziest ancient colleagues to her beloved Vee, our landlady. She could turn around and hood herself with her hands, and, when she turned back, have aged her face a century. "Don't do that!" Mama shuddered. "It's just not natural!" So Rootie did it more. It made me laugh every time.

The reunited Strom family quintet resurrected all their favorite bits of near-forgotten repertoire. With Ruth a real member now, we polished up the Byrd Mass for Five Voices, hanging on to the suspensions in the frail Agnus Dei, as if to keep it forever from the perjury of having to resolve. All my family wanted was to get each of our plates up in the air and spinning at the same time. We took our tempi from Jonah now. He had a dozen explanations why a piece should go faster or slower, places where it should broaden or swell. He dismissed the composer's written indications. "Who cares what some poor sucker hundreds of years ago thought the piece meant? Why listen to *him*, just because he wrote the thing?" Da agreed: The notes were there to serve the evening's needs, and not the other way around. At Jonah's insistence, we made dirges of jigs and jigs of dirges, for no better reason than the pulse in his own inner ear.

He made us sing several of Kimberly's treasures. My parents were game for any excursion, however otherworldly, so long as it somehow swung. But Jonah was not happy with simply dictating the night's program. He wanted to conduct. He corrected Da's technique, corrections that came straight out of János's mouth. Da just laughed him off and continued manufacturing pleasure the best way he knew.

One evening toward summer's end, just before Jonah and I returned to Boylston, he stopped Mama in midphrase. "You could get a smoother tone and have less trouble with the *passaggio* if you kept your head still."

Mama set her sheet music down on the spinet and just stared at him. Movement was why we'd always sung. Singing meant being free to dance. What other point? My mother just looked at my brother, and he tried to hold her gaze. Little Root whimpered, flapping her sheet music back and forth and shaking like a dervish to distract attention. My father's face drained, as if his son had just spouted a slur.

Solitude passed through my mother's mind. In her hush, even Jonah wavered. But his chance to recant was lost in silence. My mother just studied him, wondering what species she had brought into the world. At last, she laughed, through a crook in her lips that wouldn't seal. "*Passaggio?* What do you know about *passaggio?* A boy whose voice hasn't even broken yet!"

He had no idea what the word meant. Just another arcane trinket he'd stolen from the Monera girl. Mama looked out at him across the plain of estrangement he'd made, staring at her foreign offspring until Jonah wilted and bowed his head. Then she reached out and buffed his almond hair. When she spoke again, her voice was low and haunted. "You sing your song, child. And I'll sing mine."

All our heads moved through the next madrigal, Jonah's most vigorous of all. But we never danced again with the same abandon. Never again without self-consciousness, now that we knew what we looked like to the conservatory world.

In August, back at Boylston, the headmaster decreed that I should bunk with Jonah and two older midwestern boys. By rule, the younger grades slept in long wards on the building's top floor, while the smaller dorms below were reserved for the senior students. But we two had brought havoc into this orderly musical Eden. The parents of one classmate had already removed their boy from school, and two others threatened the same action if their children were forced to sleep in the same room with us. This was the year Brown allegedly beat the Topeka Board of Education. We didn't have much of a social studies track at that school.

For whatever reasons, Boylston kept us on. Maybe it was the size of

Jonah's talent. Maybe they figured how much they stood to gain down the years, if they survived the gamble. No one ever told Jonah and me that we were putting the place to the test. No one had to. Our whole lives were a violation. As far back as we were anything, that's who we were.

They put us in a cinder-block cubicle with Earl Huber and Thad West, two freshmen keener on rule busting than we ever were. Neither of those two would have wound up anywhere near such a school without strategizing and savvy stage-door parents. Thad's and Earl's parents gave the nod to their boys' new roommates: We would at least keep their sons close to the spotlight. To Thad and Earl themselves, the Strom boys were golden outsiders, mud in the eye of apostolic Boylston, their ticket to open rebellion.

Our new room was a shoe box, but to me, it felt like a virgin continent. Twin pine bunk beds left only enough space for two half-sized writing desks, two chairs, and two cedar closets with two inset drawers each. The day we moved in, Thad and Earl stretched in their stacked bunks like ecstatic convicts, waiting for their black bunk mates to arrive. From the first words out of my mouth, I perpetually disappointed them.

They both came from one of those midsized C cities in Ohio. They were mythic creatures to me, like Assyrians or Samaritans: boys from magazine ads and radio dramas, sandy, groomed, and straight, speaking with flat tractor drones that cut in straight lines all the way to the horizon. Their half of the room overflowed with die-cast P-47 Thunderbolts, bottle cap collections, Buckeye pennants, and a Vargas girl who could flip over and become Bob Feller the instant there was a knock at the door.

Jonah's and my side of the cell had only a wall shelf of pocket scores and an illustrated set of the *Lives of the Great Composers* pamphlets. "That's it?" Earl said. "You cats call that home decorating?" Shamed, we hung up a photo that Da had given us, a blurry black-and-white print from the Palomar Observatory Sky Survey, showing the North American nebula. For official housewarming and back-to-school music, Thad set his record player belting away on the finale of Beethoven's Ninth. They were bad influences on us in every way but the one they wanted. Jonah picked up a red pen, and on the matting below the cloud of stars, he scribbled the full harmonization of the chorale. We checked the score. He made just two mistakes in the inner lines.

Earl and Thad dreamed of becoming jazz musicians, driven as much by a need to spite their folks as by their twitching love of rhythm. They thought of themselves as fifth columnists, deep behind enemy classical lines. "Swear it," Earl always said. "If I ever start humming anything French? Mercy-killing time."

Earl and Thad talked in what they took for state-of-the-art Village slang, passed through so many rounds of Telephone, it always came out sounding more greenhorn than Greenwich. "You're the puma's snarl, Strom One," Earl would tell Jonah. "Absolutely top Guatemalan yellow-fingered fruit, at the moment. But you're about to go over Niagara any minute, cool cat. Then we're gonna hear you wail."

"That's right," Thad punctuated.

"What do you think, Strom Two?" Earl never looked at me when he talked. It took me much of that first September to realize who Strom Two was. Earl would lie back on his bunk, playing his thighs like a trap set, patting the air for the cymbals, hissing an uncanny imitation of brushes, his tongue pressed against his front teeth. "Huh, baby? You think our man's going to survive the Big Drop?" Earl reveled in his status as the school's lowest voice, beating all comers by two full tones. "Look around. How many of last year's thirteenies are still with us? Few and proud, my friends. Few and proud."

"That's right," added Thad in his recently minted tenor, ever on cue.

Jonah shook his head. "You two are so full of hot air, you're going to hit a power line and explode."

"That's right, too," Thad conceded.

Jonah loved our roommates, the simple adolescent doting on difference that atrophies the instant that contact ends. He scoffed at their rube-hipster predictions. But he knew better than anyone that his vocal fall was coming. His voice stayed clean and crack-free through puberty's first guerrilla uprisings, with no sign of the looming catastrophe. But his coming break was his constant terror. He stayed out of the sun, refused to exercise, ate only pears and oatmeal in minuscule portions, inventing new remedies daily in a desperate attempt to stop the unstoppable flow.

One night, he woke me up out of a dead sleep. In the derangement beyond midnight, I thought someone had died.

"Joey, wake up." He spoke in a leaky whisper, to keep from rousing Earl and Thad. He wouldn't stop shaking my shoulder. Something hideous had torn into our lives. "Joey. You're not going to believe this. I've got two little hairs growing out of my nuts!"

He took me to the bathroom to show me the development. More than the hairs, I remember his terror. "It's happening, Joey." His voice was hushed, near-petrified. He had only these few moments to get out his last clear words before he turned werewolf.

"Maybe you should pluck them?"

He shook his head. "It's no good. I've read about that. They'll just grow back faster." He looked at me, pleading. "Who knows how many days I have left?"

We both knew the truth. A boy's voice before it breaks promises very little about what it will sound like after. The most spectacular caterpillar alive might host a moth. Magnificent tenors sometimes rose up out of hopeless croakers. But consummate boy sopranos often ended up average. János Reményi's controversial program made boys sing right through the change, insisting on constant, coached use, all the way down to the settling point. I tried to assure him. "They'll keep you another year at least, no matter what."

Jonah just shook his head at me, condemned. He didn't want to live anywhere beneath perfection.

Each day I'd quiz him with a glance, and each day he'd just shrug, resigned. He went on singing, reaching his zenith even as his light was already going out. Whenever Jonah opened his mouth, the faculty within earshot sighed, knowing the end had to be near.

The end came at the Berkshire Festival. Serge Koussevitzky had died a few years before, and one of the conductor's lifelong friends now invited the Boylston Academy to sing in a massive memorial concert. To honor the dead champion of new music, Reményi had us do a few excerpts from Orff's *Carmina Burana*. Back in that era, the heyday of show-trial morality, making young students sing the lyrics of debauched medieval monks might have gotten him deported. But Boylston had for years been a bastion of Orff's teaching techniques. And no one, Reményi insisted, was better suited to sing Orff's hymns to Fortuna than those whose fates were still being formed. Reményi hired several Cambridge instrumentalists and supplemental adult voices, and we were off to Tanglewood.

I made the cut for the touring chorus. I figured they picked me to keep Jonah happy. Reményi's casting was masterful. He gave the drunken abbot of Cockaigne to Earl Huber, who sang it with the swagger of a Buckeye turned Beat poet. He assigned the song about the girl in the tight red dress who looks like the bud of a rose to Suzanne Palter, a seventh grader from Batesville, Virginia, who kept a Bible under her pillow so she could kiss it each night after lights-out. Latin was Latin, and Suzanne sang the shameless come-on with such robust chastity that even Reményi's cheeks colored.

For Jonah, János reserved the simplicity of "In trutina," that summa of ambiguous wavering:

In trutina mentis dubia	In the uncertain balance of my mind
fluctuant contraria	lewd love and modesty
lascivus amor et pudicitia.	flow against each other.
Sed eligo quod video,	But I can choose what I see,
collum iugo prebeo;	and I submit my neck to the yoke;
ad iugum tamen suave transeo.	to the delightful yoke, I yield.

In rehearsal, János coaxed Jonah up into a nimbus of sound. He took the song at half the speed it should have gone. Jonah floated into the phrase, hovering above the orchestra like a fixated kingfisher. This was two years before *Sputnik*, but the slow, lathelike turn he gave the line emanated from deep space. Any singer will tell you: The softer the sound, the harder to make. Holding back is more difficult than holding forth. But somehow, from the earliest age, my brother knew how to make a smallness larger than most singers' big. And he took his shattering piano gift to "In trutina."

Jonah hit his mark in every rehearsal except the first dress, when the ringer instrumentalists, who hadn't been warned, stumbled with listening. The rest of the chorus knew that if we could get as far as Jonah's number, we'd live. "In trutina" was the one sure spot in our overly ambitious program, the perfect, near-still climax that only music could give.

For the memorial, the Berkshires overflowed with more famous musicians than any of us had ever seen. Most of the Boston Symphony was there, as well as several composers and soloists whom Koussevitzky—via one rigged-up honorarium or another—had kept from starvation. Before the concert, Earl Huber ran over and tackled Jonah. "It's Stravinsky! Stravinsky's here!" But the man he pointed out looked more like the guy our parents paid to fix pipe leaks than the century's greatest composer.

Even the hard-core pros who performed alongside us were rattled by the caliber of the audience. Jonah stayed by me, in the wings, before we went on. He never understood nerves. It scared him to see it in me. He himself never felt safer than when he had his mouth open with notes coming out. But there on the stage at the Berkshire Festival, he learned about disaster.

Reményi launched "In trutina" at the expansive tempo he'd always taken it in rehearsal. Jonah started into his line as if it had only just then occurred to him. He ended the first stanza on a crest of wonder—lust and lewdness struggling in the balance.

His voice chose that moment to break in one crashing wave. None of us heard even a squeak in tone in his first stanza. But as he prepared to sing *"Sed eligo quod video,"* the next pitch wasn't there. Without a thought, he hit the words an octave lower, with only the slightest waver. He finished out the first stanza a soprano and came back in the second a fledgling tenor.

The effect was electrifying. For those few in the audience who knew Latin, the lyric found a depth it would never have again in any performance. Afterward, a few musicians even asked Reményi how he'd dreamed up the masterstroke.

Never again that high D, my brother's hallmark, out beyond the planet's pull. Never again the chaste mount up into airless altitudes, the ease of ignorance, the first tart rush of ecstasy, the ring of dazed bliss, as if he just that moment had discovered what climax might be and how he might bring himself to it anytime he liked. On the long bus ride back to Boston in the dark, Jonah said to me, "Well, thank God that's finally over." For the longest time, I thought he meant the concert.

LATE 1843—EARLY 1935

Delia Daley was light. In the gaze of this country: not quite. America says "light" to mean "dark, with a twist." By all accounts, her mother was even lighter. No Daley ever spoke of where their family's lightness came from. It came from the usual place. Three-quarters of all American Negroes have white blood—and very few of them as a matter of choice. So it was with Delia's mother, Nettie Ellen Alexander, Dr. William Daley's radiant conjugal trophy, his high-toned lifelong prize. He met her down in Southwark, the part of town where his family, too, had originally lived. "Originally" stretched the matter some. But the Daleys had lived there far enough back, in the scale of memory, for the place to shade off into something like origins.

William himself was the great-grandson of a freed house slave, James. James's owner, the Jackson, Mississippi, heiress Elizabeth Daley, after the death of her millionaire husband in 1843, was leveled by a revelation only a notch below the persecutor Saul's on the road to Damascus. Picking herself up after the blow, Elizabeth discovered that she'd turned Quaker. She learned the truth firsthand from the Society of Friends: Owning human beings would do to her soul, in the hereafter, everything it did so roundly to the bodies of her property in the recalcitrant here and now.

Elizabeth Daley set about dispersing her husband's plantation holdings as ferociously as he'd gathered them. She gave the bulk of the man's fortune to those scores of involuntary stakeholders whose work had, in fact, made the fortune for him. All the freed Daley slaves but one took their windfall profit shares and headed for Cape Mesurado—Christopolis, Monrovia—that diaspora in a diaspora, care of the American Colonization Society. African resettlement promised to solve all problems—holders' and slaves' alike—by exporting them to the Kru and Malinke, whose lands became the ante for cascading displacement.

The lone Daley house slave to stay behind was *light*. Almost as light as his former owner. James Daley was not a traveling soul. He suspected that near-black in Liberia would be no softer a fate than near-white in his inflicted, only home. So he chose the shorter voyage, accompanying Elizabeth to Philadelphia, William Penn's damaged experiment in brotherly love.

Elizabeth signed over to James a modest annuity. In almost every way, she treated him as her son, the sweetest available spite on the spirit of the man's father. James must have inherited the family business sense, for he turned his fair share of the Daley capital into a working grubstake. James would never have abandoned Elizabeth, except for her constant imploring that he do so. She insisted he learn a trade. He apprenticed at a Negro barbering shop that catered to whites, not far from the heart of the old town. The work was overlong and underpaid, but James found it ludicrously lucrative, given his employment history. Elizabeth wept when he finished his training. She died shortly after James set up his own shop, cutting the hair of well-off whites down in the Silk Stocking district.

There were still too few Negroes in the city then to raise white alarm. And James had been born knowing how to blunt white fear. His customers stayed loyal to him, and even tipped. He never returned to the South, or to any record of his enduring enslavement, except each night, in the dark, when work couldn't help him ward off memory. All night long, the waters cried to him.

While most of his race remained legal chattel, James Daley worked for himself, his only revenge on the ones he had once worked for. He cut hair from seven in the morning until nine at night. When the shop closed, he made deliveries, running his dray sometimes until sunrise. He did with little so that his sons might do with a little bit more. He tempered his boys in the furnace of his will. *Free to be spit on,* he taught them. *Free to be legally cheated. Free to be beaten. Free to be trapped and swindled at every turn. Free to decide how to answer such freedom.* Iron James and his steel sons fended off raids, dug in, pried open a little living space, and grew the business. After a shaky birth, it turned a modest profit every year of James's life.

Daley Barbering and Grooming Shop clung to its lot, a fair walk from the banks of the Delaware. It went from one chair to two. The sons grew up indentured to the cutting of straight, sandy hair. They could not cut their friends' or relatives' hair in their own shop or even tend the hair of one another, except at night, with the shade drawn. They could talk to and even touch the white man, so long as they had a scissors in their hands. When they put their scissors down for the day, even a graze of shoulders was assault.

James's second son, Frederick, kept even longer hours than his father. He lifted his head high enough to send his own son Nathaniel—like storming heaven—to Oxford, just outside the city, to attend the new colored college, Ashmun Institute, soon renamed Lincoln University. Nathaniel met his own tuition by singing with a jubilee. He returned, walking with a step his father couldn't fathom and his still-enslaved grandfather couldn't even see.

College didn't close up the Daleys' twoness; it tore it wide open. Nathaniel barnstormed through to his degree, talking of medicines, the healing arts—the old provenance of haircutters for centuries, when barbers doubled as dentists and even surgeons. "Doctors of the short robe," he told his brothers, to their brutal mirth. But the idea lodged deep, hushing them. "That was what we did, once. That's what we were. That's what we'll be again."

Iron James died, bewildered by the distance of his life's run. But before he passed from the earth's fact, he saw his grandson trade in the family's striped pole for a small pharmacy. This was decades before the Great Migration, when the Daleys could still sit anywhere on the trains, shop at department stores eager for their dollar, even send their children to the white public schools. Race was not yet all it would become. Daley Pharmacy served both races, each of which recognized good decoctions at the right price. Only after the southern flood did the clientele irreversibly divide.

Nathaniel Daley brought the family into the forms of legitimacy no Negro Daley had ever known. He shored up the business with the same legal tricks that crafty white folks used, folks who every now and then came by to knock the business back down some. Time passed, and the pharmacy survived every twist of white will. The Daleys began to think the game might almost be theirs to play.

William, the great-grandson, outstripped even Nathaniel's curve of hope. He ventured out to Washington, that watchtower on the Old South's border, to attend Howard. He came home almost a decade later, a doctor of medicine and certified member of the Talented Tenth. He never spoke of the years that twice landed him in a state of mental collapse. Medical school could break even those who weren't being pecked to death by Jim Crow. But William outlasted the curriculum, learning the nature of each muscle, artery, and nerve that composed the godly anatomy of every human.

William Daley, M.D., completed his internship at that same Negro hospital where his family had long suffered as model patients. Black doctor: He met all looks of surprise and alarm with cool possession. More: He fought alongside the dozens of his rank throughout the city to take up staff positions at the institutions where they served out their peonage. Advance, he insisted, was just a matter of permanent slogging. But even William, some reflecting nights, found the air at his new altitudes a little thin and dizzying.

Though James had long since passed beyond the colorless veil, Frederick lived long enough to see his grandson establish a modest family practice in a mixed residential neighborhood in the Seventh Ward, south of Center City. That's where the girl, Nettie Ellen Alexander, broke upon William like a womanly Johnstown flood. He neither searched her out nor made provision for her accidental arrival. She just appeared to torment him, merely twenty, yet finer in line than any creature of any color he'd ever properly seen. He hadn't looked at women for the eight long years he'd been in school, anatomy texts aside. Now, chancing upon this girl, he wanted to make up for his years of lost looking all in one go, squeezing them into the first afternoon he laid eyes on her.

Nettie smiled at him before she properly knew him. Flashed him a whole rank of perfect ivories, as if to say, *Took your time, didn't you?* Smiled at him *because* she didn't know him, but knew she would. A whole mess of muscles in her face squeezed together with enough pleasure at the sight of him to galvanize his own helpless mouth into foolish reciprocation. Miss Alexander's grin loosened a horde of silverfish inside him. Muscles that weren't on any anatomy exam twitched worse than those dead men's flexors on the dissection slab, brought back to life by that dry-cell practical joke beloved of medical students everywhere.

Medicine gave him no names for this condition. He found himself thinking of her upper thorax when thumping those of others. The dorsal surface of her scapula was something a sculptor might nick, sand, and polish for thirty years and still miss by a millimeter. Her sixth cervical vertebra's spinous process sprouted from the base of her neck like some starter bud for a coming set of wings. Each time the woman breathed, William tasted raspberry liquor, though she swore she never touched a drop.

The air around her shone, even in the Alexanders' parlor, where the couple sat, all the lamps doused, a conservation Nettie's father employed to make ends meet from month to brutal month. Her eyes put William in mind of fireflies, or luminous deep-sea fishes, living so dark for so long, they had to make their own light just to do a little subsistence fishing. The doctor could not fathom her glow, let alone say how she made it.

Nettie was *light*. Some days, her paleness almost frightened him away. It startled him and it nattered at his poise. He could feel folks turning to inspect them—*Those two? A pair?*—each time they stepped out together. Her lightness left him lapsing into feats of erudition, donning learning's armor each time he visited. He didn't relish the thought of adding one more twoness to his birthright. He told himself that yellow meant nothing. Said that he had to look past her tone, to the shadings of her spirit. Yes the woman was light, but it came from that lamp that she carried around inside her.

Still it dazzled him, this high-gold blaze. Whether her skin's shade or her hair's wave, whether posture, curve, carriage, or something more ghostly and finer, Nettie Ellen was the one whom William recognized, the crown he didn't know he'd been reaching out for until she stood sparkling in front of him, just past his trembling fingers.

But month after month, his hands panicked, afraid to close around so fine a thing. What if he were wrong? What if the lady's spark shot out indiscriminately, on everyone? What if the warmth Nettie showed him was more amusement than desire? That seed of gladness she set in him certainly felt like proof. But surely this woman transfixed every derelict buck that her twin beams trained upon.

Around her, William rose up into highest seriousness. He adored her with a gravity that bordered on mourning. Dignity, he imagined, was the one gift he could give her that no other man would think to offer. He alone in all Philly knew the worth of this woman, this pearl's rare price. His visits were reverential, his face creased with veneration.

Nettie thought the man a glowering rain cloud, but without the thunder or lightning. She suffered through a four-month courtship as sterile as any physician's clinic. He dragged her to lectures and museums, always adding his own elevating commentary. He walked her over every acre of Fairmont Park, both sides of the river, hobbling her with self-betterment until she begged him to take up cribbage, at which she gleefully commenced whipping him.

But William knew this cribbage queen for something really regal. He found dignity even in the way she horselaughed through a Bill Foster single-reeler picture. He described his practice to her, the work he did and hoped to do, the healthier future that modern medicine could bring to the hard-pressed folk of Southwark and Society Hill, once the poor and ignorant quit fearing it and let it in the door.

Worship needs a chapel, and William's was Nettie's parents' parlor. The room spilled over with chintz and cut-glass bowls and wing-back chairs that sprouted so many antimacassars, William finally took the hint and cut back on his own hair slicker. At his visits, Nettie's parents vanished into the back, leaving only a younger son chaperon for William to buy off with root-beer sticks or licorice. Then the room became their theater, their lecture room, their spiritual Oldsmobile, William holding forth, the solemn docent, while Nettie Ellen grinned at the man's talk as if it meant something.

He was lecturing one evening on Dr. James Herrick's recent clinical description of sickle-cell anemia—yet another scourge that plagued the black man with excess enthusiasm—when Nettie at last leaned across the backgammon board that served as their lone barrier and said to the good doctor, "Ain't you never gonna make a grab for me?" Her voice filled with simple practicality; the night was cold, and Nettie's parents were saving on the heat again. What good was a courter who wouldn't even keep you warm?

The doctor hung stunned in space, his mouth imitating his tie's opal stickpin. William Daley, uplift's agent, sat paralyzed with bafflement. So the woman did what the situation called for, leaning over even deeper and attaching the M of her upper lip to his astonished O.

Once Nettie taught the fellow what he was after, the stroll of their courtship stepped up to a canter. Dr. William Daley and Nettie Ellen Alexander were married within the year. Afterward, the lecture load was more evenly divided between them. She nudged his speeches forward with strategic encouragements. The scope and variety of her instruction never failed to amaze the doctor.

William prized his magnificent specimen even more after landing her. His new wife furnished the house on Catherine Street, with its solid bay-windowed turret, and she installed herself at the house's center, a genius of efficiency. At the end of the European war, she began to keep the books. With selfless efficiency, she set to work populating the household. She lost her beautiful firstborn, James, gave him up too quickly to God, who, after the Armistice, for His unknowable reasons, spread influenza around the world, settling into the Daleys' neighborhood with a special vigor.

Husband and wife battened down against the loss, cleaving to each other. But James's death claimed a piece of each of them. Nettie grew, if not harder, more guarded. Then strong-lunged Delia came, her mother's consolation, every wail of those stunned lungs a cause for joy. After a long and anxious gap, interpreted so differently by William and Nettie that they stopped talking about it, there came the rash of young ones: Charles, Michael, and at last the twins, Lucille and Lorene.

Over her husband's objections, Nettie had the children properly churched. She dressed and dragged them to Sunday school each week. Long before she married, she knew that William's freethinking would now and then burst out in some fresh foolishness about belief that she'd have to maneuver around. She'd raise no child an ignorant, self-ruling savage. Mother and brood went and celebrated, while the doctor stayed home and worked. On holidays, even he had to scrub and attend. He stood among the believers, singing lustily, even speaking the Creed, although he coughed at all references to the deity.

Nettie served as receptionist to William's patients, those endless processions of the ailing and infirm who passed through his office. A thriving man's wife, *and* light: The combination wasn't likely to endear her to the hard-pressed surrounding neighborhoods. But the woman had only to open her mouth and let one honeyed word trickle out for those around her to be caught.

She baked for her husband's patients. She made the rounds with him through that besieged community, administering her own doses of the listening cure at the sides of sickbeds in four adjacent districts. She kept the man attached to his patients, engaged and understandable. She remembered all their names for him. "You do what Dr. Daley tells you," she told them behind his back. "But go on ahead and mix up this little poultice, too. The Lord knows it can't kill you, and it might just help." As the doctor's reputation grew, he credited his constant efforts to keep up with the latest medical developments. But in this careful diagnosis, he was a minority of one.

She worshiped her man and also worked him. Both came to the same thing. "I marvel at you, William C. Daley," she declared, bringing a bromide to his office late one night. "What kind of studying you laying into now? *Human Nature and Conduct. The Varieties of Religious Experience. The Such-and-So-ology of Everyday Life.* James Joyce, *Useless.* Whoo-my. Fine black ship out there in all that cold white ice. Be careful you don't hit something and go down with all hands."

He rose up, a pillar of righteousness. "I am not *black*, any more than you are. The sole of my shoe is *black*. The coal we pay too much for every month is *black*. Look at me, woman. Look at yourself. Look at any brother of ours in the whole outcast race. You see *black?*"

"I see all sorts of carrying on. That's what I see."

"It's the other side that makes us *black*. The other side wants to know what it feels like to be a *problem*." For among all the treacherous white ice, he'd also read that light, mixed man, Du Bois. "Black's what the world wants us to be. How can we even see ourselves to be ourselves?"

She waved him away. As always when they talked such things, Nettie just shook her head at his notions. "You're whatever you want to be, I suppose. And whatever that is, Dr. Daley, you're my one of a kind."

In the long crescendo that stoked the twenties into a roar, everything Dr. Daley touched arose and walked. The clinic's success spread by word of mouth. New patients appeared in such numbers that he took to seeing them, against Nettie's wishes, on Sundays. He lucked into the perfect moment to refinance the house. Even with five children, even waiving every other indigent patient's payment, he found himself adding to his capital. His school debts and start-up costs melted away. He bought government bonds. His helpmate kept the books and ran the house with the old Alexander frugality. As his lone indulgence, William picked up a Chrysler Six hot off the line.

And still the country raced madly ahead of him. The white man had some covert entry that didn't even require Jim Crow to keep the Negro out. Dr. Daley studied the prosperity racket—the game of real riches, not the slow, hard-won advancement that had until then been his. The answer was there, staring at anyone who bothered to look: stocks. The country was gulping down equities like so much nerve tonic. Every thuggish son of an Irish immigrant knew the secret: Buy America. And finally, Dr. Daley did just that. He did so, over the scandalized Nettie's howls, and later, without her knowledge. Stock picking was worlds easier than doctoring. Nothing to it, really. You bought. The price went up. You sold. You found another investment, a little more expensive, to shelter the compounded cash. The whole scheme kept feeding itself, as long as you wanted to ride.

The daily fight for a reasonable existence turned by degrees into another struggle. By 1928, he found himself toying with the newly introduced De Soto, maybe even a small second house outside of town, in the country somewhere.

"Country house?" Nettie Ellen laughed. "*Country* house? With colored folks by the tens of thousands trying to get out of the country up where we already are?"

His wife fought him over his ill-gotten gains, which continued to grow. One evening in that warm, early spring of the following year, while taking his evening constitutional around the neighborhood, he was struck by the realization that dabbling—or, as had become his practice, submerging—in the stock market was wrong. Not wrong, as his wife had it, because the Lord abhorred gambling. Her Lord, after all, had staked the oldest, biggest crapshoot in existence. No: Making money on pure speculation was wrong, William now saw, for two inarguable reasons. First, every winner in this game profited from some loser, and Dr. Daley no longer desired to take anything away from another man, even a white one. Even if all he stole was opportunity, he could not profit. For the theft of opportunity was the original sin.

And further: No man in God's crapshoot had the right to profit from anything but the sweat of his brow. Labor was the lone human activity capable of creating wealth. Any other accumulation was just plantationism, disguised. That spring evening, taking the air, waving to his neighbors as they rocked themselves on their porch swings, William swore off not just the market but also banks, savings and loans, and any other institution that promised something for nothing.

Within the week, he turned his holdings into cash, bought a fireproof Remington safe, and kept his net worth stashed inside. In the fall of that year, when the whole national pyramid of speculation collapsed, he found himself standing up on a city of rubble.

Hardship saved its best for the colored man. Within two years, half of working Negro Philadelphia had no livelihood. The WPA, when it came, paid coloreds only a fraction of white wages, when it hired coloreds at all. Jobless, white America turned even more vicious than when the living had been easy. Lynchings tripled. They strung up Herndon and railroaded the Scottsboro boys. Harlem burned; Philly would be next. Catherine Street teetered, threatening to go the way of all Southwark.

Medicine, at least, remained Depression-proof, if not his patients' ability to pay. People paid in fresh vegetables, tinned fruit, errands, and odd jobs. In the deflated barter economy, the cash in the Remington safe went further, each increasingly desperate month. William and his bewildered Nettie looked around, to find themselves living up on a sheltered bluff, looking over the devastation of their neighborhood.

Their children would go to college—no more than the Daleys had enjoyed for two generations and no less than Nettie Alexander had herself once dreamed of, without hope of reaching. They fed their young on the upward hope of the oppressed: *How much we've done, from inside the tomb. How much more we might do, with just a little living space.*

Such was the squeezed hope that made up Delia's birthright. William's first child to live was his pride and religion. "You're my trailblazer, baby. A colored girl, learning everything there is to learn, a colored girl sailing through college, following a profession, changing the laws of this country. What's wrong with this idea?"

"Nothing's wrong with it, Daddy."

"Damn right, nothing. Who's going to stop it?"

"Nobody," Delia would reply, sighing.

They could stop her from seeing *Steamboat Willie* and *Skeleton Dance* down at the Franklin Cinema. They could restrict her to the Colored Players or send her away with nothing. They could stop her buying a root-beer float at the drugstore ten blocks from her house. They could arrest her if she crossed over the invisible neighborhood line. But they couldn't stop her from humoring her father.

He drilled her. "You've got a miracle to work. How's that miracle not going to happen?"

"No way it's not going to happen."

"That's my girl. Now tell me, my talented offspring. What can't your people do?"

Her people could do anything. The week never went by without some further proof. Just doing the same work as a European, the Negro already surpassed him, for the one was filling his house from the attic on down, while the other was carting his furnishings up from the cellar. Negroes hadn't yet begun to stand and deliver their full abilities. Time would spring them. The future would shake with their concerted movements.

"What are you going to be when you grow up, my girl?"

"Anything I want."

"You know it, beauty. Anyone ever tell you that you look a whole lot like your old man?"

"Ugh, Daddy. Never."

But five right answers out of six was not bad at all.

By thirteen, her race's destiny hunched the child over. Her mother alone consoled Delia. "You take your time, honey. Never you mind about knowing everything. Nobody ever knew everything yet, nor is going to, until the Last Day, when things no one can guess are going to get laid out on the table. Even your father's gonna have a few surprises waiting for him."

The girl had music in her. So much music, it frightened both parents. At Delia's birth, Dr. Daley installed a piano in the parlor, a salute to prosperity and a striding, rag thank-you to his ancestors, offered up in private, after all the patients went home. His little black pearl crawled up on the bench and picked out melodies before she even learned her letters.

She had to have lessons. Her parents found her a college-trained music teacher who served the neighborhood's better families. The music teacher marveled to the doctor that his daughter might outdo any white girl her age. Might outdo the college-trained music teacher herself, William suspected, given a few years.

Every seventh day, Delia's mother took all five of the children, climbing all over one another like crabs in a pot, to Bethel Covenant, the center of all music. In that weekly ecstatic keeping of faith and bearing of witness, Delia fell in love with singing. Singing was something that might make sense of a person. Singing might make more sense of life than living had to start with.

Delia sang fearlessly. She threw back her head and nailed free-flying notes like a marksman nails skeet. She sang with such unfurling of self that the congregation couldn't help but turn and look at the teenager, even when they should have been looking skyward.

The choir director asked her to sing her first solo. Delia demurred. "Mama, what should I do? It's not really decent, is it? To put yourself on display like that?"

Nettie Ellen shook her head and smiled. "When the people come for you, your choice is already made. All you can do is lift up the light God sets in your hand. That light don't belong to you anyway. It's not yours to hide."

That was all the answer the girl wanted. As rehearsal, she sang for the combined Sunday schools. She prepared one of the *New Songs of Paradise*, by Mr. Charles Tindley, the famous composer from over at East Calvary Methodist Episcopal: "We'll Understand It Better By and By." She took the tune at full force and let out all her stops. Here and there hands flew up—half holding back the rush of glory, half giving in, overcome by praise. After that glorious testimonial, Delia looked for something more somber. The junior choir director, Mr. Sampson, found her a piece called "Ave Maria," by a long-dead white man named Schubert.

Delia could feel them as she sang, the hearts of the flushed congregation flying up with her as she savored the song's arc. She sheltered those souls in her sound and held them as motionless as the notes themselves, in that safe spot up next to grace. The audience breathed with her, beating to her measure. Her breath expanded sufficiently to take her across even the longest phrase. Her listeners were in her, and she in them, so long as the notes lasted.

When she finished, the congregation let out their collective breath. Their lungs emptied in a mass sigh, reluctant to leave the music's sanctuary. The rush Delia felt as the last beat died outstripped any pleasure she'd ever known. Her heart pounded with the sound all earthly applause only imitated.

Afterward, she stood in the greeting line next to the pastor, still shaken, still humming. People she knew only by sight grabbed and hugged her, pumping her hand as if she'd just put them right in their own hearts. Delia told her mother on the walk home. "Three separate people said I was going to be our next Marian."

"You listen here, missy. Pride goeth . . . Just remember that. Pride goeth before every fall you can even think to fall. And believe me, you can fall in a thousand more ways than you can hope to rise."

Delia didn't press for explanations. It took some doing to exasperate her mother, but once she did, negotiation was over for the day. "You're not our next anyone," Nettie Ellen muttered, warding off the evil eye as they turned up the parkway. "You're our first Delia Daley."

Delia asked her father about the magic name.

"The woman's our cultural vanguard. Brightest light we've thrown off in a good long time. White men say we lack the skill or the will to take on their best music. This woman shows them up for fools. They don't have a singer this side of Hell, let alone Mississippi, who can touch that one. You listening, daughter? I thought you wanted to know."

Daughter wanted more than knowing could contain. But already she was miles above her father's lecture. Years. She built an image of that voice even before she heard it. When the radio finally played her the real thing, the real Miss Anderson's sound did not match the one she'd imagined. It *was* the one.

"You want to sing?" her father told her after that broadcast. "There's your teacher. You study that woman."

And Delia did. She studied everything, devouring, whole, every scrap of music she could gather. She exhausted one neighborhood vocal teacher and demanded another. She joined the Philadelphia People's Choral Society, the finest Negro choir in the city. She began going to Union Baptist, musical magnet of black Philadelphia, singing there every Sunday, rubbing shoulders with whatever enchantment had given Miss Anderson wings.

The move shattered her mother. "Taking up with the Baptists? What's the matter with your real church? We've always been A.M.E."

"It's the same God, Mama." Close enough, anyway, for human ears.

Too late, William Daley discovered what fire he'd lit in his daughter. He took to futile dousing. "You have a duty, girl. Abilities you haven't even discovered yet. You have to make something worthy of your future."

"Singing is worthy."

"It has its use. But damn it. Only as something a person does to round out a real day's work."

"It *is* a day's work, Daddy. My day. My work."

"It can't support a body. It's not enough for you." The long, careful upward Daley climb threatened to crash down all around him. "It's not a life. You can't make a living out of *singing*, any more than you can out of playing dominoes."

"I can make a living at anything I want, Daddy." She ran her fingers through the few remaining ripples of his retreating hair. He was a bull, ready to charge. But still, she stroked him. "My papa taught me that nobody's going to stop my miracle from happening."

Their battle turned fierce. He said there'd be no money for singing school. So in her junior year of high school, she got a job changing sheets in the hospital. "A maid," William said. "The kind of work I'd hoped never to see any of my offspring ever do."

He fell back on every feat of oratory he could raise. But he stopped short of forbidding her to follow the path of her choosing. No Daley would ever again have a master, even another of her own. His daughter's life was hers to advance or to squander. A part of him—a tiny, grain-sized irritant—fell back, impressed that the flesh of his flesh could run so gladly to ruin, as determined as the most affluent, willful white.

She applied to the city's great conservatory. The school scheduled her for an audition. Delia's coaches and choir conductors did their best to prepare her. She brushed up those church recital songs that best showed off her slow, sustained control. For a showier complement, she learned an aria—"Sempre libera," from *La Traviata*. She picked it up phonetically from an old 78, guessing at the more exuberant syllables.

Delia chose to sing a cappella, rather than risk being compromised by any fervent but finger-faulty accompanist. It seemed an act of bold self-confidence, of calculated risk. The professionals would doubtless shake their heads over her lack of training. But Delia could make up in pure sound what she lacked in finish. Her held high notes were her ace in the hole. They thrilled her to unleash, and they never failed to devastate every warm-up audience she tried them on, with the sole exception of her savage little brothers. She felt ready to face any trial, even the sight-singing, where she knew she was weakest.

She chose and vetoed half a dozen outfits—too formal, too plain, too sexy, too sacky. She settled on a deep blue flare-shouldered dress with white accents at the cuffs and collar: classic, with a hint of flash. She looked so good that a fretting Nettie Ellen took her picture in it. Delia showed up half an hour early at the institute, beaming at each stray body dragging through the foyer, sure that any one of them might be Leopold Stokowski. She approached the receptionist, faking a confident smile. "My name is Delia Daley. I have an audition with the vocal faculty at two-fifteen?"

She might have been the stone statue of the Commendatore, barging into Don Giovanni's front room. The receptionist flinched. "Two . . . fifteen?" She flipped weakly through random paperwork. "Do you have a letter of confirmation?"

Delia showed the letter, her arms going cold. *Not this. Not here. Not in this castle of music.* Her explanations raced ahead, while reason stayed behind in the guilty vehicle, arrested.

She handed over the letter, forcing her numbed fingers to release it. The receptionist scoured a massive file, all polite efficiency. "Would you mind taking a seat? I'll be with you in a moment." She disappeared, her high heels a cut-time clip, down the music-riddled corridors. She returned with a stocky, balding man in tortoise-rimmed glasses.

"Miss Daley?" All grins. "I'm Lawrence Grosbeck, associate dean and a professor of voice." He didn't offer his hand. "Please forgive us. A letter should have gone out to you. All the positions in your range have already been offered. It looks, also, as if we're probably about to lose one of our soprano faculty. You're . . . You . . ."

The flush started in her abdomen and spread in waves. The burning rushed up to her cheeks, her eyelids, the fluting of her ears. Futile good manners, pointless self-preservation fought down the urge to do violence to this violation. Down the hall, the soprano ahead of her struggled through her set piece. At the desk, the soprano after her handed over her papers. Delia kept beaming at this man, this squat, enormous, impenetrable power. She smiled, still trying to win him over, all the while tucking her head in shame.

The dean, too, heard the evidence, teeming all around them. "You're welcome, of course, to . . . to sing for us anyway. If you . . . like."

She bit down the urge to damn him and his kind for all time. "Yes. Yes. I'd like to sing. For you."

Her executioner led her down the corridor. She followed, stumbling and numb. She drew one covert finger along the paneled walls that she'd dreamed of. She would never touch them again in this life. Her ankles softened; she reached out to steady herself. She looked down on her body from above, her whole torso shaking. She lay in a deep snowbank under the January night, her body shivering, stupidly failing to realize she was already dead. Everything she'd worked for was lost. And she'd just agreed to give her destroyers one more chance to mock her.

As they reached the room appointed for her pointless, rigged hearing, her shaking undid her. Four white faces stared at her from behind a long table cluttered with papers, faces like clocks, each a passive mask of polite confusion. The dean was saying something to her. She couldn't hear him. Her sight shrank to a cloud no more than a foot across. She fumbled for the piece she'd prepared and couldn't remember it.

Then the sound came. Her voice faltered back to its first authority. Her singing stopped her auditioners, hushed their rustling. She slipped in pitch. She heard herself lose the consistent tone that had been hers in every rehearsal. Yet it tore out of her, her life's performance. She sang beyond their power to disgrace, and forced recall upon her judges. *This song; this one.*

The Verdi aria sounded, for once, like the indictment it was, the condemnation hiding under its crazed hymn to pleasure. When she finished, the judges answered with silence. They went through their charade, giving her an aria from Handel's *Acis and Galatea* to sight-sing: "As When the Dove Laments Her Love." Delia nailed it perfectly, still hoping to reverse reality, smiling through to the double bar.

At last, Dean Grosbeck spoke. "Thank you, Miss Daley. Is there anything else you'd like to add?"

Emptied, she had no encore. "I've Been 'Buked" rose up into her mouth, but she bit down on it. No revenge but refusal. When she left the audition room, all the soprano positions still filled, she saw the eyes of one of her examiners, a frail white woman her mother's age, spilling over, wet with music and shame.

She stumbled back across town, home. Her father sat in his study, reading in his red Moroccan leather chair.

"They turned me down before I even opened my mouth."

Across her father's face, every impotent recourse moved like a crew of migrant field hands: the blocked petitions, the denied lawsuits, the humiliating retries—next year, the year after, killed by the same standing refrain. He rose from his chair and approached her. He took her shoul-

ders and looked into her, the last lesson of childhood, fired to a hard finish in that old furnace they now shared.

"You're a singer. You build yourself *up*. You make yourself so damn
good, they can't *help* but hear you."

Delia had stood through the afternoon's ordeal. Now in her father's
caring gaze, she fell. "How, Daddy? Where?" And she broke down in that
finishing fire.

He helped her find a music school that would hear her. One at least
competent. He came to her admission audition and stood by, gripping the
air, as she passed, with a scholarship. He staked her the balance of her tuition, although she kept her job, to pay for those extra lessons he couldn't
understand. He went to her every recital and was on his feet clapping before the last held tonic could decay. But both father and daughter knew,
without ever admitting as much to each other, that she would never, now,
be schooled at the upper level of her skills, let alone the lower reaches of
her dreams.

A TEMPO

Clever Hänsel's voice has broken and won't ever be put back together.
"Breaking," Da tells him, "is the arrow of time. It is how we can know
which way the melody is running. Breaking is what turns yesterday into
tomorrow. Soprano before; tenor after. Deep physical principle!"

This is our Da's faith. All other things may change, but time remains
the same. "Growing disorder: This is how we must tell time. Lunch is not
only never free; it gets, every day, a little more expensive. This is the
only sure rule in our cosmos. Every other fact, you will one day exchange. But bet against the Second Law, and you are doomed. The name
isn't strong enough. Not second anything. Not a law of nature. It *is* nature."

He raises us to believe this. "Things fall down and get more broken.
More mixed. Mixing tells us which way we point in time. This is not a
consequence of matter or space. It's the thing that gives time and space
their shape." Who knows what the man means? He's his own independent
country. All we know is: No one breaks the Second Law and lives. Like
don't take candy from strangers. Like look both ways before you cross
the street. Like loose lips sink ships, a law I will never quite get until long
after all my ships have sailed.

And yet our father's unshakable faith is flawed. His science hides an embarrassment that absorbs him day and night, as if he's God's book-keeper and can't sleep until the columns balance. "At the heart of this beautiful system, a little heart attack. *Eine Schande.* Help me, my boy-chik!" But I can do nothing for him. The discrepancy drives him a little crazier every day. This scandal is his arrow, and shows him which way he runs.

I catch him working on it one evening, when I'm home for Christmas. He's in his cave, perched over a sheaf of paper marked off into a grid of blue squares. Drawings all over, like a comic book. "What are you work-ing on?"

"Working?" He always takes a moment to surface. "I'm not working on anything. This damn thing is working on me!" He likes to say that word, when Mama can't hear. "You know what is the meaning of 'para-dox'? This is the biggest damn paradox human beings have ever built." I feel guilty, responsible. "Mechanics, which I believe absolutely, says time can flow either way. But thermodynamics, which I believe even absolut-lier . . ." He clucks his tongue and waves a finger in the air, a traffic cop. "Einstein wants to kill the clock. Quantum needs it. How can both these fine theories be right? Right now—whatever *now* means!—they don't even mean the same thing by *time.* It looks bad, Yoseph. You can imagine. A big family fight in public. The dirty little secret of physics. Nobody talks about it, but everybody knows!"

He hangs his head in shame, leaning over his blue graph paper. Clown-ing for me, but suffering all the same. The world is full of snares. The Russians have the bomb. We're at war with China. Jews are executed as spies. Universities refuse my father as a conference speaker. His marriage makes him a criminal in two-thirds of the United States. But this is the crisis in my Da's *Zeitgeist*: this flaw, this blot on the whole clan of scien-tists, on all of creation, whose housekeeping they do. It turns him around in time.

Our family, too, is turned around. Jonah's voice has fallen an octave. It lies broken at the bottom of a well. Mine teeters on the verge of the same fall. We're home again, on what must be my second summer recess. Da's in a deep, jovial gloom. My little sister sits in his study with him, sharing his excited misery, his graph paper, his drawing tools, her hands stroking her chin, her face pretending to think. Mama teases him, which tears me up, given Da's obvious distress. Something in his proofs has gone horribly wrong.

"Why go on believing it if it upsets you?"

"It's mathematics," he thunders. "Belief has nothing to do with the numbers."

"Fix the numbers, then. Make them listen to you."

Da heaves a breath. "This is exactly what they will not do."

I'm in hell. My parents aren't even arguing. Worse. To argue, they'd have to understand each other. Our Da can understand nothing anymore. He's come to the conclusion that there is no time.

"No time for what?" I ask.

He shakes his head, stricken. "For anything. At all."

"My, my." Mama laughs, and Da flinches at the sound. "Where has the time gone? It was here just a minute ago."

It doesn't exist, says Da. Nor, apparently, does motion. There is only more likely and less likely, things in their configurations, thousands, even millions of dimensions, hanging fixed and unmoving. We put them in order.

"We feel a river. In reality, there is only ocean." And my father is at the bottom of it. "There is no becoming. There is just *is*."

Mama waves him off and heads to the front room to clean. "Excuse me. Can't keep my dirt waiting. Call me when you get the universe started up again." She chuckles from the end of the hallway, a laugh lost under the roar of her upright vacuum.

I'm alone with Da in his study, but I can give him no comfort. He shows me the undeniable calculations. Everything spelled out in meticulous detail, like a full pocket score of an inevitable symphony. He speaks less to this lecture room of one desperate student than to some hidden examiner. "In mechanics, the film can run in reverse. In thermodynamics, it cannot. You would know at once, by the feel of the current, if you were swimming against the stream of time. But Newton wouldn't. Neither would Einstein!"

"Don't let them in the water," I suggest.

He points out a tiny solo equation buried in his notes' cluttered orchestration. "This is the timeless wave function of Schrödinger."

He doesn't mean *timeless*. Who knows what he means?

"This is the only way we have. The only thing for tying the universe to subatomic pieces. The only one to satisfy the constraints of Mach. The function that must connect the too big with the too small."

It seems important to him that the thing move. But the universe's wave function stands still. The score hangs in eternity, unable to progress from start to last except in imagined performance. The piece everywhere always already is. Our family's musical nights have led him to this insight. Music, as his hero Leibniz says, is an exercise in occult mathematics by a soul that doesn't even know it's counting.

"We are the ones who make a process. We remember the past and predict the future. We feel things breaking forward. Make an order for before and after. But in the other hand . . ."

"*On* the other hand, Da." Forever teaching him.

"On the other hand, the numbers do not know . . ." He stops, baffled. But true to the sheets full of symbols, he rallies. "The laws of planetary motion say nothing about clockwise or counterclockwise. The year might be running summer, spring, winter, fall, and we wouldn't be able to say! That bat driving the ball forward comes to the same thing as the ball driving the bat back. This is what we mean by a system being predictable. By a deterministic world. Time falls away, an unneeded variable. With Einstein, too. One set of reversible equations already fixes for us the whole series of unfolding time. Plug in a value for any moment of time, and you know the values for all other moments, before *and* after. We say that the present completely causes the future. But it's a funny think?"

"*Thing*, Da. A funny *thing*."

"That's what I said! A funny think, as far as the mathematics? We can say also the present has determined the past. One path, whether you walk down it or up." His right-hand fingers cut a swathe across his left palm. Then his hands reverse. "It's not even that fate has already been decided. Even that idea is itself still too trapped in the notion of flow."

He still works on other, more movable things. He solves a thousand unsolved problems, important papers, where his name appears nowhere except in the acknowledgments. He keeps his colleagues publishing, long after his own flow stops. His colleagues marvel at him, so deep in his debt that they will never tunnel out. They say he doesn't work forward from the problems they hand him. He jumps into the future, where he sees the answers. Then works his way back to the here and now.

"You could make a fortune," they tell him.

"Ha! If I could take messages from the future, money would be the last thing I'd waste my time on!"

Mama says he can only solve problems for his colleagues, not for himself. "Oh, my love! You can't crack the ones you care about. Or maybe you only care about the ones not even you can wrap your head around?"

He's never once tried to wrap his head around what time is doing to us, to our family. He struggles, in his study, to do away with time. But the world will do away with all five of us before then, if it can. Da's score of scribbles distresses him more than any slur ever leveled at him. He studies his pile of scrawl the way he reads those letters from Europe, the endless unanswering answers to the hanging questions he rewrites and resends, every year, to changing addresses abroad. He's lost his family. His mother and father, his sister, Hannah, and her husband, who was not even a Jew. No one can tell Da that they're still alive. But no one will tell him they're dead.

Mama says they would have found us by now. If the German officials that Da writes to can't say where they are, then that says everything. But Da says, "We cannot speak about what we do not know." And beyond that, he doesn't.

In Europe, he tells me, the horse races are run around the oval backward. I think: You give your winnings to the track, then wait until the race reaches its start to see how much you bet. I love the idea: Jonah and me, already with him, over in Europe, back before Da has even come to America to meet Mama. What a surprise we'll be to her. I laugh at the idea of meeting all Da's missing relatives, of them meeting us, before we're even born, before they all go to the place Mama tells us they have almost certainly gone to.

But for the answers he needs, there is no certainty. Da gets another letter, emptied of all content but bureaucracy. He shakes his head, then starts another hopeless letter back. "Birthplace of Heisenberg," he says. "Of Schrödinger's cat." In his same study, after another year, he tells me, "We have no access to the past. All our past is contained in the present. We have nothing but records. Nothing but the next set of histories."

He holds his head while looking at the pictures he has drawn, the ones that kill time. He searches for the flaw in what he fears he's just proved. He mutters about Poincaré's recurrence, about any isolated system returning to its initial state an endless number of times. He speaks of Everett and Wheeler, of the entire universe budding off into copies of itself at every act of observation. Sometimes he forgets I'm there. He's still at his desk half a decade later. I'm in college. Mama's finished vacuuming for good, done with all cleaning. I stand behind Da, chopping his hunched shoulders. He hums with preoccupied gratitude, but in a minor key.

Time may exist again, according to the numbers. He's not sure. He's even less sure if that would be cause for celebration.

Increasingly—time's arrow—he makes no distinction between absurd and profound. His universe has begun to contract for him, time running backward toward some youngest day's Big Crunch. There are secrets buried in gravitational relativity that even its discoverer had not foreseen. Secrets others won't uncover for years to come. And he's foreseeing them. He draws a picture of what quantum gravity will have to look like. He counts up all the curled-up dimensions that we will need just to survive the four we are already lost in.

Breaking is what gives the flow direction. Broken voices. Broken traces. Broken promises. Broken lives. Broken bonds. Whether it exists or not, time has been putting in overtime.

He works a private system, trancelike, lost in some nowhen, plugging variables into a hedge spread whose complexities he no longer bothers to explain to me. "Augustine said he knew what time was so long as he didn't think about it. But the minute he thought about it, he did not know."

He turns those thickening features on me, that cheerful look of mourning, the tunnel of those eyes hollowed out by every moment they have looked through. He gazes out at me from across the chasm of his intractable paradox. His four gnarled fingers on his right hand rise up to wipe his brow, tracing the same reflex path they've followed a hundred times every day of this life. His eyes gleam with the pleasure that each day's impregnable strangeness gives them. If time, in fact, still exists, it must be a block, a resonance made by this standing wave's equation. The lives he has yet to live through are already in him, as real as the ones he has so far led.

"A curve in configuration space," he says. I don't know if he's found one, lost one, or is riding one. "Time must be like chords. Not even a series of chords. An enormous polytonal cluster that has the whole horizontal tune stacked up inside it."

No time at all has passed—none to speak of. I look down at the man's profile, the raised shield of a forehead, the prow of nose, the set chin as familiar to me as mine. The hair is mostly gone now, the eyes a sallow sag. But I can see the belief still lingering in the folds of his eyelids: The tenses are a stubborn illusion. The whole unholy trio of them have no mathematically distinct existence. Past and future both lay folded up in the mis-

93

leading lead of the present. All three are just different cuts through the same deep map. *Was* and *will be*: All are fixed, discernible coordinates on the plane that holds all moving *nows*.

I'm pushing thirty. I don't know where my sister is. My brother has abandoned me. Every large city in America has burned. The house is now some horror of a suburban Jersey tract home that none of us ever lived in. Da's in his study, hunched over still more drawings. He works away furiously on the one problem I need him to solve. But as always, he can't solve the ones he cares about. He's telling me, "There is no such thing as race. Race is only real if you freeze time, if you invent a zero point for your tribe. If you make the past an origin, then you fix the future. Race is a dependent variable. A path, a moving process. We all move along a curve that will break down and rebuild us all."

He and I can't possibly be related. No one who knows me or my family could possibly say this. But everyone else who might tell him as much has gone. Mama is dead, Jonah has emigrated, and Ruth is in hiding. It falls to me, my solo job, to remind my father of everything he has forgotten since he was my age, everything bright and obvious he's broken away from, in the run of mathematical time. His ruined family. What ruined them. The woman he married. Why he married her. The experiment they ran. The odds against him surviving his own experiment.

But I can't wrap my head around what he is trying to tell me. I bend down and drop my head on his shoulder. My hand goes up to his chest, to hold him back from this irreversible place he already half-inhabits.

He's on his last bed, before the long one. In a hospital, back in Manhattan, ten minutes by cab from the study that he will never work in anymore. He's talking to me about multiple worlds. "The universe is an orchestra that, at every interval, splits into two full ensembles, each one continuing on a different piece. As many whole universes as there are notes in this one!"

I need some proof that he's still in control, there inside the smiling, wasted shell. Some proof that he did not put our entire future on the line—worse, our pasts—on something so tenuous as arithmetic.

"Ha!" Da barks, knocking my head up off his shoulder, startling my hand back into my lap. He's found something, some disparity overlooked, some hidden term that smoothes all asymmetries. Or just some unbearable abdominal pain.

I wait for a day when there isn't much suffering, and ask, "Did you ever decide who wins?"

He knows what I mean: mechanics or thermodynamics. Relativity or the quantum. The too big or the too small. The river or the ocean. Flow or standstill. The only problem he's ever worked on. The one that occupies him, even in these last hours. He tries to grin at me, has to save up his strength for the monosyllable: "When?"

"At the end."

"Ach! My Yoseph." His wasted yellow arm tries to cuff my neck, reassuring. "If there is no beginning, how can there be an end?" I will go mad. The planes of his shoulder muscle slide over one another in a concerted churn beyond the reaches of the subtlest equation.

I'll never get closer to him than now. He looks straight at my need but refuses to comfort or deny. He's prepared for any outcome. Pleased, even, at the confusion he has created. The bets are all in. The results are unrolled. Somewhere, our future is already real, although we can't yet know just how real, stuck as we are in the specious present. He shrugs again, his hand in the air, conducting. His eyes laugh at the world's reel. His look wants to say, *How do you want things to come out? What will you do if they don't?*

"A *dead* finish," he says. "A photo finish. Down to the wire."

We live through a chunk of moments as frozen as that photo. He gets no better. Doctors mill about us in a data-seeking daze, clinicians exercising every charm they know, trying to influence the outcome, already run. Da will leave, and I'll be forever in the dark. This is my one certain prediction. The world will lead me through every available ignorance.

"Do you know what time is?" His voice is so soft, I think I'm making it up. "Time is our way of keeping everything from happening at once."

I reply as he taught me, long ago, the year my voice broke. "You know what time is? Time is just one damn thing after another."

AUGUST 1955

Now is a full summer's end. The boy is fourteen, a shining child with a full, round face. No one in creation exudes more confidence. He walks down the aisle of a long southbound train, a spring in his step that he thinks is everyone's God-given right. He glances out the slicing window, seeing the whole world strut along in the other direction, peeling away. He has grown up breathing the air of a large northern city. He imagines he's free.

In the pocket of his natty trousers, he carries a photo from last Christmas: a newly minted teen posing with his radiant mother. In the picture, his hair is cropped, like all boys his age. His snazzy white Christmas shirt, crisp and concert-ready, still bears the traces of its department-store folds. Under the arrow points of crimped collar, a bright new tie pokes out, a golden stripe running down its middle. His face glows, a three-quarter moon with the earth's shadow just slipping off its right side. His eyes light with confidence, as if he is the ring bearer at a large, loving wedding. All life lies in front of him. His boyish beauty makes him happy, or perhaps his joy makes him beautiful.

His mother, in the black-and-white photo, is in blue. Her dress is rimmed with a white lace collar and ruffled sleeves. A holiday necklace sparkles at her throat. Her hair spills in a hive of curls. Her right hand drapes across her son's neck, resting on his shoulder. The boy looks dead-on into the camera, but the woman smiles off past the photo's edge, beyond her boy, her soft, reddened lips a little lifted, her eyes sparkling, recalling the holiday surprise she has planned, later that afternoon.

This is the photo that flies along in the wallet in the trousers on the boy as he rushes down the aisle of the passenger train hurtling south. Another print sits in a silver frame on his mother's dresser back home in the city, her keepsake from that magical Christmas eight months earlier. She has sent the boy off to visit his relatives in Mississippi, a last country vacation before he heads back to school.

By the time the train reaches his destination, the child owns it. Charmed strangers wish him well when he gets off at a tiny Delta town called Money. He steps off the platform into a crowd of boys, his instant friends. He appears to them as another species, a creature from another planet. His clothes, gait, accent: He walks among them full of jokes and boasts, floating on confidence, sharing nothing in the world with his blood relations. Except blood.

His mother has told him to mind his manners, so far from home. But so far from home, he no longer knows what minding manners means. This backwater town is slow and overgrown and easy to astonish. Everywhere he walks along these melting tar roads, he's the center of a circle of boys, hungry for a performance they didn't even know existed until his arrival. They call him "Bobo." They demand a show. Bobo must sing for them, big-time songs, distant, urban kin of their own music they only barely recognize.

They want city tales, the stranger the better. *Where I live,* Bobo says, *everything's different. We can do anything we want. In my school? Blacks and whites have class together in the same room. Talk to each other, friends. No shitting.*

His southern cousins laugh at this crazy-ass foolishness.

Here. Look! Bobo shows them a picture of his school friends, from his wallet, next to the Christmas photo. The Delta laughter crumples in confusion. The picture turns them stony. They can't know that just this spring, the Supreme Court has declared that such craziness—*with all deliberate speed*—must become everywhere a fact. They haven't heard the men who run the state capital in Jackson declare themselves, just this summer, to be proud criminals. For the boys on the dusty, weed-shot street in Money, this news is farther than the moon.

Look here, the boy Bobo says. He points out a girl with the nail of his thumb. Frail, blond, anemic—in a sickly way, almost beautiful. To the boys crowding around the photo, the face is animal, foreign. You could no more speak to such a thing than you could walk through fire. *This girl here?* Bobo tells his country disciples. *This one's my sweetheart.*

The nigger's gone mad. For all that he's already overhauled their world, his audience can't believe him. Bobo and this girl of straw: It sasses God. It breaks the damn law of gravity. What kind of city—even up north—is going to let this black boy near enough such a girl long enough to more than mumble an apology?

You a soul-damned liar. You joining on us. You think we all don't know nothing.

Bobo just laughs. *I tell you, this here's my sweetheart. Who's going to lie about a thing that nice?*

His listeners can't even sneer. No point even letting this mojo into your ears. The picture, the girl, the word *sweetheart* taunt like some hopping round of the dirty dozens. Not even the north could truck with such lawlessness. The boy's got a match in one hand and a fat stick of gunpowder in his mouth. He wants to loose some real evil on them. The others step away from the picture, like it's dope, pornography, or contraband. Then, like it's all of those, they circle back for another, longer look.

They stand in the street in front of the tired brick box of Bryant's Grocery and Meat Market, twenty of them, between the ages of twelve and sixteen. It's a stale late August Sunday, hotter than human thought and drier than a dust-coated dead mule. The boy and his first cousin have come into town for a snack, taking a break from the long day of church where the boy's great-uncle preaches. The crowd he draws wants another look. The picture of the white girl passes from hand to hand. Whatever small part of them fears it might be true, they know it's just another city-boy performance.

You a jiving fool.

Uh-uh. The boy laughs. *Nothing like a fool. She look good in this picture? Looks even nicer in life.*

Get on gone with you. Truth, now. What's you doing with a picture of a white girl in your wallet?

And that round, cherubic confidence—all of life in front of him—just grins.

It drives the others wild. *You think you something, talking to white women? Let's see you go inside this store, talk up that Bryant woman who runs it. Ask that white woman what she doing tonight.*

The northern boy just smiles his world-beating smile. That's exactly where he was heading anyway. He nods at these rurals, pushes open the grocery's screen door, and disappears underneath the DRINK COCA-COLA signs on the white-pine overhang.

The boy is fourteen. The year is 1955. The store's screen door slaps closed behind him, pure child on a dare. He buys two cents of bubblegum from the white woman. On his way out, he says something to her, two words—"Bye, baby." Or maybe he whistles: a quick, stolen trophy to bring back to his friends outside, to answer their challenge, prove he's his own owner. He bolts out the door, but the hilarity he thinks is waiting for him outside skids off into horror. The others just stare at him, begging him to undo what he just did. The crowd disperses, wordless, in all directions.

They come for the boy four days later, after midnight, when time turns inside out and all-powerful force goes dreamlike. They come to the home of Mose Wright, this Emmett's great-uncle preacher. Two of them, potent, blunt. One is bald and smokes a cigarette. The other has a pressed, thin face that knows only rage and feeding. They wake the old preacher and his wife. They want the boy, the nigger boy from Chicago who did all that talking. The men have guns. The boy is theirs. Nothing in the world will stop them from taking him. They move with clipped authority, beyond the authority of states. The steady work, the cold, damp method of after midnight.

The boy's great-aunt steps up to plead. *He just a child. He ain't from around here. That boy, he didn't know nothing. He don't mean nobody no harm.*

The balding one smashes her across the temple with his gun butt. The two whites overpower the old man. They take the boy. This is how things operate. The boy belongs to them.

Bobo—Emmett—is the only one who's calm. He's from Chicago, the big city, up north. He did nothing wrong. He isn't falling for this backwoods intimidation game, these couple of crazy crackers in their summer-stock play, banging around by the only light in which they can pull the performance off. They can't hurt him. He's fourteen; he'll live forever.

The whites march Emmett across the night grass, twisting the child's arm up behind his back. He tries to straighten, to walk normally. The snub-faced one knees him in the groin and the boy doubles over. He cries out, and the snub-faced one slams his gun down on the boy's face. The skin above Emmett's eye opens and rolls back. He puts his hand to the lake of his blood welling there. They tie him like a calf and throw him into the back of their pickup. The snub-faced one drives and the bald one rides in back, his boot pressing on the boy's skull.

They ride him for hours on the potholed roads, his head banging against the metal truck bed. The boy can't be properly corrected until he knows how serious a thing he did. They stop to pistol-whip him, beating him from his legs to his shoulders, setting wrongs to right.

Who did you think you were talking to? The question fills with fascination. The questioners have gained confidence all night, as the boy dissolves into a ball of blood and moaning. *You blind? You think that woman was some black bitch?* The snub-faced one's eyes come alive under their flaps of turtle skin. *That's my wife, nigger boy. My wife. Not some little trash-black whore.*

He savors the words—*bitch, trash, whore, nigger, white, wife*—punctuating each repeat of the lesson with a blow from his rod. He works meticulously, some stubborn stain of infidelity here he cannot beat out. He strips the boy, smashes him across his bare chest, shoulders, feet, thighs, cock, and balls. Every piece of this rule-breaking flesh must be made to respect his power.

We never had a problem with our niggers till you Chicago vermin come down to rile them up. Don't you know nothing? Nobody never taught you can from can't?

The boy has stopped answering. But even his silence defies them. The two men—the husband of the soiled woman and his half brother—work away on the naked body: in the truck, out of the truck, questioning, beating, questioning, patient teachers who've started their lecture too late.

You sorry about what you did, boy? Nothing. *You ever going to do something so stupid again, the whole of what's left of your life?* More nothing. They look for compliance in his face. But by now, the impish bright oval from the Christmas photo has little face left. The boy's silence drives the whites into whatever calm technique lies past madness. They poke their barrels into his ears, his mouth, his eyes.

They will tell it all later, to *Look* magazine, selling their confession for petty cash. They meant only to scare. But the boy's refusal to feel wrong about anything drives them to their obligation. They throw him back into the flatbed and drive him out to Milam's farm. They root around in the shed and turn up a heavy cotton-gin fan. Bryant, the snub-faced husband, begins to lift the fan into the truck. His half brother, Milam, stops him.

Roy, what the hell kind of work are you doing there?

Roy Bryant looks down and laughs. *You're right, J.W. I'm going crazy. It's from not getting a good night's sleep.*

They make the boy pick it up. Bobo, who weighs little more than the fan. Emmett, whom the whites have beaten almost senseless. He staggers from the steel's dead weight but manages to lift it, unaided, into the truck.

You know what this is for, don't you, boy?

Still the boy refuses to believe. The drama is too broad, the cotton-gin fan too theatrical. They mean only to torture his imagination, to break him with terror. Yet lifting the heavy machinery is worse than everything he's suffered until now.

Bryant and Milam make him lie down in the truck, naked, alongside the scrap metal. They drive him back into the woods, down by the Tallahatchie. In those last two miles, the boy lives through all creation. His thoughts collapse; no message can escape him to forgive the living. All law has aligned against him. Fourteen, and condemned to nothing. Even God gives him up.

The night is pitch-dark and filled with stars. They pull the truck far off the road, into a thicket by the river. Even now—the whites will tell the magazine that buys their confession—even now, they mean only to administer his due. They threaten to tie the fan around the boy's neck with a loop of barbed wire. Bryant talks to him, slowly. *You understand now, boy? You see how you're making us do this?*

Till says nothing. He has gone where no human need can reach.

Milam waves over the black water. *We're taking you out there, boy. Unless you tell us you've learned how to treat a white woman.*

The boy didn't show the proper remorse, they'll tell the magazine. He refused to admit he'd done anything wrong.

Milam plays with the bloodied clothes while his half brother delivers the sermon. He wants to see what a black boy wears for underpants. He goes through Till's pockets. He pulls apart the wallet and finds the picture.

Roy. Milam's voice is metal. *Look at this.*

The men pass the photo back and forth, under a flashlight. Some unmeaning artifact. Some change in the fundamental laws. Bryant takes the photo to the riverside and forces it into the boy's smashed face. *How'd you get this, boy?*

There's not enough boy left to answer. The silence triggers another round of battering.

Who'd you steal this from? You better tell us everything. Now.

They might as well demand an answer from the earth they beat him into. Time melts like August road tar. The questions swell, each word unfolding its kernel of violent eternity. They hit him with a monkey wrench. Each blow is forever falling.

Who is this girl? What the fuck you do to her, nigger?

Emmett comes back from a place he shouldn't have escaped. The house is burned, and it would be no use to him now, even if they let him live. The life they own means nothing to him. Sense has run down to a standstill. But somehow he comes back, finds the concussed brain, the caved-in throat.

She's my sweetheart.

His crime swells past rape, worse than murder. It spits in the face of creation. What the whites must do, they do—no rage to their motion, no hysteria, no lesson. They exterminate by deep reflex, a flinch that comes before even self-defense. They put a bullet through the fourteen-year-old's brain, as they might kill a rabid animal. A desperate protection, the safeguard of their kind.

They tie the fan around the corpse's neck with the hank of barbed wire. They drop the body into the current, where it will never again threaten anyone. Then they return home to their families, a safety they've spent this night preserving.

When the boy doesn't come home, Mose Wright calls the indifferent authorities. But he calls the boy's mother, too, who phones the Chicago police. Pressed from outside, the law of Money moves. The local police arrest the two men, who say only that they took the boy but let him go after putting the fear of God into him.

On the third day, the weighed-down body rises from the river. It snags on the hook of a white boy, fishing, who thinks he has snared some primordial water creature. Landing the carcass, the fishing child needs several moments to recognize his catch as human. Every inch has been bludgeoned beyond recognition. Even Mose Wright can't identify his grand-nephew until he sees the signet ring belonging to Emmett's dead father, a keepsake the son wore on his slender finger, always.

The sheriff tries to rush a burial. But Emmett's mother fights the police to get her son's body returned to Chicago. Against the odds, she beats all obstructions. The body goes back north by train. Although the authorities order the casket permanently sealed, Emmett's mother must have a last look, even in the Chicago station. She breaks the law, glances inside the casket, and faints dead away. When she comes to, she decides that the whole world must look on what it has done to her boy.

The world wants to look away, but can't. A photo runs in *Jet* magazine and is reprinted throughout the black press and beyond. The boy has his white Christmas shirt on again, starched smooth, with a black jacket pulled over the top. These clothes are the only clue that the photo shows a human being at all. That the undertaker survived the corpse's dressing is itself miraculous. The face is a melted rubber model, a rotting vegetable, bloated and disfigured. Below the midline, there's nothing but a single flattened bruise. The ear is singed off. The nose and eyes have been returned to the face by hesitant guess.

This is the photo my parents fight over at the end, those two who never fought over anything. To a child raised on concord, every cross word is holy terror. A boy our age is dead. The fact leaves me, at most, confused. But our parents are arguing. And hearing their fight pitches me into the abyss.

"I'm sorry," the one whispers. "No boy their age should be allowed to see such a thing."

"Allowed?" the other says. "*Allowed?* We have to *make* them look."

Their voices whip back and forth like hushed scythes. These aren't my parents, those two people who have trouble even singing the word *hate* in a chanson lyric.

Jonah hears it, too, the blade in their back-and-forth. Though he'll remain a dutiful child for another year and a half, this crisis moves him to desperation. He ends their whispering the only way he knows how. While our parents argue over the photo, he goes to the magazine and looks.

So the fight sinks, weighted, underwater. We're a family again, looking together, at least the four of us. Ruth, my parents agree, is too small to see. We're all too small, even my father. But we look, together, anyway. That's what the mother of the boy—the boy in the photo—wants.

"Is this real?" I ask. "Really real?" I would rather have them arguing again, anything but this. "A real human being?" I see only a macabre rubber mask, two months too early for Halloween. My mother won't answer. She's fixed by the image, petitioning the invisible, asking the same question. But she's not asking about the boy.

My mother is crying. I can't say anything, but I must say something. I need to keep her with us. "Are you related to him?" I ask. It's just possible. I have much family on my mother's side, whom she and Da say I'll someday meet. But Mama won't answer me. I try again. "Are you friends with—"

She waves me away, mute, broken, before I can find how to reach her.

I ask my father. "Do we know this boy or something?"

But he, too, gives only a distracted *"Sha. Sei still, Junge."*

He comes for me at night, the thing they say is a boy. This happens more nights running than I can count. He lies decked out in that black suit, that perfect starched shirt, topped by the grotesque mushroom that ought to be his face. Then he sits up. His body pinches in the middle and he flips forward, his face zooming up to mine. He springs up to get me, the pulped mouth smiling, trying to befriend me, to speak. I try to scream, but my own mouth melts into another rubber mask as fused as his. I wake up wet, a moan leaking out of me, more cowlike than human. The moan wakes my brother, on the bunk above me. "Go back to bed," he snaps at me. He doesn't bother to ask what's wrong.

The child's funeral in Chicago becomes a national event. Da asks if Mama wants to go. "We could go together. I have not been out to the University of Chicago since Fermi died. I could get an invitation. We would be right there, on the South Side."

My mother says no. The funeral of a stranger? She has her students, and there's Ruth's day school to think of. But even at thirteen, I know: She can't go to this funeral, not this one, on the arm of a man my father's color.

Ten thousand people turn out to mourn a boy only a hundred of them knew. Each shows up locked in a private eulogy, humming a whole hymnal of explanations. Unlucky boy, backwoods regional madness, the relic of a nightmare history: This is the funeral white America thinks it attends. But black Chicago, black Mississippi, friends of the boy's mother, or last week's mother, or next week's, grab the mourning suit out of the closet—haven't even had time to iron it—and go to the mountain again.

The coffin stands open throughout the service. The public files by for a last look, or a next-to-last, a second-to-next. The crowds show up again, back in Mississippi, for Bryant and Milam's trial. All three infant television networks are there, and the newsreels, too, holding their audience repulsed but mesmerized.

A northern black member of the House of Representatives comes down in person to the county courthouse in Sumner. The bailiff refuses to let him in the room. *Nigger says he's a Congressman.* At last they admit him but restrict him to the back, with the press and the handful of colored witnesses the law requires.

The courtroom is an oven. Even the judge strips down to his shirtsleeves. The case prosecutes itself. The grooves in a cotton gin are unique, cut by only one fan. The fan tied with barbed wire to Emmett Till's neck belongs to the gin still sitting in J. W. Milam's barn. The prosecutor asks Mose Wright if he can see anyone in the courtroom involved in his grand-nephew's abduction. The sixty-four-year-old preacher rises up alone against the world's collected power and points at Milam. His finger arcs up and out, like the hand of God whose awful indictment created the first man. "Dar he." Two words start up the irreversible future.

Where the prosecution is direct, the defense is ingenious. The body floating up out of the river is too disfigured to recognize, too decomposed to have lain submerged for just three days. Perhaps the signet ring was placed on the mangled body by some northern colored-loving group, eager to raise trouble where they don't belong. Perhaps the boy is still alive, hiding up in Chicago, part of a conspiracy against a couple of men who wanted only to protect their womenfolk. Throughout, the defendants sit by their family, smoking cigars, their faces edged with defiant smiles.

If Bryant and Milam are found guilty, the defense attorney asks the jury, *where, under the shining sun, is the land of the free and the home of the brave?*

The jury is out for only an hour and seven minutes. They wouldn't have taken even that long, one juror tells a reporter, if the twelve whites hadn't lingered to drink a soda pop. The verdict comes down: Innocent on all counts. Milam and Bryant have done no wrong. They go free, back to their women and families. The whole trial is over in four days. The magazines run another picture: the killers and their mates, cheering their victory in the courtroom.

Jonah and I don't hear this outcome. We're back at our private conservatory, growing into our new voices, learning the lower lines in a vast choral fantasy about how all men are brothers. We're deep in our own improvised lives, carrying snapshots around in our own wallets. We set aside the nightmare boy, the unforgettable photo, too disfigured to be anything but a ruined clay model. We never ask our parents what happened at the trial, and they never tell us. For if there's one thing we need protection from, even more than this crime, it's this verdict.

I do not learn the final verdict until adulthood, the adulthood Emmett Till never reaches. One child dies, and another survives only by not looking. What other protection could they offer us, our parents, who stripped us of all protection when they chose to make us? For after this country, there is no safety.

But here is the part I can't get past. It's twelve years later, 1967. Jonah and I are in a room on the eleventh floor of the Drake, in Chicago, in town a dozen years too late for the funeral. I'm at our window, trying unsuccessfully to peer past the fire escapes to something the map calls the Magnificent Mile. My brother lies on one of the double beds, paralyzed with agitation. We're here for his Orchestra Hall debut, that night.

We've at last broken free from the wilds of Saskatchewan and the rain-leaking concert barns of Kansas. Jonah is streaking like a meteor across what is left of classical music's sky. *High Fidelity* has named him one of their "ten singers under thirty who will change the way you listen to lieder." And the *Detroit Free Press* has called him "a tenor who sings like a planet-scouting angel carrying back word of a place rich and strange." He has recorded a successful disk with a small label and is about to do another. There's talk of his signing a long-term contract with a larger house, perhaps even Columbia. He has only to keep from smoking and a triumphant life is all but guaranteed.

But triumph shows its first catch. A leading intellectual, whom Jonah has never heard of, has just ambushed him in print. It's only a passing line, in *Harper's*, not a venue likely to cause his career much lasting harm. Jonah keeps reading the line out to me until we both have it memorized. "Yet there are amazingly talented young black men out there still trying to play the white culture game, even while their brothers are dying in the streets." And the intellectual goes on to name a famous modern dancer, an internationally acclaimed pianist, and Jonah Strom. The piece, of course, makes no mention of me, nor any of the thousands of lesser-skilled but loyal little brothers.

Everything in the accusation is true. People are dying, and the streets are on fire. Newark is an inferno. A river of flame runs through downtown Detroit. From the eleventh floor of the Drake, it doesn't yet feel like civil war. But the evidence is everywhere, and my indicted brother has become addicted to it. In each new city we barnstorm through, in every pastel hotel room, we watch the bewildered news recaps—riots with the sound turned down—as Jonah runs through his scales and I tap out pantomime finger warm-ups on the tabletops.

It's August, as it was for Till, only twelve years later. The nation again looks on, wanting to believe that the worst has passed. Everything has changed, but nothing is different. A black man sits on the Supreme Court. The rest are in prison, trapped in burning cities, or dying in Asia's jungles. On the television in the Drake, a camera tracks down an avenue of commercial buildings, block after block of gutted brick. My brother stops in midarpeggio, three tones shy of the top of his usual workout range.

"You remember that boy?"

We've almost doubled in age since that day. Since my nightmares, we've never once spoken about the photo. Nor can I remember thinking about it. But the thing our parents fought over, the false hope of protection, has worked away inside us. I know in a beat who he means.

"Till," my brother says, just as I say, "Emmett." My brother falls quiet, calculating. He can be thinking only one thing. *Once upon a time, I was this boy's age. But now I'm twenty-six, and he's still fourteen.*

The dozen years since the boy's death open in front of us, like an empty concert hall ten minutes before curtain. I look on that year, the one I couldn't see when I lived there. Twelve years too late, I hear what our parents argued about that night. I hear our mother crying for this boy she didn't know. On the muted hotel TV, the camera pans across men shivering in doorways along what might as well be Lenox, a handful of blocks from the house we grew up in.

"She didn't want us to see. She didn't want us to know."

My brother stares at me. The first time he has looked me in the eye in over a week. "What do you mean?"

"The picture." I wave at the screen, where club-swinging police and their white-fanged German shepherds wade into a screaming crowd. "She thought it might damage us, to see what . . . they did to him." I snort. "I guess it did." Jonah looks at me as if I'm another species. I can't believe the idea has never occurred to him. "She was a mother, first, before . . . anything. We were her babies." My brother is shaking his head, denying. I start to gutter, so I press on, harder. "But your father, the scientist: 'What do you mean, too young? If it's a physical fact, they have to know.' "

"Your memory has totally fucked this up."

My face swells as if beaten. I'm ready to wheedle with him, to beg. At the same time, my fists clench. I've devoted myself to accompanying him, spent my whole life making sure that the real world won't defeat him. I've carried my brother for a quarter of a century. I'm only twenty-five. "Me? My memory? You're full of shit, Jonah. You don't remember them—"

"Don't try to swear, Mule. It's even less convincing than your Chopin."

"What are you saying? You think she had some other reason? You think she was—"

"You've got it backward. Da was the one. Didn't want us even to hear them arguing. Wanted to keep our dreams musical and clean. Wanted to think the boy was a fluke; deviant history. Never going to happen anymore. You and me and Rootie? Our generation? We'd be the fresh start. Don't tell us, and there'd be no scars."

I shake my head, short wipes of denial. He might as well be telling me we're adopted.

"I'll tell you what. Mama was furious. Said he didn't have the first idea in hell what was going on. I remember her wailing. 'Whatever you think these boys are, the world is going to see them as a couple of black boys.' We had to get ready. Had to know what people wanted to do to us." Jonah gazes at the TV, at the *Harper's* article, there, as always, on his bed stand, within reach. "Da tried to tell her it was just the South, just a couple of death-deserving animals. He's the one who said it would only fuck us up to look at it."

I can't wrap my head around his words. The people he describes: I don't know them. My mother couldn't have said those things to my father. My father couldn't have thought such stupidity.

"You know what happened? You know how things turned out?" Jonah looks up at me, smiles, and waves his hands in the air. "I mean, with the killers?"

My brother, the near illiterate, has been reading, behind my back. Or he's learned the facts on some civil rights documentary, the kind of show that airs at a harmless hour late at night, on educational TV, when all good citizens, like me, are safe in bed.

"The whites. The murderers. They sell their confession to some picture magazine a few months after their acquittal. The trial's barely over, and they're telling the whole country exactly how they killed the kid. Make a quick couple of bucks, pocket money. The kid forced them to do it, apparently. Of course, they can't be tried twice for the same crime." Jonah's face, in the hotel room light, looks almost white. "Did it do anything to you? That picture?"

"Nightmares for weeks. You don't remember? I used to wake you up, with the moaning. You used to scream at me to shut up."

"Did I?" He shrugs and waves, forgiving me for angering him. "Only weeks? I was seeing him for years. Fourteen, you see. That's what was going to happen. They were coming for me. I was going to be next."

I look at him and can't see. My fearless brother, who wrapped the world around his little finger. My brother lies back on the bed. He splays both palms as if to break his fall. He closes his eyes. The bed rushes up beneath him. "A little trouble breathing, here, Mule. I think I might be having an attack."

"Jonah! No. Not tonight. Get up." I talk to him like he's a small child, a puppy on the furniture. I walk him around in slow, relaxed circles, all the while rubbing his back. "Breathe normally. Nice and easy."

I walk him over to the window. The noise of the Loop, the lazy tangle of commerce below, helps ease him a little. Jonah collects himself. His shoulders drop. He starts to breathe again. He tries to smirk at me, his neck pulled back: "What the hell's your problem, buddy? What's with all the physical contact all of a sudden?"

He tweezers my hand off his shoulder, twisting my wrist to steal a look at my watch. He, of course, doesn't wear one. Nothing distracting or weighty allowed to touch his body. "Jesus Christ. We're late," he says, as if I'm the one who has been malingering. "Our big night, remember?"

He flashes a performer's bitter smile and heads toward the bathroom, where his tux has been hanging in steam. He goes through the whole ritual: hot towels around the neck, eucalyptus rub and lemon wedges, vocalizing as he ties his white tie. I pull the curtains and dress out in the room, between the two beds. Jonah calls downstairs for his concert shoes, which come up to the room reflecting light like a pair of obsidian mirrors. He tips the bellhop obscenely, and the man beats an apologetic, resentful retreat.

We go take our debut turn at Orchestra Hall, the songs of Schumann, Hugo Wolf, and Brahms. The white culture game. Nerves and overlearning get us through in a splash of color. There's an edge to Jonah tonight, the radiant glow of a tubercular patient about to die. The Chicago crowd—all North Siders and suburbans—feels present at the birth of a wondrous discovery.

Afterward, after the Schubert encore, when it seems we have more than survived, we join hands onstage and walk off to wild applause, two brothers, split at the fork in what, until today, was our identical past.

MY BROTHER AS AENEAS

To my ear, his laugh at fourteen had no bitter highlights yet. I'd swear he was still happy up in Boston, in the walled courtyard of our music school. Happy, or at least busy, proving he could get people of any hue to fall in love with him. And needing to seduce János Reményi before anyone. The Hungarian's approval meant more to Jonah during high school than even Da's or Mama's. And my brother must have meant a good deal to Reményi, as well. Once Jonah's voice broke, it became János's chief pastime in life to turn the virginal soprano into a sterling tenor.

Most adolescent males pass through months when their voices go off on spontaneous excursions, flopping like a fireman's hose with no one strong enough to hold it steady. Jonah entered this vocal purgatory. He struggled to settle into his new register and win back control over his hormone-thickened vocal cords. But in remarkably short order, one could hear the light sparkle of boyish ore coming through the cauldron of adolescence smelted down to a bright lump of gold.

Reményi's own career was now a relic, except for the occasional nostalgic gala. Throughout the thirties, he'd been a Bayreuth regular, doing the three consecutive evenings of Wotan without a waver. He was a celebrated CEO of Valhalla and tyrannical abuser of oppressed dwarves. But after the Sudetenland crisis, he stopped traveling to Germany. Later, he always refused direct questions about that decision, and the musical press inferred a self-sacrificing choice. In truth, 1938 was way late for acts of political courage.

Throughout the war, Reményi worked in Budapest, singing roles in safe pieces like Ferenc Erkel's *Bánk Bán* and Dohnányi's *Tower of the Voivod*. When the country's concert houses were bombed, he turned to teaching. He tried to return to opera, traveling through a decimated Italy, but his temperament—too stolid for bel canto and too brooding for buffa—got him molested in the Neapolitan and Milanese press. He stayed in Central Europe long enough to see Allied infantrymen of all races parading through Bayreuth in pillaged Valkyrie helmets and Brunhild gowns, even draped in his old Wotan costumes. Arranging a hasty evacuation to the States in the tidal wave of the late forties, he launched Boylston Academy, scoring points with wealthy Americans by playing on their cultural inferiority. His banquet speeches raised thousands of dollars for the school by suggesting that, in the world's cultural Olympics, vocal music was an event where the USA couldn't even take home a bronze.

At Boylston, Reményi was in his element, Wotan all over again. The students all fixed on him: *János asked me to audition for the spring chamber choir. János complimented me today on my C major scale.* None of us would have dared call the man anything but sir to his face. But in the safety of cafeteria talk, we were all on a first-name basis.

He gave lessons in the most opulent studio, tucked away in the recesses of the second story. He covered his floors with silk carpets from Tabriz and hung the walls with Anatolian kilims, to make sure that no student could count on any free resonance. Throughout lessons, he sat behind a Biedermeier desk in a wing-backed chair. If he needed to make a musical point, he strode over to the corner where two Bechsteins curled up in each other's curves.

During my lessons, he shuffled papers and signed forms. I'd finish an étude, and he'd work on for a few minutes before noticing. Coming up for air, he'd command, "Go on, go on," as if I'd stopped out of truculence. He cared only for those whose voices might lead to careers. I did not interest him except as the key to my brother's well-being. Perhaps he saw in me a clinical riddle: How could the same genes produce both brilliance and mere adequacy? He'd wonder for a moment, wave me on, and return to his paperwork.

Jonah's were the only lessons with Reményi to exceed the alloted fifty minutes. My brother would disappear into Reményi's lair and not come out for hours. I'd go nuts with worry. Reményi's studio had a pane of metal-threaded glass cut into the door, a school policy since an incident involving an ex–faculty member and a fifteen-year-old early bloomer. On my toes at the right distance down the hall, I could make out a thin slice of proceedings without being detected.

The teacher on the other side of that wire-meshed glass was no one I recognized. János, up on his feet, hands cupped, arms waving, mouth working on a stream of staccato triplets, was conducting the entire Met pit orchestra. Jonah imitated him, his chest out like a war hero. Through the glass, I looked in on a life-sized puppet-theater staging of Papageno and Papagena's duet.

Ecstatic János coached my brother's voice down into its new range. He showed the teenager how to open up his instrument and let that new power take up residence. Everything Jonah lost in pitch, he stood to gain many times over in color and sweep. The break was like one of those chance renovations, where crumbling plaster reveals glorious marble beneath it. The crushing innocence of his old high notes, the ones that made listeners want to take their own lives in shame, gave way to the richer highlights of adult awakening.

There would be years of sweat and woodshedding. But of all János's maturing students, Jonah, he said, had the least to unlearn. The Hungarian claimed he'd caught the boy while music was in him, before anyone could trample him. The truth is: We and music are not unified. Nothing in our animal past calls for anything so gratuitous as song. We must put it on, wrap it around us like the dark, cold firmament. Some part of Jonah's sonority came from his great lungs, the softness of his larynx, the fluting of his vocal cords, his skull's chambered resonance. But the heart of his gift was learned. And only one violating couple could have taught him so deeply as they did.

Jonah might have flourished under almost any teacher. Once away from our family's charmed evenings of motets, he became a sponge, using people for whatever he could steal from them while reserving, even in happy compliance, the right to second-guess anything anyone fed him.

Jonah stole the best of everyone—Reményi's experience, Kimberly Monera's precocity, Thad's and Earl's hipster avant-gardism, my feel for harmony—until all of these became his own annexed domain. But in the story he invented for himself, Jonah made this journey alone, whoever his passing sponsors might have been.

The teenager's voice stepped out from the boy's wreckage. Within months, János could hear the hint of adult wonders to come. This boy's raw material—shaped by early immersion—pointed toward places beyond those Reményi himself had reached. The only question was how far beyond his own ability any teacher could teach. So long as Jonah stayed dutiful, all was well. His lessons with Reményi progressed, the master's one hand flinging my brother outward, the other, unconsciously, holding him back.

Jonah humored his teacher's enthusiasms and even returned them. I'd hop past the room on my toes, catching glimpses of them in arcane training rituals, exercises coming out of a teacher I never saw do anything more vigorous than shuffle papers. There was János, dropping to his knees to pantomime the falling larynx, turning his hands in precision catcher's mitts for Jonah's pitches to hit, shaping his arms into tubes through which Jonah threaded his thirty-second-long pianissimi.

The Boylston master was a monster about tone. Only Jonah had any idea what the man meant by the word. Once, during social studies class, fifty yards down the hall from where my brother worked in Reményi's lair, I heard the man bellow, *For God's sake! Let the tone ride upon your breath like a ball on a fountain of water.* More curse than command. My fellow social studies students turned to me in sympathy, their heads hung, as if Jonah's fall chastened us all. Then we heard a sustained high forte such as no teenager had ever produced. The Hungarian bellowed, even louder, *Yes! That's it!*

Even in rapture, the man was guarded. Most often, he affected cool neutrality. His pedagogical method was both archaic and iconoclastic. He fed my brother buffets of scales out of Concone and tortuous workouts from García: triplets, four-note scales, arpeggios. He made him sing fast, wordy passages while biting down on two fingers. Jonah never took the tongue for granted again. János made him do legato melismata as machine-gun sforzando. Jonah had to land each tone dead on its mark or start the whole sequence over. Teacher and student joined together to birth up chunks of sensation, lost to the sheer sense-heightened pleasure of the chase.

Our Wotan believed no student could master vocal technique except as part of a greater cultural mastery. He told us as much, at our winter assembly, 1955. "Singing is heightened speech, in a language beyond human languages. But if you want to speak in the words of the cosmos, you must train on earthly words. To prepare yourself to perform the *Missa Solemnis* or the Mass in B Minor—those summae of Western art—you must start to read all the European poetry and philosophy you can lay your hands on." Reményi's transcendental humanism lit up our skies like a nova. We couldn't know that, like a nova, the star throwing off the blaze was already dead.

János Reményi's Grand Masonic approach hurt Jonah less than other artificial technique-building programs might have. For all his shouting about tone, Reményi knew he could do nothing better for my brother's voice than release it. The boy was the older man's golem, his American Adam, his Enlightenment-haunted tabula rasa, a seed perfectible under greenhouse conditions. Europe had just offed itself again, its rococo opera houses gutted in high culture's final flare-up. But in this charmed monastic backwater, whose leading novitiate surpassed anything Reményi had worked with in the Old World, the aging bass-baritone saw his chance for one more shot at *Erhabenheit*, no matter his disciple's skin tone.

This was the year János implemented the school's first vocal competition. He made Jonah compete in the senior division. He chose my brother's piece—Handel's "Süsse Stille"—and tried to choose his accompanist, as well. But Jonah refused to perform without me. By the time the first round ended, even those gladiators who'd gone into the arena with the fiercest ambitions pleaded no contest.

A week later, someone painted our bedroom door. A premeditated midnight raid: No other way the painters could have done it. The art was a grotesque portrait, thick liver lips and Brillo hair, a bastard son the Kilroy family sent guilty child support. The artists must have spooked themselves with their voodoo, because the caption beneath the picture only got as far as an *N*, an *I*, and a jagged *G*. The medium was red fingernail polish.

Thad discovered the portrait on his return from breakfast. "Holy Shetland sheepdogs."

Earl managed an awed "Whoa!"

Jonah and I saw the thing at the same time. Jonah recovered faster. He laughed maniacally. "What do you think, fellas? Realism? Impressionism? Cubism?"

He and Thad hunted down some finger paint and added a beret, a pair of shades, and a hand-rolled cigarette hanging out of the ample lips. They named their beatnik Nigel. Nothing could have thrilled our roommates more: tarred with the same rouge brush, with a little property damage thrown in to boot.

Stony adults came to remove the door from its hinges and replace it with a virgin one. Jonah put on a show of disappointment. "Nigel's deserting us. Nigel's graduating."

"Nigel's gonna blow this peanut stand," Thad added. "Nigel's gonna go make the *real* scene." The scene our roommates dreamed of making.

For a long time after, I woke up an hour after falling asleep, hearing scratching at the door.

Something in János almost seemed to like the fact that his star pupil wasn't white. The dissonance only added to his thrill at presenting to the world something so rare and novel. Like most champions of Western culture, Reményi pretended race didn't really exist—giants, dwarves, and Valkyries aside. He could grasp the obscurity of *Parsifal* more easily than he could imagine what humiliations our mother had lived through, just to sing European music at all. János Reményi had no more idea of his adopted country than did the rest of the white Boylston faculty. He thought music—his music—belonged to all races, all times, all places. It spoke to all people and soothed all souls. This was the same man who'd sung Wotan right up until 1938, never glimpsing the coming twilight of the gods.

He clung to this imperial idea: One trained the singular voice only by releasing the universal spirit. From the ruins of this bombed-out creed, Reményi drilled my brother. But in the fall of 1955, my brother's spirit began to grow in ways his teacher would have strangled in the cradle had he been able to see them.

When Jonah's voice broke, the wall between him and Kimberly Monera gave way. After his transposition to tenor, the baffling *What now?* dividing the two prepubes came tumbling down, answered. One summer had changed Kimberly, too, beyond recognition. She came back to school radiant. She'd spent the break in Spoleto, her father's summer base. There, she'd somehow learned to sing. The freakish albino, in act two, had gone swan.

She returned with a shape so changed, it must have frightened even her. Her body, a narrow, backward thing the previous spring, now tapered with newfound power. I sat behind her in music history, wondering why her mother didn't buy her larger clothes. Under that surprised binding, the new surface of her skin readied itself for use. Through the lime or columbine of her taut blouses, I stared for eternities at the little bandage of her bra, the three raised welts of its metal hooks, miracles of engineering. Whenever she crossed her nylon legs, I heard fingers sliding up and down a violin's strings.

Around her, Jonah grew protective, gallant, stupid. The solitary solidarity of our rooftop club dissolved forever. Earl and Thad tried to lure him into games of Truth or Dare. But loyal to his Chimera and overnight wise, Jonah said nothing. And still, nothing was all we needed to reach the wildest conclusions.

Thad rode him, his grin of vicarious delight glowing in the dark. "What the hell have you been up to, Strom One?"

"Nothing. Just practicing." The feathers of the canary all over his chin, even as he wiped it with a quick backhand.

"*Practicing*, Strom One? I dig."

Jonah snickered. "Practicing singing."

"First base?" Earl could rise from a coma, ready to shoot the breeze all night long.

"First *base*?" The question outraged Thad. "Huber, you gone cat. Does this look like a man left stranded on lowly bag one? First base on a hardline drive. Takes second on a wild pitch. Throwing error into short center sends him . . ."

"You've all lost your minds." Jonah caught my eye, a back-off warning. "You're all flipping nuts."

"That's cool," Earl decided.

Jonah disappeared on us, all Halloween evening. He didn't come back until after midnight. I don't know how he slipped the evening head count without getting caught. Long after curfew, he scratched the door to be let in. He was dizzy but mum. Earl Huber berated him. "Don't get the girl in trouble, Strom."

Jonah held his stare. "You don't have the slightest idea what you're talking about."

Thad intervened. "Strom One, man, we're your loyal subjects and vassals. We'll do your bidding for all time. I'm begging you. What's it like?"

My brother stopped pulling off his blue-black school trousers. "What's *what* like?"

"Strom, man. Don't do this. You're killing us."

"It's . . . like nothing you can know."

Thad lay back in bed, kicking the air and howling.

My brother held up a silencing hand. "It's like total, continuous . . . It's like Wagner."

Not a name we'd dared bring up before coming here.

"Thank *God*," Thad shouted. "I'm not missing anything, then. I hate that shit."

"It's like beating off on somebody," Earl explained, "who happens to be beating off on you."

Jonah went so dark, his color became definitive. If he was doing anything wrong to her, I'd kill him. Close my fingers around his golden throat and stop his sound for good.

Whatever they were doing in their few moments by themselves, their trysts made Kimberly glow. Even Thad West noticed her transfiguration. "Is this some kind of light operetta, Strom One? I mean, what the hell? Look at her. She didn't look like that before Halloween."

Jonah wouldn't be baited. The Chimera was no longer a fit topic for our running commentary. He and his chosen one made themselves invisible, moving in a secret subplot, awaiting the sunlit modulation to E major that would turn them from outlaws to inheritors.

Then a teacher surprised them, seated on the grass behind the trellises at the Rose Garden in the Fens. They were parked over a score—Massenet's *Werther*. But their exact condition at the moment of discovery became a matter of endless speculation. Students came up to me for days to settle their raging bets.

Following the scandal, Kimberly relapsed into her congenital anemia, sure the two of them would both be thrown out of school. But even the faculty couldn't imagine the two of them actually committing such transgression. They escaped without reprimand.

Kimberly was so scared, she dashed off a preemptive note to her father, then in Salzburg, explaining her side of things. The great man laughed it off. "*Sempre libera*," he told her, jotting a few notes of the aria on a scribbled staff in the letter's margin. "Pick your mates of the moment wisely, and make them value whatever small favors you choose to bestow. *'Di gioia in gioia, sempre lieta!'* " She showed Jonah the letter, swearing him to solemn secrecy. Jonah told me, because I didn't count.

János reprimanded my brother for his extracurricular Massenet. The dressing-down was dry and lofty; Jonah probably didn't even know how sharp it was meant to be. Reményi began taking Jonah along with him on conducting engagements around the city. He wanted my brother occupied at all times.

Not long after the Rose Garden incident, my trial came. Thad West pushed me into it. "That Malalai Gilani has the swoons for you, Strom Two."

"That's right, hep cat," faithful Earl added. "She does."

Their words were an accusation, a police raid on innocent bystanders. "I didn't do anything. I've never even said hello to her."

"Oh, you're doing something to her, Strom Two. This much, we know as a matter of factation."

I knew nothing about the girl except the obvious. She was the darkest child in school, darker than Jonah and I combined. I never knew where she came from—one of those mythical countries between the Suez and Cathay. The whole school wanted us paired: two troubling ethnics, safely canceling each other out.

The girl had a solid alto, clear as a carillon in winter. She could count like mad, always entering on time, even in tricky twentieth-century work. She had the kind of voice that stocked decent ensembles. And she'd noticed me. I lay in bed mornings, crippled with responsibility.

From the moment our roommates opened my eyes, mutual knowledge sprang up between Malalai Gilani and me. In choral rehearsals, on performance tours, in the one large class I shared with her, a pact hardened between us without our exchanging more than a single, deniable glance. But with that one look, I signed my name to a contract, in blood.

The day I sat down next to her in the cafeteria, driven by my peers, she seemed not to notice. The first words she spoke to me were, "You don't have to." The girl was fourteen. It bound me to her with worse than chains.

We never did things together. She didn't do anything with anyone. Once, on our way to a performance in Brookline, we shared a seat on the school's bus. But we took so much abuse on that short ride, we never repeated the mistake. We didn't talk. She seemed not to trust English much, except in movies and songs. It was weeks before—brief and damp—we even brushed hands. Yet we were a pair, by every accepted measure.

Once, she looked at me, apologizing. "I'm not really African, you know."

"Me neither," I said. Easier to misunderstand. All the school wanted was that we not trouble them.

I asked where she came from. She wouldn't say. She never asked me—not about my home, my family, my hair, nor how I came to be at Boylston. She didn't need to. She knew already, better than I.

She read about the strangest things—the House of Windsor, Maureen Connolly, the Seven Sisters. She loved fashion magazines, homemaking magazines, movie magazines. She studied them furtively, with an astonished head tilt, puzzling out the artifacts of a fabled civilization. She knew all about the Kitchen of the Future. She loved how Gary Cooper started to tremble a little in *High Noon*. She suggested I might look good if I grew my hair out a little and slicked it down.

Ava Gardner fascinated her. "She's part Negro," Malalai explained. This was when Hollywood could stage a mixed-race musical, but not with a mixed cast. My father believed that time didn't pass. He must have been right.

Thad and Earl were relentless. "What does she want from you, Strom Two?"

"Want?"

"You know. Have you discussed the terms? What she expects?"

"What are you talking about? She just kind of blushes when we pass in the hall."

"Uh-oh," Thad said. "Commitment."

"Mortgage time," Earl agreed, giving the syllables a bebop syncopation.

"You better get yourself a good job, Strom Two. Support and all."

Just before Thanksgiving, I bought a bracelet for Malalai Gilani in a drugstore on Massachusetts Avenue. I studied the options, taking hours to settle on a simple silver chain. The price—four dollars and eleven cents—was more than I'd paid for anything in my life except my beloved pocket scores and a set of the five Beethoven piano concertos.

My hands shook so badly as I paid for the bracelet, the cashier laughed. "It's okay, dear. I'll forget you bought it as soon as you're out the door." Half a century later, I still hear her.

I put off giving Malalai the gift. I needed to tell my brother first. Just broaching the topic of Malalai Gilani seemed disloyal. I waited until an evening when Thad and Earl were off listening to jazz in the common room. Jonah and I were alone in our cell. "Have you bought anything for Kimberly for Christmas?"

Jonah snapped to. "Christmas? What month is this? Jesus, Joey. Don't scare me like that."

"I just bought a bracelet . . . for Malalai." I looked up and awaited my punishment. No one else could understand the size of my betrayal.

"Malalai?" I saw my face falling, reflected in his. He shrugged. "What'd you get her?"

I handed over the square white egg of a jewelry case. He looked in, controlling his face. "That's fine, Joey. She'll have to like that."

"You think so? It's not too. . . . ?"

"It's perfect. It's her. Just don't let anyone see you give it to her."

It took me days to make the presentation. I carried the thing around in my pocket, my leaden penance. I ran into her in the courtyard, long before the holidays, but far and away the best chance I was going to get. My throat rode up into my skull. Stage fright hit me, worse than anything the stage could produce. "I bought you . . . this."

She received my trembling gift, her face pinched between pleasure and pain. "No one ever gave me anything like this before."

"Like what? You haven't opened it."

Malalai opened the box, the hush of her pleasure horrible. An animal cry escaped her lips at the flash of silver. "It's so beautiful, Joseph." The first time she spoke my name. I flipped between pride and annihilation. She held the bracelet up. "Oh!" she said. And I knew I'd bungled things.

I grabbed the trinket. It looked flawless, just as it had in the drugstore. "There's nothing on it." Her eyes shot downward, my lightning education in intimacy. "This is an ID bracelet. They usually have names."

The very idea of engraving had never occurred to me. The clerk had said nothing. My brother had said nothing. I was a pitiful idiot. "I . . . I wanted to see whether you liked it. Before I put your name on it."

She smiled, flinching at my words. "Not *my* name." The magazines must have told her. She knew more about my country's ways than I ever would. My name was to be chained to her wrist from now until the day all scripture was overthrown. And I'd done nothing. Nothing wrong.

Malalai placed the flashing bracelet around her near-black wrist. She played with the bare faceplate, its purpose now so obvious, even to me.

"I'll get it engraved." I could borrow cash from Jonah. At least enough to spell out J-O-E.

She shook her head. "I like it this way, Joseph. It's nice."

She wore the blank bracelet like a prize. It gave the girls more to mock her with: unengraved ID jewelry. Malalai must have thought I didn't want anyone seeing her wearing my name. But the bracelet was already more connection than she'd ever hoped for, in such a place. Little changed between us. We managed to sit near each other during one school assembly and a special holiday meal. She was happy with our silent link. When we did talk, all I could talk about was concert music. She loved music as well as the next Boylston student. But it didn't grip her like movies or magazines or the Kitchen of the Future. She grasped it long before I did: Classical music wouldn't make you American. Just the opposite.

It slipped out one day, after one of her quiet confidences—something about how wonderful she found the 1950 Nash Rambler convertible. I laughed at her. "How did you ever land in a place like Boylston?"

Her hand strayed to her mouth, effacing and erasing. But she couldn't make my question disappear or mean anything but attack. She didn't cry; she got away from me before sinking to that. Still, she managed to avoid me for the rest of that school term. I helped with that. In late December, before the vacation, she sent me the white mausoleum box back, with the blank bracelet in its tomb. Also a record, *Music of Central Asia*, with a note: "This was going to be for you."

The school performed our string of annual holiday concerts. These were, for Boylston, what exams were for ordinary schools. Jonah and Kimberly headlined the recitals with prominent solos. I rowed in the galleys. János Reményi took us on tour to area schools—Cambridge, Newton, Watertown, even Southie and Roxbury. Kids our age sat in darkened school gyms, as stunned by our music as they might have been by a band of organ-grinding, hat-tipping monkeys. One or two of the local principals seemed to want to make some special mention of Jonah, some object lesson in tolerance or opportunity in the speeches they delivered after the music ended. But our last name, combined with Jonah's inexplicable coloring, left them fumbling and mum.

Before our show in Charlestown—the first time any of us had been to the wrong side of Boston Harbor—the chorus was milling in our usual preconcert jitters, when János came looking for me. I thought he wanted to reprimand me for the two notes I'd dropped at the Watertown concert, the day before. I was all set to assure Mr. Reményi that the inexcusable wouldn't happen again.

But Reményi cared nothing about my performance. "Where is your brother?"

He scowled when I said I had no idea. Kimberly Monera was missing, too. János blasted away as quickly as he'd blown in, his face clenched the way it was when he conducted triple fortes. He darted off, determined to stop catastrophe before it started. But that required speeds János could never reach.

More versions of my brother's disgrace exist than there are operatic treatments of Dumas. János found his star pupil and the great conductor's daughter back behind the stage flats, fumbling underneath each other's clothes. He hauled them out of a supply closet, in the late throes of heavy petting. They were locked in a back dressing room, naked, about to do it standing up.

Of *it*, I guessed only the barest, mangled logistics, inferred from off-stage goings-on in Puccini matinees. When Jonah reappeared, one look warned me off ever trying to ask. I knew only that all three principals fled the scene in one of those explosive third-act trios: János enraged, Kimberly broken, and my brother humiliated.

"That bastard," Jonah whispered, four feet from the thrilled knot of our buzzing schoolmates. I died at the sound of the word in his mouth. "I'll finish him."

He never told me what the man said, and I never asked. I didn't even know my brother's crime. All I knew was that I'd failed him. All life long, we'd kept each other safe from everyone. Now I was on the outside, too.

The Charlestown concert didn't live in anyone's musical memory. Yet the student audience might have mistaken our sound for joy. János beamed and bowed, and with that easy harvest of his hands, he made the chorus do the same. Kimberly somehow pulled off her solo. When Jonah rose to take the flourishes we'd heard him do a hundred wondrous times, it shot through my head, the slow-motion preview given those about to have an accident: He was going to take revenge. All he had to do was hold his breath. Nonviolent resistance. That little ritard he loved to take prior to plunging in, the slight pause awakening his audience that even our conductor knew to back off from, spread wide. Silence—the motor drive of nothingness underneath all rhythm—threatened to last forever, a spell of sleep cast over the entire kingdom of listeners.

In panic at Jonah's stunt, my brain began dividing and subdividing the beats. János just waited out the endless hesitation, hands poised in the air, refusing even to blanch. Jonah neither caught his eye nor looked away. He stayed inside his perfect silence, hung on the stopped, forward edge of nowhere.

Then, sound. The web tore, and my brother was singing. Familiar melody drew me back from the end of the world. No one in the audience felt anything but heightened suspense. János was there, alongside Jonah, bringing the chorus in from my brother's silent cadenza right on the downbeat.

By the end of the piece—one of those myopic medleys of English folk tunes that spelled, for 1950s America, the height of holiday nostalgia—the whole choir caught fire. Jonah's spark of defiance awoke their showmanship, and the final chord brought down the house.

János wrapped his arm around his prodigy's shoulders and embraced him in front of everyone, the boy's protector, the idea of any falling-out between them as silly as the bogeyman.

Jonah smiled and bowed, suffering his master's hug. But as he turned from the applauding audience, his eyes sought mine. He locked me in a look past mistaking: *You heard how close I was. Easiest thing in the world, someday.*

In the postconcert bedlam, I tracked him down. Charlestown kids were coming up to him to see if he was real, to touch his hair, befriend him. And Jonah was cutting them dead. He grabbed my wrist. "Have you seen her?"

"Who?" I said. With a click of disgust, he was gone. I chased after him, through the assembly. He kept racing out to the waiting academy busses and darting back into the school building, like a fireman trying for a medal or seeking his own immolation. One of the Boylston students finally told us he'd seen Kimberly hustled off in János's car.

Jonah looked for her back at school. He was still looking when the night proctor came through, declaring lights-out. Jonah lay in the dark, cursing János, cursing Boylston, words I'd never heard before out of him or anyone. He thrashed until I thought we were going to have to restrain him with the bedsheets.

"This is going to kill her," he kept saying. "She'll die of shame."

"She'll live," Thad called across the blackened room. "She'll want to finish what you two were doing." The jazzers reveled in the drama. Jonah's scandal was the scene. It was now. Opera for the new age—all juke, jive, and gone. Nigel and the blonde. What more show could anyone want?

In the morning, Jonah was a twitching nerve. "She's gone to hurt herself. The adults haven't even noticed she's missing!"

"Hurt herself? How?"

"Joey," he moaned. "You're hopeless."

She turned up the next afternoon. We were in the cafeteria when she came in. Jonah was a wreck, ready to spring toward her, his boyhood's north. All eyes in the school were on them. Kimberly never even glanced toward our table as she cut through the room. She sat as far from us as the room allowed.

My brother couldn't stand it. He crossed to her table, indifferent to all consequence. She flinched, cowering from him, when he was still yards away. He sat down and tried to talk. But whatever they'd been to each other two days before had passed into another libretto.

He stormed back across the cafeteria. "Let's get out of here," he said, more to himself than to me. He fled upstairs. I scrambled behind. "I'll kill the bastard. I swear it." His threat was an operatic prop, a collapsible tin knife. But from my seat up in the second balcony, I was already gasping as the silvery thing disappeared to the hilt in his mentor's chest.

My brother didn't kill János Reményi. Nor did János mention the incident again. Disaster had been averted, decency preserved, my brother cuffed. Reményi just went on assigning more phrasing exercises from Concone.

Jonah went after Kimberly. He tracked her down late one afternoon, curled up in a stuffed chair in the sophomore lounge, reading E.T.A. Hoffmann. She tensed to run when she saw him, but his urgency held her. He sat down beside her and asked her a question in the smallest possible voice. "Do you remember our promise?"

She squeezed her eyes shut and breathed from the base of her gut, the way János had worked on them both to breathe. "Jonah. We're just children."

And at that moment, they no longer were.

He'd have thrown away all his skill to get it back: the childish secret engagement, the shared listening and sight-singing, huddling over scores, planning their joint world tour. But she'd closed up to him, because of something the adults told her. Something she'd never considered. She listened to him once more, but only as penance. She even let him take her marble hand in his, although she wouldn't squeeze back. For the pale, white European Chimera, all the sweetness of first-time love, all their shared discoveries were dirtied with maturity.

"What are you saying?" he asked her. "That we can't be with each other? We can't talk, touch one another?"

She wouldn't say. And he wouldn't hear what she wouldn't say.

He tormented her. "If we're wrong, then music is wrong. Art is wrong. Everything you love is wrong."

His words would kill her before they convinced her. Something had broken in Kimberly. Something sullied the secret duet they'd perfected in front of an empty hall. Two weeks before, she'd imagined herself opening in her life's debut. Now she saw the piece from the back of the auditorium, the way the public saw, and she panned her own performance.

Jonah wandered the school like some favored family pet punished for doing the trick he'd been trained to do. His movements grew slow and deliberate, as if what he settled on here, in his first dress rehearsal, would seal the rest of his life. If this could be taken from him, then nothing was really his. Least of all music.

By week's end, Kimberly Monera was gone. She'd gathered her belongings and vanished. Her parents withdrew her from Boylston in the middle of the school year, the last days of fall term. My brother told me, in a crazed falsetto giggle. "She's gone, Joey. For good."

He stayed awake for three days, thinking that at any minute he'd hear from her. Then he concluded that she must have already written, that the school's storm troopers were destroying her letters before they reached him. He turned over the nonexistent evidence so many times, it atomized under his touch. His explanations grew florid with appoggiaturas. I was supposed to listen to every ornament.

"János must have told her some lie about me. The school must have written her father. Who knows what slander they told him, Joey? It's a conspiracy. The maestros and the masters had to get together and hustle her away before I poisoned her." Jonah even tortured himself with the possibility that Kimberly herself had asked to be withdrawn. He disappeared into a cloud of theories. I brought him every scrap of thirdhand gossip I could gather. He waved away all my offerings as useless. Yet the more worthless I became, the more he wanted me around, a mute audience for his ever more elaborate speculations.

Late in December, he signed us out at the front office, saying we were heading to the Fine Arts Museum to see a European photography exhibition. The day was chill. He wore his green corduroy coat and a black-furred Russian cap that came down over his eyes. I can't remember what I wore. All I remember is the bitter cold. He walked alongside of me, saying nothing. We ended up in Kenmore Square. He sat me down on the curb at the T-stop entrance. The cold from the subway steps seeped up through my pants, and my underwear held the frost against my skin.

Jonah felt nothing. Jonah was on fire. "You know what this is about, Joey, don't you? You know why they're keeping her away from me?" *You know.* I knew. "The only question is . . . the only question is: Did she decide?"

But I knew that one, too. She'd been his. They'd learned scores together, unfolding each other. Nothing had changed except that they'd been caught in a supply closet. "Jonah. She knew . . . who you are. For as long as she's known you. She had eyes to see."

"A Moor, you mean? Could see I was a Moor?"

I couldn't tell who he was attacking: Kimberly, me, or himself. "I'm just saying. It's not like . . . she didn't know." The ice I sat on burned me.

"Her father didn't know. So long as her father assumed the Boylston Academy of Music's prizewinner was a harmless little white boy, he was just fine with her little puppy crush. Told her to enjoy herself. *Sempre* . . ."

He sounded old. Knowledge, like some disease, had come over him in the night, while I was sleeping. I put my arm on his shoulder. He did not feel it, and I took it off. I didn't know anymore how he felt about my touching him. Every sure thing was lost in the nightmare of growth. "Jonah. You don't know. You can't be sure that's what it was."

"Of course that's what it is. What else could it be?"

"Her father didn't want her . . . didn't want the two of you . . ." I couldn't bring myself to say what her father hadn't wanted. I hadn't wanted it, either.

"He wrote her a teasing letter. Told her to live life to the fullest."

"Maybe he thought . . . Maybe he didn't really know how . . ." I wanted to say *how far*.

"Joey. Stupidity's over."

I looked away, at the forked intersection, the newspaper shill's stand pitched against the subway railing, the diner across Beacon Street with its tawdry Christmas tinsel strung across the plate window. It had begun to snow. Maybe it had been snowing for a while.

"She left too fast for it to be anything else. Only one thing in the world makes people that crazy. János must have called Monera up. Told him the score. World-famous conductor can't have his prize girl running around with a little brown half-breed."

My brother had always been my private freedom, my basement-level safety of willful unconcern. People and their blindness had been put on this earth strictly for his amusement. He'd always declared how others

1 2 5

would see him. Every ambiguous slight, every veiled lynching had rolled off him until this one. Now the fever was in my brother's face: the prick of our childhood's vaccine, gone inflamed.

"Look at us, Joey!" His tone issued from a throat that had closed long before his had even opened. "What are we doing here? Couple of freaks. You know what we should have been?"

His words scattered me under the feet of the crowds that kept disgorging from the subway. We were homeless. We'd taken up living on this curb, no warmth, no sheltering inside to return to. Everything I knew to be certain was dissolving as fast as the fat flakes of snow landing on my brother's face.

"We should have been real Negroes. Really black." His lips were frozen; his words were a runny egg. "Pitch-black. Black as the sharps and flats. Black as that guy over there." His thumb flicked up a little trigger, and his finger targeted a man cutting diagonally across Brookline. I grabbed his hand. He turned and smiled. "Don't you think so, Joe? We should have been simple, straight-up. Black as Ethiopia in a power outage." He looked around, picking a fight with all of indifferent Kenmore Square. "We'd know where we stood, anyway. Our self-serving little rich kid friends would have stoned us to death. János wouldn't even have taken me into his fucking school. Nobody would've bothered using me. I wouldn't have to sing."

"Jonah!" I held my head and groaned. "What are you saying? They wouldn't expect a black person to *sing?*"

Jonah laughed like a crazy man. "See what you mean. Not without dancing. And not the shit they make me sing now."

"Shit, Jonah? *Shit?*" Everything we loved, everything we'd grown up on.

Jonah only chuckled. He raised his palms, the innocent victim. "You know what I'm saying. We wouldn't be . . . where we are."

We sat in our unreal lean-to, curled against the crowd. Snow accumulated in drifts around our feet. My mind raced. I had to keep us here. Classical music was all I knew how to do. "Real black . . . very black people sing what we sing."

"Sure they do, Joey."

"Look at Robeson."

"You look at Robeson, Joey. I've had enough of looking."

"What about Marian Anderson?" The woman our parents claimed had brought them together. "She's just cracked the Met. The door's open now. By the time we're . . ."

Jonah shrugged. "Greatest alto of the twentieth century. And they throw her a little second-scene bone, fifteen years past her prime."

I plunged ahead, down a path I couldn't make out. "What about Dorothy Maynor? Mattiwilda Dobbs?"

"You done?"

"There's more. Lots more."

"How many is lots?"

"Plenty," I said, drowning. "Camilla Williams. Jules Bledsoe. Robert McFerrin." I didn't need to name them. He, too, had them all memorized. Everyone who'd ever given us something to go on.

"Keep going."

"Jonah. Black people are breaking into classical music all the time. That woman who just played *Tosca* on national television."

"Price." He couldn't help smiling in pleasure. "What about her?" He flung his arms at me. "Look at us. Two halves of nothing. Halfway to nowhere. You and me, Joey. Out here in the middle of . . ." His hand swept the angular plaza, the people hurrying through the snow. "We'd have been better off. Nobody's going to want what they can't even—"

"She wanted you." I couldn't bring myself to say the bloodless girl's name. "She knew who you were. She knew that you . . . weren't white."

"Did she? Did she? She's twenty-five jumps ahead of me, then."

"Don't torture yourself, Jonah. You don't know. They might have taken her out of school for any—"

"She would have *written*." Furious at my trust, my blindness. "Joey. You know how they got the word *mulatto*?"

I was a long time answering. "You think I'm stupid, don't you? You think I'm a tagalong idiot." I tried to stand, but couldn't. My legs were a statue's. My butt was frozen to the curb. When I managed to rock forward and rise, his hand held me down. His face was full of wonder at realizing how much I'd stored up for years, in silence.

"I don't think anything of the sort, Joseph. I just think your parents brought you up in a dream."

"Funny. I was just thinking that about *your* parents. So tell me. Where'd the word come from?" The one I hated, whatever its origin.

"It's Spanish for 'mule.' Know why we're called that?"

"Cross between a horse and a . . . whatever."

"City boy." He reached out to pull my hat down over my eyes. "They call us mules because we can't reproduce ourselves. Think of it. No matter who you marry—"

"You'd never have married her, Jonah. It was just a game. Neither of you ever believed you were going to . . . Just a little operetta the two of you were dabbling in." Yet their ending, written by another.

I'd never talked back to him before. I sat still and waited for death. But he didn't even hear me. He started up again, resigned. "You and me, Mule. The two of us: one of a kind." What she'd always called us, our mother. Our secret bond of pride, all the years of growing up. "Couple of damn bears on roller skates is what we are."

A pair of ankles appeared to my left. I looked up at a policeman, staring down at us. His badge name looked Italian. He was as dark as either of us. Darkness was never really the issue.

The dark Italian scowled. "You boys are blocking traffic."

Jonah looked up at the man, all earnest attention, just waiting for the lift of his baton to stand and deliver an aria.

"You hear me?"

I nodded dumbly, for all of us.

"Then get the hell out of here, pronto. Before I cuff and print you."

Jonah did a three-point round-off, pushing back up to his feet. "I can't move," I bleated. I'd frozen into place. I'd have to go on sitting, freezing to death, like some doomed Jack London hero.

"You hear me?" the officer said. "You deaf?" Darker than olive. Maybe he had a secret Turkish ancestor hiding out in the family tree foliage. He grabbed me by one shoulder and dragged me to my feet. He twisted my arm so roughly that, had I been my own grandson, I'd have had grounds for a lawsuit.

Jonah raved at the policeman. "I'm a mulatto bel canto castrato with a legato smorzato." I pushed him away. He pushed back, leaning toward the cop and waving his finger. "That's my obbligato motto, Otto."

"So gesundheit, already." The man turned away from Jonah without a thought. He'd seen crazier. Every working hour: the sinkhole of human illness, on every block of his repeating beat. He threatened us vaguely with the back of his hand. "Get lost, hoodlums." We hobbled off, my limbs still stiff with the season. From a hundred yards, he yelled, "Merry Christmas." Anxious to thank him for his lenience, I returned the greeting.

One of my legs was cement. I called out to Jonah to slow down. We walked back along Yawkey Way, past the ballpark. Sometimes, in the early fall, from our room in the conservatory, we could hear the shouts of the desperate stands. Now the Fenway sat abandoned, a nuisance winter slum.

Jonah walked two steps ahead of me, hands in his pockets. His words formed frozen vapor puffs on the air. "I'm worried about her, Joey. Her parents . . . Her father might have . . ."

I wanted to tell him. But I was his brother, before anything.

By the time we got back to the conservatory, the snow had crusted us both in white. The roads lapping the Fens had that low, gray, angled, cloudy light of civil defense drills. Cars padded along at half speed on the strewn wadding. We couldn't even see the school until we were in it.

We stepped back into hushed excitement. Students backed away from us in the corridor where we entered. For a moment, we were that sterile cross-species my brother had said we were. A boy we didn't know addressed us. "You're in trouble. They're looking all over for you."

"Who?" Jonah challenged. But the boy just shrugged and pointed toward the office. His eyes shone a little at the thought of the angel-voiced Jonah Strom taking a fall.

We shook the crust of white from us and headed for the office. I wanted to run; the faster we owned up, the lighter the sentence might be. But nothing could move Jonah from his usual hallway pace. In the office, even the adults shied from us. We'd somehow gone beyond them on our short walk, traveled to a place they weren't ready to reach.

The assistant head laid into us. "Where have you been? We've torn the whole school apart looking for you."

"We signed out," Jonah said.

Our scolder was distraught beyond the scale of our offense. "Your father's waiting for you. He's upstairs in your room."

A look passes between us, pinning us where we stand. A look we'll exchange forever. We take the stairs in a sprint, two at a step. My brother shoots up ahead, landing after landing, still in full breath when I'm already sucking air. He could stop and let loose a high A for fifteen seconds, without strain.

I reach the summit, gasping. My brother already dashes down the hall. I follow Jonah into our room in time to hear him ask Da, "What's going on? What are you doing here?" He has his theories, already. He sounds more thrilled than winded.

The man sitting on Earl Huber's bed is not our father. This man is bent, shrunken, more bag man than mathematical physicist. His skin is drained. Under his clashing cardigan, his chest heaves. The face swings up to me, some shrill claim at blood relations. But this is not a face I've ever had to meet. Behind the tortoiseshell glasses, under the cubed forehead, the muscles fall slack. Our father thinks he's smiling at us. A beseeching smile, gone begging. A smile that expands and settles in me, driving me from childhood.

"How are you boys? How are you two?" The German accent has thickened to a gruel, the *how* broadening to *who*. I thank God that we're alone, no boys from the *C* cities in Ohio to explain things to.

"Da?" Jonah asks. "What's wrong? Everything okay?"

"Okay?" our father echoes. Empirical reductionist. *Okay* has no measurement. *Okay* is a meter stick that shrinks with the speed of the measurer. He inhales. His jaw flops open to form a word. But the puff of consonant clutches on his throat's thin ledge, a suicide wanting to jump, wanting to be coaxed back in. "There was *ein Feuer*. An explosion. Everything . . . burned. She's . . ." All the words he auditions and rejects hang in the air between us. And my father still smiles, as if he might somehow be able to accept what he can't even name.

"What's happened to her?" Jonah shouts. "Where did you hear this?"

My father turns to his eldest son. He tilts his head like the puzzled mutt hearing his master's voice coming out of the gramophone. He reaches out a hand to pierce the confusion. The hand, too small for anything, drops back into his lap. He's still smiling: Everything everywhere already *is*. He nods his head. "Your mother is dead."

"Oh," my brother says. And an instant too late, his relief turns to horror.

APRIL–MAY 1939

She was back in Philly on the 2:00 A.M. train. That very same night. No time at all for anything to have happened while she was in D.C. Yet she slipped back into the sleeping house like a criminal, bearing a secret wider than the Potomac. And she was still up, after four hours of feigned sleep, dragging out of bed to make her morning classes, and, after that, her job at the hospital, if she lived that long.

Her mother met her in the kitchen, the question on her lips, although all Philadelphia already knew the answer. So many radios had tuned to last night's broadcast, it was a miracle the city hadn't fished the wavelength dry. Every listener had hung on the sound of her own private Marian, singing from the steps of that most public Mall.

"How was your concert?" Nettie Ellen asked, as if Delia herself had been the singer. Something in the woman knew, as sure as history: If her daughter hadn't performed the night before, she was clearly performing up a storm that Monday morning.

"Oh, Mama. The biggest recital in the history of singing. The whole country was there—a dozen times more people than turned out for Jesus's loaves and fishes thing. And Miss Anderson fed everybody on even less than he did."

"Uh-huh. Good, then?" Nettie Ellen had heard every note of the shattering performance, cramped over the living room crystal receiver, that voice sailing up crisp and clear over the crackles of static. She, too, had swallowed down the bruise rising in her throat, the burning bile taste of hope—hope *again*, such foolishness, after all the corpses that had lined the way to that day. She'd read, before her daughter was out of bed, this morning's headlines, lobbed by Monday's paperboy over the porch into the burning bush: AMERICA THRILLS TO COLORED VOICE. Nettie hadn't time for America. She was up to her wrists in baking powder, flicking the bits of egg-wetted flour around in the stoneware mixing bowl. She beat at the recipe with a force her daughter couldn't fail to read. Nothing short of Judgment Day justified a grown woman coming home at 2:00 A.M., waltzing in like the whole world had turned itself inside out and hollering lawless.

But the lawless girl had gone strange to her, docile and awed. "Mama. Mama. I don't have time for biscuits." Nettie just glared, and Delia set about, helpless, to help make them. In her sleep-starved daze, Delia even got the children up and pointed them toward their school clothes while her mother kneaded and punished the recalcitrant dough.

The mystery rose up between them, too thick for naming over biscuits and gravy. Not that Nettie Ellen needed any names spelled out. Seventy-five thousand lovers of fancy singing all gathered in a single place, and of course her Delia was going to cross paths with one who'd keep her out until all hours of creation. Clear as the features on her face: The girl was love's zombie. Sighing like a chicken on an open fire. Setting the table in a dream, laying out the silverware as if spreading flowers on a grave.

Nettie Ellen had been waiting some time for this, braced for the spell that would turn her oldest child into another creature. She knew it would eventually settle in, as rapidly as spring—one minute, the lawn ratty and bare; the next, rolling in banks of aconite the color of condensed sun. It would as ever be the last, great test of selfless mothering: how to lay all her care down and let her own flesh and blood grow strange to her.

From the start, Nettie had vowed to rise to that last parental sacrifice before her girl forced her. But she hadn't foreseen this pure foolishness, her own daughter turning shy on her, as if Nettie hadn't spent years attending to the girl's body—sick, naked, and needy—as if a girl's *mother* didn't already know all about the need flesh was made for. Silly timidity, the mother had expected. But this, her daughter's frightened, inward flowering, was past all understanding.

Charles and Michael burst into the kitchen, filled with that good night's sleep Delia would never again enjoy. They launched their industrious breakfast torments, warbling at her, throwing their noses and pinkies in the air. Big sister just cupped their closely cropped heads to her, one in each palm, and gazed at them, as if memorizing their faces before stepping off remembrance's dock into oblivion. It scared them witless, and the boys took their chairs without another word.

Lucille and Lorene made their grand entrance, twinned displays of bows and shoe polish. Toward her little sisters' prim show, too, Delia turned bravely weepy. Over the ranks of plates and glasses, all Nettie's children bowed their heads in grace. Delia took her turn with the words: "Thank you God for all good things." The syllables rumbled through the kitchen, each a lumbering boxcar in foreboding's freight. All through her daughter's breakfast prayer, Nettie's lips worked away, moving to her own unheard incantation. One concert, and her girl would be forever strange to her? But even before her Delia had had anything to hide, the girl had always refused to be cornered.

Thanks given, Nettie raised her head and appraised her zombie saint. And over the steaming mounds of biscuit, some phantom movement caught her eye. The motion lasted only the barest second, if it moved at all. A whole family seemed to sit around the half table, lit in the lightning flash before her sight settled. A brace of faces, strangers to her, yet familiar as the ones who sat to this breakfast, *this* one. These spirit faces were not hers to name or know, yet somehow they seemed to belong, at one remove. Two or three, at first. Then, while Nettie turned her head to take them in, the faces multiplied. Before the glimpse dimmed and went out: more than she could count. More than could fit in her overflowing kitchen.

My line. The notion hit her with the force of foregone proof. *My grandchildren, come back to see me.* But something as thick and impenetrable as years held them clouded and soundproof, the far side of unreachable.

"Mama?" something called, and she fell back into now. "Mama?" That infant's first question, wanting no answer but *Here I am.* Her hands felt splotchy, weak with heat. The saucer below her trembling cup filled with a liquid the color of skin. She was spilling, shaking like the old woman she'd just been, only an instant before.

"Eat up now," she said, ignoring her eldest's alarm. Delia had been dishing out her own bright doses of fear all morning. It wouldn't hurt her to take a little. "Eat up, all of you. The world ain't going to hold up school, just so y'all can dawdle."

The children scattered at the sound of their father's descent. The doctor appeared, resplendent in serge, his shirt's iron whiteness shining out from underneath his suit like a bolt of ancient raiment. In his rich bronze voice, a tessitura that every time thrilled Delia to despair—*And the trumpet shall sound!*—he announced, "Seems she came through for us. Our Miss Anderson."

"She was perfect, Daddy. She sounded like God singing to Himself, the evening before the very first day."

"Hush," Nettie said. "Don't you go blaspheming."

William just nodded. "Good concert, then? Everything we could have hoped for?"

Hope had been so far outstripped, it now seemed too meek a preparation. "Good concert." Delia giggled and shook her head. "Good concert." She was far away, as far as the concert houses of Europe. Vienna. Berlin. Farther. "I think it changed my life."

The doctor's beam clouded to a scowl. He took his seat at the table's head, where a place setting materialized by magic in front of him. "What do you mean, 'think,' girl? If it changed your life, wouldn't you *know* it?"

"Oh, she knows it all right." Nettie Ellen fired her salvo from the sink, scraping at the child-savaged plates, her back to them both. Dr. Daley swept a look from wife to child. Delia could only shrug and hide in whatever scrap of protective foliage her parents deigned to leave to her.

The doctor devoured his breakfast. The steam off the brown-capped biscuit crusts, the thick smell of the gravy's suet roux pleased him. He spread the newspaper around him, his fixed routine. His face stayed impassive as he scoured the momentous headline. He commenced filleting both the gravy-strewn biscuits and the news into clean, digestible portions. He partitioned and consumed the account of the epochal concert with the same appetite he applied to Hitler's reinterpretation of the Munich Pact and insistence on Danzig. He dismantled the first section of the paper, flattening each sheet back with care, and scanned the stories through the final paragraph.

"It seems our nation's capital wasn't prepared for what hit it last night." He spoke to no one, or to everyone in earshot. "Is this performance the start of something, do you think?" He looked up at his daughter. Delia looked down, too fast. "Let's imagine, for a moment, they finally *heard*?"

Delia caught her father's eye. She stood waiting for the question. But it seemed he'd already asked it. She tried to nod, just a fraction of an inch, as if she followed him.

He shook his head and set to restoring the paper's front section to mint condition. "Who can say what it will finally take? Nothing else has worked. Why not try a little old-time singing? Though it's not like we haven't been doing a heap of that all along."

At the doctor's pronouncement, Nettie Ellen, still at sinkside, began humming to herself, her husband's cue to get along with the earning of the daily bread. On his way out, William cast his daughter one more look: concession, congratulation, as if the triumph of the night before had been hers.

The doctor decamped to his clinic and the day's first patients. That left just the oldest game going: mother and daughter, mutely reading each other, evading, trading, knowing before knowing. Nettie washed, and Delia stood by, drying. The proper cleanup. Air drying left streaks. You had to get to the dishes right away, with a towel and two elbows.

They finished. Both stayed in place, fussing and straightening. "I have to go," Delia said. "I'll be late for class."

"Nobody's keeping you."

Delia shoved her towel back on the rack. Her hands said, *Be that way, then.* She broke for the doorway, and made it as far as the stove. "Mama. Oh, Mama." Relief was easier, words were more obvious than she'd thought possible.

Her mother crossed the tiles to her, reached out one hand, and fixed the wave of hair that fell down across Delia's face. Hair whose curl looked different now to each of them.

"Mama? How long before . . . How soon did you know?"

Her mother reached up to fix Delia's heaving shoulders. "You take your time, child. The longer the making, the better the baking."

"Yes, Mama. I know. But how fast? Was there one clear thing that . . . made you realize?"

The daughter tried on a slant, scared smile. At that look, her mother saw her kitchen fill up again with invaders. Grandchildren. Great-grandchildren, relentless and multiplying, underfoot. They schooled around Nettie Ellen Daley, at once the oldest American woman still standing upright.

"How I felt about your father? Child. I'm *still* figuring out what I got going on with that man."

Delia fought for breath. She'd done nothing wrong. Nothing had happened. Nothing that meant anything. She was turning herself into a mad mooncalf for no reason. Giving herself pointless fits, over pure invention. Yet in the last night's rareness, the press of that record-setting crowd, up too close to history, something had turned in her. Some ancient law had split apart. Drunk on the godlike Miss Anderson, the voice of the century, a feather floating on a column of air, Delia made a separate journey, traveled down into the briefest crack in the side of sound. A widening in the day had opened up in front of her, pulling her and her German stranger into it. They'd traveled together down into long time, along a hall without dimension, to a place so far off, it couldn't even really be called the future, yet.

Now, in her mother's kitchen, it shamed her to think how she must have invented the whole trip. Nothing had happened. She'd traveled nowhere. And yet, the man had traveled to that nowhere with her. She couldn't have invented that. His eyes, as they said good-bye, already remembered the place in detail.

By that afternoon's bed-making shift at the hospital, Delia managed to put the dream behind her. By the next day's vocal lesson, she'd put it so far behind her, it was staring her in the face again. Lugati was going on about support, appoggio, that abdominal combination of tightening and relaxing too complicated for any but a medical student to follow. "A singer has only so much mileage in her," Lugati said. "If you drive yourself wrong, you'll spend your voice in ten years. Used right, your equipment can last as long as you do."

At those words, the German was there again, alongside her. Together, as they'd been in Washington, on the Mall. Using each other right. Lasting as long as they needed to.

By week's end, Delia had a letter from him. He asked if he might come to Philadelphia. She wrote back a dozen different answers, mailing only one. She met him out in front of Independence Hall—neutral territory. As in Washington, they lost themselves in a mixed, indifferent crowd.

Strangers turned to look. But none of them stranger than he. Again, that unreachable future opened up in front of them through a crack in the air. Again, they drew near to enter it. The wilder her feelings, the more she doubted. The man's visit was brief, lucky, mad. But anything more than one illicit afternoon outside Independence Hall would be impossible. Surely he saw that.

"When can we do this again?" he asked.

"We can't," she answered, squeezing his arm like a hank of emergency rope.

When he left, she felt empty again, criminal. It encouraged her, how quickly his accent fell away in her ear, how hard it was to re-create him in silence. His alien face grew amber, less pallid, when dissolved in her memory. She wouldn't see him again. Her life would return to her, simple, obvious, and pointed toward its goal.

She went to meet him in New York. She told her parents she had an audition—the first lie of any size she'd ever told them. Inside a month, she was telling larger. Her secret grew, even with poison waterings. She'd have to confess, or lose herself to duplicity. She had to make this wrong thing good again, as good as she sometimes imagined it was when they were together, alone, the sole curators of that long, dimensionless passage, the first visitors to that world they'd somehow shortcut to, diagonally, across the field of time. He knew all her music. He loved how she sang. She was herself with him.

She tried to tell her mother. Shame and disbelief prevented her. Once or twice, she started, then fled down another topic. Any words she tried to give it turned it evil. Like perfect fruit, it went rancid when exposed to the air. After some weeks, Delia stopped looking her mother in the eye. The lie spread into her daily doings, tainting routines that had nothing at all to do with the man. Her most innocent comings and goings slipped under the growing cloak of concealment. Even her little brothers and sisters began shying away from her.

Her mother kept still and waited for her to return. Delia could feel her, patient, kind, horribly wise, trusting to her gut, where motherhood lived. And in her trust, driving her daughter away.

Her mother stayed good, until goodness began to strangle them both. Then Nettie went upstairs one evening, to the little attic room that served as Delia's provisional studio. Delia stood in her posture of forced comfort, working a chunk of chromatic scale across the higher of the two passage points in her voice. She stopped at the knock on the door. Her mother stood, hands cupped as if around a coffee cup or a prayer book. Neither of them spoke for a quarter minute.

"You keep on singing. I'll just make myself hid and listen."

She hunched over, already old, her shoulders weighted down into an unanswered question mark by a hundred years of unanswered need.

"Mama" was all the girl could say.

Nettie Ellen stepped into the attic and sat. "Let me guess. He's poor."

Delia's private prize rushed upward, flushed out of the underbrush. She flared up, the righteousness of the guilty. Then anger dissolved in tears, easing into a relief she hadn't felt in weeks. She could talk to her mother. All distances might close again, in words.

"No, Mama. He's . . . not exactly poor. It's . . . worse than that."

"He's not a churchgoing man."

Delia bowed her head. The bare floor filled with sea for drowning in. "No." Her head made one slow, leaden swing. "No. He isn't."

"Well, that's not the end of the world." Nettie Ellen clicked in the back of her throat. The sound of all things that needed enduring. "You know we've always had our problems with your father on that count, and he sure don't seem about to jump up and reform anytime soon."

Nettie smiled at her daughter, mocking her own long-suffering. But she got no smile in return. Delia stood mute, her whole body begging, *Ask me some more. Please, please, keep asking.*

"He's not from around here, is he? Where's he from, then?"

The animal scare in her mother's eyes killed any chance Delia had of cleaving to the truth. "New York," she said, and slumped still lower.

"New York!" A glow of foolish hope in her mother celebrated the reprieve. "Thank the Lord. New York's nothing. We can *walk* to New York, girl. I thought you were going to say Mississippi."

Delia forced herself to laugh, heaping lie on lie.

Her mother heard the note at once. Her mother's golden ear, the one Delia had inherited. "Have pity on me. You got to tell. No way I'm going to guess. What could be so wrong with the man? He have three legs or something? Been married five times already? He don't speak English?"

A giggle tore from Delia, hollow and horrible. "Well. There is that."

Nettie Ellen's neck jerked back. "He don't? Well, what's he speak, then?"

Then a look. A wide-eyed, overdue dawning. Sorrow, fear, incredulity, pride: all the colors of the rainbow, bent out of the white light of incomprehension. The question she'd climbed up into this attic studio to ask died on her lips. *Do you love him at least?* no longer had any bearing.

"You're saying he's not one of us?"

The full force of that mad simplicity. Hundreds of years lifted off Delia. Centuries of evil and worse, waiting for their answer. She felt the long-sought appoggio well up under her breath. History was a bad dream that the living were obliged to shake. The world—right use—could start from now.

"That's right, Mama. He's not . . . entirely one of us."

In the centuries that sprang up between them, neither, anymore, was she.

BIST DU BEI MIR

We went back home with Da. I say "home," but the place was gone. We stood in front of the gutted building, staring at the rime of frost that coated our blackened freestone. I stood in a mound of rubble, looking for the place I'd grown up in.

I kept thinking that we were one street too far south. The fire had charred the two entrances on either side of ours. Our building looked like the target of a stray artillery shell. Wood, brick, stone, and metal— things that couldn't have come out of our house—lay heaped up in a twisted mass. But everyone—our neighbors, our invalid landlady, Mrs. Washington, even Mrs. Washington's Jack Russell terrier—had gotten out alive. Every living creature but my mother.

We stood in front of the ruin so long, we were in danger of freezing. I couldn't look away. I looked for the little spinet we'd always sung around, but nothing in that pile of slag remotely resembled it. Jonah and I huddled together, stamping, our breath steam. We stood until the cold and the pointlessness grew worse than our need. At last, Da turned us away from the sight for good.

Ruth didn't come with us for that last look. She'd already had hers. Rootie had been the first, coming home to a house in flames. Her local grade school's bus, unable to turn into our barricaded street, let her off at the corner. She didn't know until she walked into the mob of firemen just whose house was burning. The men had to drag the screaming ten-year-old girl away from the blaze. She bit one of them on the hand, drawing blood, trying to fight free.

She screamed at me, too, as soon as we saw her. "I tried to find her, Joey. I tried to go in. They wouldn't let me. They let her die. I watched them."

"Hush, *Kind*. Your mother was already dead a long time by the time you came even close." Da meant it as consolation, I'm sure.

"She was burning up," Ruthie said. "She was on fire." My sister had become another life. The oldest child on earth. Air rasped in and out of her. She started at something none of us could see. I put my arm on her and she didn't even register.

"Shh. No one could be inside a flame like that and still feel." Da had lived too long in the world of measurement. To him, even a ten-year-old girl wanted only the truth.

"I heard her," Ruthie said, though not to any of us. "They trapped me. They wouldn't let me reach her."

"The *Heizkörper* exploded," Da explained.

"The what? The hot body?"

"The boiling," Da said. "The heating." He'd forgotten how to speak the language. Any language.

"The furnace," I translated.

"There had been a leak, most likely. The furnace exploded. This is why she could not get away from this fire, even though it came on her in the middle of the day."

This was the theory that best fit all evidence. For weeks, in my dreams, things exploded. And in full daylight, too. Things I couldn't name or outrun.

We moved into a tiny apartment down in Morningside Heights that a colleague loaned my father for the length of our emergency. We lived like refugees, dependent on the gifts of others. Even our classmates from Boylston sent us boxes of castoffs, not knowing what else to do.

My father arranged a memorial service. This was the first and last complex social act he ever managed to pull off without our mother's help. There was no casket for viewing, no body left for burial. My mother had already been cremated, on someone else's orders. All of our pictures of her had burned, alongside her. Friends contributed what keepsakes they had, to make a remembrance table. They propped them up on a sideboard by the hall door: clippings, concert programs, church bulletins—more mementos of my mother than I'd ever see again.

I didn't think the little rented hall would fill. But people kept coming until they couldn't get in. Even my father had underestimated, and he needed to call in more folding chairs. It stunned me to discover my mother had *known* so many people, let alone could bring them out on a bleak midwinter Sunday afternoon. "Jonah?" I kept asking under my breath. "Jonah? Where did all these people come from?" He looked and shook his head.

Some of the gathering turned out for my father's sake. I recognized several of his colleagues from the university. Here and there, black yarmulkes clung to the crowns of balding skulls. Even Da briefly wore one. Others in the crowd came for Ruth, kids she went to school with, neighbor children we never really knew but whom Ruth had befriended. But most of the room turned out to send off my mother: her students, her fellow church circuit singers, her improbable assortment of friends. In my child's mind, I'd always thought of Mama as an exile, barred from a country that should have been hers. But she'd furnished exile and thrown it open wide enough to make a life in.

From up front in the room, mourning's showcase row, I turned around to sneak a look at her crowd. I scanned the range of colors. Every hue I'd ever seen sat somewhere in that room. The faces behind me shone in all gradations, shades split and glinting like the shards of a light-splashed mosaic. Each one insisted on its own species. Flesh casts slanted off everywhere, this way mahogany, that way walnut or pine. Clumps of bronze and copper, pools of peach, ivory, and pearl. Now and then, some extreme: bleached paste from out of the flour bin of a Danish pastry kitchen, or a midnight cinder from down in the engine room of history's ocean liner. But in the spectrum's bulging middle, all imaginable traces and tinges of brown packed onto folding chairs against one another in the crowded room. They gave themselves up by contrast, taupe turning evidence on ambers, tan showing up tawny, pinks and gingers and teaks giving the lie to every available name ever laid over them. All ratios of honey to tea, coffee to cream—fawn, fox, ebony, buff, beige, bay: I couldn't begin to tell brown from brown. Brown like pine needles. Brown like cured tobacco. Tones that might have been indistinguishable by daylight—chestnut, sorrel, roan—pulled away from the tones they sat next to under the low lamps of those close quarters.

Africa, Asia, Europe, and America had slammed into one another, and these splintered tints were the shards of that impact. Once, there were as many shades of flesh as there were isolated corners of the earth. Now there were many times that many. How many gradations did anyone see? This polytonal, polychordal piece played for a stone-deaf audience who heard only tonic and dominant, and were pretty shaky even picking out those two. But all the pitches in the chromatic scale had turned out for my mother, and many of the microtones between.

This was my stolen, forbidden look back. Next to me, Jonah kept craning his neck, twisting in his chair, scanning the audience for someone. At last, Da told him, as sharply as he ever spoke to us, "Stop, now. Sit still."

"Where's Mama's family?" Jonah's voice reverted to soprano. A field of welts marked his face where he'd tried to shave. "Is that them? Are they here? They have to come for *this*, don't they?"

Da hushed him again, lapsing into German. His words floated out without bearing, spreading across all the places he'd ever lived. He spoke rapidly, forgetting that his sons had a different mother tongue. I made out something about how the people in Philadelphia would have their own service, so everyone could attend without having to make the journey. Jonah didn't catch any more than I did.

My father wore the same style of double-breasted gray suit already years out of date when he'd gotten married in one. He studied his knees with the same baffled smile with which he'd told us our mother was dead. Ruth sat next to Da, tugging at the sleeves of her dress's black velvet, whispering to herself, her hair a tent of snarls.

1 4 1

A well-meaning but bewildered minister told my mother's life story, which he didn't know from Eve's. Then friends stepped in to salvage the wreck the eulogy made of her. They told stories about her girlhood, a mystery to me. They named her parents and gave them a past. They brought to life her brothers and sisters, and recalled their three-story house in Philadelphia, a family fortress I pictured as an older, wooden version of our brownstone, which had burned down around her. The speakers seemed almost ready to fight over what they had most loved in her. One said grace; another said humor. Another said her foolish belief that the worst in us was fixable. No one said what they wanted. No mention of being spit on in elevators, no threatening letters, no daily humiliations. No talk of fire, no explosion, no being melted alive. People in the audience called out aid at every pause, joining the refrains like those congregations my mother once sang for. I sat up front, nodding at each testimonial, smiling when I thought I was supposed to smile. I would have spared them all, told every speaker to sit down, said that they didn't have to say anything, if it had been in my power.

My mother's student, a bass-baritone named Mr. Winter, told how she'd been refused by the school where she first wanted to study. "Not a lesson went by for me when I didn't bless those sorry bastards for putting Mrs. Strom on another path. But if I were a federal judge, I'd sentence them to one afternoon. Just one. Listening to the sounds that woman could make."

It came my father's turn to speak. No one expected him to, but he insisted. He stood, his suit flying outward in all directions. I tried to straighten him up a little as he rose, which sent a nervous laugh through the whole congregation. I wanted to die. I'd have given all our lives for hers, and come out ahead.

My father walked up behind the podium. He bowed his head. He smiled out across the audience, a pale beam aimed at other galaxies. He took off his glasses and wiped them with his handkerchief, the way he always did when overcome. As always, he succeeded only in smearing around his eyebrow grease. For a moment, he blinked, sightless, a bloated, poached whitefish lost in this sea of real color. How could my mother have seen past such a skin?

Da slid his glasses back on, and became our Da again. The thickness of his spectacles made him cock his head. The raised side of his face went up in a horrible grin. He held out his right hand and shook it in the air, about to start one of his lectures on relativity by telling a funny story about clocks on moving trains or twins on rocket ships traveling near the speed of light. He shook his hand again, and his mouth fell open, preparing the first word. A dry clicking came out of his throat. His voice spread across thousands of staggered attacks, all the part-songs he'd ever started with her. He floundered on the upbeat.

At last, the first word cleared the hurdle of his larynx. "There is an old Jewish proverb." This wasn't my father. My father was out standing in the face of some terrible bare wind. "A proverb that goes, 'The bird and the fish can fall in love . . .' "

The jaw dropped and the clicking came on again—dry reeds on a riverbank scraping one another. He held still for so long, even my embarrassment, in that dry clicking, scattered, along with the room's every discomfort, into silence. My father lifted up his chin again and smiled. Then, with a crumpled apology, he sat down.

We sang: the only part of the day that might have pleased her. Mr. Winter delivered "Lord God of Abraham," from Mendelssohn's *Elijah*. The best of my mother's amateur women took a run at the Schubert "Ave Maria," Miss Anderson's hallmark, so loved by my mother that she herself had not sung it since girlhood. The student singer couldn't control any note above her second E. Grief tore up her vibrato, and yet, she'd never again come so close to a perfect rendering.

One by one, then in groups, the voices my mother once sang with took their turn singing without her. They littered the room with fragments of *Aida*. They sang Russian art songs whose words were a wash of phonetic watercolor. They sang spirituals, the only folk music that always harmonized itself out to four, five, even six abandoned and abiding parts. They stood and sang spontaneous bits of gospel, all the available scraps of improvised salvation.

For the briefest, thinnest moment, I heard it again, the game of Crazed Quotations—my parents' eternal courtship ritual and their children's first singing school. Only here, the counterpoint slowed and drew itself into a single thread. Deep turned to wide, chords to lines. Yet something of that old melodic piling up remained. And the something that remained was my mother. She'd come from more places than even her hybrid children could get to, and each one of those clashing places sang its signature tune. Once, those competing strains had fought to pass through the ear all at once. Now they gave up and took turns, polite, at last, in death, each making way for the other, lengthwise down the testament of time.

My father didn't try to sing. He was too smart for that. But he didn't stay silent, either. He'd written out a three-minute quodlibet, a record of our old evenings together, nights that had seemed endless, once, but had more than ended. Into those three minutes, he packed every quote that fit the seed harmonic progression. He could not, in any conceivable universe, have composed the piece in the few days since her death. Yet if he'd written out the piece in advance, it could only have been with this occasion in mind.

He'd scored it for five voices, as if we were still the singers. He might as well have written an aria for Mama herself to perform. An ad hoc quintet of her friends and students stood in for us, while we sat in the mute audience. On short notice, they worked a miracle. They reassembled Da's crazed pastiche, giving it the virtuosity of an airy good-bye. Had they heard the thing for what it was, they'd never have gotten through it: our family's nightly musical offering, thanks for a gift we thought would always be ours.

Da performed a feat of musical reconstruction. All our old quotation games had died and burned, as sure as every family album. Yet here was one intact again, exactly the collage we'd sung one night, in everything but the particulars. Da somehow recovered that name, too familiar to retrieve. He was the transcriber, but he could never have composed this piece alone. She was there in counterpoint, laying down line on line. Note by note, he pulled her back from the grave. Her "Balm in Gilead" careened into his Cherubini. Her Brahms *Alto Rhapsody* bickered with his growled klezmer. Debussy, Tallis, Basie: For the length of that collage, they made a sovereign state where no law prevented that shacking up, such unholy harmonies. This was the only composition Da ever wrote down, his one answer to the murderous question of where the fish and the bird might build their impossible nest.

My brother and I were slated to go on after Da's piece. I stole a look at Jonah as the group headed toward the work's surprise, inevitable home. His face was a nest of wasps. He didn't want to stand and perform in front of this audience. Didn't want to sing for them. Not now, not ever. But we had to.

The piano in that rented room played damp and wayward. My brother's voice was wrecked with refusal. He'd chosen a song he could no longer sing, one pitched up a childhood above his highest note. I'd tried every way possible to talk him out of the choice. But Jonah wouldn't be moved. He wanted to do that Mahler he and Mama had once auditioned together. "Wer hat dies Liedlein erdacht?" Who thought up this little song?

This was the way he wanted to remember her. Two years after their joint performance had gotten him into the academy, Jonah had asked that she not come pick him up at the holidays. Now the source of all his love and shame had died before he could release her from that banishment. He'd carry this fact with him for the rest of his life. Not even singing would be able to expel it.

Two nights earlier, he'd come up with the monstrous idea of singing the whole song in falsetto, up in the original soprano of *The Boy's Magic Horn*, like some grotesque countertenor straining for the unreachable return. I made him hear the absurdity. We took it down an octave, and except for that jarring dissonance—the innocent words sung in his exiled range—we got through it. The mourners must have found the tribute inexplicable. What did this darling girl in her mountain house have to do with the matter-of-fact, irreverent black woman from Philadelphia, burned alive before the age of forty? But the girl in the song was Mama. Who could declare how her sons saw her? Death mixes all the races. Now more than ever, she was that girl, looking out forever on the original green meadow.

Our house had burned and our mother was dead. But we had no body to prove it. I wasn't old enough to believe, without the evidence of seeing. To me, all these people had gathered to sing, rehearsing for some future first anniversary of the missing one's return. Who thought up this little song? Only when the hidden mountain girl took my mother's face did she at last appear to me. And only in my father's tortured, fairy-tale language could *wund* rhyme with *gesund*:

> My heart is sore.
> Come, Treasure, and heal it!
> Your black-brown eyes
> Have wounded me.
>
> Your rosy mouth
> Makes hearts healthy,
> Makes boys wise,
> Makes the dead live . . .

Who, then, thought up this pretty little song?
Three geese carried it over the water,
Two gray and one white.
And for those who can't sing this little song,
These geese will whistle it.

I pressed the keys that her fingers once had pressed, in the same order she'd once pressed them. Jonah whistled his way through the tune, inventing it in midflight. I stayed with him, beat for beat. The extra octave in his thickened cords disappeared. He sang the way others only thought to themselves. His voice came to the notes like a bee to a flower, amazed by the precision of its own flight: light, true, unthinking, doomed. Everything was over in a minute and a half.

Your voice is so beautiful. I want you to sing at my wedding. She never knew how much the joke terrified me. *So I'm married already. That can't stop me from wanting you to sing at my wedding!* Maybe even being dead would not stop her wanting. Maybe this was the wedding she wanted us to sing for.

Her brown-black eyes might have made us healthy, might have made us wise. Might have raised us all from the dead, had she not died first. Who can say why she loved that pretty little song? It wasn't hers. It was some other world's. This life wouldn't let her sing it. Mama's three geese—two gray and one white—carried the song back over the water for her, to the place where she never got to live.

I played once more that day, a final accompaniment to finish out the service. Throughout all the speeches and songs, Rootie sat on the wooden chair next to Da, picking at her stocking knees, peeling her shoe soles, her wayward hands daring her mother to come from out of the burning house and slap them. For nights after the fire, Ruth had gone to bed wailing and awakened in screams. She'd choke on her spittle, demanding to know where Mama was. She wouldn't stop weeping until I told her no one knew. After a week, my sister settled into a hard, safe cyst, turning her secret over and over. The world was lying to her. For unknown reasons, no one would tell her what had really happened. The grown-ups were setting her a task, a test for which she was completely on her own.

Even at the memorial, Ruth was already working on that mystery. She sat in her chair, twisting her hem into ribbons, turning over the evidence. Daytime, at home, and everyone escaped but one. Ruth knew Mama.

Mama would never have been caught like that. All during the remembrances, Rootie kept up a steady subvocal dialogue, quizzing and tea-partying with her now-vaporized dolls. Now and then, she scribbled into the palm of her hand with her index finger, indelible notes to herself on her ready skin, all the things she must never forget. I leaned down to hear what she was whispering to herself. In the smallest voice, she was repeating, "I'll make them find you."

However unforgivable, we saved my sister for last. Ruth was our mother's best memory, the thing most like Mama in the world. At ten, she'd already begun to show the voice Mama had. Ruth had all the goods—a pitch that matched Jonah's, Mama's richness, a feel for phrase beyond anything I could produce. She might have gone beyond us all in music, given a different world.

She sang that learner's song, by Bach and not by Bach, the simplest tune in the world, too simple for Bach himself to have written it without help. The tune appeared in Bach's wife's notebook, the place where she scribbled down all her lessons. Ruth had learned it from Mama, without a lesson at all.

> Bist du bei mir, geh' ich mit Freuden
> zum Sterben und zu meiner Ruh'.
> Ach, wie vergnügt wär' so mein Ende,
> es drückten deine lieben Hände
> mir die getreuen Augen zu!

> If you are with me, I'll go gladly
> to my death and to my rest.
> Ah, how pleasant would my end be,
> with your dear hands pressing
> shut my faithful eyes!

Root sang as if she and I were the only two souls left alive. Her sound was small but as clear as a music box. I kept off the sustain pedal, sounding each chord almost tentatively, not with the press of my fingers but with the release. Her held lines floated above my stepwise modulations like moonlight on a lost, small craft. I tried not to listen, except to stay inside the throw of her beam.

The simplest tune in the world, as simple and strange as breathing.

Who knows what the room heard? I'm not even sure Rootie understood the words. They may have been meant originally for God. But that's not where Ruth sent them.

We sat down to a silent room. Ruth never again sang in her father's language, never again performed her mother's beloved European music in public. Never again, until she had to.

The room sang itself out with "On That Great Gettin' Up Morning." The song wasn't listed in the program, but it came off almost as if by plan. My mother's friends let loose with the sunniest syncopated major. One exchange of glances was enough to set the send-off tempo. Voices with voices, rich, rolling, knowing we'd never have any other account but this. The ad libs grew dizzy, and I checked Jonah to see if we might add some ornaments to the fray. He just looked at me, swollen, and said, "Take it away, if you want."

Afterward, the group visited over little square-cut sandwiches, tucking into the food with an appetite that made me hate them all. The few children in attendance sniffed out Ruth, who couldn't bring herself either to play or stand off. Jonah and I held up the wall, just watching people smile and enjoy one another. When anyone came by to say how sorry they were, Jonah thanked them mechanically and I told them it wasn't their fault.

A man came up to us. I hadn't seen him during the service. He seemed as negligent with age as any adult. He was in his early thirties, ten years older than was decent in anyone. He seemed to me the perfect color, just the cinnamon side of clove. He walked up to us, shy, certain, curious, his eyes rimmed with red. "You boys cook," he said. His voice struggled. "You boys really hum."

He couldn't smile. He kept looking around the room, ready to bolt. I couldn't understand how someone I didn't know could feel such grief for my mother.

"Is that good or bad?" Jonah asked.

"Real good. Good as it gets. You remember I told you that." He bent down, his blood-streaked eyes at our level. He stared at us, himself remembering. "You," he accused Jonah, index finger out. "You sound like her. But you." His hand swung around in a slow quarter circle. "You *are* like her. And I'm not talking shade."

The man straightened up and peered down on us. I felt Jonah turn fierce, even before I heard him. "How would you know? Do you even know us?"

The man held up his disarmed palms. They looked like mine. His palms would have looked no different had he been white.

"Hey, hey. Keep cool, cat." He sounded like what Thad and Earl would have died to be able to imitate. "I just know is how I know."

Jonah heard it, too. "You were close to her or something?"

The man only looked at us, his head sliding from side to side. We amazed him, and I couldn't say how. He couldn't accept our being, but he found it wonderful, even comic. He put his hands on each of our heads. I let him. Jonah shook free.

The man backed off, still shaking his head, filled with sad wonder. "You two really hum. Remember that." He looked around the room again, afraid of being caught, or maybe wanting to be. "You say hello to that Da of yours. From Michael, okay?" Then he turned from the sorrowing party and left.

We found our father drawing Feynman diagrams on the back of a napkin for two of his Columbia colleagues. They were arguing about the reversibility in time of elementary colliding particles. It seemed obscene, that they should be talking about anything other than death or Mama. Maybe, for Da, they were talking about both.

Jonah broke up the session. "Who's Michael, Da?"

Our father turned away from his colleagues, a blank across his face. We were simply the next people intent on getting him to solve a problem for them. "Michael?" Failing to recognize the name of this new elementary particle. He looked at us, registered who we were. Something engaged. He grew frightened and excited, all at once. "Here?" Jonah nodded. "A tall man? About a hundred and ninety centimeters?" We looked at each other, frightened. Jonah shrugged. "A fine-looking man? Narrow face? One of his ears does this?"

Da flipped down his right ear flap to mimic the fold we'd both noticed. He never mentioned the cinnamon. First thing anyone else would want to know. Our father never even asked.

"Yes?" he asked. "This is him?" Still happy, still scared. He looked about the room, matching Michael's own furtive look. "Where is he?"

Jonah shrugged again. "He's gone."

"Gone?" Da's face drained as pale as the day he came up to Boston to tell us about Mama. "Away?"

I nodded at the imbecile question. Something had gone wrong, and it was Jonah's and my fault. I nodded, trying to right things. But Da never even saw me. Our father was never at home in his body. The thing was squat and his soul was slender. When he moved, he slumped along next to himself like an overpacked suitcase. But at least this once, he ran. He moved through the rooms so quickly, the surrounding conversations were sucked up into his wake. Jonah and I scrambled to chase after him.

Da ran outside, on the street, ready to dash on through the passersby. He got as far as the first cross street. I watched him from half a block back. He didn't belong in this neighborhood. He fell off the edge even of this street's broad spectrum.

The buzz of conversation kept spilling from the little rented hall behind us. Da turned and rejoined us, beaten. The three of us went back in. The hum hushed at our entrance. Da looked around at the gathering, still trying to smile.

Jonah asked, "He was somebody we know or something?"

"He said I look like Mama." I sounded like a child.

"You both look like your mother." Da refused to look at us. "All three of you." He took off his glasses and pressed his eyes. He slipped his glasses back on. The smile, the grin of disbelief, the slow shake of the head left him. "My boys." He wanted to add, *My JoJo*, but couldn't. "My boys. That was your uncle."

SPRING 1949

I'm seven years old when our father tells me the secret of time. We're halfway up the steps from 189th Street, climbing toward the next way camp along our route, a place called Frisch's Bakery on Overlook Terrace. Pick a Sunday near Easter in the spring of 1949.

My brother Jonah is eight. He climbs the stairway like a tank, two stairs to my labored one. In this year, Jonah's hips still come up near my sternum. He climbs as if he wants to leave me in his distant past. He probably would if Da didn't hold us together, one boy in each whitened hand.

Our father has worked on time since time began. He was working on it even before my brother was born. I can't get enough of the idea: Jonah nothing, not even a speck of dust, and my father already at work, not even missing us, not even knowing that company is coming.

But now, this year, we're here with him. We make this long pilgrimage to Frisch's together, stopping to catch our breath. "To catch up with ourselves," Da says. Jonah has already caught up with whoever he is, tugging at the leash of our father's arm, smelling adventure just up this stone-paved hill. I'm winded and need the rest. All this is half a century ago. The day has brittled in the interim, like a box of old postcards from Yellowstone and Yosemite laid open in a spring-cleaning purge. Anything I remember now must be half invention.

We pass people who recognize my father from when he used to live here. "Before I met your mother." The sound of this frightens me. My father greets some of them by name. He says hello as if he just saw these strangers the day before. These people—older than the moon and stars—are cool to him, distant in a way Da doesn't see. They flick us a look, and we are all the explanation they need. Already I'm used to seeing all that Da won't notice.

Our Da watches his old neighbors walk along Bennett Avenue in stunned persistence. The war is four years over. But even now, Da seems unable to figure how we've all been spared. Spring 1949, he and his boys, moored halfway up the steps to Overlook. He shakes his head, knowing something none of his former Washington Heights neighbors would ever believe, now or in a lifetime of Sundays. Everyone is dead. All those names no more than myths to me—Bubbie and Zadie and Tante—everyone we never knew. All of them gone. But all still here, in the shake of our Da's head.

"My boys." Da says the word to rhyme with *voice*. He smiles, lamenting what he must say. "*Now* is nothing but a very clever lie." We should never have believed in it, he says. Two twins have dismantled the old illusion. Somehow the twins have our names, although twins are the last thing my brother and I are. "One twin, call him Jonah, leaves the earth forty years before, traveling in a rocket near the speed of light. Joey, the other twin, stays home on earth. Jonah comes back, and this you cannot guess: The twin brothers aren't the same age anymore! Their times have run at different speeds. Joey, the boy who stays at home, he is old enough now to be his brother's grandfather. But our Jonah, the rocket boy: This one has jumped into his brother's future, without ever leaving his own present. I tell you: This is, every word, true."

Da nods, and I see he is serious. This is the secret of time that no one can guess, that no one can accept, except that they have to. "Every twin has his own tempo. The universe has as many metronomes as it has moving things."

The day in question must be fine, because I no longer feel it. Perfect weather disappears, in time. Even back now, the world already seems outdated. The war is over; everyone who isn't dead is free to do anything. At eight and seven, my brother and I wait for the stream of breakthroughs that will revive the planet and make us feel finally at home. Mechanical stairs, to lift us up to Overlook without moving. Visual telephones on your wrist. Floating buildings. Pellets that change into any food you want—just add water. Dial-up music, everywhere on demand. This brick and iron city is something I'll remember in old age, with the same head-wagging smile of bewilderment my father resorts to, here in this foreign country, in this false now.

I see my impatience mirrored in Jonah's eyes. This whole place is backward, outmoded. There aren't even rocket ships yet, except for the one those twins use to split time in two. We know what they'll look like already, and what planets we'll take them to. The only thing we don't know is how long it'll take until they finally arrive.

I look at Da and wonder if he'll live to see them, these speed-of-light ships he tells us about. Our father is obscenely old. He has just turned thirty-eight. I can't imagine what fluke has let him live so long. God must have heard about his work, all the different-speed clocks, and given our Da a clock with a mainspring all its own.

We reach the stairs' crest, the sidewalk on Overlook Terrace. We bear left, toward Frisch's Bakery, past a steel mesh trash can I remember better than yesterday. In front of that can, there's a dead bird. We can't be sure what kind, because it's coated in a chocolate swarm of ants. We walk along, past that paint-scabbed bench where, one night a quarter of a century later, back in a Washington Heights I'll no longer recognize, I'll tell the kindest soul I'll ever meet that I can't marry her. Today, an old man—maybe twenty—owns the bench. He slings one arm over the backrest and points his shoulders toward eternity. He has on a banded hat and thick, pilling suit. I look at the man, and remember him. He looks back at us, jumping from boys to father and back, his eyes confused—the confusion we produce everywhere but home. Before he turns to deliver some hostile greeting, Jonah yanks Da guide-dog style across the street, toward Frisch's, and further explanation.

With each step that he pulls away from me, Jonah's clock slows down. But if his clock slows, it only makes him more impatient. Jonah races and slows; Da dawdles and speeds up. He's still talking, as if we can follow him. "Light, you see, always flies around you at the same speed. Whether you run toward it or away. So some measure must shrink, to make that speed stand still. This means you cannot say when a thing happens without saying where, in what frame of motion."

This is how he talks. He has gone a little crazy. This is how we know it's Da. He can look down this length of Sunday street and see no single thing at rest. Every moving point is the center of some hurtling universe. Yardsticks shrink; weight gets heavier; time flies out the window. He pokes along at his own pace. I try to keep our three hands linked. But there's too much difference. Jonah flies and Da drags, and soon Da's time will run so fast, we'll lose him to the past. He doesn't really need us. He doesn't need any audience at all. He's with Bubbie and Zadie, with his sister and her husband, working on a way to bring them back.

I try to make him laugh, humor him. "The faster you go, the slower your time?"

But Da just hikes up his face, approving my silliness.

A car races past, faster than Jonah. "That car's clock is wrong? Too slow?"

Our father chuckles, a loving-enough dismissal. He doesn't say, *The difference, at low speeds, is insignificant.* The difference, for him, is monumental. "Not too slow. Slower than yours. But fast enough for himself!"

I don't have a clock. But I don't bother reminding him. He'll give me one for Christmas, later this year. And he will warn me, so gravely that I can't tell if he's joking or not, never to set it backward.

"The driver of that car," he says, although the car is long gone, "gets older slower than you."

"So if we all drove around fast . . ." I begin. My father watches me work through it, his face all encouragement. "We'd live longer?"

"Longer, by who?"

He's asking me. Really asking. But the question must be a trick. Already I'm searching for the trick answer.

"Remember that for us, in our frame, our own clocks slow down not at all!" He speaks as if he knows I won't catch up to this message for years. I'm the receiver and messenger all in one, expected to carry the message to myself, somewhere far from now. "We cannot jump into our own futures," he tells the future me. "Only into someone else's."

I look down the street onto this slurry of moving times, and it's too crazy. Clocks and yardsticks softer than taffy. Time all fractured and oozing, sliding at different rates, like an excitable choir that cannot set a tempo. If now is really so fluid and mad, how can we even meet here, Da and I, long enough to talk?

Jonah's gone, disappearing into the doorway of what must be Frisch's. I have a daymare, seeing myself round the corner and enter the shop, fifty years old, a hundred, even older than Da, but not knowing how old I've become until Jonah looks at me in horror.

"The faster you go, the stranger measurement gets." Da sings the words. He rocks his head while he walks, like a conductor. "Close to the speed of light, very strange indeed. Because light still passes you at light speed!" He whips his hand through the now-warped air.

"If you speeded up past the speed of light . . ." I start, happy at the thought of going back.

"You cannot go past the speed of light." His voice stings with displeasure. I've done some wrong, offended him. My face crumples. But Da doesn't notice. He's off somewhere, measuring with a yardstick that shrinks to zero.

Jonah waits for us in Frisch's. He's caused a clamor that falls silent as soon as we enter. In the bakery, Da turns foreign. He and Mr. Frisch speak in a language not quite German, one I follow only in ghostly outline.

"Why are they numbered?" I whisper.

"Numbered?" Da, the numbers man, asks. I tap his arm to show him where. Da hushes me, which he never does. "*Sha.* You ask me again, this time next year."

But he's just said that there is no *this time next year*.

Mr. Frisch asks me something I can't understand.

"The boy doesn't speak," Da says. Although I speak fine.

"Doesn't speak! How can they not speak? I don't care what they are. What they look like. How are you raising these boys?"

"We are raising the best we can."

"Professor. We're disappearing," the baker says. "They want us everywhere gone. They almost have succeeded in this. Our people need every life. Doesn't speak!"

We leave, nodding and waving, making our peace with Mr. Frisch, Da carrying our magic foreign substance, *Mandelbrot*, under his arm. This is a food Mama can't make. Only Frisch's sells the exact *Mandelbrot* that Da used to eat before he came to the United States. To Jonah and me, it looks like a good, sweet bread, but hardly worth the long trip north. To Da, it's from another dimension. A time machine.

We hoard our treasure in a bag of greasy paper, hauling it up to Fort Tryon. My father can barely contain himself. He snitches two pieces by the time we sit on the benches lining the park's snaking path. We sit by ourselves. Other people sit, too, but never next to us. Da doesn't notice this. He's busy. His face, when he puts the magic substance in his mouth, is like light racing itself to a standstill.

"This is *it*," he shouts, crumbs flying outward like new galaxies being born. "This is the same *Mandel* bread I'm eating when I'm your age."

The idea of my father at my age makes me feel ill.

"The same one!" Pleasure stops my father from saying more. *Mandelbrot*, that rare substance only available in Germany, Austria, and Frisch's Bakery on Overlook, goes into his mouth and transforms him. "Oh. Oh! When I was you . . ." Da begins, but memory overwhelms him. He puts a hand on his stomach, closes his eyes, and shakes his head in grateful disbelief. I see a small child, me, devouring the bread just now entering his mouth. The same one.

Da is still that child, the one I'm already ceasing to be. His mind races at such a speed, his clock has all but stopped. Not a day goes by when he doesn't ask us twice as many questions as we can answer. It's exhausting. *Could time be matter, sideways? Might it have joints, like the grooves in a brick wall? Might there come a time when water will flow uphill?* With thoughts like that, he could easily dissolve like a lump of sugar in the hot tea of his own ideas.

"Every moving person has his own clock?" I ask knowing the answer. But the question keeps him seated. It keeps him eating the *Mandelbrot*, for the moment, out of danger.

Da nods, and the motion makes his next bite miss his mouth.

"And nobody sees their own clock running funny?"

He shakes his head. "Nobody's clock *is* running funny. When you speed past another, they think *your* clock runs slow." He draws a corkscrew sign for *crazy* in the air. The sign most others would draw for him.

"Both people think the other is slow?" The thought is too outrageous even to dismiss.

Jonah loves the idea. He giggles and juggles three wadded-up dough balls of *Mandel* bread, a little solar system. Da applauds, scattering

155

crumbs in all directions. Every pigeon in the five boroughs is on us in a pack. Jonah lets loose a high B, the delighted screech of childhood. The pigeons scatter.

If Da is serious, the universe is impossible. Every chunk hurtling loose, all its measures liquid and private. I take my father's arm. The ground squishes under my feet like pudding. I'll have nightmares for weeks—drooping people zooming up and contracting before my eyes, pleading incoherently like those caramel voices from our record player as Jonah and I drop nickels on the turntable. I feel myself going nuts, and all because of my father's pet experiment: Can you free a mind to think in relative time, before it has set into absolutes?

"But if everybody's on their own clock . . . ?" My voice scatters. My courage, too, like the pigeons from my brother's screech. "What time is it, really?" I sound like my own frightened child, a small flood-tossed boy who can't get past his first timeless question: *Is it tomorrow yet?*

Da beams. "Ah, you have it, boychik. I knew you would. There is no single now, now. And there never was!"

As if to prove the ridiculous claim, he walks us up the last little neck of island to a hidden valley in the Heights. Behind a rim of trees is an ancient monastery. "The Cloisters," Da says. Behind that, the even older river, which he doesn't bother naming. We push through a hole in the side of the air and go back six hundred years.

"Here is the fifteenth century. But if we turn here, we go into the fourteenth." Da points to the centuries, like places. I'm turned around, like Mama sometimes gets when we go down into the subway and wind up on the wrong platform. If the past is older than the present, then the future must be younger. And we must all go backward with each passing year.

"This building is not a real building. It is a nice big . . . hmm?" Da jumbles his hands together, looking for the word. "A mixed-up puzzle picture. Bits and pieces, from places with all different ages. Cut up in the Old World and shipped off to the New for rebuilding. Brought together into one museum, like a little index. A *versammel*ed word book of our past!"

He says "our," but that's the salad he makes of English. We always have to figure what his words really are. This is not *our* past. No American, I know, has ever set foot here, except by getting lost. It seems to me that every spot on earth must be a diorama, like the kind Jonah and I make with Mama: Apollo giving Orpheus his first lyre, or Handel sitting at his desk and writing the *Messiah* in twenty-one days. Each spot its own now, its own never.

"It collects, here, five different abbeys from France," Da says. He names them, and the names pass into the empty future.

"How did they get the buildings over here?" I ask.

My brother shoves me. "Stone by stone, dummy."

"How did they get them?" Da is gleeful. "Rich Americans *stole* them!"

A guard glares at us, and Jonah and I hustle Da down the walkway to safety. We turn into a courtyard of arches that shelters a garden. It reminds me of a place, the school I'll live in, years from now. Holding up each arch are two stone columns. Each column sprouts a crown of stone vines, strange snakelike ropes and coils, ancient creatures in the undergrowth. Some of these figures do things small boys shouldn't see and adults don't. Jonah and I race, high-speed heel-toe, around the courtyard, giggling at the taboo messages sent by stone carvers seven hundred years dead. Around us are scores of brutal paintings on wood. We're in some stone-carved children's tale, the world's rough boyhood.

Da reins us in with a palm to each of our shoulders, keeps us from knocking over Europe's priceless baby pictures. How many museums we'll dash or drag through—Modern Art, Indian, Jewish, Met, Cooper-Hewitt, Hall of Fame for Great Americans—how many exhibits we'll absorb, rapt, obedient, or bored, on our way to meeting our future selves. But for some reason, this museum grabs Jonah even more than the giant toboggan of dinosaur bones down on Eighty-first. He stands in front of a suit of armor, ready to take it on in personal combat. I don't know what he sees—some kings and catapults fantasy, knights slaying dragons, a boy's bedtime tale. He's giggling, ready to move into some secret wing hidden in time that no one has yet discovered.

Da steers us on. I'll always obey that hand. We enter a room, dark, gray, and cold, the stone heart of some fantastic castle, cut out and transplanted to this place, hidden at the tip of our island. "Will you see this picture?" Da asks. He points to a wall-sized curtain of heavy cloth, a huge green rug filled with flowers. I look for a picture in the monster thing. There are millions of them, hiding in the vegetation.

"What is there? What do you see?" Da waits, happy, for my answer. "An *Einhorn*, yes? What does English name him?"

"Unicorn," Jonah says. The word is everywhere, on all the signs. Da doesn't read them.

"Unicorn? Uni-corn!" The word delights him.

The beast is huge and white, filling the entire frame. Da cocks back and looks. He stares at a point through the unicorn, behind the tapestry, beyond the wall it hangs on. He takes his glasses off and leans in. He mutters something in German I can't make out. He asks, "What is this picture of?"

Jonah is looking, too. But he's not as desperate to answer as I am. My eye runs a loop-the-loop. The wall carpet is too big to take in whole. I can't put the parts together, can't even see them all from my eye level. The unicorn sits in a makeshift prison, a round three-rung fence it could step over politely if it wanted. A fancy green belt hangs around his neck, something Mama might put on for church. The thing I think is a fountain is really the unicorn's tail. A dancing midair ghost turns out to be the beast's beard. He sits or he lies or he rears up; I can't figure it out. His horn looks as long as his entire body. Behind him is a tree with letters floating in it—*A* and *D*, or *A* and a backward *E*. Maybe these are the unicorn's initials.

Then I see it: the chain. One end of the chain is clamped to the tree, and the other is fastened to the unicorn's collar. The collar is a cuff, and the unicorn is caught, a prisoner, forever. All over his body are wounds, stab marks I didn't see at first. Spurts of cloth blood pour out of his side.

"He's captured. The humans got him. He's a slave." I tell Da what the picture is, but he's not satisfied.

"Yes, yes. He's trapped. They have him in their craft. But what is the picture *of*?"

I feel my face starting to cry. I stamp my feet, but a look from Jonah stops me in my steps. "I don't know. What do you mean? What are you trying to say?"

"Look up close." He nudges me. I step. "Step closer."

"Da!" I want to cry again. "The guard will get me."

"The guard will not get you. You are not the guard's slave! If this guard tries to get you, I will get this guard!"

I step as close as I dare, ready at any second to be caught and sentenced. All three of us will be chained forever, imprisoned in old gray stone.

"Good, so, my Yoseph. What is the picture of?" I still don't know the answer, let alone the question. So Da tells me. "Knots, boychik. The picture is of knots, no less than every picture we live in. Little knots, tied in the clothing of time."

He doesn't mean *clothing*, I'm almost sure. But for a moment, I see what he sees. Every now, made from every motion on earth, is a little tied colored thread. And if you can find a place to see it from, all the threads combine, tied in time, into a picture, bound and bleeding in a garden.

Jonah loses interest in Da's lessons. Clocks, knots, time, *Einhorns*: My brother is past all of it, already leaping clean into his own future. He wanders into another room, where Da and I must track him down. He fidgets in front of a golden music stand in the shape of an eagle. On the stand is a book, and in the book, antique music. It looks nothing like the music I've known how to read for as long as I've known how to read words. It's unlike any music we've ever seen. It has no bars, and not enough lines per stave. Jonah works at the notes, humming away furiously. But he can make nothing that sounds like a tune. "I can't get it. It's totally crazy."

Da lets the two of us puzzle awhile before giving us the key. Or not the key, since this is music before there were such things. He gives us the secret of pitches in time. The click of counting, back when the world beat to another pulse. The shape of duration, before measures existed.

The three of us stand in this cold stone room, chanting. I don't know the word for it yet, but I can do it as easily as breathing. We huddle in this pastiche of jumbled-up monasteries, this American treasure-grab, trapped inside a knot in the cloth of time as snarled as a fraying sweater, a Jew and his two light black sons, singing *"Veni, veni,"* Europe's wake-up tune, sung to itself before it woke up and took over the globe. We chant softly but audibly, even as people filter into the room around us. I feel their disapproval. We are too free, in this museum of good breeding. But I don't care what they think of us, so long as this thread of music continues to unravel and the three of us keep drawing it outward, around ourselves.

When we get to the end of the parchment, we stop and look. People are sitting in banks of wooden chairs that have been set up for a concert. Some of them turn to glare at us. But Da beams, rubbing our tufts of hair. "My boys! You know how to make it, now. The language of time."

He leads us to the front of the block of chairs, where we sit. This is the reason we've come. The magic *Mandelbrot* was just a stopping point, fuel to get us here. All along, we've been heading toward this free concert, this stolen and rebuilt ruin of history.

Sunday, spring 1949. The world is older than I ever imagined. Yet each year that it has ever lived through hides out somewhere in an arch-lined courtyard. This room smells of moss and mold, lacquers and shellacs, things stored too long in linty pockets, brittle paper returning to reeds. I don't share this room's *when*, even though I sit in it. Only by some miracle that Da doesn't explain to me can I see it at all. Every spot on earth has its own clock. Some have reached the future already. Some not yet. Each place grows younger at its own pace. There is no now, nor ever will be.

Now that a concert is coming, my brother stops jittering. He ages as I watch, and soon he's sitting stiller, straighter, more eager than any adult. But he jumps up from his chair and claps like crazy the minute the singers walk out. The singers are all in black. Their stage is so small, they crowd in almost on top of us. Jonah leans forward in gladness to touch one of the women, and the singer touches him back. The whole audience laughs along with her, until Da's arm settles Jonah back into the seat.

Silence falls, erasing all separateness. Then the silence gives way to its only answer. This is the first public concert I will remember ever hearing. Nothing I've already lived through prepares me for it. It runs through and rearranges me. I sit at the center of a globe of sound pointing me toward myself.

It doesn't occur to me, at the age of seven, that a person might luck upon such a song only once a lifetime, if ever. I know how to tell sharp from flat, right singing from wrong. But I haven't yet heard enough to tell ordinary beauty from once-only visits. I will look for this group through-out my life—on vinyl, then tape, then laser pit. I'll go to performances in hope of resurrection and come away empty. I'll search for these singers my whole life, and never come any closer than suspect memory.

I could track the group's name down, in the museum's records for that Sunday concert fifty years ago, twenty years before the idea of reviving the first thousand years of European music had occurred to more than a curatorial few. I could look all the singers up: Every year we pass through is hidden away, if not in a cloistered scriptorium somewhere, then in a bank of steel filing cabinets and silicon chips. But anything I'd find would only kill that day. For what I thought I heard that day, there are no names. Who knows how good those singers really were? For me, they filled the sky.

There is a sound like the burning sun. A sound like the surf of blood pumping through my ears. The women start by themselves, their note as spreading and dimensionless as my father says the present is. *Keee*, the letter-box slots of their mouths release—just the syllable of glee little Ruth made before we persuaded her to learn to talk. The sound of a simple creature, startling itself with praise before settling in for the night. They sing together, bound at the core for one last moment before everything breaks open and is born.

Then *reee*. The note splits into its own accompaniment. The taller woman seems to descend, just by holding her pitch while the smaller woman next to her rises. Rises a major third, that first interval any child any color anywhere learns to sing. Four lips curve upon the vowel, a pocket of air older than the author who set it there.

I know in my body what notes come next, even though I have nothing, yet, to call them. The high voice rises a perfect fifth, lifting off from the lower note's bed. The lines move like my chest, soft cartilage, my ribs straying away from one another, on *aaay*, into a higher brightness, then collapsing back to fuse in unison.

I hear these two lines bending space as they speed away from each other, hurling outward, each standing still while the other moves. Long, short-short, long, long: They circle and return, like a blowing branch submitting again to its shadow. They near their starting pitch from opposite sides, the shared spot where they must impossibly meet back up. But just before they synchronize to see where they've been, just as they touch their lips to this recovered home, the men's lines come from nowhere, pair off, and repeat the splitting game, a perfect fourth below.

More lines splinter, copy, and set off on their own. *Aaay-laay. Aaay-laay-eee!* Six voices now, repeating and reworking, each peeling off on its own agenda, syncopated, staggered, yet each with an eye on the other, midair acrobats, not one of them wavering, no one crashing against the host of moving targets. This stripped-down simple singsong blooms like a firework peony. Everywhere in the awakened air, in a shower of staggered entrances, I hear the first phrase, keyed up, melted down, and rebuilt. Harmonies pile up, disintegrate, and reassemble elsewhere, each melody praising God in its own fashion, and everywhere combining to something that sounds to me like freedom.

All around me in this room, listeners fly back into their pasts. I won't see, until I'm much older, how they're airlifted back before the Berlin crisis, nestled in their beds before the A-bomb, hiding as yet uninventoried from the numbering authorities, back before everyone has died, back before the unicorn lay chained in its pen of flowers, back before that now that never was, even with so many listeners needing to flee it. But I'm not brought back. Just the opposite. This music flings me forward, toward the speed of light, shrinking and slowing until I stop at that very spot where all my future selves put down.

It has been years now since I've been to the northern end of Manhattan. I say *now*, though my father taught me long ago, when my mind was still dilatable, not to be taken in by such things. Frisch's Bakery has disappeared, deported, replaced by a video-rental store with a game-cartridge sideline, or one of those neighborhood stalls sealed up behind an accordion grate for longer than anyone remembers. Last time I visited, half a decade ago, the neighborhood streets were still in upheaval—this time from Jewish to Dominican—the turning tide of immigration, forever advancing on a shore it can never reach. Forty thousand islanders were settling in to their new, desperate nation, with Fort Tryon up on the colony's old Heights protecting them from well-off Jersey and the ravaged Bronx.

And underneath the fortress, at the island's very tip: that imitation, changeless garden. I've been up to the Cloisters only once since Jonah sang there in the late sixties. The image sickens me: a hodgepodge of bottom-dollar Romanesque and Gothic fragments, assembled paradise, a stone's throw from forty thousand Dominicans trying to survive New York's inferno. The ancient pasteup job must feel even more ancient now that the world has descended into endless youth. It must still draw its audience, the bewildered and dying, those who slip through their shell-shocked urban nightmare for a glimpse of a world before the crash of continents, when art still imagined us as one.

We're walking back toward 191st Street, and the subway home. I don't know how we got from the Cloisters here. A piece is missing, frames clipped from the final cut. The concert has ended, but the sound goes on growing in my ears. It happens again, just as it did in the piece itself. No sooner do the clear, high voices bring in the melody than the low foundations pick it up and multiply.

We walk back a different way than we came. For a moment, I'm panicked. Then I'm just amazed that south followed by east can so perfectly undo north followed by west. Jonah laughs at me, but Da doesn't. He finds it amazing, too. "Space is commutative. It does not matter in what order you take the axes. Why this should be, I have no good reason!"

We pass a building that has gone wrong. "What is this, Da?" I'm glad Jonah asks. I'm frightened to.

Da stops and looks. "This is a shul. A synagogue. Like the one I took you to on a Hundred and——"

Da will not notice. But this is not like the one he took us to. I try to read the words scrawled across its front door, but they've been scrubbed almost invisible. Da won't help me sound out the missing ones. All he'll say is, "Christian Front. Who could believe such people can come back now?"

"Da said *now*," I tease, and Jonah picks up the taunt. But Da only gives us the crooked edge of his grin. He takes our hands, one each, and walks on. He studies the sidewalk where we step, as if the cracks he always swears are safe might be more dangerous than he thought.

We're a block away when he says, "Hitler called it a Jewish plot."

"What?" Jonah asks. "What's a plot?"

"Relativity."

"What's relativity?" I say.

"Boychik! What we're just talking about! All those different-running clocks."

For me, a lifetime has intervened. But I want to keep him talking, forever, if possible. So I ask, "Why?"

"What why?" he answers.

"Da! Why, what you just said." *Just* does not mean just, to my father, the professor of liquid time. "Why did Hitler say the clocks were Jewish?"

"Because they *were*!" His eyes glint with laughing pride, which they almost never show. "The Jews were the only people who figured out that everything we think is true about time and space isn't! The Jews were everywhere, looking at what the world really looks like. Hitler hated that. He hated anyone smarter than he was."

"Da was plotting against Hitler!" Jonah shouts. Da shushes him.

I can't tell yet—I can't tell *anymore*—whether Da is serious. I can't even tell what he's talking about, except for the Hitler part. Hitler, I know. On those torturing afternoons when Jonah and I are banished from the house and made to play with the neighborhood boys, it's always the war—Normandy, Bastogne, crossing the Rhine. The world war lives on in small boys, still happily vicious, four years after the adults give it up. Somebody has to be Hitler, and that somebody's always the Strom boys. One of us must be Uncle Adolf, and the other his demented officers. We two make the best Hitler, because we talk funny, die well, and lie so still for so long, it scares everyone. We lie still until the day our playmates re-create the fall of Berlin by setting us on fire. After that, for a long time, we get to stay home.

We walk along Overlook, my father bobbing his head at all the passersby. Twenty blocks and sixteen years away—depending on your clock—is the Audubon Ballroom, where Malcolm X will die. Already, a million lifelines lead there. Already, that murder is happening—on this block, the next, a mile away, more distant prisons. The strands of the killing tighten for decades, and my own threads weave around them.

We duck down the subway steps to the rank center of the earth, the scent of vomit, newsprint, cigarette stubs, and pee. Da is talking again, about mirrors and beams of light and people at the ends of oncoming trains, trains that could take us to Berlin in seconds. There's a scuffle down on the platform. Da leads us away to safety, talking all the while.

"I had been already born for four years," he says, "four whole years be-fore anyone saw space-time as one single thing. I already lived *four whole years* before anyone saw gravity could bend time! It took the Jews!" The family he's told us so little about. All dead.

Years pass. More than thirty of them. I'm in a train station in Frank-furt. We're touring with Voces Antiquae. Jonah asks me to buy him some nuts at the snack stand. "Almonds." It surprises me that, half-German, I've never learned so common a word. Then it surprises me worse: I have. I've known the magic substance my whole life. The stuff's every-where, as common and cheap as years.

If there is no single now, then there can't have ever been a single then. Still, there is this Sunday, the spring of 1949. I'm seven. Everyone I love is still alive, except for the ones who died before I met them. We sit to-gether on the hard subway seats, Jonah and I, with Da between us.

"Did you take pleasure, my boys?" He rhymes the word with *choice*. "Did you enjoy?"

"Da?" I've never heard Jonah so dreamy, so distant. He's on a rocket ship, leaving this poor backward planet behind. But when he comes back, the world has aged away and he alone remains. "Da? When I grow up?" Not really asking permission. Just making sure to let us know well in ad-vance. "When I'm an adult?" He waves back behind us, toward the Clois-ters, falling away from us as fast as we fall forward. "I want to do what those people do."

My father's answer startles me, though not so much there and then. From here, half a century on, I can't make it out. His every blood relation but us is murdered, killed for spreading relativity's plot. He, too, should be dead, but he's still here. A dozen years an immigrant, and in no time, he's become pure American. "You two," he tells us, grinning, his lone answer. "You two will be anyone you want."

MY BROTHER AS ORPHEUS

The fire didn't kill her, Da said.

"She would have lost awareness a long time before. You must remember the rate of rapid oxidation for so large a blaze." The fire would have sucked all the air from our house long before the flames touched her. "And then there was the explosion." The furnace, that time bomb. "She would have been knocked unconscious." That was why she never got out. The middle of the day, Mama quick and healthy, and no one else killed.

She couldn't have felt a thing. That's what Da meant, trying to comfort us. The fire did burn her. It did turn her to char, nothing but ash, bone, and her wedding ring. Da's consolation was infinitely feebler: The fire didn't *kill* her. She was dead already by the time she burned.

Still, he reminded us whenever he thought we needed it. *The fire didn't kill her.* Jonah heard: Dead before the firemen even got there. I heard: Death by suffocation, her lungs getting nothing, just as bad as flames. Ruthie heard: Still alive.

For a long time, the four of us did nothing. Time, for us, was another facedown corpse, knocked out in the explosion. We must have spent five months in that little apartment that my father's colleague loaned us. I didn't feel the weeks pass, although most days I was sure I'd die of old age before the clock advanced from dinnertime to bed. We never sang, at least not all together. Ruth hummed to herself, scolding her dolls and telling them to shush. Now and then, Da put something on the record player. Jonah and I spent long afternoons listening to the radio. Broadcast seemed somehow less sacrilegious, inflicted on us, rather than chosen.

After a while, Ruth went back to her neighborhood school. She screamed on the first day, refusing to leave the apartment. But we three men stood firm with her. "You have to, Ruthie. It'll help you feel better." We should have known that was the last thing she wanted.

Jonah refused to consider returning to Boston. "I'll never go back. Not for all the private lessons in the world." Da only shrugged in acquiescence. So, of course, I didn't go back, either. The possibility of my returning alone never even arose.

Da resumed his classes at Columbia, after what must have seemed an eternity to him. Jonah raged to me. "That's it? Everything's normal again? He just waltzes back to work, like nothing's changed?"

But I could tell by the way Da's shoulders ground now when he walked how badly everything had. He had nothing left but work. And from the moment Mama died, even his work altered. Time, that block of standing evers, that reversible dependent variable, had turned on him. He no longer knew how much was left. From the moment of the fire until his own death, he gave himself up to finding time and breaking it.

We lived in that cramped borrowed apartment until its owner finally had to ask for it back. Then we evacuated, without much plan, to another, slightly larger one, also in Morningside Heights. We were as close to invisible there as we could get, on a street that teetered right on the color line. Or not on the line, but in the many moving ripples. For the university stood like a huge rock in the surf of changing blocks, the churning populations beyond math's ability to calculate. With the insurance, Da bought new furniture, bright blue dishes that Mama would have liked, and a replacement spinet. He even started rebuilding our sheet-music library, but the project was hopeless. Even among the four of us, we couldn't remember all the music we'd owned.

Ruthie changed schools—to one, like her, that split down the middle, almost half and half. She made new friends, new nationalities every week. But she never brought them home. She was ashamed of her men, the three of us living like there was no tomorrow and even less a yesterday.

At first, Da came home most afternoons. But his need to lose himself in work soon outweighed his need to work through our loss. The equations swallowed him. There was a woman, Mrs. Samuels, who came by to keep house and watch after Ruth when she got home at 3:30. Mrs. Samuels's only instrument was the chord organ. So there were no lessons. Da must have paid her well for the time she put in, but she did it, I think, out of love. She would have liked to be his children's friend.

Jonah spent most days scribbling into his notebooks. Sometimes he wrote words, other times, notes on ledger lines. He wrote a long letter on all different kinds of paper and posted it abroad, to Italy, with lots of exotic airmail stamps. "So she can't say she didn't know how to reach me," he said. The letters I wrote, I kept in my head, with no other place to send them.

When he wasn't scribbling, Jonah listened to the Dodgers, "Dragnet," "The FBI in Peace and War," all the shows of delayed boyhood. He even had a favorite big-band station, when he really needed to keep himself from thinking. He let me listen to the Saturday Met broadcasts, following along while pretending not to.

When Ruthie came home from school in midafternoon, I read to her or took her out to a safe corner of the park. I hadn't spent more than a few weeks with my sister in two years. She was a stranger, a wound-up little girl who spoke to herself and who cried herself to sleep because we couldn't fix her hair the way Mama did. We tried. We got it just the way we all remembered it, except Ruth.

Some days, I'd sit with her at the piano, the way Mama used to sit with me. Ruth learned anything I gave her faster than I'd learned the works myself. But her fingerings were never the same twice. "Try to be consistent," I said.

"Why?" She lost all patience for the instrument, and most days we ended up fighting. "It's dumb, Joey."

"What's dumb?"

"The music's dumb." And she'd rip off a parody Mozart sonatina, brilliant in its improvised burlesque. She mocked it, sneering through the keys, the music we were brought up on. The music that killed her mother.

"What's so dumb about it?"

"It's ofay."

"What's ofay?" I asked Jonah that night, when Ruth couldn't hear.

My brother was never at a loss more than an eighth note. "It's French. It means up to date. Means you know how things are done."

I asked Da. His face turned stern. "Where did you hear this?"

"Around." Evading my own father. Everything honest in our home had died the day our mother did.

My father removed his glasses. He was blind without them. Blinking, helpless, a flounder on ice. "Do they still say that?"

"Sometimes," I bluffed.

"It's not good. It's pork Latin."

I burst out laughing. He should have slapped me. "Pig Latin."

"Pig Latin, then. For white people." *Oe-fay*. Foe.

I didn't confront Ruth. But we didn't go back to Mozart, either. My sister was not quite eleven, at least a year from childhood's end. But she'd already changed. It took those many weeks together for me to see that little Root had vanished along with Mama.

"What do you want to learn?" I asked her. "I can teach you anything." The offer came out of my unlimited ignorance. Had I the first idea of the ways of playing—swings and jolts, bends and bops, slaps and tickles, restless, headlong fence rushes, resilient hybrid strains, the twists of tonality, the quotes, thefts, arrests, and reparations, all the modes and scales torn out of the mere two that my music stuck with—had I even once considered the bottomless invention all around me, I'd have been unable to teach my little sister a C major chord in root position.

"I don't know, Joey." Ruth's left skittered up and down, walking a bass at a trotter's pace. "What did Mama like to play?"

It had only been months. She couldn't have forgotten already. She couldn't think memory was lying to her.

"She liked it all, Ruth. You know that."

"I mean, other than . . . you know—before you all took up with . . ."

For my part, I practiced at least four hours every day and soon went back to formal lessons. Music was no longer a game, nor would it ever be pure pleasure again. But it was all I knew. One of my mother's students, Mr. Green, took me on. Every few weeks, he'd give me a new movement from another Beethoven sonata and get out of my way. Each week, I'd try not to outgrow him too quickly.

I learned to cook. Otherwise, we might have all gotten rickets, scurvy—last century's diseases, still rampant just a few blocks north and east. I read somewhere that potatoes and spinach, served with a little ground beef, had all the nutrition a body needed. All Mama's recipes, written in pen on three-by-fives that she kept in her green metal box on the kitchen sill, had burned. Nothing I ever made did more than apologize to the feasts that once had poured out of her oven. But my audience knew it was this or oatmeal.

The month our mother died, Rosa Parks refused to move back. While I was cooking for my family and my little sister was walking to her integrated school, fifty thousand people in Montgomery laid down their yearlong walking siege. The movement had started. The country I'd been born in was edging toward showdown. But I never heard a word. Da must have followed the story in detail. But he never brought the subject up in all his dinner-table ramblings.

Jonah spent his days in feverish passivity. He listened to the radio. He took walks or, on days when he went to campus with our father, sat motionless at the music library at Columbia. He was trying to race backward, just by standing still. A decade later, he'd tell an interviewer that these were the months that turned him into an adult singer. "I learned more about how to sing by keeping silent for half a year than I ever learned from any teacher, before or after." Except the teacher from whom he learned even silence.

Da couldn't let us stay home forever. "Come on, my boys. The world is not gone, yet. If you don't want to study physics with me, then you must choose some other school."

This was the last *must* Jonah ever listened to. "What the hell, Mule. Robinson's going to retire. They've taken "The Shadow" off the air. We might as well go back to the slammer."

He settled on Juilliard—the next-closest thing in the world to staying home. At Juilliard, we could almost vanish again, into the one thing we knew how to do. Da got Jonah a vocal coach from the Columbia Music Department, and Jonah started woodshedding again a month before auditions. Maybe he was right about how much he'd learned through silence. Juilliard took him into the prep program without probation.

At the premier performance school in the country, not even a singer of Jonah's caliber had any leverage. He could hardly make his acceptance contingent on mine. The pressure of my own admission lay wholly on me. "Not going if you don't," Jonah said just before I had to play. I'm sure he meant it as emotional support.

I took my audition, my brother's future pressing down on my shoulders and almost forcing my face into the keys. I hiccupped through the first movement of opus 27, no. 1, my runs turning to rancid butter. I could hear myself condemning my brother and me to a lifetime of lassitude in my father's suffocating apartment. After I played, I went to the toilet off the rehearsal room and threw up, just like the boys Jonah once marveled at, years before. Our musical education had been more rapid and comprehensive than our parents could have anticipated. I'm glad Mama hadn't lived to see where I'd landed.

My acceptance came attached with two sheets of red-inked faultfinding. The last comment on the list was a double-underlined word: "Posture!" Jonah never let me forget it. He barked the word with a German accent each time we sat at dinner. Walking along the street, he'd grab and force my shoulders back. "Posture, Herr Strom! Do! Not! Slump!" He never guessed that the weight slumping me over was him.

Branded with my red-inked acceptance, I followed my brother into the Juilliard prep division. If Boylston was music's provincial outpost, Juilliard was its Rome. Walking down one hallway, I lived through three hundred years of Western concert music trickling through the doors in fantastic cacophony. Jonah and I were children again, the lowest rungs on a ladder of experience that stretched away from us, out of sight.

From the building on Claremont, we were an easy stroll from home. We didn't have to live with anyone, a reprieve that gave me unspeakable relief. In that independent nation of music, we were no one's problem, no one's scandal, no one's trailblazer. No one much looked at us at all. Sight counted for nothing there. There, everyone was all ears.

Our fellow students put the fear of God in us. Jonah may have learned more about singing from seven months of silence than he did from any teacher after our mother. But he learned more about the world of professional music making from two weeks in its North American capital than he'd ever cared to know. The academic side of our education was even more perfunctory than it had been in Boston. That suited us. We were there for one thing. The only thing either of us had any heart left to do.

Jonah didn't stay long in the prep division. As soon as they could, his teachers hustled him upstairs. He was far from the youngest to start college there. The school was rotten with prodigies, some who'd completed the program by sixteen, the age Jonah entered it. But he was surely the least prepared to enter adulthood early.

He started the year of Little Rock, three years after *Brown* became the reputed law of the land. Jonah studied the same news pictures I did: nine kids threading through the 101st Airborne paratroopers, just to go learn about Thomas Jefferson and Jefferson Davis, while we sashayed in the front door of our conservatory to learn about sonata-allegro form. I sneaked into the school library each day to see the newspapers. Kids our age, marching to school through riots, just one step ahead of getting strung up by the rabid crowd, skipping up the army-lined stairs along the gauntlet of bayonet-fixed M1's of their all-white protectors following their own gunpoint orders. Army helicopters landing on the school football field, establishing a perimeter. Governor Faubus invoking the National Guard, canceling the court orders, squaring off against the federal forces, taking the insurrection to television: "We are now a country under occupation." And General Walker answering, "The sooner the resistance ceases, the sooner normalcy will return to the school area." The whole country stood ready to resume civil war a hundred years on, over nine kids my age, while I struggled with Chopin études and Jonah breezed through Britten.

The conservatory was my country. Arkansas was no more than a distant nightmare. I don't know what Jonah thought about Little Rock. We spoke of it only once, sitting in front of Da's first black-and-white television, watching a news clip while waiting for a thriller that didn't last past the following summer. On screen, a thin, white, bulldog crew-cut teen nosed up to a beautiful girl in sunglasses and whispered a muted threat. Jonah, next to me in the dark, said, "He touches her and he pays."

We, in our new world, lived like princes. Every afternoon had another free recital, the highest caliber of pleasure performed for mostly empty houses. Every few weeks—as often as we could talk Da into letting us stay out—we could have a symphony or even an opera for a student pittance.

I studied and practiced, needing eight more hours in each day. I had my first run at repertoire so mythic, I almost rebelled at stroking the notes. With my teacher, George Bateman, I went back and relearned opus 27, no. 1, this time properly. *The Well-Tempered Clavier* was my daily bread. I read my way through a chunk of book one, keeping to safe tempi on the tricky fugues.

Mr. Bateman was an accomplished accompanist. He still performed often and canceled as many lessons as he kept. He moved through my lessons in a state of distraction. But he could hear like hell's watchdog, and he did with two fingers of his left hand what I couldn't do with my entire right. His crumbs of praise fed me for weeks.

He tucked his criticisms so deeply amid that praise that I often missed their bite. I played Chopin's Mazurka in A Minor for him. Its trick is that little dotted rhythm—how to make it lilt without listing. I got through the first repeat without incident. Then I made that turn into C, the burst of relative major—the most predictable surprise brightening on earth. Mr. Bateman, eyes closed, maybe even dozing, jumped forward. "Stop!"

I jerked my hands off the keys, a dog whacked with the newspaper he has been trained to fetch.

"What did you just do, there?" I was afraid to look up. When I did, Mr. Bateman was waving. "Do that again!" I did, crippled with self-consciousness. "No, no," he said, each rejection oddly supportive. "Play it the way you did the first time."

I played it exactly as I always played it. Each time, Mr. Bateman's face rose and fell in whole storm systems. Finally, he lit up. "That's it! That's beautiful! Who taught you that?" He waved his arms around his head, happily warding off a swarm of fact. "Don't tell me. I don't want to know. Just keep doing it, no matter what else I tell you to do!"

For days afterward, I wondered if I might not, after all, have a gift I didn't suspect. I knew what Mr. Bateman was trying to do: move me from fingers to feeling, from mechanics to mind. He called a little Schumann fantasy piece I played "brilliant," and all that afternoon, I thought I could change worlds. I wanted to tell Mama what Mr. Bateman had said, as soon as I got home. Then, remembering, the pleasure of accomplishment turned to a bitterness deeper than I'd felt at her death. Nothing made sense. My crippled tune dragged through more unprepared keys than I knew how to survive. I was the most contemptible teenager alive, to feel such elation, so soon after elation should have ended for good. To go on shamelessly growing, while Mama would not.

That leaden pointlessness fell away when I practiced. Still, I hated myself for letting it go, even for a minute. I don't know how Jonah survived. We saw little of each other once he started the college track. He needed me less. Yet when we strolled back through Morningside Heights at the end of a day, he'd recap his hours, irritated that I hadn't been there to experience it all with him firsthand. On weekends, as we bummed around the music shop on 110th, he could go exultant again over nothing, launching into the horn blare from the third movement of Beethoven's Fifth, expecting me to be right there, in tempo, a third below him in the second horn, no later than the score's marked entrance, as if no one had died.

Juilliard was so big, even Jonah shrank in it. The cafés around school babbled like a musical UN. Until Juilliard, we'd only noodled away at little Dittersdorf duets. Now we'd landed somewhere in the middle risers of an international *Symphony of a Thousand*.

There were even a couple of Negro students. Real ones. The day I saw my first—a wide, preoccupied grad with dark glasses and a sheaf of scores under his arm—I fought the urge to greet him like a long-lost cousin. He caught me out of the corner of his eye and called, "Hey, sol-dier," flicking me a two-fingered salute of shared, unlikely membership. White people never knew for certain. They took us for Indian or Puerto Rican. They never looked. Blacks always knew, for the simple reason that I looked back at them.

The second time I saw the man, he stopped. "You're Jonah Strom." I corrected him. "Heaven's sake. There's two y'all?" He was from the South, and harder to follow than even János Reményi. He was a bass named Wilson Hart. He'd gone to a black college in Georgia, a state I'd never even considered before, where he'd graduated in teacher training. "Only line of work I thought a black concert bass could follow." A visiting professor had heard him sing and persuaded him to think otherwise. Wil-son Hart was not yet convinced.

I could hear, even in his speaking voice, what resonance the man had. But Wilson Hart had a dream that went beyond singing. "Tell you what I'd do, if the world was well?" He opened the portfolio he always carried un-der his arm and spread the cream-colored pencil-filled staffs in front of me, right there in the corridor. I sounded out the notes, notes this man had written. However derivative and dreamy, they had riches.

He wanted to *compose*. It filled me with wonder, to my lasting shame. Yes, because he was a member of my mother's race. But more because he was *living*, here, talking to me. I stood looking out over my own life. Composing had never occurred to me. New music was every minute streaming into this world, from every quarter. We could do more than channel it. We could write our own.

Wilson Hart looked at me like God's spy. "They always asking you how a black man got interested in this line?"

"We're mixed," I said.

The word came back to me, turned around in his face. "Mixed? You mean like *all* mixed up?" He saw me die. "That's okay, brother. Isn't a horse alive who's a purebred."

Wilson Hart became the first friend I ever made all by myself. He'd smile from down long hallways and sit with me in crowded concert halls. "You stop crucifying me with this 'Mr. Hart' business, now. Mrs. Hart's the only one I'm gonna let call me Mr. Hart, once I find her. You, Mr. Mixed, you call me Will." When he passed me in the corridors, he'd pat his portfolio of freshly penciled music. It was our private conspiracy, this stream of new notes. *You and me, Mix. They're gonna hear our sounds, before we're done with this place.* The thrill of his singling me out to stand with him oppressed me worse than any racism.

Will and Jonah finally met, although I was in no hurry to introduce them. They were like fur and fire. Jonah had exploded with the avant-garde, the making and unmaking of new freedom. The first time Jonah heard the Second Viennese School, he wanted to round the rabble-rousers up and execute them. The second time, he just sneered. By listen three, the smoldering threat to Western civilization started to rise like its star shining in the East. Time's arrow, for Jonah, now pointed mercilessly forward, toward total serialism or its paradoxical twin, pure chance.

Jonah looked over Wilson Hart's scores, singing out lines with a voice as forceful as the instruments they were written for. For that treatment alone, Will would have shown him everything he'd ever written. But at the end of a bravura sight-sing, Jonah tossed up his hands. "Will, Will! What's with all the *beauty*? You'll kill us with kindness, man. Single-handedly drag us back into the nineteenth century. What did the nine-teenth century ever do for you, except wrap you up in chains?"

I'd sit between them, waiting for the world to end. But they both loved the fight.

"This here's nothing about the nineteenth century," Will said, gathering in his wounded troops. "This is your first look at the *twenty-first*. Y'all just don't know how to hear it yet."

"I've *already* heard it. I know all those tunes by heart. Sounds like a Copland ballet."

"I'd give twice my eyeteeth to write a Copland ballet. Man's a great composer. Started out messing with that chicken-scratch music of yours. Got tired and gave it up."

"Copland's okay, if you dig crowd-pleasers."

I prayed to Mama's ghost to come pummel him, as she should have done so often while she was alive.

"And here I was, thinking pleasure was what music's all about."

"Look around you, man. The world's on *fire*."

"That's right. And we're looking for a nice big ocean to douse it in."

"You study with Persichetti?"

"Mr. Persichetti studied with Roy Harris, just like our own Mr. Schu-man."

"But Persichetti's gone *past* all that. No more recycled folk and jazz. He's gone on to richer things. So should you. Come on, Wilson! You should be listening to Boulez. Babbitt. Dallapiccola."

"You think I haven't wasted hours listening to that? If I want noise, I can stand in the middle of Times Square, get me some. If I want chance, I can play the nags. God told us to *build this place up*. Make it better, not tear it down and feed it to the dogs."

"This *is* building. Listen to Stockhausen. Varèse."

"If I want police sirens, they're right outside my apartment every night."

"Don't be a slave to melody, man." Jonah didn't even hear the word.

"There's a reason we invented melody, brother Jon. You know the best thing Varèse ever did? Teach William Grant Still to find himself. Now there's a composer who knew how to sound. You ever ask yourself why no one plays that man's music? Why you never even *heard* of a Negro composer until you came nosing around me?"

Jonah shot me conspiratorial grins. I stood between them, band-sawed down the middle.

Will worked on me when Jonah wasn't around. "I've spent years listening to your brother's deaf gentlemen. Nothing new down that way, Mix. Certainly not the freedom brother Jon hopes to find. You listen to me. That brother of ours gonna come running back to us, ears covered, soon as he tires of the squeaks and bangs."

Will showed me every new piece that came out of him—dressed-up concert cadences flirting with swing and cool, reverent gospel quotes buried in Dvořák-driven lower brass. He made me swear to him that I'd never forsake melody just because of some bad dream of progress. "Promise me something, Mix. Promise me that someday you will write down all the notes that are inside you." It seemed a safe-enough vow. I was sure there couldn't be more than a couple of half-note measures in there, all told.

He had this thing about Spain. I don't know where it came from. Sancho and the Don on horseback. Low, arid hills. Will was going to travel there as soon as he could pay for the trip. Barring Spain, Mexico, Guatemala—anyplace that sparkled after midnight and slept at the peak of the day.

"Must have lived there once, brother Joe. In another life." Not that he knew the first thing about the place or spoke a word of Spanish. "My people must have paid that land a little visit once. Lived there for a couple of centuries? The Spaniards are the finest Negroes north of Africa. Germans wouldn't know what to do with this much soul except lock it up." His hand flew up to sinning lips. "Pay me no mind, Mix! Every people have their notion of what this world's after."

Wilson Hart wanted to bridge Gibraltar, to reunite Africa and Iberia, those twins separated at birth. He heard one coiled in the other, where I never could hear any relation at all. What little I learned about African music at Juilliard confirmed that it was an art apart. But Will Hart never gave up trying to get me to hear the kinship, the rhythm joining such disparate rhythms.

I often found Will in one of the cubicles off of the library, hunched over a 1950s turntable with its stylus arm the size of a monkey's paw, listening to Albéniz or de Falla. He grabbed me one visit and wouldn't release me. "Just the pair of ears this piece was calling out for." He sat me down and made me listen to an entire guitar concerto by a man named Rodrigo.

"Well?" he said as the third movement sailed triumphantly into harbor. "What do you hear, brother Joe?"

I heard a dusty, tonal archaism, wanting to be older than it could honestly admit to being. It flew in the face of history's long breakdown of consonance. Its sequences were so formal, I completed them before I heard them. "It sure dances." The best I could do.

His face fell. He wanted me to hear some *thing* in particular. "What about the man who made it dance?"

"Besides that he comes from northern North Africa?"

"Go ahead and fun me all you want. But tell me what you know about him, now that he's told you everything."

I shrugged. "I give up."

"Blind from the age of three. You really couldn't hear?"

I shook my head, reaping his disappointment.

"Only a blind man could make this." Will placed his right hand on his own closed portfolio. "And if God would let me make something even one-tenth as beautiful, I'd be as glad as a—"

"Will! Don't. Not even in jest." I think I frightened him.

I asked Jonah if he'd ever heard the piece. *Concerto de Aranjuez*. He scoffed before I could finish the title. "Total throwback. Written in 1939! Berg had been dead four years already." As if the true trailblazers would be ahead of anyone, even in dying. "What's that Will doing to you, man? He's going to have you whistling to transistor radio by the time we're out of this joint. Music and wine, Joseph. The less you know, the sweeter you need them."

"What do you know about wine?"

"Not a damn thing. But I know what I don't like."

Jonah was right. Will Hart lived on the school's suspect fringe. Juilliard still dwelled in that tiny diamond between London, Paris, Rome, and Berlin. Music meant the big Teutonic *B*'s, those names chiseled into the marble pediment, the old imperial dream of coherence that haunted the continent Da had fled. North American concert music—even Will's adored Copland and Still—was here little more than a European transplant. That this country *had* a music—spectacularly reinventing itself every three years, the bastard of chanted hymns, spirit hollers, cabin songs, field calls and coded escape plans, funeral rowdiness gathered by way of New Orleans, gutbucketed and jugged, slipped up the river in cotton crates to Memphis and St. Louis, bent into blue intervals that power would never recognize, reconvening north, to be flung out everywhere along Chicago's railhead as unstoppable rag, and overnight—the longest, darkest overnight of the soul in all improvised history—birthing jazz and its countless half-breed descendants, a whole glittering Savoy ballroom full of offspring scatting and scattering everywhere, dancing the hooves off anything whiteness ever made, American, *American*, for whatever that meant, a music that had taken over the world while the classical masters were looking the other way—had not yet dawned on these Europe-revering halls.

Jonah's friends were white, and my friends, aside from Will, were Jonah's. Not that my brother sought white friends out. He didn't have to. Dr. Suzuki's movement was just ten years old; several years would pass before the Asian tsunami hit the States. The handful of Middle Eastern students there had come by way of England and France. Juilliard's cosmopolitan sea was still more or less a restricted swimming hole.

My brother hung out at Sammy's, a coffee shop just north of the school. Jonah chose the venue, knowing, as his new friends didn't, where he could sit with his buddies and still get served. The dive had a state-of-the-art Seeburg jukebox, its little claw grabbing the vertical records and slapping them down for a nickel a play. The highbrow student singers claimed to hate the thing, even while guzzling down all the pop culture it served up. After practice hours, half a chorale would hole up at Sammy's, carrying on in a back booth. Jonah held forth at the singer-infested table, and his friends would always squeeze out a little room for his kid brother.

At Sammy's, the angelic performers sat for hours playing some variation of the musical ratings game. Who could hit the highest highs? Whose lows were the richest? Who had the cleanest passage points? It was worse than the TV quiz shows they all watched in secret, and just as rigged. The rating judges were never so blatant as to rank one another by number, and they'd only rate singers who weren't present. But in the constant pegging and scoring, each figured out his own place in the pecking pyramid.

The group's clown was a deadly eared baritone named Brian O'Malley. With a few tremulous semiquavers, he'd have the others rolling on the linoleum. He could imitate anything, bass through coloratura, without ever needing to tell anyone whom he was mocking. His listeners laughed along, even knowing they'd be next as soon as they were out of earshot. Hands clasped primly in front of his chest, Brian launched into a nightmarish Don Carlos or Lucrezia Borgia, taking a friend's familiar, small vocal blemish and magnifying it to horrific scale. Afterward, we'd never hear the hapless target the same way again.

O'Malley's gift mystified me. I asked Jonah one night, from the relative safety of 116th Street. "I don't get it. If he can reproduce anybody, down to the pimples, why . . ."

Jonah laughed. "Why can't he make a voice of his own?" Alone among Juilliard voice students, O'Malley's voice was featureless beyond parody. "He's making himself as small a target as possible. He'll have a career, you know. He'd make a great Fra Melitone. Or a Don Pasquale kind of thing."

"Not for the voice," I said, horrified.

"Of course not."

Jonah could sit for hours and listen to the clique's ranking games. Their need to evaluate was every bit as great as their need for music. For these athletes in training, the two things were equivalent. Song as competition: fastest, highest, hardest—the soul's Olympics. Hearing them made me want to lock myself into a practice room and refuse to come out until I'd tamed some snarling Rachmaninoff. But I stuck close to my brother among his friends, the two of us swinging together in the deadly breeze. Jonah picked up their idiom like a native speaker. "Haynes's middle five notes are just about perfect," or "Thomas has a girl in every portamento." His verdicts always had an innocent wonder to them. He never sounded like he was slandering anyone.

As for his own vocal reputation, even Jonah's detractors knew they had to go after him with both barrels if they were foolish enough to go gunning. I overheard students in the back rows of the darkened auditorium declaring his sound too pure, too effortless, too light, claiming it lacked that muscular edge of the best concert tenors. No doubt on winter nights after we headed home, the Sammy's crowd slammed him with worse. But as long as we sat with the others over phosphates, they treated him with a resigned shake of the head. They'd go through an afternoon's list of finest, brightest, clearest. "Then there's Strom," O'Malley would say. "A species unto himself."

We sat at Sammy's one afternoon, just before I passed out of prep and began degree work. Talk turned to Jonah, who was just then working up his first go at Schubert, the Miller's Beautiful Daughter, an assault on white womanhood that drew O'Malley's awe. "Strom here's our ticket to fame. We might as well admit it. The boy's going all the way. Ride his coattails we shall, if he'll but let us. If not, we'll watch him ascend from afar. Laugh not! See how the conquering he-he-he-he-hero comes!"

My brother put his wadded-up straw wrapper in his nose and blew it out at the speaker.

"You think I jest?" O'Malley carried on. "Barring accident, our boy here's going to become the world's most famous half-breed. Our illustrious school's next Leontyne Price."

The country's most thrilling new voice, after half a decade, had just been granted her stage debut, in San Francisco. The school was abuzz with its newest headliner alum. But at O'Malley's invocation of the name, the booth at the back of Sammy's lurched, their laughter like wet firewood. Jonah arched his eyebrows. He opened his mouth, and out came absurd falsetto. "Gotta brush up my spinto, don't you know, honey." A silent hiccup passed through the group. Then fresh, forced hilarity.

I didn't talk to him for the longest time, heading home. He heard my silence and met it head-on. We were halfway to the Cathedral of St. John the Divine before either of us said anything.

"Half-breed, Jonah?"

He didn't even shrug. "What we are, Mule. What I am anyway. You be what you want to be."

Juilliard's highest talent thought of themselves as color-blind, that plea bargain that high culture employs to get all charges against it dropped. I didn't yet know, at fifteen, everything that *color-blind* stood for. At Juilliard, color was still too successfully contained to pose much threat. With a few crazy exceptions like the lovable Strom boys, the Negro's scene was elsewhere. Race was a southern crisis. O'Malley treated us to his pitch-perfect Governor Faubus: "What in God's name is happening in the United States of America?" My brother's friends rose to righteous indignation over every crime against humanity, each one, like the folk song, five hundred miles from home.

"People, people," O'Malley challenged. "Who am I?" He covered one ear with a cupped hand, tucked his chin into his sternum, and sang in mock Russian at the absolute nadir of his range. It took us a few beats to recognize "Ol' Man River." O'Malley's test glance never lasted more than a quaver. One of this country's greatest men was living under government-conducted house arrest, forced to sing to European audiences over a telephone, and here was O'Malley going into a whole routine mocking him. Robeson speaking in best Rutgers Phi Beta Kappa accent: "Mr. Hammerstein the Second, sir. Far be it from me to criticize, but your lyrics seem to partake of a few errors in subject-verb agreement."

The vein in my brother's temple flickered as he considered flipping the booth over and never coming back. Not over race; over Robeson. No one was allowed to touch such a voice. For a moment, he looked set to send this group to hell and return to the solitude of real music. Instead, as everyone's eyes fought to stay off him, Jonah just laughed. Harsh, but participating. All other moves were a losing game.

Race was just a bagatelle. The curators of proper singing saved their real firepower for the clearer, more present danger: class. It took me years to decode the Sammy's scoring system. I'm not sure Jonah ever cracked it. I remember him challenging a unanimous decision that bewildered me, as well. "Just a minute. You're saying you'd rather hire Paula Squires to sing Mélisande than hire Ginger Kittle to sing Mimi?"

The chorus was merciless. "Perhaps if La Ginger agreed to a wee change of name . . ." "You have to love her diphthongs, though. That *aeyah* of hers? At least you can be sure it'll play in Peoria." "And those synthetic blends she wears? Every time she climbs above a B-flat, I expect her blouse to spontaneously combust." "Miss Kittle *embodies* the Mimi of her generation. Always radiantly dead by act four."

Jonah shook his head. "Have you all gone completely deaf? So she could use some finish. But Kittle has Squires beat hands down."

"Maybe if she *kept* her hands down . . ."

"But *Paula Squires?*"

"Jonah, my boy. You'll figure it out as you ripen, don't you know."

Ripening came over us both. I spent my days in a perpetual state of arousal I mistook for anticipation. Everything curved or cupped, any tone from lemon to cocoa excited me. The vibrations of the piano, seeping up my leg from the pedal, could set me off. Sparks would start in an innocent glow, one warm word from anything female, and cascade into elaborate rescue fantasies, ultimate sacrifice followed by happy death, the only possible reward. I'd restrain myself for a week or two, channeling all pure things—the middle movement of the *Emperor*, my mother hugging us on a windy Eighth Avenue, Malalai Gilani, our family evenings of counterpoint a decade before. Even as I fought temptation, I knew I'd eventually succumb. I waited in patient irritation to be alone in the apartment. The revulsion of the slide only intensified it. Each time I gave in to pleasure, I'd feel as if I'd sentenced Mama to death again, betrayed every good thing she'd ever praised or predicted for me. Each time, I swore to renew myself.

Maybe Jonah did better with lust—another rush to add to the rushes that drove him. Maybe he found some willing nymph to touch him when and where he needed. I didn't know. He no longer reported his body's developments to me, though he did still share his latest enthusiasms. "Mule, you have to see this girl. Like nothing you've ever seen. Marguerite! Carmen!" But the objects of his desire were always plainness incarnate. I thought he must be mocking me. Any beauty he saw in them lay beyond the visible spectrum. "Well? Isn't she the greatest thing you've ever laid eyes on?" I always managed a vigorous nod.

His body was a seismograph. Even sitting in an auditorium chair became a free exercise routine. He settled on altos. Whenever one passed within a hundred feet, his head rose up on his neck like a U-boat periscope. For the first time in his life, singing acquired an ulterior motive. He sang like a greyhound who'd slipped the leash, running around Morningside, peeing on any hydrant that would hold still for his mark.

I hated him for betraying Kimberly. I knew it was crazy. There I was, in the middle of my own solitary hormone storm, rubbing off to the image of everything that moved. But I wanted my brother to preserve the memory of our past, and that included the albino wraith. Here in New York, Boylston's sheltered, fake Italianate courtyard seemed a cheap operetta set. I'd spent my childhood like one of those polio-stricken kids in photo magazines, trapped in an iron lung, kept alive by artifice and invention. All that exploded with our leaking furnace. I needed something from our stripped-away past to survive, if only that anemic ghost.

Jonah flirted with every vocalist at Juilliard. And every flirtee, safe in the absurdity of his appetite, flirted back. His voice could turn the yellowest head. To a twenty-year-old elite female in the late 1950s, he offered all the thrill of transgression, all the more exciting by being harmless, of course. Unthinkable.

I found something to praise in his every new drab goddess, raising the same enthusiasm I mustered for his recitals, whose repertoire now baffled me. The simple trip from tonic to dominant and back now bored Jonah. Only the most jagged music still promised him a real workout. Tritones and the devil's other intervals, weird new notational systems, poly-rhythm, microtones: He only wanted to keep growing, a thing the world rarely forgave.

Jonah fell deeper into the avant-garde, a group the mainstream singers called "the Serial Killers." The Killers wore the badge proudly, worship-ing at the shrine of their imported saint of rigor, Schoenberg, canonized the instant he died at UCLA, of all places, a few years before. They de-clared everything outside the twelve-tone row to be mere ornament, a fate worse than beautiful.

The Serial Killers talked idly about going to see the first full staging of *Moses und Aron* at the Zurich Stadttheater. When that pipe dream fell through, they vowed to do their own read-through. Jonah was Aaron, the silver-tongued spokesman for his speech-impaired brother. He wasn't yet twenty, but already he could pick up, in quick study, the thorniest music. He grasped the complex systems the same way he'd learned preadoles-cence's simple diatonic pleasures. He made atonality sound as light as Offenbach.

Jonah talked Da out of the apartment for the performance. "*Moses und Aron?* Stories of the patriarchs? I raise my children to be good God-fearing atheists, and this is the thanks?" But the read-through delighted Da. All night long, he nodded at the revival of a story he never thought to pass along to us. He beamed at his son's otherworldly ability to hold his pitch amid a cacophony of signs and wonders.

I never understood Schoenberg. I don't mean just that unfinished opera libretto, the unsolvable enigma of divine will. I mean the music. I couldn't feel it. Da wasn't much better. He ribbed Jonah all the way home. "Do you know what Stravinsky said at the first *Pierrot?*"

"I know the story, Da."

" 'I wish that woman would stop talking so I can hear the music!' Hey. You should laugh, boychik. It's funny."

"I laughed the first time, Da. A hundred years ago.

"Ruth didn't come to the read-through." Jonah, forced casual.

"She is starting on the funny age," Da explained.

Jonah snorted. "When does the funny age start?"

"Right around 1905," I said.

"I embarrass her. She's ashamed of me. Doesn't want to see her brother in greasepaint. A stooge of the elite."

His voice had a note I'd never heard. Da waved off his injury. "The girl is just twelve years." But Jonah was right. Ruth stayed home increasingly now, whenever she could, preferring her girlfriends to her family. She had her ear pointed elsewhere—other voices, other tunes.

Not long after the Schoenberg, Da, Jonah, and I chanced to catch a radio news broadcast of a faint signal from outer space. The signal came back from the first human thing to escape the earth's surface. I thought of that star map, Jonah's and my only decoration at Boylston, in the sealed room of our childhood. We sat with one another around the family radio, listening to the regular beep, the first word from *out there*, the future.

Jonah heard just the opposite. His ears were tuned to further frequencies, the groundbreaking past that all signals were rushing to join. "Joey. You hear that? Schoenberg's Second String Quartet. It's happening, little brother. And in our lifetime! 'I feel the air of another planet.'"

"'*Ich fühle Luft von anderem Planeten.*'" Da spoke to himself, remembering, in a distant orbit.

That ethereal, beeping metronome drew Ruthie from her room, where she now hid out. "A signal from space?" My sister's face filled with awful hope. One hand flew up to the side of her eyes, blocking her peripheral sight. I knew what possibilities she was turning over. "That's coming from somewhere else?"

Da smiled. "The first space satellite."

Ruth waved, impatient with his denseness. "But someone is out there? Sending . . ."

Da formed the corrections to his corrections. "No, *Kind*. Only us. Alone, and talking to ourselves."

Ruth retreated to her room. I tried to follow, but she closed her door on me.

Those cycling beeps from outer space confirmed Jonah's iconoclasm. He studied new notation systems at night, asking my help in decoding their hieroglyphs, even as his teachers gave him Belle Epoch salon songs. In the future that his progressive music was making, all objects bathed in the same blinding light. When the time came, he'd be free, released to deep orbit, signaling the earth from out of the endless vacuum.

I heard him at school, sailing up his aerial chromatic scales, a few practice rooms down from mine. My own practice hours were more plodding. Mr. Bateman gave me Grieg's *Lyric Pieces*. Each time I played for my teacher, he'd nudge my fingers, wrists, elbows. I felt my body extending the piano, those tripping hammers replayed at large in my more intricate muscle.

I worked through the *Lyric Pieces*, one every two weeks, a dozen bars every afternoon. I'd repeat the phrase until the notes dissolved under me, the way a word turns back to meaningless purity when chanted long enough. I'd split twelve bars into six, then shatter it down to one. One bar, halting, rethreading, retaking, now soft, now mezzo, now note for staggered note. I'd experiment with the attacks, making my hand a rod and striking each machine-coupled note. I'd relax and roll a chord as if it were written out arpeggio. I'd repeat the drill, depressing the keys so slowly, they didn't sound, playing the whole passage with only releases. I'd lean on the bass or feel my hands, like an apprentice conjurer extracting hidden interior harmonies from the fray.

The game was leverage, control. Speed and span, how to crack open the intervals, widen them from on high, raise the body's focus from finger into arm, lengthen the arm like a hawk on the wing. I'd coat the line in rubato or tie every note into a legato flow. I'd round the phrase or clip it, then pedal the envelope and let it ring. I'd turn the baby grand into a two-manual harpsichord. Play, stop, lift, rewind, repeat, stop, lift, back a line, back a phrase, back two bars, half a bar, the turn, the transition, the note, the thinnest edge of attack. My brain sank into states of perfect tedium laced with intense thrill. I was a plant extracting petals from sunlight, water wearing away a continent's coast.

I'd chink away for hours, moving my spine less than four inches in either direction. Then I'd stand, pace around my cubicle like a zoo wolf spinning in his pen, head down the hall, and stick my head under the arc from the drinking fountain. The halls filled with glorious racket. All around me, bursts of broken-off melody bled together like an Ives symphony. Crusts of Chopin collided with fractured Bach invention. Ostinato Stravinsky attached itself to Scarlatti fragments. Earnest, industrial-grade laboring here and there delivered strains more gorgeous than anything I'd ever heard in concert, snippets so beautiful they plunged me into depression when they broke off in midphrase. Down this monastic clubhouse hall came a mass version of my parents' old Crazed Quotation game: hymns pressing up against honky-tonk; high Romantic philters elbowing rigid fugues; funerals, weddings, baptisms, sobs, whispers, shouts: everyone at this party talking at once, beyond any ear's ability to unravel.

I'd return to my cage for another two hours of dismantling and rebuilding. My body threatened to collapse and my brain tried to slip into a permanent coma. The drill was maddening, dulling, grueling, thankless, exhilarating, addictive, consuming, consummate. It felt like love, like a refiner's fire. I was a child at the beach with a sieve, improving the infinite expanse of sand. In the focus of my will, the sheer hammering repetition, I could burn off all of the world's impurities, everything ugly and extraneous, and leave behind nothing but a burnished rightness, suspended in space. I closed in with microscopic steps on something I couldn't see, something clean and unchanging, pure form and purer pleasure, a delivering memory, music, some glimpse of a still-unmade me.

But even such a focused blaze couldn't burn off the teenage body that fueled it. I'd sit rolling the stone up the hill for half an hour before admitting the stone was rolling back over me. When every key press felt like mud, I'd hunt down someone else to distract—Jonah, or, more often, Wilson Hart.

When he wasn't off in his mind's dusty Spain, Will, too, spent his days in a practice room. But he never practiced as much as he should. He had that splendid muscular bass, overflowing the resonators of his chest and head. But it slipped in and out of control as he drew it through scales. His low-range power alone might have landed him a teaching job at a college like the one he had left to come to Juilliard. At his best, he might have held any stage on either side of the Mason-Dixon. But he only hit his best around half the time.

Will's vice was his wanting to *make* music, not just be someone else's messenger boy. He'd start to air out those magnificent pipes of his, but the piano in the practice room corner proved too much temptation. I ambushed him one day, working at the thing that was not his work. He sat at the keyboard, the indicting evidence of a new score spread around him. "You should be in the composition program. You know that?"

Something in my joke went wrong. "Yes, I do." Then, forgiving me my ignorance, his fingers broke into a quotation of the Rodrigo guitar concerto's middle movement, a tune sad enough to deflect my stupidity. He scooted over on the bench. "Sit down. We're going to make something happen."

I sat to his left and awaited instructions. None came. Will went on teasing out the Spaniard's phrase, all there was to know about abandonment. His hands found their marks on nothing but foreknowledge. I sat still for a few measures until a nod from Will pointed out the obvious. I was supposed to fill out the lower lines, on nothing but the same.

I'm cursed with a near-perfect musical memory. One listen, plus my sense of the rules of harmony, and I can find my way to just about any lost chord. I'd only heard the Rodrigo once before, when Will played it for me. But the thing was still in me, intact. Under Will's melodic promptings, I recovered the spirit, if not the full letter, of the thing.

Will laughed out loud as we fell into line. "Knew you could, brother Joe. Knew you had it in you." So long as he didn't expect me to chat back, we were in business. We got through the stray modulations, then started to head back to home and the theme's recap. Will flicked his head and said, "Here we go, now, Mix." Before I knew what was happening, his fingers dropped into bottomless places. They untied the long, mournful melody and lifted out the contents hidden inside.

I saw the moves and heard each sound he built: clusters that weren't in the score, yet might have been, in some world without a Mediterranean. The core of Will's chords came from Rodrigo. Yet the blind romantic could never have written them. The line that Will unrolled shared its parent melody, but his hands bent the slow troubadour tune into another arc, away from Iberia, down old, forced Atlantic crossings. He challenged that fake antique tune, like some unacknowledged half brother come knocking on your front door one afternoon wearing your nose, your jaw, your eyes. You don't know me, but . . . Mixed. *All* mixed up. Wasn't a horse alive with a clean pedigree.

My fingers were clubs. I heard each thing Will did before he did it. But I tagged along behind each change, getting there only after Will had already left me in his harmonic wake. I knew the shape of the music he made. You couldn't live in this country and not breathe it. But I'd never learned the rules, the laws of freedom that kept these improvisations aloft, just out of reach of a clean conservatory death.

I felt myself tracing pitiful clichés. My left hand reached out for the safe cartoon, no closer to Will's outpouring than a minstrel show to a spiritual. He cracked Iberia open and freed every Moor who had ever strayed into it. I bobbed in the Strait of Gibraltar, looking for a sandbar or a splinter of driftwood. The clash of his intervals traced dark, intricate places. Mine were just gratuitous dissonances. Mistakes.

Will chuckled at me over his improvised waves. "Witness? Can't I get a witness here?" He figured I'd ease in after a few bars. When I didn't, he went grim. He slowed, surprised. His disappointment made it harder for me to find the elusive groove.

I gathered myself and dove forward, drawing on every scrap of theory I'd ever squirreled away. I thought my way into the modulations. For a few phrases, I came alive. Will settled into a sequence I grasped, and I quit my little cheater's stagger-syncopated tagalong and headed out to meet him in the open seas. I pegged his wanderings and we were there together, skimming along in concert a few feet above the swells. I don't know how long we flew along together—maybe no more than a dozen bars. But we were really there. A rumble in the back of Will's throat opened up alongside us. Over the blanketing sadness of notes, he laughed a muffled, chamois laugh. "You got it, Mix. Go on, tell me!"

Will nudged me on, moving me out of sight of shoreline, into the coldest currents. His modulations held back, waiting for me to take over. He handed me the rudder. Like that novice pilot who has just shot through the most dangerous shoals and now faces only openness in all directions, I turned from exhilaration into panic. I hung there, treading water, until Will took over again. But he wasn't done with me yet. He eased out on the line, and I heard, in a burst of thirty-second notes, just how far he'd taken in the boundaries, to keep me alive. Snippets of familiar songs bubbled up to the surface of his bouillabaisse, hints of anthems I recognized by reflex, tunes I knew everything about except for their names. He took us on a giant-step, lightning tour of subterranean America, the rivers just now percolating up into the main stream—the music I'd shied away from all my life, crossing the street to avoid the threat of its oncoming silhouette.

Now and then, Aranjuez itself poked back through his inventions and struggled for sunlight. Everything we'd done—the free-form quotes, the random wandering—was just a huge unlimbering of the harmonic journey hidden in that original material. But the Spain we made was rocked by that same Civil War that Rodrigo had fled to write his piece. Will stacked up the chords, widening his palette of surprise intervals. He was sure I could free myself, find my way forward into a new song by thinking myself back, back to forebears who'd discovered the secret of this flight. Will cut me a path, note by note, sure I could get there with him. His faith in me felt worse than death.

I stumbled and fell back on cheap banalities, slopping up wallpaper sounds like a hack in a Bourbon Street bar, grinding out twelve-bar seventh chords to please the tourists. Every shred of technique I'd ever mastered held me shackled to the block. I was a drain on him. He could do more with his two hands than the two of us could do with four. I fell back on skeletal fills. My riffs thinned out. I pulled back into a long diminuendo and stopped.

Will finished out solo, and with an ingenuity even greater than he'd shown on the voyage out, he brought the key back to tonic and led his fingers home to Aranjuez. He looked at me. "You can't make it go, on its own? You need it out there in front of you, on the page?" He meant to be kind, but his every word made things worse. My face went hot. I couldn't look at him. "Don't make no difference, brother Joe. Some folks need the notes. Other folks don't even care what the notes are called."

He stirred the keys again. The chords were fading comments, trickles under his fingers, his latest reflections on the matter.

I wanted to make him stop. "Where did you learn to do that?"

Will smiled, as much at his hands as at me. His fingers crawled over the keys like puppies in a giveaway wicker basket. He was as amazed by their freedom as anyone. "Around, Mix. Same place you're gonna learn it."

Same place I could have. Should have.

He let out a train of staccato block chords, a parody of the opening of the Waldstein, my current nemesis. Will Hart was surprised at me. I'd lost my inheritance. If I could do everything Beethoven wanted of me, I ought to be able to please myself. I didn't even know what such a thing might mean. But I could still hear the sounds he'd just unleashed, rolling in my ears, humbling the material they came from. "Why don't you . . . write music like that?"

He stopped and stared. "What you think we two just *did*?"

"I mean, write it down. Compose it, instead of . . . I mean, not instead of . . . Along with?" His academic, written-out music felt almost wilted and window-boxed, compared to the music he'd just grown out of his head. If a person could do what he'd just done, launch raw possibility out of the empty air, why would he waste a minute writing down well-behaved conservatory music that stood little chance of being played even once?

"Some songs are for writing down. Some songs are for freeing from writing."

"What you just made? That was better than the stuff you made it from."

He just grimaced at the blasphemy. Nobody was better than that blind Spaniard. He scooted through another elaborate sequence of chords that took me a moment to recognize as a hotted-up, cooled-out circle of fifths. He lifted his hands and offered me the keyboard. I brought my claws toward the keys, knowing, before I closed with them, that it was no good. There was nothing in my digits but *Lyric Pieces*. Nineteenth-century northern Europe's airbrushed studio portrait.

"I can't." He'd caught me out. Exposed me. My hands fell to the keys but did not press them.

His left hand grabbed my neck as if it were the root of his next wild chord. "That's okay, brother Joe. Let every soul praise God in his own fashion."

I jerked at the words. But I was old enough, now, not to ask where he'd learned them. He'd picked them up the same place my mother had: around.

I set aside a few minutes each day, at the end of my practice, when further repetition of the day's passage would do more harm than good. Ten minutes—a prayer to myself, an exercise in remembering how Wilson Hart made music on the fly, out of emptiness. My fingers began to turn without any notes to propel them. But the hardest printed music came easier for me than the simplest indigo riff.

I told Jonah. "You have to hear Will Hart improvise. Out of this world." My words damned my friend with understatement. Something in me was protecting both men, hiding out where neither could ask anything more of me.

"Not surprised. How come he doesn't hang out with the jazzers?"

Jonah couldn't have heard, then, even if he had come listen. His own musical sea change preoccupied him. He came to me one day, swollen with nonchalance. "They're setting up lessons for next term. William Schuman wants me to study with Roberto Agnese. *Schuman*. The president of the school, Mule. I didn't think he knew undergraduates even existed."

Agnese, old workhorse tenor, was among the most venerable of the vocal arts faculty. "That's fantastic, Jonah. You're on Easy Street." I had no idea what borough I thought that street ran through.

"Small problem, honorable baby brother. Number-one son also desired as student by Mr. Peter Grau." Grau, the Met star, who never took more than a few of the most promising graduates.

"You're joking. How?"

"He *came and asked me!*" The punch line to a dirty joke. We giggled at the inanity, our old conspiracy of two. "He must imagine I'm still teachable!" My brother, who at seventeen, knew more than he ever afterward would.

"Jesus. What are you going to do?"

"What the hell *can* I do? It's not like I can say no to either one."

"You're going to study with them both?"

Jonah gave a doomed stage cackle.

He spent a season in hell. He took a lesson each week from each great man, putting in twice the hours, struggling to remember which teacher had asked for what. He kept each one in the dark about his rival. The whole thing played out like some sordid French farce, Jonah dashing from one studio to the other, hiding the evidence, changing his sound depending on the day, swearing fidelity to two contrary approaches. "I'm fine, Mule. Just gotta make it until the end of term. Few more weeks. Then I'll figure something out."

"No one can keep this up, Jonah. You'll break down."

He glowed. "You think? A nice sanitarium on the top of some snowy mountain?"

His two mentors were each other's spiritual opposites. Agnese was all touch and feel, the bodily mechanics of sound, his hands perpetually sculpting my brother's jaw, practically moving his lips, his Neapolitan mass forever exploding in vast semaphores of grief or ecstasy. "The guy squeezes my gut while I'm singing. 'Come, Strom. Everything comes from low down inside you.' Pervert. Like I'm in basic training or something."

Grau, at his antilessons, made the body disappear in a cloud of thought. He'd never dream of touching Jonah. He stood as far away as his studio allowed, speaking in a motionless haze. "Feel your head backward and up. No! Do not push. *Think* it so. Think the larynx down. Do not move it! Do not use the muscles. The muscles must vanish. You must become a ghost to yourself, full of the power of not doing."

Musicians speak of bliss, but that's just to throw the uninitiated off the scent. There is no bliss; there is only control. All the orphic gymnastics that each coach demanded of Jonah pushed down into his nervous system, hitched to the traces of every emotion Jonah had ever felt. Both coaches believed that a given muscle set *was* the emotion that produced it. The symbol produced the thing, and the ability to reverse create, by muscle movement, the full spectrum of human feeling represented the ultimate artistic power.

His mentors differed violently over how to produce this power. Agnese ran about the studio, flapping his massive wings, shouting, "Move your sound. Above the upper lip. Out in front of the teeth. Put the brain away. Let the pitch correct the vowel. *Ah, eh, ee, oh, oo.* We must hear joy! Love! Desolation! Ma-je-sty!" Grau stood still, a pillar of transcendence, musing. "Draw in your breath with your thighs. Drop as you rise. Sing on the air, not with it. Conceive the sound before you make it. Start your sound before your throat, in your mind!"

Roberto Agnese gave Jonah his first crack at reading a famous role. He toyed with the experiment, settling on Donizetti's *Elixir of Love*—the poor, swarthy Nemorino, in particular the devastating cavatina, that one fat, famous, secret tear stealing down the lead's cheek in the dark. Jonah took a stab at the part, penciling up his expensive foreign edition with articulations.

Then Peter Grau hit upon assigning him the same role. Jonah came to me in a panic. "There *is* a Supreme Being, Joey. And He's after my mulatto ass!"

He didn't have the cash to spare for a second copy of the music. So each week before each lesson, he'd erase every pencil mark given him by the one teacher and replace them with the carefully archived marks of the other, down to the slightest scribble. He was like a plagiarist, constantly tripping up, begging to be caught. The labor was herculean. Every recopying took him the better part of a night.

Each teacher's "Furtive Tear" was the other's opposite. Agnese wanted it wet, wide, and scooping. Grau wanted it dry as the winter Sahara. Agnese told Jonah to wallop the first note of each phrase and swoop down a fifth to nab the rest of the line in his talons. Grau had him clamp on the attack, then swell from nothing. The Italian wanted the sorrow of all mankind. The German wanted a stoic rejection of human absurdity. Jonah just wanted to escape alive.

They had him going like Joanne Woodward in *The Three Faces of Eve*, the previous year's multiple-personality Oscar winner. Jonah couldn't remember who'd ordered what. He got so he could switch interpretations in midnote, given the tiniest tremor in his current teacher's eyebrow. Then one week, Mr. Grau leaned down to examine my brother's penciled articulations. "What's this? Sostenuto, *here*? Surely I told you no such thing."

Jonah mumbled something about a friend's joke, and fell to furious erasing.

"Who would *dream* of sostenuto at such a moment?"

Jonah shook his head, appalled at such an outrage.

"*You* surely don't think that's the way to do these lines?"

Jonah looked scandalized.

"Well, why not. Go ahead and try it that way."

Nothing if not limber, my brother did, trying to make it sound as if he hadn't rehearsed it that way, every other session, for the last three weeks.

"Hmm." Grau scowled. "Not uninteresting."

When Agnese stopped him at the same passage and told him—just a crazy whim—to try it staccato, Jonah knew the gigue was up. For a week, both of his teachers raked him with antiphonal silence. My brother apologized to each.

Grau wagged his head. "Whom did you imagine you were fooling?"

Agnese chuckled. "You think this stereophonic 'Furtive Tear' was what you Americans call a *coincidence*?"

My brother didn't inquire how long they'd seen through his sham. But, as abjectly as possible, he did ask, "Why?"

"Consider it your education in the politics of performance," Grau said. "Believe us: From here on out, such things will cause you far more tears than any passage in Donizetti."

So ended my brother's attempt to two-time the school's finest. Jonah's escapade briefly made him the conservatory's Brando. Outside the school, the cranked-up youth uprising geared up to break open the world. But inside our soundproof practice rooms, tempo violations were still the worst imaginable crime. We simply had no idea where we lived. The Sammy's crowd traded murky tales of reefer and horse, potent substances that by all accounts made Village jazz musicians schizophrenic and turned the Harlem underclass into killers. They worried the question for hours. "Say it made you play better for a while, and then it killed you. Would you take it, for your art?"

Sex was the much closer transgression. Rumors of hand jobs, even mouth jobs performed in darkened practice rooms for standing-room-only recipients abounded. One slim blond ingenue flutist—everyone's fetish—had to leave school under circumstances ripe with inventive explanation. The hint of vice filled the halls, a broken scent bottle no amount of ammonia could scrub out. My brother's friends argued forever about which female vocal students, with their various techniques, would best serve their needs—the fast, high passage-workers, the deep embouchures . . . We were such children as this country will never produce again. Long past the age when our old Hamilton Heights torturers were being sent off to their first prison terms, Jonah and I held on to a naïveté we mistook for sin. But when the time for real sinning finally came, we had all the advantage of the late starter.

With the settling of his voice, Jonah landed most of the plum parts he set himself after. Two years into the bachelor's, he was singing with graduate productions. If the part called for weightless precision, all pretense of democratic auditions broke down. He had a flair for the comic—the eighteenth-century page boy whose ditsiness is surpassed only by his heartbreaking zeal. He sang a Bach Evangelist that had half the agnostics in the house ready to convert, at least for an evening. He learned how to act. By nineteen, he'd mastered that devastating sucker punch, the one that lulled audiences into thinking they were watching some *other* poor bastard's life, only to zap them at the flick of an invisible switch into realizing just whose story this was.

He performed hungrily. He'd sing anything written since the war. He had his pick of premieres, as few other students wanted to kill themselves learning new, extended techniques for a one-shot deal. But he'd also sing little bits of French fluff he could have ripped through at age six. Up on Claremont, he sang everything from Celtic folk songs to Russian liturgical monody, with Sturm und Drang, buffa, and High Renaissance hankie flirtations littered along the way. He couldn't distinguish between a funeral mass and a flippant encore. He sang every tune as if it were his swan song. He could make stones weep and guiltless animals die of shame: the Orpheus that Peri, Monteverdi, Glück, Offenbach, Krenek, and Auric had in mind.

In life's opening few years, everything you hear, you hear for the first time. After a while, the ear fills in, and hearing turns back from the future and into the past. What you've yet to hear is outstripped by what you already have. The beauty of Jonah's voice lay in its running backward. With every new phrase that came out of him, old notes lifted off of his listeners and they grew younger.

People actually turned up to hear his degree recital. He insisted I accompany him. We worked for weeks on the pieces, mostly mainstream nineteenth-century German lieder. He mocked the melodramatic crowd-pleasers we had to do: "Aural Novocain." At our dress rehearsal, we scrambled to put the last desperate touches to the "Will-o'-the-Wisp" from Schubert's *Winterreise*. I was halfway into the second verse, the almost nihilistic

> Bin gewohnt das Irregehen,
> 's führt ja jeder Weg zum Ziel:
> Uns're Freuden, uns're Leiden,
> Alles eines Irrlichts Spiel!

All our joys and sorrows a will-o'-the-wisp, when I heard Jonah singing:

> Pepsi-Cola hits the spot-ta,
> Twice as much for a nickel, too.
> Twelve full ounces, that's a lot-ta,
> Pepsi-Cola's the drink for you!

I slammed down the lid and shouted over the last words. "Damn it, Jonah. What the hell do you think you're doing?"

He saw my face, and couldn't stop cackling. "Joey, it's a fucking school recital. We can't let them bust our nuts with it."

I was sure he'd repeat the stunt in recital, if not deliberately, then by practiced accident. But he sang the words as written, an old man twice Da's age, who knew from bitter experience that every path leads to the same sea and every urgent joy and sorrow are just phantom lights on the far side of an uncrossable channel. He passed the recital, with honors.

The Sammy's crowd threw him a little bash a few days after our performance. My brother still hung with that crowd, for whatever sense of freedom they gave him. I'd fallen away, out of disgust. I preferred running through the coda of my current Beethoven sonata another thousand times to hearing my competitors evaluated even once more.

But Jonah wanted me to put in an appearance at this celebration. When I arrived, Brian O'Malley was holding forth, the way he had for most of our college career. His routine turned toward race at my entrance, as it often did when I was around. Proof of O'Malley's enlightenment. For our amusement, he launched a burlesque of the shit-kicker soda jerks behind the Woolworth counter in Greensboro: "Seein' as how y'all are gonna be settin' here a spell, you want somethin' cold to drink? Y'all will have to drink it outside, of course, but you can come on back in soon as you're done!"

I stared out the window with a deflecting smile, doing my best to outlast this humor. Across the street, a woman stepped from behind a delivery truck and passed uptown. She was wearing a navy blue midcalf-length dress with wide, pointed shoulders, decades out of date. Her hair was a wren's nest of soft black thread. I had only a glimpse of her face. She was a tone I'd given up on ever finding. Seeing her like this, at large, heading north, free to be anything, I knew she'd been put there for me to discover.

I tripped getting up, wrecking O'Malley's punch line. I faked some excuse and bolted. Outside, I found her again. She was sailing uptown, a beautiful navy blue cutter against the afternoon current. I followed her up Broadway, where she made a right on LaSalle. She turned again up Amsterdam, a hundred yards ahead of me. I tried to close, but she walked so fast, I worried that she was fleeing me.

Still chasing her up toward City College, I felt myself start to dissolve. I looked on myself from above, a teenager chasing a total stranger. Each step added to my abasement. What drove me wasn't lust, but some need simpler than I'd felt in my life. A woman whom I knew better than I knew myself had been walking around Claremont, the blocks around my school, looking for me. She couldn't have known I was sitting in a nearby coffee shop, the captive of fools. She'd given up trying to find me. It was up to me to redeem myself.

The buildings alongside me closed into a tunnel. I could no longer feel the air against my skin. I urged myself on, from miles above myself in space. I was my own marionette, the central character in my own life, a story whose plot had just revealed itself to me. I hadn't felt so focused, so alive, since earliest childhood's music evenings. Everything was well. All lines would finally resolve and reach cadence. Every person on this packed street had some note to hand the chord.

195

All the while, my tow bobbed in front of me, her walk tailored and purposeful. So long as I kept her in sight, I had no other needs. I drew close enough to make out her neck underneath that perfect fall of hair. For a moment, in the thinning afternoon light, I panicked. Her skin shifted, as if by some trick of protective coloration. The tinted glass window at Sammy's had misled me. My sense of recognition vanished. Then she turned and looked my way. So much certainty filled me that I almost called out. Her face inhabited that place I thought I lived in alone.

She bore right and I followed, so focused, I forgot to notice the cross street. Runners in the middle of a turf war tensed as I slid past them. Two heavyset men glared at me from their doorway lookout. All eyes up and down the block picked me out as an intruder. Ahead, that navy blue coat moved deeper into this injured neighborhood like a ghost over a battlefield.

She veered twice more, and I kept to her trail. Some nearby motion distracted me. When I looked back ahead, the navy-dressed woman was gone. She disappeared into a doorway that I searched for but couldn't find. I stood on the corner, stupidly waiting for destiny to return and claim me. People pushed past, impatient and indifferent. Busses disgorged their contents a hundred feet away. The neighborhood turned malevolent, smelling my fear and sensing I had no right to be here. The intersection closed in around me, and I bolted.

The streets I fled back down felt more hostile than the ones I'd come up. I turned west too early, on a street that, after a block, veered diagonally through the grid, back uptown. I stopped, turned, took a few steps, and turned back again, confused. I clipped along the edge of a long, scorched parkway. My body took over, and I sprinted back toward what I hoped was Amsterdam.

All at once, I wasn't in New York. I felt myself in a herd of people not from around these parts, moving too slowly for 1960. I can't say how long I stood there. The question had no measure. I was out on the streets of a city I didn't recognize, in a crowd of people who weren't mine, on a day I shared with no one around me.

I cursed myself for losing everything. The woman still felt so present that I felt sure I'd find her again, as soon as I was supposed to. I knew her neighborhood, where she walked, how she moved. My finding her could not have been a one-off chance. I was eighteen years old. And I'd waited until that moment to fall in love with an image even more fleeting than music.

Jonah lit into me when I got home. "What the fuck do you think you were doing back there?" It took me a while to remember: the scene at Sammy's. Jonah was merciless. "What was that all about? Were you deliberately trying to humiliate me with those people?" He needed an answer. I had none.

"Jonah. Listen. I just saw the woman I'm going to spend the rest of my life with."

"Oh?" All those classes in dramatic presence. "Your whole life? Starting when?"

"I'm serious."

"Of course you are. Little Joe is no kidder. You will be sure to let the woman know, right?"

I went to Sammy's the next day, and every afternoon at that hour for two weeks. I suffered through the worst that high culture had to offer. Jonah thought I was doing penance, and he doled out little verbal awards. But I was keeping my vigil, as regular and necessary as sleeping or eating. She'd have to be back. She couldn't have been dangled in front of me, only to disappear for good. That afternoon, or the next, by month's end at the latest . . .

When she didn't appear again, I grew edgy. Impatience became confusion. Confusion turned desperate without any help from me. After a week, I tried to retrace my route north, through blocks I couldn't resurrect. I stopped going to Sammy's, stopped doing anything except sitting in a practice room, paralyzed, the last holdout case of polio, brought on by a glimpse of this girl, whose name I had no chance in hell of discovering.

After a month of seeing me like that, Jonah began to believe me. One night, from nowhere, he asked, "What did she look like?"

I shook my head. "You'd know her. You'd know her the minute you saw her."

This is how the dream of the 1950s ended for me, before I could wake myself from it. Around us, in New York and farther, the whole key signature changed from one measure to the next, as if that swap of digits really meant something. The year the decade changed, I turned adult. Revolutions sprang up everywhere, except inside my brother and me. At the flick of that invented calendar switch, the world went from black and white to colored. And by some law of conserving physics, Jonah, Ruth, and I went from colored to black and white.

The bald general gave way to the thick-haired, hatless boy. The superpowers edged toward the nuclear brink, each one willing to go down without blinking. The arms race moved into space. Black students moved into white establishments. I spent less time inside my practice room fall-out shelter and more hours above ground, waiting for the perfect-toned, navy-dressed woman to come claim me before the world went up in mushroom clouds.

The nation—the white part anyway—sang along with Mitch, following a ball that bounced across the lyrics at the bottom of the television screen. People really did this. Maybe not New Yorkers, but out over the Hudson, to all points west: the entire country, singing out loud in front of the TV, a chorus of millions of living rooms in one vast, last, if isolated, sing-along, where nobody could hear one another, but where, for a final moment, everyone kept to something like the same key.

Lenny Bruce played Carnegie Hall, performing my brother's all-time favorite routine. Jonah bought the record, his first comedy disk, listening to the shtick until the vinyl wore out. He studied the inflections with his perfect ear, cackling at the cadences no matter how many times he listened:

I'm going to give you a choice, your own free will, of marrying a black woman or a white woman, two chicks about the same ages, same economic levels . . . whatever marriage means to you—kissing, and hugging and sleeping together in a single bed on hot nights . . . fifteen years . . . kissing and hugging that black, black woman, or kissing and hugging that white, white woman . . . Make your choice, because, see, the white woman is Kate Smith. And the black woman is Lena Horne.

Jonah played it for me, joining in on the punch line. "You dig, jig? The whole thing's not really about race after all. It's about ugliness! So let's go string up all the *ugly* people, huh?" But Jonah repeated the routine only in private performance. For the better part of thirty years—and the worse part, too—he never recalled the joke for anyone but me.

Down in the Village, music was having quintuplets. From the insidious Seeburg jukebox at Sammy's, from little trickles of radio on our way to the Met broadcasts, and from wilder dispatches in the streets all around us, we finally heard. Something had been happening, for years. At last, Jonah wanted a listen. We went downtown, sat in on two progressive jazz sets, had the tops of our heads taken off, then headed back home. Jonah waved the whole scene away. Then, a month later, he wanted to go back.

We fell into a semiweekly ritual, sneaking into the hot spots I wasn't legally old enough to enter. The bouncer saw that hungry musician's gaze and looked the other way. We'd hit the Village Gate one week, the Vanguard the next. While the jazz giants gathered at the Gate, the folkies took up across the street at the Bitter End: two furious scenes that couldn't have been further apart in every way except distance. The mind-warping Vanguard sound had rumbled around for years, old inland blues swelling, flowing, coming back east to get cool and urbane. The older club regulars told us we'd already missed the peak. They claimed that the real gods had already passed from the face of the land, and that 1960 was already nothing but an echo. But to Jonah and me, here was the air of a planet newer than Schoenberg, with an atmosphere far more breathable.

I couldn't hear it then, the re-creation in our recreation. That sound had filled the house once, pouring out of the radio on Sunday mornings. We had never eaten one of Da's elaborate experimental omelettes except to jazz. It was never really ours, not like the stuff we sang every other day. Never home to us; more like a wild two-week summer rental on the Strip. But our parents had listened. Only Jonah and I had fallen away. We didn't feel our prowling around the Village as a return. We thought we'd stumbled onto a place we'd never been.

Da didn't want us staying downtown all night. He'd lost track of us, vanishing into his work, coming up for air only to blunder through parenting. He surfaced long enough to say that he wanted us home by midnight, too early to hear the stuff that the regulars talked about in hushed tones. Those sets never got started until early morning. The heavy players were still going—zipped up and cooking on fuels I'd never heard of—by the time Jonah and I dragged back into the conservatory the next morning. We could have skipped Da's curfew anytime without his noticing. But for whatever reasons, we obeyed this law, staying out to the last possible minute the clock allowed, Jonah going through a beer or two while helping himself to my seltzers. By the time we headed back uptown, we'd be reeling like the worst of hard-core drunks, Jonah pale with the darkness, the smoke, the wonder of it, as pale as any Semitic fellow traveler. And all anxious explanations.

"They're stealing the wild stuff from the thirties avant-garde. Paris, you know. Berlin." It reassured him, somehow. But from what I'd read, the Europeans had stolen their best bits from New Orleans and Chicago. Music, that vampire, floating around for centuries, undead, wasn't at all picky about whose jugular it sucked. Any old blood line would do, any transfusion that kept it kicking for another year.

I loved how the jazzers prowled around the streets with their horns, looking for the next quick place to unpack, scouting for like-minded cats, with no other long-range program except to sit back and blow. Their engine was pure self-delight, self-invention. Their sound had no motive, no beginning, no end, no goal but the notes, and even those they looked at only in order to look past. All a body really wanted was to play.

We caught Coltrane one night, tearing the roof off what felt like someone's living room in a street shorter than a Tinkertoy, on a stage the size of a cheese Danish. He'd been standing in a nearby alley, leaning on the end of his tenor case, when the drummer and pianist of that night's session went to have a smoke. They waylaid 'Trane, or he had nothing better to do. Sources varied. In any case, Jonah and I sat with our ears in that giant upturned bell, hearing the cups clapping his tone holes, listening to a game of Crazed Quotations beyond our ability to follow.

For all my grounding in theory and harmony, I couldn't hear a third of what that pickup quartet did that night. But here was music as it had been, once, in the beginning, when my family first gave it to me. Music for the sheer making. Music for a while.

I loved to watch Jonah when the best of the Village's singers adventured onstage. He favored the sets of a southern woman named Simone who'd started out studying piano at Juilliard with Carl Friedburg. Her voice was harsh, but she took it into unknown places. His other goddess was another dark woman, from Mama's Philly, who could scat wilder than a Paganini pizz. Jonah sat like a spaniel at a rabbit farm, leaning forward, mouth open, body ready to bolt onstage and join the fray. I had to keep a hand on his collar sometimes. Thank God I did, for on the long ride home—the two of us, north of Fifty-ninth, breaking into the obligatory "Take the A Train"—I heard how gelded his whole concert-hall, full-voiced precision would have sounded on any stage south of Fourteenth.

His keepers at Juilliard didn't know about his after-hours flirtations with the island's lower regions. After his senior recital, the school prepared to grant my brother their degree. His teachers split over what he should do next. Agnese wanted him to enter the graduate program, attacca, without pausing for breath. Grau, who loved my brother more ruthlessly, wanted him out in the world, getting a taste of the brutal arena of auditions, the quickest way to toughen that voice that still held on to an unnatural innocence.

The Rome-Berlin axis compromised on a trip to Europe. They conveyed their plans to Jonah. If Jonah put up a token sum, they could arrange a scholarship, free accommodation, and a superlative teacher in Milan. Italy was the voice's home, the hajj every singer made, the dream world with which Kimberly Monera had once fed Jonah's childish imagination. He'd had four years of the language and could say things like "To love one another eternally—that is the curse coursing through our blood!" and "Even the gods' indifference will not delay me" with all the ease of a native speaker. There was no question: He would have to make the pilgrimage to vocal music's promised land. The only question was when.

My brother had gone to Juilliard purely as an alternative to grief. And now he started planning for Milan only as an alternative to hanging around Claremont forever. Da was sure this was the proper next step. "My boy, I wish I were traveling with you." Ruthie used her baby-sitting money to buy a set of conversational Italian records so she could jabber with him at breakfast in the weeks before his departure. But after a few go-rounds with Jonah correcting her pronunciation, she broke off the attempt and condemned the records to our piles of opera LPs.

Jonah was booked to leave just after graduation. The night before commencement, he came into the kitchen to help me wash dishes. He seemed transfigured, lighter than he'd been in weeks. I thought it was his approaching departure.

"Mule, you go. I'm sitting tight for a while," I laughed. "Serious." My mouth sagged, waiting for him to come clean. "Serious, Joey. I'm not going. You know why. You know everything, brother. The last few years have been perfect hell, haven't they? For both of us. You knew that all along, while I waltzed around, pretending . . . "

"Jonah. You have to go. It's all arranged. They've put themselves out for your sake."

"Help a colored boy see the Vatican."

"Jonah. Don't do this. Don't throw this away."

"What am I throwing away? They're throwing *me* away, damn it. Everybody has plans for me but me. Imagine what I'd be after six months of Europe. Their charity case. Their trademarked act. Indebted to my sponsors forever. Sorry. Can't do it, Joey."

He looked away, avoiding my eye. A muscle in his cheek twitched at a hundred beats a minute. For the first time in his life, my brother was afraid. Maybe not of failing: Failing would have been a relief. Afraid of who he'd be, if the problem of who he was was solved for him.

His teachers were furious. They had pulled strings for him, and he was walking away from their protective benefice. Agnese wasn't accustomed to having his generosity trashed. He threw my brother out of his studio and refused to talk to him. Grau, the longer-term architect, sat him down, hostage for a few more minutes, and made him say just what he wanted to do instead.

Jonah threw his palms in the air. He was just that age, emerged adult, with adolescence's pupa still clinging to him. "I thought I might sing a little?"

Grau laughed. "And what have you been doing for the last four years?"

"I mean . . . sing for humans."

The laugh went sharper. "Humans, as opposed to teachers?"

"Humans as opposed to, you know, people who are *paid* to listen?"

Mr. Grau smiled to himself. He folded his hands in front of his face and said with theatrical neutrality, "By all means, go and find your humans." Neither blessing nor curse. Just: Go see.

Da was more confused than I'd ever seen him. He kept shaking his head, waiting for reality to clear itself up. Then the disappointment set in. "If you want to stay in this apartment after graduating, then you must look for work." Jonah had no idea what such a thing might mean. He typed up a ridiculous résumé and peddled it to a few low-skill employers—midtown department stores, uptown restaurants, even Columbia Operations and Maintenance. He managed to list just enough of his cultural attainments to sabotage any interest.

He decided to go out for auditions. But no ordinary tryout would do. He combed the music trade press, hunting down the perfect coming-out opportunity. He found a contest tailor-made to showcase him. He came to me with the listing. "This is the one we're doing, Mule."

He held the paper under my nose. America's Next Voices: a national competition for singers with no prior professional recognition. The thing carried a jewel of a prize. Trying for it seemed reasonable enough. The first round was months away, just before I was slated to do my own senior recital.

"I'm with you, brother. Just let me know when you want to get started."

"When? No time like now."

Then I knew what plans he had for me. "Jonah." I put my palms out to slow him. "My lessons. My recital." My degree. My life.

"Come on, Mule. We've already worked up the whole program, for my recital. You're the only player who knows me, who can read my mind."

"Who's going to coach us?"

Jonah got that manic twinkle he usually saved for the stage. "No coach. You're going to be my coach, Joey. Who else is going to do that blood-brother thing? Who else can I depend on to be absolutely merciless? Think of the stakes. If we come from nowhere and walk away with this?"

"Jonah. I have to graduate."

"Jesus. What do you take me for? I'm not going to thwart your education, for Christ's sake. You're a growing boy."

I never did graduate. But I suppose, technically, Jonah never thwarted my education.

He told Da we needed a place to rehearse. "What's wrong with here? It's just your sister and me. We know all about you."

"Exactly, Da."

"What's wrong with your home? Home is where you always made your music, since you were little."

"We're not little anymore, Da." Da looked at me as if I'd changed sides.

Jonah outdid me. "This isn't home, Da." Home had burned.

"Why don't you rehearse at school?"

Jonah hadn't told Da the details of his break with Juilliard. "We need privacy, Da. We have to nail this contest."

"This is just another audition, my boys. You've taken these before."

But it wasn't just an audition. It was our entry into the deadly horse race of professional music. Jonah didn't mean merely to enter this contest. He meant to walk away with it.

Da understood nothing, except what Jonah said he needed. He sat us down at the kitchen table after Ruth went to bed. "A little money came to us when your mother . . ." He showed us some papers. Jonah made some pretense of decoding them. "This is not a fortune I'm speaking about. But enough to start you. This is what your mother would want, what she always believed for you. But you must know: When this sum is gone, no more comes along after it. You must be sure you're doing what you need with it."

Certainty was always Jonah's vice of choice. He found a studio ten blocks from our apartment, on the edge of Harlem. At considerable expense, he rented a piano and had it moved in. It suited me: The room sat just a few blocks from where I'd seen the woman I was going to spend my future with. During our breaks, I could go stand on the corner where she'd disappeared and wait for her to materialize again.

Not that Jonah planned many breaks. He figured that once we set up the space, we'd pretty much camp out there. He picked up a half-sized refrigerator and a couple of old Boy Scout sleeping bags secondhand from some real boys. He planned to work straight through until the first rounds of the competition, that fall.

I had my own lessons, with Mr. Bateman. To Jonah, my continuing to study with the same teacher proved I wasn't learning anything. It came down to a choice: Jonah or school. Mr. Bateman was the best teacher I'd ever have. But Jonah was my brother, and the greatest musical talent I had any chance of working with. If he couldn't bring Mama back alive, what hope had I?

I applied for a leave of absence. I told Mr. Bateman it was a family emergency. He signed off without any question. Wilson Hart was the only one I leveled with. My friend just shook his head at the plan. "He know what sacrifice he's asking you to make?"

"I think he sees it as an opportunity."

It took all the man's judgment not to judge me, not to say what he should have. "More like a gamble, far as I can see."

Worse than a gamble. But so was singing. Will and I both knew one thing: With this much riding on one throw of the die, I wouldn't be coming back to school, whatever the outcome.

"You listen here, Mix. Most men?" Wilson Hart reached out and cupped my chin. I let him raise my head. His fingers grazed my Adam's apple. I wondered whether a blind person could tell race by touch. "Most men would kill for a brother like you."

He made me sit and play, while I was still in the neighborhood. Who knew when I'd be back through? We played through a four-hands version of the chamber fantasy he was working on, an eerily consonant, sepia-toned piece full of tunes I should have recognized but didn't. Jonah would have called the piece reactionary. But Jonah didn't have to know.

This time, Will gave me the upper lines. I watched my friend's face during the rests. We broke off where the piece did, at the introduction of a surprise new theme, a broad-willed subject that wasn't exactly "Motherless Child" but might have descended from it, somewhere down the orphaned generations. The song broke away under our fingers, unfinished. We hung in space over the keys, listening, after the fact, to all the things it had sounded like while we were too engaged to hear.

After a silence as noisy as any, I started playing again. I revived the first theme from his exposition. I made a point of refusing the page. After the motive unfolded, I couldn't have used the page if I'd tried. Will Hart's tune went down my arm, through my wrist, into my hand, and out my fingertips. Then it took off, with me just within earshot behind it. I heard a sharp intake of breath beside me on the piano bench as I did a number on his number. Then that breath came out a deep bass laugh, one that traveled down Will's own fingers to freedom. Will ran alongside and hopped on the freight I'd hijacked, shaking his head in amazement at discovering where I'd been spending my weekends.

His surprise subsided, and we flew along side by side. We commenced poking our souls into time signatures the tune on the page had been too shy to try out. Will howled at the change I showed since our last outing. He wanted to stop and razz me, but our hands wouldn't let him. I dangled dares in front of him, calls whose responses he couldn't help but pick up and flip back at me. He tested me, too, drawing me deeper into the shade of each idea I launched. Where I couldn't equal his inventions, I at least embroidered them with curls of counterpoint ripped off from my études, handfuls of bloom to fit the vase he handed me.

He laid down a solid floor with his chords, on which I did my best to spin lines that had never before existed. For a while, for at least as long as our four hands kept moving, the music for writing down and the music for letting loose found a way to share a nest.

I be-bopped us into a three-point landing, stealing a great alto sax riff I'd heard unleashed one night at the Gate. Will was laughing so hard at my full-body, adult baptism that his left hand had to hunt around for the tonic. We needed only a trap-set release, which we jumped up and performed in unison on the piano lid.

"Don't sue me, Wilson," I said when we'd caught our breath. "I didn't see no copyright symbol anywhere on your score."

"Where in God's creation you learn to do that, Mix?"

"Oh, you know. Here and there. Around."

"Get away! On out of here!" He waved me out of his sight. As if only the throwaway gesture guaranteed I'd be back. From a distance, he called, "And don't forget: You promised me." I looked back, a blank. Forgotten already. He mimed a scribbling motion. Composing. "Get that all down on a score someday."

By summer's end, Jonah had us on a regimen. We left the apartment every morning by the time Ruthie went to school, and returned too late to say good night to her. She complained about our being away, and Jonah laughed at her. Every so often, he sent me home to tell Da we were staying overnight, to hammer out some resistant passage.

We found our rhythm. Jonah's appetite for work outstripped the available hours. "The man wants something," I baited him. "He's hungry."

"What else are we supposed to do all day long?"

"You've never worked this hard in your life."

"I like working for myself, Joey. More future in it."

We went deep underground, where music must always go. We went down into places untouched by anyone. We put in such strange, extended hours that the days began to dissolve. Jonah wouldn't let me wear a watch. He banished any ticker with more memory than a metronome. No radio, records, newspapers, or word from the outside. Only the growing list of notes we made on a canary yellow legal pad, the curl of the sun's slatted shadow across the floorboards, the frequent sirens, and the muffled battering from the apartments below proved that the seasons still moved.

Harlem wrapped around us. The street outside drowned out our noise with its indifferent survival cries. Sometimes neighbors thumped on the walls or pounded on the door to get us to quit. Then we switched to pianissimo. For longer than the metronome could say, we were dead to the world.

Jonah obsessed on placement, those minute locations of tone that the tiny rented room made audible. He cleared out the uncertainties at each end of his range. We spoke to each other in bursts of pitches, shaping, bending, imitating. Before my eyes, Jonah pushed into an agility in his upper notes that rivaled the precision of my keys.

We were too young to travel alone. Overtrained by any measure, neither of us really knew anything. Great singers sing their whole lives and still want a teacher to hear and herd them. But here was Jonah, who'd barely sung in public, training for the first crucial contest of his life, with no one to correct him but me.

We grated on each other's nerves. He wanted me to be his harshest critic, but if I faulted his execution, he'd hiss. "Listen to the piano player, will you!" Three days later, he'd be doing what I suggested, as if it had just occurred to him. If I dropped a clunker or struggled with a passage, he assumed a patience so long-suffering that I'd start seizing up on the simplest dotted figure.

Sometimes I couldn't count to four the same way twice. But now and then, I held up a mirror to his interpretation or brought out some interior ripple he'd never heard. Then Jonah walked behind me at the bench and wrapped his arms around my shoulders in an anaconda squeeze. "Who else but you, brother? Who else could give me everything you do?"

The hours passed, motionless in their expanse. Some days, we seemed to go for weeks before darkness sent us home. Other days vanished in half an hour. In the evenings, both of us punchy with exertion, Jonah grew expansive. "Look at us, Joseph. At home on our own forty acres. And the pair of mules is free."

We weren't the only ones singing. Just the only ones locked up, singing to ourselves. Above our "Erl-King" and Dowland, tunes broke in on us from all directions. Don't forget who's walking you home. Who's coming for you, now, when you're all alone. Soft and clear like moonlight through the pines. Dry and light, like you like your wine. Darlin', please. Only you. Something you know, and something you do. Come on, baby, let's do the twist. Take me by my little hand and go like this. Takes more than a robin to make the winter go. You got what it takes, Lord, don't I know. Come on, baby, now, I'm needing you. Just an old sweet song, the whole night through.

I listened to these tunes on the sly, even as Jonah launched his own bottomless columns of air. Each note that bled into our apartment exposed us. We were some extinct, flightless bird, or that living fossil fish hauled up from the primordial deeps off Madagascar. Da had told us that once we burned the insurance money, there'd be no more. Cash, like time, flowed in one direction: away. If we barreled into this contest and stumbled, we were finished. If we came up empty, we'd have to face the music. The same music everyone else now sang.

Ours was worse than the wildest juvenile fantasy, the ten-year-old on a glass-strewn empty lot behind the condemned tenement, practicing his major-league swing. Worse than a preteen crooner singing into the mike stand hidden in a sawed-off parking meter, the next Sam Cooke, his friends the next Drifters or Platters. Jonah couldn't distinguish between long shot and shoo-in. Singing was what he did best in this life. Singing outdid the best the world had to give, better than any drug, any sedative. It was in his body. His baseline blood chemistry pumped it out like insulin. Doing something else was never an option. The pleasure of flight was too great in him.

Our preparation was pure tedium, worse than any I'd ever spent. Sometimes I sat silent, stock-still for twenty minutes as Jonah tamped out a dimple in an appoggiatura. Sometimes I stepped outside, killing time on the corner or walking a few blocks, hoping to stumble upon the woman with the wide navy blue shoulders. Then Jonah would come out after me to haul me back, furious at my desertion.

Sometimes he crawled down a well of despondence and wouldn't come out, certain that every note coming out of him sounded like dried dung. He'd try singing into a corner. He'd lie flat on his back on the wooden floor, singing to the ceiling. Anything to get his two hundred singing muscle groups to agree. He'd lie there after I stopped playing, crushed under an ocean of atmosphere. "Mule. Help. Remind me."

" 'You two boys can be anything you want.' "

He started to suffer from occasional shortness of breath. He: Aeolus's walking pair of lungs. In the middle of an E-flat major scale, his throat clamped shut as if he were in severe anaphylaxis. It took me three beats to realize he wasn't goofing around. I broke off on a leading tone and was on my feet, walking him around the room, rubbing his back, soliciting. "Should I get help? Should I call a doctor?" But we had no phone, and no doctor to call.

He put out his arm and beat time like the conductor of a volunteer community orchestra. "I'm fine." His voice came from under the polar ice caps. Two more spins around the room and he was breathing again. He walked over to the piano and built a little cadence to resolve my broken-off leading tone. "What on earth was that?" I asked. But he refused to talk about what had happened.

It struck again ten days later. Both times, he came back quickly from the attacks, his voice clearer than ever. Some film had lifted from it, one I didn't notice until brightness peeled it away. I even had the guilty thought, *If we could only time this . . .*

One evening, walking home, he stopped and grabbed my arm. He stood there on a rough corner of 122nd, his mouth forming a thought, just waiting to be mugged. "You know? Joseph. There's nothing in the world—*nothing* . . ."

"Like a dame?"

"Whiter than singing Schubert in front of five impotent, constipated judges."

"Shh. Jesus! You'll get us killed."

"Nothing whiter in creation."

"How do you know they're constipated?"

"Nothing."

"Oh, I don't know, Jonah."

"Name one."

"How about five impotent, constipated judges judging singers of Schubert?"

"Okay. Name another."

I was eager to keep moving, placate the street. But Jonah was deep in a kind of interrogation I'd never seen in him. "You know the funniest part of this? If we win . . ."

"*When* we win . . ." One of us had to be him.

"Think how much darker we'll seem, to the judges. To everybody but us. If we walk away with their prize."

The contest rules were mailed weeks in advance. There would be a scale exercise supplied by the judges and a sight-singing exercise of average difficulty. Beyond that, we had to prepare three pieces of varying character, from which the judges would ask for one. Jonah ended up assembling what anyone else would have considered an eccentric lineup. First, we brushed up a Dallapicolla song on a text by Machado; Jonah still lived for the twelve-tone idiom, and he imagined the judges would fall in love at their first whiff. Then, we tamed the Erl-King, Jonah turning that old warhorse into Pegasus. And lastly, we polished Dowland's "Time Stands Still" until it vaporized. He knew that few, if any, of the other contestants would reach that far back. With that simple song, he planned to bring stones to life and change lives into mute stones.

The local round for the contest was held at the Manhattan School of Music. We walked across the island that day, Jonah muttering stern encouragements to me. The thing was a cattle call, a fair number of first-timers unrolling their showstopper from *Guys and Dolls*. Thankfully, the

Juilliard faculty had all been shipped out to judge rounds in Jersey and Connecticut.

We were six weeks overprepared. For the first time in his life, Jonah held back onstage. He was almost marking, compared to the full voice he'd given rehearsals. Still, we made it through to the citywide round. His sight-singing alone almost guaranteed it. It would have taken a catastrophe for us to have been scratched from that preliminary screening. But as soon as we were alone, I lit into him.

"What were you thinking? We've been at this for months, and that's the worst I've ever heard you do that stuff."

"Last-minute decision, Joey. We don't want to stand out too much at this point. That just increases the odds of some judge going on a leveling vendetta." He'd learned much at the conservatory.

"Give me a little advance warning next time you go changing the game plan."

"Thousand pardons, Mule. You played like a dream. Come on! We're in round two, aren't we?"

We had two weeks for adjustments and made two months' worth. We'd heard good singers at round one, including the best of our Juilliard acquaintances and a few impressive unknowns from upper Manhattan. Most had half a dozen more years of experience than Jonah. Aside from a voice that could make lifelong fugitives surrender themselves, all we had was unbroken time.

In Queens for the citywide round, he almost disqualified us. Jonah, drunk on more ability than a twenty-year-old should be allowed, sang through the allotted time. We gave them Dallapicolla, which impressed but did not delight. Then one of the judges asked for a verse of the Dowland, to clear the palate before they dismissed us. We discharged the first verse, but when we reached the double bar, Jonah, shooting me a larcenous glance, pressed on through the end of the song. That tune's second verse scans like a battered reverse translation, impossible to phrase inside the melody that works so brilliantly with the first stanza. But in Jonah's astonished tone, the words swung open like a political prison after its illegal regime falls.

We'd clearly violated contest protocol. The judges could have thrown us off the stage, but after an initial murmur, they sat still. When we finished, you could hear the silence hurt them. Had there been a third verse, they'd have suffered it.

They waved us through to the regionals. Many of our Juilliard acquaintances didn't go forward, even some whose voices could have cured anyone's need for beauty. Contests, like snapshots, don't always show their subjects in the best light. They slice time into too thin cross sections. You practice ten hours a day, month after month, in the hopes that a few seconds onstage go something like they did in a year of rehearsal. It rarely did. We happened to sound good, in that vanishing slice of time. We were the judges' chosen ones, at least for another few days. Back in our rented studio, we allotted two minutes for a postmortem.

"Why do you suppose they love us, Joey? Can we really sound that much better than the others? Or are the judges just grateful we're the kind of Negroes who won't beat the shit out of them on the street?"

I ground out a bit of our Dowland, strewn with Parker. "They don't really know that for sure, do they?"

"You are *right*, brother. Just because we can do 'The Erl-King' doesn't mean we aren't out to rape their loved ones. You never know."

You never knew what was being given you and what taken away. You never knew who the thoroughbreds were seeing when they looked at you. Even I didn't know anymore who I saw when I saw the two of us.

"So there're these three guys on death row," Jonah said, edging us back into the repertoire. "An avant-garde Italian, a Romantic German, and an Elizabethan Englishman . . ."

For the regionals, we traveled to Washington. We'd reached the stage where even a loss would be bankable. Jonah was the youngest singer left in the running. But Jonah had his eyes on a single distant prize. And the America's Next Voices competition was just a hostage in that vaster campaign.

The semifinals were held at the auditorium at Georgetown. We stayed in a cheap hotel a good hike to the northeast. Any hotel at all was still a novelty. The clerk at the check-in asked whether we wanted the afternoon rate.

That evening, without a word to each other, we rolled out and found ourselves near the Mall. We'd heard our family's founding legend so often in so many ways that we had to see the place where our parents had met. *The same place, only later*: We still believed, despite a lifetime of our father's lessons, that where and when were independent variables.

I never imagined that a spot so filled with landmarks could feel so empty. Hundreds of people walked out on the nation's front lawn, even at that hour. Yet it looked deserted. I'd imagined crowds—tens of thousands. But this green openness felt evacuated, a civil defense drill. We crossed the long rectangle, neither of us saying much, both looking for something we couldn't find: The thing that had caused our parents to keep seeing each other, after that day when they should have gone their separate ways.

We played the next day, for more ghosts than there were healthy bodies in the audience. For the first time in my life, my arms locked in stage fright. I knew the disease had always been there, waiting like an aneurysm, terror ticking toward its debut. It chose that moment to step out. The two of us, in black tie, walked to center stage, a dozen football fields from the wings. We bowed our shallow, synchronized dips, like two water-drinking toy birds. I went to the keyboard and Jonah took up his post, grazing the crook of the piano. I looked out on the audience, who were clapping curiously on the strength of our rumor. Suddenly, I couldn't hear anything. Not even an echo.

I sat down in front of the empty music rack—I always played from memory. I rubbed my knuckles for emergency circulation. The judges asked for "The Erl-King." A dozen other composers besides Schubert have set Goethe's fake medieval ballad, and all their settings are dead. Only this one has stumbled onto forever.

We set out on our customary gallop. Once Jonah and I had rehearsed a tempo, we rarely varied more than two beats a minute. You could have set anyone's Swiss watch to us, except maybe that of the Bern patent clerk who got us into this. Perfect pitch served Jonah well over the years. But perfect meter had been even more useful. We took off running in the all-stakes darkness:

> Who rides so late through a night so wild?
> It is a father, holding his child . . .

Midway through that second line, I seized up with memory lapse. I hit a rock, and my body went on sailing so far away, I couldn't even see it land. The rich, definitive harmonies under my fingers spun out in a horrible Tristan chord. I stopped, leaving my brother galloping along in the dead of night over a yawning expanse of nothing.

When he realized I wouldn't be coming back anytime in this lifetime, Jonah reined in, although, in his air-bound scamper, he briefly considered bolting a cappella through the rest of the piece. The hall reeled from the shock of his voice and its violent silencing. Jonah never turned from the crook of the piano to look at me. He glanced at his shoes, a rude joke playing across his face. He took a crisp step forward and said, "We're going to take this again, from the top. Once more with feeling!"

The house tittered, with spatters of mortified applause. Even then, Jonah didn't turn to see if I'd recovered. He placed his right hand back upon the piano, just as before we were thrown. Then he inhaled and floated back into place, past certain that I'd join him. His sureness crucified me. The landscape beneath my fingers turned to bog. When the keys firmed, I watched them snap into a crazy chorus line, gapped where they shouldn't have been.

Nothing of the piece remained. Not the key signature, the melody, the first note, nor the name. It had to be one of three songs, but which three, I had no clue. All I could grab onto was my forgetting. Panic cheered me on, every hint of the notes I needed skidding off, a floater just to the right of my chasing eye.

I saw the hall empty out, a big vaudevillian hook extending from stage left to extract us. I sat and unlearned every piece I'd ever memorized, the film running backward, reversing Juilliard, undoing Boylston, wiping out Hamilton Heights, until I touched bottom at my very first memory: the sound of my mother singing.

Then, my mother's voice grew into my brother. Jonah was aloft again. All I had to do was sit quietly and listen. I must have been playing along, racing the wild late night, because I heard the piano there, underneath. But I was pure audience. Under my oblivious fingers, the line galloped as it never had. The cause lost, Jonah sang with death incarnate sitting on his shoulder, the ride that much wilder because of the heart-stopping stumble. We hit that state performers live for: unforgiving eternity, nothing between the notes and the instant past they rushed toward.

Rivers didn't turn in their course to track his sound. Animals didn't fall dead or stones come to life. The sound that came out of him made no difference in the known world. But something in that hall's listeners did stop, flushed out of hiding, exposed for two beats, naked in a draft of daylight, before bolting again for cover.

Afterward, a judge broke the confidentiality rules and told Jonah they'd written us off. "Then you came out for round two and annihilated them." That was his word: *annihilated*. The more deadly music was, the better.

I gave him my ultimatum on the train back north, heading home with an engraved plaque and a date for the national finals, in Durham, at Christmas. We sat side by side, without touching. Jonah's hands fidgeted with freed energy, conducting a silent symphony into the dark.

"Get rid of me, Jonah."

"Are you mad? You're my rabbit's foot. My shrunken-headed voodoo doll." He reached over to rub my hair, his good-luck charm, one degree nappier than his. He knew I hated that.

"We got a break we shouldn't have. I was finished. Total amnesia. I could be lying there still."

"Ach. I knew you'd recover."

"You knew more than I did."

"I always do, Joey."

"I'm dragging you down. Even when I'm on the mark, I'm just ballast."

"Ballast is good. Keeps ships steady."

"You need someone who's your equal."

"I have that."

He talked me back to myself, just like rehearsal: over and over, the same passages, smoothing, interrogating, dismantling, reassembling. But in my shame, I needed to torch everything and elevate quitting to something noble.

Desperate, Jonah fought dirty. "We're in the finals. All the marbles. December. There's no chance in hell I can find someone . . ."

"I'll play for the finals. God help me, I'll do whatever I can do for you. But after that . . ."

"After that, we'll talk."

My brother is standing, as alone as birth, just to the right of center stage in the old music building at Duke, Durham, North Carolina. He towers in place, listing a little bit toward starboard, backing up into the crook of the grand piano, his only safety. He curls forward, the scroll on a reticent cello. His left hand steadies against the piano while his right cups itself in front of him, holding some now-lost letter. He grins at the impossibility of being here, breathes in, and sings.

These few minutes are the sole point of our long self-burial. We've spent our adolescence underground just for this, this *winning*, dragging the prize back up to the light of day. The sweet release comes out of his mouth as if he has just found it. But under his breath——that fountain of air on which this prize floats like a ball on a plume—his skill is burnished to the hardest finish. His sound is automatic, autonomic, so honed, we could walk away and leave it out here onstage alone: music perfect to the point of absentee, exuberant, flexing all the musculature of joy, without the slightest visible effort.

This is how I see my brother, forever. He is twenty; it's December 1961. One moment, the Erl-King is hunched on my brother's shoulder, breathing the promise of a blessed deliverance. In the next, some trap-door opens in the warp of the air and my brother is elsewhere, teasing out Dowland of all things, a bit of ravishing sass for this stunned lieder crowd, who can't grasp the web that slips over them. He touches his tongue to his hard palate, presses on the cylinder of air behind it until his tongue tips over his front teeth with a dwarf explosion, that fine-point puff of *tuh* that expands, pulling the vowel behind it, spreading like a slowed-film cloud, to *ta* to *tahee* to *time* to transcend the ear's entire horizon, until the line becomes all it describes:

Time stands still with gazing on her face,
Stand still and gaze for minutes, hours, and years to her give place.
All other things shall change, but she remains the same,
Till heavens changed have their course and time hath lost his name.

He sings that gaze, the one the heart tried to hang on to but couldn't. His eyes shine with the light of those who've freed themselves to do what they need. Those who see shine back, fixed at this moment, arrested, innocent. As he sings, Elizabeth's ships sail out to sudden new continents. As he sings, Freedom Riders one state away are rounded up and jailed. But in this hall, time stands still, afraid to do so much as breathe.

Jonah wins. Half a dozen years too young to walk away with a prize this size, my brother leaps into the inheritance he's always known was his. In the chaos afterward, the other singers hating him, the remembering audience still in the throes, wanting just to stand near him, he seems complete. He can't notice our sister well enough to feel the scope of her misery here, at this last public concert of his that she will ever attend. He and my father dance a little dance around the near past, their growing awkwardness. Da faults Jonah's German, calls him a Polack. Says he almost was one, in another life.

"I could have been a Polack?" my brother asks.

"You are a near Polack. A counterfactual Polack."

"A Polack in one of many alternate universes?"

My sister and I try to hush them. But my brother is past hushing, past even hearing the likes of us. For a moment, he has everything that singing can give him. When we're out of earshot, I beg him again to ditch me, to get an accompanist worthy of him. And again he refuses.

An old gentleman of the landed, tobaccoed countryside interrogates us. I smell hostility on his affronted breath. "What exactly *are* you boys?" And my brother sings to him, smart-mouthing, the prize in hand granting him liberty to ignore how the world sees him:

> "I am my mammy's ae bairn,
> Wi' unco folk I weary, Sir . . ."

The word he sings in mockery draws me back, down into that ending we passed through only moments before. We're onstage again, centered in that stillness he brings on simply by chanting about it. At the keyboard, I force my fingers to their marks, imitating the flourishes of a Renaissance lute. I concentrate, try not to listen, keeping off the reef he has arranged for me. But I stray close enough to that stilled spot to hear what prize my brother means to win. All music is just a means to him, toward that one end. In the timeless time it takes him to reach the cadence, the song starts to work. She rises up behind him, following, just as the gods promised. But in the thrill of his tune's victory, Jonah forgets the ban, and looks back. And in his joy-cracked face as he turns around, I see him watch as Mama disappears.

NOT EXACTLY ONE OF US

Nettie Ellen takes the news in silence, as she does everything that the white world has inflicted since the captivity. Not a hateful silence, just a dead one. 'Nother sorrow coming. 'Nother piece of flesh stripped away.

All the questions she climbed up into the attic to ask her daughter mean nothing now. She doesn't sharpen her silence for the kill. But it does the job, blunt, just as well. She sits motionless. And motionless, outside of time.

Her daughter, too late, repents this thing she never asked to feel. But love outlasts repentance, three falls out of five. Something scrabbles in Delia Daley, wanting the old, first absolution. *Mama, don't leave me. I'm still your girl.* She knows that also is a lie: a lie, most of all, about who's leaving whom.

Delia, too, keeps still. But in that standing stillness, she reaches out to cover her mother's arm. The arm feels nothing but added weight. Her mother looks out on this new trial she should never have had to look on. Here it is, the old master of the lash, the one they'd almost outlived, coming round and letting himself in the side entrance.

The woman, Nettie, looks up at the flesh of her flesh. She can't ask that the cup be taken away, now it's already spilled down the front of her best Sunday dress. Can't even ask why Delia's done what she's done. Her girl has already wrecked herself with explanations. When Nettie Ellen can talk again, all she says is, "You best go tell your father."

The doctor rises up righteous at the news. He paces and wheels, the danger there in the room with them, spitting distance from where his daughter struggles to tell him. "What kind of self-satisfying . . . What in the name of God Almighty do you think you're doing?"

"Daddy," she guns. "You're getting religion."

"Don't get smart with me, daughter. Or you'll live to regret how smart you are."

She crumples through the middle, her *Yes, sir* dying in darkness. Yesterday, she'd have had the man grinning like an imp at her impudence. Today, he's stone. Stone of her making.

He paces the book-lined study, thinking. She has seen him this way, with patients whose poverty of body and mind turns him from healer to killing messenger. "What ever possessed you to side with those who've done your own—"

"Daddy. I'm not siding with anybody."

He whirls about. "What exactly are you doing?"

She doesn't know. She'd hoped he might.

"You're a colored woman. Colored. I don't care how high-toned you are. I don't know what the world of that white music has been leading you to—"

"Daddy, you've always told me it's whiteness makes us black. Whiteness that makes us a problem."

The sole of my shoe is black. *The coal we burn too much of is* black.

"Don't you dare turn my words against me. And don't you dare pretend you aren't doing what you're doing. A public proclamation that none of the eligible, accomplished men of your own race——"

"This isn't about race."

He stops pacing and sinks into the red Moroccan chair. He fixes her in his eyes, as if she's a malingering patient. "Not . . . ? Tell that to the whites. And you'll have to, young lady. Every minute of your life. In ways you can't begin to imagine."

She tries to hold his gaze, but his unmasks her. She must look away or burn. Defeating hers, his eyes take on four hundred years of violence coming from all directions.

"Not about race? What *is* this about?"

She wants to say *love*. Two people, neither of them asking for this. Neither of them knowing what to do or how to make a home wide enough for the fear they now must live in.

He turns his face away from her, toward his books. He throws open the agenda on his desk and takes his pen, as if to sign a final severance. His hand hovers, then slams down on the blotter. He swings around to face her again. His voice drops, its menace multiplied by an awful, collaborator's confidence. "What *is* this about, then? You tell me, seeing as how you're the expert. What do you imagine you're trying to *prove*?"

Whatever she might prove, he has already refuted. Still, he stares at her, blameless confusion, begging her to restore him. *Have you no pride? All these years, have I taught you nothing?*

"A colored girl," she says, giving up on placement, projection, support, her sound collapsing. "A colored girl growing up, going to college, learning what she wants, taking what she needs, being anything she cares to be, changing the laws of this country." Her voice falls to nothing. But it does not break. "Who's going to stop her? What's wrong with that?"

His words come back, in her voice. He hears what it costs her, to risk this echo. A spine in this girl he never put there. He falls still, a captive audience. Up in the front row, watching his life in review, events strange but familiar, scripted yet open. Her voice hangs in the air. How much music that voice might make. How much work that music might do. His shoulders fall. The clamp of history slips loose. He doesn't stoop to forgiveness, any more than whiteness will ever forgive him for remembering. "Nothing," he says, and looks away. "Nothing's wrong with that."

The worst isn't over; nothing of this nightmare will ever be *over*. The weight will ever be on her, of proof and its opposites. But still, she'll live.

Her flesh will keep her. Blood will not disown. So much gratitude tries to escape her all at once that it comes out liquid, in her sobs. Her mouth moves in wordless, frozen thanks, and she breaks down under that burden, belonging.

He offers her a handkerchief but no shoulder. The threat is all around them, still. Only the immediate crisis has passed. When her crying fades, he asks, "What does this man do?"

She snorts. She can't help it. "Daddy, I wish I knew."

The rage flashes back. "Am I to understand the man is some kind of trash-picker? Or an Ivy League playboy who's never had to work an hour in his life?"

Her snickers die in childbirth. "No, Daddy. He's a professor at Columbia University. A scientist. He makes a living studying time." She fights to keep her face straight, free of those self-swallowing curves her David claims inhabit even the straightest lines. "He works on the General Theory of Relativity."

Her cultivated father registers the same kind of disbelief she felt on hearing this was one of the world's accredited professions. Doubt and awe, old half-blood brothers, mix in Dr. Daley's face. The secrets that obsess him are as subtle as the ones he would ignore. "I thought only half a dozen men in the world are able to understand that."

"Oh, probably." She fights to hide her hope. There will be a meeting. Her father, the autodidact, has a few questions to ask the authority. "However many there are, David's one of them."

"David?" Her father wrestles with the physics. The optics. For generations now, it's been their secret scale, the pull that led him to her mother. Light as you can, right on up to the invisible edge, but never over. *Over* is unthinkable betrayal, even though loyalty never asked questions along the graded way. His eyes consider: Suppose it were anyone else but him, laying down the law, preventing such a match. Anyone else declaring that the upper echelons of whiteness, its mental mysteries, were off-limits to his offspring. Then he'd die for her right to this foreign man, clearly unfit to hold his daughter's hand. "What does his family say?" Brittle, flinching from the answer, the eternal beating down.

"About what?" she bluffs. But she drops her eyes.

The man doesn't know where his family is. They've fled from Rhineland to Zeeland, buying, at most, months. He has written to Europe several times, getting no satisfactory reply. The news of David's choice of mate will reach his family, if at all, as news from another galaxy—freezing, airless, irrelevant.

"He's a Jew, Daddy."

The fact operates upon her father. "Does your mother know?"

Delia moans low. "A Jewish atheist foreigner."

"Covering all your bases, aren't you? Where in hell did you meet this man?"

This is what she'd like to remember. One moment, she was singing along to herself, passive oracle to the goddess Miss Anderson, and the next, she and the German had known each other for decades. No: There'd been a moment between those two, one of his geometrical figments she can't wrap her head around—finite but infinitely dividable.

Something happened to her, to her country, as the contralto sang it into being. The continuous carpet of crowd absorbed her, one pulsing, breath-holding creature made up of 75,000 single cells, fused by that voice. The man stood next to her the whole time, and she never saw him. Hadn't seen any separate spot of pigment in this mile-long swath until this one grazed her on the shoulder.

Are you a professional?

Delia thought he was speaking in German. The inflection, the unmistakable cadence of that language that had been her special torment these last three years.

Professionell . . . The first word she ever spoke to him.

Her pronunciation must have passed, for he responded, *Sängerin?*

She beamed. *Not yet.* Looking down, fumbling for the words: *Noch nicht.*

But you would like to be? In the future?

She caught up to his words. *How . . . Oh, help me. You could hear me? The whole time?*

He tried not to, then let himself smile. *Not . . . the whole time. I couldn't hear "O mio Fernando." Noch nicht, vorläufig.*

I was singing out loud?

He pushed out his chin: *Never let the world worry you. Sotto voce. I had to bend to hear.*

My God! All these people around!

Very few could hear.

Why on earth didn't you hush me up?

He shrugged, feeling the peace only music can give. *Miss Anderson . . . sounds like paradise. But she was far away, and you . . . were right here.*

He introduced himself. So great was her undying shame, she introduced herself in turn. No one in the dispersing crowd stopped to look twice at them. The thousands who swept past were still lost in the sound that had joined them. Discrete humanity had not yet sedimented back out of solution.

The press of people forced them to move. She waved good-bye to the most intimate conversation with a white she'd ever had. But this man, David Strom, fell in alongside her in the flow. She heard him say, *I have heard Miss Anderson sing already. In Vienna, some few years ago.*

You heard her? In her excitement, Delia forgot she'd just enjoyed that unforgettable pleasure herself. With a burst so easy that it still mystified her, they were talking voice. Was Flagstad as good a Sieglinde as the magazines claimed? Who was his favorite Norma, his choice for Manon? She sounded like the most shameless striver, but something even worse drove her. Her questions opened parentheses faster than he could close them. If one could only buy two new recordings this year, which should they be? How big a voice did a woman need in order to fill, say, La Scala? Had he ever heard the legendary Farrar?

The man chided her. *Farrar stopped singing in 1922. I am a little younger than you must see.*

She stopped to examine his face. He wasn't her father's age at all, but at most ten years older than she. He had on a gray suit, white shirt, and a narrow burgundy tie, poorly tied. He held his gray-blue felt hat, crushed down to a porkpie. Brown socks and shoes, poor soul. He might have thrown on the whole concoction in the dark. Not handsome, by any race's measure. His rounded forehead crested a little, in the planning stage of balding's evacuation, and the bridge of his nose rode up too high, as if broken.

His eyes, too wide, left him looking permanently baffled. She combed her own hair with two fingers and brushed a quick palm check across her cheeks. The muscles in her lips tensed, the way that always annoyed Mr. Lugati, her teacher. Inside those too-wide eyes, the man looked out, seeing her. *Her:* nothing larger. No sign but herself. She, at most ten years younger than he.

She let the man see. The need to flee had run off somewhere, giving up on her. She'd dropped her guard somewhere back in the crowd, ceased watching out for herself in this public place. Miss Anderson's fault. *Sotto voce,* the man had said. But clearly not sotto enough. Singing out loud, of all imaginable crimes. Still in his gaze, taking too long to get it out, she articulated, *Verzeihen Sie mir.*

Could there be whites who might not, after all, hate her on sight for the ungivable forgiveness they needed from her? Clearly this man knew nothing of her country, except what it felt like to be here. Here, on the Mall, this Easter, not for history, not to see what came from centuries of making heaven of the readiest hell. Just here to hear Miss Anderson, the voice he'd heard in Vienna, a voice one is lucky to hear once every hundred years.

He looked again, and she lost herself. What marker could his map hold for her? His gaze seemed free of anything but itself. She felt herself unbound in it. He saw her only here, in the rolling, open territory Miss Anderson had sung no more than an hour ago. *My country. Sweet land.*

The square mile of federal land around them thinned out. The nation of listeners slipped unwillingly back home, as they, too, would now have to. But the German had a hundred questions for her first. What was the best way to broaden the notes at the top of the range? Who were the best present-day American vocal composers? What exactly was this "Gospel Train," and did it stop anywhere nearby?

She asked if he were a musician. *Perhaps, in another lifetime.* She asked what he did in this one. He told her, and she broke out giggling. Absurd, making a living studying something so obvious, something one could do so precious little about.

They moved up the long reflecting pool in silent agreement, toward the monument, where the crowd still pressed in on that spot so recently graced. They chattered of Vienna and Philadelphia, as if they'd been sent their long, separate ways so each could scout out all the concerts the other couldn't get to. She made a note to remember this coda to a day she'd never be in danger of forgetting. Their talk didn't turn awkward until they reached the monument, their invented destination, the edge of their shared world.

She looked at the man again. She felt her look returned, emptied of history. *Thank you for talking music,* she said. *It's not often . . .*

It's less than not often, he agreed.

Wiedersehen, she said. *Lebewohl.*

Yes, he answered. *Good-bye.*

Then they saw the child. A lost boy, no older than eleven, keening, sprinting back and forth around the edge of the indifferent crowd, making the panicked forays of the lost. He ran to one side, calling out incoherent names and scouring the faces of those adults drifting past him. Then, terror rising, he ran back to search again in the opposite direction.

A colored boy. One of hers, she thought, and wondered if this German gentleman thought the same. But it was David Strom who called to the child. *Something is wrong?*

The child glanced up. At the white face, the clipped German sound, the boy bolted, looking back over his shoulder at his motionless pursuers. Just as instinctively, Delia called out, *That's all right, now. We ain't gonna hurt you.* She fell through some hole into her mother's family's Carolina past, on no stronger prompting than the curve of the boy's forehead. The boy might have been from South Chicago, Detroit, Harlem, Collingwood, Canada—the last terminal on the Underground Railroad. He might have been far better off than she. But that was how she called to him.

The boy stopped and looked at her, squinting. He stepped closer, a skittish, starving creature eyeing the food-baited trap. His suspicious fascination appraised the white man next to her. He looked at Delia. *You come from around here?*

His accent startled her; it came from no place she could identify. *Not far,* Delia answered, pointing vaguely. David Strom proved his intelligence by keeping silent. *How 'bout you?*

The boy's voice turned wild at the words. Delia thought she heard *California,* but between the unlikeness and the boy's sobs, she wasn't sure. *Everything's going to be all right. We're gonna help you find your people.*

The boy brightened. *My brother's lost,* he told her.

Delia sneaked a look at David Strom. She fought down her own cheek muscles. But on the scientist's face, no stray amusement. No trace of anything but problem solving. And in that moment, she decided: She might share nothing else with this man in the rest of invented existence, except for trust.

I know he is, honey, she said. *But we're gonna help you find him.*

It took some time to talk the boy down. But at last, his blanket panic began to lift. He was able to tell them, without too many contradictions, how disaster had struck. But the open lines of the place and the dispersing crowd mazed him. *We were over there!* he shouted. But when they drew close, joy broke down. *This not it.*

Delia kept him talking, damping his terror. She took his hand, and the boy, in the fickleness of childhood, took it as if he'd held it all his life. *What's your name?* she asked.

Ode.

Jody?

Ode.

Really! She tried not to sound too surprised.

It means I was born on the road.

Where does it come from?

He shrugged. *My uncle.*

They walked back along the reflecting pool. Distance played tricks on Ode, revising his geography every fifty paces as the landscape curved away from him. But every minute the three of them walked, his fear subsided by an hour. The white man fascinated him. Ode kept stealing glances at David Strom, and Delia added theft to theft. She watched the child struggle to fit the man. Each time the German spoke, the boy fell off, bewildered.

Where're you from? he demanded.

New York, Strom said.

Ode lit up. *New York? My mama's from New York. You know my mama?*

I haven't been there long, Strom apologized.

Delia hid in a coloratura coughing fit. Ode grinned, willing to be the butt of her delight. He looked up at the white man. *You don't have to take that from her, you know.* Something he'd heard some adult say once.

Strom smiled back shyly. *Oh, but I do!*

Without thinking, the boy took the man's hand in his free one. They walked along, two agitated adults flanking a frightened child.

Ode jabbered to them so nervously, Delia had to hush him to keep him on the search. She couldn't make out more than half the boy's panicked argot. They tacked back and forth across the Mall, a skiff becalmed.

I would like very much to see you again, David Strom said over Ode's head. His voice shook with a fear all its own. Through the child's arms, Delia felt the man tremble, making his own winter.

He didn't know. He couldn't. *Forgive me,* she said. Unforgivable: twice since meeting him. *It's impossible.*

They walked beneath the flanking trees that formed a colonnade of pillars in this roofless church along a nave too wide to span. Her *impossible* thickened in the air around them. Each step harder than the last. She couldn't tell him. She didn't care to prove the impossibility, either now or later.

Whatever the word meant to a physicist, the physicist did not say. David Strom pointed toward the boxlike monument. The crowd clinging to the spot of Miss Anderson's miracle had thinned. *That is where we need to go. Where we can see everyone, and they us. Underneath the statue of that man.*

Delia laughed again, the weight now suffocating her. Ode laughed along, at the foreigner. *You don't know who Lincoln is?* The boy twisted his head clear sideways. *Where you been all your life?*

Ah, Strom said, assembling all American history.

Lincoln was a nigger-hater, the boy told them.

Strom glanced at Delia Daley. *Ein Rassist?* Delia nodded and shook her head, all at once. The German looked up at the monument, confused. Why would any country want to immortalize . . . ?

That's right, a racist.

He was not! Delia scolded. *Who ever taught you that?*

Everybody knows it.

What are you talking about? He freed the slaves.

He never did!

Delia looked at the white man, who fought to understand. The hand-joined trio kept walking toward that monument, the nearest available one. They skirted the day's makeshift stage and stepped up to the mass of marble. That is when they must have fallen through the side of time, some trick of physics the scientist set in motion, one of those laboratory black arts a conservatory student could never hope to know. Time dilated and took them with it. They climbed up as close to the enormous seated statue as the remaining crowd permitted. They built a scouting outpost on the white stone steps, fixing the boy up high, where he could look out, conspicuous, on the whole visible world.

There they fell into the gravity of that "impossible," a force not even time could escape. Delia didn't feel her clock alter. They talked—minutes, hours, years—though no longer about music. They talked around the impossible, in improvised code, to keep the boy from understanding. But the boy understood, better than they. The boy and the man sat on the marble steps, discussing the planets, the stars, laws of the expanding universe. The sight of the two hunched forms undid her. And when the lost boy jumped up and called out, the sound of his voice restarting time, whole lifetimes had rolled away.

The boy saw his brother before his brother saw him. Then Ode was running, this day's message, undeniable. Delia and David called to the boy, but he was safe now, beyond them. They drifted to the edge of the monument, craning to see the child reclaim his own and losing the reunion in the crowd. They stood on the white steps, abandoned, without thanks or reassurance that all would be well.

The two of them, then, alone. She couldn't look at him. She couldn't bear to see if his face confirmed that fluid future they'd just come through. Already the place closed to her, and she had no heart to find it again. She felt him studying her, and she looked away.

It's getting late, Delia said. *I've got to get back, or I'm going to catch a licking.*

That is not good?

No. Not good in the least. She shot a look at her watch. *Oh my God. It's not possible!*

She shook her watch, held it to her ear to hear the movement that escaped her. They hadn't been with the child for more than fifteen minutes, from finding to reunion. She'd thought it hours. Felt them in her body. Just on the steps of the memorial alone, they'd been far longer.

Yes, he said from a great distance. *It does that, sometimes.*

How? She looked up at him, despite herself. Yes: He'd been there, too. The trace of that long passage. She saw it in him, still. Independent proof.

He turned up his palms. *We physicists talk about time dilation. Curving. Dirac even suggests two different scales for time. But this one*—he bowed his head, the fragile freight—*is more a question for the psychologists.*

My God. I can't believe it.

He laughed a little, but just as baffled. *Since it is earlier than you thought? Maybe we could find a coffee shop to sit?*

I'm sorry. That is the first of the impossibles.

They walked down the last few steps, each harder than the last, driven together out of the vanished place.

Forgive me, she said a third and final time. *I have to get home.*

Where is home? Your nest?

At this word, its reference to where they'd been, she went hot again. *Home is where I have to go back to.*

Home is where she has to bring him now, if she is to survive.

That they've made it even this far is its own miracle. She can't explain to her father what she can't explain to herself. Where in damnation did she meet this man? Where indeed.

"I met him at . . . a voice recital, Daddy."

"And how did you manage to miss the obvious?"

She plays dumb. "We love all the same things." This, too, a lie made of literal truth.

"Oh? Whose things are these?"

"Music, Daddy. Nobody owns it."

"No? And are you going to eat music when you're hungry?"

"He's a professor at one of the best—"

"Music's going to protect you when they start throwing stones? You are going to sing when the world strings you up?"

She bows her head. The world's hatred is nothing. But this man's slightest scorn will kill her.

Her father rests his weight against the arms of the red leather chair. His right hand explores the first patch of pattern baldness on his close-sheered crown. He sinks back in the chair. She knows this expansiveness, his last stage of resistance when there's nothing to do against bitterness but name it. He regards her, a dullness worse than any anger he might show.

She hurts him, irreversibly, a hurt more damaging than hate. Defeat plays in the folds of his faraway eyes. She hurts him worse than the famed Philadelphia conservatory once hurt her. Worst of all, she's used his own words against him, coming into her own.

William Daley holds his hand in front of his face and twirls it: front, back. Front, back. He forms a loop of fingers, almost praying. "You think your physicist music lover is going to be comfortable walking into a Negro home?"

Her physicist music lover has never been comfortable anywhere inside the earth's gravitational field. "He doesn't see race, Daddy."

"Then he needs an optometrist. I'm a family doctor. I don't do eyes." He rises and leaves the room. The first time he's ever walked out on her.

She sets up the dinner for three weeks on. Three weeks: long enough for all involved to catch up with the present. On the evening of the meeting, her parents move about the house stricken and stiff. They're both dressed hours before David Strom's scheduled arrival.

"He . . . he doesn't take much care in his clothes," Delia tries to tell them. But it makes no difference. Over her Sunday finest, Nettie Ellen lashes two aprons, front and back. She heads into the kitchen, where all day she has perfected food from the Alexander ancestral recipe trove: pig and greens and pungent dark sauces from old Carolina days.

Brother Michael crinkles his nose. "What are you *making*? This supposed to be *Jewish* food?"

In truth, it's such a meal as William Daley rarely lets on his table. But today, the Philadelphia doctor is right there in the kitchen, spicing and steeping alongside his helpmeet. And for once, the woman doesn't shoo the man away.

Charles checks the saucepots. "Man's getting both barrels, huh?"

His mother swats at him and misses. Charles puts his arm around his sister's shoulders, half comfort, half torture. "You don't mind if I play a little banjo before we eat?"

"Yeah," Michael cheers. "We need the Charcoal show!"

Delia swats and hits. "We need the Charcoal show like we need the plague. And you call him Charcoal while Mr. Strom is here, I'll tie you up and put you in the cedar chest."

"How come he can't call me Charcoal? That's my name, lady."

Nettie Ellen points the wooden spoon at her eldest son. "Your name's what's printed on your birth certificate!"

"Tell him, Mama." Delia swipes again at Michael, who stands just out of arm's reach, mouthing, Char-*coal,* Char-*coal.* She steps toward him, threatening.

Michael tears away. "*Achtung, Achtung.* The Germans are coming!"

Lucille and Lorene follow Delia around from room to room. "Is he tall? What's his hair like? He speak English?"

"Do you?" she shouts. She shoos them away, then clamps her temples to keep her head from spilling open.

She picks Strom up at the station. They can't linger; Nettie Ellen wants them to come right home or call if there's trouble. There will be trouble from now until death. The first taxi driver flips them the finger. The second drives off without a word. The third, a Negro, loses no chance to roll his eyes at Delia in the rearview mirror. David doesn't notice. As it has every other hour for the last four months, Delia's nerve fails her.

She tries to warn him in the cab about what's waiting at home. She starts several times. Each attempt sounds more disloyal than the last. "My family . . . they're a bit unusual."

"Don't worry," he assures. "Life is unusual." He squeezes her hand, down below the seat, where the cabbie can't see. He whistles a tune for her ears only, one he knows she'll recognize without asking. Purcell's *Dido and Aeneas*: "Fear no danger to ensue; the hero loves as well as you." The tune cheers her and she smiles, until she remembers how that story ends.

When they get to Catherine Street, her family has turned into saints. Her father greets the guest a little verbosely but ushers him into the foyer. Her brothers stick their hands out to shake, bobbing awkwardly, but without minstrelsy or goose-stepping. Only the twins seem remote. They glare at their sister, betrayed. They pictured some other white man, Tarzan maybe, that Flash Gordon, or even Dick Tracy. Anything but this grinning, four-eyed Dagwood Bumstead with the bumper already sprouting around his middle.

Nettie Ellen flashes about like heat lightning, getting the man's coat, seating him on the good front room sofa, charming the feet from out beneath him. "So this is the man we been hearing so much about. Finally get to meet you, sir! Ain't that a dandy tie you got on! How you liking it here? It's a *big* country, don't you think? Now, I'd like nothing better than to sit and chat, but we got a beautiful roast waiting in the oven just two rooms beyond, and if I don't go keep my eye on it, we'll all be eating cinders tonight!"

Nettie Ellen laughs, and David Strom laughs a dotted eighth note after her. Something in that delay and in the game look he flashes Delia tips her off: He can't understand a word her mother says.

Fortunately, her father overcompensates. Where Nettie Ellen's speech steals richly back home, William's crisps. He makes a magnanimous show of sitting his daughter down on the sofa next to David. Then he takes the armchair facing them.

"So tell me, Professor Strom. How do you find life in the Apple?"

Now the visitor understands every word. But putting them together produces only a bizarre image of decomposing fruit. Delia fumbles for a shame-free way to play interpreter. But her father follows up before she can.

"My daughter tells me you're close to Sugar? These are hungry times for the Children of Ham."

David Strom determines the general dietary topic, but beyond that, *nicht*. He shoots Delia a look of happy befuddlement. But she's lost in her own surprise at her father breaking the ancient law. Every dinner conversation her family sits down to brushes against the topic, but no outsider must ever be allowed to hear. Now here he is, leading with the private theme. Delia sits mute, waiting for the smoke to lift, by which point rescuing her guest will be impossible.

"Desperate in all neighborhoods, I understand. But our kind have again been chosen to bear the brunt. One out of every two of our own on relief. Now don't misunderstand me." There isn't, Delia knows, a chance in hell of that. "I'm not a Communist. I'm closer to Mr. Randolph on these issues. But when half of one's people can't put food on the table, one begins to heed the rioters, wouldn't you say? Where exactly are you living, Mr. Strom?"

David brightens. "New York City. I like it there, very much."

William shoots a look at his daughter. Delia considers excusing herself to go take her own life. Her father surveys the extent of the wreck. It's easier to abandon ship and start fresh on another vessel. "What do your people back home make of this so-called nonaggression pact?"

"I don't . . . I'm not sure what you . . ."

"The one between Mr. Hitler and Mr. Stalin."

Strom's face darkens, and he and Dr. Daley are both, briefly, on the same band. After race and politics, Delia decides, they'll move on to the third great arena: sports. She gives the two least athletic men she knows a total of five minutes to get onto the last Olympics, in Berlin. They reach it in three. Each for his own reasons is ready to kiss the ground Jesse Owens flies over. She begins to hope, against all reason, that the two men might make enough common ground between them for her to live in.

Her mother calls her from the kitchen. Delia hears at once the premeditated plot in it. "Taste this glaze," Nettie Ellen tells her. "I just don't know what it's missing!"

After a breadline of rejected suggestions, mother allows daughter to convince her that the glaze is missing nothing at all. Nettie then lets Delia return to the front room, to whatever carnage of cross-examination that remains. But if the men have been probing delicacies that required her absence, it doesn't show. Her father is asking the man she, well, call it *loves*, "Have you ever read *Ulysses*, by James Joyce?"

The scientist answers, "I think that writer was Homerus?"

Delia wheels and heads back into the kitchen. The sooner food is on the table, the faster the torture will end. On the way back to her mother's kingdom, the thought occurs to her. Those monuments of white culture that her father assaults are not pilgrim stations, but pill-boxes, strategic emplacements in a prolonged battle against an invading foreign power that doesn't have the first notion of what's being contested.

She rounds the corner of the kitchen into fresh disasters. Her mother stands by the stove, crying. Charles waves Delia over to inspect the damage. As Delia draws near, her brother turns on her. "How come *you* didn't think about this before?"

"Think of what?"

Nettie Ellen raps the wooden spoon against the rim of the cook pot. "Nobody told me. Nobody told me not to."

"Now, Mama," Charles rides her. "You know the Jewish people don't eat pork. That's all over the Bible."

"Not *my* Bible." Whatever provocations she has stirred into this recipe, this one wasn't planned.

"You should have told her," Charles scolds his sister. "How come you didn't tell her?"

Delia stands crumbling. She knows nothing of this man she's dragged here. He doesn't eat pork: Can that be? That weekly sustenance, a poison to him. What others? The man she brings home is all alleys and cellars, strange smells and closeted, robed rituals barred to her, rites that will keep her always on the far side of knowing, skullcaps and curls, silver engravings hung up in door frames, backward-flowing letters, five thousand years of formulas passed from father to son, codes and cabalas whose chief historical goal is to scare and exclude her. How much can she change her life? How much does she want to? The bird and the fish can fall in love, but they share no word remotely like *nest*.

Then she hears his voice from the other room: *David*. Her David. We are not born familiar. At best, familiar waits for us down the run of years. Familiar is what he can become to her only through life. But familiar to herself, already, looking on him.

There will be strangeness. They'll hit places far more alien, gaps they cannot close. But this, at least, is not a fatal one. She rubs her mother's back, between those thin-winged shoulder blades. "It's all right, Mama." Covert, and open, deliberate and secret sabotage: all of it, all right. The meat sauce will test the man harder than the meat source. Yet the meal is still a gift, steeped in all the flavors of indigestible difference. "It's all right," she repeats, soothing, petting. "A lot of people in his line of work? They'll put anything in their mouths."

This much will always translate: This much, they'll each always recognize. She and the man both—nations inside nations. They may share nothing else but this, and music. But already, it's enough. Already they've tried on the idea together. And that act of pretending becomes a fact all its own, too late to retract: a nation inside a nation inside a nation.

David is a wonder at dinner. Too quickly, he learns enough of the local dialect to follow each Daley, or at least seem to. Already he can tell her father's send-ups from his oracular insights. He holds Charles captive with the tale of his flight from Vienna. He fascinates the twins, who scowl happily at how he works his knife and fork, keeping hold on both pieces, sawing and scooping at the same time, never letting go. He eats with enough zeal to overcome her mother's first wave of wariness.

"This is amazing," David says, pointing to the pork with his knife. "I've never tasted anything like it!"

Delia almost spits her mouthful across the table. She gags, hands in the air. David is first on his feet to whap her on the back and save her. The simple act of contact, even in emergency, stuns everyone. He *touched* her. But David Strom is first, too, back to the sacrament of food, as if no one at this table has almost choked to death.

Delia lasts out the meal. From afar, she makes out the music of her family's speech, a thing she's never heard, from inside it. Tonight, the words of that seven-member celebration are subdued, stopped down, toned up. She hears them in their hiding, all the sheltering clan construction in a place that would prefer you dead. Her blackness sits on her like a tight slip, something she's never noticed, so wrapped in it is she. What can she look like to this man?

And still the meal goes better than she could hope. Ease would be too much to ask. But at least there's no bloodshed. Everyone's best efforts wreck Delia to look on. She would never be able to survive these two split worlds colliding were it not for the memory of the lost boy, their Ode. Without the mercy of those words traded on the monument's steps, that glimpse of long time, this meal together would kill her.

After dinner, David entertains Michael with coin tricks. He shows the boy how to hang a spoon from his nose. He improvises a Cartesian diver, a spectacle that enthralls even Charles and the twins.

Nettie Ellen does her best: all that her religion asks of her. "You are a musician, too, Mr. Strom?"

"Oh, no! Not a real one. Just a—hmm?—a love-haver."

"An amateur," Delia says. "And he's a good piece more than that."

The amateur objects. "I can't match your daughter. She is the real one."

Nettie shakes her head, a puzzlement as deep as the one she was born into. "Well, we don't have that piano sitting over there for nothing. You two sit down and make some music for us while me and the girls do the washing up."

Delia objects. "We'll wash the dishes, Mama. You made the meal, you give yourself a rest."

"Nonsense. Let everybody serve God in their own fashion."

She'll not hear otherwise. So the two music makers sit, each, in their fashion, love-havers. They split the bench between them, careful not to touch each other. They play from Nettie's hymnal: "He Leadeth Me," the antique psalm, thunked out four-hand, SATB, straight from the page until David gets hold of the idiom. Little by little, warming to the old inheritance, Delia edges him down to the lower confines of the keyboard, absorbing first the tenor, then the bass, then all sorts of lines Strom didn't realize were hiding in there. She lets loose, heading upward, stoking and embellishing, working into a swell that she knows, even as she strays into full-out gospel, is its own test: *Are you sure?* She probes to see just how he sees her, and yes, she checks to see if he can carry the chords for her while she spreads and flies.

Her father wanders through the room, pretending to be looking for things. At one point, Delia swears she hears him humming along. Maybe it could work after all, this act of total madness. Maybe they could make an America more American than the one the country has for centuries lied to itself about being.

Her mother comes into the parlor from the kitchen, dish towel in her hands, two aprons again flanking her Sunday-best dress. "Now that sounds just beautiful." Delia hears, *I know that sound. Now that is still my daughter.*

When they lead "He Leadeth Me" into all the pastures it will willingly go, they negotiate a final cadence and turn to inspect each other. David Strom beams like a lighthouse, and she knows he would ask her, right then and there, to share all time with him, were it not for the warning her face beams back.

"Do you have this one?" he asks. And sparsely but musically, he lays down the outlines of a song she learned her freshman year, a tune simple enough to be among the hardest things she's ever tried. His fingers clip through the chords, realizing only the simplest figured bass.

"You know this, too?" she asks. Then ashamed to hear herself. What membership is strong enough to keep them from *having* this same tune? All ownership is theft, and melody above all.

He stumbles through to the end of the first phrase. Without signal, they're back at the beginning. She lands from above, square upon the first note, knowing he's there underneath her. She sings with no chest at all. His fingers on the keys grow accurate, in her light. She imitates those pure resonators, a perfect tube of brass or wood. Her vibrato narrows to a point, thin enough to thread the eye of heaven. She floats in an aerial piano, motionless above the moving line:

> *Bist du bei mir, geh' ich mit Freuden*
> *zum Sterben und zu meiner Ruh'.*
> *Ach, wie vergnügt wär' so mein Ende,*
> *es drückten deine lieben Hände*
> *mir die getreuen Augen zu!*

If you are with me, I'll go gladly to my death and to my rest. Together, they come back to tonic, dropping into held silence, the last element of any score. But before the quiet dies a natural death, a third voice punctures it. Brother Charlie sits on the arm of the sofa, his own makeshift balcony, shaking his head in admiration.

"Ain't that the same song the whites used to sing, right after spending the day whipping us?"

"Hush up," Delia says, "or I'm gonna whip *you*."

"How far you planning to drift, sister Dee?"

"I'm not drifting, brother. I'm rowing, hard as I know how."

Charlie nods. "When you get to the far shore, you think they're going to fish you out?"

"Nobody needs to fish me out. I'm going to hit land and keep on moving."

"Till you get to safety?"

"Not safety we're talking about, Char."

"Uh-uh. Mind your mama, now. Don't call me Char."

"Is this serious?" David says, two steps behind, by every measurable measure. "People used to sing this song while . . . Can this be so? This song was written . . ."

"Don't pay the man any attention." First time she's ever called her brother a man.

Her father returns, saving them all from themselves. "Dr. Strom?" Dr. Daley says. "Would you mind answering an amateur's questions? I almost hate asking . . ." Delia spins from one threat to the other. Her father hates asking like the rabbit hates the brier patch. "But I can't wrap my thinking around this one little thing."

Delia braces. Now it will come: the mighty blow of Things as They Are, blasting the dream she and this stranger have been hiding in. Not even love can survive the facts. She holds still and waits. How foolish to think the angel might pass over them, to imagine they could escape this, her father's one little question. The question is out there, running through the streets of the Seventh Ward, over in Harlem, across the Black Belt that rings South Chicago. The question the workless half of her race, annihilated at every turn, wants to ask. The question no person of David's race can answer or even hear. She hangs her head and mouths the words, knowing them already—the one little thing her father can't wrap his thinking around.

"Suppose I'm flying past you near the speed of light . . ."

Delia's head jerks upright. Her father has gone mad. Both of them: madder than anything in this country's whole toxic drugstore could make them. David Strom leans forward, for the first time this evening, in his element. "Yes." He grins. "Go on. I follow."

"Then according to relative motion, *you* are flying past *me* at the same speed."

"Yes," Strom says with all the delight he just gave their playing. Here at last is something he can talk about. "Yes, this is exactly correct!"

"But that's what I can't understand. If both of us are moving, then we both think the other's time slows down, relative to ours."

"This is good!" David's glee is spontaneous. "You have made a study of this matter!"

William Daley's teeth clench. His eyes test the other's for condescension, a level gaze that would expose all patronage. But here is only pleasure, mind pushing through loneliness to a surprise meeting.

"Your time is slower than mine. Mine is slower than yours. It makes a joke out of reason."

"Yes." The man actually giggles. "That, too, is true! But only because our reason was created at very slow speeds."

"It smacks of utter nonsense." Dr. Daley stops short of saying *useless parasitism* or *Jewish plot*. But his outrage is more than public. "Which one of us is right? Which one of us really ages faster?"

"Ah!" David nods. "I understand. This is now a different question."

Delia listens to the closest thing she'll ever hear to a teatime chat in the monkey house. The light-speed slowing of time is easier to believe than these two men. The room goes liquid. She must key on either the speech or the speakers, though both are hopeless. Her father has indeed made a thorough study, but the man she drags home will never know why. And yet David, too, is locked in a contest she can't understand. His work feels stranger to her, in this moment, than the most closed tribal ritual. It smells of unguents and incense. It sits like a prayer shawl pulled around the man's shoulders.

She studies the white one, then the black. Their animated battle is too much for her. Her father's disbelief knows no bounds. "The laws of physics are the same," the foreigner insists, "in any uniformly moving system." Her father sits still, forgoing reason, trying to embrace the impossible.

They strike a truce of mutual awe, a truce that alarms Delia more than open warfare. Forgotten by them both, she retreats to the remaining domain of common sense. Maybe she's lost her citizenship there, as well. Maybe her mother will bar her entry.

But Nettie Ellen is standing in front of the stove, as she was before dinner, when Charlie drove her to tears. Now her face is dry. She holds a towel, although the dishes are done. She looks down into a space in front of her, one that Delia, too, can see. She seems not to hear her daughter enter. When she speaks, it's to the pit in front of her. "You two seem strong together. Like nobody can hurt you. Like you already lived through a bunch more days than you have."

Her mother has stumbled onto her incredible truth. The man's alien notions, his curved space and slow-running time, that Easter afternoon on the Mall have somehow given them time enough to find each other. The bird can love the fish for no other reason than their shared bewilderment, turning in the blue.

"That's the crazy thing, Mama. That's what I can't figure out. More days than we . . ."

"That's good," Nettie says, wheeling around to face the sink. "You're gonna need all the preparation time you can get."

If she means it as a reprimand, it still can't match the pain Delia has already sown. She wants to hug her mother for this blessing, however backhanded. But the blessing has damaged them both enough already.

Her mother looks up, fixing Delia's eye. From ten years away and another city, the daughter is saying, *She's so small. Thin as a bar of soap at the end of the wash week.* "You know what the Bible says." Nettie Ellen works her mouth to citation. "You know . . ." But nothing more comes from her moving lips than a whole "cleave" and half an "unto."

Not for the last time, they trade things too hard for speaking. Delia takes the idle dish towel from her mother's hands and returns it to the rack. She turns her mother's shoulders, and together they head out front to reclaim the male strangeness assigned to them. They don't link arms as they might have, once. But still, they walk together. Delia makes no effort to prepare her mother, for that would insult them all. All must watch the others fly past, each to his own clock.

They find the men turning from contest to outright pact. William and David hunch toward each other, hands on knees, like they're pitching pennies out in the alley. They've formed an alliance in the face of the universe's fundamental law. Neither looks up as the women enter. The doctor of medicine still scowls, but a scowl wrestling with the angel of insight. "So you're saying that my now happens before your now?"

"I am saying that the whole idea of 'now' cannot travel from my frame of reference to yours. We cannot talk of 'instantaneous.' "

Nettie shoots her girl a frightened look: Is the man speaking English? Delia just shrugs: the vast futility of the male race. She settles down into that time-crafted dismissal, one that rejoins her to her head-shaking mother while all the while drawing her closer to her betrothed-to-be.

"In case you gentlemen have failed to notice, it's getting late." Nettie Ellen shakes her finger at the window, the undeniable outside. Telling time by darkness: nothing to it.

"This is what you call our legendary hospitality." William winks at David.

Strom scrambles to his feet. "I must go!"

Nettie Ellen throws up her hands. "Now that's just the opposite of what I'm telling you. I'm saying, You sure you want to be jumping on a train at this hour?"

Delia watches her mother struggle mightily to be spontaneous. The offer she'd make without thinking, in any world but this, crawls up in her throat and sticks. Nor is Delia wholly ready for her mother to extend it. To lodge the man under the same roof as her parents . . . She stands at attention, wincing. Her foreigner, too, waits politely, trying to brake from the speed of thought, to slow the moment enough to see what's happening. The three hosts stand nodding at their guest, each waiting for the other to say, *There's a spare bed in the downstairs room.*

They stand forever. Then forever stops. Michael and Charles burst into the room, too excited to speak. The little one gets the words out first. "The Germans have invaded Poland. Tanks, planes—"

"It's true," Charles says. "It's all over the radio."

All eyes turn to the German in their midst. But his search out the woman who has brought him here. Delia sees it, faster than the light from his face can reach her: a fear that leaves him her dependent. Everything this man's culture touches, it sets alight. His science and music struggle to take in this war they've let happen while away in their playful, free flights. And in a single blitzkrieg, all that the man has ever cared for burns.

She sees, in that flash, what this news means. And she never stops to question. His family is dead, his country unreachable. He has no people, no place, no home now but her. No other nation but their sovereign state of two.

MY BROTHER AS OTELLO

Carolina asks, "What exactly *are* you boys?" And our answer drops on us, overnight: America's Next Voice. Not current; just next. Not fame, exactly, but never again the freedom of obscurity.

We don't get out of Durham without a deck of business cards, people who want us to call them. Ruth says, "So look at my brothers. Does this mean the two of you are big-time?" Jonah ignores the question. But her words are the most professional pressure I'll ever feel.

Jonah's in the catbird seat: People in big cities all across the country ask him to come sing, sometimes even offering to pay enough to cover expenses. All at once, he has a future to decide. But first, he must find a new teacher. He's thumbed his nose at Juilliard, pulled off his parting snub by winning a nationwide competition against countless older and more experienced singers, all without any vocal coach. But even Jonah isn't crazy enough to imagine he can move much further on his own. In his line, people keep studying until they die. And maybe even night school, after that.

His new prize credential gives him a shot at working with the town's better tenors. He toys with the idea of Tucker, Baum, Peerce. But he rejects them all. As far as he's concerned, his greatest asset is his tone, that pointed silver arrow. He's afraid the famous males will turn him grotesque, wreck his growing sound. He wants to stay clear, fast, light. He wants to try the recital route, honing his chops in various halls, returning to his deferred dream of opera when he figures out how to fatten up while keeping the purity intact.

He picks a woman teacher. He picks her for all sorts of reasons, not least her aggressive strawberry hair. Her face is a boat's prow, cutting through rough seas. Her skin is a curtain of light.

"Why not, Joey? I need a teacher who can give me what I don't have yet."

The thing he needs, the thing Lisette Soer can give him, is dramatic instruction. A lyric soprano sought after in San Francisco, Chicago, and New York, she's not yet in permanent orbit. But the rockets are firing. She's just a few years younger than Mama was when she died. Just a dozen years older than Jonah.

If her voice can't match the leading divas, she has begun to land those roles whose sexiness is usually confined to insistent program notes. She's more an actress who can sing than a singer trying to act. She walks across a room like a statue turning flesh. Jonah comes back from his first lesson, raising his fists underhand to his eyes, growling with bliss. He finds, in his new redheaded trainer, the intensity he's after. Someone who can teach him all he needs to know about the stage.

Miss Soer approves her new student's general plan. "Experience is all," she tells him. "Go out and play every stage you can. East Lansing. Carbondale. Saskatoon, Saskatchewan. All the places where culture is auctioned piecemeal on the spot market. Let them see you naked. Learn your grief and fear in situ, and what you don't get under your belt on the road, your teacher will feed you upon your return."

She tells him straight out: "Leave home." He passes the command on to me, as if he's invented it. You can't expect to sing yourself forward while still rooming with your family. Can't get to the future while living in the past. The arrow of growth points one merciless way.

She'd do away with me, too, I'm sure. But Lisette stops short of planting that idea in Jonah. Together, they decide I'm to leave with him, find a place where we can grow into our promise. Ruth sits in the kitchen, pulling her pigtails. "It's stupid, Joey. Move downtown when you can live here free?" Da just nods, like we've deported him, and he's seen it coming all along. "Is it because I bring my friends home sometimes?" Ruth asks. "Are you trying to get away from me?"

"How about our studio?" I ask Jonah. But it's way too small to live in. "How about a larger unit in that building?"

"Bad location," he says. "Everything's happening in the Village." And that's where we find our new quarters. The Village is pure theater, the greatest practice in what Madame Soer, in her favorite refrain, calls "living at maximum need."

Maximum need is Lisette's most teachable skill. She keeps it deep in her body. Her voice is a beam that cuts through the thickest orchestral fog. But voice alone can't account for her success. The dancer's body doesn't hurt. She oozes anticipation, even in trouser roles, her blazing hair balled up under a powdered peruke, charged, prehensile, ambiguous. Her most casual stroll across the set is satin hypnosis. Even her fidgets are a leopard's. This is what she means to give my brother: a tension to gird up his muscle-free tone.

At Jonah's third lesson, she walks out on him. He's left perched over the black music stand, trying to guess his sin. He waits for twenty minutes, but she never returns. He comes back to our new one-bedroom down on Bleecker in a cloud of wronged innocence. All weekend long, it's my job to tell him, "It's just a misunderstanding. Maybe she's ill." Jonah lies in bed, tensing his abdomen. He's deeper inside the shock of his body than I've ever seen him.

Lisette floats into the next lesson, beatific. She crosses the room and kisses him on the forehead, in neither forgiveness nor apology. Just life in its inexplicable fullness, and "Can we take the Gounod from your second entrance, please?" He lies in bed that night in another riot of feeling, working his muscles in long-unexercised directions.

Singing, Soer tells him, is no more than pulling the right strings at the right time. But *acting*—that's participating in the single, continuous, million-year catastrophe of the human race. Say, for argument, that the gods have conspired against you. There you are, alone, front and center, on the bare stage, in front of five hundred concertgoers who dare you to prove something to them. Hitting the notes is nothing. Holding a high, clear C for four measures can only go so far toward changing anyone's weltanschauung. "Go where the grief is real," she tells him. Her right hand claws at her collarbone in remembered horror. *Is there a place yet, in your young life, where you've known it?*

He knows the place already, its permanent address. Better than she can know. He has spent years trying to escape every memory of it. But now, under Lisette, he learns to revisit it at will, to turn the fire against itself and fashion it into its only answer. Under the woman's fingers, his voice lays itself open. She readies him for the Naumburg, for Paris, for whatever awards he might care to shoot for.

She introduces us to the agent Milton Weisman, an old-school impresario who signed his first talent before the First World War and who still works on, if only as the least offensive alternative to death. He demands to see us in his cluttered warren on Thirty-fourth. The eight-by-ten glossies Lisette takes of Jonah are not good enough; he wants to see us in the flesh. I've lived my whole life under the illusion that music is about sound. But Milton Weisman knows better. He needs a face-to-face before he can begin to book us.

Mr. Weisman is wearing a double-breasted pinstripe suit with shoulder pads, almost Prohibition era. He ushers us into the office, asking, "You boys want a root beer? Ginger ale?" Jonah and I wear black lightweight jackets and narrow ties that would seem conservative to anyone our age, but which, to Mr. Weisman, brand us as beatniks or worse. Lisette Soer wears some diaphanous Diaghilev fantasy of Mogul India. One of her lovers, we think, is Herbert Gember, the hot costume designer at City Center, though the affair may be a mere convenience match. She's one of those opera personalities who must dress down when they're onstage.

We chat with Mr. Weisman about his client lists from the golden age. He's worked with half a dozen front-rank tenors. Jonah wants to know about these men: what they ate, how much they slept, whether they talked at all the morning before a concert. He looks for a secret formula, that little extra leverage. Mr. Weisman can vamp on the topic for as long as he has listeners. All I want to know is whether these famous men were kind, whether they cared for their families, whether they seemed happy. The words never come up.

While talking, Milton Weisman roams his decrepit office, fiddling with the blinds, edging around us from all angles. He rarely looks us in the face, but even his sidelong glances find their mark. The old booking agent gauges how we'll look under the footlights, drawing up his map's out-of-bounds lines: Chicago, *sure*. Louisville, *perhaps*. Memphis, *no chance*.

After half an hour, he shakes our hands and says he can find us work. This puzzles me; we already have offers coming in. But Lisette is ecstatic. All the way back downtown, she keeps pinching Jonah's cheek. "You know what this means? That man is a force. People listen to him." She stops short of saying, *He'll make your career.*

They send us on recital barnstorming tours. "Lieder," Lisette insists, "is harder than opera. You must turn emotions loose upon your audience, with no props but sound. All your gestures take on handcuffs. As the words fill your throat, you must feel your body moving, even though it can't. You must model the invisible movement, so your audience will see it."

This is the incantation she sends us out with, and it works. Audiences in our off-circuit towns respond more like sports fans than the usual stiff-necked classical crowds. They come backstage. They want to know us, to tell us the tragedies that have wrecked their lives. The attention works on Jonah. I have to watch him more closely now as we play. Even in pieces we've drilled down into our marrow, he's likely to lace passages with a surprise slight caesura or rubato, nothing the careful ear would register, unless I fail to be there with him.

Mr. Weisman has a knack for getting us in and out of towns without incident. Sometimes, in bigger places, he finds local cultural lights who actually compete to have us under their roofs. In smaller towns, we get good at picking hotels that won't hassle well-groomed young men with collegiate accents. Jonah handles the check-ins, and I wait offstage. When we sense a problem, we beat a quick retreat, someplace a little farther from the concert halls where we do our Schumann *Dichterliebe* to ovations.

We're playing Tucson, Arizona—a pink adobe hall whose balcony might as well be cathouse rooms above a saloon—the night we hear about James Meredith trying to enter Ole Miss. The army rolls in again, that part of the army not already engaged in propping up the earth's collapsing dictators. Twenty-three thousand troops, hundreds of people injured, and two people killed, all to get one man enrolled in college.

We're in the dressing room—cinder blocks actually painted green—when Jonah hands me a sheet of music and says, "Scratch the Ives. Here's our encore." Never doubting there'll be an encore. Never doubting I can play the substitute from sight. In fact, compared to the tricky, polytonal Ives—a piece that satisfies Jonah's hunger for the avant-garde while giving the audience a nostalgic scrap of "Turkey in the Straw"—this new piece is trivial.

"You're kidding," I say.

"What? You don't know the tune?"

I know the tune, of course. I've even seen this arrangement: the great Harry Burleigh setting of "Oh Wasn't Dat a Wide Ribber?" Jonah must have been carrying it around in his valise for just such an emergency. The setting is straightforward, and very pianistic. It stays close to the familiar melody, but it's laced through with inspired passing tones that trick the song into a different country. One look, and I could play the thing without looking.

"I know the damn tune, Jonah. I just don't know what the hell you plan to do with it."

"I'll tell you what I'm thinking. Right now." He takes the sheet back and peppers it with markings.

"We're not going out there and doing this thing cold."

"It's Tucson, Arizona, brother. Wyatt Earp. The O.K. Corral." He pronounces the word *chorale*. He goes on marking the score. "The Wild West. We can't be caught actually *practicing* stuff."

I take back the sheet, now filled with his scribbles. I look at the markings and see the day's headlines all over them. "You coming clean, Jonah?" Cheap shot. He's never tried to hide anything. Never anything other than he was: a swarthy, vaguely Semitic, loose-curled, mixed-race kid who happens to sing European art songs. I'm sick of myself as soon as the words leave my mouth. It's the stress of touring, the sleepless haul down from Denver the night before. He needs an accompanist who *likes* performing, who actually enjoys trying to get halls full of strangers to love him.

But Jonah just smirks. "I wouldn't exactly say *clean*, Mule. It's only an encore."

I know what he wants without his having to talk me through. After the standing ovation and our second curtain call, my brother glances at me as we come out of the bow: *You ready?* I play from the music, afraid to tempt fate, but also letting the audience know this isn't the standard order of business. I know what Jonah wants: all those sweet dissonances brought out into blithe daylight. He wants me to lean into the shadings that hide in this cheerful expansiveness, to throw the upbeat tune into full relief. Maybe even toss in some clashes of my own. He wants the tune bright, cheery, major, and flooded with jarring disaster.

The place we make tonight is too small for Lisette Soer to enter, too small and hard and shining for anyone but me and my brother even to see. Shout, shout: Satan's about. One more river to cross. Shut your door and keep him out. One more river to cross. There's this man Meredith trying to go to school, and there's the U.S. Army, and people dead, same as last year, same as next. We'll never reach ourselves. One more river; one more wartime Jordan. And one more after that.

No one in the audience suspects the source he sings from. The things that are happening abroad tonight all happen over in someone else's state. Satan is nigh, but nobody sees him. One more river to cross. Yet the crowd hears the song: something brutally American after all the undecipherable Italian and German fare we've served up at this evening's concert. Baking out here in the hundred-degree desert, with even the ocotillo and saguaro dying of drought and the streams all dry for so long that there's six feet of bramble in their beds, the audience takes this ancient headline home, to their stucco haciendas and transplanted Kentucky bluegrass lawns, their city carved out of neighboring reservations, twice-stolen land. And as they lie there, the cultural artifact keeps them awake. One more river to cross.

Jonah's singing does nothing for Mississippi. Nothing to help make an America, or unmake one. Meredith probably would have hated our version. But the spiritual does do one invisible thing, for an infinitely smaller nation. "How did it sound?" Jonah asks me in the wings.

And I tell him. "Wide."

He feeds Lisette Soer the story when we get home. Her face turns the color of her hair when she learns we changed the program without consulting her. She softens, though still miffed, when she learns the details. There are powers that even Method acting won't dare tap. Powers she knows not to tamper with.

They grow dependent on each other, my brother and Madame Soer, joined in a way Jonah hasn't been with any teacher since Reményi. Close in a way he hasn't been with anyone since the fire. She asks him to sing in an open master class, along with four promising females. She wants to keep him out in front of other aggressive East Coast ears. They listen to old recordings together, great dead tenors—Fleta, Lindi—late into the evening, until one of her famous competing consorts comes by and sends the boy home.

They listen on a stereo fifty times more expensive than the one our parents bought us years ago. My brother comes home after these listening excursions, shaking his head in wonder. "Mule, we never even heard those bastards. You won't believe what they're really doing!"

Lisette doesn't talk through these performances, the way Jonah and I used to, listening in the dark. She forbids speech while the music plays, and for some minutes afterward. She restricts all commentary to squeezes of his upper arm, her long, lyric fingernails sinking into his flesh proportionate to the power and pure drama of the moment, relived through electricity's séance medium.

She knows whole lifetimes of music, having lived several already in her third of a century. She builds up my brother's sound without much changing it. But the change she works on Jonah is dramatic. She opens his throat, fills his vowels with color, and smoothes them across his range. She's the first teacher to teach him the shape of his own tongue and lips. The first to teach him that too much perfection will kill you. But her chief lesson is far harsher. Miss Soer teaches my brother hunger.

I hear it before I see it. He's restless down in the Village. Things don't happen fast enough. Beat is dead. The jazz scene, he declares, is falling into retreads. He exhausts his fascination with the classical avant-garde. "Those jokers haven't produced anything truly new since Henry Cowell." Cage and the Zen crowd just bore him, and even quadrupling the boredom doesn't help. When we aren't on the road, he prowls the streets, listening for other voices, breaking into other rooms.

The hunger she sows shows up onstage. We're in Camden, Maine, singing on a makeshift stage that shakes a little with every pound of the nearby surf. He's singing "When I am one and twenty," pressing into it as if diction alone could turn the peat lyric to diamond. He wants something from the words, the pitches, the audience, me. Lisette has taught him the rule that keeps all drama from going mawkish. At the top of the phrase, at the song's maximum need, pull back. Don't get big and messy; draw yourself inward around the unbearable, until it glows with the smallest light.

His hunger focuses. He starts to read again—Mann, Hesse—those works János Reményi made him read, decades before Jonah could hope to understand them. Even now, he's years too young to make them out.

But he totes them under his arm to lessons, thinking they'll please Soer. They horrify her. She finds them repugnant, Germanic. She wants him on Dumas, Hugo at the very least.

"Did you know Dumas was a black man?" This is news to Jonah. He wonders why she feels the need to tell him.

He must see what's coming. The white iceberg must condense for him soon, even out of his whiter fog. But I keep still; the woman is doing too much for us. I'm learning volumes from her, secondhand—whole worlds about music, and even more about the musical world.

We're at a stand-up pizza place on Houston, pretending to be students, enjoying the night, how it fuzzes into that passing crowd. "Mule? You ever sleep with anyone in college?"

He sounds for a moment like an ancient wife confronting her husband at the end of the day with a suspicion that's too old to be anxious about anymore, now that everything is past mattering.

"Aside from the actresses, Gypsies, consumptives, and courtesans with hearts of gold?"

He jerks up and stares, then flips me the finger. "I mean for real. Not your diseased imagination."

"Oh. For *real*." I wonder if I even wanted to, with anyone *real*. My one moment of love—the woman in the navy blue dress followed for twenty blocks—was free of any such compromising risk. "You think I could even have *thought* about it without your knowing?"

His lips twitch a little, and he hides them behind a wedge of pizza. He chews and swallows. "You ever *almost*?"

I pretend to deliberate, blood racing. "No."

"How about since?"

"No." Haven't left your sight. "But since we're on the subject—"

"How many . . . men do you think she has?" Only one *she* in our lives now. He doesn't really want me to count them, and I don't.

The shortness of breath he suffered during our preparation for the America's Next Voices competition returns. It happens before a Sunday afternoon recital in Boston, the first time we've been back since Boylston. Ten minutes before we go on, he starts wheezing so badly, he almost passes out. I tell the house manager to cancel and call a doctor. Jonah objects, although it almost suffocates him. We go on, twenty minutes late. As performances go, it's ragged. But Jonah sings at maximum need. The audience flocks backstage afterward. There's no sign of Reményi, any Boylston teachers, or our once friends.

Back in the city, Lisette forces him to get a checkup. She even offers to loan him the money for it. I bless the woman for making him do what I can't. Nothing wrong, the doctor says. "Nothing wrong, Mule," Jonah repeats, eyes darting around the waiting room, as if the walls were closing in.

I'm better with his panic attacks now that I'm sure they pass. Calmer, I can bring him out faster. He manages them, almost seeming to time them to avoid total disaster: early in the afternoon before a concert, or at the reception just following one.

We play eight venues in January of 1963 alone: big cities looking for new blood, midsized cities pretending to be big cities, small cities looking for affordable culture, small towns that, through historical accident, hold on to their European roots. Maybe their grandfathers once bought standing-room tickets at the *Stadtschauplatz*, or loved the free *Rathaus* affairs on public holidays. So the descendants preserve the forms after all context has washed away, the way people turn massive old radio consoles into knickknack cabinets.

We don't even know about Project Confrontation until we see it on a lobby television in a two-star hotel in Minneapolis. A police commissioner named Bull Conner releases fire hoses and attack-trained German shepherds on protesters for singing "Marching to Freedom Land" without a license. Most of the marchers are years younger than we are. Jonah looks on from Minneapolis, humming to himself, "Way down south in Birmingham, I mean south in Alabam," not even hearing.

The country on television isn't ours. The streets on film are mobbed, as in some jackboot-crushed Eastern European uprising. Police club fallen kids, dragging them off in paddy wagons. Bodies roll in the spray, pounded into clumps against brick walls by vicious water jets. Everywhere is spray and chaos, limbs gashed and beaten, two white policemen smashing a boy in the face with billy clubs, until the hourly wage Minneapolis bellhop, black, is told by management to turn the channel, and Jonah and I head off to a last-minute auditorium test prior to charming the Twin Cities.

Tonight, we do another encore. Jonah whispers it to me as we take a curtain call. "Go Down, Moses," in D minor. He doesn't even have the sheet music this time. We don't need it. An old friend of mine has taught me how to improvise, to pull notes out of the air that serve as well as any written down. Jonah doesn't quite know the words, but he finds them, too. He sings them at the same moment as the children in their cells down in Birmingham jail sing, "Ain't gonna let nobody turn me round . . ."

The audience, too, has seen Birmingham, served up by Cronkite, earlier that evening. They know what's happening way down in Egypt land. They hush when Jonah finishes, hard, luminous, and piano. But they aren't sure how to see this mix, this _cause_ creeping into the confines of beauty. Even supportive applause seems wrong.

Our bookings increase, and so do the protests. They tear through hundreds of cities north and south, even passing through the towns we tour. Yet we always miss the marches, blowing through a day before, two days after. We polish our new encore and add it to the standing repertoire. Jonah doesn't tell Lisette.

She's increasingly eager to groom our public look. "Jonie"—and yes, he stands for it—"you're getting noticed. You're earning a name for lightness. You have to watch out for anything lugubrious. Find work that lets you *sail*." She squelches attempts to sing anything written later than 1930. She arms him with an arsenal of shiny pellets, each one finished in two minutes. She feeds him Fauré. She goes through a Delius kick—"Maude" and "A Late Lark." He sings them, like appearing onstage in pastel tights.

Lisette sands down the cheats he's developed to hide his thinner notes. She pushes him to get a single burnished arc out of all three of his voice's regions. No one has ever heard in him what she hears. No one has ever dared him on as she does. At his lessons, she sings back to him. When she sets him aside and takes up the notes, it's like brass after bronze. His instrument is more magnificent than the one she's been dealt. But her presence blows my brother's away. She merely has to *think* the notes; they fall from her in the effortless afterthought of inner recall. Her singing draws him to his fate. Even I can't turn away.

She huddles up to him as he sings, pressing on his sides, patting his flank, resting her cool palms against his neck. It's a loving cruelty, torturing him with touch. But this is how they learn best now, locked in a constant clinch, passing information through the siphon of skin.

"Grow huge," she tells him. "Not in mass; not even in volume." He must learn to place not just his sound but his very soul into the dark back corners of the most cavernous halls. One day, she'll have him storm the arenas of drama and demand a hearing. Until then, he must perfect the high, clear force of lieder, a different matter altogether.

She wants us to hear how opera is really done, in the trenches, under fire. She gives us two tickets for her coming performance—Fiordiligi in *Così*, for Mr. Bing. "Mozart?" Jonah teases her. "What nationality was he again?"

She tucks him under the chin the way Maria Theresa once coddled the boy composer. "He sure as hell wasn't German, darling. He loved those Italian libretti, you'll notice. And he'd have lived in Paris forever, by choice."

Her coolness betrays how much is at stake. A role in *Così*, at the Met. She seems, at most, a little harried. "Lives don't come down to one moment," she claims. We know she's lying.

She gives us the golden tickets and shoos us away. "Have a good time, boys. I'll be the one in the big wig and white petticoats."

We wear our concert clothes for the event. It's overkill, but it preempts trouble at the door. We head down to Broadway and Thirty-ninth, hoping to slip in without a scene. The seats Lisette gives us are magnificent, a few rows back from the block she gives her family. Jonah waits for the curtain, biting his cuticles until they bleed. He's in agony, worse than anything he's ever felt before going onstage himself. Here at eye level, he can see what his teacher cannot, up there behind the blinding lights.

"You feel that?" he asks. I nod, thinking he means the electricity. "They want her blood. They want her to fall to pieces."

It's crazy. We're talking a midsized role in Mozart's "problem" opera, the one nobody quite gets. Disaster will, at worst, send her back to San Francisco for a few seasons. Triumph will, at best, win her another chance to prove herself to Bing.

"That's paranoid, Jonah. Why would anyone want her to fail?"

"What do you mean? For the excitement. The drama missing in their own lives. Look around. These people would love a good wipeout. Now that would be *real* opera."

As soon as the curtain rises, Jonah stops worrying about whether his teacher's going to die and starts worrying about whether she's going to stay faithful to her feckless lover. He's lost from the overture's first theme. Doesn't she love her officer? Why doesn't his departure destroy her? How can she fail to see through these turbaned Albanians, gotten up like fifty-cent Turks?

In the intermission, he's ruined for talk. He has it in for Despina and Alphonso. Only sheer, faithful concentration can hold their devious plot at bay. But all around us, the audience is deep in appraisal. They weigh the orchestra, the conductor, the leads, Mozart—deciding who should live and who needs to die for humanity's sins. I know enough not to cough, lest they train the fire hoses on me. The matron next to me ruffles through her program. "Who *is* that gorgeous thing playing the faithful one?"

Her cadaverous escort coughs. "You mean Soer? She's been around. Up-and-comer. Second lead sort of thing. Could go all the way."

"She's good, don't you think?" I look to Jonah, but he's busy fending off the first act's dangers, guarding his teacher's chastity. "The note doesn't say where she's from. Is she French or something?"

The cadaver just snorts. "Lisa Sawyer. Hails from Milwaukee, where, I understand, her father makes what passes for beer. Emphasis on *passes*." He flips through his own program, frowning. "Hmm. They don't mention that?"

The woman raps his shoulder. "Nasty. Is that her real color?"

" 'Does she or doesn't she?' Apparently, only half of the city knows for sure."

She slaps him on the wrist with her rolled-up program.

Jonah comes out of his trance. "What do you think of the tempi?" I ask. He corrects them all, from memory.

The curtain rises on the second act, plunging us back into life or death. Jonah grips the armrest throughout Lisette's second big aria, anticipating the octave-and-a-half swoops, sure she's going to give in and get laid by this pseudo-Albanian, her sister's fiancé, her betrothed's most trusted friend. *Everybody does it.* Does she love this *other* man? Why is her fall so much sweeter than her earlier sworn chastity? His whole body sighs with her thrilling debasement.

Lisette doesn't always soar. Some of the highs lack support, and her rapid, dipping passages take cover. Still, she's supernatural. She inhabits the stage, never having lived anywhere but in this story, never experiencing any time but this one renewing night. Fiordiligi has waited patiently for just such a supple body to reawaken in after long hibernation. Never has a singer taken such shameless physical pleasure in a role. Lisette is wayward, consumed, consummated by the unlikely luck of this part. By her "Per pietà," Jonah is lost, and even I forgive her anything.

"She *is* fun to watch," the cadaverous man concedes in the extended applause. "A real piece. Piece of work, that is." His consort smacks him again, this time with her knuckles.

From the "toast" quartet through the fumbling denouement, Lisette glows, divinely human. She radiates the *social*, unable to exist except through the grace of those out front, in this hall, from the pit to the upper balcony. She needs society, feeds off others, and yet her art lives in the most sealed of vacuums. The struggle of 1963 is nothing to her, not even unreal. This might be the Burgtheater, Vienna, 1790: a dress rehearsal in paradise, the morning after the last revolution.

Tonight, she is the privileged world's darling. Applause brings the cast out again and again. Sheaves of roses float up to her onstage, more than for Dorabella and Despina combined. During her bows, she finds us and locks our eyes: *You see now? Living maximum need?* An old trick, a staple for those who live by an audience's love: She knows how to gaze so that everyone in the house feels singled out.

We don't even consider the receiving line. Lisette Soer is the toast of New York tonight, until tomorrow replaces her. She wouldn't even recognize us in the adoring fray. The couple alongside me declines, as well. But they're still talking about her as they file out ahead of us, on their way to whatever postopener postmortem their people retire to.

In the lobby, Jonah's voice veers. "She'll have her pick tonight, won't she, Mule?" He doesn't want an answer. He only wants me to get him home, down to Bleecker. "Let's take a cab."

"Sure," I say. But I steer him to the subway.

When Jonah goes to his Wednesday lesson, she rages at him. "I give you tickets to opening night, the biggest role of my career, and you don't care enough to come backstage to tell me what you think? Go on. Get out of here. Just get out!" She slams her studio door on him and will not open it.

He comes back home in agony. He sits me down and dictates a review of her performance, note by note, muscle by electrifying muscle. His letter is a masterpiece of exacting musicology. Its observations surpass anything that newspaper reviewers can even hear. His judgments are so closely grounded in musical specifics, they take on the air of universal truth.

"I was afraid to come see you afterward," he has me write. "I just wanted to feel your transcendence a little longer, before rushing it back to earth."

She writes him back. "Your letter is going into my first-rank scrapbook, next to the note from Bernstein. You are right: We must sustain the aura as long as we can. I wish I could have done so, with you. Would my greatest student accept a special lesson as my apology?"

Dignity has never meant much to Jonah. Now it's not even an impediment. "Tell me she's evil, Mule." We're trying to practice. His concentration is shot. He'll wander off and mark pitches for several measures, before remembering what we're doing. I've learned to play through his vacancies. But when he talks, I stop. "Tell me the woman's no damn good."

"She's not evil. Just manipulative. She knows everything there is about . . . performing. But she doesn't know much about people."

"What do you mean by that?" He sounds hurt, ready to charge out of his corner swinging at the sound of the bell.

"She wants you to adore her. She'll do everything in her power to keep you on your knees in front of her."

He studies me over the music rack. His face is a mask. Another thing she's taught him: Never telegraph emotions. "What the fuck do you know about anything?"

"Nothing, Jonah. I don't know anything."

I stare at the keyboard, he at me. We sit for a long time, a fair rendition of John Cage's *4′33″*. I only wish we had a tape recorder; our first take would have been a wrap. I won't speak first. I think he's staring me down. Then I realize he's just elsewhere. At last, he murmurs, "Wouldn't mind being on my knees in front of her, come to think."

I hammer out a little Scriabin, an on-the-fly *Poem of Ecstasy*. He doesn't need the program notes. His head bobs up and down, his grin private. "Know what the problem is, Mule?"

"What's the problem, Jonah?"

"The problem, since you asked, is she's manipulative."

I start a slow, seductive "Dance of the Seven Veils," ready to throw on an overcoat at the first wrinkle in his brow.

"I know, I know. I have to get a handle on my life. Otherwise . . ." He raps the music stand, our shattered rehearsal. "Otherwise, we might never be able to perform Schubert in good faith again!" He giggles like a lunatic. For an awful moment, I think I'm going to have to call Da, or Bellevue. My alarm only makes him worse. "Yeah, I'm a goner," he says when he comes back. "I've got to get the woman out of my blood."

"There is a way. Call her bluff."

"Oh." Pianissimo. "Turns out . . . it's not a bluff." He mitts my shoulder, contrite now, inspecting the damage. "I'm sorry, Mule. I wanted to tell you. I tried a while back. I didn't know how."

"Are you . . . How long?"

"I don't know. Weeks? Look. I said I'm sorry. Don't try, Mule. You can't make me sorrier than I already am."

But I'm not angry. Not even betrayed. I'm cut free, lost in the inconceivable. My brother has learned how to act. He wanted to tell me. Tried but couldn't. He's slept with a thing fresh out of a sinister fairy tale, nearer our mother's age than ours. I've been denying everything: his finicky distraction, our growing tension over the last weeks. He gives me the details, the ones I should have guessed weeks ago. Most of them float by in my disbelief.

The first time, it's just like part of his lessons. She's showing him Holst's "Floral Bandit," as always, with her hands. Pushing here, rounding there. Let every muscle serve the needs of the words. Well, the words are musty and suspect at best. She knows he doesn't buy them. "Mr. Strom." She pinches his flank, an aggressive sneer on her lips. "If you don't believe the song, what right do you have to ask a roomful of people to believe you? Yes, I know. It's sentimental rubbish, already archaic when the man wrote the words five thousand years ago. But what if they weren't? What if the sun rose and set around this poetry?"

"That's what you call this?"

"You don't get it." She stands six inches in front of him, grabs his armpits, and shakes him like a terrified mother might shake a child who has just survived death. "And you won't be more than a pretty-throated boy until you do. Your personal taste means nothing. What you think of this frilly twaddle doesn't count. You must make yourself someone else's instrument. Someone with different needs and fears. If you're trapped in yourself, screw art. If you can't be someone more than yourself, don't even think about walking out onstage."

She draws him closer, placing both palms on his breasts. She has done so before, but never so tenderly as now. "Music is something we aren't. It comes from outside and must go back there. Your job is notness." She shoves him, then yanks him back by the shirt as he reels. "It's why we bother to sing at all. Ninety-nine point nine nine nine"—she brutalizes his chest with each digit—"percent of everything that has ever happened, happened to someone who isn't you and who's centuries dead. But ev-

erything lives again in you, if you can clear enough room to carry it."
She jabs him in the sternum, and he catches her hand. "Ah!" she says, delighted, twisting back against his grip. "Ah! Want to fight me?"

He drops her wrist, surprised.

"Aw! Not this time?" She takes up his hand again, lifts her eyes, looks
about the room, distracted. " 'Have you seen her? What is her name?' "

He thinks she has gone mad, another weak-gened Ophelia wracked up
on the fey waywardness of Western high culture. Then he places the
words: the damn Floral Bandit. The pathetic, pale, wilted thief of spring.

She closes his hand into her soft cushion. The scent of jasmine is her
sweat. She snares his gaze. Her eyes, incredible, are jade against the amber of her hair, green as the words of the song she now degrades him
with. " 'Who is this lady? What is she? The Sylvia all our swains adore?' "
She smiles up at him, on her toes, drawing one finger down the cliff of his
throat. She pinches his chin jut, swings his hand in hers like a little girl,
the innocent, anemic girl he once was bound to.

This is a slaver's game. This art only works by denying the desperate.
But he feels her breath on him and stays as silent as the condemned. She
puts that denying finger on his lips: " 'For human tongue would strive in
vain to speak the buds uncrumpling in it.' "

Laugh lines light up every corner of her. She draws up level to his
face. He hears her add, "Do you want me?" She'll deny ever saying this,
though there are no words in the poem he might have mistaken for them.

This is her lesson in making songs real. And what happens next is just
another. When he folds into her, he thinks it's his own daring. She'll draw
away, outraged. She doesn't draw away. Her mouth is waiting, an old familiar. He holds his skin on hers, moist-to-moist. Any taste of her would
seem forever, and he gets twice that. When they stop, he turns his head
away. She draws his face around, forces him to look. It's her. Still her. Still
smiling. See?

He's too small for his shock. He can look at her. All her laugh lines
look back, cheering his victory, daring him, asking him, *How much would
you like to see?* All yours, for the gazing and grazing. If his fear were any
less, his joy would kill him. The lessons move to her daybed, an antique
Viennese unfolding fern whose function in her studio he has always
dreamed about. She shows him how to unwrap her. All the while, she
babbles senseless things, half-sung phonemes, droplets of words from the
damn poem. " 'For no one knows her range nor can guess half the phrases
from her fiddle.' "

She is more perfect than he imagined her in his best renditions. As fair as that first anemic girl he never got to see. Her flanks surprise him, the cup of breasts, the dimpling high up on the back of her thighs. She needs to be examined in her studio's full sun. He feels callow, his slender arms, his tawny, hairless chest, his boyish explosiveness in her hands. No sooner does she take him, body swaying, an impulse gurgle in her throat, than he flows all over her. Even this, she marvels at, and her delight dissolves his shame. "Next time," she promises. "Next lesson!" She presses his lips, shushes and dresses him, for she has another student coming. *This lady who 'fore ev'ry man, breaks off her music in the middle.*

She invites him to her apartment, an evening appointment he must clear with no one but me. He wants to tell me but doesn't. That's music. That's his job. To be someone else, someone not him. If you can't be someone more than yourself, don't even think about walking out on-stage. Her lair is filled with musical conjuring. The walls are covered with documents—her Paris triumph, a Verdi manuscript page, a photo of Gian Carlo Menotti with his arm around her young waist. The furnishings feel like some museum Da might long ago have dragged him to. She shows him the eighteenth-century virginal with painted underlid and plinks out a gentle, deceptive cadence.

He feels these chords' coy come-on and reaches for her there as she stands plinking. She recoils, hands up. "You haven't even sung for me!" Her head tilts back, chin challenging. "How do I know what you're worth?"

He sings the Holst again. But now he sings as if his life hangs on these words. She rewards him by seeming to reward herself. Something in him that she wants: It works on him, like her creed of maximum need.

She's his first. It stuns me. For years, I've imagined him enjoying a string of casual throwaways. But he's been saving himself, faithful to this woman in advance of meeting her. They get better, lesson by lesson. They work at it, from the first burst of open throat down to the smallest details of support. They get so good, they must study more. She shows him goodness he never expected: all of life in front of him. They find out places that never were. She turns into his maker, his keeper, his ladder. Teaching him how to touch her, she tenses and subvocalizes, tenders into his hand, sforzando, as if she's waited all her life to be performed only like this.

His first: She can't remember what that landmark means. She's too far down the path of experience. She's refined all her pleasures already. All her surprise discoveries, long ago lost in perfecting. Or rather, this boy helps her remember—that ambush in his face, sweating, glowing above hers. His body lowers onto hers and freezes, overwhelmed by this prize. His freed gratitude returns her, once more, to that moment when everything might still turn out other than you think. Other than what it has so solidly become.

"Do you hear?" she asks him one night before dressing and sending him home. "Do you hear how big this is making you?"

He snickers, a child. "I didn't know you could *hear* it."

She spanks him. "I mean your voice. We're growing it."

He twists between the impossible and the unbearable. Too much; too little: the few minutes of play she restricts him to after every coaching session. His eyes can't adjust to her. Her arctic whiteness blinds him. He is her puppy, sniffing her thighs, inhaling her hair's jasmine until she giggles—"Quit tickling!"—and swats him away. His hands explore her skin's unlikelihood: the rise of her foot, the gather behind her knee, the sag beneath her buttocks, the plates of her shoulder blades jutting from the continent of her back. He can't stop verifying every inch of her. She takes to dimming the lights, a small shield from the glare of his gaze.

In the half dark, he places his arm along hers. Hers shows him what he looks like to her. And yet his wrist differs from the back of hers less than brother from sister. Where the bruises of their hips come together in the dark, no difference at all. Except for the difference in their passages here.

She sees him measuring, and rolls over on top of him in her joy. "You! How can I show you?" She's childlike with him. She licks him down like a kitten, working distractedly, as if he won't notice or isn't there. Then she tenses, shudders, going off again. She does so easily now, needing little more than the feel of him. She lies with her face in the pillow, talking, her words effaced. Impossible to say what audience she speaks to. He hears her say, "I love your people."

He freezes. He wants to say, *Say that again?* But he doesn't dare.

She talks into the gag, muffled, drunk, liking the words' blur. His arm, a whipped cord upon the back of her neck, loosens again in her stream of nonsense. She flips over, ready to play some more, one palm on his slight bare chest, staying him. "How can I keep you this way?"

"Potions," he tells her. "Spells and elixirs."

"Can you take me home with you someday?" His hand, straying between her legs, stiffens again. "Not as . . . Nobody would have to . . . I am your teacher, after all." He pulls his hand away like a wire off a battery. The current goes dead. She doesn't notice or admit. "You have a place that we . . . can't get to. So rich, so full. I'd just like to sit and savor it awhile."

What place? What riches? What *you*? He makes her out in a glint of lamplight: a famine tourist. A slumming succubus, feeding on her victim's victimhood. He reels from her, but not hard enough to break free. In the moment he pulls away, he feels how cold and airless any escape would be. Where could he go if he stood up now, dressed, walked out of this apartment with its baroque furnishings? Her sickness is also opera's, the world he has trained for. What other place would even take him in?

He is, to this woman, some thrilling brown thing, an adventure denied her. He can't tell her how wrong her reading is. The people she loves are not his people. He hates her already for loving any people at all in him but him. But he fails to rise to his hate, to be the nation of one he knows himself to be.

He waits for another night, when she's naked and satisfied, in his arms. "You said you might want to come home with me someday?"

She turns around, grazes his lips. She can't remember. Then: *Oh. That home.* She says nothing. She's graduated to studying for a different role, some remote Asian beauty, some frail chinoiserie.

"We can. If you want."

"My Jonie." His pulse pounds. "Where's home?"

"Uptown," he answers vaguely. She nods, knowing. He feels her working up to ask his neighborhood. What rich brown streets might he lead her into? "It's . . . only my father now. And I should tell you. He's—not from around here."

"Really?" Her enthusiasm revives.

"He's German."

The news catches her across the face. Even the actress can't recover fast enough. "Is he? What city?"

He feels himself losing her, like an audience that comes for Canteloube and gets Shostakovich. She asks what brought his father here. "The Nazis," he says. Now she's a lacquered mask.

"You're not Jewish?"

This is what makes him tell me, at last. He falls back on the bond bigger than any secret link the two of them could grow. "Tell me she's evil, Mule. Tell me the woman's no damn good."

I do. And he ignores me.

"She's going to stab me," he says. "I'm going to blunder around for half an hour in act four, spewing blood from my gut."

"Just be sure you do it with breath support." I don't know what else to give him. His eyes fill. He tries to laugh and flip me the bird at the same time. We go back to practicing. Somebody else's music. Some other people.

The effect on his voice is electrifying. He can harrow now, leave you for dead. His passage work is as clean as ever. But his phrases push into new, awful places. On tour, he sings the same numbers as ever, each time stumbling on some further climax. He no longer settles weightless onto Brahms's long, dark suspensions from above. He severs them, leaving them helpless, in midair.

We perform "The Floral Bandit"—a piece of time-marking fluff before the intermission. One night, camped out in a small campus hall in the guts of Ohio, we drop through a hole in the stage and lay open the song's veins. I'm still pressing the keys. Sounds must still be exiting the instrument, but I can't hear them. There's only Jonah, that fleshed-out voice drawing remorse out of lifelong repeat offenders. His pitches float in the ether, hovering at sound's motionless center.

"What the hell was that?" I ask afterward, hiding in the wings from the applause. He only shakes his head, stumbles back out onstage, and takes another bow.

Those reviewers who a year ago faulted his cold precision now proclaim his passion. Sometimes the notices mention me: "a synchrony that could only exist between blood relations." But often they write as if Jonah could sing lieder to a ballpark organ. "Emotional, profound," the *Hartford Courant* says, "giving a precocious insight into the depths and heights in each of us." All this, Lisette does for him. No teacher ever gives him more.

But his education isn't finished yet. She moves his lessons back to the studio, saving the apartment for special invitations. The invitations come syncopated now. He may go dancing, but she calls the tune. Still, she goes on dancing with him. Something in him still wakens her. She needs him to help her remember what *only* feels like, what *always* was. The force of his desperation is what so moves her.

She still touches him while he sings, still locates muscles he didn't know he had. She dangles new parts in front of him: Don Carlos, Pelléas, juicy tenor roles men ten years older are afraid to tackle. One afternoon, she tells him, "We need to find you someone."

"Someone for what?"

"Someone for *you*, Jonie."

His voice deserts him. "You mean another teacher?"

She mews back in her throat, puts a hand on his. "You'll probably teach *her* a few things."

"I don't understand. What are you saying?"

"Oh, *caro*! Don't worry." She leans in toward his ear and whispers. "Whatever you learn from her, you'll come show me."

He's worthless for a week. It takes me until noon to get him out of bed, then another two hours to get him to the breakfast table. I have to call Mr. Weisman with two cancellations. I tell him Jonah has a bronchial infection. Weisman is furious.

Soer calls. I almost refuse to put her through. But Jonah knows even before I can say two words to her. He's on his feet and bowling me over for the receiver. He's dressed and at the door in minutes.

"We need to rehearse," I say. "We're in Pittsburgh next week."

"We are rehearsing. What do you think I'm doing?"

When he comes back, after midnight, he's ready to kill giants again. When we do rehearse, the next day, his voice sounds strong enough to heal the sin-sick world.

But the world doesn't want healing. In June, while fishing for the Philharmonic radio broadcast, we hear Kennedy make a belated speech for civil rights. Four hours later, the NAACP's Mississippi field secretary is shot in the back and killed in front of his home by a waiting gunman. He'd been working on a voting drive. The killer goes free. The state's governor enters the courtroom during the trial and shakes the man's hand.

This time, Jonah and I sing no special encores. "Tell me what we're supposed to do, Mule. Name it and I'll sing it." I don't know what we're supposed to do. We go on doing what we've trained for. Holst and Brahms.

Jonah and Lisette fight over his auditioning for opera roles. The money from our mother's insurance, which supplements our meager concert fees and helps pay our rent, is running out. Jonah grows restless with nineteenth-century German lieder recitals.

"Not yet, *caro*. You're getting there. Right now, you have the perfect lieder sound."

"But it's getting fuller, fleshier. You said so yourself."

"You're building an audience out there. Getting good notices. Take your time. Enjoy it. You only begin life once."

"My voice is in bloom."

"And it will be for another thirty years, with care. You're almost ready."

"I'm ready now. So ready, I can't tell you. I need to audition. I don't care where. I can land some stage part."

"You're not singing 'some stage part.' Not while I'm your teacher. When you make your debut, you'll do it right."

"You're afraid I might land a plum, aren't you?"

"You *are* a plum, chum. Jonie? Train for the day."

He chafes, but he does as she tells him. He trusts this woman, after everything. "She's my only real friend," he tells me.

"I see," I say.

The two of us, constantly in transit, parading in front of rooms of people, are at the mercy of her slightest shift. Jonah's old Juilliard cronies—those who have stayed in town, those who haven't trickled into education or insurance—try to drag him up to Sammy's for reunions. Brian O'Malley, singing in choruses at City Center, still presides. Jonah is that circle's only remaining lottery ticket to real fame. But they feel the change in him as well, the darkening. We see no one else close to us aside from Da and Ruth, only rooms full of admiring strangers. Our only calls are from Mr. Weisman and Lisette Soer.

We do socialize with strangers. Lisette drags us to parties—massively cultured affairs where whole social solar systems of spinning planets spread through the rooms, orbits that range from the day's reigning sun at the center to the furthermost icy asteroids. Jonah and I are usually banished out somewhere between Neptune and Pluto. At one, a guest addresses us in blundering Spanish, assuming we're two self-improving Puerto Ricans.

We're dressing for one of these pointless parties, a reception for *The Ballad of Baby Doe*, when I balk. "What the hell are we going to another one of these for, Jonah? Three hours, minimum. That's three hours we could be learning new rep."

"Mule, jobs come from these things."

"Jobs come from people who hear us perform."

"These parties are crawling with the most powerful musical people in this country." He could be Lisette talking. "They need to see us up close."

"Why?"

"To make sure we're not savages. They don't want us sneaking up behind Western civilization and mugging it at gunpoint."

"I'm a whole lot darker up close, you know."

My brother, in black jacket, fiddles with his tie. He smoothes down his lapels and inspects the results. He turns and glides my way until his face hovers inches from mine. He peers at me, inspecting the problem. "Huh! Would you look at that! How come you never told me this, Joey?"

"You've got a lot of confidence in folks with a bad track record."

"Come on, brother. We're *uplift*. We're moral advancement. The coming fashion."

"Don't want to be the coming fashion, Jonah."

He cranes his neck back. "What *do* you want?"

"I just want to play the music I know how to play."

"Come on, Joey." He grabs my strip of tie out of my hand, wraps it around my neck, and begins tying. "We'll tell them you're my chauffeur or something."

At one evening gathering in late June, I'm standing in a corner, smiling preemptively, counting the rests until Jonah's ready to leave. Over the burr of the conversation, like a radio station bleeding through static, something hits me. The party's sound track switches in my head from ground to figure. The jazz coming through our host's expensive speakers is state-of-the-art Village, the innovations Jonah and I so recently learned to follow.

I listen, the melody slipping me, like a name too familiar to recover. I close my eyes and surrender to this agonizing sense of known unknown. I'm sure I've heard the piece, tracing in advance its every modulation, but just as sure it's nothing I could have heard before. I drift to the turntable. The prospect of cheating kills all chance of naming that tune.

A tall guy in green jacket and plastic horn-rims, skinny and pale even by these parties' standards, stands by the hi-fi equipment, nodding in time to the music. "What *is* this?" I surprise us both with my urgency.

"Ah! That's my man Miles."

"Davis?" The trumpeter who dropped out of Juilliard ten years before we started and who went on to turn bebop cool. The man who, just a few years earlier, was beaten by police and jailed for standing outside a club where he was slated to play. A man so dark, I'd cross the street if I saw him coming.

"Who else?" Green Jacket says.

"Friend of yours?" First-name basis. A fair assumption, at this party of music's elite.

But the face behind the horn-rims turns hostile. "I dig the music, man. You have problems with that?"

I back off, palms up, looking around for my big brother. Who does this skinny, pale guy think he is? Even I could beat him senseless. My rage builds, knowing all it can do is back off. This punk owes me an apology, one he expects me to offer him. But all the while, it eats at me: more grating than my humiliation by this white Negro. The music. I need to know how I know it. I've heard lots of Miles Davis, but never this. Yet these scorched chord clusters, modal, atavistic, play through my head as if I wrote them. Then it dawns on me: *transcription*. The piece is not for trumpet; it's for guitar. It isn't *Miles* I recognize. It's Rodrigo.

I take the record sleeve from the pale guy's hands. My excitement keeps him from taking a punch at me. I fumble with the cardboard, wondering if two independent people can stumble on the same fact independently, like those souls wandering in the scientific wilderness Da used to tell us about over dinner. The sleeve calls the music *Sketches of Spain*. I'm the last man on earth to hear of it: a Juilliard School dropout's treatment of Aranjuez. Music has to sit around for at least a hundred years before I get it. It feels to me at least that long since Wilson Hart and I sat down to see what was hiding in this tune, more than a century since we played four-hand and I learned to improvise.

Will was right about the Reconquista, right about the uses this tune could be put through. Yet everything about these trumpet-led sketches is different from what Will and I made that day—everything but the theme. The lines play back and forth from Andalusia to the Sahara and southward, all cultures picking one another's pockets, not to mention the pockets of those who only stand and listen.

I listen, in tears, not caring if this white Negro sees me. I hear the loneliest man I'll ever meet, transcribed from his world into another, loving a music that had no home, huddled in a practice room writing orchestral suites he knew would be the ridicule of any group he showed them to. And he showed them to me. A man who made me promise to write down the tune inside me. And to date, I've written down not a single note—exactly what's in me.

I hear the fact in every reworked Spanish note: I failed to become my friend's friend. I don't know why. I haven't tried to contact him since our good-bye, and I know I won't, not even when we go home tonight, my heart full of the man. I don't know why. I know exactly why. *That's okay, brother Joe. Let every soul praise God in his own fashion.* This is my way: lieder recitals in Hartford and Pittsburgh, and Upper East Side dress-up balls full of the musical elite. The cardboard record sleeve shakes in my hands. Andalusia via East St. Louis washes out of the speakers, the trumpet discovering its inevitable line, and all I can do is stand here, shaking my head, sobbing. "It's okay," I tell Green Jacket, his glare turned to fear. "It's cool. There isn't a horse alive that's purebred."

We see Da and Ruth at least once a week, up in Morningside, for Friday dinner, if we're not on the road performing. Ruth's growing up fast, under the care of our father and his fifty-year-old housekeeper, Mrs. Samuels, against whom Ruthie now wages continuous war. She has a pack of girlfriends I can't keep straight, who've tried to fix her hopelessly hybrid hair into a slightly limp globe and who dress her up in a shiny, vinyl way that Mrs. Samuels calls "criminal."

Ruth's all set to go to college in the fall, over at NYU Uptown, in University Heights, where she's planning to study history. "History?" Jonah asks, surprised. "What possible use is there in studying that?"

"Not all of us can be as useful as you are, Jonah," she mimics in her best FM announcer style.

We meet most of her inner circle one night, when they come by to drag Ruth to the movies, three black-dressing girls. The lightest of them makes Ruthie look vaguely Latina. They can barely contain their mirth at me and Jonah, and they start shrieking the moment Ruth follows them out the apartment and pulls the door shut. Ruth grows tighter with them until, over Da's objections, the weekend outings become regular and she's rarely there anymore when Jonah and I do make it uptown for Friday dinner. Over the course of the summer, we manage a full reunion only three times. But all four of us, and Mrs. Samuels, too, are sitting eating together in the same room in early August when Da announces, "We are going to Washington!"

Jonah is eating latke off the tip of his knife. "Who do you mean 'we,' Da?"

"We. Us. This whole family. Everyone."

"First I've heard."

"What's in Washington?" I ask.

"Lots of white marble," Ruth answers.

"There will be a great objection movement."

Jonah and I exchange shrugs. Mrs. Samuels clucks. "You boys haven't heard about the march? Where have you been keeping yourselves?"

Turns out everyone has been alerted but us. "Jesus, you two. There are leaflets all over town!" Ruthie shows off a little metal button, which cost her twenty-five cents and which is funding the enterprise. She's bought one for each of us. I put mine on. Jonah does coin tricks with his.

Da holds up ten fingers. "The one-hundred-year marking of the Emancipation."

"Which freed no one, of course," our sister says. Da lets his gaze fall.

Jonah raises his eyebrows and scans the table. "Someone? Anyone? Please."

Ruthie volunteers. "The March on Washington for Jobs and Freedom. Mr. A. Philip Randolph has organized—"

"I see," Jonah says. "And might anyone here know exactly when this manifestation is planned?"

Da lights up again. "We go down on the twenty-eighth. You come stay here the night before, so we can catch the early bus they are sending down from Columbia."

Jonah flicks me a look. Mine confirms his. "Can't make it, Da."

Our father, the solver of cosmic puzzles, looks more confused than I've ever seen him. "What do you mean?"

"They're busy," Ruth sneers.

"We're booked," Jonah says.

"You have a concert? There's no concert for August twenty-eighth on the list you gave to me."

"Not a concert, really. Just a musical obligation."

Da scowls. He looks like the famous bust of Beethoven, only angrier. "What kind of an obligation?"

Jonah doesn't say. I could break rank, say I have no obligation. I'll march for jobs and freedom. The instant lasts so long, all my crossed loyalties turn murderous. Then it passes, and I lose my chance of saying anything.

"You should give up this musical obligation. You should go with us for this March on Washington."

"Why?" Jonah asks. "I don't get it."

"What's not to get?" Ruthie says. "Everybody's going."

"This is civil rights," Da tells him. "This concerns you."

"Me?" Jonah points at his chest. "How?" Trying to force Da to say what he has never, in our lives, come out and said.

"This march is the right thing to do. I am going. Your sister is going." Ruth fiddles with her twenty-five-cent Freedom March button, incriminated.

"Da!" Jonah says. I stand and start stacking dirty plates. "Are you getting political on us in your old age?"

Da looks past us, a quarter of a century. "This is not political."

"And your father isn't old," Mrs. Samuels says.

Ruth glares at the woman. "What's wrong with politics?"

A week after the disastrous dinner, Jonah comes back late from Lisette Soer's. Something has happened. He stands in our doorway, wavering. At first, I think he's told her we aren't going to her little gathering after all, that we have to go to Washington with our family for a march that concerns us. Perhaps they've fought over this, even broken. I want to support him, to tell him how good he has always been. As good as his voice. Maybe even better. But his stare stops me.

"Well." His voice sounds shaky and untrained. "It's happened. She's having a kid."

I think, *She's seduced someone even younger than he is.* Then I figure it out. "She's pregnant?" Jonah doesn't even acknowledge. I'm just distraction while he scans the apartment for a surface that will hold his weight. "Are you sure that you're . . ."

He stops me with his eyebrows. "You trying to save my good name, Mule?"

I make him lime juice in hot water and sit on the floor across from him. It's not what I think.

"A *baby*, Mule. Can you imagine!" He sounds like the boy who once scribbled the "Ode to Joy" under a photo filled with stars. "I told her, 'The perfect thing about marrying me is that I can pass for the father, whatever color the kid is.' " His eyes gleam as if he's onstage. His nostrils flare with that crazed intensity she has taught him. "You can't say that about everybody, Joey!" He snickers and drops the cup. It shatters, and he laughs even harder. I clean up the mess while Jonah keeps talking. "She's gone insane. Off her nut. She just kept screaming, 'Do you know what this will do to my voice?' "

He calls her repeatedly over the next few days but gets no answer. "She's doing *Così* again. I'm going to go wait for her afterward."

"Jonah. Don't be crazy. A black guy waiting out on the street by the Met stage door? We don't have the bail money."

I talk him into waiting for her soiree, that intimate gathering of one hundred of her closest friends that keeps us from marching on Washington with Da and Ruth. By the time we arrive at the Verdian nightmare, things are in full swing. Lisette moves around the room in a violet strapless sheath that hangs to her by animal magic. She looks as if she's never been touched by man. She flits from guest to guest, spreading license and joy—all but belting out the aria that will fatally break her weakened heart.

I know with one look into the room. We should never have come. We slink to the drinks table, keeping together. A black man in black-tie regalia stands behind the table. He takes our orders, all three of us avoiding eyes. Jonah's glance keeps darting out to his walking secret, waiting for a chance to corner her. She hits a lull in her rounds, and, cutting through the room's cocktail haze, he materializes at her side. Her hands go out to push on his chest, but I can't read the gesture. The room is riddled with conversation on all sides: a dozen manic topics crawling over one another. But raised on counterpoint and drifting near, I pick his tenor line out of the chorus of noise.

"Are you okay?"

"Brilliant. Why do you ask?"

"Do you think you should be—"

"That's Regina Resnik over there. Isn't she lovely? I'm so glad she's gone over to mezzo. It so suits her. Come with me, boy. I'll introduce you."

"Lisette. Stop it. I'll kill you. I swear it."

"Ooh. Where'd you learn all that fire?"

They lean against the wall, each aping casual. Both whisper, but even the whispers of a trained voice carry. He grips her wrist. On the wall behind Lisette hangs a photo of her as Dido, singing "When I Am Laid in Earth." "Talk to me," he orders.

"Relax. There's nothing to worry about. Drink up. Enjoy yourself."

"Lisette. You're not going through this by yourself. I can take care of the child while you enter your prime. Then I'll be hitting my own stride while you . . ."

"While I what? Say what you were going to say, little boy. While I go into my decline?"

"You've told me yourself: There're no limits to the career I might have. I'm a good bet, Lisette. I can keep you comfortable."

"You'll protect me—is that what you're saying? You'll take care of me and watch out for my poor little offspring when I'm old?"

"I know you think I'm still a child. But someday, we'll be the same age."

"Someday you'll be the age I am now. And you'll hear how young you sound."

"Marry me, Lisette. I can be a good husband. I can be a good father to this child."

"Husband? Father?" She gags on his words.

A trio of riotous high voices approaches them, all talking at once. "What do we have here? Private lessons? Tête-à-tête? You two look like you're about to go do something illegal."

Lisette breezes off, turning the trio into a quartet. I cross to Jonah. "Let's get out of here."

His head wobbles. But he's not ready to go yet. He stalks her through the crowded apartment, clumsy, upwind, spooking the prey every time before he can close in on her. I stand on the edge of the gathering, drowning in the general hilarity. There's no saving him. He catches her at last, by accident, when she turns in the wrong direction. He takes her by the upper arm. "We can do this any way you want. But I told you, Lisette. I'm not leaving you to deal with this yourself."

"And I told you, Mr. Strom. Everything's fine. There's no problem. Do you understand me? *No problem!*"

I'm no longer the only one listening. Nearby conversations fall quiet. Lisette makes a comic show of patting Jonah's head, to chuckles all around. Jonah does his best to grin. As soon as we can do so without disgrace, we run. He swears at her all the way home.

He wants to call her first thing the next day. I make him wait three hours, until 9:00 A.M. She tells him again, over the phone: There is no problem. She has to say it a few times and ways for him to understand. No problem: no baby.

He takes longer to hang up the phone than Mahler takes to resolve a chord. He calls my name, although I'm standing right there. "Joey. I don't understand."

"False alarm. You both should be relieved."

"That's not it. She'd have said that."

I'm not slow. Just stupid. "She lost it." I hear the words. Lost it, in her carelessness.

"When? Thirty minutes before the party? That's what gave her the halo glow?" He wants me to shut up, to never say anything again. But silence will drive him mad. "She's going to get somebody to do it, Joey. If she's not on her way to do it right now. She loves my people. But she'd rather kill my baby than—"

"Jonah. Look. Even if it is yours—"

"It's mine."

"Even if . . . You still don't know that she . . ."

He knows everything. Knows where we've lived our whole lives.

Da calls to tell us what we missed down in Washington. "The whole world at once, walking down Independence Avenue!" Jonah listens to every detail, indifferent, frantic for distraction.

Time confirms Lisette Soer. No problem: no baby. "Taken care of," Jonah tells me. Something in him has been taken care of, too. The gap in their ages closes, faster than he predicted to her. He sits on the piano bench, chin on his knees, fetal. But older than she is.

"She didn't want to lose her peak career years," I say. Every word makes him hate me. "She didn't want hormones wrecking her voice." Didn't want a baby. Didn't want a husband twelve years younger. Didn't want a husband. Didn't want him.

He nods, rejecting my every sop. "She doesn't want black. She doesn't want a kid with lips. Why take chances with your life? Once black is in the blood, it's Russian roulette."

At night, he smashes things. He hurls a plate of spaghetti I've made out the window. It shatters in the street, almost hitting a pedestrian. Now that we need a road trip, we have no bookings. Not that he could sing. The top of his range drops two full steps. He goes out alone and returns reeking of reefer. I chat with him until bedtime about nothing. Jonah, his slack face unrecognizable, sits and giggles. I jabber to a man who can't talk back, all the while terrified that the smoke he's inhaling has already ravaged those vocal cords.

A week later, the Sixteenth Street Baptist Church in Birmingham explodes. We see it on the television, then in the two newspapers we buy the next day. The church is a spew of brick and slag, glass and twisted metal. I'm standing on the scorched, frozen sidewalk outside our house that day eight years ago, while the car waits, trying to recognize my life. I stare at this new photo, swallowing down the taste that rises into my throat, half memory, half prediction.

The bombers have waited for the church's annual Youth Sunday. The explosion rips out the church basement, where the children practice their parts in the special ceremony. Four girls are killed, three fourteen-year-olds and one eleven-year-old. My brother can't stop staring at their photos, running his fingers over their beaming faces until he smears the newsprint. He's a boy of ten, singing a euphoric duet for a church so pleased to have a little Negro singing Bach for them. He's seeing his own little girl a decade from now, the one just taken away from him. Seeing these four dead girls: Denise, Cynthia, Carole, and Addie Mae.

Seven bombings in six months. Bloody battles roll through the streets of Birmingham, like something the United States ordinarily exports abroad. The Reverend Connie Lynch tells the world, "If there's four less niggers tonight, then I say 'Good for whoever planted the bomb!' " Two more black children are killed, a thirteen-year-old shot by a pair of Eagle Scouts and a sixteen-year-old murdered by a state trooper.

The nation I lived in is dead. The president speaks of law and order, justice and tranquillity. He calls on white and Negro to set aside passion and prejudice. Two months later, he, too, is dead. Malcolm says: *The chickens have come home to roost.*

Lisette Soer calls my brother but gets me. She wants to know why he's missed three lessons. She wants him to call her back. The first time, I tell her Jonah's laid up with a virus. She sends him daisies. The second time, I tell her he's gone to Europe and won't be back for a long time. My brother sits ten feet away, barely able to nod. Miss Soer takes the news with stunned rage. Lisa Sawyer, the brewer's daughter from Milwaukee, calls me a lying monkey.

"I don't know what you mean," I tell her. But by now, this monkey has a fair idea.

They gather at the base of the Washington Monument. People pour in from wherever there is still hope of a coming country. They rumble up from the fields of Georgia on broken-down grain trucks. They ride down in one hundred busses an hour, streaming through the Baltimore tunnel. They drive over in long silver cars from the Middle Atlantic suburbs. They converge on two dozen chartered trains from Pittsburgh and Detroit. They fly in from Los Angeles, Phoenix, and Dallas. An eighty-two-year-old man bicycles from Ohio; another, half his age, from South Dakota. One man takes a week to roller-skate the eight hundred miles from Chicago, sporting a bright sash reading FREEDOM.

By midmorning, the crowd tops a quarter of a million: students, small businessmen, preachers, doctors, barbers, salesclerks, UAW members, management trainees, New York intellectuals, Kansas farmers, Gulf shrimpers. A "celebrity plane" airlifts in a load of movie stars—Harry Belafonte, James Garner, Diahann Carroll, Marlon Brando. Longtime Freedom Riders, veterans of Birmingham, Montgomery, and Albany, join forces with timid first-timers, souls who want another nation but didn't know, until today, how to make it. They come pushing baby strollers and wheelchairs, waving flags and banners. They come straight from board meetings and fresh out of prison. They come for a quarter million reasons. They come for a single thing.

The march route runs from Washington's needle to Lincoln's steps. But as always, the course will take the long way around. Somewhere down Constitution are jobs; somewhere down Independence is freedom. Even that winding route is the work of fragile compromise. Six separate groups suspend their differences, joining their needs, if only for this last high-water mark.

The night before, the president signs orders to mobilize the army in case of riot. By early morning, the waves of people overflow any dam the undermanned crowd-control officers can erect. The march launches itself, unled, and its leaders must be wedged into the unstoppable stream after the fact, by a band of marshals. There's agitation, picketing, a twenty-four-hour vigil outside the Justice Department. But not a single drop of blood falls for all the violence of four hundred years.

Television cameras in the crow's nest of the Washington obelisk pan across a half a mile of people spilling down both sides of the reflecting pool. In that half mile, every imaginable hue: anger, hope, pain, new-found power, and, above all, impatience.

Music breaks out across the Mall—ramshackle high school marching bands, church choirs, family gospel groups, pickup combos scatting stoic euphoria, a funeral jubilation the size of the Eastern Seaboard. Song echoes from staggered amplifiers across the open spaces, bouncing off civic buildings. A bastard mix of performers work the staging area—Odetta and Baez, Josh White and Dylan, the Freedom Singers of SNCC and Albany fame. But the surge of music that carries the marchers toward the Emancipator is all self-made. Pitched words eddy and mount: *We shall overcome. We shall not be moved.* Strangers who've never laid eyes on one another until this minute launch into tight harmonies without a cue. *The one thing we did right was the day we began to fight.* The song spins out its own rising counterpoints. *The only chain we can stand is the chain of hand in hand.* All past collapses into now. *Woke up this morning with my mind on freedom. Hallelujah.*

David Strom hears the swelling chorus in a dream. The sound bends him back upon his past self, the day that first took him here, the day that made this one. That prior day is here completed, brought forward to this moment, the one it was already signaling a quarter century before. Time is not a trace that moves through a collection of moments. Time is a moment that collects all moving traces.

His daughter walks beside him, eighteen, just two years younger than her mother was then. The message of that earlier day travels forward to her, too. But she will need more time, another bending, before it will reach her. His daughter walks two steps ahead of him, pretending that this pale face tagging along behind her is nothing she knows. He humiliates her, just by being. He trots and stumbles to keep up with her, but she only walks faster. "Ruth," he calls her. "You must wait up for your old man." But she can't. She must disown the day he carries. She needs to deny him, if she's to have any chance of signaling to her later self or remembering her way into the future she will make, the next time here.

He can't see why he so shames her. He's far from the only white here. Whites turn out by the tens of thousands. He moves through the gathering, the same one that he saw massing at the end of Virginia Avenue that day he came down from Georgetown, only far larger. The crowd has more than tripled since that first outing. Strom looks west and sees himself, a young man, fresh with twenty-eight-year-old immigrant ignorance, about to collapse into his own destiny. Which way did she come that day, his Ruth's mother? He looks to the northeast, piecing back the woman's vanished coordinates as she rushed from her Philadelphia train. Barely older than this girl who walks ahead of him, recalling herself toward some menacing, misread future, the life that life held out for her. "Impossible," she told him several times. She knew already. *Impossible.*

The crowd pushes forward, like that first crowd. He shouldn't think *first.* Strom stands at the curb as this parade passes. Then shortcutting across the hidden radius of time, the same parade circles past him again. There will be another march, one that will, in time, turn this later day earlier again. The crowd will surge on, downstream, and he'll rejoin it there.

They sing, "We shall not be moved." He knows the tune, if not the words. But the words, too, he remembers from somewhere as soon as he hears them. The words arose before any melody at all. *Just like a tree that's standing by the water. We. We shall not. We shall not be moved.*

Rhythm, Strom hears, is a closed, timelike loop. The chorus dies and lifts up again, above the heads of its participants. It circles and reenters, canonic, the same each time, each time embroidered into a new original. Just like a tree. A tree standing by the water. He quickens his pace past the meter of the song. He gains on the moving march, draws abreast of his daughter. She is her mother's profile, only more so: the same bronze in a brighter light. He looks on the girl, and the shock of memory knocks him forward. Every remembrance, a prophecy in reverse. His Ruth moves her lips, singing along, her own inner line. Time stays; we flow.

He sees it at last, after a quarter century: This is why the woman sang that day. Why she stood next to him, voicing under her breath. Why he leaned in to hear what sound those moving lips were making. "Are you a professional?" he asked. And she answered, *"Noch nicht."* Not yet. Moving her lips while another woman sang: This was the thing that made him talk to her, when all the world would have prevented their ever trading a word. The thing that made them try a life together. That makes this later girl, their flesh and blood, walking alongside him, pretending she isn't, move her lips in silent song.

For two years now, she has sung nothing with him. Since her brothers left, she's refused all duets. She, the quickest of them all, the girl who read notes before she could read words. Once, he and her mother couldn't put this one to bed if any voice anywhere north of Fifty-ninth Street was still singing. Now, if she sings at all, it's away from the house, with friends who teach her other tunes, out of her father's hearing.

Ruth was their peace baby, born three months after the eternal war ended. From birth, she had that soul that thought all things were put here

for her to love. She loved the mailman with all her heart for his daily gen-
erosities. She wanted to invite him to her fourth birthday party, and she
cried until they promised to ask him. She loved their landlady, Mrs.
Washington, for giving them a house to live in. She loved Mrs. Washington's terrier as she might have loved God's angel. She sang to total
strangers on the street. She thought everyone did.

At eight, an older boy in the park called her a nigger. She ran back to
her mother on her bench, asked what it meant. "Oh honey!" Delia told
her. "It means that boy is all confused."

She ran back to the boy. "How come you're all confused?"

"Nigger," the boy mumbled. "Monkey girl."

Ruth, the peace baby, child of certainty, scolded him in delight. "I'm
not a monkey girl! This is a monkey girl." And she improvised for him a
chimp dance, something out of her own *Carnival of the Animals*, cupping
her lips and aping primate joy. The boy broke into a nervous laugh, standing there entranced, ready to be wrong, ready to join in until his own
mother came and yanked him away.

"Is Joey a nigger?" Ruth asked on their way home. "Is Jonah?" In her
mind, she'd formed three categories. And hers was the smallest and most
dangerous.

"Nobody's a nigger," Delia answered, stripping the loving girl of all
defenses.

Ruth made friends while her parents weren't looking. She found them
at the mixed school David and Delia sent her to, their belated admission
of how little good they'd done the boys through home schooling. Ruth
brought them home before her mother died, friends of all shades. Sometimes they even came back, after the shock of the first visit. And through
these friends, she learned all those melodies her parents had failed to
teach her, the melodies that drove her into David's study one night, asking, "What am I?"

"You're my girl," he told her.

"No, Da. What am *I*?"

"You are smart and good at whatever you do."

"No. I mean, if you're white and Mama is black . . ."

The answer he gave her then: also wrong. "You are lucky. You are
both." Wrong about so many things.

Ruth just looked at him, a shame bordering on scorn. "That's what
Mama said, too." Like she'd never be able to trust either of them again.

Their children were supposed to be the first beyond all this, the first to jump clean into the future that this fossil hate so badly needs to recall. But their children do not jump clean. The strength of the past's signal won't let them. Strom and his wife, so lost in time, guessed wrong—too early, too hopeful by decades. In every future that his Delia's lips mouthed on that day, she dies too soon and leaves her daughter hearing only how wrong their music was. But they are right, Strom must still believe, about how the double bar will sound. Right that the world will someday hear what its cadence must be. Like a tree by the water. His girl's lips move silently. Two hundred meters and twenty-four years away, off where his Ruth can't hear, her mother's silent lips answer back.

The crowd moves them on. He and Ruth float down this living river, silting out in front of the Lincoln Memorial. Everything horribly the same: same day, same statue, same thrilled hope signing the air, same brutal truth waiting just off the Mall. More posters, more banners, more protests. People have more words now for what they don't have. The sound of these thousands of voices billows, eerie and reverberant, the song of a continent that didn't exist when he was here last. But this is the same human carpet stretching over the curve of the horizon. Strom gauges where he and his daughter stand. He figures where he and his wife were. Dead reckoning, distances at sea.

The mass elation overwhelms him. His sight blurs and his knees start to give, a middle-aged man, faint with heat and excitement. He stumbles for his daughter. She props him up, as anxious about him as she is humiliated. He points a finger at the ground. "We were here. Your mother and I."

She knows the lore: how Strom met Daley, how she came to be. She hushes him, smiles sheepishly at the circle around them. No one cares. Half a million eyes are on the speaker's stand, a quarter mile away.

"Here," he repeats. "Right *here*." She stares at the ground. His certainty shakes her.

A flurry on the podium, and the singing falls hushed. Only when the tunes stop can they hear how many melodies were running at once. The PA's rumble takes a full second to pass over them. The crowd comes to order, fusing into a city-sized camp meeting. One by one, speakers take the stand, each a different shade, each telling this otherworldly crowd where they're heading. The first counsels compromise; the second scorches with fact. The measureless congregation calls out *"Go on, tell it, now!"*

Cameras and microphones capture chapter and verse. Even ABC cuts away from its scheduled soap operas to give the nation its first full look at itself.

Ruth slumps and straightens during the speeches. Her body registers changes in pressure Strom struggles to interpret. She twitches through the white preachers' catch-up bandwagoning. She comes alive for John Lewis, the SNCC spokesman, five years older than she, hurling his indictments down the length of the reflecting pool. He speaks of living in constant fear, a police state, and Ruth applauds. He asks, "What does the government do?" and she joins the piercing response: *"Nothing!"* He speaks of immoral compromise, of evil and evil's only answer: revolution. The mile of people carry him onward, and Strom's daughter is with them, cheering.

Fear of suffocation comes back over Strom. If this crowd turns angry, he's dead. As dead as his own parents and sister, killed for being on the wrong side of a crowd. Dead as his wife, who died for making a life with him. Dead as he will be anyway, when the signal of the past at last remembers him.

The sun turns brutal and the speeches turn long. Someone—it must be Randolph—introduces the women of the movement. An older woman on the dais gets up to sing, and Strom lifts up through his own skull. Still he looks, and still he chides himself for believing the hallucination. There is some resemblance, but only enough to tease the credulity of an old man. The differences are greater. The sheer age, for one: This woman is a generation older than the one he confuses her with.

Then the past swamps him, like pavement swimming up to slam a falling man. "My God. Oh my God. It is her."

His daughter jerks up at his voice. "Who? What are you talking about?"

"There. This one, up there. That is her." The hat is bigger, the dress more colorful, the body weighed down by twenty-four more years. But the sound is the same, at its core.

"Who, Daddy?"

"The woman who married your mother and me."

A pained laugh comes out of Ruth, and they fall silent in the music. The girl hears only an old woman, no voice left, years past her prime, warbling "He's Got the Whole World in His Hands." Banal tune, with even sadder lyrics. Ruth sees what she saw when they taught her the song in third grade: solar system–sized hands cupped around the globe as if it were a prize cat's-eye. What color, those hands? If he ever had the planet cradled, the better part of it has long ago slipped through his cumbersome fingers. The wind and the rain. The moon and stars. You and me, sister. For eight years, ever since she stood screaming to break free from death's fireman grip, Ruth has known what this old lady hasn't yet admitted.

Strom is lost in other songs—"O mio Fernando." "Ave Maria." "America." The voice one hears only once a century—what Toscanini said of her, in Vienna, back in another universe, before that sick metropolis was leveled. And he was right. For it has been a century since Strom heard this voice, if it has been an hour. And even longer since he's had someone to listen with.

The moment passes, father and daughter frozen in separate forevers, waiting for the song to end. Ruth looks over at her father, her face curdled by catching up to the past. This is the woman, the mighty myth she was raised on. Strom feels her disappointment. He holds still in this coda to his wife's shortened tune. He shouldn't have lived long enough to hear this voice again, when his Delia cannot.

More singers follow, with harder memories. Mahalia Jackson releases a mighty "I've Been 'Buked," her unaccompanied voice rolling across the mile of people, parting the reflecting pool like the Red Sea. Then come more speakers. And more after that. The day will never end, nor ever come again. The crowd chafes at the moment, a promise unfilled. Too many speeches, and Ruth dozes. In her dream, she meets her mother in a teeming train station. People crash into them, keep them from reaching each other. Ruth's children have disappeared somewhere in the crowded hall. Her mother scolds her: *Never take your eyes off the little ones.* But Delia sings the scold, up high in her range, in a ghostly accent.

Then the song turns back to speech, and the accent turns to German. Someone is shaking her, and that someone is her father. "You must wake up. You must hear this. This is history." She looks up at him in rage, for once again taking her mother away. Then she swims awake. She hears a swelling baritone, a voice she has heard before, but never like this. *We also have come to this hallowed spot to remind America of the fierce urgency of now.*

Now: the reason why her father wakes her. But the thought nags at her between the rolling baritone thunder: Her father couldn't have known the words were coming until after he shook her awake. Then she forgets, posting the question to a later her. Something happens in the crowd, some alchemy worked by the sheer force of this voice. The words bend back three full times in staggered echoes. Her father is right: history. Already she cannot separate these words from all the times she'll hear them down the years to come.

The preacher starts to ad-lib, stitching together Amos and Isaiah with snippets of Psalms that Ruth remembers from old anthem settings her family once sang together. *Unearned suffering will redeem.* She'd dearly like to believe him. *One day this nation will rise up and live out the true meaning of its creed. I have a dream that my four children will one day live in a nation . . .* She sees herself with children of her own, and still no nation.

Every valley exalted. Every hill laid low. God help her: She can't keep from hearing Handel. Her parents' fault; a birthmark stain. She could sing the whole text from memory. *The rough made plain . . . and the glory of the Lord shall be revealed.*

With this faith we will transform the jangling discords of our nation into a symphony. She lifts her eyes and looks out—brown on brown, all the way to the edges of sight. A massive music, beyond all doubt, but nothing like a symphony. Ruth looks back at her father beside her. His white skin looks sick to her, alien. The thinning gray hair, tangled by the wind, is nothing of hers. The words of this speech roll down his cheeks like waters. She can't remember her father ever crying, not even at her mother's funeral. Back then, he was only bewildered smiles, his theory of timeless time. Now he weeps for these words, this abstract hope, so desperate and obvious, so far past realizing. And she hates him for waiting so long. For refusing to look at her.

Strom feels his daughter's eyes on him, but he will not turn. So long as he doesn't turn his face square on that face, his Delia is still more than half there, at the concert they once shared. When the preacher starts in on those words, the words the voice of the century sang that first day, Strom is waiting for them. He knows in advance the moment when they must start, and when they do, it's because he wills them.

He's known the tune forever. British imperial hymnody. Beethoven wrote a set of variations. Half a dozen European countries have their own flag-waving versions, his fallen Germany included. Yet he'd never heard the American words before that day. He did not, then, get them, but he gets them now, after a quarter century in this place. *Land where my fathers died.* A million times more this preaching man's land than Strom's. But handed out to Strom in New York Harbor, with less question.

Let freedom ring. From the prodigious hilltops of New Hampshire. From the mighty mountains of New York, the heightening Alleghenies, the snow-capped Rockies, the peaks of California. From Stone Mountain, Lookout Mountain, every molehill of Mississippi. From every mountainside.

The words spark like the first day of creation. Now they might join to do it: Now this crowd could roll down this green fairway, an unstoppable army, and take their Capitol, their Court, their White House by soul force. But they are too joyous now for force, too lifted up.

Free at last, the speeches end. Then the crowd, too, is free. Free to go back to their rotting cities and caged lives. The mass disperses, as it did that earlier day. Strom is afraid to move off the spot, knowing that the edge of revelation must still be there, nearby, waiting for him to cross it. The crowd curls past, annoyed at these two snags of flotsam in the stream. Ruth smolders at the man. His reverie maddens her. She sees him missing the evidence. The Black-Jewish alliance is crumbling all around them. It won't even survive the bus ride home.

Ruth starts walking, alone. She has been alone too long. Her brothers are too busy to bother with the present. Her father too trapped by the past. She strides off, sure of her bearing, nursing a phrase from the baritone preacher's speech: "this marvelous new militancy." It feels to her the only useful future, the only one where she won't be forever alone. She heads back to the lot where the Columbia busses dropped them off. Even her father will know to come find her there.

David Strom stands dissolved, populating every spot in this public openness. Here's where his woman freezes in shame, learning she's been singing out loud. Here's where she asks if he's ever heard the legendary Farrar. Here's where she begs his forgiveness, and where they say good-bye forever. Here's where they find the lost boy. There, up there, is where she explains how it's all impossible, their seeing each other again. A mistake, to think any story ever finishes.

When he looks up to locate his daughter, she's gone. His body goes cold. He has expected this. A sick fascination grips him, and the fifty-two-year-old begins to trot, bolting several steps one direction, then banking away toward another. He's more panicked by the pattern than by the prospect of any real danger to her. She's safer on this Mall with these marchers than she is in New York, walking home from school. She's eighteen; the capital is crawling with police. And yet, he knows the threat is infinite, as large as time. She's gone: nowhere, anywhere. He turns on the straightaway along the front of the monument, running, calling, propelled by prophecy.

He jogs to the spot where they found the lost boy. His girl isn't there. He retraces their steps—not his and Ruth's, but his, Delia's, and the child's. He moves toward the giant statue. He looks up at Lincoln, the figure he didn't recognize then, the one who the boy said never freed the slaves. Every speaker at this rally confirms him. Strom gets as close to the steps of the monument as the press of bodies allows. She must be there. She isn't. She's been and gone. She'll swing past a minute from now. Ten minutes. How can any two paths ever intersect in time? The field is too great and our wakes too small.

He does the probabilities in his head: two random walks, at staggered starts. The odds of finding her are best if he stays within a narrow radius of this spot. For this is where they returned the boy, back in time, back before the war, back when love between him and his wife was still impossible.

This is where his daughter finds him, thirty minutes later. He's the easiest mark on the Mall to find: a white, scattered man tacking at random across an ebbing sea of brown. She'd have found him ages ago, but for her certainty that even the brilliant scientist would eventually stumble onto the obvious. She strides up to him, shaking her head: helpless, hopeless.

He's wild at the sight of her. "I knew I'd find you here!" He trembles in the face of explanation. "Where were you? Who have you been with? Did you speak with anyone?"

His need is so great, she can't even rebuke him. "For God's sake, Da. I've been sitting on the bus, waiting for you. They're going to leave without us."

She drags him back as fast as his legs can manage. Only once does he stop and cast a glance behind them. No revelation. Nothing to see. A man on roller skates in a sagging red sash. Volunteer crews sweeping up the litter. He feels the past's signal dim and slip away from him: free at last.

SPRING 1940–WINTER 1941

David Strom married Delia Daley in Philadelphia on April 9, 1940. As the two exchanged vows in the dingy Seventh Ward courthouse, the Nazis swarmed over Denmark and Norway.

The ceremony was small and apologetic. The twins wore matching tan crocheted vests over light burgundy dresses. Charles put on his Sunday best. Michael's limbs stuck an inch too far out of the blue suit that had fit him at Christmas, just four months ago. Dr. Daley's majestic black tux showed up the groom, who nevertheless outdid himself in double-breasted gray. The bride's mother wore the shining green silk dress she wanted to be buried in. The bride was radiant in white.

Whatever else she thought about this marriage, Nettie Ellen had assumed it would take place in Bethel Covenant, where she and William had married. The church she'd raised her children in. The church where Delia learned to sing.

"They won't do it," Delia said.

"Reverend Fredrick? 'Course he'll do it. That man baptized you."

"Yes, Mama. But he didn't baptize David."

Nettie Ellen considered this technicality. "He can do that first, then take care of the two of you after."

"My mother wants you to convert." Delia groaned the eleventh-hour warning while holding her fiancé in the dark of his tiny Washington Heights apartment. She tried to laugh it off, and failed. "So we can marry in her church."

His answer, when it came, unmade her. "Once, I almost made a religious conversion. When I was a boy. My father taught mathematics in a special high school. My mother made clothing, at our home. Before the world war, they were lucky to work at all. But under Weimar, for a little while, times were better to the Jews. Rathenau became foreign minister. Israelites were burning new paths."

"Blazing."

"Yes. Then times were not so good again. People said the Jew lost the war for Germany. 'Sold it down': Do you say it so? How else could Germany lose such a conflict? Even my father was becoming anti-Jew. He had no patience for the old ways. Everything was reason and formula. His family was German, for two hundred years. For a long time already, they had been students of fact and reason, not the shul. Then, when I turned eleven, anti-Jews forced Rathenau's auto off the road and filled him with bullets. They even bombed the auto to be certain."

Delia gripped him tighter about the wrists. He returned her grip: all he had in this life, except ideas.

"After that, the way is blocked for most Jewish people, even the non-Jew Jews, like my father. They can only advance in jobs without interest or value. Like theoretical physics! And even here, the paths are often closed. My father wanted every chance for our future. My sister became an office worker. He hoped for me to finish Gymnasium. Even such a dream was tempting the gods to strike us. I finished Gymnasium two years early, but here I am: still in school. And Max Strom, who was finished with Judaism forever, and his Rebecca, they are . . ."

He lapsed into a dark place, hiding in a neutral country. Delia followed him, knowing the way from long remembering.

"So it always has been, for us! A funny thing, though. When I was still young? My father said, Go: convert. Advance. Become something. I read your Gospels. I found much truth in them. 'Do not gather up treasures in this world, but gather them up in the next.' These words moved me deeply. But they left me in a paradox."

She shook her head, up against his chest. "I don't understand."

"If I want to get ahead, I must become a Christian. But if I use Christianity to get ahead, I lose my soul!"

She laughed a little with him, against him. "Light gain makes heavy loss."

"*Light?* This is what you say?" He sat up and scribbled the phrase into his dog-eared notebook, along with a diagram. To show his father someday, on the other side of light.

She watched him, fascinated. "The notebook industry's going to explode after you marry me, Mr. Strom."

"You are Christian?" he asked. "You believe in the Gospels?"

No one had ever asked her point-blank. It had never struck her to ask herself. "I believe . . . there must be something bigger and better than us."

"Yes!" His whole face celebrated. "Yes. This is what I believe."

"But you don't call it God."

His eyes worshiped her. "It's bigger than my name. Better."

She felt his forehead with the back of her hand, teased up his eyelids with her finger, and gazed in. "I thought mathematics ruled everything for your people."

"My people? My people! Yes, surely. But what rules mathematics?"

Later, just before she left to spend the night at her cousin's on 136th and Lenox, he asked, "How will we raise our children?"

Nothing would ever be a given again. From now on: slow, tentative, experimental, at best an hour ahead of what they knew for certain. The bird and the fish could fall in love. Building the nest would go on forever.

Every answer seemed a death. At last, she said, "We can raise them to choose."

He nodded. "I can become a Christian."

"Why?" She straightened his glasses and pushed his limp forelock back on top of his head. "So we can marry in a church? That's light gain if ever there was one!"

"Not for the church. For your mother."

It sounded to her more than the Gospels. She wanted to say, *You out-Christian the Christians.* But in that year, the compliment would have damned him. "No. Let's get married by a justice. We'll get the earth part straightened out first. Plenty of time for heaven later."

They married in a courtroom as his Europe burned. He wasn't sure how many Stroms might have come, even if he could have found them. Years ago, while he was at university, his sister, Hannah, had married a Bulgarian intellectual. Their mother had to be dragged to the wedding. *An atheist socialist Slav: The man's not anything! Where will they live? Who will they be?*

The Daleys turned out for them in force, all the way out to Delia's cousins. The courtroom filled with a forced merriment that the justice, an old Spanish exile darker than Delia, scowled at. Was the couple sure? he asked. But that's what he had to ask everyone. And everyone, the judge's sagging, defeated shoulders attested, was always sure.

Three of Strom's Columbia physics colleagues—all Central European émigrés who shared Strom's passion for music—came out together. "To console your unfortunate bride." The happy, napkin-scribbling wizard had helped each of them with some intractable problem in multiple dimensions, and they owed him. A day in Philadelphia was almost a vacation. But seeing them arrive, Strom wept in gratitude. They sat in the back of the court during the lightning ceremony, sparring with one another in something like Greek, hushing only when the justice glared.

Franco Lugati, Delia's teacher, was the only other white, if Jews and scientific Gypsies were granted that category. He even went back to the Daleys' home for the reception. For his gift to the newlyweds, he brought a chamber group—oboe, bassoon, two violins, viola, and continuo—to accompany him in Bach's wedding aria, "O Du angenehmes Paar." The blessed pair were far too keyed up to hear the music. Dr. Daley stood at attention in front of the instrumentalists, guarding them. The players left in a rush, one quick glass of punch after the final cadence. Lugati, mixing excuses with blessings, departed soon after.

Once the musicians left, the real music began. The twins launched into a semirehearsed burlesque of their sister's chosen art, complete with lavish costume changes, their parody so broad even David Strom figured out when to laugh. Then, knowing their father could hardly forbid it in such a crowd, they laid down a shimmering, sulky, piano twelve-bar while Michael improvised on the sorrows of matrimony and the end of freedom. Charles ran upstairs and returned with his tenor sax. By then, Delia Daley Strom was too blissful to pretend to moan. She even shoved her sisters on down to the lower lines and did some freewheeling, high-note riffing of her own.

A hum began from somewhere in the gathered group. Nobody in particular started it and everybody in general moved it along. Strom caught a few words—bits and pieces from the Song of Songs, overhauled in a place as far from Canaan as this world got. But into this, the world's earliest wedding song, there came words he'd never heard. "Brother, are you here to help her? Give me your hand and pray. Sister, are you here to help him? Give me your hand and pray."

Without consultation, the knot of wedding well-wishers became a chorus, a five-part soul swell edged with a remembering minor seventh that even in happiness would never go away. For the first time in his life, Strom felt surrounded by a nimbus of comfort. Before the tune ended, the song worked itself up into a wave of pure pulse, repeat on repeat, every ornament beyond duplication.

Throughout the singing, Strom's colleagues huddled on the Daley sofa, their side plates of rolled meats teetering on their laps. "You are being rude," David told them. "This is a wedding. *Kommen Sie.* Go right now, and talk to the others before I throw you all out on your ear."

But they turned to him in wonder, recounting fresh stories of the Berkeley cyclotron and its brand-new assay—traces of an element that took matter beyond nature's terminus, uranium. Strom's new wife had to come drag him out of the heated speculation and back into his own party.

Dr. Daley, his eyes on the knot of whites, overheard the news. "You gentlemen are saying that we've succeeded in transmuting matter? Mankind is finally making new elements?"

Yes, the Europeans told him. Everything had been rewritten. The human race had entered on a whole new day of creation. They made a space for the doctor on the sofa, drawing him diagrams, sketching tables of atomic weights and numbers. And so the room divided, not white against black, not native-born against newcomer, not even woman against man, but singers versus sculptors, with no one knowing which art was more dangerous or which had more power, at last, to reverse the world's hurt.

The food ran out and the guests started to disperse. A peace settled on the remaining party, peace shattered only when Nettie Ellen let out a toe-curling shout. She vanished into her kitchen pantry, bringing back an elaborately decorated broom. "We were supposed to do this as soon as you two entered this house!"

She formed the guests into a ring, making even the groom's Promethean friends flesh out the circumference. She grabbed her husband. "You make yourself useful for a change." She shoved the broom into his arms.

Everyone laughed except the astonished bride. The broom—a loose handmade straw scimitar—was braided through with flowers and ribbons of all colors, the handiwork of Lorene and Lucille, under their mother's guidance. On the ribbons hung dozens of magic charms: infant Delia's spoon, a lock of her ten-year-old hair, the ring she wore throughout grade school, a picture of her pushing twin baby buggies, a tin eighth note, the curled-up program of her first church recital. The broom bore a few bits of her husband, too: the hands from a broken wristwatch fixed at three o'clock, a single Columbia University cuff link gotten off him by conjure, and a tiny plate Star of David just like the one he'd never worn, picked up in a secondhand shop in Southwark.

Dr. Daley began the invocation, his throat a wide, cold river. "Every couple needs their friends and family if they're to make it through together to the end of the day. This couple . . ." He waited in silence for his voice to return. "This couple will need everyone they have."

While the doctor spoke, husband and wife were made to grasp the broom handle and sweep through the circle's arc. They spun around twice, touching all the hours of a full day. The bristles of the decorated broom summoned each person present to witness.

"A couple can't be just a couple if they want to stay a couple."

Someone in the circle said, "Go ahead."

"A couple has to be less than two and greater than two, both at the same time."

"That's right," Nettie Ellen said, the broom coming around to her.

"This is the strange mathematics—this is the non-Euclidean geometry of love!"

David Strom looked up at his father-in-law, his grin pulling in his ears.

Delia, too, appraised her father, her head hanging like a screen door that had lost its spring. Her doctor father, the man of reason, was a closet preacher.

"These two could be put away for what they're doing. But not in this state!"

"No sir!"

"And not in the state where they choose to live."

"State of grace," someone called.

"Bless and keep," William Daley ended, so quietly that neither newly-wed realized he'd finished. The freshly minted husband was made to lay the broom down lengthwise in front of his bride. On the count of three, they leapt over and landed together on the far side.

All sound gave way to laughter and applause. "What does it mean?" the groom asked.

The bride's mother answered. "It means you're all swept out. It means the house you're moving into is clean, top to bottom. All the bad past that ever happened to you—swept away by this broom!"

Her daughter shook her head, for the first time in her life, truly disobedient. Her eyes were wet and hunted, pleading *no*. "It means . . . It means we couldn't, we couldn't even . . ."

David Strom stared at the floor, the bangle-woven stick of straw. His bride's words came clear to him. Centuries outside the law, barred from the sight of God, stripped of even this most given human right: *to marry*. He stared down at the floor, this court, this church, this broom, this makeshift promise witnessed and sealed in the eyes of those who were also denied, this secret, illegal agreement, this unbreakable clause stronger than any signed contract, more durable than the most public pact, a vow to match in hardness the swept soul . . .

The last of the guests vanished, leaving only their wishes. Then the Daley children grew shy and sullen, the size of their sister's deed only then dawning on them. Dr. Daley and Nettie Ellen sat the couple down on the front room settee and drew, from nowhere, a decorated envelope. Delia opened it. Inside was a Brownie print of a spinet.

"We're having it shipped to you," Dr. Daley said. And his daughter broke down, sobbing.

They took their leave in a series of sober hugs. Together, the new couple left their parents' house, David carrying their luggage and Delia clutching the broom. In a rented car, they drove back to New York. They could go nowhere for their honeymoon but his bachelor's apartment. No place on the map would take them in. But in their shared horizon that first night, their gladness outfell Niagara.

They moved through marriage with careful bewilderment—a little allegro duet of solicitude. Shared life was nothing either could have predicted. It fascinated them, all their assumptions so comically wrong. They watched each other at table, over the dishes, in the bathroom, the bedroom, the apartment's entryway, all custom upended. They laughed sometimes, sometimes incredulous, now and then standing back in belated revelation. In the better part of love's rough negotiation, they got lucky, for what was ironclad rule to one was often, to the other, a matter of no difference at all.

Learning each other was steady work, but no harder than the work of being. Misunderstandings seemed always to leave the harmed one strong enough to comfort the harmer. The disgust pressing in on them from outdoors only drew tighter the shelter they made. Singing, they spoke the same language. In music, they always found their pitch. None of their circle of musical acquaintances ever heard them speak harshly to each other. And yet, they never called each other anything but their given names. Simple recognition: the best of available love. They could be silly with each other, full of sass and mock laments. But their deepest endearments were not words.

Two months into their joined life, they were evicted from their apartment. They'd waited for the blow. Delia sailed forth in her finest flare-shouldered blue dress, threading the blocks around City College, looking for a place that would let them live. She carried on searching, farther north, through neighborhoods of ambiguous boundaries. Her husband had glimpsed something. "The bird and the fish will build their nest from nothing!" And for a little longer, the thought comforted her.

The nest appeared by magic. A woman Delia met while singing in a poorly paid choir steered them toward that saint of all mixed species, Mrs. Washington, and her Jersey freestone house in Hamilton Heights. Grateful Delia fell at the woman's feet, offering free service—floors stained, walls replastered—until the day that even their delighted landlady couldn't, in good faith, allow her to labor anymore.

For months, they lived in a blessed, stilled present. Then Delia came back from the doctor's with a terrified smile. "Three of us, David. How?"

"You have already seen how!" he said. And she had.

She sung to her firstborn in the womb. She made up whole operas of nonsense syllables. At night, she and David sang part-songs at the spinet that her parents had given them. She pressed her midsection against the vibrating wood, letting the harmonies spread in waves through her.

David put his ear to her roundness and listened for whole minutes at a time. "Already busy in there!" He heard frequencies beyond the ear, making time's transforming calculations. "Tenor," he predicted.

"Lord, I hope so. They get all the best parts."

In their bed, under the gray wool blanket, in such darkness that not even God could spy them out, she told him her fears. She spoke to her husband of permanent doubt, that daily, ingrained wariness so thick in her she couldn't even see it. She spoke of turning away from baiting, of smiling at concealed slight, of never knowing, of the drain of having to stand, every minute of her life, for everything but herself. Her dread, as she named it, was more swollen than her belly. "How can we hope to raise them?"

"Wife. My beautiful woman. No one knows how to raise children. Yet people seem to have done this from the very beginning of the race."

"No. I mean, what will they *be*?" And then, what won't they?

"I don't understand." Of course not. How could he?

"Bird or fish?"

He nodded and opened his arms to her. And because there was nowhere else now, she let herself be held.

"Do we really get to say?" he asked. She laughed into his collarbone. "The child will have four choices." She jerked back to arm's length, looking at him, astonished. "I mean, this is just mathematics! They can be A and not B. They can be B and not A. They can be A and B. Or they can be neither A nor B."

Three more choices than this child would ever get. Choice and race were mortal opposites, more distant than Delia and the man she'd married. Another mathematics came upon her: Their child would be a different race from at least one parent. Whether they had a choice or not.

Delia went back to Philadelphia for the birth. Her father's house was ample, and her mother's experience ampler still. Her husband followed, the moment his university duties permitted. Luck brought David there in time for the delivery, at the end of January 1941, in the hospital where William practiced, three-quarters of a mile from the better hospital where Delia had once worked.

"He's so light," the awed mother whispered when they let her hold her baby.

"He'll darken up," Nettie Ellen told her. "You wait and see." But her firstborn never did what he was supposed to do.

David wrote his parents the news, as he had after the wedding. He told them all about their new daughter-in-law and grandson, or almost all. He looked forward to the day they would all at last meet. Then he dispatched the letter into the growing void. Fortress Holland had fallen. Rotterdam, where his parents had fled, was leveled. He wrote to Bremer, his father's old headmaster in Essen, asking everything in coded phrases, using no names. But he heard nothing in return, from any quarter.

The Nazis took the Continent, from Norway to the Pyrenees. France and the Low Countries were gone. Every week, silence fell across a new theater—Hungary, the Balkans, North Africa. At last, word came—a scribbled note from Bremer, smuggled past the censors, through Spain:

I've lost track of them, David—Max and Rachael. They're back in Germany, if they're anywhere. An NSB neighbor in Schiedam, where they had gone into hiding, turned them in for *Arbeiteinsatz*. Nor can I reach your sister; she and her Vihar may have escaped. But wherever they've gone, it's only a matter of time . . . This is the end, David. It doesn't matter what you say you are. You'll all be rounded up and simplified. Not one left, and you don't even get your moment of Masada.

David showed his wife the note—everything he'd long suspected. Each now held a part of the other's destruction. In that stripping away— *Your family, gone*—they became each other.

And the boy, in turn, became his parents' reason for being. Terrified by the uncountable minute threats in every gust of wind, warming his milk to within half of a half degree, they weekly learned that children survive even their parents' best intentions.

"He's here already," Delia marveled. "Already a little man! A whole self all figured out, no matter what our plans. This whole baby act is just to humor us. Isn't it? Yes, it is, isn't it?"

The baby gurgled in the face of all his parents' fears. They took him back to Philly when he was three months old. The boy performed for his grandparents, babbling on pitch, reducing his grandfather to a heap of proud anxiety. The old family practitioner paced and fretted. "Watch! Watch out for his head!"

"You ought to be thinking about getting him baptized," Nettie Ellen said. "He's getting awful big awful fast. Oh, yes you are!"

Delia answered simply, the result of weeks of practice. "He can get baptized when he's older, Mama. If he wants."

Nettie raised her hand, fending off strange denominations. "How you going to raise him up, then? You going to raise him Jewish?"

"No, Mama. We're not."

Nettie Ellen held her grandson to her shoulder and looked around, ready to run with him. "He's got to hear something about God."

Delia smiled across the room at her husband. "Oh, he hears about God almost every night running." She didn't add, *In Lydian, Dorian, German, and Latin.*

The doctor deferred the question that Delia knew was coming. She fended him off by pure will, until she was ready with an answer. Delaying until that day when her new family's strange mathematics invented a fifth choice.

We're all four home for Christmas, Ruth's second winter vacation since starting college. This is a third of a century ago. The sixties have just started turning fab. The *Billboard* charts are overrun by shaggy Anglo-Saxons in Edwardian suits who've just discovered all the taboo chords that black Americans worked their way through decades ago. A black poet dances his way to the world heavyweight title. Ruth gives me a fan magazine devoted to this poet boxer for Christmas, and she laughs insanely when I open it. After, she gives me my real present: a picture-book history of the blues. I give her a black pullover that she asked for and that she won't take off for the next two days, even to go to sleep.

She runs her fingers through my hair. "Why do you comb it down like that?" she asks.

"Comb?" Jonah snickers.

I don't know what to say. "That's the way it grows."

"You should pick it out. You'd look much better."

Jonah scoffs. "You got another job for him lined up?"

Something has blown up between the two of them. I blame it on the times. The hatless boy president is dead—all his delays and explanations spattered across the back of a top-down convertible. Our father is still mourning the man a year on. The man's successor has signed civil rights into law, but way too late to head off the first of the long, hot summers to come.

Harlem starts it, and my sister is there. Five months back, a white policeman killed a Negro boy two years younger than Ruth, fewer than a dozen blocks from where our family once lived. CORE organized a protest, and a group of undergrads from NYU Uptown turned out, Ruthie, my new collegiate activist sister, among them. They started to march up Lénox, the model of peaceful demonstration. But something went wrong when the leading protesters met the police rear guard. The march came apart and madness was everywhere, before Ruth or anyone else knew what was happening.

The way she tells it to us, over Christmas dinner, it took just seconds for the street to scatter in screams. The crowd cracked open. Ruth tried to run back to the parked busses, but in the chaos, she got turned around. "Somebody shoved me. I bounced off this policeman—totally panicked—who was slipping around on the sidewalk, clubbing everything that moved. He came down with his baton, smashed me right here." She shows me, grabbing my upper arm.

More terrified than hurt, she plunged into a sea of twenty-year-olds, all running for their lives. Somehow, she ran through bedlam and found her way home. Even five months afterward, she can't say how. One more Harlem child dead, and hundreds of marchers wounded. For two days and nights, the streets overflowed. Then the fire spread to Bedford-Stuyvesant and, down the following weeks of a bad summer, to Jersey City and Philadelphia. All of this has come to pass just a year after a quarter of a million people—Da and Ruth lost among them—descended on the Mall to hear the greatest act of improvised oratory in history. " 'I have a dream,' " my sister says, shaking her head. "More like a nightmare, if you ask me."

After the riot died out to nothing, Ruth took her smashed upper arm back to University Heights, where she promptly changed her major from history to prelaw. "Only law can leverage what's coming, Joey." History could no longer predict what was happening to her.

History, today, is just the four of us. Da paces in his study. Jonah lies on the floor playing with a new sliding puzzle Da has given him for Christmas. I sit on the couch next to Ruth, who has been gearing up toward some question all day. "What do you remember about Mama?" she asks me at last, still trying to fix my hair. Like requesting an old dance number. *What do you remember?* She really wants to know, although she's already decided.

Jonah and I have scheduled this break in our barnstorming—eighteen stops in every drafty auditorium across the Pacific Northwest—to try to reconnect with our family. It's been months since I've sat and talked to Ruth. She's lived through a riot, changed her major, taken to dressing exclusively in tight, dark clothes. She's exploding with ideas she's picked up at school. She's reading books by famous social theorists I've never even heard of. She's passed me by in every way but musically. She feels like my unknown, exotic, well-traveled cousin. Once she was almost my age. Now she's amused by my doddering senility.

"About Mama?" I answer. Mama's old trick: Always repeat the question. It buys you time. "You know. Nothing you wouldn't recognize."

Ruth stops fiddling with my hair. She picks up the blues book, my present from her, and flips through it. "I mean from before my time."

"You should ask the man." I point my thumb at our father, who paces with excitement in an oval between the sterile dining room and his chaos-infested study in a state of quantum perturbation. Ruth just rolls her eyes. She's right: Da is already unreachable, halfway back to whatever dimension Mama now occupies. He knows every message our mother's memory might have for us, but he can't give them to us. Now and then as he paces, he calls out a few private syllables of insight for no one, then collapses at his desk to jot down a stream of hostage symbols. Recently, his age-old enigma has thickened. Fitch and Cronin, two Princeton-based acquaintances of his working over in Brookhaven, have just shattered the past: Temporal symmetry is violated at the subatomic level. The world's equations are not cleanly reversible. Da paces about the first floor of this new, alien house in a wide, closed loop, shaking his head, singing, "Ah, sweet mystery of life!" The tune has started to grate on our collective nerves.

It's just the four of us now, in a house belonging to no one. The old home in Hamilton Heights is banished to some planet of memory none of us can reach. Our father has bought this place, just over the Washington Bridge, in Fort Lee, New Jersey, on the colossal miscalculation that we children might take this transplanted nest to heart. He can't see us anymore. This neighborhood makes all three of his offspring look like a foreign exchange program. Ruth, in particular, looks like a UN delegate from one of those newly decolonized countries no one's heard of.

Even this holiday reunion is a sad fabrication. Ruth has found a wreath and a few lights, but no one had the heart to decorate. The first night of Hanukkah descended into TV dinners. For Christmas, we order take-out Chinese. The day's angel messengers are off on some other hillside, miles up the Palisades, announcing the mysterious birth to those flock-watching shepherds who've managed to remain more easily taken in by good news.

This is the last time we'll be together like this. Every time is something's last, but even I can feel this holiday's scattering. Ruth sits on the couch, nursing her arm, the bruise still tender almost half a year on. Something I can't name has been happening to her while she's been away at college. Something happening all across the country, and already it's moving too fast for me to see. The country's clock has slowed to a stop, and mine races on. Mama always said I was born antique. "This one's born ancient," she once whispered to Da, after she thought I was asleep. "And he's going to get older and older every time humanity turns him around."

Now I've become Ruth's grandfather. She looks at me, begging for memories only I am aged enough to reach. I'm her only reliable link to a room that time's sliding walls have sealed her off from. She's changed while we've been touring. Never again Ruthie, Root. She has on tight black jeans and that black V-necked pullover, her fine curly hair combed out unsuccessfully on her head, as if she's swum halfway across some fast-running stream of fashion before panicking and swimming back. Her body has turned perfect since the last time I saw her. I look away now when she leans toward me, asking, "What were we all like, when I was small?"

"You could sight-sing before you could see. You were the best, Ruth. You could sound like anyone."

We've not sung together, as a family, this entire vacation. It's all any of us have thought about, but no one's brought it up. Jonah and I practice daily, but that doesn't count. The only other notes are Da's, his million looped refrains of "Ah, Sweet Mystery": "Ah, sweet mystery . . . of life . . . At last I've found you!" To which we kids add no harmonies.

"Joey, you dope!" Ruth's accent has drifted over the river toward

Brooklyn, as if other people have brought her up. Which they have, I guess. "I don't need to know about me!"

The two of us look to Jonah, the only one truly old enough for solid data. He lies on the floor, toying with the sliding puzzle, humming to himself the glimpse of arpeggiated paradise from the end of Fauré's *Requiem*. Jonah's eyebrows go up at our aimed silence——*Hmm?*—as if he hasn't heard us. He has registered every word. "Altos!" he explodes. "Vee need more altos!" Time-honored mockery of Da, from our earliest years. The accent is so good that even Da himself stops pacing around the dining room to smile at us from out of what was once his body.

"Altos!" I come in, a dutiful imitation. "Ven, voman, you are going to make me some altos?"

Ruth, the real mimic, grins at the canonic gag. But she adds no line of her own. Ruth, the alto, hasn't sung a note since she went away to school. She pinches up her cheeks in frustration. "No! No, you stupid crackers." She slaps the sofa with an open palm. She grabs my forearm, leans in, and bites it. "What do you remember about *Mama?*"

This is my sister's only holiday question—my sister, who was barely ten when the world she wants to know about came to its early end. She was the first to discover the blaze, where all our photos burned. Now every memory she has has drifted, unreliable, except for her memory of the fire itself. She thinks Jonah and I still have entry rights. But she's not even wrong. Our sister wants back in to a place with no dimension, no place of entry, not even the one she asks us to invent for her now.

I wait for Jonah to answer. Ruth prods him with her toe. But he's gone back to humming Fauré's sickly sweet burial Mass and sliding around his puzzle squares. It falls to me, in this life, to make sure no one I love goes unanswered. This Christmas, more than ever, that is a losing proposition. I need to start looking for a better job. "You want stories from before you were born?"

"Before. After. I'm not in a position to be picky." My sister talks to her hands, which dethread a tasseled pillow that she picked out for Da as a gift. It's gold and burgundy, nothing she'd let near her own apartment. "God's sake, Joey! Give me whatever you have!" Her voice is a jagged alto gasp. "Mama's blurring on me. I can't hold her."

The things I know for sure, my sister doesn't need. The things she needs from me, I'm unsure of. I root through the jumbled shoe box of the past, all my own snapshots burned. A midday shadow falls across the couch, between us. Mama's here. I can see her: that face I once mistook for my own reflection, its mouth the idea of mouths, its eyes, all eyes. But she has blurred on me, too. I'm no longer certain of her features. With nothing to check against, I can't be sure what I've done to her. "She looked like you, Ruth. A slightly taller, fuller you."

Jonah just grunts. Ruth looks down, upset and skeptical. "What did she sound like?"

The timbre of her voice is in the bones of my skull. It's packed so close, I can't get to it. The sound is second nature, but to try to describe it would be worse than a cheap recording. Not this; not that. I can't say what my mother sounded like, any more than I can hear myself sing. Not even Jonah could reproduce her.

"She . . . I don't know. She used to call us 'JoJo.' The two of us." I kick my motionless brother. "Like we were one child with two bodies."

"I remember." Ruth squirms in place. This isn't what she wants.

"She was a fantastic teacher. She used to praise and correct us in the same breath. 'JoJo, that's wonderful. That sounded just about perfect. Try it a few more times, and I bet that octave leap will be right there.' "

Jonah just nods. He has never been big on *comprimario* roles. When he's not center stage these days, he doesn't bother coming onstage at all.

"Did she have students?"

"All the time. Talented adults, coming back to music. Teens and older kids, from around the neighborhood."

"Black or white?" All my sister asks is what the world asks her. It's the only question of any interest, over in the Bronx, at NYU Uptown. In the twitchy streets of Harlem. The old neighborhood.

I turn on the sofa, sidesaddle, to look out the front bay window. No whiter street. I imagine myself a child of this neighborhood, a suburban boy, biking through its manicured blocks, tossing a pigskin across its tracts, party to a fantastic mass evasion. Our parents couldn't have lived here if they'd wanted. I couldn't have walked down these streets as a boy and lived. Even now, for this briefest family visit, some neighbor is already on the phone to the police. Tonight, if I walk around the block, they'll stop me for questioning.

It strikes me how rarely Jonah and I left our house, even in the city. We stayed home, huddled over the piano, radio, and record player. Mama had to force us out. I count up how many of our childhood tormentors were black, how many white, how many as ambiguous as we were. We covered most bases. "Both, I think. Mostly black?"

I glance at Jonah, the only real authority. That one-year difference between us was almost an eon back then. Jonah sets down his puzzle and, in a deep gospel bass, intones, "Red and yellow, black and white, they are equal in His sight. Jesus loves the little students of this world."

Ruth laughs, despite herself. She leans over him and slugs him in his softening underbelly. "You're a complete asshole. You do know that?"

It's supposed to be playful. He looks up at her impassively. I blunder forward, before there's an incident. "She was still taking lessons herself, you know. At Columbia, when we were little. She even studied for a little while with Lotte Lehmann."

"Is that supposed to be something special?"

I fall back, mouth open. "Lotte Lehmann?" All I can think to say. A name I know better than my own blood relatives. "You don't . . ."

"Naw," Jonah says, standing and stretching. "Nothing special. Just some famous diva bitch."

Ruth's ignoring him. It's the most productive thing she can do with him these days. "What made Mama get interested in classical? Can you think of any reason why she would choose . . ." Ruth circles the question, unwilling to go to war over something she's not sure she can win. "How good was she, anyway?"

I want to say, *How dare you ask?* "Don't you know? You must have heard her just about every night for a decade!" The words come out harsher than I mean them. Ruth takes them across the face. I start again, softer. "She was . . ." The voice against which I measure every other. The sound that my sound strove for. A richness not even Jonah has learned to produce, one that came from giving up everything. "Her voice was warm. High and clear, but full-blooded. Never a hint of a slavishness." I hear the word before I can suppress it.

"Sun coming up on a field of lavender," Jonah says. And I remember why I'll always do anything for him.

It almost satisfies Ruth. But she nurses a bigger demon, one that only gets hungrier when the smaller ones are fed. "What was she *like*?"

Even Jonah looks up, hearing the edge in her voice. I know just what Ruth wants one of us to say. But I can't give her the Mama she needs. "When we were little, she used to walk us around, each of my feet on top of hers. Each step we took was a beat of a favorite tune. As if the song she sang was the motor of this enormous walking machine."

My sister's face is a spoiled watercolor. "I remember. 'I'm *Tram-pin*'. I'm *Tram-pin*'.' "

"She cut out little stars from silver paper and stuck them up on our bedroom ceiling, in the shapes of constellations. She got us growing potatoes and lima beans in water glasses. She was a perpetual sparrow-rescuer. We had an eyedropper always filled with sterilized milk, ready for every maimed creature between Broadway and Amsterdam."

"She used to beat us boys with nail-studded planks," Jonah confides. "She'd softened a good deal by the time you came along."

"That's not true," I say. "Never anything longer than carpet tacks."

Ruth throws up her arms in disgust and stands up to leave. I hold her and bring her back down. She sits, with a little persuading. There's no place else for miles around for her to go.

I stroke her bruised arm. "She'd fret for two days if the subway attendant looked at her the wrong way while she was putting her dime in the turnstile. But she was tougher than Jesus. She could hold her breath longer than she could hold a grudge. She loved having people over. At least to sing."

None of this is any use to Ruth. "How black was she?" she asks at last. She studies my face for any cheating, a pitiless external examiner.

Black is now the going term. Ruth started using it not long after hearing the young John Lewis at the March on Washington. *Negro* is for gradualists, appeasers, and Baptist ministers. *Black* means business, and it's taken hold, after what's happened this year in Harlem, Jersey City, and Philadelphia. The country keeps changing the problem's name every few years, like a liar elaborating his excuse. I'm not sure what the word for mulatto is at the moment. It'll be something new a year or so from now.

I don't even glance at Jonah. I know his answer. "How black?" *One drop,* I want to tell her. That's the going rule. No scale, no fractions, no *how much.* Not something this country lets you have degrees of. The only shade Americans see: One spurned size fits all. Ruth's known as much since the age of ten. But now she's decided there's more to know. Another scale, one that measures degree. I meet her gaze. "What exactly are you asking?"

"What do you think I'm asking? Don't be a fool, Joe."

"Fool?" I pull my arm off her. "You can sit here asking these questions about your own mother, and *you* call *me* . . ."

Ruth turns her head. Her neck is the shade of beautiful polished walnut. She waves her hand, casting a fishing rod. "Okay, I'm sorry." She won't fight me. I'm the peacemaker, the conciliator, the crossover, the thing she won't, yet, call me. I reach out and take her slender fingers. She turns to fix me, shaking her head a little, hurt, puzzled, needing me to be with her on this. *Like,* her look says, *you were once.*

Jonah stops his humming, but his words are almost chanted. "You mean did she talk Gullah before you were born? Did she cook chitlins and pone?"

She doesn't even turn to look at him. "Who asked you, Tuxedo Boy? Do you have a hang-up with this? Does my asking about this make you uptight?"

Hang-up, uptight: the terms of the hour. My sister is, as ever, ahead of her time. Or at least ahead of me. A part of me, the white, simplifying part, wants to keep Da from hearing us. But I won't hush her; I won't drop my voice. We died when Mama did; no one left to protect.

A supplicant hang of my sister's head, and I'm her brother again. Ruth needs from me what no one else in the world can give. From those few extra years I lived with our mother, she thinks I might know the secret of what black *is.* She knows Jonah won't hand it over. But me: She imagines I can show her how to slip into it, like an old chemise of Mama's Ruth has found hanging in a closet of her dreams. My refusal to tell her is simple perversity.

"What can I tell you, Ruth? Her father was a doctor. One of a couple dozen in all of Philadelphia. More broadly educated than Da. Her family was better off than his. You know what they lived with, Ruth. What's the secret membership? What else do you want me to say?"

I'm telling her, saying already, by all I can't say. Very black. Blacker than her mule sons can enter into. Black inflicted and black held on to. Black by memory and invention. The daily defensive backing off and smiling, twenty generations of remembered violence that doubled you over even when you thought you weren't doubled. Black in the way that is the sole property of high yellow. The day never passed when she didn't store it up, when she didn't have to touch its protecting core. But every bit as light in skin, hair, features, and all things visible as her mixed-race daughter, who hates herself for not being simpler.

"Black, Ruth. She was black."

"Black's all right," Jonah says. "Some of my best genes are black."

Ruth says nothing. She's turning over the possibility: The truth is too monochrome and stupid to make it out. She makes some massive reverse Middle Passage, getting no closer to that coming future our parents imagined than this starter bungalow in the suburban desert of New Jersey, where none of us can live.

"You don't know, Joey. A year and a half, back and forth across the

Harlem River from University Heights . . . I sit there in those classes full of crew-cut white business majors, all set to carry their fiancées back home to Levittown. The nice ones look at me like I'm neutered, and the cretins come on to me like I'm some kind of exotic barnyard lust machine. Or they want to know why I talk the way I do. They ask me if I'm adopted. If I'm Persian, Pakistani, Indonesian. Or they're afraid to ask, afraid to *offend* me."

"Tell them you're a Moor," Jonah said. "Works every time."

She's looking at me, her eyes welling, like I can help save her. Save her from America, or at least from her oldest brother. "Nobody at school knows what to make of me. Gangs of those Irish-Italian-Swede dumpling girls talk to me slowly, through foot-long smiles, swearing how close they've always been to their domestic help. But at the Afro Pride meetings, there's always some sister grumbling out loud about infiltration by funny-featured, white-talking spies." She nods her head, quizzing me: *Right? Right?* Whatever our parents taught us to recognize in ourselves must have been wrong.

This is what she's learning at school. Every day, she braves a neighborhood that's fleeing from her and her nonexistent kind. Last year's residents are halfway to White Plains by now. The university has tried to salvage the uptown campus, hiring Marcel Breuer to stamp it with pedigreed European high modernism. But all the slabs of brutal concrete, grafted onto McKim, Mead & White's Italianate arcades, only make it obvious to everyone that the game is over. Soon University Heights will sell its buildings to a "transitioning" community college for pennies on the dollar.

And my sister knows she's to blame. I put my hand on her shoulder, the safe top knob of the collarbone. Five inches up from where that policeman grazed her. "Ruthie. Don't let them beat you up. You aren't the one, you know."

"Don't patronize me, Joey. What would you know about it?"

"Joey?" Jonah says. "Joey's an authority. He wrote the damn book. *Gray Like Me.*"

Ruth just snorts. My sister thinks I'm over the line, right up there as light as Jonah, just because I trot out onstage with him night after night, to the applause of near-blind octogenarians. It doesn't occur to her that Jonah makes me look darker than I've ever made her.

"What would I know about it? Nothing, Ruth. Totally ignorant."

"Well, where the hell were the two of you, then, while I was growing up? You could have run interference for me. You could have told me what . . ."

I can't answer. More time has passed than I can account for.

"Ron yoor own race," Jonah says. "Ron yoor own race." I jerk up and shush him, hoping Da hasn't heard him go this far. My family is coming undone, faster than it did that first time. Ruth's words swing in the air in front of us. She's past the first accusation and is on to a new one, below skin, up against bone. Where *were* we when she was growing up? Off somewhere, singing. Who said we should spend our childhoods away? Why can't I remember her between the ages of eight and eighteen? This woman disappears into no place I recognize. Worse by far than the one I lived through. The identical place, changed by the run of a mere few years.

My sister opens her throat, but nothing comes out. She tries again. At last, the rasp catches. "Jesus Christ. It gets so old."

"It was old when Mama was young."

"What were they *thinking?*"

Jonah says, "I'm not sure *thinking* is the operative word."

I inhale. "They wanted us to grow up believing . . ." But that's not quite right. "They thought they could raise us beyond . . ."

The bile in her throat spits out in an acid laugh. "*Beyond?* They got that one right, didn't they?"

My eyebrows work away on nothing. "I must have been seven before I saw how different Da's and Mama's tones were."

"You, Joey, are beyond *beyond*." My sister shakes her head, mourning me. But around her eyes, the folds of recognition.

"They wanted us to be what happens next. To transcend. They didn't want us to see race. Didn't even want us to use the word."

"*Da* didn't," Ruth says.

Jonah's gone back to his slider puzzle, to Fauré. It makes Ruth cover her ears and shriek. When she stops, I say, "They were very big on the future. They thought the thing was never going to get here unless we leapt into it with both feet."

"We leapt into something all right." Ruth wrinkles her nose. "Soft, warm, foul-smelling? Is that the future we're talking?"

"Parents have done worse," I say.

"What did she do with her blackness? After she married. After she had us three."

This *blackness*, a misplaced trinket—a ring of keys, a scribbled note. Jonah hears what I do. "It's probably still around here somewhere."

Ruth presses her head. "Well, you two seem to have set it down somewhere you can't find."

My fault, everything I can't deliver to her. But she's my sister, every drop, and there's nowhere she can go without my finding her. I circle around the one thing, that fact I ought to tell her, even though she may read it totally wrong. Yet whatever Ruth might make of it, I have to give it over. For it's already hers.

"It's true. She used to laugh more, early on. Dance around. Like there was music all the time, even when there wasn't."

Ruth bobs her head, taking my concession, for which she gives thanks. Neither of us owns this woman's memory. But as Ruth's head bobs its short, shallow dips, I see pure Mama. She enters into our mother without knowing it, reincarnating her, body for body, nod for nod. She moves the way Mama used to move on those nights when our family sang, five lines flying in all directions.

Then Ruth holds still. "What happened to her?" Her voice falls off to nothing. For a beat, I misunderstand. This is the question I've dreamed of asking *her*, a hundred times a year since our mother's death. Dreamed of asking Ruth, the one who had to look on it, up close, with a ten-year-old's eyes, seeing the evidence, watching the house while Mama burned alive. Then I come back. She means: What happened to her, *before* what happened to her?

"I think . . ." Two notes in, I have to stop. Breathing has always been my downfall. Jonah can go for huge phrases and never break for air. I'm already gasping after a measure and a half of moderato. "I think it wore her down. Hammered from all sides, every waking minute, even when nobody said anything out loud. Her crime was worse than being black. Destroying the barriers, marrying: the worst any two people can do. This woman spit on her once, as we were coming out of the elevator to the dentist's. Mama tried to make us think it was an accident. Can you imagine?"

"I think it was an accident, Joey," Jonah says. "I think the woman was trying to hit you."

"She gets spit on, *and* she has to keep us from thinking there's anything wrong. Wore her out finally. More shit than even she could survive."

"Joey sa-id 'shi-it,'" Ruth calls out, singsong. The best Christmas present I could give her. And her burst of delight: the best she could give me, or ever again will.

"Her face changed, when we were older. What would you call it, Jonah? Punch-drunk. Like she'd never imagined it could be so hard. She couldn't even take us into a clothes store to outfit us for school without a security guard cornering us. No right course left, except to send us away."

Ruth's own face glows at the notion, as if these horrors vindicate her. She leans back on the sofa, her body relaxing into confirmation. She savors the record of our mother's blackness, the first description of that shade where Ruth can go join her. She turns her full brown eyes on me. "How many sisters and brothers did she have? All together."

I look at Jonah. His hands go up and his eyebrows down, Pagliaccio-style, a burlesque of innocent ignorance.

"Where do they live?"

Jonah's on his feet. His muscle-twitch walk leads him into the kitchen for what's left of our sesame chicken Christmas dinner. Ruth turns at his sudden departure, and I see it for a second in her face: *Don't leave me. What have I done?*

"Most of them still in Philadelphia, I guess. She took us to see her mother once. Right after the war. We met in a diner. We weren't supposed to be there. That's all I can remember."

Jonah comes back from the kitchen, his mouth full of chicken scooped straight out of the white cardboard delivery carton. Ruth won't even glance at him. She speaks only to me, now. "Was that the only time?"

"Her brother was there at her funeral. You remember."

"For God's sake. Look at us! How can we not know our own grandparents?"

Her pitch shatters Jonah's Buddha smile. I say, "You'd have to ask Da."

"I've asked him for ten years. I ask him once every three months, and he never does anything more than grin at me. I've asked him every damn way I know how, and get nothing but detached, evasive crap. 'You've met your grandparents already. You'll meet them again.' The man's out there beyond the Crab Nebula. If the three of *us* disappeared for twenty years, he wouldn't even notice until the day we showed up again. The man doesn't care what's happened to us or where we're headed. He's lost in scientific mumbo-jumbo. 'Time isn't a flow. Nows don't succeed one another; they simply are.' What kind of arrogant, intellectual, self-satisfied . . ."

Jonah sets down the carton of sesame chicken. Maybe he needs both hands to talk to her. Maybe he's just finished eating. "Hey, Rootie." Her turn to flinch at a taboo word. "Hey, squirrel." Jonah, too, somehow believes all nows simply are. He sits down on the couch again, on Ruth's other side. He shoves her right shoulder, an old team sport where he and I, our little sister between us, volley her body back and forth like a metronome. The game once occupied the three of us for endless stretches: a slow increase of speeds, Jonah calling out tempi, me keeping the beat, Ruthie giggling in the life-sized accelerando until we hit a crazed "Prestissimo!" Jonah pushes her now, and, caught off guard, Ruth gives a little. So I shove back, but even with this first nudge, we feel her stiffen. She isn't playing anymore. It takes Jonah halfway to andante to give the game up for lost. I see his face, too, flash an even briefer fear: *I'll hurt you before I'll let you refuse me.*

Ruth lays an open palm on each of us, a last secret handshake of non-belonging. As little as we look or feel like siblings now, she must take us in, the only ones on this earth her exact internal shade. She pats me on the shoulder: nothing in writing, just the quick attempt to get past all this. The pat turns into a riff, one beat per syllable—the whiff of the irrepressible dotted Motown she's been listening to exclusively these days. "How did she start fooling with music that, music that . . ."

"That didn't belong to her?" Jonah's voice floats a lazy challenge. He's ready to go at it if she is.

"Yeah." That showdown courage born in terror. "Yeah. That wasn't hers."

"Whose is it? Who owns it, girl?"

"White German intellectual Jewish guys. Like you and Da."

Our father, back in his office, thinks we're calling him. He calls back in mock long-suffering, "Yes? What is it this time?"

Jonah appraises Ruth, almost shaking. A Brahms vibrato. "You could chant before you could speak. You read music before you could read. You think that because somebody dragged our great-great-great-grandfather onto a European ship against his will, a thousand years of written music is off-limits?"

Ruth holds out her palms. "Fine. Cool it."

"What music do you think she should have—"

"I said *cool it*. Shut the—" She breaks off. She won't go to the brink with him. Not this vacation. Not this year. "Just tell me." She looks away from Jonah and, by elimination, toward me. "Why did she stop singing?"

I start. "What are you talking about? She never stopped singing!"

"If she got that far in, if she was as good as you two say, if she trained . . . If she went through all that grief, why did she stop halfway? Why didn't she have a career?"

"She did have a career," Jonah says.

"Churches. Weddings." The words issue from my sister's mouth, dismissals. I want to tell her, *If those mean nothing, you'll never know the woman.* "I'm talking about a real career. Recitals. Like the two of you have."

"I suppose that was our fault. We kids came along and put an end to recitals." I feel it for the first time: We curtailed her. "I'm not sure she ever felt the loss. 'The praise is in the doing.' That's what she used to say."

"What are you saying? Of course she would have felt the loss." But before Ruth can ramp up, Da staggers out of his study, grinning, a pale, paunchy vacationer at one of those Catskills resorts, who has just shoved a perfect game of shuffleboard. His once-creased pair of black slacks, maroon argyles, gray loafers, brown belt, light blue shirt, white tee, and rust-colored cardigan mimic the clothes Mama bought for him fifteen years ago. Great loops of yarn unravel from the sweater around the indifferently patched edges. He has made himself a home in a world without other comfort. He lurches toward us, pure excitement, expecting—no, *knowing*— that his children will share his pleasure in this new revelation. He doesn't make many errors in calculation. But when Da misses, he misses big.

His hands speak. Mirth spills from him, a jowled elf of empiricism. He tries out on us, his last three contacts with the outside world, the latest, most outrageous shaggy-dog story his physics has yet concocted. "It's incredible!" His outrage and delight are children of the same mixed marriage. The silverware is mounting a sprawling performance of *Faust*. His eyes moisten with the thought of this latest bizarre twist to the quantum world. "Nature is not invariant with regard to time. The mirror of time has broken!"

Jonah raises both hands. "We didn't do it, Daddy-o. We didn't break nothing."

Da nods and shakes his head at the same time. He takes off his glasses, daubing his eyes. He's like a bachelor suffering the toasts of his friends the evening before his wedding. "You can't believe this." He holds out both palms to keep the invisible forces of nature from rushing him to the punch line. "The electrically neutral kaon."

Jonah pinches his smirk between thumb and index finger. "Ah, yes! The Electrically Neutral Kaon. The latest British beat group, right?"

"Yes, of course! A rock group!" Our father waves his hands in front of him, canceling all jokes. He removes his glasses again and starts over. "This kaon flips between particle and antiparticle in a way that should be reversible in time. But it *isn't*." As the terminology gets more technical, the accent thickens. "Imagine! A strange particle, an *antistrange* particle, that can somehow tell forward from backward. The only thing in the universe that knows the difference between *past* and *future*!"

"The only thing in *your* universe."

"Ruth? Again, please?"

"Everything in *my* universe knows the difference between past and future. Except you."

Da nods, humoring her. "Let me explain this to you."

Ruth is on her feet. She's Mama, only a shade darker. Faster. "Let me explain *this* to *you*. I'm sick of this total self-absorption."

Da looks at Jonah, his lay-world touchstone. "What's eating her?" The slang, wrapped in his Teutonic accent, sounds like a big-band leader in a Beatle wig.

"Ruthie wants to know if she's a *Schwarze*, a half *Schwarze*, an anti-*Schwarze*, or what?"

"Fucker."

Da doesn't hear, or pretends not to. Particles decay, irreversibly, all over my father's face. But he remains a study in rapid calculation. He looks at his daughter, too late, and sees. "What's this about, sweetheart?"

She's desperate, begging, full of tears. "Why did you marry a black woman?"

Their eyes lock. He denies this sneak attack. "I did not marry a black woman. I married your mother."

"I don't know who you think you married. But my mother was black."

"You mother is who she is. First. Herself, before anything."

Ruth recoils from his present tense. She would rush into his arms for safety. "Only white men have the luxury of ignoring race."

Da wheels, danger on all sides. This is not the route down which his mind inclines. His face works up an objection: "I'm not a white man; I'm a *Jew*." The hands illustrate, start to rise like a flock of meanings. But he's smart enough to strangle them in flight. His words inch over this landscape, looking for cover. "Abraham married a black concubine.

Joseph . . ." He points at me as if I were my namesake's keeper. "Joseph married an Egyptian priestess. Moses said the stranger who comes to live with you, who takes up as your family, will become as one who is born in your own country. Solomon, for God's sake! Solomon married Pharaoh's daughter."

I don't know this man. Whole vanished generations, ancestors whose existence I've never imagined rise up from their pebble-strewn graves. My father, the protector of no doctrine, the believer in nothing but causality, turns before my eyes into an interpreter of the Torah. I can't bear Ruth's silence. I blurt out, "Goodman. Goodman and . . . Schwerner." I surprise myself, remembering the names, even though they died just last summer—Freedom Summer, when Jonah and I were performing in Wisconsin.

"What about them?" Ruth challenges.

"Two white men. Two Jews, like Da. Like us. Two men who didn't have the luxury . . . you're talking about."

"You wouldn't know anything about luxury, would you, Joey? These men were no older than you two. Your age, out there on the front line. Chaney died for being black. Those other two were in the line of fire."

My throat would make sounds, but I can't shape them.

"The Jews can't help us," Ruth says. "It's not their fight." Her voice betrays the universe she needs from Da. The one he can't give her.

"Not our fight? Not *our* fight?" Our father teeters on the edge of the irreversible. "If one drop makes a *Schwarze*, then . . . we're all *Schwarzen*."

"Not all of us." My sister falls away. She is ten again. Breaking. "Not all of us, Da. Not you."

This is how my family spends Christmas of 1964. I would say our *last*, but the word means nothing. For every last breaks forward into a next. And even last things last forever.

MY BROTHER AS FAUST

Fame caught Jonah when he was twenty-four. It felt as if he'd been singing lifetimes. In fact, he was still a child, by every measure but skill.

The skill had solidified, each one of his teachers handing him some piece of foundation. Jonah's trick was to keep the skill as fresh as that moment fifteen years before, when he startled our parents by joining their quotations game. He walked out onstage bemused, in front of growing audiences who'd heard through the musical mill that something remarkable was happening. He looked around the hall as if about to ask directions from the nearest usher. My hands touched the keys, and he opened up, amazed.

And somehow Jonah would convince each audience that he, too, was discovering the purity of his tone that very night. His face lit up, ambushed by this wondrous accident. The room would draw in a collective breath, witnesses at the birth. He ran a kind of devout, aesthetic con game, all in the higher service of the notes. *I can fly!* He pulled off the stunt four dozen times in the course of a year, and every time, it took my breath away.

His fast passages hung motionless in flight, every note audible: one of those stop-action photographs—a bullet halfway through the width of a playing card, or a corona of milk after the droplet hits. He had more power now, but his pitches were still so focused, they could pierce cloth. He found the mystery of tone that all his teachers had carried on about, each one meaning something different. His sound was secure. He never faltered, never made you feel you needed to stave off disaster with your own concentration. Even at the top of his range, he floated for measures without strain. His warmth passed into your ears like a whispered confidence, a friend you'd forgotten you had.

Maybe splendor is nothing but convention. Maybe the corroded soul can still mimic a saint. Who knows how we hear care or decode comfort? But all these things were Jonah's when he sang, even when he sang in languages he didn't speak. Singing, he owned what his speaking voice disowned. For the space of an hour, over the run of three octaves, my brother constructed grace.

In February of 1965, three black men gunned down Malcolm X a few blocks from where Da fed us *Mandelbrot* and taught us the secret of time. We performed the night of his murder, in Rochester, New York. While thousands marched from Selma to Montgomery, we were driving from East Lansing to Dayton. The night Rochester exploded, we sang in St. Louis. When Jacksonville burned, we played Baltimore.

Every one of those nights, Jonah used Da's secret of time. Leave the earth at unthinkable speed and you can jump into another's future. His beauty in that year came from freezing out everything that wasn't beautiful. While he sang, nothing else mattered.

I could have lived that life forever—college towns paying on arts sub-sidies, midsized cities building cultural capital by bringing in obscure first-rung talent at third-rung prices. It was enough for me. With sound pouring out of us, night after night, I had no other needs. But Jonah wanted more. Onstage, he could sing:

> Ah me, how scanty is my store!
> Yet, for myself, I'd ne'er repine,
> Tho' of the flocks that whiten o'er
> Yon plain one lamb were only mine.

But offstage, his eyes caught every glimmer in professional music. Ca-reers were taking off all around him. Teenage André Watts soloed with Bernstein and the New York Philharmonic. "Jesus, Mule. What does he have that you don't?"

"Fire, edge, passion, speed, beauty, power. Aside from that, I play just like him."

"He's a halfie, too. Hungarian mother. Tell me you couldn't pace him. You can do everything that guy does."

Except soar. But Jonah was one of those people who assumed everyone could soar who chose to step off the cliff.

Grace Bumbry led his list of career obsessions, especially after *Die schwarze Venus* scandal broke at Bayreuth. We heard her interviewed for German television about the hubbub. "Jesus, Mule. She speaks better German than both of us put together." Jonah hung a stunning photo of her on his closet door. "At last, an opera star as sexy as the roles she plays. Carnegie at twenty-five. Met debut at twenty-eight. I've got four years, Joey. Four years, or I'm history."

But that fabulous woman was miles from anyone who attracted Jonah in real life. She was the polar opposite of the woman whose memory he drew on every recital night to drive his harsher passages into dissonance. Since his break with Lisette, we were off the party circuit, working as we hadn't worked since being named America's Next Voice. Jonah was pulling himself inward, culling, smoothing, focusing, building a revenge by the only means he had.

For all his hunger, Jonah was smart enough never to push Mr. Weis-man. Our agent knew more about the music business than the two of us ever would. He knew how to start a rumor, feeding it week after week.

Our bookings multiplied. We sang in cities I thought would never let us sing. We sang in Memphis, as far south as we'd yet gone. I was sure we'd be canceled, all the way up to the moment we walked out onstage. I kept looking into the hall, waiting for my eyes to adjust, to see the audience's hue. They were the same color they always were.

Memphis blurred into Kansas City, the Quad Cities, St. Louis. We walked down to Beale Street, where the baby Blues was left out howling in the rain. The street felt self-conscious and short—two blocks of music bars looking like a theme park, the Colonial Williamsburg of the one true American art.

Like America, we had to be discovered again and again. Mr. Weisman, a patient conductor building a long crescendo, edged us back to our hometown for a cleverly orchestrated theatrical revelation. Over months, he laid the groundwork for our breakthrough. He booked us into Town Hall for early June. We paid expenses ourselves. Ticket sales wouldn't defray more than a portion of costs. We scraped up what remained of Mama's insurance legacy and gave it to the hall managers. Not enough remained for more than perfunctory advertising. Jonah wore the thin, crazed smile of a gambler as he handed over our check. "One blown entrance and we'll have to look for real jobs."

We blew no entrances. The Schubert had gone better out west, and the Wolf never reached the intensity it had on his greatest nights. But his Town Hall concert stood above anything Jonah had achieved. Right before the curtain, my brain spun with adrenaline. But Jonah never looked so calm, so expansive as when desperation was on him. To me, the stage lights of Town Hall felt like interrogation lamps. Jonah walked into them beaming, scouting the auditorium like an adventuring boy.

We'd gone back and forth over the program, waffling between safety and danger. We started with "The Erl-King." We needed something certain to open with, and we'd done that piece so many times, it could have galloped along by itself after throwing both of us. Then, with Goethe as a bridge, we went with Wolf's three *Harfenspieler* settings, every pitch in those complex textures a dare to disaster. Then we did three of the Brahms opus 6.

"What's the link?" I asked during the planning.

"What do you mean, 'What's the link?' Wolf hated Brahms's guts. They're joined at the hip."

That was connection enough for him. In fact, Jonah mapped out the whole recital as an enormous arc of death and transfiguration. Part one was our retreat from the world into aesthetic solitude. Part two was a full-blooded race back into the mess of living. His Brahms brought down the first curtain with that last word on nineteenth-century beauty. We led the audience back from intermission by resurrecting "Wachet auf." Jonah had the idea that this old chorale prelude—always performed with a wall of singers—would make the perfect solo. The tune's sailing self-evidence was my brother's birthright. "Zion hear the watchman singing."

In his inner ear, Jonah heard the watchman call so slowly, it sounded like a bell buoy in the night. At his tempo, those four pitches topping the opening triad turned into the universe's background radiation. Most listeners never know how much harder it is to make a soft sound than a loud one. The breakneck tear will always upstage the legato sustain, but the latter is harder to pull off. Slowed to stopping, Bach's huge, expanding hover held more terror for me than any other piece in our concert. Jonah wanted my prelude to unfold so gradually that the audience would forget about his chorale lines until his next shocking entrance. We passed our parts back and forth, swapping figure and ground. His nine stark phrases flowed over my intervening elaborations like ice sheets across a forgotten continent.

From glacial Bach, we jumped off into our trio of Charles Ives show-stealers. We did them in flat-out New World roughness. He turned the last, "Majority," into a hooting lark. By the time the audience rolled back off their heels, they were too deep into raucous Americana to be alienated. Jonah pegged the persona of the pieces so perfectly, we actually drew laughs and whistles as we pulled up at the end of the bygone parade.

Then we sprinted to the finish and sent them home humming. He wanted to do a crossover, partly to show he could and partly to do at least one number we'd never done in public. "Good for our moral character. Gotta keep you fresh, Giuseppe." The two of us arranged "Fascinatin' Rhythm," sprinkling it with all the crazed quotations we could remember our parents singing as counterpoint to the hackneyed song. Our gimmick was a steady accelerando, slow enough to seem wayward at first, but winding up, by the last verse, with Jonah riding through the syncopations so fast, he wrapped his lips around the syllables only by miracle. Out of pure nervousness, I goosed it even more than we meant to. But Jonah shot me a dazed smile of thanks during the applause.

We closed with "Balm in Gilead." The audience wanted him to finish with some aerial tenor feat, strange, difficult, and dazzling. He gave them the simplest tune he'd ever sing, pitched smack in the fattest part of his range. The choice mystified me. Mama had sung the song when we were young, but no more often than she sang a million others. Only at the concert did I figure it out. He'd picked the song for Ruth. But Ruth wasn't there. Da was front and center, next to the patient Mrs. Samuels. Ruth's seat next to them was empty, and only I knew how much her absence rattled him. "There is a balm in Gilead to make the wounded whole." He sang tentatively, testing to see if it were still true. By verse two, the verdict seemed a toss-up. He ended in a place beyond judgment, his singing itself the only thing close to a proof of that promise.

The softest possible ending, the simplest kind of start. The house erupted before my last chord died away. We hadn't planned an encore; Jonah refused to tempt fate. So it wasn't until the applause died down and we were alone on the brutal stage that Jonah whispered, "Dowland?" I nodded without registering. Thank God he also chose to announce the choice to the house, so I could hear. And time stood still again, as it did each time my brother said so.

Without doubt, Jonah's was one of the strangest New York debuts ever. I'd have called it courageous had I thought he knew what he was risking. He simply picked what he liked to sing.

I saw Lisette Soer in the back of the hall as we took our bows. It's impossible to make out faces when the lights are trained on yours. But it was her. She wasn't applauding. She was holding one hand over her mouth and with the other, on her breast, flashing an awed victory. If Jonah saw her, he made no sign.

Backstage was giddy. I'd stumbled into a documentary film about myself. Every year of our lives was present in cross section. At one point, I stood pumping the hand of a stranger who praised me at length before I registered him as Mr. Bateman, my longtime piano teacher at Juilliard. Jonah did worse: A middle-aged woman cornered him, repeating, "You don't know who I am, do you? You don't recognize me!" Jonah stalled, wagging and grinning, until the woman started to warble. Her shot voice hinted at a vanished glory, ruined by nothing but accumulated days. She burbled up the line *"Wir eilen mit schwachen, doch emsigen Schritten."* We rush with faint but earnest footsteps. Jonah still didn't remember the name Lois Helmer, even as her voice's imprint came rushing back to him. He remembered that first public performance but couldn't remember the boy who had sung it. The joy, the trust, the total ignorance: Nothing visible remained, from this distance. All he had left were the lines of that great duet. So the two of them stood and sang through the first four entrances from memory, under the noise of the buzzing, embarrassed crowd, one voice headed toward gravel, the other sailing past the furthest point that the first had reached in her prime.

A thin man with sparse but luxurious goatee wandered around on the edges of the gathering, standing out among the sea of dark suits in his tight black jeans and a headache-inducing green-and-blue paisley shirt. In a lull, he crossed the room toward me, smirking behind the facial hair. "Strom Two. What's on, brother?"

"My God. Thad West!" He felt like some supporting opera buffa figure squirreling off the stage to greet me in my aisle seat. I clutched him by his elbows, which hung cool and loose. "Jesus, Thad. What the hell are you doing here?"

"Had to come hear you cats play. You two stomped. Have to tell you. Really stomped."

"Where are you living?"

"You know. Here and there. Mount Morris Park."

It flashed through me: He meant *in* it. "You're living in New York? And you've never . . . What are you doing with yourself?"

"Oh. Making music. What else?"

"Really? What are you playing?"

He laid some names on me I'd never heard. He mentioned some clubs, gave me addresses. I didn't know how to respond. I stood staring at my old childhood roommate. Adulthood sat on me like a toad. "We'll come listen soon." In some other, better-executed life.

"That's right. Come soon. We'll blow you something cool."

"Has Jonah seen you yet? Does he know you're here?" I looked around the room and spotted him, surrounded by old Juilliard classmates already working him.

"I'll catch up to the master when he's not so mobbed." He didn't say it cruelly, but I was getting my lie back. Thad still loved my brother. But plainly, he no longer cared for him.

I felt myself grinning too much. "So where the hell is Earl when we need him?"

"Earl's in Nam, man."

"*Viet*nam?"

"No, man. The other one."

I couldn't grasp it. Earl the irreverent, the invincible, caught up in something so stupidly real. "They drafted him?"

"Oh, no. Earl enlisted. Wanted to see the world. He's seeing it now, I guess."

The joy of smacking facefirst into my own past ground to a standstill. "Thad, Thad, Thad. I'm going to come hear what you've got going."

He smiled, unfooled. Then, from nowhere, he said, "You remember that thing they painted on our door? The red fingernail polish?" Buried in childhood, and yet the drawing was still there, after a decade, defacing the door we shared. "Remember? *Nigel*." I didn't even have to nod my head. "That your first time, for something like that?"

I shrugged and flipped my palms. Every time's the first. It was still a thrill to him, that anonymous assault. A badge of honor. Downtrodden by association. Thad didn't have a clue. He didn't want the everyday human idiocy. He wanted some darker, more soulful suffering, some grand affliction to redeem his fatuous Ohio past. Now he had that, living in Mount Morris Park, blowing cool, scraping by. The only thing was, he could have his fill and walk away anytime.

Thad gestured around the room at all the old folks in suits. He shook his head. "Look at you, Strom Two. What the fuck, huh? What would Nigel say?"

I looked down at the shine of my Italian shoes. I wanted him to be proud of me. He wanted me to be my color. He, too, wanted me to leave Town Hall to its owners.

"Do me a favor, Strom Two?" He looked around the room, smiling through the side of his mouth. "Keep this scene hopping, will you? Shit's dying on the vine."

"Hopping."

"That's right." Thad slapped my proffered hand and vanished.

Jonah and I made it home after 3:00 A.M., worthless and still wired. There was nothing left to do but try to sleep and hope there'd be a newspaper notice. Not even necessarily a good one. Just some acknowledgment that something had taken place. Jonah might have sung the stars down from heaven, but if the house critic had been suffering from reflux, the lifeline unrolling in front of us would have unraveled. My job that next day was to venture outside and buy every newspaper I could find. Jonah's was to lie in bed and come up with how we were supposed to make a living now. He kept returning to the idea of night watchmen.

He was still planning when I threw the crumpled-up *Times* on top of his prostrate form. "*Wachet auf*, you bastard. Arts section, page four. Howard Silverman."

"Silverman?" He sounded frightened. *No*, he'd claim later. *Only groggy.* He tore through the pages and found the short review. "'A near-perfect voice, and Mr. Strom's 'near' is no cause for regret.'" He looked at me over the newsprint. "What the hell does that mean?"

"I think it's supposed to be positive."

It sounded, in fact, as if the man were writing with an eye toward the blurb on Jonah's first recording. "'While wrapped in consummate technique, this young man's sound has something deeper and more useful in it than mere perfection.'" Jonah's eyes glinted with total larceny. "Holy shit."

"Keep reading. It gets better."

Silverman went on to note our buckshot programming, calling the second half "a breath of New World fresh air, and a convincing rejection of today's too-predictable approach to the art song." He threw in the obligatory cavils—something about occasional eccentric phrasing, something about losing a little velvet in the fast passages. The core reservation came just before the end. According to Silverman, the youthful magic needed more real-world run-ins, more headfirst tangles with experience to ripen into full emotional complexity. "'Mr. Strom is young, and his slightly callow loveliness wants maturing. Lovers of voice will wait eagerly to see if the freshness of this remarkable sonority can survive the deepening of years.'"

Then Jonah hit the windup. "'That said, Mr. Strom's painterly highlights, his crisp articulation, and his brilliant, if dark, purity already stand up well alongside the best of contemporary European lieder singers his age. Predictions are always risky, but it is not difficult to imagine Mr. Strom becoming one of the finest Negro recitalists this country has ever produced.'"

Jonah dropped the pages to the bed.

"Let it go," I told him. "It doesn't matter. The rest of the article is a total love letter. He's handed you a career on a platter!"

He tried to wrap his head around the generous insult: "Predictions are always risky." He worked each word, turning the promise of the phrase into menace. My brother had never tried to pass, but it staggered him to discover that he couldn't. I braced for Jonah's contempt, knowing it would spill over in my direction.

But he was lost to contempt, working on that word, that one fat adjective hanging there in the paper of record, describing something, something as real as *lyric*, or *spinto*, or *tenor*. He was balancing the slap-down qualification against *finest ever*. *Finest this country has ever produced.* He wavered between tenses, feeling, for the first time, what it meant to kick open doors that kept closing, no matter how many legends had already passed through. Feeling what it meant to be driven out of the self-made self, forced to be an emblem, a giver of pride, a betrayer of the cause. Feeling what it meant to be a fixed category, no matter how he sung.

"Da and Mama should have named me Heinrich."

"It wouldn't have made any difference."

He'd been "niggered" before, more brutally. But not from a major music critic in the country's leading paper. He lay in bed in his red-and-green-plaid bathrobe, covered in newspaper, shaking his head. Then perplexity turned to rage. "Of all the condescending . . . Who does this bastard think—"

"Jonah! The thing is a triumph. Howard Silverman's talking you up in the *New York Times*."

He stopped, surprised by my force. He went back to staring up at the ceiling, at all the people who'd never get through even that separately labeled door. He saw our mother coming home from her conservatory audition. The finest recitalist he'd ever know. He rolled his head through a weary arc. He looked at me, doing that performer's trick with his hazel eyes. They don't get close enough to check your eye color when they come to burn down your house. "You're one of those big-smile, Satchmo gradualists, aren't you?"

"You're the one who wanted to close with the damn spiritual."

There was an awful pause while we searched for the tempo. He could have killed me by saying nothing. For a long time, he did. When he spoke, it was with full Dowland flourish. "Don't argue with me, human. I'm one of the finest Negro recitalists this country will ever produce."

"'Has ever produced.' Big difference. Ask your father." We both resorted to jittery giggles. "Finish the article. The condescending bastard saved you a big finale."

Jonah worked through the last sentences aloud with his studied diction. "'If this exciting young tenor has a limit, it is perhaps only that of size. All the other fundamentals are in place, and his every note rings with exhilarating freedom.'"

Exactly the kind of hedged praise critics loved to deal in. Who knew what it was supposed to mean? It was more than enough to launch a career with.

"I'm the Negro Aksel Schiotz. I'm going to be the Negro Fischer-Dieskau."

"Fischer-Dieskau's a baritone."

"That's okay. I'm liberal. Some of my best friends are baritones."

"But would you want your sister to marry one?"

Jonah appraised me. "Know who you are? You're the Negro Franz Rupp." He swiped up the article and poured through it again. "Hey. He doesn't even mention the accompaniment."

"Good thing. If you have to mention the accompaniment, there's something wrong."

"Mule! I owe you so much. I wouldn't even have been out there if . . ." He considered the thought and didn't complete it. "How can I repay you? What do you want? My Red Ball Jets? My old seventy-eights? All yours. Everything."

"How about you get dressed and buy me breakfast. Okay, make it lunch."

He crawled out of bed, doffed the robe, and padded around the uncurtained room, showing off his welterweight body to every passerby. As he threw on briefs, chinos, and a golf shirt, he asked, "How come Ruth wasn't there?"

"Jonah. I don't know. Why don't you call her?"

He shook his head. Didn't think he should have to. Didn't want to know. Couldn't afford the answer. He sat back down on the unmade bed. "Dark purity: *C'est moi*. Only question is: Who's going to be the white Jonah Strom?"

"Put your shoes on. Let's go."

He never got his shoes on, and we never went. While he was puttering, the phone started to ring. The *Times* was detonating in a million kitchens, reaching every acquaintance we'd ever made. Jonah fielded the first thrilled congratulations. The second wave rolled in as soon as he hung up. The third call came before he could recross the room. It was Mr. Weisman. He'd received a recording offer. The Harmondial label wanted our recital pressed into vinyl, exactly as we'd performed it.

Jonah called out the details to me as Mr. Weisman gave them. My brother hooted at the invitation, ready to sign and do the recording that afternoon. Mr. Weisman advised against it. He suggested that we do two more years of concertizing, make a few high-profile appearances, then try for a longer-term arrangement with a better recording company. He mentioned RCA Victor as within the realm of possibility. That slowed Jonah for a moment.

But Jonah was zooming away from earth at speeds old Mr. Weisman couldn't gauge. He was set on jumping into other people's futures, and recording gave him the chance. To turn the moment permanent, spread the dying *now* out lengthwise into forever: Jonah didn't care who was offering. Harmondial was a young, small company, two strikes against it in Mr. Weisman's book, but a selling point for my brother. He and they could break into the game together. At twenty-four, Jonah was still immortal. He could crash and resurrect as often as he liked, drawing on endless time and talent.

"You only start once," Mr. Weisman kept saying. But Jonah could make no sense of the warning. Harmondial's bid went beyond anything Jonah imagined. None of Mr. Weisman's objections could change Jonah's sense that the offer had no downside. It was a giveaway, a lottery prize that cost him nothing to try.

We flew to Los Angeles to record. Harmondial used their California studio mostly for their catalog of pop and light classics. Jonah said it would give him exactly the presence he wanted. We flew out at the beginning of August, two kings in coach, giggling like criminals all the way across the continent.

We crossed L.A. in a waking daze, driving around Hollywood and Westwood in a rented Ford Mustang. Kids were everywhere, glued to their transistors as if to news of an alien invasion. The invasion, in fact, was already in its advanced stages. We'd missed the signs, back east in our barnstorming. Now we cruised down Ventura, paralyzed latecomers to an epidemic. The sound was everywhere, past our ability to take in.

"Jesus, Joey! It's worse than cholera. Worse than communism. The absolute triumph of the three-chord song!" Jonah trolled the car radio dial for the same tunes we could hear beating from every corner, in a hurry to sample the thrill so long kept at bay. Some of the songs were venturing far beyond tonic, subdominant, and dominant. Those songs were the ones that scared him. Those were the ones he couldn't get enough of.

He made me drive, piloting me around town to the hits of 1965. *Stop! In the name of love. Turn! Turn! Turn! Over and Over!* And when he got us completely lost: *Help! I need somebody. Help!* By the time we found the studio for the first session, Jonah was riffing on tunes he'd absorbed on a single hearing. All we need is music, sweet music. In Chicago. New Orleans. New York City. They're dancin' in the streets. The sound engineers heard him and went nuts. They made him do level checks by singing *My baby don't care* in every cranny of his register, from up above countertenor to down below baritone.

"What the hell are you doing singing Schubert?" one of them asked. "With power like that, you could be making real dough."

Jonah didn't tell them the twelve-hundred-dollar Harmondial advance felt like a small fortune. And nobody pointed out the problem: he made the Supremes' "I Hear a Symphony" sound, well, symphonic: a one-off novelty act, my brother, the one-hit wonder of precision-pitched, breath-supported R & B lieder, the single-handed Motown Mo-tet.

We stuck to Schubert, and by the fourth take, the sound engineers changed their tune. In Jonah's throat, all these dead tunes were once again someone's popular song. Something in his voice on those tracks insists, *We are still young.* Something in that near hour of songs, recorded over the course of days, says the centuries are just passing tones on their way back home.

I can hear it on the record, still. My mother's voice is there inside his, but my father's is, too. There is no starting point. We trace back forever, accident on accident, through every country taken from us. But we end everywhere, always. Stand still and gaze: This is the message in that sound, rushing backward from the finish line it has reached.

When he heard his first takes, my brother couldn't stop snickering. "Listen to that! It's just like a real record. Let's do it again. Forever."

Jonah could hear things on the tape the engineers couldn't. We spent two increasingly tense days battling between cost and inaudible perfection. The producers would be knocked out by the first several takes, each of which left Jonah wincing. They told us about how they could splice in a measure to fix a lapse. Jonah was outraged. "That's like pasting eagle feathers on your average slob and calling him an angel."

Jonah learned to seduce the microphone and compensate for its brutalities. Under the pressure of compromise, our takes took on the edge of live performance. In the baffled, soundproofed room, Jonah grew incandescent. He sang, posting his voice forward to people hundreds of years from now.

The third night, after we got the Wolf within a few vibrations of how it sounded in his mind, we sat down with the Harmondial publicist. The girl was fresh from summer camp. "I'm so glad you two are brothers!"

I flopped around like a fish on the dock. Jonah said, "We are, too."

"The brothers thing is good. People like brothers." I thought she might ask, *Have you always been brothers? How did you come to be brothers?* She asked, instead, "How did you get interested in classical music?"

We went mute. How did you learn how to breathe? It hit me. The story this girl already imagined would go into press releases and liner notes, unhindered by any data we gave her. Even if we told her about our evenings of family singing, she wouldn't hear. Jonah left it to me to create some facsimile. "Our parents discovered our musical ability when we were young. They sent us to a private music school up in Boston."

"Private school?" The fact flustered our publicist.

"A preconservatory boarding school. Yes."

"Did you . . . get scholarships?"

"Partial ones," Jonah said. "We washed dishes and made beds to pay the rest of our way. Everyone was very generous toward us." I snorted. Jonah shot me an offended look, and the poor girl was lost.

"Was the music you learned at school . . . a lot different from the music you grew up on?"

Jonah couldn't help himself. "Well, the tempi dragged at Boylston sometimes. It wasn't the school's fault. Some of those kids were coming from musically backward homes. Things got a little better once we were at Juilliard."

She scribbled into a canary yellow legal pad. We could have told her anything, and Jonah pretty much did. "Did you have any role models? I mean, as far as singing . . . classical music?"

"Paul Robeson," Jonah answered. The girl scribbled the name. "Not for his voice so much. His voice was . . . okay, I guess. We liked his politics."

She seemed surprised to hear that a famous singer could have politics. Mr. Weisman was right. This wasn't RCA Victor. You only start once. I watched Jonah's answers drop into the permanent record, where they would last as long as the sounds we'd just laid down.

The girl asked for publicity photos. We gave her the portfolio, complete with clippings. "So many reviews!" She picked the photo I knew she would, the one emphasizing the novelty that Harmondial had just bought. Something to distinguish their catalog from all the other burgeoning record labels: a brother act, black but comely. She looked for just the right pose of comfort and assurance, the one that said, *Not all Negroes want to trash everything you stand for. Some of them even serve as culture's willing foot soldiers.*

In the car, heading to the hotel, Jonah sang, "I wish they all could be California girls."

"God only knows what she wishes we were." We both knew, now, just which sentence in the *Times* had sealed this offer. The upstart record label wanted this up-and-coming Negro voice, the next untapped niche. Civil rights meant ever larger, integrated markets. The same thinking had just led *Billboard* to combine their R & B list with their rock and roll. Everyone would finally sing and listen to everything, and Harmondial would capitalize on the massive crossover.

We finished recording on a Wednesday night, two days later. The producer wanted Dowland to be the record's last track. I picked the studio's backup piano, a rare combination of covered sound and stiff action that helped me fake the frets of a lute. Today, you'd never get away with piano anymore. A third of a century ago, authenticity was still anything you made it. *Time stands still.* But never the same way for long.

Jonah's first take felt flawless. But the engineer working the board was so entranced with his first-time taste of timelessness that he failed to see his meters clipping. Take two was leaden, Jonah's revenge for the first's destruction. The next five takes went belly-up. We'd reached the end of a difficult week. He asked for ten minutes. I stood up to take a walk down the hallway outside the recording booth, to give my brother a moment alone.

"Joey," he called. "Don't leave me." Like I was abandoning him to oblivion. He wanted me to sit but not say anything. He'd fallen into a panic at sending a message out beyond his own death. We sat in silence for five minutes, and five stretched to ten: the last year that we lived in that would leave us still for so long. The engineers returned, chattering about the recent *Gemini* flight. I sat down, Jonah opened his mouth, and out came the sound that predicted everything that would still happen to him.

"Time stands still with gazing on her face." As my brother sang, a few minutes' drive from the studio, a white motorcycle policeman stopped a black driver—a man our sister's age—and made him take a sobriety test. Avalon and 116th: a neighborhood of single-story houses and two-story apartment blocks. The night was hot, and the residents sat outdoors. While Jonah put stillness's finish on that opening *mi, re, do*, a crowd gathered around the arrest. Fifty milling spectators swelled to three hundred as the policeman's backup appeared on the scene.

The young man's mother arrived and started scolding her son. The crowd, the police, the man, his mother, his brother all closed on one another. More police, more pull, the crowd restive with history, and the night turning warm. There was a scuffle, the simplest kind of beginning. A club in the face that lands in the face of everyone looking on.

The crowd grew to a thousand, and the police radioed for more help. This was around 7:30, as we were listening to the tape: "Stand still and gaze for minutes, hours, and years to her give place." The producer was crying and cursing Jonah for laughing at him.

Over on Avalon, all music stopped. Someone spit on the officers as they hauled the man, his mother, and his brother off to jail. Two patrolmen waded into the crowd, guns in the air, to arrest this next wave of offenders. By 7:40, as Jonah and I stood on the hot sidewalk in front of the studio, the police were pulling away under a hail of stones.

We chanced onto the news on the car radio as we left the studio. Reports of the gathering riot broke into the Top 40 countdown. Jonah looked at me, connecting. "Let's have a look."

"A look? You've got to be kidding."

"Come on. From a distance. It's over by now anyway." I was driving. Something in him made me. He pointed me south, navigating by a combination of news report and acute hearing. He got us on South Broadway, then over onto eastbound Imperial Highway. He made me pull over and then got out. He stood there on the pavement, just listening. "Joey. You hear that?" I heard only traffic, the usual background of shouts and sirens, routine urban insanity. But my brother heard whole bands of the spectrum I couldn't, just as all week long he'd heard sounds on our tapes hidden to the rest of us. *"Listen!* Are you deaf?"

He packed us back in the car and steered us northeast. We hooked right, where madness materialized in front of us. Crowds of people lined the streets of the tinderbox neighborhood, just waiting for the match. We crept another block east. I pulled over and checked the map, as if the outbreak might be marked there. The Mustang was a death trap, as stupid a car as we could have chosen to drive. Straight through our windshield, down the street, a mass condensed, drifting from block to block, stopping cars by force and stoning them, the only alternative to justice. The streets were the same as most in L.A.—white-walled arroyos of small one-family dwellings. Only, down this one, a creature lumbered out of some filmic dream. The laws of physics bent the air around us. It was like watching a flock of starlings twist and blot the sun. Like watching a funnel cloud dissolve the house across the way.

The crowd hit a pebble in its path and veered. Jonah was hypnotized by the movement, thrilled. They were going after any moving cars, pelting them with stones. At any minute, they'd smell the last notes of Dowland still clinging to us, and charge. I should have turned the car around and fled. But this drifting, methodical mob was so far beyond the rules of ordinary life that I sat paralyzed, waiting to see what happened. The crowd was like stirred bees. They surged and attacked a police outpost. The officers broke and scattered from the advance. No one gave orders, but the mass moved as if under single command. The forward edge swung west, toward us. I came out of my spell and turned the car around hard, cutting across the bewildered trickle of traffic.

"What are you doing?" Jonah yelled. "Where do you think you're going?" For the first time in my life, I ignored him. Somehow, I got us back on the northbound Harbor Freeway. Our hotel, back near View Park, felt more unreal than the trance we'd just witnessed. Neither of us slept.

The morning papers were filled with the story. But the thing they reported was not the thing we'd seen. The official accounts were stunted, deluding, clinging to the unreal. The radio performed feats of heroic denial. Everyone in the hotel was buzzing. The streets that Thursday morning wore a bright, forced cheer that barely masked the rush of expectation. Even as the city tried to talk itself down, it braced for the night to come.

We checked in with the studio at noon for last-minute touch-ups. But all was well: Yesterday's takes sounded even better in the light of day. I blessed our luck; Jonah couldn't have recorded the piece again, not after the previous night. Even the Harmondial people saw how shaken he was. No one could assimilate the news. The engineers joked nervously with us, as if we might turn, in front of them, from Elizabethan troubadors to looters. By four o'clock that afternoon, the producers sent us off with hugs and great predictions for our debut release. We were all set to head back to LAX for an evening flight. We had a couple of hours.

"Joey?" His voice was more spooked by itself than anything. "I need another look."

"Another . . . Oh, no, Jonah. Please. Don't be crazy."

"Just a detour on the way to the airport. Joey, I can't get it out of my head. What did we see last night? Like nothing I've ever come close to in my life."

"That doesn't mean we have to get close to it again. We were lucky to get out without incident."

"Without *incident?*"

I hung my head. "I mean to us. The rest—what were we supposed . . . ?" But Jonah wasn't interested in my defense. He was already going after the missing bit in his education, the thing that no teacher had yet given him. He felt the years still ahead trying to signal him. He needed to go back, to hear. He no longer trusted anything but the sense that would finally kill him.

Jonah drove, a concession to my rage at him. We reached the previous night's neighborhood just after five o'clock. The blocks off the expressway should have satisfied him. The streets sparkled with smashed shop windows, a carpet of fake diamonds. Here and there, the soot of extinguished fires coated the stucco and concrete. Knots of teens edged up and down the sidewalks. The only visible whites were armed and uniformed. Jonah pulled the Mustang into a deserted lot. He shut off the engine and opened his door. I made no objection; you can't object to what you don't believe is happening.

He didn't even look at me. "Come on, brother." He was out through the other end of the scrap-strewn lot before I could yell at him. I locked my door—ridiculous to the end—and raced to catch up. The crowd had swelled again to thousands, double the night before. Already that ranging group mind was taking over. The police were lost, worse even than the newspaper accounts. You could see it in their faces: *We've given them so much; why are they doing this?* Their strategy was to set up a perimeter, contain the violence to the immediate neighborhoods, and wait for the National Guard. Jonah scouted the police border, finding a gap in it between a package store and a burned breakfast dive. After twenty-four years of hiding indoors, my brother chose that night to come outside.

We passed down the alley, through the break in the police cordon. The street cutting just in front of us flowed with running hallucination. Three cars, rolled over onto their carapaces, poured blackened flames into the air. Firemen fought to get close enough to douse the fireballs, but the crowd beat them back with rocks and stood over the blazes, tending them.

No one scored out the chaos. It just unfolded around us in a horizon-wide ballet. Three dozen people materialized in front of us to trash a greengrocer's. Their bodies worked at the task, neither excited nor functional. They cohered around the job, a band of tight improvisers handing one another supplies—hammers, axes, gas cans—as if passing so many relay-race batons. The cadence was eerie, a slow, resistant, underwater, paced rage, workmanlike, as if the plans for apocalypse had been perfected over generations.

Jonah yelled over the deafening sirens. "Pure madness, Mule. Dancing in the streets!" His face shimmered, at last up close to whatever he'd been looking for. Two thousand rioters swept past. Four steps ahead of me, Jonah slowed to a walk. All I could think, with hell erupting all around, was, *He's too light to be here.* He was a frail, vulnerable boy, listening wide-eyed to the Valkyries riding through our radio.

Jonah hovered, turning to inspect the flames that shot up fifteen feet to his left. His hands cupped unconsciously, lifting from his sides, beckoning to the roving packs, cuing their entrances and attacks. He was *conducting.* Beating time, phrasing the chaos the same way he always did when listening to the music that most moved him. I came alongside him; he was *humming.* At his command, a drone rose up behind us, pitched but variable, matching his throb, a hybrid of rhythm and melody. The sound multiplied through the spreading human mass. I'll remember that sound until I die.

The police concentrated their power on making sure the violence didn't spill over into white neighborhoods. The firemen were getting the worst of it. They gave up extinguishing the overturned cars and focused on containing the burning commercial buildings. The blast of hoses and the hissing crowd fused into a single chorus. Jonah watched, deep in some interpretation I couldn't make out. The stress intoxicated him. Total collapse: lives ricocheting past us, handmade explosions going off, all the rules of reason worse than flaccid.

He stopped in front of a pawnshop, where half a dozen children were slamming a mesh garbage can through the plate-glass door. They threw and ran back, walked up, threw, and ran back again. The entrance fell in a hail of shards. One by one, the looters disappeared into the cave. Jonah stood still, waiting for revelation. After a sickening moment, the excavators returned, carrying a television, a stereo, a brass floor lamp, new hats for all, and two handguns. Three centuries' worth of reparations.

I stuck to myself, two shops away. Jonah was out ahead of me, twenty feet from the door. He stood with his feet spread, leaning into the chaos. He watched the actors run out of the store, as if all history depended on their grabbing these denied goods, here at the denouement. From out of the synchronized dream, one of the newly armed boys saw my brother staring. He ran toward Jonah, waving his snub-nosed gun like a Ping-Pong paddle. My body turned worthless, fifty yards, a continent away. I tried to yell but couldn't find my throat. The boy shouted as he ran. His words broke in the air into harsh, incoherent rivets. His scattering friends turned to meet the challenge. The other armed boy began waving his own gun at Jonah. It weighed down his arm, too heavy for him, a bad prop.

"What you want here?" The first boy reached Jonah, who stood dead, his arms lifted from his sides. "Get the fuck out. Ain't no place for white." The boy waved the barrel side to side, charming a snake. His hands shook. Jonah just stood the way he did onstage, draped on the crook of an imaginary grand piano, ready to launch into a huge song cycle. *Winterreise*. He stood as though I was right behind him, at the keyboard.

The second boy was on them in an instant. He fell out of orbit, slamming into Jonah's flank and knocking him to the pavement. My brother crumpled in pain, then lay still on the concrete, his arm scraped open.

"Motherfucker hurt you?" the second boy shouted at the first. Both boys stood over him, aiming, shaking, jumping. "Back to the Hills, motherfucker. Back to Bel Air!" As if that were where even death would send this intruder.

I found my voice. "He's black. The man's a black man." I was too far away. They couldn't hear me over the riot. My voice cracked and broke. I never did have much projection. "The man's my brother."

The two armed boys stared up at me. One aimed his gun in my direction. "This? This ain't no brother."

"The man's a black man."

Jonah, picking his moment, as if the largest part of him really did want to die, relaxed his head onto the pavement. He looked up into the smoking sky. His lips began to work. He might have been pleading with them, praying. No sound came out of him but a weird monotone moan.

I knew then that one of the shaking boys would shoot him. Murder here would be nothing: one more randomness at time's end. Jonah worked his lips, moaning, preparing his finish. But that burst of monotone, coming from that body stretched out on the pavement, unnerved his assailants. The two teens backed away from the voodoo wail. Behind them, their friends with the television and stereo screamed for them to scatter. The Man was *here*, and shooting. The two gunmen looked over at me, down at Jonah, even up in the air at the stream of funereal smoke that my brother sung to. Still staring, they turned and ran.

I fell to my knees on the pavement beside him, sobbing and pulling at his ripped shirt. He nodded. My relief flooded over into rage. "What the hell are we *doing* here? We gotta get out. Now." It took all I had to keep from kicking Jonah in the ribs, where he lay.

He looked up at me, in shock. "What?" Blood seeped up his sleeve and down his arm. The scraped-open skin filled with cinders. "What? Practice, Joey. Rehearsal." He snickered, wincing.

I sat him up, still shouting at him. I wrapped his arm in a piece of shirt. "Jesus Christ. They were going to kill you."

"I saw." His jaw was trembling, out of control. "Right there. But you told them, didn't you?" His throat closed and his breathing shut down. He laughed and tried to apologize. But a choking fit prevented him.

I got him to his feet and made him walk. Two hundred yards to our left, a line of police advanced against a makeshift emplacement of stone-throwers. I took Jonah to the right, doubling back west past Albion, where we'd entered the inferno. The air was a kiln, and the concrete under our feet melted into tar. Jonah's breathing worsened. We had to slow. He pulled up at a corner and put out his hand, reassuring me, staving off suffocation. "Keep walking; keep moving."

I leaned him up against a wall so he could catch his breath and slow his heart. While we stood, Jonah bending forward and me holding him, a light-skinned middle-aged man walked past and brushed our backs. I spun around and saw the gray-haired man walk placidly away, carrying a can of house paint and a brush. On Jonah's bare back, and on the tails of my shirt, he left a spotty brown stripe. The man disappeared into the crowd, leaving his brand on anything that held still long enough.

Jonah could see my shirt but not his back. "Me, too? He got me good?"

"Yes. He got you."

His breathing eased. "We're all set then, Mule. Passport stamped. Visa. Safe passage." He started up again, humming. I took his good arm and walked him on. He felt even more wobbly than reality. We headed west along 112th Street, to safety. But we'd never be safe again. From two blocks away, I saw the police perimeter we'd crossed on our way in. It had thickened. A line of officers three deep fought back the rushing stone-throwers. Burning bottles arced upward and fell to earth in splashes of flame. Watts was trying to spread the pain to Westmont, Inglewood, Culver City. Someplace where the fires had something expensive to burn.

"Come on, Mule." He sounded drunk. "Keep going. We'll talk our way through." By then, he could barely form a sentence. I knew what the police would do if we got even close. Nobody was getting out across this line. The whole township was ringed by a thousand policemen, herding it at gunpoint. Behind the police wall was the National Guard. And behind the Guard, the Fortieth Armored Division. We were sealed off, trapped inside the permanent pen. My brother was too light to survive inside, and I was too dark to get us out.

I dragged Jonah south, along a weed-shot alley that dead-ended in a street running diagonally along a railroad track. Scattered gunshot echoed off the flanking buildings, spattering from all directions at once, unreal, like cap pistols fired off into garbage cans. I steered us southwest, then realized we were running straight toward Imperial Highway. We came out in the middle of bedlam.

A band of rioters had broken through the police salient and were fanning into the streets beyond. Retaliating, the police waded into a group of bystanders and beat whomever they could reach, tearing them up like dogs catching squirrels. People thrown to the sidewalk and slammed into walls, guns popping off, glass shattering, and the crowd, everywhere routed, shrieking and running.

Jonah fell back, choking, into a covered doorway. He leaned forward to ease the pressure in his chest. His left arm nursed his damaged right. He pointed in awe at my leg. I looked down. My right trouser was torn and blood oozed from my shin. We stood there, bodies whipping past like planets in broken orbit, close enough to touch.

A scream broke toward us. One white policeman, swinging a nightstick, chased two middle-aged, bloodied blacks, who cut in the direction of our door before seeing us and swerving. The slow-heeled cop stood mired for a second before spotting us. I saw how we looked to him: my gouged leg, Jonah doubled over, half-shirtless, his arm scraped open, both of us panting, marked with a brown stripe of paint. He charged us, stick raised. I put up my hands to break the blow. Jonah, choking, delirious, fell back on instinct. He swung upright and shouted a kind of high B. The pitched cry brought the cop up short. His voice saved us from having our faces beaten in.

The cop scrambled backward, one hand feeling for his gun. I got my brother's hands into the air. More stunned than we were, the cop handcuffed us together. He marched us two blocks to a police van, prodding us with his stick, still in control, keeping us out in front of him, his captives. Jonah regained his voice. "Wait until your sister hears this. She's gonna love us all over again. Old times."

The officer jabbed us on. He was still wondering why he hadn't clubbed us senseless. Still trying to figure out why the voice had stopped him.

We were taken by van with a dozen others to an auxiliary jail in Athens. All the ordinary facilities were filled. Arrests poured in by the thousands. All of black L.A. was locked up, but the riots kept flowing. We sat all night in a narrow cell with twenty men. Jonah loved it. He stopped complaining about the throb in his arm. He listened to every inflection, every seditious word as if this were rehearsal for some new dramatic role.

Talk in the cell was a grim mix of threat and predictions. The most articulate of the group were testifying. "They can't stop this anymore. They know they can't. We've won already, even if they lock us all away and destroy the key. They had to call out the *army*, man. They need the *army* for us. The whole world knows now. And they'll never forget."

We were held until late the following afternoon, when our officer showed up and admitted that all we'd done was cower in a doorway. Half of those still held had done no worse. Our story checked out—the record company, the rented car, Juilliard, our agent, America's Next Voice—everything except the reason why we'd been at the scene of a riot in the first place. We must have been inciting, part of a conspiracy of educated, radical, near-white blacks filtering into the tinderbox and encouraging it to set itself alight. The way the police went at us, we'd done something far worse than looting, arson, and assault combined. We had everything—advantage, opportunity, trust. We were the future's hope, and we'd betrayed it. Our crime was sight-seeing, coming by to watch while the city went up in flames. The booking officers verbally abused us, pushed us around a little, and threatened to hold us for trial. But finally, they discharged us in disgust.

The law couldn't waste its breath on us. By Friday evening, it was clear that Thursday night had been just a prelude. Friday was the real fire. The violence started early and built without respite the entire day. By Friday night, Los Angeles descended into the maelstrom.

We heard it on the radio on the way to LAX. Nothing that night was flying in or out, for fear of getting shot out of the sky. We sat glazed in front of the reports, watching the blaze spread. Nothing in Southeast Asia could match it. The firefight moved out of Watts into the southeast city. Snipers fired on police. Police shot at civilians. Police shot themselves and blamed the mob. Six hundred buildings were gutted; two hundred burned to the ground. Dozens of people died of gun wounds, burns, and collapsing walls. Thousands of National Guardsmen swept through the streets, shoulder-to-shoulder, sowing still more anarchy. Jonah listened to the reports, his lips like lead.

We stayed in the airport all night, sleeping less than we had in our cell. We didn't fly back to New York until late Saturday night, by which time thirteen thousand Guardsmen roamed the streets of Los Angeles. The rebellion would roll on for another two days.

On the long flight, Jonah played with the gash on his arm. He stared at the back of the seat in front of him and shivered. We were over Iowa when I finally found the nerve to ask him. "When you were lying there on the ground? Your lips were moving."

He waited for me to finish, but I already had. "You want to know what I was singing?" He looked around. He leaned in and whispered, "You can't know. The whole score was right there in front of me. I was looking up into it. It sounded good, Joey. *Real* good. Like nothing I've ever heard."

His voice never again sounded as it had before that night. I have the recordings to confirm me.

SUMMER 1941–FALL 1944

She's known the song her whole life. But Delia Daley never heard the full voice of human hatred until she married this man. Until she bore her first child. Only then does the chorus of righteousness pour down on her, slamming her family for their little daily crime of love.

She's guilty of the greatest foolishness, and for that she must be punished. Yet she will wake startled in the middle of the night, wondering whom she has injured so badly that they must come after her. What future unforgiving accusers? Every time she tallies up her sins, it comes to this: to think that recognizing means more than its opposite. To think that race is still in motion. That we stand for nothing but what our children might do. That time makes us someone else, a little more free.

Time, she finds, does nothing of the kind. Time always loses out to history. Every wound ever suffered has only lain covered, festering. Some girlish, unenslaved part of her imagined their marriage might cure the world. Instead, it compounds the crime by assaulting all injured parties. She and David say only that family is bigger than guilt. And for this, guilt must rise up and punish them.

Great spaces of life have always been closed to her. But the spaces remaining were larger than she could fill. Now even her simplest needs become unmeetable. She'd like to walk down the street with her husband without having to play his hired help. She'd like to be able to hold his arm in public. She'd like to watch a movie together or go for dinner without being hustled out. She'd like to sling her baby on her shoulder, take him shopping, and for once not bring the store to a standstill. She'd like to come home without venom all over her. It will not happen in her lifetime. But it must happen in her son's. Rage buckles down in her each time she leaves the house. Only motherhood is large enough to contain it.

Once, she thought bigotry an aberration. Now that she ties her life to a white's, she sees it for the species's baseline. All hatred comes down to the protection of property values. One drop: just another safeguard of ownership. Possession, nine-tenths of the law.

Negroes, of course, make room for them. Her family, her aunt in Harlem, the church circuit, her friends from college. That saint Mrs. Washington, who keeps a roof over their heads. Nobody's exactly thrilled with the arrangement, of course. But if whiteness depends on those who can't belong, blackness is forever about those who must be taken in. Her boy is nothing special. Three-quarters of her race has white blood. Age-old rights of the plantation: the disclaiming owner, the disowning father. The difference this time is just that her child's father sticks around.

Not every white they must deal with is certified hopeless. Her husband's band of émigré colleagues see her as no more irrelevant than any wife. They've witnessed more suspect matches, couples more wildly crossed. Those musicians among them will show up at her house at the mention of a soiree, ready to make music in any key. With them, she can relax. They no longer appraise her, waiting to see how long she can walk on her hind legs without wobbling. But then, these men are not quite of this world. They live down in the interstices of the atom, or up among the sweep of galaxies. People are to them irreducible complications. Most of these men have fled their own homes. By and large, they're big on being allowed to live. Every other one a refugee: Poles, Czechs, Danes, Russians, Germans, Austrians, Hungarians. More Hungarians than Delia knew existed. A big self-knit international nation of the dispossessed, the bulk of them Jewish. Where else could this hapless group live except where her David does—in the borderless state that recognizes no passports, the country of particles and numbers?

There's Mr. Rabi, who hired David and who David says will turn Columbia into a commuter suburb of Stockholm. There are Mr. Bethe, Mr. Pauli, Mr. Von Neumann—a trio of mad foreigners. And Mr. Leo Szillard, who may truly be crazy, who doesn't work anywhere, but lives out of a suitcase at the King's Crown, the hotel where David stayed when he first arrived. Mr. Teller, with his eyebrow thicket, who plays Bach so beautifully, he must be good. Mr. Fermi and his wife, the dark, beautiful Laura, who got lost on their way back to fascist Italy after picking up his Nobel in Sweden and wound up in New York, at Columbia, another of her husband's revered colleagues.

Delia dreaded these men for months, hated even meeting them. She'd shake their hands and mumble stupid, earthbound things as they sized her up, and she'd struggle hopelessly to make out what they mumbled back. At the first musical gathering she and David hosted, Delia spent the evening in the kitchen, hiding out with the door closed, inventing labors, while these men talked shop in terms her mama would have consigned to the devil. She banged around with pots and pans—the hired kitchen help—until a quartet of them burst in, wine and cracker crumbs all over their jackets, saying, "Come. The music is starting."

Now she only pities them, the ones who apologize for moving through the room, the ones—like that Mr. Wigner from Princeton—whose every movement is humbled by mysteries they can't penetrate. It's as David tells her, sometimes, while their flanks press against each other's in the dark: "The deeper you look, the more God's plan recedes. At the edge of human measurements, infinite strangeness." Pitching tent in a place so strange must blunt a man's tribalism.

The foreign scientists are easy around her, an ease born in ignorance as much as anything. They aren't pinned underneath the weight of that old crime that cripples the country they now inhabit. They don't look at her and flinch by reflex. They don't need to defend themselves to her. They share, a little, her tacit exile. Yet, even these upended Europeans carry the disease. Empirical skeptics one and all, they still run their built-in statistics, invisible but sight-driven, that universal assumption, so deep that they don't even know it's assumed. The fact is, every one of them is shocked the first time they hear her sing.

And what if they're right? Right to look on her as on a trout sprouting wings. Twenty generations, and the difference goes real. This is the soul-destroyer, the one no one gets around. Not a day goes by that she doesn't have to account for the tunes she chooses.

Her husband can't begin to understand. She feels that now, her distance from him. She'd never have married him but for the lost boy, the hidden future they fell into together at the stray boy's words, that day in Washington. She knew what it would cost this man to take on her citizenship, to share her birthright. She could not hope to preserve him from whiteness's revenge. So it stuns her, night after night, to rediscover: The harder that the offended orders press them, the closer they huddle.

He loves her so simply, so free from belief and prior category. She has known unconditional love—her parents' fierce care, more dogged in the wake of where they've been, grittier in the face of where she's going. With David, she just *is*. She likes the woman he sees when he looks at her—a favorite winter constellation, the steady alignment of stars he always knows how to find.

She loves his amazement at her, his mindful explorations and grateful surprise. His tenderness matured in the cask of being. The awe of his fingers tracing her round, resistant belly when it contained the capsule of their union. Around him, she feels a bashful calm, the lightness of a tinker's plaything. When they lie next to each other, the boy in his crib at the foot of their bed, their shyness multiplied by this drop-in company, this humming third party, they are not anything. Nowhere but here. Their tune together is constant modulation, distant keys always falling back to *do*.

In the daily hard work of getting along, he holds his own. Not much of a housekeeper, his hygiene more random than his irregular verbs. His habits madden her. He can leave a quart of ice cream on the counter and be shocked, two hours later, to find it sticking to his soles. But he laughs readily. And for a man of theory, he's remarkably patient. For a man: as kind as memory is long.

It helps that he's older than she, more able to tell real worry from its many free riders. It saves them, a hundred times a month, that he has so little fixed investment in how things ought to be done. Their surprise divergences at every hour delight him. He picks up a favorite phrase from her, the one she exclaimed the first time she saw him write the number seven. Few weeks go by—watching her cook a stew or pay a bill or hang a picture—when he won't need to say, "Would you look at that!"

Any less joint astonishment and they'd never have reached their first Labor Day. Melting pot New York puts them through a blast furnace; five minutes out on the sidewalk threatens to melt them down to slag. But indoors, all ore belongs to them. They can sing any tune going, and, more often than not, make any two of them fit together. They've come to love the same composers, along routes so different that each confirms the other's divergence. Their chords take their beauty from the surrounding dissonance.

They made love for the first time just before they married. It surprised her, after all those months of nerve-racking abstinence, their dizzy, stifled necking. His choice—God knows, *she* wasn't waiting for any ring. Once she'd committed, she was in with all limbs. All those nights, when she visited in New York and he sent her back to her aunt's, she'd go away thinking, *Can he really be that otherworldly? Or is he holding out for me?*

And then, the week before the wedding, they never broke off. David whispering while he touched her beyond the highest limits of his prior touch, "Next week, we promise to the state. Tonight, I make my promise to just you." When they were finished and she lay coiled back up inside herself, wondering whether it was all that she'd expected, unable to remember just what that had been, he smiled, so full of confusion that she thought for one awful eternity something was wrong.

He waved his hand behind him, at yesterday. "I feel a little boy sitting on my shoulder. He's heavy. Like an old man. He wants me to go somewhere!"

"Where?" she asked, touching his lips.

"The way we're going!"

Then that little boy was here. And now another on the way. The more of them they become, the safer they'll be. David is just as awed by her pregnancy the second time around. Both of them—amazed by her moods and cravings. She grows imperious, placid, animist, alert to every creak in the floorboards. She wants only to curl up with her firstborn against her, her second inside her, her husband standing watch over the apartment as over a dark, soft underground den.

How different expecting is this second time. Jonah kicked and roared in the womb at all hours. This one makes no trouble. The first time, the two adults were alone. Now they have this walking, talking golden thing to keep them company and comment their astonishment. "Mama big. Make new Jonah. Baby come."

David is a wonder with the baffled boy. They sit together on the front room rug in the late afternoon, building cities out of oatmeal boxes and food cans, explaining to each other how things work. She can watch them forever. The boy has his father's eyes, his father's mouth, his father's puzzled amusement. David can understand even Jonah's most cryptic, pre-earthly thoughts. He holds the child entranced with two wooden clothespins and a piece of string. But when her boy is restless or scared, loose in too large a place, nothing will do but curling into his mother, ear against her chest while she sings.

The war has come to them at last. Pearl Harbor is almost an anticlimax, she and David have been waiting for it for so long. That cataclysm, too, neatly divides these births. Delia must remind herself daily that they've joined the world catastrophe, so little has changed in her life since the President made his declaration. Her country is at war with her husband's, although he's given up his citizenship and taken hers. David, sworn in with a roomful of grinning immigrants, with their freshly scrubbed knowledge of executive, legislative, and judicial. David insisting she teach him all the words to the unsingable national anthem, words that make her blush, even as she tries to explain them. David, the logician, struggling for a gloss on the self-evident Declaration of Independence. "But would that not mean . . . ?" She has to warn him not to try to argue the matter with the citizenship judge.

They decide to speak only English to the children. They say it's to prevent confusion. There will be time for other lessons later. What other choice for now? Her brother Charlie enlists. Her father and Michael would, too, in a heartbeat, if the army were taking old men and children. She anguishes nightly that David might be drafted. They wouldn't send him against Germany, but they could ship him to the Pacific. They're taking men with even worse eyesight.

"Don't worry, treasure," he says.

It maddens her. "Don't you tell me not to worry. They'll take every-one. It's bad enough having a brother sent to North Carolina. I'm not los-ing you."

"Don't worry. They will not take me."

The way he says it hushes her. Some privilege of rank. Surely univer-sity professors won't be exempt. His colleagues, the ones who come by for music evenings, men who shuttle among a dozen universities as if they all worked for the same employer, sharing nothing but wild, broken En-glish, a love of mysteries, and a hatred for Hitler: Won't they go, along with everyone?

"They're needed here," David tells her.

How can that be? He has always told her that there's no work more worthless, more abstract than his. Except, perhaps, music.

The last three weeks of Delia's second pregnancy leave her lumbering to the finish. Her voice drops to tenor. She stops her lessons and gives up even her church choir jobs. She can't sit, lie, or stand. She can't hold her child on her lap. She's huge. "My wife," David teases, "she goes from a Webern bagatelle to a Bruckner symphony." Delia tries to smile, but she has no spare skin left.

Thank God he's there when it happens. The contractions start at 2:00 A.M. on June 16, and by the time David gets her to the hospital a dozen blocks away, she almost delivers in the lobby. It's a boy, another beautiful boy. "Looks like his mother," the nurse remarks.

"Looks like his brother," says the mother, still in that far place.

"We have four of us," the father repeats. His voice is dazed. "We are a quartet."

Once again, the state puts "Colored" on the birth certificate. "How about 'Mixed' this time?" she asks. "Just to be fair to all the parties?" But Mixed isn't a category.

"Discrete and not continuous." Her husband the physicist. "And the two are not symmetrical?"

"No," she answers. "They are not."

This perplexes her husband. "Whiteness is recessive. Black is domi-nant."

She laughs. "I wouldn't put it quite like that."

"But look. Whiteness is lost. They are the exception category. The *sogenannt* pure case. Black is everything that isn't white. It's whites who decide this, yes?"

Whites, she hears her brother Charlie telling her, *decide everything.*

"So the white race should see this is a losing idea, over time? They write themselves out of the books, even at a fraction of one percent every year!"

She's too exhausted, too sedated, too ecstatic to have this conversation. Her baby's her baby. His own case. Race: Joseph. Nationality: Joseph. Weight, length, sex: nothing but her baby, her new JoJo.

But the hospital also gets the eye color wrong. She tells them to fix it: green, for her son's safety. Just in case the error comes back to haunt him in later years. But they won't. They can't see the green. Leaf and bark are to them all the same color.

The baby comes home for Jonah to inspect. Older brother's disappointment is infinite. This new creature doesn't want to do anything but sleep and suckle, suckle and sleep. Total perversity, and what enrages the seventeen-month-old most is that both parents are entirely duped by the act. They are both careful to take turns with Jonah, while relieving each other with the new baby.

It's as Delia wants. Everything she can imagine wanting. If they could freeze time right here. Humming to each child, listening to them hum. Plunking out the basic melody of days.

This one does darken up a little, as her mother again predicts. More than his brother, but stopping right around cream with a little coffee. Even before he can walk, he's a helper. He doesn't want to put his mother out, even to feed him. It wrecks her to watch. Even before he can talk, he does everything anyone asks him.

They pack up the children every few months and take them to Philly. It's not enough for her parents. "They're different little men every time I get to see them," Nettie Ellen chides. The twins dress the boys up and take them, one each, around the block, showing them off to any neighbor who's fool enough to stop. Even Dr. Daley—his own Michael barely out of short pants—turns into a foolish old grandfather, cooing and calling to his descendants.

Delia and David time a visit to coincide with Charlie's first leave since his transfer. Her brother bursts into the assembled room in uniform, to a collective gasp. He has gone down to Montford Point a second-class citizen and come back a marine. Marine in training anyway. Fifty-first Defense Battalion. He makes the choice not out of any romantic, boyish attachment to that branch of the service. Just because, until a few months ago, they said he couldn't. Dr. Daley rises to shake his son's hand. They stand a moment, clasped, and break off wordlessly.

"My Lord, My *Lord*!" Nettie Ellen fingers the uniform.

"That's the one," Charlie says. "The one and only. Same old threads they said we'd never wear. Yes in-*deedy*. You're looking at a walking, talking incarnation of Mr. Frankie Dee's Executive Order Eight-eight-oh-two!"

"Watch your mouth," his mother says. "I didn't raise you up to bad-mouth the President."

"No, Mama." Pure contrition, with a wink for Delia. "You did not."

The twins swoon over him. "You're so fine." "So divine." "You are the one." "Fancy as they come!"

"Notice how surprised my sisters sound," Charcoal tells David.

Only he's not Charcoal anymore. This man has disowned the boy who left home. He's passed by David in age now, by an easy decade. Aged overnight by sights even Philadelphia has never seen. Over dinner, he entertains them with tales from the hell of basic training. "Then they dropped us down in the middle of a swamp at night. Two days, with nothing but a pocketknife and a piece of flint." William Daley eyes his son with fierce regard, an esteem bordering on rivalry. Little Michael dies of envy by agonized degrees.

"You look up your aunt and uncles yet?"

"Not yet, Mama. They don't let us off base much. But I will."

After dinner, he steps out back with his sister to sit on the stoop and smoke a cigarette.

"Marines teach you that, too?" she asks.

"Taught me how to bring it home anyway." His face is grim. Like it used to be when white people crossed the street rather than pass alongside them.

"So what is it, Char? What aren't you telling them?"

He flashes her a look, ready to deny everything if she can't pin him. But she can. He stubs out the butt against the concrete walk. "It's a joke, Dee. A sick, bad joke. We're at war already, and we haven't even left the parade ground."

She bobs her firstborn on her knee. Little Joey's safe inside with his grandmother and aunts. She cups Jonah's ear against his uncle's anger, deflecting and protecting. She watches Charlie put out his cigarette, her hopes for the goals of this good war stubbed out with it.

He sucks in empty air. "You think Philadelphia's fucked up? North Carolina makes this place look like Brotherly Love. How did Mama's family survive it down there all these years? Can't get a lunch anywhere outside the base. Can't even go onto Lejeune, even in full dress, without a white man taking me in with him. White general comes over to Montford Point to address the first Negro marines in history? Ends up telling us, right to our faces, how shocked he is to see a bunch of darkie upstarts wearing his heretofore-unspoiled uniform."

Charles takes off his cap and rubs his close-cropped skull. "You want to see my enlistment contract? It's stamped COLORED, in big block letters. Case you might miss the fact. Know what that's all about? Means the President can make them take us, but he can't force them to make us real marines. Guess what they have planned for the Fifty-first? We're going to be stewards. Ship us out to the Pacific so we can be the damn Pullman porters for the white battalions. The enemy will be firing at us. And we'll be hiding behind oil drums and shooting back at them with baked beans."

Little Jonah breaks free from Delia's grip and makes a dash for a gray squirrel. The squirrel heads up a tree. So the child, baffled and empty-handed, breaks for wider freedom in the fenced-in yard. Charlie studies his nephew, a level gaze. The child is small distraction. "Even with all the shit we've always been through up here? With everything we've lived through, I'd never have believed this. Life in this country is a waking nightmare. Hitler's got nothing on the United States, Dee. I'm not even sure that everyone on this side of the ocean really wants to take the motherfucker down."

"Oh, hush up, Charlie." He does, but only because she's his big sister. "Don't talk crazy." She wants to give him something, some countering truth. But they're both too old now for reassurance. "It's the same fight, Char." And who knows? Maybe it is. "You're in it. You're fighting. One war."

A grin breaks out on Charlie's face, nothing to do with her. "Speaking of war. Your little Brown Bomber there takes out any more of Mama's roses, we're all dead." Before she can move a step toward Jonah, Charlie whistles. The piercing, pure tone stops Jonah in his tracks. "Hey, soldier. Fall in. Report for duty!" The boy smiles, gives his head a slow, sly shake. Charles Daley, Fifty-first Battalion, U.S. Marine Corps, nods back. "Kid's awfully light, ain't he?"

They don't get out to Philly as often as they should. She marks the weeks by her boys' bursts of growth. She tries to slow the changes in them but can't. Her mother's right: different little men, each time they rise to breakfast. David, too: scariest of all. Changing faster than she can figure out. It's not that he's cold, only preoccupied. Every human in the world, he tells her, runs on his own clock. Some an hour or two behind, some as much as years ahead. "You," she tells him, one of the sources of her love, "you are your own Greenwich."

Now he's running out ahead of her—not much; maybe five minutes, ten—just enough for her to miss him. She looks for the reason in herself. Her body has changed a little, after the boys. But it can't be that; in those moments when they still catch each other, his palm against the small of her back, his nose still buried, astonished, in her neck, his clock returns to hers, entraining, lingering in their sweet after-the-fact. She worries it might be the boys, somehow, their constant need. But he's as devoted to them as ever, reading Jonah endless repetitions of nursery dimeter, entertaining Joey all Sunday long with a pocket mirror's dancing sunbeam.

He travels too much. She has memorized the Broadway Limited schedule to Chicago. His beloved Mr. Fermi has set up a lab there, at the university. David makes so many trips, he might as well be on salary.

"Are we moving out?" she asks. Trying to be good, trying to be a wife, managing only to sound doleful.

"Not if you do not wish." Which somehow frightens her even more. She's never been one to let her imagination run away from her. But it doesn't have to run; it has so much free time now, it can cover any distance in a leisurely stroll.

David is called out to Chicago the evening before Jonah's second birthday. The news astonishes her. "How can you miss this?" The most acid she's shown him since they married.

He hangs his head. "I told them. I tried to change. Fourteen people need me there on this day."

"What fourteen people?"

He doesn't say. He won't talk about what's happening. He leaves her to her worst guesses. He holds out his palms. "My Delia. It's tomorrow already, on the other side of the dateline." So they have a leap-ahead birthday party, complete with newspaper hats and an orchestra of combs and wax paper. The children are thrilled; the adults guarded and miserable.

She sits alone with the boys the next day. They plunk on the piano,

Joey on her lap, reaching for the keys, Jonah next to her on the bench, hitting the tonic to match her right hand's "Happy Birthday." She bobbles more notes than her boy does. She knows what it is. It's something white. No man in this world will choose to stay with somebody dark if he doesn't have to. She falls asleep that night to this thought, and the same certainty shoves her up from sleep at 3:00 A.M. It's a white woman. Maybe not lust. Just familiarity. Something that just happens to him, comfortable, known. After almost three years, he's discovered that his wife's blackness is more than circumstance. The distance doesn't close up just by naming.

Or maybe it's not even a woman. Maybe just white doings, white flight. Things she doesn't understand, things white life has always locked her out of. What has that world ever done but run from her? Why should this man be any different? He has seen some blemish in her, some crudeness that confirms the law. She has been a fool to think they could jump the broom, jump across blood on anything so feeble and handcuffed as love.

These thoughts nest in her at that weird hour, the time of night when even knowing that a thought is pure craziness doesn't help banish it. The fear is under her skin, crippling her. Even feeling that crippledness proves that the two of them shouldn't be together, should never have tried. But her boys: her JoJo. They prove something, too, just the look of them: proof beyond any earthly proof. She rises to watch them in their beds. Their simple act of breathing in their sleep gets her through until morning.

By daylight, she vows to wait until her husband brings it up himself. Anything less would be unfaithful. He'll tell her. And yet, he hasn't. They vowed when they married that no lies would ever come between them. Now she makes this smaller vow, only to let him break the larger one.

"What is it?" she asks, cornering him. He's barely off the train. "Tell me what's going on out there."

"Wife." He sits her down. "I have a secret."

"Well, you better let me in on it, or you'll be sharing your secret with Saint Peter."

He curls his forehead, trying to decode her. "By law and by oath, I'm not permitted to share this. Not even with your Saint Peter."

Where I come from, I'm your oath. In my country, we save each other from the law.

He hears her, in her silence. He tells her what she already knows. "War work. Work of the highest possible security."

"David," she says, near flattened. "I know what you study. How could your work be of even the least . . . ?"

He's laughing before she frames the thought. "Yes! Useless. My specialty, absolutely useless. But they don't use me for my specialty. They use me to help with the next related idea."

Everything, related. It's how he even has a job to begin with. His legendary ability to solve others' problems, to sit in the lunchroom and scrawl on the backs of napkins the clues his stumped colleagues have been seeking for months.

"Let me guess. The army's making you build a time bomb." His face's startle is worse than any 3:00 A.M. fear. "Oh my God." She covers her mouth. "It can't be." Ready to laugh, if he'll let her.

He doesn't. Then the law is just the two of them. He tells her the secret he can't tell anyone. He leaves no evidence, draws no pictures. But he tells her. Yes, it's a white thing. But it isn't his. He has been brought into it, along with hundreds of others. A monster thing, a time-ending thing, built in secret places, here and out west.

"I don't do much. Just mathematics."

"Do the Germans know about this?"

He tells her about his old friends from Leipzig, Heisenberg and the others, the ones who didn't emigrate. "Physics"—he shrugs—"is German."

He must travel, whenever they need him. No question. It could end the war. It could bring Charlie home, and all the others. Keep her boys from harm.

"Now I am your prisoner. Because I've told you this. Anytime you want to have me . . ." He draws a finger across his throat and makes a slurping noise. She stops his hand. *Don't even joke.* He sits with her a little longer, neither of them going anywhere.

"Someday?" he says. "You must tell me something back. Something you can not tell anyone."

"I already have."

Joey turns one. This time, David's home. The whole family sits down at the piano bench to explore "Happy Birthday," one hand from each player, with the birthday boy joining in and squealing in delight.

David is in and out of town the whole summer, gone that first night of

August, when police shoot a Negro soldier in uniform over at the Brad-
dock Hotel. Delia has the radio tuned to classical music—the station she
uses to put the boys to bed. They don't go down easily in this wilting
heat. They need a fan, the music, and an open window to pacify them.
She's asleep herself, well past 11:00 P.M., when a knock at the door
awakens her. She stumbles upright and throws on a robe. The knock
grows frantic and a voice spasms on the other side. She pads toward the
door in terror, calling out, "Who is it?" Her brain scrabbles up from out
of sleep, fleeing some country under occupation. The door starts to open
and she screams. The boys wake; Joey begins to cry. "David?" she yells in
the dark. "David? Is that you?"

Her heart revives when she makes out Mrs. Washington, their landlady, even more panicked than Delia. "Oh, Lord, Mrs. Strom. It's all
over. The city's on fire!"

Delia calms the woman and brings her into the parlor. But Mrs. Washington won't sit. If the world is ending, she wants to be vertical. By now,
the boys are up and clamped to their mother, wailing. This has some
blessing, as it forces Mrs. Washington to compose herself and help comfort them. But whispering, as if to keep it from the boys, she tells Delia,
"They're coming this way. I know it. They're going to go after the nice
houses. Come tear down what we got."

No use asking who. Even a sensible answer would be insane. The laws
outside have broken down. That's all they are allowed to know. Delia
goes to the front window and pulls back the curtains. A few people mill
in the street, shocked, in robes and dressing gowns. Delia starts to pull
on a few hurried clothes. Mrs. Washington shouts, "Don't you go out
there! Don't you leave us." The boys scramble up, ready to protect her.
But another child calls her outdoors, a quieter, more frightened sound.
Someone in trouble, a girl whose voice she knows but can't yet recognize. One voice out of the anarchy, calling her by name, pulling her from
safety, and she has no choice.

Delia steps out, just down to the sidewalk, the same few steps she
takes every day. But everything outside the freestone house is wrong. She
walks into a wall of heated air, a chorus of sirens going off at all distances,
wailing in spectral waves like wounded animals. She looks eastward down
the street at a pale orange halo pasted against the sky. A plume rises behind it, toward the south. She hears a murmur like surf, and when her
ears attenuate, the sound turns into people shouting.

Large buildings are on fire. The glow comes from the direction of

Sydenham Hospital. Police, fire, and air raid sirens all blare, the first real wartime sounds she's heard these last twenty months. Harlem's going up, giving back a taste of everything it's ever gotten. She asks anyone who stops to answer, but no one knows. Or everyone does, only no two accounts are the same. The police have killed a soldier who was defending his mother, shot him dead in the back. A group of armed defenders have the Twenty-eighth Precinct surrounded. It's a thousand people. Three thousand. Ten. A gun battle on 136th. A crowd overturning cars, crumpling them with baseball bats. The destruction is moving southward, street by street. No—north. The burning is headed her way.

She watches as the crowd down her block starts schooling. Even on this street, so far untouched, clumps of mesmerized bystanders turn in tight, frightened circles. Some younger men trot in the direction of the flames, their years of pressed rage now turning them diamond. Others flee toward some dissolving city, west of here. Most stand still, all faith betrayed. The night is a cauldron, the air like fired brick in her mouth, the taste of torched buildings. She spins and looks at their row, sees their house burned to the ground. The image is so real, she knows it has already happened. She adds her voice to the shriek-filled air and runs, not stopping until she's back inside, the door bolted, her curtains drawn.

"Away from the windows," she tells the children. Her calmness astounds her. "Come on, everyone. Let's sit in the kitchen. It'll be nicer there."

"They're coming this way," Mrs. Washington cries. "They're going to come up here and get the nice places. That's what they're after."

"Hush. It's miles away. We're safe here." She nurses the lie even as she serves it up. The thing she has seen—her house torched and gutted—is as real in her now as any fixed past. They shouldn't be cowering here, in this death trap, waiting for the end to come find them. But where else can they go? Harlem is burning.

The boys aren't frightened anymore. The night's a game, a bright breaking of rules. They want lemonade. They want shaved ice. She gets them whatever they ask for. She and Jonah show Mrs. Washington how they sing "My country, 'tis of thee" in two-part harmony, with little Joseph keeping time on an overturned quart pot.

A quick listen in the front room confirms her fears: The night's cries are coming nearer. She swears at David for choosing this night to be so far away. She couldn't reach him now, even if she knew how. Then she remembers, and blesses their luck. His presence here tonight would finish them all.

"Nothing's ever gonna change for us." Mrs. Washington speaks like praying. "This is how it's always gonna be."

"Please, Mrs. Washington. Not in front of the boys."

But the boys have curled up, each on his own oval rag rug, cushioned islands on the hardwood sea. Delia keeps vigil, ready to rush them out the back if the crowd reaches their door. All night long, she hears someone out there in the cauldron calling for her. This is how the four of them sit, the tide of violence lapping at the corner of their street, cresting in a fury of helplessness before subsiding just before dawn.

Morning breaks, silent. The fury of last night has spent itself to change exactly nothing. Delia rises to her feet, bewildered. She walks out to the front room, which is still, astonishingly, there. But she saw it. The house was gone, and now it's still here, and she doesn't know how to get from that one certainty back to this other.

Mrs. Washington draws Delia to her in a wild departing hug. "Bless you. I was dying of fright, and you were here. I'll never forget what you did for me."

"Yes," Delia answers, still dazed. Then: "No! I did nothing." That's what must have saved them. Holding still, waiting for judgment to pass over.

When David returns, two nights later, she tries to tell him. "Were you frightened?" he asks. The weight of foreign words hobbles him so badly, he doesn't even try for the thing he needs to know.

"We just sat there, the four of us, waiting. I knew what was going to happen. It all felt decided. Already done. And then . . ."

"Then it did *not* happen."

"Then it did not happen." She gives a soft shake of the head, refusing the evidence. "The house is still here."

"Still here. And all of us, still, too." He takes her in his arms, but their bafflement grows. He asks, "What has caused this riot?" She tells him: a hotel arrest. A soldier trying to keep the police from arresting a woman. "Six people dead? Many buildings burned? All this from one arrest?"

"David." She closes her eyes, exhausted. "You can't know. You simply cannot know."

She sees this sting him across the face: a judgment. A rebuke. He tries to follow her—the rational scientist. But he can't. Can't know the pressure, millions of lives sharpened to a point, the blade that skewers you every time you try to move. He can't even start to do the math. It's something you come into, centuries before you're born. To a white: a drunken woman breaking the law. But to those that the law effaces: the one standing, irrevocable death sentence.

David takes off his glasses and wipes them. "You say I cannot know. But will our boys?"

Two days after the riot, the boys have already forgotten. But something in them will remember hiding in the kitchen one night while still too young to know anything. Will they know the riot the way *she* knows, the way their father cannot? "Yes. They'll have to. The largest part of them will know." As if it had parts, this knowledge.

David looks up at her, pleading for admission. His sons will not be his. Every census will divide them. Every numbering. She watches the world take his slave children away from him to a live burial, an unmarked grave. We do not own ourselves. Always, others run us. His lips press together, bloodless. "Madness. The whole species." She sits through this diagnosis in silence. Her man is in agony. The agony of his family, lost in bombed Rotterdam. The agony of his family, hiding in the dark in burning Harlem, while he is gone. "Nothing ever changes. The past will run us forever. No forgiveness. We never escape."

These words scare her worse than that night's sirens. It will end her, a blanket condemnation coming from this man, who so needs to believe that time will redeem everyone. And still, she can't contradict him. Can't offer him any hideout from forever. She sees the mathematician struggle with the crazed logic that assigns him: colored there, white here. The bird and the fish can build their nest. But the place they build in will blow out from underneath it.

"Perhaps they do not have four choices after all. These boys of ours."

She touches his arm. "Nobody gets even one."

"Belonging will kill us."

She hides her head from him and cries. He places one hand on her nape, her shoulders, and feels the boulder there. His hand works softly, like water on that rock. Perhaps if humans had the time of erosion. If they could live at the speed of stones. He talks as he rubs her. She doesn't look up.

"My father was finished with all of this. 'Our people. The chosen. The children of God.' And everyone else: not. Five thousand years was enough. A Jew was not geography, not nation, not language, not even culture. Only common ancestors. He could not be the same as a Jew in Russia or Spain or Palestine, who is different from him in every way that can be different except for being 'our people.' He even convinced my mother, whose grandparents died in the pogroms. But here is the funny thing." Her lips contract involuntarily under his rubbing fingertips. She knows; she knows. He doesn't need to say. "The funny thing . . ."

His parents are chosen anyway.

She lifts her head to him. She needs to see if he's still there. "We can be our people." Renewing their first vow. All its break and remaking. "Just us."

"What do we tell these boys?"

She is bound to him. Will do anything to lift up the man, his solitary race of one. Anything, including lie. So she signs on to her downfall: love. She puts her hand on his nape, sealing the symmetry he began. "We tell them about the future." The only place bearable.

A groan breaks out of him. "Which one?"

"The one we saw."

Then he remembers. He takes hold again on nothing, a tree on a rock face, rooted in a spoonful of soil. "Yes. There." The future that has led them here. The one they make possible. His life's work must find them such junctures, such turnings. What dimensions don't yet exist will come into being, bent open by their traveling through them. They can map it slowly, their best-case future. Month by month, child by child. Their sons will be the first ones. Children of the coming age. Charter citizens of the postrace place, both races, no races, *race* itself: blending unblended, like notes stacked up in a chord.

America, too, must jump into its own nonexistent future. Nazi transcendence—the latest flare-up of white culture's world order—forces the country into a general housecleaning. The Tuskegee Airmen, the 758th Tank, the Fifty-first and Fifty-second Marine Corps divisions, and scores of other Negro units are shipped out to all the choke points of the global front. Whatever future this war leaves intact, it will never again be yesterday's tomorrow.

Delia gets a letter from Charles in January of 1944. He's been assigned to the Seacoast Artillery Group.

We're starting our first major offensive—a drive across fortified enemy concentrations in Georgia, Alabama, and Mississippi. Should we succeed in forming a beachhead and breaking out, we plan to sweep through Texas, New Mexico, and Arizona—dangerous territory—and press on to establish a forward perimeter in San Diego. From there, we'll ship out and meet the Japanese, who ought to be a cakewalk in comparison to the folks down this way.

He sends another note in mid-February, from Camp Elliott, California:

Greetings from Tara West . . . We've a ninety-mm gun crew here who can hit a towed target in less than a minute. Show me the white crew that can do better. But last night, when the brass decided to throw us an open-air movie, that same crew, along with the whole Fifty-first, was sent to the back, behind thousands of white boys, who, I suppose, had to keep themselves between us and Norma Shearer so there wouldn't be any race mingling. (Nothing personal, sister.) Well, we particular marines didn't much feel like heading back. We wound up getting thrown out all together. The place turned into a free-for-all, with a couple dozen good-sized bucks ending up behind bars. We ship out tomorrow on the *Meteor*, not an hour too soon, as far as I'm concerned. I'm so ready to leave these shores and try my luck in the savage, uncivilized islands that I can't begin to tell you. Keep an eye on the home front, Dee. I mean, watch out for it.

Delia talks to David, in bed that night, before his next trip out west. "Hurry up with that work of yours." The one quick jump into the future that will save everyone she cares for. The idea forms in her, in that place before idea. She must protect her boys from the present, preserve their unlabeled joy, refuse to say what they are, teach them to sing through every invented limit the human mind ever cowered behind.

So it feels like a message from space—one night in midyear, spring cracking the crust of a winter grown unbearable, as she bathes Joey in the bassinet and David listens to the New York Philharmonic in the overstuffed chair, his arm around Jonah—when a piece for full orchestra called *Manhattan Nocturne* seeps through the crystal set into their rented home. The piece is lovely, sonorous, and tinged with anachronism.

Singable. She hums along by the end, buzzing the primary theme into a giggling Joey's belly as if her baby boy's body were a kazoo.

She notices the music without really noticing. But the polished announcer's words afterward hit her like an omen. The composer is a thirteen-year-old girl named Phillipa Duke Schuyler. And if that wasn't impossible enough, the girl is of mixed race. Delia almost puts a safety pin through her boy, and even then, Joey suffers her. She thinks she misheard, until David wanders slack-jawed into the room. His eyes fill with frightened vindication. "One hundred piano compositions before her twelfth year!"

Delia looks at her husband, feeling as if they've escaped the prison that the laws of a dozen American states would still sentence them to. The girl has an IQ of 185. Played the piano at three and began the concert circuit by the age of eleven. Their boys have an advance scout in this newfound land. The continent exists already, and it's inhabited.

The girl's father is a journalist, her mother a Texas farmer's daughter. The father has written a meticulous account of his prodigy in the *Courier*, which Delia tracks down. The principles are simple. Raw milk, wheat germ, and cod-liver oil. Intensive education—a two-parent home schooling scheme of around-the-clock instruction. But the real secret is that old western farming trick of hybrid vigor. The basics of agricultural breeding. Twin-race children—that genius girl proves it—represent a new strain of crossed traits more robust than either of their parental lines. Mr. George Schuyler goes on to claim even more. Sturdy crossbred children are this country's only hope, the only way out of centuries of division that will otherwise grow wider with the run of time. Just writing as much would land Mr. Schuyler behind bars in Mississippi, according to a law no older than his daughter. But the words reach Delia like food falling from the desert sky.

Raw milk and wheat germ, mixed blood, daily doses of music, and the girl has become an angel. Her *Manhattan Nocturne* for one hundred instruments awes wartime America. Mayor La Guardia even declares a Phillipa Duke Schuyler Day. The sound of the past vanishes at the little girl's playing. Delia buys copies of all her available sheet music. She leaves the *Five Little Piano Pieces*, composed at age seven, out on the music rack. Her boys stare, rapt, at the picture of little Phillipa on the cover, seeing something in her that will take them decades to recognize. The pieces are among the first the boys learn—the foundation stone of the new Strom schoolhouse.

Others have been this way: It makes all the difference in the merciless world. Home lessons begin in earnest. The boys leap through every little melody she sets them. David rolls around on the floor with them, playing games with blocks that only an older, sadder child would suspect to be the basis of set theory. David and Delia even try the wheat germ and cod-liver oil, but the boys aren't taking.

"Kein Problem," David says. "We don't need one hundred and eighty-five IQ."

"True. Anything over one hundred and fifty will do just fine." In fact, it begins to dawn on Delia that every child who learns to walk and talk has the genius of whole galaxies engineered in them, before hate begins to dull them down.

It thrives, this school of four, without anyone thinking *school*. Outside their house, life sends them a sign, confirming their leap of faith. The Supreme Court deals a blow to all-white elections. The Allies land in France and push eastward. The endless war will end, and melting pot America will be the force that ends it. The only question is how soon. No day will be soon enough. For four years, they've had no word of David's parents. His sister and her husband have disappeared, too, most likely lost in Bulgaria when it went under. Month after month, Delia props up her man, telling him in every possible way that silence proves nothing. But finally, gradually, it does. All the messages escaping that continent converge on the same conclusion.

She feels him protecting her in turn. He already knows where his family must be, in the absence of opposing evidence. But he won't say as much to Delia. "You're right. Everything must remain possible." Until it isn't.

Her husband turns his private grief toward a response unthinkably large. As the Americans break out across the French *bocage*, David tenses. He hints at his fear to her, all the while trying to honor the government oaths he has sworn. She knows his anxiety. Some crossed trip wire on the map—the Meuse, the Rhine—will bring forth a pillar of elemental German fire. German physics. Some world-sized quantum experiment: two futures, either one of which must birth an outcome that will swallow the other forever.

The fall turns bitter. The Allied advance reaches Belgium. The Brits and Canadians crack open Antwerp to Allied shipping, and still they suffer no cosmic retaliation. Not a hint that Heisenberg is even close. The evidence builds that the greatest scientific power on earth—David's world-changing colleagues from Leipzig and Göttingen—have taken a wrong turn somewhere.

But any moment can alter every other. Rumors collapse back into fact the moment they are released. Some days, Delia feels her husband turning fatalistic, with nothing to do but shrink and wait, the passive inheritor of events too long in the making for him to influence them. On others, the urge to act possesses him, bending him almost double in further, more obscure efforts. These are the moments when Delia most loves him, his need for her so great, he can't even see it. What comfort can she give him, trapped in salvation's footrace? She gives him *here, now*, the sheltered fortress of their rented home.

One night, the air still heavy with heat and the boys tossing in sleep on the sofa in front of the steel-caged floor fan, the phone rings. It's a rare enough event in any week, and so startling at this hour that Delia almost sears her scalp with the pressing comb. David answers. "Yes? Who? Operator. Ah! Hello, William."

She's on her feet. Her father, who hates the telephone. Who believes the instrument is driving people schizophrenic. Who makes his wife place all his calls. Who doesn't believe in long distance. She crosses to David in two steps, hand out for the receiver, while her husband lapses into mumbled German. She takes the phone, and far away, tinny in her ear, her father tells her Charlie is dead. Killed in the Pacific. "On a coral atoll." Her father wanders. "Eniwetok." As if the name might keep her from screaming. "They were garrisoning the air base."

"How?" Her voice isn't hers. Her breath presses, and the smallest thought takes forever. She imagines death from the air, the enemy singling out her brother, his darkness a target against the white sand of paradise.

Her father's voice waits for a collection that's more like collapse. "You may not want . . ."

"Daddy," she moans.

"They were unloading a gun battery off a ship. A restraining cable broke. The snap caught him . . ."

She doesn't stop him, but she doesn't hear. She races ahead with management. Undo by doing. "Mama. How is Mama?"

"I've had to sedate her. She'll never forgive me."

"The children?"

"Michael is . . . proud. He thinks it was combat. The girls don't understand what it means, yet."

The girls? The girls don't? Yet? As she clings to that word *understand*, she closes down. Blood beats into her face and her eyes break open. Sobs come out of her that couldn't have been in. She feels David take the phone, make some hurried arrangements, and hang up. Then she's being comforted, held up by the ghost white arms of this man who'll never be more to her than almost recognizable, a stranger to her blood, the father of her children.

They go to Philadelphia. All four of them take the train that once smuggled her to New York, hidden from everyone but Charlie. Delia stands in the front of the house, under the tree Char fell out of at eight, the fall that left him with the bent nose and jutting collarbone. Her mother comes out of the house to meet her. She's falling already, twenty feet before they reach, and Delia must catch her. Nettie Ellen holds her hand to her mouth, stilling a thousand shaking prayers. "He can't be done yet. Too much more he's still got to do."

The doctor stands behind Nettie, blinded by daylight, his hair gone white overnight. They retreat into the house, Dr. Daley propping his wife, Delia holding her little one, and the white man leading his subdued but adventuring oldest boy. Michael is inside, wearing a jacket emblazoned with the Marine Corps insignia that his brother smuggled him from North Carolina. Lucille and Lorene bicker softly on the couch, barely lifting their heads as their sister enters.

Her brother Charlie, stopped forever. No more bitter-laugh letters, no more razz, no more improvised Charcoal show, no more rounds of sounding or toasting, no more fate-dismissing shrug. The new silence of this house closes in on Delia, swallowing all their sound.

There's no body for a burial. What's left of Charlie rots on a Pacific atoll. "They won't send it back," Dr. Daley tells Delia, out of the others' earshot. "They're going to leave him in a sandy hole with a six-inch salt-water table. Shark food. My country. I was here before the Pilgrims, and they won't send me my boy back." He points at the gold star Nettie Ellen has mounted in the front window. "They did, however, pay for that."

That night, they hold a makeshift service. No one but family. The net around them is large and strong. Many have been by already, feeding, helping out, talking and holding quiet. But tonight, there is just kin, the only people that boy never had a choice but to trust. Their grief knows no cure but memory. Each of them has something to recall. Some stories need only two words to play out again in front of all of them. Michael gets his brother's old sax and shows off the riffs he has stolen just by watching. Dr. Daley sits at the piano, tries a left-hand stride like the ones he used to chide his son for pounding out. For six full bars, he finds the swell. Then, hearing what his fingers want to do, he crumbles.

Mostly, they sing—wide, spectral, full-chorded things, the intervals cutting through generations. Sorrow songs. Songs about abiding and getting away and crossing over. Then the tunes that seem more wedding than funeral, thanking the dead boy for yesterday, for a joy it will kill them to ratify. The family finds their lines, one each, with no one assigning. Even Nettie Ellen, whose speech has shut down, finds the harmonies slated to her, keeping time—the beat of deliverance—with a hand on her thigh. Bound to go. Bound to go. I can't stay behind.

Jonah sits rapt on his mother's lap, mouth open, trying to join in. Joey fusses, and David picks him up and carries him outside, into the yard. That's best, Delia decides. God help her, but it's easier that way. More Canaan, more comfort, without having to make the perpetual explanations. Without having to look at the color that Charlie used to say was too light for pain.

"Folks will want to come. They're making a mountain of food." Nettie Ellen's barest request to her daughter: Stay a few days. We need to keep together now, sing that boy home. *Just stay*—the old racial certainty, comfort to be had only here, in the safety of *we*. All other places betray us. But hearing those wordless words, Delia can't bear it. Not another day. Belonging crushes her shoulders so she can't even stand. Run by histories laid down centuries before her own past had the chance to write itself. She'll suffocate here, in her mother's dining room, with its scent of wood soap and molasses, work and sacrifice, belief and resignation, and, now, dead children. She needs to fly, back home, back to the project of her family, back to the freedom her nation of four has invented. Get free tonight. Tomorrow is too late.

She starts to tell her mother she must go. But the woman hears her before Delia can speak a word. A low keening tears from Nettie's throat, a flood of whatever comes before words, whatever thicker thing words are made from. Her mother sobs rhythm, her narrow chest a drum. The river of loss dam-bursts out of her, up from a world Delia knows only in shadow, bits of ground-up ancestry refusing to be shed, a tongue not yet

English, older than Carolina, older than the annihilating middle passage of this life that cages them all. Delia's mother comes through, the way she has never once let herself come through in any church. Comes through to the beginning, and this death is already there.

Then she is in Delia's arms, the daughter flailing to give comfort. Awful turnaround, nature running backward. Her mother's mother now. The younger children look on, terrified at this twist. Even William's face pleads with his daughter to undo what has been done. Her whole family turns toward Delia, searching, until she sees. They're grieving the death that hasn't happened yet, alongside the one that has. Five faces beg Delia to reverse the thing she has set in motion. Her mother gasps for breath in her arms. English returns, but thick and low, scrabbling for syllables, cursing her native tongue. "Why did that boy die? All they'll ever want from us is dying."

Dr. Daley covers his face with one great fist. His children swing round upon him, and he looks up, horribly visible. He finds some refusal in him that stands in for dignity. He rises to his feet and heads from the room. "Daddy," Delia calls. "Daddy?" He will not turn.

The back door slams. Then the front opens. David and her baby, her second compensation, return. Her mother asks again. "Tell me a reason. Give me just one."

David surveys the faltering family. Joseph, too: the solemn child just turning, staring. Delia sees knowledge rise into her husband's face, that look she must carry around on hers, every waking hour. *This isn't yours. You're not welcome here.* He looks to her for the slightest guide. Her eyes flick up, toward the back door. This colorless man, this man she somehow married, this man who can understand nothing here, understands her. He gives the child to the twins and slips off, the way her father left, Delia fighting the urge to call him back.

She hums to her mother, cradling her head, as if all her years of receiving the same were simply training to give it back. She says nothing, speaking in the old, discarded accent that comes back so easily. She reminds her mother of heaven, courage, and other foolishness, of plans beyond anything so small as a human ever being able to second-guess. But her thoughts are on the men. As soon as she can, she signals Lorene to go check. Her little sister comes back, nodding. Delia wrinkles her brow but gets no more clarification from the girl than a puzzled grimace.

Delia stands and cranes, trying to see out the back hall window. Nothing. She makes some pretense—checking the cooling pies—to duck out to the kitchen. She looks through the bowed screen, the one her own mother spent years glancing through, keeping track on her children at play outdoors. Delia approaches the screen and peers sideways down the steep wooden stoop.

Both men sit motionless on the ground, their backs to the thick red maple. Now and then, their mouths move, forming words too soft to hear across the yard. One speaks and the other, after a long interval, answers. David punctuates his words with hand sweeps, illustrating on the air some halting geometry of thought. Her father's face folds up in struggle. His muscles dart through all the feints of a cornered animal: first rage, then barricade, then playing dead.

Her husband's face, too, pulls up lame, looking for some gloss it can't reach. But the hands keep moving, tracing their equations in space, drawing their only conclusion. The fingers form closed loops, lines lying inside themselves, running back along their point of origin. Her father nods—near-motionless head bobs. Not agreement, not acceptance. Just acknowledgment, bending like the top of the maple as it fits the day's breeze. His face slackens. She could call it calm, from where she stands, this far away, behind the gauze of the screen door.

They stay the night. That much, Delia gives her mother, who gave her everything. Who gave Charlie everything, and wound up paid by a gold star in her front window. But when people start arriving the next morning—the hunched aunts and uncles; neighbors with pans of crisp, pungent fowl; Dr. Daley's lifelong patients; those patients' children, many older than Charlie—when every soul who ever knew the boy and half of those who couldn't have told him from his nickname wander into the Daley living room, assembling like the choir of some suppressed sect, Delia gathers her boys and bolts. She's an impostor here, an intruder at her own brother's wake. She won't inflict that on the others, too charitable to name what has already happened to their little Dee.

This day, Nettie Ellen doesn't weep. Doesn't even protest her daughter's desertion except to say to her, just before the Stroms head for the station, "You are what's left of him, now." She kisses her grandchildren, and watches them leave, stone-still, waiting for the next blow.

Dr. Daley pecks Delia good-bye and shakes the hands of his sobered grandsons. To David, he says, "I've thought about what you told me." He pauses a long time, stuck between doubt and need. "It's madness, of course." David nods and smiles, his glasses sliding down the cantilevered bridge of his nose. That's enough for the doctor. He does not press for reason, but only adds, "Thank you."

The four of them are on the train, the boys running down the aisle, delighted again, released from death, when Delia asks David. The whole car stares at them, as it always does, disguising their curiosity or telegraphing their disgust. Only Delia's lightness keeps the threatened purebreds baffled enough to let her family pass home safely. Her thoughts have no time for these outsiders. Her father's parting words to David obsess her. *Madness. It's madness, of course.* Part of her wants to let it go, allow her father and husband to have at least this one secret between them. But more of her needs whatever broken comfort they've traded. Her father has never suffered consolation gladly. But this one seemed to give him room. She contains herself the whole ride. Then, as the train pulls into Penn Station, Delia hears herself ask, from high up in the atmosphere, "David? Yesterday?" She can't face her husband, too shockingly close on the seat beside her. "When you were talking to my father? I saw you. The two of you, through the back door. Sitting under that red tree."

"Yes," he says. She hates him for not volunteering, not reading her mind, not answering without making her spell out her need.

"What were you talking about?" She feels his head turn toward her. But still she can't look.

"We talked about why my people had to be stopped."

She swings round. "*Your* people?" He only nods. She'll die. Follow her brother. Become nothing.

"Yes. He asked me why I was not . . . fighting in the army."

"My God. Did you *tell* him?"

Her husband spreads his hands upward. Saying, *How could I?* Saying, *Forgive me: yes.*

The train slumps to a halt. She gathers her boys, the whole car still turning covertly to check if her children are really hers. Her Jonah pranks and sings, struggling to escape his mother's hand and dash out the train door onto the platform. But her Joey looks up at her, searching for reassurance, as if the trip to Philadelphia, his dead uncle, has just come home. His eyes lock on hers, darting diagonally, early into old age, nodding at her, the same huge motionless nod her father succumbed to only yesterday.

She must know. She waits until they're standing on the platform, an island of four in a swarming sea. "David? Was there more?"

He studies her as they follow the departing passengers. More. There's always more. "I told him what . . . *my people* think." He twists the words, through the corner of his mouth. She thinks he has turned on her, gone cruel. He shepherds the boys through the crowd, out onto the street and their next public humiliation, talking as he walks. "I told him what Einstein says. Minkowski. 'Jewish physics.' Time backward and time forward: Both are always. The universe does not make a difference between the two. Only we do."

She grabs his elbow, pulling until he stops. People flow past them. She doesn't hear their curses. She hears only what she heard the day they met—the message from that long-ago future she's forgotten.

"It's true," her husband says. "I told him that the past goes on. I told him that your brother still is."

MY BROTHER AS LOGE

I listen to Jonah's recording, and the year comes back intact. *Comes back*, as if that year had hurtled off somewhere while I stood still. The needle has only to touch down onto that circle of black vinyl and he's standing in front of me. Aside from the scratches and pops, the scattered flyspecks in amber that accumulate over years of listening, we're back on that day we laid the tracks down, two boys on the verge of the big time, the night before Watts exploded.

Da liked to say you can send a message "down into time." But you can't send one back up. He never explained to me how you could send *any* message, in *any* direction, and expect it to reach its mark. For even if the message arrives intact, everything it speaks about will have already changed.

My brother's debut recording, *Lifted Voice*—a title he hated—was released, to several favorable and even a few excited reviews. Purists found the recital miscellany more suited to a midcareer singer than to a first-timer. Some reviewers called the sampler approach "light," saying Jonah should have done a whole lieder cycle or a single-composer collection. This boy's attempt to show he could sing anything somehow overreached. Yet for most reviewers, the reach took hold.

The record jacket showed a late brooding landscape by Caspar David Friedrich. The back of the jacket had our black-and-white head shots and a midrange shot of Jonah onstage in concert dress. A silver medallion on the front bore a quote from Howard Silverman's *Times* review of the Town Hall recital: "This young man's sound has something deeper and more useful in it than mere perfection . . . His every note rings with exhilarating freedom."

The disk sold quietly. Harmondial was pleased, banking on long-term return on investment. They considered Jonah a buy and hold. We two were stunned that anyone bothered to listen to the thing. "Jesus, Joey! Thousands of people have added us to their record collections, and we don't even know them. My picture could be pressing up against Geraldine Farrar's kisser somewhere, even as we speak."

"You'd like that, wouldn't you?"

"One of her early pub photos. A nice little Cho-Cho-San."

"And somewhere else, you're pressing up against the tip of Kirsten Flagstad's spear point."

Jonah imagined that, having made a good recording, we had only to sit back and wait for the jobs to pour in. Mr. Weisman did book us more regularly into bigger cities, and we could just about live now on what we made. But week to week, our life was still the same university concert series and festival-dredging it had been before the record appeared.

I drop the needle onto the first track—Schubert's "Erl-King," a Marian Anderson standard—and I circle back into that closed loop. The record spins; the piano gallop resumes. Jonah and I send out the song's surging message, unchanged. But the people to whom we thought to send it are gone.

The same president who passed the Civil Rights Act forced through Congress a blank check for widening the war in Asia. Jonah and I carried around our draft cards, nothing if not law-abiding. But the shadow of the call passed over us. We slipped through the minefield, exiting out the far side, too old to be tapped. The summer after our record, Chicago erupted. Three days later, Cleveland followed. It was high July again, just as it had been when we'd laid down the tracks. And once again, the bewildered reporters tried to blame the heat. Civil rights was heading north. The chickens, as Malcolm had said, were coming home to roost. Violence accompanied us, nightly, on our hotel televisions. I stared at the collective hallucination, knowing I was somehow the author of it. Every time I put our record on the turntable to hear what we two had done, another city burned.

"They'll have to declare nationwide martial law." The idea seemed to appeal to Jonah. This was the man who'd lain on the sidewalk of Watts, moving his lips to some ethereal score, waiting to be shot. *High Fidelity* had just run a feature, "Ten Singers Under Thirty Who Will Change the Way You Listen to Lieder," naming him to their number-three spot. My brother's country was just fine. Martial law might even help stabilize our bookings.

I looked out from the upper stories of antiseptic hotel rooms onto a carousel of cities whose names bled into one another, watching for the next new trickles of smoke. The music that year was still in denial—"I'm a Believer"; "Good Vibrations"; "We Can Work It Out." Only this time, tens of millions of twenty-year-olds who had been lied to since birth were out in the streets saying *no*, singing *power*, shouting *burn*. I drop the needle down on the tracks of our Wolf songs and hear for the first time where the two of us were. My brother and I, alone, were heading back into that burning building that the rest of the country was racing to evacuate.

We called Da from San Francisco just before the High Holidays. Not that he ever kept track. Long distance, back then, was still a three-minute civil defense drill, saved for funerals and machine-gunned best wishes. Jonah got on and did a prestissimo recap of our recent concerts. Then I got on and greeted Da with the first few lines of the Kol Nidre in Hebrew, which I'd just learned phonetically out of a book. My accent was so bad, he couldn't understand me. I asked to talk to Ruth. Da said nothing. I thought he still didn't understand my English. So I asked again.

"Your sister has broken with me."

"She *what*? What are you talking about, Da?"

"She has moved away. *Sie hat uns verlassen. Sie ist weg.*"

"When did this happen?"

"Just now." To Da, that might have meant anything.

"Where'd she go?" Jonah, standing nearby, quizzed me with a look. Da didn't have the faintest idea.

"Did something happen? Have the two of you . . . ?"

"There was a fight." I found myself praying he wouldn't give me details. "The whole country is rebellion. Everything has become revolution. So of course, it's finally come your sister's and my turn."

"Can't you get her address from the university? You're her father. They'll have to tell you."

Shame filled his voice. "She has dropped out of school." More grief than when he told us, that December day at Boylston eleven years before, that our mother was dead. The first death still fit into his cosmology. This new disaster pushed him over into a place no theories could accommodate. His daughter had disowned him. She had torn loose in some astral discontinuity Da couldn't comprehend, even as it broke over him.

"Da? What . . . what happened? What did you do?"

"We had a fight. Your sister thinks . . . We had a fight about your mother."

I looked at Jonah, helpless. He held out his hand to take the phone. I gripped the receiver, ready to take it to my grave.

"I am the evil one." Da's voice broke. He'd seen the future, and his children were it. But this disaster had somehow hijacked his vision. "I am the enemy. There is nothing I can do." All our lives he'd told us, "Run your own race." Now he knew just how worthless that advice had always been. No one had their own race. No one's race was theirs to run. "I killed your mother. I ruined the three of you."

I could hear my own blood coursing in my ears. Ruth had told our father this. Worse: He'd reached the same conclusion. I felt my lips moving. Any objection I could make would only confirm him. At last I managed to say, "Don't be crazy, Da."

"How did we come here?" he answered.

I handed Jonah the phone and went to the hotel window. Down in the square below, in the gathering dusk, two street people argued. Jonah talked on to Da for several sentences. "She'll show up. She'll be back. Give her two weeks, tops." After a little gap of listening, he added, "You, too." Then the call was over.

Jonah didn't want to talk about it. So for a long time, we didn't. He wanted to rehearse. I sounded like shit pushed through a sieve. At last, he smiled at me and gave up. "Joey. Cool it. It's not the end of the world."

"No. Just of our family."

Something in him said his family had ended years ago. "Mule. It's done. It's not your fault. What are you going to do about it now? Ruth has been working up to this for years. She's just been waiting for the moment when she could punish us all for being who we are. Bust us for all the things we've done to her. Haven't done. Whatever."

"I thought you told Da she's coming back. You said two weeks."

"I meant two weeks in Da years." He shook his head in a controlled fury. The rage of confirmation. "Our own little sister. She's resented us for years. She hates everything about us. Everything she thinks we stand for." Jonah paced in place, trying to breathe normally. He shook his shoulders and shot his clenched fist into the air. "Power to the purple. Light brown is beautiful."

"She's a good deal more than light." Before he could shut me down, I rushed on. "Poor Rootie."

Jonah looked at me, rejected. Then he put his fingers to the bridge of his nose and nodded. "Poor all of us."

We went to Jersey to see Da as soon as we were back in the city. We went for dinner, which he insisted on making. I'd never seen the man so shaken. Whatever reason Ruth gave for quitting school and cutting Da off without a forwarding address had destroyed him. Da's hands shook as he passed the plates to put out on the table. He slumped about the kitchen, apologizing for being. He tried to make the tomato and chicken stew that Mama had loved to make. Da's smelled like a damp terry-cloth towel.

Jonah cued up a stack of Italian tenors to accompany dinner. When that distraction didn't work, he did his best to set the topics. But Da wanted to talk about Ruth. He was a total mess. "She says I am responsible."

"For what?"

Da just waved my question into the ether.

Jonah lectured at us both. "Let her go where she needs to go. Get out of her way, and she'll stop blaming you. That's all she wants. Remember how Mama raised us? 'Be whatever you want to be.' " I could hear how betrayed he was.

"That is not what your sister wants. She has told me to my face that your mother died . . . because she married me."

I slammed my fork down on my plate, splattering the stew. "Good God. How can she even . . ."

Da went on, talking to no one. "Have I been in terrible error all this time? Did your mother and I do wrong by making you children?"

Jonah tried to laugh. "Frankly, Da? Yes. Some other set of parents should have made us."

Da said only, "Maybe. Maybe."

We blasted through what was left of dinner. Jonah and I made short work of the dish cleanup while Da stood by, waving his arms. We talked a little about upcoming concerts. Jonah told Da he was planning to do a Met audition early in the spring. First I'd heard. But then, he'd gotten used to his accompanist reading his mind.

Ruth came up again only as we readied to leave. "Tell us when you hear from her," Jonah said. He tried not to sound too eager. "Trust me. She'll surface. People don't just cut off their own flesh and blood." He must have heard what he was saying. But Jonah never even flinched. His acting skill now matched his singing. My brother was ready for any audition he cared to take.

As we got our coats, Da broke down. "Boys. My boys." The word, after all his years in this land, still rhymed with *choice*. "Please stay here tonight. There is so much room in this place. It must be too late to take the train."

I checked my watch. Quarter past nine. Jonah was for going. I was for staying. We had two programs to perfect by next week, without enough hours to perfect them. But I wasn't budging, and Jonah wouldn't go by himself. Da put Jonah on the living room's foldout sofa and me on a bedroll on the floor of his study. He didn't want either of us staying in Ruth's room. You never knew when the girl might come home in the middle of the night.

I woke at no hour. Someone had broken into the house. In my half state, I heard the police searching down a tip they'd received about illegal fugitives hiding in the neighborhood. Then it sounded like a conversation, hushed voices in the hours before dawn, planning the day. Then I thought the radio was on, tuned to some lightly accented FM announcer. The accent was my father's, and I was awake. Da was talking to someone on the other side of the wall, in the kitchen, ten steps away from me. Amber seeped in under the crack of my room's door. For a moment, Jonah and I were spying on our parents where they whispered together in the old kitchen in Hamilton Heights, the night Jonah's first boarding school application had been rejected for unstated reasons. Now my father whispered with his firstborn son, while I did the eavesdropping, alone. I pictured Da and Jonah, head-to-head across the breakfast table. I couldn't figure it: My brother never woke up in the mornings without vast external encouragement. I checked the window: still hours from morning. They weren't just waking; they hadn't yet fallen asleep. By some secret signal, they'd arranged to stay up after I went down, to discuss in private things not meant for me.

I listened. Da was explaining himself. "How has it become greater than family?" I lay in the dark, listening for Jonah's reply, but there was none. After a pause, Da spoke again. "It cannot be bigger than family. It cannot become bigger than time. I could have told her what we saw.

Should I have told her about the child?" I had no idea what he was talking about. Again, I waited for Jonah to answer, and again he didn't. He'd grown completely helpless without me.

There was a sound, eerie and grating. At three o'clock in the morning, even "Happy Birthday" sounds terrifying. It took me a few rasps to decide: Da was laughing. Then it wasn't laughter. Our father was breaking down, and still Jonah said nothing. My hearing swelled until I realized: Jonah wasn't there. One padded set of footsteps, one clinking spoon against a single teacup, one muffled course of breathing. Da was alone, in his kitchen, in the middle of the night—one of how many nights running?—talking to himself.

He said, "I did not foresee this. I never saw this would come." Then he said, "Have we made a mistake? Maybe we have understood all wrong?"

I froze in my bedroll. There was only one person he could be talking to. Someone who couldn't answer. I fought down the urge to fling the door open. Anything out there would have killed me. All I could do was lie still in my makeshift bed, afraid even to breathe, straining to hear what answer he might receive. After a while, I heard my father change. He seemed, through the door, to grow lighter. He said, "Yes, that's so." In a voice awful with peace, he added, "Yes, I could not forget that." I heard him stand and move from the table to the sink. He set the dishes onto the porcelain. He stood there for some time, no doubt gazing out the darkened window above the sink. A groan escaped him. "But our little girl!" He didn't wait for an answer now, but padded out of the kitchen and down the hallway, to his room.

I never fell back asleep. I dressed at last with dawn and went out into the transformed kitchen. There, in the sink, were two of everything: two cups, two saucers, two spoons.

The whole bus ride back to the city, I sat next to Jonah, needing to ask if he'd heard, not wanting to ask, in the event that he hadn't. Our father talked to a phantom. He set out a coffee cup for her. Perhaps he talked to her all the time, nightly, when we weren't there, as if they both still had full days to compare. So long as neither Jonah nor I said anything, I might have invented everything. When we got off at Port Authority, Jonah said, "He'll never hear from her again." Only when he added, "She might as well be dead" did I realize he meant Ruth.

I figured that she would have to call us. Whatever Ruth imagined that Da had done to her, he'd done to us, as well. Only now did I see how out of touch we had drifted the last three years, while Jonah and I were on the road. I called so infrequently, usually just birthdays and holidays. I'd always been able to reach Ruth, even if I rarely did. I could not believe that she really wanted to hurt any of us. But with each day out of touch, I began to see how badly I'd refused her, just by living as I lived.

Weeks went by and we heard nothing. It occurred to me that she must have gotten into trouble. There was something in the papers every day. People were constantly getting arrested for making speeches, holding rallies, printing pamphlets—all the things Ruth excelled at and had so taken to since starting college. I had nightmares that she was being held in an underground cell where the guards wouldn't let me see her because the name I gave them didn't match the one they had on the list.

Jonah took his Met audition. I was to play for him, quavering piano reductions of pit orchestra tutti. I felt like an Italian organ-grinder. "Let me get this straight. I'm supposed to help you put me out of a job?"

"I get a contract with these people, Mule, and we'll make an honest man out of you."

"Tell me again why you want to do this?" His voice was about light, air, and upper altitudes, not about power, mass, and histrionics. He sang lieder as if Apollo were whispering into his ear on the fly. Opera seemed perverse. Like forcing a magnificent racehorse into armor for a joust. Not to mention that he hadn't studied it in years.

"Why? You're kidding, right? It's Everest, Mule."

By which he meant high, white, and cold. Then again, it was steady work. We'd been breaking hearts on the recital circuit for years, and we'd run through all our mother's insurance legacy. Maybe he was right. Maybe it was time to make a living.

Jonah must have imagined he'd be singing for Mr. Bing himself. Sir Rudolph, however, had other things on his plate the day Jonah did his fire walk. But alerted by Peter Grau, Jonah's old teacher, the casting people did give him a special listen. Jonah spent the better part of an afternoon passed from one merciless set of ears to another, singing in spaces in the bowels of the new Lincoln Center that ranged from gym-squeaky to bone-dead. Sometimes I played for him. Sometimes he sang a cappella. They ran him through a gamut of sight-singing. Sitting at the keys, I knew that if I played well, my reward would be never to accompany my brother again.

I played well. But not as well as my brother sang. That afternoon, he sounded as if he'd been sandbagging for all our last six months on the road. He did more to seduce these judges than he'd done for full houses in Seattle and San Francisco. He sailed up to the roundest sounds he knew how to make. The jaded New York set squirmed, trying to pretend there wasn't something special going on. People kept asking where he'd sung, what roles, under whom. Everyone was dumbstruck with his answer. "You've never soloed in a choral work? Never sung in front of an orchestra?"

It probably would have been shrewd to stretch the truth a little. But Jonah couldn't help it. "Not since childhood," he admitted.

They gave him da Ponte Mozart. He romped through it on a lark. They gave him meaty Puccini breast-beaters. He aired them out. They didn't know how to position him. They passed him up to a senior casting director, Crispin Linwell. Linwell studied my brother like a man regarding a rack of magazines, the heels of his black leather boots apart, horn-rim glasses pushed up on his forehead, the arms of a cardigan tied around his neck. He made Jonah sing the opening strains of "Auf Ewigkeit," from *Parsifal*, cutting him off after a few bars. He sent his aides upstairs on a raiding mission to steal a favorite soprano, Gina Hills, out of a closed rehearsal. The woman came into the room cursing roundly. Crispin Linwell waved her down. "My dear, we need you for a noble experiment."

Miss Hills calmed a little when she learned that the experiment involved the first love duet from act two of *Tristan*. She wanted Isolde, and thought this trial was hers. Linwell insisted on playing the piano reduction. He set them a smoldering tempo, then let the two of them loose.

My brother, of course, had often looked at the score. He'd known the scene by ear for a decade. But he'd never sung a single note of it anywhere outside of lessons and our apartment shower. Worse, it had been ages since he'd sung anything *with* anyone. When Mr. Linwell announced his experiment, I knew the jig was up. Jonah would be exposed as just another pretty voice, unable to work and play with others. Another over-reaching recitalist, stumbling in his bid to make it onto the big stage.

After about two minutes, it dawned on Miss Hills that she was playing a love scene with a black man. Realization rippled through her with the floating chords. I saw the uncertainty turn into revulsion as she scrambled to figure out why she'd been set up for this ambush. She flubbed an entrance, and we lived through an awful moment when I was sure she was going to run screaming from the room. Only the thought of her career held her in place.

Then the old musical philter did its trick again. Something came up out of my brother's mouth, something I'd never heard him do. Eight measures later, Gina Hills was smitten in midphrase. She wasn't a homely woman, but she was built like an opera singer. Her face was like her voice: best sampled from the middle of the house. My brother somehow turned her into Venus. He invested her with his full power, and she took it. The traction of his phrases drew her into his orbit. They started out on opposite sides of the piano, fifteen feet from each other. Four minutes in, they locked gazes and began dancing around each other. She wouldn't touch him, but reached out as if to. He wouldn't close that last gap between them that their duet so completely destroyed. The wonder of flaunting in broad daylight in front of a handful of listeners the last great taboo only stoked her sound.

Jonah started out with the score in front of him. But as they surged through the scene, he needed it less and less, singing over the top of the lowered page, finally jettisoning it altogether. Gina Hills hit the top of a sustained phrase, her face filling with blood. Jonah kept building, wave on wave, until the knot of listeners disappeared and this couple stood alone, naked and lifted, turning need into the most sublime delay available to the human body. This was 1967, the year the Supreme Court made it legal, even in that third of the country where it was still forbidden, for Jonah to marry a woman of this Isolde's color, a woman of our father's race.

Linwell rolled out with a gliss, stood up at the keys, and waved his fingers. "Yikes. All right, people. Air raid's over. Back to your normal lives." He snagged Gina Hills, who, in some private game of musical chairs, once the music stopped, refused to look at my brother. Linwell pinched her shoulders. "You were on some other planet, love." Miss Hills looked up, glowing and crestfallen. She'd wanted the role more than she wanted love. Then, for ten minutes, she'd inhabited it, the ancient tale of chemically induced disaster. She wobbled, still under the drug's residue. Linwell could have promised her an opening night in the next season, and she'd still have left that rehearsal room subdued.

When the room cleared, Linwell turned to us. His English eyes narrowed at me and wondered whether he could get away with asking me to wait in the hall. But he let me ride, then turned to absorb my brother. "What are we going to do with you?" Jonah had a notion or two. But he kept them hidden. Linwell shook his head and examined his clipboard of notes from the afternoon. I could see him making the calculation: Was it still too soon? Would *ever* be too soon, on such a country's stage?

He set down the scribbles and looked my brother in the eye. "I've heard about you, of course." It felt like a police shakedown. *Don't lie to us, boy. We know you're up to something.* "I thought you sang lieder. Not even that. I heard you did *Dowland*." He couldn't mask his distaste.

"I do," Jonah said. Just that: *I.* I was dispatched to whatever family would have me.

Linwell sat silent, fighting embarrassment. "Would you . . ." he began, seeking out some sordid favor. "Would you mind . . ." He gestured toward the piano. It took me a moment. He didn't believe us. He wanted proof.

Jonah and I took up our battle stations so routinely, I almost slipped and bowed out of sheer habit. Jonah made the massive turn without even thinking about it. He looked at me, inhaled, lifted imperceptibly, and on the downbeat we were there, tied together, on "Time Stands Still." We finished into the silence that the music named. I patted the piano lid and looked at Crispin Linwell. His eyes were wet. This man, who hadn't listened to music for pleasure for longer than I'd been alive, remembered, for three minutes, where he came from.

"Why would anyone want to give that up?"

Jonah blinked, deciding how real the question was. He'd have smiled right through, but Mr. Linwell waited for an answer. Someone doing what he was born to do, someone who could bring down a little corner of eternity onto earth wanted to throw it all over for pumped-up, gaudy spectacle. I could think of no reason big enough, except one. *You boys can be anything you want to be.*

Jonah leaned against the piano and drew his hand along the back of his neck. His eyebrows played with the question, still innocent. "Oh, you know." I winced and dug down into the piano stool. "It's more fun to sing with other people." He slipped down into a basso profundo. "Ahm-a *tarred* of livin' alone."

Crispin Linwell didn't laugh. He didn't even smile. He only shook his head. "Be careful what you wish for." He pulled his glasses from his forehead and tapped the tip of his pen on the clipboard's clip, a rapid motor rhythm. His whole body drew up in his chair and professionalized. "We can find something for you. You will sing with us. With . . . other people. Your agent's number's on the vita? . . . Fine. Tell him to expect a call." He shook our hands and dismissed us. But before we could go, Linwell stopped Jonah with one hand to the shoulder. I knew what he was going to say before he said it. I'd heard it often, impossible lifetimes ago, although, back then, always in the plural. "You are one of a kind."

Out on Broadway, in the late-winter air, Jonah whooped like a banshee. "'One of a kind,' Mule. 'Expect a call.'"

"I'm happy for you," I told him.

We expected the call through the whole spring. Mr. Weisman called with festivals, competitions, and concert series—Wolf Trap, Blossom, Aspen—but nothing from the Met. When Jonah bugged Mr. Weisman to nudge someone over in Linwell's office, our agent just laughed. "The wheels of opera grind exceeding slow, and not all that fine. You'll hear when you hear. Meanwhile, find something more useful to worry about."

Weisman did call with word from Harmondial in early summer. On slow but steady sales of the first recording, they were turning a profit. The record had gone into a fourth reprinting. There'd be a royalty check, not enough to pay for phone bills, but cash all the same. Harmondial wanted to talk about a follow-up. Two days after Jonah agreed in principle to a new contract over the phone, central Newark burned down. That industrious city just a handful of minutes by the PATH train from where we lived; gutted, as bad as the Hanoi neighborhoods Johnson had been targeting. It was July. Central Detroit followed the week after. Forty-one people dead and fourteen square miles of the city in cinders.

I went to Jonah in a panic. "We can't do this record. Tell them we're out."

"Mule! You nuts? Our public needs us." He shook me by the shoulders, a slapstick attack. "What are you worried about? You're not losing your nerve, are you? Not afraid of a little eternity? So what if people will be listening to you after your death? We can fix anything, on tape."

"That's not it."

"What is it, then?"

"Tell them we can't. Tell them we need to just . . . wait awhile."

He laughed me off. "Can't, Joey. It's all agreed to. Verbal contract. You're legally bound and gagged already. You don't own yourself no more, brother."

"Did I ever?" It didn't often happen that he looked away first.

Around the time Jonah began preparing for the second record, we started getting hang-up calls. He'd answer the phone, thinking it was

Weisman or Harmondial or even Crispin Linwell. But the moment Jonah said hello, the line would go dead. He had as many theories as there were walk-ons in *Aida*. He even thought it might be Gina Hills. I was home alone one afternoon in August when the phone rang. Jonah was out vocalizing in a practice room at NYU downtown. I answered, and a voice more familiar than my own asked, "Are you alone?"

"Ruthie! Oh, God, Ruthie, where *are* you?"

"Easy, Joey. I'm all right. I'm just fine. Is he there? Can you talk?"

"Who, Jonah? He's out. What's wrong? Why are you doing this to us?"

"Doing? Oh, Joey. If you don't know by now . . ." She fought for control of her voice. I don't know which of us was worse off. "Joey, how are you? You okay?"

"I'm good. We're all good. Da and Jonah. Everything's . . . moving along. Except for worrying about you, Ruth. We've been sick to death—"

"Stop it. Don't make me hang up on you." I heard her holding the mouthpiece away, fighting sobs. She came back. "I'd like to see you." She asked to meet at a bar on the northwest corner of Union Square. "Just you, Joey. I swear, if you bring anyone else with you, I'll run."

I left a note for Jonah, saying I wouldn't be back for dinner. I scrambled over to Union Square and hunted down the place she'd named. Ruth was there, sitting in a back booth. I'd have fallen all over her, but she wasn't alone. She had brought a bodyguard. She sat on the same side of the booth as a man a couple of years older than Jonah and several shades darker. He had a two-inch picked-out Afro and wore a denim vest, paisley shirt, and a silver neck chain with a little fist clenched around a dangling peace symbol.

"Joseph." My sister fought for a breezy neutral. "This is Robert. Robert Rider."

"Nice to meet you."

Robert Rider lifted his gaze, half a nod. "Same here," he said through a hard smile. I reached out to shake his hand, but his fingers wrapped up around my thumb, forcing mine to do the same.

I slung into the booth across from them. Ruth looked different. She had on a bright green minidress and boots. I tried to remember how she was dressed when I saw her last. I wore the tan dress shirt and black slacks I'd been wearing for two years. There was something odd about her hair. I nodded what I hoped was approval. "You've changed. What did you do?"

She snorted. "Thanks, Joey. It's not what I did. It's what I'm not doing. No more hot iron. No more relaxants. No more nothing but what I got."

Next to her, Robert grinned. "That's right, baby. Nappy and happy." She leaned into the man, touched her palm to his.

A waitress came by to see what I wanted. She was black, pretty, and about twenty. She and my sister had already made friends. "My brother," Ruth said. The waitress laughed, as if that could only be a joke. I ordered a ginger ale, and the waitress laughed again.

"You look great, Ruth." I didn't know what else to say. She did. She looked good and strong. She just didn't look like my sister.

"Don't sound so surprised." I could tell by her glance: I looked pale. She wasn't going to say anything.

"Are you all right? Where are you living? How are you making ends meet?"

Ruth stared at me, twisting her mouth and shaking her head. "Am *I* all right? How am *I* making ends meet? Oh, Joey. I'm not the one you should be worried about. There are twenty million people in this country whose lives aren't worth your monthly take-home." She glanced at the man next to her. Robert Rider nodded.

"I don't take home . . ." I let it drop. I saw myself, a double agent. My sister wanted to talk to me. I could hear in her voice the new worlds opening up all around her. She wanted to give them to me. I had to listen with enough approval and enthusiasm to keep her going, trick her out of her current address, and take it back to my father and brother.

She turned to Robert, who was studying the beer in front of him. "Joey here plays a mean Grieg. If blacks could vote, they'd want to elect him their cultural ambassador."

Robert hid his curled lips behind his lifted glass.

"Are you still in the city, Ruth?" I waved out the plate-glass window. "Have you moved downtown?"

"Oh, we live all over the place." I glanced at Robert. But that "we" seemed to mean more than just the two of them. "Town to town. Just like you and Jonah. Maybe not quite as deluxe." I felt myself grinning too much. "Joey stays in hotels," Ruth told Robert. "They ever have trouble finding a room for you, Joey? They ever have to send you to some other establishment?"

I said nothing. I didn't know what I'd done to her, except live. Above her challenge stare, Ruth's cheeks wavered. "So how's tricks, Joseph? You doing okay?" She hadn't come to fight. She'd come because she needed me.

"I'm fine. Aside from missing you."

She looked away, anywhere but at me. Her face twitched all over. Robert handed her a large black leather satchel. Ruth rooted through the bag and took out a manila envelope. She placed it on the booth in front of me. "Robert has been helping me look into the fire."

Bizarre angles played out in me. My sister had joined a religious cult. She was mixing in something illegal. But as I reached out for the envelope, I knew what fire. Inside the envelope was a sheaf of xerographic copies of dozen-year-old documents. While I examined them, Ruth held her breath. Something was on trial here—me, the two of them, the nation, the entire compounding past. I read as best as I could, unable to concentrate with those eyes appraising me.

"We've been staring at this our whole lives. I know you've thought the same thing, many times. But it wasn't until I met Robert, and I told him all about Mama . . . It's so obvious, Joey. So obvious, I had to have it pointed out to me."

I handled the copies, police reports of our gutted house in Hamilton Heights, the house we grew up in. The prose sank into leaden detail: measurements, times, charred inventories. I read over the destruction of my life as written by a committee of public servants. The ten-year-old girl who'd bitten the restraining fireman's hand while trying to break free and rescue her mother could not have survived one paragraph without outside support. I skimmed the last two pages and looked up. Ruth was staring at me, hopeful, afraid. "You see? You get what this means?"

She swirled the pages and found the one she was after. She turned it toward me, fixing the indictment with her fingernail. In so many stories about mixed-race people in fiction, their fingernails always identify them as really black. Ruth's fingernail hung on the word *accelerants*. Presence of trace accelerants throughout the foundation level.

"You know what those are?"

"Oily rags. Half-empty gas cans. The kind of stuff Mrs. Washington kept in her basement."

She wavered and glanced at Robert. She rallied. "Things deliberately planted to speed the rate of burn."

Robert nodded. "Somebody accelerating."

"Where . . . How do you . . ." I looked back down, reading furiously. "Nothing here says anything like that."

Robert bit into his words. "Now that's a fact."

"Accelerants mean arson," Ruth said.

I sat there shaking my head. "It doesn't say that anywhere. This report doesn't even——"

A one-note, mirthless laugh from Robert cut me off. I was a hopeless naïf. Worse: a classical musician. With brothers like me, the fire would have stayed an accident forever, just like the authorities wanted it to.

"And if it's arson . . ." Ruth was waiting for me to follow her. But her eyes knew this was a losing proposition.

Robert focused on a grim horizon. "If it's arson, it's murder."

I looked down at the smudged photocopies for some fact to steady me. "Ruth. Listen to what you're saying. There's no way. It's insane."

"It's at least that," Ruth agreed. Robert Rider sat still.

Then the fire that took my mother rose up through my spinal fuse and burst in my brain. The floor softened beneath me. I reached out and braced my hands against the booth, a block chord spread across the keys but making no sound. My decade-old nightmares of Mama's suffocation flooded back, in full, adult daylight. I couldn't let myself think the thought. The thought I was thinking.

I looked up at Ruth. Her face smeared. She saw my animal panic. "Oh, Da didn't have anything to do with it." Her voice held some fraction of pity, behind the disgust. "The man's not clever enough to know what started the fire. But he's responsible for her death, just as if he had."

The craziness of her words brought me back. "Ruth. You've lost your mind." She stared at me with something ready to protect itself at any cost. I dropped my eyes down to the nonexistent evidence. "If the police report found evidence of arson, why didn't they say it was arson?"

"Why bother?" Ruth looked out over the crowded room. "Nobody was hurt. Just a black woman."

"Then why bother even to mention the accelerants in the report?"

Ruth just shrugged and stared into nothing. But Robert leaned forward. "You have to know how these people work. They put in the barest minimum of fact, so they can't get busted if it ever comes back to them. But they're never going to put down one single word that might turn the thing into a case. Not if they don't have to."

"I just don't understand. How could it have been deliberate? Who could have wanted . . ."

Ruth held her head. "White man married to a black woman? Six million people in New York were holding that bomb."

"Ruth! There was no bomb. The furnace exploded."

"The fire was helped along by something somebody put there."

There *had* been violence. Steady, lifelong. Words, muffled threats, shoves, spit: all the confusions I'd seen in childhood and refused to name. But not this level of madness. "Listen. If this was an attack against a mixed-race couple, then it was an attack on Da, as well. Who's to say the attacker was . . ."

"Joey. Joey." Ruth's eyes filled with liquid. She grieved for me. "Why are you hiding from this? Don't you see what they have done to us?"

Robert lowered the edge of his enormous hand to the table. "If the police had had a black suspect for this thing, the man would have fried six weeks after the crime."

I looked up at this stranger. How long had they been working on this theory together? Where had they gotten these photocopies? My sister had said more about her mother's death to this outsider than she'd ever shared with me. I sat rubbing water droplets off the outside of my glass. We'd been born in the same place, within a few years of one another, of the same parents. Now my sister lived in another country.

"Da collected on Mama's life insurance." I studied her as I spoke. I only now realized how criminal we'd been toward her. Most of that insurance money went into launching Jonah and me into performing orbit. Ruth had gotten only a fraction, for college tuition. And now she'd quit school. "If the insurance company had even a shred of evidence to make them doubt . . ."

Ruth looked at Robert, their proof wobbling. I'd wanted only to relieve her. I'd done just the opposite. Robert shrugged. "I'm sure the insurance company looked into it, as far as they were able to. They couldn't prove fraud. Once that wasn't the issue, they couldn't be bothered with how the woman died."

"Ruth. Listen to me. You know that Da would never have let this go by without an investigation. Not if there had been the smallest thing to go after. Any suggestion at all."

Ruth stared back. I was failing her, attacking. But she still needed me for something I couldn't understand. "The man is a white man. He has no concept of such things. He needed it to be an accident. Otherwise, her death is on his conscience."

And Ruth: she needed the opposite. Mama murdered, and by someone we'd never know. Someone who might not even have known us. It was the only explanation that left her anyplace in the world to live. I lifted up the sheaf of copies, their body of evidence. "What are you planning to do with this?"

They looked at each other, too tired to enlighten me. Ruth shook her head and lowered it. Robert grimaced. "Black person's never going to get a case like this looked into."

I had the bizarre sensation they wanted me to get Da—some white person—to press the case. "What on earth do you want from me?" I heard the words leave my mouth and could not take them back.

Ruth pressed her clenched fingers against her lips. "Don't worry, Joey. We don't want anything from you." Robert shifted in the booth. He looked down on the bench between them as if he'd dropped something. I felt a surge of admiration for the man, based on nothing but his willingness to be here. "We just thought you'd want to know how your mother . . ." Ruth's voice turned liquid. She took the copies away from me and slid them back into her satchel.

"We have to tell Jonah."

Some mix of hope and hatred rose in my sister's eyes. "Why? So he can call me crazy, just like his little brother did?" Her lip trembled, and she bit it in, just to make it stop.

"He has a better head for . . . He'll want to know what you think about this."

"Why?" Ruth said again, her tone now pure self-defense. "I've been trying to tell him something like this for years. I can't say shit to him without him busting my ass. The man despises me."

Her mouth crumpled like a rear-ended car. Her eyes welled over and one glinting thread started down the walnut of her left cheek. I reached over and took her hand. It didn't pull away. "He doesn't despise you, Ruth. He thinks you don't—"

"Last time I saw him?" She flipped her hand up toward her new hair. "He said I looked like a doo-wop backup singer. Said I sounded like Che Guevara's diary. He just laughed in my face."

"He was probably laughing in pleasure. You know Jonah . . ." I wasn't halfway through the sentence when it hit me. "Hold on. You mean you've seen him recently?" She looked away. "He never told me . . . You never said anything!" I took my hand away from hers. She scrambled for it back.

"Joey! It was only five minutes. It was a bleeding disaster. I couldn't say anything to him. He started shouting me down before I even—"

"One of you two might have told me. I thought something had happened to you. I thought you might be in trouble, hurt . . ."

She hung her head. "I'm sorry."

I looked at her. The little girl who'd sung "Bist du bei mir" at her mother's funeral. "Ruth. Ruth." Another syllable and I was finished.

She didn't look at me, but rooted around in her satchel for her wallet. Pay and run. Then she stopped and blurted, "Joey, come with us."

My eyes widened and my right hand pointed downward: *Now?* I turned to Robert. His face set into that look: *If not now, when?* The fire—their theory about it, our argument—was just a passing item on a more sweeping agenda. "Come . . . Where are you going?"

Ruth laughed, a good alto laugh, from the gut. She wiped her eyes dry. "All sorts of places, brother. You name it, we're headed there."

A grin like the sun broke across Robert's face. "It's all happening. Anything we work hard enough at."

I kept still. I was just happy, for a second, to have my sister back.

"We need you, Joey. You're smart, competent, educated. People are dying, in Chicago, down in Mississippi. My God, over in Bed-Stuy. People dying by miles, because they refuse to die by inches anymore."

"What are you . . . ?"

"We're working for the day, brother. It's easy. We're everywhere."

"Are you with some kind of organization?"

Ruth and Robert traded glances. They made an instant negotiation, appraising my file and deciding on discretion. Robert may have made the call, but my sister agreed. Why should they trust me, after all? My side was clear. Ruth reached across the table and took my elbow. "Joey, you could do so much. So much for people like us. Why are you . . . ?" She glanced at Robert. He wasn't going to help her. I blessed the man for refusing, at least, to judge me. "You're stuck in time, brother. Look at what you're peddling. Look who's buying. You don't even see. How can you play that jewelried shit while your own people can't even get a job, let alone protection under the law? You're playing right into the power-hoarding, supremacist . . ." She checked her volume. "Is this the world you want to live in? Wouldn't you rather work for what's coming?"

I felt a million years old. "What's coming, Ruth?"

"Don't you feel it?" Ruth waved at the plate-glass window behind me—the world of 1967. I had to keep from turning around to look. "Everything's shaking loose. It's all coming down. New sounds, everywhere."

I heard Jonah singing, in a funky falsetto, "Dancin' in the Streets." I raised my head. "We play a lot of new music, you know. Your brother is very progressive."

Ruth's laugh was brittle. "It's over, Joey. The world you've given your life to has played out."

I looked down at my hands. I'd been playing some piece on the tabletop. As soon as I noticed my hands, they stopped. "What do you suggest I do instead?"

Ruth looked at Robert. Again, the warning flash. "There's more work to do than I can begin to tell you."

An awfulness came over me. I didn't even want to look at the evidence. "You two aren't involved in anything criminal, are you?" I'd lost her already. I had nothing more to lose.

My sister's smiled tightened. She shook her head, but not in denial. Robert took a chance far bigger than mine. "Criminal? Question doesn't mean anything. You see, the law has been aimed against us for so long. When the law is corrupt, you no longer need to treat it like the law."

"Who decides this? Who decides when the law—"

"We do. The people. You and me."

"I'm just a piano player."

"You're anything you want to be, man."

I backed into the corner of the booth. "And who are you, *man*?"

Robert looked at me, ambushed, reeling. I'd gone for anger; I got pain. I heard my sister say, "Robert's my husband."

For a long time, I could produce no answer. At last I said, "Congratulations." All chance of feeling glad for them was lost. I'd have played at their wedding, all night long, anything they wanted. All I could do now was accept the news. "That's great. How long?" Ruth didn't answer. Neither did her husband. The three of us twisted in place, each sentenced to a private hell. "When were you going to tell me?"

"We just told you, Joe."

"How long have we been sitting here?"

Ruth wouldn't look at me. Robert met my eyes and murmured, "Actually, we weren't going to tell you at all."

My back slammed into the booth. "*Why?* What have I done to you?"

Ruth swung her face toward me. Her look said, *What have you done* for *me?* But she saw me, and broke. "It isn't you, Joey. We didn't want the news . . . to get back."

"Get *back*? You mean to Da?"

"Him. And . . . your brother."

"Ruth. Why? Why are you doing this to them?"

She folded into the man and put her arm around him. He hugged her back. My brother-in-law. Her protection against my words. Against all that the rest of us had done to bust her ass. "They've taken their stand. I'm not their business anymore."

Everything in the declaration sounded forced and wrong. From across the booth, my sister's *marriage*—I could hardly think the thing—seemed doomed before it started. "They'll want to know. They'll be happy for you." I didn't even sound feeble.

"They'd find some way to insult me and my husband both. I wouldn't give them the pleasure. Don't you dare tell them. Not even that you saw me."

"Ruth. What's happened? What's gotten into you?"

"Nothing's got into me, brother. Everything was in me already. From birth." She put her arm out on the table for me to examine. Physical proof.

"How can you treat Da like this, Ruth? The man's your father. What has he ever—"

She tapped her satchel, the manila folder. "He knew. The man knew all about these reports, a month after it happened."

"Ruth, *you* don't *know* for—"

"He never said a word to us. Not then. Not when we got older. Everything was always just an accident. Just fate. He and his so-called house-keeper—"

"Mrs. Samuels? What does Mrs. Samuels have—"

"The two of them, raising us like three sweet little white kids. See No Race, Hear No Race, Sing No Race. The whole, daily, humiliating, end-less . . ." Her body started to shake. Robert Rider, her husband, rested his hand on her back, and she collapsed. She curled into his open hands. Robert just sat there, patiently petting her burst of uncoiling hair. I wanted to reach across the table and take her hand. But it was no longer my place to offer comfort.

"That was their answer, Ruth. Move the world forward. Shortcut into the future, in one generation. One jump—beyond tribes."

"That's not a place," she hissed. "That's not a future." I waited for her to finish the thought. She already had.

"If Da thought for one minute that someone . . ." I wasn't sure what I meant to say. "Whatever he told us or didn't tell us about the fire, I'm sure he was just trying to honor her memory."

Ruth put her palms out to stop my words. She'd had enough of me and my kind. She pulled away from her husband's petting, ran her hands through her globe of hair, and blotted both eyes with a wadded napkin. When she took the napkin from her face, she was composed again. Ready for all the world's work her parents had failed to tell her about. She grabbed her satchel and rose, speaking more to her wristwatch than to me. "You've got to give the man up, Joey."

"The man? Give him up?"

"He's done nothing but exploit you. From the beginning of time."

"Da? *Exploit* me?"

"Not Da!" Her mouth twisted with agony. She wouldn't say his name.

"Jonah?" I waved toward her satchel, the evidence. "Jonah doesn't know anything about this. He can't reject your theory if you never even—"

"Jonah," she enunciated like a Met radio announcer, "doesn't know much about anything beneath his perch." Robert chuckled. I would have, too. Little Rootie had always been the perfect mimic.

"He's doing what he can. What he does best in the world."

"Being white, you mean?" She waved me off before I could counter. "You don't have to defend him, Joey. Really, you don't. So he's got a secret. I ain't gonna tell no one!"

"We could use a voice like that." The way Robert said this made me guess: She'd slipped him into a concert. He'd heard his new brother-in-law sing, and the memory of that sound left even him a little ashen. "Whole world's on fire. We could use everyone."

"He'd end up using us," Ruth said. She hated him. I couldn't even admit it long enough to ask why. "Well, brother?" She pulled out her wallet and rooted for some dollars. I wondered what she was doing for money. I didn't even know what my new brother-in-law did for a living. "You've heard all the evidence. The facts of what really happened to us. Make your own choice."

"Ruth. What *choice*? You make this sound like some kind of cosmic showdown." She tilted her head at me and lifted her eyebrows. "What choice am I supposed to make? I can play the piano, or I can help you save our people?"

"You can make a difference. Or not."

"For God's sake. You won't even tell me where you're living. You won't even tell me what you're involved in. Are you running guns or something? Bombing buildings?"

Robert's massive hand came across the table and landed on my wrist. But softly, certain. Too graceful to frighten. He'd have made a magnificent cellist. "Look. Your sister and I have joined the Party."

"The Party? The Communist party?"

Ruth chuckled. She pressed her palms into her cheeks. "Hopeless. The boy is hopeless."

A Morse code smile flicked across Robert's face. "Panthers." He leaned forward. "We're helping set up a New York chapter."

Ruth was right. I was the white man's nigger. Just the sound of the word scared me. I sat for a while, turning the name over in my head until it disintegrated. "Where's the black leather jacket?"

"Left it at home." Robert grinned, released my wrist, and waved outside. "I thought it was going to rain."

Had she grown radical out of love, or fallen for the man out of politics? "You going to shoot at people?" I asked my little sister.

I meant it as a nervous joke. Ruth answered, "They're shooting at us." I couldn't talk. I couldn't even breathe without betraying some blood relation.

My sister saw my agony. She stiffened, ready to go to war. But her husband shifted between us, softening. "Land, bread, education, justice, and peace. That's all we're talking."

"And the right to carry loaded weapons in public."

Ruth laughed. "Joey! You've been reading the newspapers. White newspapers, of course. But still."

Robert nodded. "We're fighting that bill, yeah. We have to. Police want us empty-handed. Whites want us to be the only ones without arms. Then they can keep doing anything they damn please to us." It sounded like madness to me. As terminally mad as the streets of Watts. And yet, aside from that one nightmare evening, I knew my life to be a far crazier, far more sheltered dream. "A man has a right to defend himself," my brother-in-law was saying. "So long as the police go on killing us at will, I'm holding out for that right. They've got the choice: the Whited States of America or the Ignited States."

His words were empty of theater. The sound died in the room's background chatter. I saw what Ruth responded to in the man. I, too, needed his approval, and I didn't even know him. Ruth pulled at her husband. "Come on, Robert. Joey's busy. Too busy for the facts. Too busy for what's coming."

"Ruth!" I pressed my fists into my eyes. "You'll kill me. What does any of this have to do with . . . ?" I waved at her satchel.

"With how your mother died? I thought it might help you decide whose son you are. That's all."

My mammy's own bairn. I spoke slowly, trying to find the beat. "My mother married my father. They raised us as they thought right. She died in a fire." *The fire didn't kill her.*

"Your mother died in what was more than likely an act of racial hatred. Every day, someone somewhere dies the way she did."

"Your mother . . ." And I couldn't anymore. Neither of us owned her. She was lost to us both. I looked at Ruth for a last moment. "Mama sang a mean Grieg."

She didn't reply. A look crossed her face. I saw it clearly, but I couldn't read it. She threw too much money down on the table and the two of them left. I wanted to stand up and follow them, at least for a street or two. But I was stuck to the booth, worthless, without belief.

I didn't tell Jonah I saw her. If he guessed, he never said as much. I never asked about his seeing her. I never even hinted at the meeting to Da. My loyalty to Ruth was greater than anything I owed either man, if only because I'd betrayed her so badly already. Each time I spoke to my father now, I saw a sheaf of photocopied police reports hidden away in his memory's files. Did he know what they contained? Could he say what they meant? I couldn't even form the questions in my head, let alone ask him. But Da sounded different to me now, filtered through all the things he'd never told me, whether they were his to tell me or not.

The year has become an operatic blur. Three astronauts burned alive on the launchpad. A South African surgeon put one man's living heart in another man's body. Israel ran through the assembled might of the Arab armies in six days, and even my anti-Zionist father feared something biblical in the lightning victory.

A play where a turn-of-the-century black boxer kissed his white wife onstage scandalized audiences worse than the real-life boxer had, half a century before. Tracy and Hepburn struggled with the prospect of a black son-in-law. A black man took his place on the Supreme Court, and I wondered if my sister's husband took any pleasure in the event. Marshall's appointment seemed, even to me, too little too late. Seventy separate riots spread through more than a dozen cities over the course of the year. The country turned upon itself, twisting on two simple words: *Black Power*.

Jonah, surprisingly, loved the phrase. He loved the disarray it sowed in the ranks of those good Americans, just minding their own business. He thought of it as guerrilla theater, just as aesthetically unsettling as the best of Webern or Berg. He walked about the apartment brandishing a dark tan golf-gloved fist over his head, shouting, "Mulatto Power! Mulatto Power!" for no one's benefit but mine.

And still the year's music beat on, cheerful, love-crazed, sun-drenched for a day. White music went black, stealing funk's righteous refusal. The Motown sound migrated even to cities whose cores had not recently burned down. At the same time, Monterey sent pop into places even my brother couldn't ridicule. Jonah brought home the first rock album he ever paid real money for. The Beatles, in high-camp Edwardian military band regalia peeked out from the cover with a cast of dozens, including effigies of their former selves. "You have to hear this." Jonah parked me under two cantaloupe halves of padded earphones and made me listen to the last cut, its slow, cacophonous orchestral climb to a forte major triad that spread into eternity. "Where do you think they got that idea? Ligeti? Penderecki? Pop ripping off the classics again, just like Tin Pan Alley used to do Rachmaninoff."

He made me listen to the whole record, pushing his favorite bits. From English music hall to raga, from sonata quotes to sinkholes of sounds that hadn't happened yet. "Trippy, huh?" I'd no idea where he learned the word.

The year split into vapor trails as tangled as those cloud-chamber traceries Da studied. Fashion went mad. Safari dresses, cossack blouses, aviator coats, Victorian velvet, silver metallic vinyl space-age miniskirts, Nehru jackets, combat boots with fishnet stockings, culottes with capes: a grandiose splintering into all years and places but this one. Fifty thousand people took to the Mall to protest the war, and three-quarters of a million strolled down Fifth Avenue in New York supporting it. Coltrane died and the U.S. government officially recognized the blues by sending Junior Wells on a goodwill tour to Africa. Che Guevara and George Lincoln

Rockwell both died violent deaths. Jonah and I lived our days between flower children and nurse slayers, decolonization and defoliants, Twiggy and Tiny Tim, *Hair* and *The Naked Ape*.

We'd be in some hotel room in Montreal or Dallas, watching the news, trying not to drop off the face of the earth, and some story would come on, a space shot or a riot, a love-in or mass strangling, an emperor's self-coronation or Third World insurgency, and Jonah would shake his head. "Who needs opera, Mule? No wonder the damn thing's dying. How can opera go head-to-head against this circus?"

We watched that year's performance race through its acts, all the while waiting for the Met to call, the call that would be Jonah's delivery and my death sentence. "They're nervous that I've never really sung over an orchestra." He decided to plump the vita with whatever symphonic solo appearances he could land. He told a bewildered Mr. Weisman to find him anything, with any body of instrumentalists. "I've got volume. You know that."

"This isn't about your volume, son." Mr. Weisman, whose fifty-year-old daughter had just died of breast cancer, had taken to calling us his sons. "This is about positioning you. Making people hear what it is you do."

"I'll do whatever the audience wants. Why do they need a brand? Can't they just listen?"

He couldn't understand the lead time on finding orchestral jobs. "It takes two years to do anything! Jesus, Joey. A read-through, a dress rehearsal, and a performance. Keep the thing fresh."

He picked up a substitution for a flu-stricken tenor who'd been slated to sing *Das Lied von der Erde* at Interlochen. The conductor couldn't find anyone else willing to step in on such short notice. Jonah mastered the treacherously craggy tenor songs in under five weeks. "I was born singing this stuff, Joey." I sat in the audience with the rest of the weeping public. Da came out for the debut. He sat and listened to his son sail drunkenly on the silent winds of outer space and make a mockery of human misery: *Dunkel ist das Leben, ist der Tod.* Dark is life, is death. A voice that knew nothing but its own fire veered about in wild precision, fueled by a skill equal to the music's extremes: *Was geht mich denn der Frühling an? Laßt mich betrunken sein!*—What can springtime mean to me? Let me be drunken!

People who'd never heard of Jonah's lieder performances suddenly discovered him. The audience clapped as if they wanted him to come out and do *Symphony of a Thousand* as an encore. The *Detroit Free Press* ran that review calling him a "planet-scouting angel." In truth, they were right. He didn't live here. His voice was on a long, sweeping search for any part of this backwater galaxy where it might put down for an eon or two.

Just before Chicago and our Orchestra Hall debut, the disastrous piece in *Harper's* appeared, calling him a flunky of the white culture game. Jonah thought his career was over. Orchestra Hall would rescind the engagement when they found out. He couldn't stop reading me the passage that fingered him: " 'Yet there are amazingly talented young black men out there still trying to play the white culture game, even while their brothers are dying in the streets.' That's me, boy. Big time back-stabber. Cut you and leave you for dead, if I need to."

Orchestra Hall didn't rescind. Despite our preconcert argument about our parents and Emmett Till, and despite a suffocation fit only an hour before the performance, Jonah hit the stage singing—the songs of Schumann, Wolf, and Brahms—and came away to raves.

The *Harper's* accusation chewed him up. He'd been passing, and it had never even occurred to him. All those boys his age, ground down, locked out, threatened, beaten, killed, while he'd been granted the safe passage of lightness. All those men, locked up, held down, digging civilization's ditches, taking the blows, while he was up onstage spinning florid doilies, making time stand still. He'd read the article and cock his head: could it really be?

He canceled two weeks of engagements, claiming the flu. Truth was, he was afraid to show his face in public. He no longer knew what that face looked like to his audience. Not that he'd ever much cared how others saw him. Music was that place where look fell away and sightless sound was all. But here was someone insisting the opposite: Music was just what we put on, after we put on ourselves. How a piece sounded to its listeners had everything to do with who was up there making the sounds.

After a while, Jonah's horror at the *Harper's* piece turned to fascination. It amazed him to think that the article's writer considered him worth slandering. The attention promoted him to a level of interest he'd never commanded, a player in a drama bigger than any he'd ever starred in. Amazingly talented black man playing the white culture game. Even *winning*. He turned the formula over and over. Then, in the kind of modulation he excelled in, he threw a little switch in himself. After days of chafing against the label, Jonah decided to revel in it.

He returned to the concert circuit, now blessed by the condemnation.

And when the calls from Mr. Weisman came in, with significant symphonic and choral solo offers among them, Jonah's about-face seemed borne out. People smelled an opera, and they wanted tickets. *Harper's* was going to make him notorious.

"Thank the Lord God Almighty for the revolution, Mule. The movement's opening doors. Providing for our people. Gonna get us a call from the President Lincoln Center." He rubbed my close-cropped head the way I always hated. "Huh, bro? Culture works. Uplift and elevation. Even the black man's Al Jolson gotta eat."

He took to reading the magazine accusation over the telephone to anyone who'd listen. "Where's your sister when we need her?"

He knew better than I did. "She's seen it. I'll bet you anything."

"You think?" He sounded pleased.

I saw him wondering how to get the article to Lisette Soer, to János Reményi, even to Kimberly Monera, who, in another lifetime, once asked if he was a Moor. I waited for notoriety to change his sound. I couldn't see how he could get up onstage, week after week, so twisted up, and still manufacture that silk perfection. He sang Beethoven's Ninth, again at short notice, with the Quad Cities Symphony. When the chorale came—that discredited dream of universal brotherhood, the same notes he'd once scribbled, by ear, underneath the photo of the North American nebula we'd hung on our bedroom wall—I half-expected him to open his mouth and turn hideous, to bray a quarter tone sharp, tremulous and imperial, like those pompous Teutonic goose-honk voices we used to ridicule when we were boys.

Just the reverse. He gave himself over to the classical's full corruption. Only death, beauty, and artistic pretense were real. Limbered, his notes floated up into a clerestory treading in light. He entered completely into that blackballing country club, the heaven of high art.

For the second recording, he got it into his head to do a cycle of English songs—Elgar, Delius, Vaughan Williams, Stanford, Drake. Harmondial talked him out of it. The aura of decadent sweetness that clung to his voice left the tunes sounding freakishly pure, like some choirboy who'd gone through every part of puberty except the crucial one.

The label wanted something darker, to capitalize on Jonah's controversy. They settled on Schubert's *Winterreise*. That was a piece for grown men, to sing when the singer had traveled far enough to describe the journey in full. But no sooner did they suggest the idea than Jonah took it up and sealed it.

This time, we did the taping in New York. Jonah wanted a harder, more exposed finish. He'd sung many of the individual songs at one time or another. Now he assembled them into a plan that still takes my breath away. Instead of starting out the journey in innocence and ending in bitter passion, he began in a wry romp and ended far off, stripped bare, gazing motionless over the lip of the grave.

Even now, I can't listen to the thing straight through. In five days at the end of his twenty-sixth year, my brother jumped into his own future. He posted the message of 1967 forward to a year when he would no longer be able to read it. With total clairvoyance, he sang about where we were headed, things he couldn't have known as he sang them, things I wouldn't recognize even now except for his explanation waiting for me, telegraphed from an unfinished past.

This time out, Jonah had two more years of control. He knew exactly what he needed each note to do within the larger phrase. He heard in his head the precise inflection of each song in the cycle, every nuance. He was a relentless mechanical engineer, bridging life's winter trip, cabling up the starting block with the finish post in a few sweeping suspension swags and joining the whole into one coherent span. His voice was surer, better worked. We were singing in our own town, heading home each night to a certain bed, before the uncertainties of the next day's takes. He adored the studio, the sterile glass cubicle sealing him off from outside danger. He loved to sit up in the control booth, listening to himself sing over the monitors, hearing the magnificent stranger he'd been just minutes before.

He spoke about it during one long break. "You remember that *Sputnik* signal, ten years ago? What's this going to sound like, after I'm dead?"

The day we lived in was sealed. The message of where we were going would never reach us. His tone was so expansive, it felt like the moment to ask. "Did you ever think there was anything strange about the fire?" A dozen years after the fact, and I still couldn't name it.

But he needed no more. "Strange? Something unexplained?" He ran both hands backward against his scalp. His dark hair was long enough now to furrow. "Everything's unexplained, Joey. There are no pointless accidents, if that's what you mean."

I'd lived two decades thinking that skill, discipline, and playing by the rules would bring me safely in. I was the last of us to see it: Safety belonged to those who owned it. Jonah sat sipping springwater with a little lemon. I had wrapped my hands in hot towels, bandaged, as if just injured. I hunched forward, groping for some light in Jonah's eyes. We'd drifted too far to rely on the old boyhood telepathy anymore. Onstage, still, yes; but in another year or two, we'd understand nothing in each other but music. That afternoon, one last time, he thought my thoughts, as if they were his.

"I used to think about it every night. Joey, I always wanted to ask you."

"Why didn't you?"

"I don't know. I thought if I asked you, I might make it real." He massaged his neck, exploring under the ears, scooping up into the chin, working, from the outside, the cords that he lived by. His throat was tan, a color that hid the way he'd come. No one could say, by that one cue alone, just what time had done to him. "Does it matter, Joey? One way or the other?"

My hands spasmed, scattering the hot towels. "Does it *what*? Jesus. Of course it matters." Nothing else did. Murder or accident? Everything we'd thought we were, everything my life meant hung on that fact.

My brother stuck his fingers into the lemon water and rubbed a trickle into his neck. "Look. Here's what I think. I've thought about this for twelve years." His voice was gaunt, from somewhere that had never known song. "You want to know what happened. You think that knowing *what happened* will tell you . . . what? What the world's going to do to you. You think that if your mother was killed, if your mother *really* died by chance . . . Say it wasn't some random furnace. Say it had human help. That answers something? That's not even the start of what you need to know. Why were they after her? Because she was black? Because she was uppity, sang the wrong stuff? Because she crossed the line, married your father? Because she wouldn't keep her head down? Because she sent her mutant children to private school? Was it a scare tactic, intimidation gone wrong? Did they even know she was home? Maybe they wanted Da. Maybe they were trying for us. Somebody helping to return the country to its original purity. You want to know whether it was a crazy person, some neighborhood committee, some clan from some other neighborhood, twenty blocks north or south. Then you want to know why your father never . . ."

He stopped for a breath, but not because he needed one. He could have sailed on forever on that fountain of air.

"Or say it was the furnace, all by itself. Nobody helping it along, nobody's historical mission. Why that furnace? Why were we living in that house, and not some other? Don't they inspect those things, in the good neighborhoods? How would she have died if she'd been living over on some burned-out block between Seventh and Lenox? They're dying of tetanus up there. They're dying of flu. Illiteracy. Dying in the backseats of cars when the hospital won't take them. A woman like Mama dies in this country, at her age—it's somebody's fault. What do you need to know? Listen, Joey. Would it change the way you live if they told you all the answers, beyond doubt?"

I thought of Ruth. I had no answer for Jonah. But he had one for me.

"You don't need to know if someone burned her alive. All you need to know is whether someone wanted to. And you know the answer to that one already. You've known that one since—what, six? So somebody did what everyone's thought of doing. Or maybe not. Maybe she died a race-less woman's death. Maybe furnaces explode. You don't know, you can't know, and you're never *going* to know. That's what being black in this country means. You'll never know anything. When they give you your change and won't put it in your hand? When they cross the street a block down from you? Maybe they just had to cross the street. All you know for sure is that everyone hates you, hates you for catching them in a lie about everything they've ever thought of themselves."

He did that head-rolling shoulder heave singers do to loosen themselves. Ready to return to recording, get on with his life. "I got Da talking once. God knows where you were, Joey. I can't keep track of you all the time. Before they were married, apparently, he listed four possibilities for us, like a logic problem: A, B, both A and B, neither A nor B. He didn't like the fixed categories. No element of *time*. What did he know about us? No more than we know about him. Neither of them liked race trumping everything. Wasn't that how history screwed us in the first place? They both thought family should trump race. That's who they were. That's why they raised us how they did. Noble experiment. Four choices, all of them fixed. But even fixed things have to move."

He stood and put his arms over his head, bent them back behind him and touched his shoulder blades, the sockets of his pruned wings. When I listen to that second disk now, this is how I see him. A glow in his eyes, about to launch into some tune that will mean the end of self.

"But you know what, Mule? They don't. Don't move. White won't move, and black can't. Well, white moves when black buys a place in the neighborhood. But beyond that, race is like the pyramids. Older than history and built to outlast it. You know what? Even thinking there are four choices is a joke. In this country, choice isn't even on the menu."

"Ruth's married a Panther." This, too, he somehow already knew. Maybe she'd told him when they'd met. All he did was nod. I carried on, stung. "Robert Rider. She's joined, too."

"Good for her. We all need to find our art."

I flinched at the word. "She has the police reports. No, I mean for the fire. She and her husband . . . They're sure. They say if the—if Mama had been white . . ."

"Sure of what? Sure of everything we already knew. Sure of what killed her? You'll never know. That's blackness, Mule. Never knowing. That's how you know who you really are." He did a horrible little minstrel-show shuffle. Years ago, I might have tried to talk him down, to bring him back from himself. Now I just looked away.

"If Mama and Da both wanted family more than . . ." The bile backed up my throat. "Why the hell don't we even *have* our family?"

"Who? You mean Mama's?" He held still, scanning the past. He alone was old enough to remember our grandparents. "Same reason Ruth took off, I guess."

"Not the same reason."

Jonah smiled at my open treason. His folded hands, steeple-style, touched his lips. "There was an argument. You remember. I told you, Mule. We can't know. Didn't I tell you? Race trumps family. It's bigger than anything. Bigger than husband and wife. Bigger than brother and sister . . ." Bigger than objects in the sky. Bigger than knowing. And still there was one thing so small, it could slip past race without notice. Jonah put his arm around my shoulder. "Come on, brother. We've got work to do."

We went back into the studio and recorded "The Crow" in one take—the only time in the entire recording session we hit a song perfectly on a single try. Jonah listened to the master tape again and again, probing for the smallest flaw. But he could find none.

> A crow was with me
> As I made my way from town.
> Back and forth, all the way to now
> It has flown around my head.

Crow, you strange creature,
Won't you leave me be?
Are you waiting for prey here, soon?
Do you mean to seize my corpse?

Well, there isn't much farther
To go upon this journey.
Crow, let me finally see
A faith that lasts to the grave.

He kept his laser-guided pitches, but all the while his voice dissolved the notes, sliding into them with a whiff of Billie Holiday wandering across the remains of a lynching. He sang the words into their final mystery.

The night we finished taping, we shook hands with the technicians and stepped out into the strangeness of our hometown. Midtown was a blaze of fossil fuel. We walked down Sixth Avenue through the thirties, mixing into the brittle after-hours crowd. A siren cut through the air from ten blocks away. I grabbed Jonah. I practically jumped on him.

"Just a cop, Joey. Nabbing some second-shift robber."

My chest was wound up tighter than Schubert's organ-grinder. I'd been conditioned. I was waiting for the return loop, for some part of the city to ignite. I knew what happened whenever we laid down his voice into permanence. We walked all the way from the studios to the Village. New York had as many alarms that night as any. I flinched at every one, until my brother's amusement turned into disgust. By the time we hit Chelsea, we were quarreling.

"So Watts was my fault? This is what you think?"

"That's not what I said. That's not what I think."

At Fourth Street, he gave up on me and took off alone. I went to the apartment and waited up for him all night. He didn't show until the next day. When he did, the topic was off-limits. I wasn't to ask him anything of consequence, ever again. Nor did he ever ask how I knew about Ruth. She, too, was now off-limits. All the things we couldn't talk about left me endless time to replay the things I'd told him. I convinced myself I hadn't betrayed Ruth. She wanted me to tell. She'd sworn me to secrecy the way Jesus banned his disciples from telling anyone he was going around working miracles.

Every time the Panther Party made the news, I had the sick feeling she or Robert was going to be a footnote casualty. Huey Newton, the Party's founder, was arrested for killing a police officer in Oakland. Ruth had about as much connection to the man as I had to President Johnson. But I dragged through two weeks, feeling as if she'd somehow helped to pull the trigger. *A man has a right to defend himself. So long as the police go on killing us at will.* Part of a state government building up in Albany collapsed, the result of building-code violations. No one was hurt, and there was no sign of tampering. But jumpy politicians tried to tie the collapse to a shrill call for rights put out by the New York Panther chapter, the group Robert and Ruth Rider were helping to organize.

The world had never made much sense to me, much less my life. But now it was Meyerbeer without subtitles. My sister would write me. She and her husband, after a tour of the militant battlefield, would remember themselves. They'd go and work for Dr. King. So I fantasized, most days, without ever daring to believe. But other days, performing fey hundred-year-old music for well-off folks who loved hearing two Negroes staying out of trouble, I thought Ruth must be waiting for a letter from me.

Mr. Weisman called Jonah a month after we'd finished recording. He had an offer from the Met. Jonah took the news over the phone, as if he'd known all along it was coming. "Great." He might have just been offered half off on his next dry-cleaning bill. "What are they thinking about?"

Weisman told him. Jonah repeated the offer out loud, for me to hear. "Poisson, in *Adriana Lecouvreur?*" I shrugged, clueless. The opera was some vehicle for stupendous sopranos. Diva Drivel, we'd always called the genre. Neither of us had ever bothered to listen to it. "What's the part?" Jonah called into the phone, his voice rising.

The part, Mr. Weisman told him, didn't matter. My brother, at twenty-seven, would be singing on the same stage with Renata Tebaldi. He, a lieder singer with almost no orchestral experience, had wanted to break into opera. And the world of opera was willing to let him try.

Jonah got off the phone and interrogated me. I was worthless. We pulled the *World's Greatest Opera Librettos* off the shelf. We ran out to the Magic Flute record shop and grabbed a remastered 1940s budget recording with a distinguished cast and listened to the whole thing at one go. The music ended. "You call that a role?"

I didn't know how to handle him. "Other people have to break in, you know."

"Other people can't do what I do."

"They start elsewhere. You could be singing out in Santa Fe. You could be singing at the Lyric in Chicago, or at the Boston Opera, or San Francisco."

"Plenty of folks start in New York."

"City Opera, then. The point is, you've never *sung* opera. And you want to break in at the top. You're not going to star first time out."

"Don't need to star. Just don't want to hold spears."

"So take this one and make it shine. If they notice you, they'll offer—"

He shook his head. "You'll never understand, will you? There is no future in chickenshit deference. The collective thing. Start a little fish, end a little fish, only eaten. They see you servile, and that's how they'll see you forever. Who owns you, Joey? The chickenshit collective will, unless you refuse. That's all they want: to decide who you are and what kind of threat you represent to the pecking order as they maintain it. The minute you let someone own you, you might as well go and off yourself. Your life—*your* life—is the only thing you ever get to decide."

He told Mr. Weisman to tell the Met that Poisson was not, in his opinion, the right vehicle for his operatic debut. "A fucking insult," he said to the dignified, old-world Mr. Weisman in his pinstripe zoot suit on the other end of the line. Jonah hung up. "They're afraid my voice is too pure. They're afraid I can't fill a hall with my little lieder instrument. What does that sound like to you, Joey? I'll tell you. My voice is too light, and I'm too dark. *Poisson.* Fuck them."

Something in me lifted at the decision. Nobody turned down the Met and got another chance. We could go on doing the only thing we'd ever done. Somehow, we could make touring and festivals and contests pay. The Naumburg competition was coming up; he could win that one, if he had half a mind to. Something else would break for us. I'd wash dishes on the side, if need be.

But Jonah was right. The Met got back to him, and faster than even he could have imagined. His gamble seemed to pay off, to pique the interest of the musical powers. They returned with a vastly upped ante. He could have his vehicle after all. They wanted him for a grandiose center-stage showstopper. The Met offered him the lead in a brand-new opera by Gunther Schuller called *The Visitation*.

We'd once met Schuller, in Boston, when we were children. Years later, Jonah went through a third-stream phase, his enthusiasm actually lasting several weeks. An opera by the man was bound to be riveting. A North American premiere amounted to more self-creation than even Jonah could ask for. As gambles went, this one had his number.

"You must have pulled a real Svengali number on that Linwell," Mr. Weisman said when he called with the offer. "What in the world did you sing for him anyway?"

"What's the opera about?"

The libretto, Weisman explained, was spun off from a Kafka fable, transplanted to the underside of the contemporary United States.

"And the part?"

But Mr. Weisman didn't know anything about the part. He didn't even know the name of the character. Perhaps Jonah didn't understand: This was the lead, in a premiere of a new piece by a major composer, a piece that had electrified Hamburg audiences for a whole year.

What was with all the questions? A singer could sing rings around Gabriel, score triumph after triumph at midsized opera houses, be sleeping with Saint Cecilia herself, and would still have to count such an offer as the lucky break of a lifetime.

But Jonah wanted to see a score before committing. It seemed a reasonable precaution. After years of struggling with borderline stage fright, I was reduced to terror even thinking about Jonah taking on something this size in front of that many people. Some part of me hoped that by asking for a score, he'd irritate the producers so much that they'd withdraw the offer. For that matter, the country itself might fall apart before the score actually arrived.

But the United States hung on for another few weeks, and Jonah got his copy of *The Visitation* to peruse. We spent a marvelous two days reading through it. I'll have that pleasure to answer for, at day's end. God forgive me, but I always enjoyed sight-singing. Jonah was a wonder to watch, breezing all the parts as I plunked out a two-hand reduction. The score had everything: serialism, polytonality, jazz—a wild grab bag of sounds, purely American. "Crazed Quotations," Jonah said at one point, the two of us sitting shoulder-to-shoulder on the piano bench. "Just like the folks used to play."

And its story, Kafka aside, was pure American, as well. A young sensualist university student is arrested and forced to stand a surreal trial for mysterious crimes he has no knowledge of committing. He's found guilty and then lynched. The man is never named. Throughout the score, he's identified only as "the Negro."

We read our way through, realization hitting early. Neither of us felt much need to talk about it. He'd probably made up his mind before the end of the first act. But we read all the way through without Jonah making any sign. I didn't know which way to hope. When we got through the last system of staves, he announced, "Well, Mule, that's that."

"It's good music," I said.

"Oh, the music's wonderful. A few real showcase moments."

"It . . . might be important." I don't know why I bothered saying anything.

"*Important*, Mule?" He circled for the kill. "Important musically? Or important *socially*?" He gave the word a pitch that wasn't quite contempt. Contempt would have betrayed too much interest.

"It's timely."

"*Timely?* What the hell's that supposed to mean, Mule?"

"It's about civil rights."

"Is it? I knew it had to be about something."

"It's sexy." The only word that gave him pause.

"There is that." He teetered, as if considering asking Mr. Weisman to find out whom he'd be playing opposite. Then all compromise crumbled, and he was whole again. "No way. No way in creation."

"Jonah," I said to slow him. But he was flying.

"Professional suicide. Maybe the Europeans ate this thing up. But it's going to bomb here. It's going to end up looking just . . ."

"Suicide? Your chance to sing in front of thousands of people? To be reviewed across the entire country? Jonah, people know how to separate the performer from the piece. If they don't like the show . . ."

"They won't. I know what they're going to say already. It's not what people pay good money to see. Art can't beat this country at its own game. Art shouldn't even try."

I didn't ask what art should try to do. I kept wondering about Ruth, what she'd say about her brother playing the Negro, how it would sound to her, compared to yet more criminal Schubert. Nothing Jonah might sing would ever have a bearing on the cause. I wondered what music the Panthers listened to, in their cars, out on the hot street, in their beds at night. No doubt Ruth and Robert, like my brother, knew exactly what art shouldn't do.

"It could be something," I told him. "Something good. You could make . . . a difference."

Air burst out of his mouth. "A difference? A difference to what?" I bowed my head. "No, really, Joey. A difference to who? You think there's a single operagoer who's going to think differently about herself because of *music*? They're not listening to themselves, Joey. They're listening to the performance. Connoisseurs about everything that's not them. That's where this piece falls flat. It's too good. It's too serious. It gives the audience too much credit."

"So you're saying if they offered you Rodolpho or Alfredo—"

"Or Tristan. Yes. That's what I'm saying. Let me sing what I've given my life to learning."

"Rodolpho? When have you given one hour—"

"Let me sing the things I could sing better than anyone in this world. The roles any other tenor of my caliber would be given. Who am I hurting by doing that?"

"Who are you hurting by taking this part?"

"Which part? *The Negro?*"

"There's a difference, Jonah."

"No doubt. Between what and what?"

"Between . . . chickenshit deference and artistic cooperation. Between deciding your own life and making the world follow your own rules." I was going to humiliate myself in front of him, all to get him to take a role I didn't even want him to take. "Jonah, it's okay. Okay to be a part of something. To choose to be one thing or the other. To come home, somewhere. Belong."

"Belong? Belong with all the other Negro leads? A leading light unto my people, maybe? An exemplar?" His voice was horrible. He could sing anything now. Any role or register.

"To be something other than yourself."

He nodded, but not in agreement. I wasn't to talk until he'd decided the best way to annihilate me. "Why is the Met offering me this part? I mean *this* part?"

You'll never know. That's what being the Negro means. I dug in. "Because you can sing it."

"I'm sure they have several dozen limber leads in their stables who can *sing* it. Men with operatic experience. Why not use them? They do *Otello* in blackface, don't they?"

I heard a tiny, translucent, almost blue little girl ask, *Are you two Moors?* She never existed. We'd invented her. "Would you take Otello if they offered it?" They'd have to darken Jonah's face, too, just to make him believable.

"I refuse to be typecast before I've sung a single role."

"Everyone's typecast, Jonah. Everyone. That's how the human brain works. Name a singer who doesn't stand for some . . . No one is just himself."

"I don't mind being a Negro. I refuse to be a Negro tenor." He reached down to the keyboard and felt out four measures of what sounded like Coltrane. He could have played piano like a king, if he hadn't sung so well.

"I don't get you."

"I won't be the Caruso of black America. The Sidney Poitier of opera."

"You don't want to be mixed-race." I was sitting with him at the top of the subway stairs in Kenmore Square, Boston. "That's what you mean."

"I don't want to be *any* race."

"That—" I was going to say, *That's your parents' fault.* "That is something nobody but a purebred white person could want to get away with."

" 'Purebred white person'?" He laughed. "Purebred white person. Is that like a well-modulated soprano?" He prowled around the cage of our front room. It might have been a concrete cubicle in the Bronx Zoo, a mat of straw, a watering trough. He scraped his fingers back and forth in the mortar lines between the wall bricks. He might have rasped them raw if I hadn't grabbed his wrist. He slunk back to the piano bench. The instant his mass touched wood, he was up again. "Joey. I've been an absolute idiot. Where are all the men?"

"What men?"

"Exactly. I mean, we have Price, Arroyo, Dobbs, Verrett, Bumbry— all these black *women* pouring out of every state in the union. Where the hell are the men?"

"George Shirley? William Warfield?" It sounded like clutching at straws, even to me.

"Warfield. Case in point. Brilliant voice, and opera's basically locked the man out. Start out singing *Porgy*, and that's all anybody's going to be able to hear you do."

"It's not in the culture. Black man wants to be an opera singer? I mean, really."

"It's not in the culture for the *women*, either. And they've come up from nowhere—from Georgia, Mississippi, One hundred eleventh Street. They're stealing the show, out of all proportion . . ."

"There's the whole diva thing. That doesn't work for men. Think of you at Juilliard. The recital stuff was fine. But nobody there was helping you over into the opera theater."

"Exactly, exactly. Exactly my point. And why? The door's kicked in, and the Man's finally dealing with the whole thing, and there they are up onstage, this white guy and this black woman, kissing and cooing and, well, that's kind of yummy, in a nice old-fashioned, time-honored plantation way. Same old domination by another name. Then there's this big black man and this white woman, and what the hell? Who let this happen? Blow the whistle, wave the play dead. It all comes down to who's doing the fucking and who's getting—"

"Jonah." All I could do was blink at him. "What difference does it make? Why do you need this role? You already have a career. More career than most singers of any color even dream of."

He broke out of his pacing and stood behind me. He rested his hands on my shoulders. It felt like the last time he'd ever do that. "What do I have, Joey? Maybe fifteen years of prime voice left?" The figure shocked me, a crazy exaggeration. Then I did the math. "I just thought it might be good to go make some noise with other people. A little harmony, while I'm still in form."

He turned down the offer to play the Negro. He was the one who said no, in the full knowledge that no one ever got a third try. But then, saying yes might have left him even more enslaved. This way, he kept at least one of his hands on what he thought was the rudder.

He was right about everything. The Met, their first choice gone, ended up not producing *The Visitation*. The opera did come to town, with the premiere cast that had triumphed with it in Hamburg the year before. Just as Jonah predicted, the New York critics slaughtered it. They accused the libretto of irrelevance at best and of stilted falseness at worst. If one wanted civil rights, one should read the papers or hop a bus down south. One came to the opera, on the other hand, for the passion and drama of the tragic self. The tickets were too expensive for anything else.

The first American staging of *The Visitation* went west, to the San Francisco Opera. They mounted their premiere with a tenor named Simon Estes in the leading role. They performed the expressionist drama just across the Bay from where Huey Newton and the police had had their shoot-out. Every staging of a work is a new universe. San Francisco was farther from New York than Kafka was from civil rights. The West Coast critics adored the show, and it launched Mr. Estes, several shades darker than my brother, on his distinguished, singular career.

Not that Jonah's career stood still. Only time did that. Our second record came out, and for weeks afterward, I waited, flinching. I didn't give a damn about critics or sales: I wanted the whole thing to sink without notice. Jonah heard me holding my breath and just laughed. "What is it, Joey? What evils have we unleashed on the world this time?"

A month went by, and nothing happened. No earthquake from our own trivial tremor. The Kerner Commission released its report on the violence across the country: "Our nation is moving toward two societies, one black and one white, separate and unequal." But this time, even the cities where our record sold well remained quiet.

Gramophone magazine reviewed the new LP, proclaiming that a man so young and callow had no earthly right to sing Schubert's wintry trip "until he's within earshot of that season." The reviewer was that great judge of vocal talent, Crispin Linwell. Linwell's review was so dreamily brutal that it touched off what passed, in classical musical circles, for a street brawl. The controversy fed on itself, and the record got written up in more big-city dailies than I thought possible. A few outraged protectors of world culture hid behind the Linwell name and dismissed Jonah's effort as at best premature and at worst impudent. A few other writers, themselves too young to know what they were wading into, found Jonah's youthful rethinking of the cycle as thrilling as it was spooky. One reviewer, reviewing the battle as much as the recording, pointed out that Jonah Strom was only a few years younger than Schubert was when he wrote the thing. When these reviewers talked about the singing at all, they tossed around the word *perfection* as if it were a mild reprimand.

The first to mention race was a writer in the *Village Voice*. The proper way to serve up Schubert was hardly that paper's stock-in-trade. The reviewer admitted up front to being a jazzer who could listen to lieder only under the influence of artificial enhancement. But Schubert, the writer said, wasn't the issue. The issue was that the white cultural establishment was trying to skewer a gifted young black singer not because he was too young to sing the masters but because he was too uppity. The reviewer proceeded to list half a dozen European and American white singers who'd tackled the work to acclaim at ages even younger than Jonah's.

I showed the piece to Jonah, expecting rage. But when he got to the end, he just cackled. "Is it him? It has to be. The smart-aleck style? The bit about being able to listen to lieder only while stoned?" I hadn't even checked the byline. Jonah handed me back the issue. "T. West! Who else could it be? Thaddy boy. That white Negro bastard."

"Should we call him? I've a number for him from . . . awhile ago." Old broken promise. But Jonah shook his head, reticent, almost scared.

T. West's accusation blew our little winter's journey wide open. Crispin Linwell was all over himself in a *Gramophone* response, hotly denying that race had anything to do with the way any classical performance is received. He'd worked with tens of black artists and even hired one or two. The papers that ran follow-up squibs generally made the same claim: Race simply wasn't an issue in the concert scene. Talent was all. The monuments of classical music were color-blind, never troubling with such ephemera. Anyone who wanted to could worship at the altar.

"That's what your father and mother believed," Jonah said, and kept reading.

An editorial in the *Chicago Defender* thanked the white cultural establishment for being so color-blind: "And it must be so, for the cultural elites to be able to look out on classical music audiences and declare that race is not an issue when dealing with eternal verities. But then, nobody can see much color when the lights are down so low." Even this editorial didn't talk about Jonah's singing, except to declare it, for whatever the phrase meant, "a constant astonishment."

For weeks, our record sold as well as if it had been released on a major label. We got letters telling us to stick to jig music. We got letters—militant, enthusiastic—from faceless, raceless listeners who told us to keep reviving the dead stuff, forever. But by then, who knew what music anyone was hearing in our sounds? I hated the notoriety, and still thought that once the fuss blew over, we could return to the realm of simple performance. Right up to the last, I imagined such a place existed.

But the Linwell flap also seemed to break our curse. I'd been braced for riots, our repeat punishment for trying to stop time again. This precious little tempest, played out in small-circulation magazines catering to a dying art, was all the riot our recording would touch off this time. I was a slung-assed fool. I felt the size of my vanity, the old animistic belief that the world lived or died by what cracks I stepped on.

Then King was killed. He died on the balcony of the Lorraine Motel in Memphis, a few blocks south of Beale Street, the day after he went up to the mountaintop. That voice for reconciliation met its only allowable end. He'd been leading a strike by garbage workers and now he was over. *How long? Not long.* I heard the news on FM radio while cleaning the apartment. The dazed announcer broke in on the highlights from Donizetti's *Lucia di Lammermoor.* He forgot to fade the music down, instead just clipping it off and tearing into the garbled news. He didn't seem to know what to do next. Going back to Donizetti was impossible, even though it was one of Dr. King's favorites. The silence grew so long, it made me wonder if the station had gone off the air. In fact, the announcer had simply walked away, into the station's record library, to root around for the right eulogy. For whatever private reason, he settled on William Billings's crude, haunted originary wail, "David's Lamentation": "Would to God I had died for thee, O Absalom, my son, my son."

I shut the radio off and went out. It was already evening. I turned, by instinct, uptown. The streets seemed so matter-of-fact, so unchanged, though most of the passersby must already have known. I walked at random, looking for Jonah, hurrying to tell him.

The firebombs started in Memphis, an hour after the shooting. By the end of the week, 125 cities were at war. The fires in Washington burned worse than they had since 1812. The Battle of Fourteenth Street required thirteen thousand federal troops to suppress it. The city set a curfew and declared martial law. Chicago's mayor ordered his forces to "shoot to kill." The governor of Maryland announced a lasting state of emergency as a quarter of Baltimore burned. In Kansas City, police lobbed gas canisters into a crowd enraged by the decision to keep schools open through Dr. King's funeral. Nashville, Oakland, Cincinnati, Trenton: uprising everywhere.

Four straight summers of violence: The revolution had come. And Jonah and I stood by watching, as if from mezzanine boxes at a matinee performance of Verdi's *Requiem.* Our concerts in Pittsburgh and Boston were canceled and never rescheduled, casualties in a conflict where music wasn't even the smallest thing at stake. How could a little song and dance compete against the country's supreme art form?

For some months, our life had looked increasingly unreal. Now I lost all sense of what *real* was supposed to look like. Jonah knew. "Here we go. All out in the open now. Straight-up tribalism—everything anyone wants. Something solid to believe in. We've been killing one another over imaginary membership for a million years. Why change this late in the day?"

My brother's take on the human species had never been complicated. Now it was simplifying down to a single perfect point. People would rather die in invented safety than live in invigorating fear. He'd seen enough. Jonah turned his back on the whole time frame of earthly politics, and I could no longer call him back. Every passing day only confirmed him. None of us knew how to live here, at the rate of life we were given.

The two of us were running up to an engagement in Storrs, Connecticut, in a borrowed Impala—just a shade too pale to be pulled over and frisked—when Jonah, in the passenger seat, leaned toward me and confided, "I know why they killed him."

"Who's 'they'?"

"They killed him because he was coming out both barrels against Vietnam."

"Viet— That's insane."

He waved his hand in front of the dash, the whole panorama of interstate. Danger on all sides. "His attacks, last year. 'America's the world's greatest purveyor of violence.' Sending out blacks to kill yellows. Come on. You show me the person in power who's going to let some darkie preacher shut down a game like that."

I checked my speed. "You're saying the government . . . The CIA . . ." I felt like a fool just pronouncing the letters.

Jonah shrugged. He didn't care which acronym had pulled the trigger. "They need the war, Joey. It's like housecleaning. Forces of good. Making the world safe. Onward, upward, oneward."

The skin on my neck turned to scales. He'd gone the way of the country at large. My brother, always grandiose, had taken that last little baby step upstream. But something in me relaxed at his words. If he'd arrived here, too, then there was no conflict. Ruth could come back. I could tell her what had happened to him. We could be together, the three of us again, as we had never been. No enemies, aside from everyone. I'd believe whatever the two of them told me.

I had no strong feelings about the war, except to avoid it. Now this spillover was killing people across 125 cities. On every long car ride now, Jonah spun through the dial, searching for counterculture songs. He'd weave a Dies Irae cantus firmus around the melodies, that same gift for counterpoint that had stunned my parents during our music evenings and made them think they had a duty to send him away to boarding school. The fatal facility that stunted his life. And when the three or four predictable funk or folk guitar chords failed to accommodate the harmonies he spun, he'd curse the tone-deaf arrangements and threaten to firebomb the nearest record store.

The war took us over. Everything became a referendum on it. Love-fests, pot parties, sit-ins, draft-card bonfires, Upper West Side benefits that threw together militant radicals and shameless philanthropists: Everything became the war. My brother sat next to me on an upholstered Chevy seat, weaving counterpoint around the words, "There's something happening here." The old order was taking its last twilight gasp; some spiraling hope was breathing its first. My brother hummed along, obbligato, above "Stop, hey: What's that sound?" But no one could say what that sound was or just what future it was trying to buy.

The war took Phillipa Schuyler. That wonderous little girl, the daughter of hybrid vigor, the celebrated heroine of Phillipa Duke Schuyler Day, whose *Five Little Piano Pieces* were among the first keyboard works Jonah and I ever learned, died in Da Nang. The musical prodigy burned to death in a helicopter crash in a war zone, on her way back from Hue. Her country had loved the girl for the shortest moment, until she passed through puberty and lost her status as a freak of nature. When precocity failed her, all those whom hybrid vigor threatened with extinction turned the full force of purebred unity against her. She fled to Europe, playing to acclaim from crowned families and heads of state. She toured internationally as Felipa Monterro, racially, nationally, and historically ambiguous. She published five books and wrote articles in several languages. She became a correspondent. And she fell from the sky and died on a bungled humanitarian mission to rescue schoolchildren whose village was about to be overrun. She was thirty-seven.

The news devastated Jonah. He'd loved the girl, on nothing more than her sheet music and our parents' accounts. He'd imagined she'd hear of him someday, that they would meet, that anything might happen between them. I, too, had always thought so.

"Just us now, Mule," he told me. Just us, and the tens of thousands just like us, whom we'd never come across.

From Hue and Da Nang—hamlets no atlas of ours carried—the war came home. At Columbia, what started as an SDS-led demonstration ended with a unit of twenty-year-olds taking over the president's office in Low Library, where they set up an autonomous people's republic. Across that postage stamp of campus where our father worked, the latest American revolution played out in microcosm. Half a dozen buildings were occupied, besieged, and sacked over the course of a war that lasted longer than the latest one between the Arabs and Israel.

Da had no lab to worry about losing. He'd always carried his science

399

around with him in his head. But even this much he failed to protect. He didn't even know about the battle for Morningside Heights until two days in, when he strolled across the south end of the Campus Walk and noticed a disturbance in the distance. Good empiricist, he investigated. Within minutes, he was enveloped in bedlam. The thousand police President Kirk had summoned to drive the protesters from campus were achieving their only possible result: tear gas, stones, clubs, and bodies flying in all directions. Da saw an officer laying into the legs of a prostrate student and ran up to stop the beating. He took a club in the face and went down. He was lucky the jittery policeman didn't shoot him.

His cheekbone collapsed into the back of his face and had to be rebuilt. I had no way of reaching Ruth, nor did I know whether she'd care. Jonah and I went to see Da in the hospital after the surgery. In the hall to his room, a nurse blocked our path until we convinced her we were the man's sons. We couldn't be his sons, she thought. We weren't the same color. Maybe she thought we were the thugs who'd put him here, come back to finish the job.

Da still bobbed under the anesthetic. He looked through the gauze wrappings holding in his face. He seemed to recognize us and tried to sit up in the hospital bed to sing. He flipped a weak hand up to his mummified head and droned, *"Hat jede Sache so fremd eine Miene, so falsch ein Gesicht!"* Hugo Wolf's "Homesickness," a song Jonah used to sing, before the words meant anything. Everything had so strange a countenance, so false a face.

Jonah saluted. "How's our cheekless wonder? You feeling better? What do the docs say?"

The question set Da to singing again, Mahler this time:

Ich hab' erst heut' den Doktor gefragt,	Only today I asked the doctor,
Der hat mir's in's Gesicht gesagt:	And he told me to my face:
"Ich weiss wohl, was dir ist, was dir ist:	"I know exactly what's wrong with you:
Ein Narr bist du gewiß!"	You are surely a fool!"
Nun weiss ich, wie mir ist!	Now I know what's wrong with me!

He sounded like a flock of geese rushing south. The performance went right through my intestines. Jonah cackled like a crazy man. "Da!

Cut it out. Quit with the jaw movements. You'll collapse your face again."

"Come. We sing. We make a little trio. Where are the altos? We need altos."

Jonah only egged him on. After a while, Da settled down. He craned up and said, "My boychiks," as if we'd just arrived. He couldn't rotate his head without shattering. We sat by his bedside for as long as Jonah's attention permitted. Da perked up again as we got ready to leave. "Where are you going?"

"Home, Da. We have to practice."

"Good. There's a cold soup in the refrigerator. Chicken from Mrs. Samuels. And *Mandelbrot* in the bread box, for you boys. You boys like that."

We looked at each other. I tried to stop him, but Jonah blurted, "Not that home."

Da just blinked at us through his bandages and waved away our jokes. "Tell your mother I'm just fine."

Outside, on the street, Jonah preempted me. "He's still doped up. Who knows what they have him on?"

"Jonah."

"Look." His voice swung out at me. "If he loses his job, we can start worrying about him." We walked in silence toward the subway. At last he added, "I mean, it's hardly the kind of job where craziness is a liability."

We performed in Columbus, at Ohio State, a pocketbook auditorium paneled in dark wood. There couldn't have been more than three hundred people in attendance, half of them at student prices, scoping out the object of controversy. We'd have lost money on coming out if we hadn't had bookings in Dayton and Cleveland, too. Jonah must have felt something, some sense of what was already racing to happen to him. There, in that random hall, in front of an audience that didn't know what hit them, for an hour and ten minutes, he sang like nothing living.

Once, when I was a child, before Mama died, I dreamt I was standing on the front stoop of the house in Hamilton Heights. I leaned forward without stepping and lifted off the stoop, surprised that I could fly. I'd always been able to, only I'd forgotten. All I needed to do was lean forward and let it happen. Flying was as easy as breathing, easier than walking through the neighborhood where my parents put me down. That was how Jonah sang that night in the middle of distant, dislodged Ohio. He landed on the most reticent pitches from a fixed point in the air above, like a kingfisher catching silver. He hit attacks and came off every release without a waver. Each note's edges tapered or sustained according to innermost need. His line bent iridescent, a hummingbird turning at will and hovering motionless, by the beat of its wings, even fusing air and flying backward. His sound spread to its full span, huge as a raptor, all taloned precision, without a trace of force or tremor. His ornaments were as articulate as switches and his held notes swelled like the sea trapped in a shell.

Technique no longer dictated what sound he could or couldn't make. The full palette of human song was his. Every protection racket he'd lived through gave him something to sing about, something to escape. He'd always been able to hit the notes. Now he knew what the notes meant. In his mouth, hope hung, fear cowered, joy let loose, anger bit into itself, memory recalled. The rage of 1968 fueled him and fell away, amazed by the place he made of it.

His sound said, *Stop everything. The votes are in. Nothing but listening matters.* I had to force myself to keep playing. I stumbled, pulled along in his wake. To do him justice, to match what I heard, my fingers turned extraordinary evidence. For the shortest while, I, too, could say everything about where we'd come from. Playing like that, I didn't love Jonah because he was my brother. I loved him—would lay down my life for him, already had—because, for a few unchanging moments onstage, backing up into the crook of the piano, he was free. He shed who he was, what he wanted, the sorry wrapper of the self. His sound traveled into sublime indifference. And for a while, he brought back a full working description for anyone to hear.

That's how the music came out of him. Silk slid across obsidian. The tiniest working hinge in a carved ivory triptych the size of a walnut. A blind man, lost at a street corner in a winter city. The disk of affronted moon, snagged in the branches of a cloudless night. He leaned into the notes, unable to suppress his own thrill in the power of making. And when he finished, when his hands dropped down flush to his thighs and the bulge of muscle above his collarbone—that cue I always watched like the tip of a conductor's baton—at last went slack, I forgot to lift my foot off the sustain. Instead of closing the envelope, I let the vibrations of that last chord keep traveling and, like the sign of his words on the air, float on to their natural death. The house couldn't decide if the music had ended.

Those three hundred midwestern ticket holders refused to break in on the thing they'd just witnessed or destroy it with anything so banal as applause.

The audience wouldn't clap. Nothing like it had ever happened to us. Jonah stood in the growing vacuum. I can't trust my sense of time; my brain still ran that tempo where thirty-second notes laze through the ear like blimps at an air show. But the silence was complete, soaking up even the constant coughs and chair creaks that litter every concert. It grew until the moment for turning it into ovation was lost. By silent agreement, the audience held still.

After a lifetime—maybe ten full seconds—Jonah relaxed and walked offstage. He walked right past me on the piano bench without looking my way. After another frozen eternity, I walked off after him. I found him in the stage wing, fiddling with the sash ropes that ran up into the theater's fly tower. My look asked, *What happened out there?* His answered, *Who cares?*

The spell over the audience chose that moment to break. They should have gone home in their chosen silence, but they didn't have the will. The clapping began, halting and stunted. But making up for the late start, it turned into a riot. Bourgeois normalcy was saved for another evening. Jonah resisted going back and taking a bow. He'd had enough of Columbus. I had to shove him out, then wait a step and follow along behind him, smiling. They brought us back four times, and would have gone five except that Jonah refused. The third curtain call was the point when we always trotted out an encore bonbon. That night made an encore impossible. We never even looked at each other. He dragged me out to the loading dock before anyone could come backstage to congratulate us.

We headed to our campus guest room at a trot. Five years ago, we might have giggled in triumph the whole way. But that night, we were grim with transcendence. We got to the student guest house in silence. The all-reaching creature became my brother again. He undid his tie and took off his burgundy cummerbund even before we entered the elevator to our room. In the room, he lost himself in gin and tonics and televised jabber. For a while, he'd hovered above the noise of being. Then he nose-dived back in.

The world we returned to likewise fell apart. I could no longer tell cause from effect, before from after. Robert Kennedy was shot. Who knew why? The war—some war. Chickens roosting. Impossible to keep track of what futures were being decided or what scores were being settled. Thereafter, all crucial decisions would be made by sniper. Paris boiled over, then Prague, Peking, even Moscow. In Mexico City, two of the world's fastest men raised their black fists in the air on the Olympic medal stands in a silent, world-traveling scream.

Toward the end of summer came Chicago. The city hadn't yet recovered from "shoot to kill." We were supposed to perform at a summer festival up at Ravinia, on the eighteenth of August. Jonah, on a hunch, canceled. Maybe it was the hippies' threat to lace the city water supply with LSD. We stayed in New York and watched the show on television. The presidential nomination turned into a bloodbath. It ended as every recent battle for our souls had: with an airlift of six thousand troops equipped with every weapon from flamethrower to bazooka. "Democracy in action," Jonah kept repeating to the flickering screen. "Power of the vote." Filled with his own helplessness, he watched the country descend into the hell of its choice.

In October, he bailed. He came to me waving an invitation to a monthlong music residency in Magdeburg starting before Christmas and running past New Year's. "You gotta love this, Joey. The one-thousandth anniversary of the establishment of the archbishopric. The town is gung ho on reviving their one brief moment at the center of civilization."

"Magdeburg? You can't go."

"What do you mean 'can't go,' bro?"

"Magdeburg is in East Germany."

He shrugged. "Is it?"

I may have used the term *Iron Curtain*. It was a long time ago.

"So what's the big deal? I'm an invited guest. It's a special occasion. Practically a state function. Their foreign service or whatever it's called will get me a visa."

"It's not about getting in over there. It's about getting back in over *here*."

"And why, exactly, would anyone want to?"

"I'm serious, Jonah. Aid and comfort to the enemy. They'll hassle you over this for the rest of your life. Look what they did to Robeson."

"I'm serious, too, Joey. If there's a problem coming back, I don't want to." I couldn't bear to look at him. I turned away, but he spun a little impish pirouette to keep his face in front of mine. "Oh, for Christ's sake,

Mule. This country's totally fucked up. Why would anyone want to live here if he didn't have to? What choices do I have? I can stick around and tote bales, and if I stay out of trouble long enough, they'll let me be a certified black artist. Or I can go to Europe and *sing*."

I grabbed his flailing wrists. "Sit down. Just. Sit. You're making me nuts." I took his shoulders and shoved him down on the piano bench. I chopped at him with my index finger—performers' obedience school. "Europe is fine. Musicians . . . like us have been going that route forever. Germany? Why not, for a little while? But go to Hamburg, Jonah. Go to Munich, if you have to go."

"Munich hasn't offered to pay my way and put me up with a healthy honorarium."

"Magdeburg's doing all that?"

"Joey. It's Germany. *Deine Vorfahren, Junge!* They invented music. It's their life's blood. They'd do anything for it. It's like . . . like firearms over here."

"They're using you. Cold War propaganda. You're going to be their showpiece for how America treats its—"

He laughed out loud and doused his hands into the keyboard for a Prokofievian parody of the "Internationale." "That's me, Joey. Traitor to my country. Me and Commander Bucher." He looked up at me, both corners of his mouth pulled back. "Grow up, man! Like the United States hasn't been using us our whole lives?"

The United States had offered him the lead in a premiere of a new Met opera. Yet he could be an artist only if he'd wear the alien badge. Music was supposed to be cosmopolitan—free travel across all borders. But it could get him into the last Stalinist state more easily than it could get him into midtown. I looked at him, begging, a black accompanist, an Uncle Tom in white tie and tails, willing to be used and abused by anyone, most of all my brother, if we could only go on living as if music were ours.

He rubbed my head, sure that we'd always bond over that ritual humiliation. "Come with me, Joey. Come on. Telemann's birthplace. We'll have a blast." Jonah detested Telemann. *The man's greatest claim to fame is turning down a job they then had to give to Bach.* "You wouldn't know it from our bookings in this country in recent months, but we two do have a salable skill. People will pay good money to hear us do what we do. It's state-subsidized over there. Why shouldn't you and I get in on a little of that action? Rightful descendants, huh?"

"What are you thinking? Jonah?"

"What? I'm not thinking anything. I'm saying let's have an adventure. We know the language. We can amaze the natives. I'm not getting laid anytime soon. *You're* not getting laid, are you, Mule? Let's go see what the *Fräuleins* are up to these days." He examined me long enough to see what his words were doing. It never occurred to him I might say no. He changed keys, modulating faster and further afield than late Strauss.

"Come on, Joey. Salzburg. Bayreuth. Potsdam. Vienna. Wherever you want to go. We can head up to Leipzig. Make a pilgrimage to the Thomaskirche."

He sounded desperate. I couldn't figure out why. If he was so sure of Europe's embrace, why did he need me? And what did he mean to do with me once the requests started pouring in for concert work, solos with orchestras, and even—the grand prize he'd set himself—opera? I held up my palm. "What does Da say?"

"Da?" His syllable came out a laugh. He hadn't even thought to tell our father. Our father, the least political man who'd ever lived, a man who'd once lived a hundred kilometers from Magdeburg. Our Da, who vowed never to set foot in his native country again. I couldn't go. Our father might need me. Our sister might want to get in touch. No one would be here to take care of things if I let my brother drag me away for months. Jonah had no plan, and he didn't need one. He didn't really need anything except, for reasons that escaped me, me.

I weighed how much he expected me to throw away. When I didn't step forward with a ready yes, it seemed to confuse him. His look of friendly conscription rippled with panic, then narrowed to a single accusing question: "How about it?"

"Jonah." Under the pressure of his gaze, I slipped out and looked down on the two of us. "Haven't you jerked me around enough?"

For a second, he didn't hear me. Then all he could hear was betrayal. "Sure, Mule. Suit yourself." He grabbed his cap and corduroy jacket and left the apartment. I didn't see him for two days. He came back just in time for our next gig. And three weeks after that, he was packed and ready to go.

He had his visa, and an open ticket. "When are you coming back?" I asked.

He shrugged. "We'll see what comes down." We never shook hands, and we didn't now. "Watch your back, Mule. Keep away from the Chopin." He didn't add, *Decide your own life.* He'd do that for me, as always. All he said on that score was, "So long. Write if you get work."

AUGUST 1945

Delia's on the A when she sees the headline. Not by law a Jim Crow car, but the law's just a tagalong. Car color changes with the blocks above ground. Safety, comfort, ease—the cold comforts of neighborhood chosen and enforced. Choice and its opposite shade off, one into the other, so fluidly these last days of the war. She has come to know, close up, the blurred edge between the two—things forced upon her until they seem elected; things chosen so fiercely, they feel compelled.

Tuesday morning. David is home with the boys. She runs out, just for a minute, to buy an ice bag for the little one. He has fallen down the front steps and hurt his ankle. Not one cry from him after the first. But the ankle is a swollen dark stain, thicker now than her wrist, and the poor child needs the comfort only cold can bring.

She rides two stops, to the pharmacy she knows will serve her. They know her there—Mrs. Strom, mother of small boys. Two stops—five minutes. But she reads the headline in a flash, no time at all. Three fat lines run across the length of the page. They're not as large as the headlines last May, declaring an end to Europe's Armageddon. But they come off the page in a more silent burst.

A deep sable man sits next to her, poring over the words, shaking his head, willing them to change. The night has brought a "rain of ruin." One bomb lands with the force of twenty thousand tons of TNT. Two thousand B-29's. She tries to imagine a ton of TNT. Two tons. Twenty—something like the weight of this subway car. Now ten times that. Then ten times, and ten times that again.

The gaze of the man next to her freezes on the headline. His eyes keep scanning back and forth, the lines of text forcing his head through a stiff, refusing *no.* He struggles, not with the words, but with the ideas they pretend to stand for. Words don't exist yet for what these words brush up against. She reads in secret, looking over his shaking shoulders. NEW AGE USHERED. His gaze remains unchanged. IMPENETRABLE CLOUD OF DUST HIDES CITY. Delia thinks: This city. SCIENTISTS AWESTRUCK

AT BLINDING FLASH. SECRECY ON WEAPON SO GREAT THAT NOT EVEN WORKERS KNEW OF THEIR PRODUCT.

They heard last night on the radio. Confirmation of what her household long ago knew. But the story goes real for her now, seeing the words in print, in this Negro subway car. The DAY OF ATOMIC ENERGY begins for this unchanged underground train. The jet-black man next to her shakes his head, mourning tens of thousands of dead brown skins, while for the rest of the car, life passes for what it had passed for the day before. A woman across from her in a red silk hat checks her lips in a compact mirror. The boy in a smashed fedora to her left studies his *Racing Form*. A little girl, ten, out of school for the summer vacation, skips up the aisle, finding a shiny dime some unfortunate has dropped.

She shouts at the whole car, in her skull. *Don't you see? It's over. This means the war is over.* But the war isn't over, not for any of them. Never will be. Just one more story on a weary, turning page. JET PLANE EXPLOSION KILLS MAJOR BONG. KYUSHU CITY RAZED. CHINESE WIN MORE OF "INVASION COAST." One more numbing war report, after a lifetime of war.

NOT EVEN WORKERS KNEW. How do the reporters presume to know that, a day after the blast? She knew. She's known for almost a month, since the secret desert testing. SCIENTISTS AWESTRUCK AT BLINDING FLASH. She knows just how awed the scientists are, lit by the flash of the work they've done. In the cloud enveloping her, Delia Strom almost misses her stop. She dashes through the train doors as they start to close. She wanders up to the surface, then into her familiar pharmacy. A moment ago, she was filled with purpose. But when the clerk asks her what she wants, she can't remember. Something for her hurt child. The smallest imaginable hurt, and its even smaller comfort.

Something the shade of melted clay. Tough gray rubber and hard white cap. She grips it to her all the ride back. The bottle is a skinned lapdog, half as large as her little one, and twice as resilient. At home, she covers his wounded foot with it. The day is so hot already, they've made his invalid's bed right inside the window casement, his little swollen foot practically hanging out the screens. Her Joey can't understand why his mama wants to inflict him with freezing cold. But he suffers the torture with a smile meant to absolve her.

Her husband, the awestruck scientist, finds her in the kitchen, laying furiously into the bottom of the saucepan with copper cleaner. "Everything is good?"

She drops the scouring pad and grips the lip of the sink. She's pregnant again, in her fifth month, past the early spells of bodily revolt. This is a different dizziness. "Everything," she says, "is what it is."

Two years ago, when Charlie was still alive, when it might have kept her flesh and blood from harm, she wanted this bomb. Now she only wants her husband back, the world she knows. Those hundred thousand brown bodies. How many of them children, as small or smaller than her JoJo? Hundreds of men involved: scientists, engineers, administrators. He can't have contributed anything. Nothing the others wouldn't have figured out on their own. He's never told her just what part he worked on. Even now, she can't ask.

At night, in bed, she wants to whisper, *Did you know?* Of course he knew. But what her David knows, she can only guess at. He's never done anything but play with the world, that bright hypnotic bauble. Like Newton, he says: gathering pretty shells on the beach. His life's work, chosen because it is more useless than philosophy. Avoiding trouble, evading detection, expelled anyway. *Jews and politics do not mix.* She remembers his interview with that national academic honor society: "Are you a practicing Jew?" How he almost lied, on principle, just to force them out of hiding. And how they rejected him anyway, claiming, "We don't accept people who renounce their given faiths."

She watches as he undresses, hanging his rumpled trousers on a chair, exposing his shocking whiteness, a strangeness even greater than she'd suspected before they married. Stranger, even, than the strangeness of men. This white, this man, this unpracticing Jew, this German shares her room with her. But the room they share is stranger than either of them.

He can't have contributed much to this bomb. You can't turn an atom into twenty thousand tons of TNT on anything so imaginary as time. He's explained it to her, his accidental expertise, his spin-off ability to imagine what goes on inside the smallest matter's core. Still she can't see his connection. His colleagues have kept him around—through Columbia, Chicago, New Mexico, all those epic train rides—as nothing but their puzzle-solving, happy mascot. The one who helps others find what they're after.

Four months before, he became the least-published member of his department ever to make permanent faculty. His colleagues bent the rules, granting him tenure largely for the one paper he published while still in Europe, the one his friends say will keep his name around for years. She has tried to read it, slipping down its pages as down a glass mountain.

Then, only two more papers since his arrival, and those got written only because he was bedridden with glandular fever. The American work simply never materialized. The stream of follow-on discoveries exists only in his mind.

Still, the department has given him security for life, if only for selfish reasons. Even those who believe David's own lifework will forever come to nothing have never profited more from any other colleague. First, there are the students. The shy ones, the ones with no English, even when it's their native tongue. The ones who go out in public as if climbing the scaffold. The ones who wear the same white short-sleeved shirts and cotton pants, even in the dead of winter. They adore the man and crowd his lectures. They'd lay down their lives for him. Already they land sterling jobs—Stanford, Michigan, Cornell—their work fueled by tricks of insight derived from their beloved teacher.

"What's your secret?" she asked him once. She, with students of her own.

David shrugged. "The ones without talent can't be taught. The ones with talent need not to be taught."

The department might have kept him on for his teaching alone. But there's more—far more. He wanders the halls of the building with a fountain pen and a pocket score of *Solomon* tucked under his arm, waiting for offices to open at the sound of his step and pull him in. Or he'll sit in the coffee room, scanning his score, humming to himself until some stumped colleague slumps down next to him and bemoans the latest obstinate equation. Then, for the price of a cup of coffee, he leads them to answers, scribbling out the groundwork on a paper napkin. Not that he ever *solves* the problem. His mastery of any but his own small corner of time is dusty at best. He has no great skill at formulas, although he loves that game of estimation they all call "Fermi problems": How far does one crow fly in the course of a lifetime? How long would it take to eat all the bowls of cereal made from a hundred-acre cornfield? How many notes did Beethoven write in his life? Whenever he pesters her with such questions, she replies: "Far." "A heap of days." "Just enough for us to listen to."

But for the price of a cup of coffee, he gives them something invisible. They leave clutching the magic napkin, staring at the scribbles before they fade, sure that they could have seen the way forward themselves, given a little more time. But this way is faster, cleaner, lighter. No one can say exactly what David does. Nothing rigorous. He just displaces them. Moves them around the sealed space until they find the hidden door. He scribbles on the white napkin, relying more on pictures than equations. His colleagues complain that he doesn't really use reason. They accuse him of jumping ahead in time to that point where the researcher has already solved his problem, then coming back with some rough description of solutions yet to come.

His pictures are the flattened traces he brings back from later worlds: imps climbing up and down staircases. Snaking queues of moviegoers waiting to enter a theater by two separate doors. Zigzag arrows with heads and tails hooking up in tangled skeins: the experimental, extended notation. Those whose work he helps dislodge must then pester him, needing to know how he always finds, in single lightning flashes, the angle that aligns.

"You must learn to listen," he says. If particles, forces, and fields obey the curve that binds the flow of numbers, then they must sound like harmonies in time. "You think with your eyes; this is your problem. No one can see four independent variables mapping out a surface in five or more dimensions. But the tuned ear can hear chords."

His colleagues dismiss this talk as mere metaphor. They think he's hiding something, storing up his secret method until it delivers the one blinding insight he's after. Or perhaps he's in it for the endless free cups of coffee.

Delia, though, believes him, and knows how it is. Her husband hears his way forward. Melodies, intervals, rhythms, durations: the music of the spheres. Others bring him their deadlocks—particles spinning backward, phantom apparitions in two places at once, gravities collapsing on themselves. Even as they describe the hopeless mysteries, her David hears the rich counterpoint coded in the composer's score. This, she sees, lying in bed watching him undress, is how he helped them build their bomb. He did no real work except to free up the thoughts of men who made the design. All of them boys, caught up in pure performance. The permanent urge to find and catch.

Her husband undoes the collar of his shirt and struggles out of its sleeves. The flaps of fabric go slack onto their haphazard hanger. She will turn his closet right again after he leaves for school in the morning. He moves across the room in T-shirt and boxers, this night's peace in his eyes. The war is over, or it will be soon. Work can begin again, free from nuisance politics, the showdown of power, the assorted evils that he, a secular Jew in love with knowing, would never have chosen to mix in. Life can resume, safe at least, if never again the way it was before such safety. This is her husband, padding over the floorboards to their August bed, across a distance harder to guess than any Fermi problem.

She wants to ask, *Is this what you thought?* One cog in the largest engineering project ever. Nothing. She wants to ask him exactly what he did, what subsection of this invention he made possible. But he closes the distance to her before she finds the nerve. He bends his weight onto the bed, and just as every night, their two adjacent hues shock each other into being. His eyes drop to the greater mystery. He puts his hand on her thickened middle, the third life they've started there. He says something soft she can't catch, neither English nor German, but in a language far older than both, an earliest benediction.

It's August, too hot for the slightest touch. He rubs her with a little alcohol on a cotton rag that they keep on the bed stand. For a minute, she is cool. "You have not felt sick today?"

Because she does not lie to him, she says to the road-map ceiling, "A little. But it wasn't the baby."

He shoots her a look. Does he know? Always the same question. And no one can give her an answer that won't, itself, go forever begging. He looks away from her ripened belly. He swings his feet onto the bed. He lifts the undershirt above his head, bares the chest she can't quite learn. He lies back on the mattress, his shoulders pressed down into the sheet and his hips lifted, like a wrestler bucking free of a pin. In one smooth motion, he draws his boxers down his legs. A final fish wiggle and he's naked, his undershorts a soft missile arcing onto the chair. How many nights has she seen him undress? More than the miles a crow lives to fly. How many more will be given to her? Fewer than the notes in a Beethoven allegro.

She lies in bed, six inches from a man who has helped—what? Begin a new age. Helped his awe-blind friends think the unthinkable and place it squarely into this world. She might ask him, and gain only his confusion. She can come no closer than flush alongside him. Every human a separate race. Each one of us a self no one can enter. How has this man found his way to this bed? How has she? Here they are, a little more than five years on in their marriage, and already there's no hope of saying. Even less chance of saying where another five years will leave them. She casts herself—her solitary, sole race—forward another five years into this new age. Then fifty more, and further. She sees herself blocked, breaking out, becoming something new. She feels what this unknowable man next to her so often insists: "Everything the laws of the universe do not prohibit must finally happen."

He lies naked along her nakedness. He on top of the flat sheet, she half under. She can't sleep, however hot the night, without some cover. A hundred thousand people gone in one airborne flash, and she needs a sheet to sleep. She, too, wanted this device. She, too, asked him to hurry. An evil large enough to end the larger evil. Now the war is over, and life—whatever they might yet make of it—begins again. Now peace must rise to the horrors war has left. Now the world must become one people. If not one, then billions.

The one person who is her husband lies back in his own body. He slips his palms behind his neck, elbows protruding into a ship's prow, his face the figurehead. In profile, he grows strange, another species. Would he have taken on this marriage had he known what the days would bring? Their endless battle just to step out of the house, walk down the block, go shopping. The times they must pretend to be strangers, slight acquaintances, employer and servant. The passive attacks and murmured violence he came to this country to escape. The low-grade war no blinding flash will ever end.

She should never have let him, knowing what he didn't. How much she's dragged him into. How much she's made impossible. And yet, the children: as inevitable as God. Now that they live, they had to, all along. Her two little men, her JoJo, who could never not be. And this new third life on the way, sleeping in her, soft and round as an Indian mound: already a story that always was. She and this man are here only to ensure these three.

Her husband turns to her. "What will we do for schooling?"

He reads her mind, as he has once a day since the mind-reading day they met. She needs no other proof that this war is theirs, the one they were meant for. School will kill them. The daily bruise of their lessons will make grade-standard schoolyard assaults look like ice-cream socials. Her JoJo, like those magazine illusions: paper white against one crowd, lamp black against the other. Already, they belong nowhere. Their oldest has perfect pitch. She's tested it already: infallible. He seems to be training his brother in the same. They play together, paint, hold their lines in complex rounds. They love themselves, love both their parents, see no shades between. All this will die in school's brutal curriculum.

"We could school them at home." Writing her mind, reading his.

"We could school them ourselves. You and I, the two put together."

"Yes." She shushes him. "Between the two of us, we can teach them a great deal."

He lies back quiet, content in their plans. Maybe that is whiteness, manness. Safe within himself, even on a day like this day. Even with all that has happened to his own family. In a minute, his contentment leads to what it always does. His night to start tonight: He hums a tune. She can't say what it is. Her mind is not naming yet, but keeps inside the phrase. Something Russian: the steppes; onion domes. A world as far away from hers as this world permits her. And by the time his slow Volga tune comes into its second measure, she's there with the descant.

This is how they play, night after night, more regular than sex, and just as warming. One begins; the other harmonizes. Finds some accompaniment, even when she has never heard the tune, when it comes down out of the attic from some musty culture no one would claim to own. The secret's in the intervals, finding a line half free of the melody, yet already inside it. Music from a single note, set loose to run in unfolding meter.

Humming in bed: softer than love, so as not to wake their two sleeping children. This third, as close as her abdomen, won't mind hearing. She sings, tuning with a man who has as little sense of her past as she has of these haunted Czarist chords. His whole family has vanished, leaving behind no hard fact to mourn. He's left his handprints on a bomb that takes a hundred thousand lives. It's August, too hot for the lightest touch. But when they fade and settle down to sleep, no angels watching over them out of the newly stripped skies, his fingers brush against the small of her back and hers reach out behind him to rest, for the next half hour anyway, upon the familiar strangeness of his thigh.

Her father writes David a long letter, started the day after the second bomb and finished three weeks later. "Dear David." How their letters always begin: "Dear William." "Dear David."

This incredible news explains everything you couldn't tell me over the last two years. I've come to appreciate what you must have carried inside you, and I thank you for giving me as much of a sense of this as you were able.

With the rest of America, I give praise to whatever power there is that this chapter in human history is at last over. Believe me, I know how much longer it might have dragged on had science not succeeded in producing this "cosmic bomb." If nothing else, I thank you for Michael's sake. But so much else about this development eludes me that I feel I must write you for clarification.

Delia watches her husband read, blinking the way he does when baffled by words.

I have no trouble in accepting the first explosion. It seems to me politically necessary, scientifically triumphant, and morally expedient. But this second blast is little more than barbaric. What civilized people could defend such action? We have taken tens of thousands more lives, without even giving that country a chance to absorb the fact of what hit it. And for what? Merely, it seems, to project a final superiority, the same world dominance I thought we were fighting this war to end . . .

David Strom gapes at his accuser's daughter. "I don't understand. He means I'm to answer for this?" He hands the paper to his wife, who speeds through it. "I am not the one to talk about this bomb. Yes, I've done work for the OSRD. So did half of our scientists. More than half! I did a little thinking about neutron absorption. A little later, I helped people to figure a problem surrounding the implosion. I did more work on electronic countermeasures that were never developed than I did for this device."

Delia reaches out and grazes her husband's arm. What can her touch feel like to him? His words relieve her a little, suggest the answers beyond her asking. But here: this letter, a sheet between them. Her father's question has weighed on her for weeks. And her husband, she sees, has not yet asked it of himself. David takes the page back from her, resuming his penance at the pace of the foreign reader:

This country must know what it's in danger of pursuing. Surely it sees how this act will look to history. Would this country have been willing to drop this bomb on Germany, on the country of your beloved Bach and Beethoven? Would we have used it to annihilate a European capital? Or was this mass civilian death meant, from the beginning, to be used only against the darker races?

Too much for David. "Yes," he shouts. She has never heard this strain in him. "Surely. Of course I would use this against Germany. Think what Germany has used against everyone who is my relation! We have bombed all the German cities, by daylight and by nighttime. Flattened all the cathedrals. We were racing to make this final bomb before Heisenberg. *Alle Deutschen . . .*"

She nods and cups his elbow. Her father, too, cheered David's war work, what little David could tell him. The doctor, too, urged all speed to ring in the American future as quickly as possible. But her father was backing a thing invisible to him.

Know that I don't blame you, but only need to ask you these few matters. You have seen up close what I can only speculate about. I had in mind a different victor, a different peace, one that would put an end to supremacy forever. We were fighting against fascism, genocide, all the evils of power. Now we've leveled two cities of bewildered brown civilians . . . You may not understand my racial-izing these blasts. Maybe you'd have to spend a month in my clinic or a year in the neighborhoods near mine to know what I wanted this war to defeat. I'd hoped for something better from this coun-try. If this is how we choose to end this conflict, what hope can we have for peacetime?

No doubt this extraordinary turn of events looks different to you, David. That's why I'm writing. If you could show me what I've failed to understand, I'd be much obliged.

Meanwhile, rest assured that I do not consider you to be su-premacy, power, barbarity, Europe, history, or anything else but my son-in-law, whom I trust is taking care of my girl and those as-tonishing grandsons of mine. May Labor Day find you all well. I look forward to hearing back from you. Ever, William.

David finishes and says nothing. He's *listening*; this much she must al-ways love in him. Holding out for a hint of harmony. Waiting to hear the music that will answer for him. "I can get on a train." His voice is a frayed rope. "Go out to Philadelphia and see him."

"Don't talk crazy," she tells him, trying for comfort and missing by a wide margin.

"But I must speak with him. We must try to understand this, face-to-face. How can I do this thing, through writing, when nothing of what I must say is in my language?"

She takes him in her arms. "The doctor can come pay us a house call if he wants to talk. When was the last time we had him out here? He can come see his boys and have a listen to this little bun in the oven. You men can drink brandy and decide how best to fix civilization's future."

"I don't drink brandy. You know this." She has to laugh at the droop in him. But he does not lift at her laughing.

Her idea is inspired. She floats an open invitation just as Dr. Daley debates whether to attend the big postwar conference on the latest developments in sulfa drugs and antibiotics hosted by Mount Sinai and Columbia. Mixing pleasure and business appeals to the doctor's efficiency. He arrives at the house on a September evening. Jonah and Joseph are on their feet and flying to the door at his knock. They sing "Papap" at the top of their voices, primed all day for the man's arrival. Delia peers down the corridor as they bang into each other, each reaching for the handle to let their grandfather in. Joseph still favors his twisted ankle. Or maybe she imagines it. She has her hands full with basting bulb and ladle, but she towels clean in a moment and is off to the door, two steps behind her boys.

She reads the violence as her father steps into the room. She thinks at first, *This bomb, this matter of morality he comes to discuss with David.* But something nearer has happened. He doesn't lean down to embrace the boys or carry them. He barely lets them cling to his legs before he brushes past down the corridor, radiating fury.

She's seen this before, more times than she cares to remember. Seen it first when she was no older than Joseph. In her boys' faces, the seed of that poison tree: *What did we do?* The question she herself could never answer. Now it's her boys' turn to suffer the inheritance she can't keep them from.

Her father nears her, and she tries to hug him. He pecks her on the chin. She feels him struggle, with that last scrap of dignity so powerful in him, to bite down this rage and swallow it whole, a cyanide capsule they give to agents caught behind enemy lines. She knows he won't be able to. He'll wrestle and fail, no less spectacularly than the world has failed him. Meanwhile, she cannot ask, can't do anything but play along, a show of cheer while waiting for all hell to break.

It takes until after dinner. The meal itself—turkey, broccoli, and creamed corn—is polite, if strained. David doesn't notice, or he's

shrewder than Delia ever supposed. He asks about the sulfa-drug conference and William answers in Western Union. William tries instead to
rehash the mess at Potsdam and Truman's doomed slum-revitalization
program. David can only grin, hopeless on both scores. Delia feels them
both fighting to stay off Japan, the atom shadow, the dawn of the new cosmic age. The case this night's meeting was meant to hear.

After the apple compote, her sons drift from the table to the spinet,
that wedding gift from Dr. Daley, far and away their favorite toy. They
tinker with octave scales. "Play me a nice old-time song," Dr. Daley tells
them. "Can you do that? You boys play a little tune for your grandpap?"

The two boys—four and three—smash down onto the bench and play
a Bach chorale: "O Ewigkeit, du Donnerwort." Jonah gets the melody, of
course. Joseph holds down the bass. This is how it goes: two boys discovering the secret of harmony, delighting in passing dissonance, tumbling
over the jumble of moving lines, romping through the transformed scale.
"O Eternity, you thunderous word! You sword boring into the soul! Beginning minus ending, Eternity, time without time, take me whenever it
pleases you!" Nobody in this room knows the words. It's notes only in
here tonight. The boys weave their runs, butt wrists, kick each other's
shins where they dangle in the air, lean away in the swell of progressions,
come back playfully on the smallest slowing, home. The music is in them.
Just *in* them, this opening chrysanthemum of chords. It makes them
happy, each juggling lines utterly separate that nevertheless fall one inside
the other. Breathing in this perfect solution to a day that belongs to no
one.

Some night, a life will arise that has no memory of where it came
from, no thought of anything that has happened on the way here. No
theft, no slavery, no murder. Something will be won then, and much will
be lost, in the death of time. But this night is not yet that night. William
Daley looks on these small boys, doing their chorale tumbling act. In that
look lies every chord that music doesn't speak. He shakes his head in
wide, fact-denying arcs. The boys think he's pleased, maybe even amazed,
as every adult who has ever heard them has been. They lower themselves
off the bench and toddle off to other discoveries. William turns to his
daughter and stares at her, the way he once stared at his son Charles for
playing coon songs on the parlor upright back home. The look sinks into
her: accomplice, accuser. *Anything you want.* Wasn't that the creed? *The
equal of any owner. The owner of all you would equal.* Dr. Daley's head shakes

to a terrible stop. "What are you going to *do* with them?" He might mean anything. Anything you want.

Delia rises and starts to clear the table. "David and I have decided to school them at home." She's almost in the kitchen by sentence's end.

"Is that so?"

"We've thought about it, Daddy." She swings back to the table. "Where can they get a better education? David knows everything there is to know about science and math." She waves toward her husband, who bows his head. "I can teach them music and art."

"You going to give them history?" In the whip crack of his voice, there's all the history he means. His fingers clamp around his water glass to keep his daughter from stealing it from him. "Where are they going to learn who they are?"

She slips back into her seat without a sound. She wraps herself in this role, the way Mr. Lugati trained her to do onstage. *We work hard during countless rehearsals, so we can be inside ourselves, free for that one performance.* She reaches down to find that column of breath. "Same place I learned, Daddy. Same place you learned."

His eyes flash gunmetal. "You know where I learned who I am? Where *I* learned?" He turns toward David, who learned elsewhere. And that, Delia sees, is his unforgivable crime. "You asked about the conference? You wanted to know how the *conference* went?"

David just blinks. No longer sulfa drugs. No more antibiotics.

"I wish I could tell you. You see, I missed the better part of it. Detained downstairs in the lobby, first by the hotel dick, and later by a small but efficient police escort. A slight misunderstanding. You see, I couldn't, in fact, be Dr. William Daley of Philadelphia, Pennsylvania, because Dr. Daley is a real medical doctor with genuine credentials, while I'm just a nigger busting his woolly head into a civilized meeting of medical professionals."

"Daddy. We don't use that word in this house."

"You don't? Your boys are going to have to learn it, between their pretty four-part hymns. Full dictionary definition. Count on it. Home school!"

Her walls are in flames. "Daddy, you . . . I don't understand you. You raised me . . ."

"That's right, miss. I raised you. Let's agree on that."

She sees her lightness in the almond of his eyes. Has he forgotten?

Does he think she has *gone over*, over to something as invented as the one laid down upon them?

" 'You are a singer,' " she says. " 'You lift yourself *up*. You make yourself so damn good that they *have* to hear you.' "

His palms flash outward. *Look!* "You've been out of school for half a decade. Where's your career?"

She falls back from him, smashed in the face.

"She has been very busy," David answers. "She is a wife and a mother of two. With one more coming."

"How has *your* career been? Family obligations haven't kept *you* from tenure."

"Daddy." The scale of the warning, in the back of Delia's throat, startles even her.

He won't be humbled, not again this day. He wheels on her. "I'll tell you where your career is. It's waiting out back of the concert hall, in the alley. The Coloreds Only entrance. Which just happens to be boarded up for the foreseeable future."

"I haven't really taken any auditions."

"What do you mean, 'haven't really'? Either you haven't or you have."

"I'll do more after the boys are older."

"How long does a voice last?"

So many accusations come at her at once that she loses count. Smartest baby ever born, either side of the line, and she hasn't become a lawyer, run for Congress, become even a mediocre concert artist. Hasn't moved the race down the line. All she has done is raise two small boys, and that, apparently, not well.

Her father drops into deep bass, a tone she's never heard him use. The sound silts up with her mama's yellow clay-bed Carolina, a place he's not been, aside from one unwilling visit, for more than fifteen years. Forget tobacco, forget cotton: land too bleak for anything but the most pitiful beans and peanuts. Land too poor to pay its own rent. His voice comes out a note-perfect mock of his own battered-down father-in-law, the one Delia met just three awkward times in this life. Only the voice isn't mocking. "Those people ain't *never* gonna let you sing."

"They let Miss Anderson sing."

"Sure. They let her sing, up at the Big House, on Novelty Night. Do a little dance, too, if she likes. Entertainment! Dogs on bicycles. Just make sure she gets back down to the darkie quarters when the act is over."

Delia sits, hands frozen on the half-cleared table. Some street gangster has taken over her daddy, the man who worked his private way through *Ulysses*, who corresponds with university presidents, who demanded David's explanation of Special Relativity. The man who has spent his adult life easing the sick. Stripped of his clinic, separated from his wife, taken from the neighborhood where he has for years been a healing god, fingered in a hotel lobby and held like some petty crook or dope fiend. What the world sees will always destroy what he rushes to show it. There is no counter but that collapse that, in time, takes everyone. Identity.

Dr. Daley walks over to the spinet. He plays the boys' chorale from memory. He gets the first four bars, more or less as the backwoods cantor wrote them. It shocks Delia how good he is. He plays like one who has lost his native tongue. But he plays. She has never heard him play much of anything but snippets of Joplin. "That baby's crying seemed to be,/Somewhere near the Sacred Tree." A little broken boogie-woogie at Charlie's memorial. Now this. By ear. Nothing but ear.

William's hands pull away from the saw-toothed Lutheran chords as if the piano lid just bit them. "You know what I hear when I hear that music? I hear, 'Cursed be Canaan.' I hear 'White—all right: Brown—hang around: Black—get back.' "

His daughter raises her blasted eyes to his. She tries for piano. Soft is harder than loud, as Lugati always said. "I'm sorry they were idiots at the conference, Daddy." *More reason,* she wants to add, *to beat them at what's theirs.*

"Mount Sinai. Not idiots. Best there is." His eyes test the extremes of punishment not yet visited on him. Stripped so easily, he knows no bottom. Held and humiliated for an hour: It cost him nothing. Laughable. Dust yourself off and walk away. But if that, why not locked up in the coat check, chained to the shoe-shine stand in Penn Station, kept illiterate, driven out of the polling place, beaten up for turning down the wrong alley, or hung from a ready sumac? Even the most stubborn self in time will be identified.

From under his prayer shawl of silence, David speaks. "I have been thinking. What has been done to you today. This is an error of statistics."

William bolts up. "What do you mean?"

"These are men who will not calculate while flying."

Dr. Daley stares at the man. He turns to his daughter, dumbfounded. Her lips pucker. "On the fly."

"Yes. On the flight. They are taking shortcuts in the steps of their deductions. They do not see the case, but only make bets on the basis of what they think likelihood tells them. Category. This is how thought proceeds. We cannot alter that. But we must change their categories."

"Likelihood be hanged. This is nothing but animal hatred. Two species. That's what they see. That's what they're intent on making. And damn us all, that's what we're going to be. They couldn't see my clothes. They couldn't hear my speech. I was quoting whole chapters from the seventh edition of the mother*fucking Merck Manual* . . ."

"My father told me it happens." Her voice spinto, sailing on the shakes. She needs only ride this out. "My father taught me to live through it. To make a *me* too big to take away."

"And what will you tell your children?"

Jonah chooses this moment to reenter the room. And where he strays, Joey isn't far behind. Two preschoolers wandering in the woods, the pointless thicket of adulthood. William Daley clasps his eldest grandson's shoulders. In this room's light, the boy's beige throws him. Somewhere between *hang around* and *all right*. A bent harmonica note, neither sharp nor natural. Between: like a rheostat, the slow turn of a radio dial receiving, for the slightest subtended turn, two stations at once. Like a coin landing freakishly on its edge, before the laws of likelihood condemn it to fall on one face or the other. He looks at this boy and sees a creature from the next world. Something comes back to him, an unusable aphorism he found while wasting his time trespassing in Emerson: "Every man contemplates an angel in his future self."

"Joseph," he says.

"Jonah." The boy giggles.

The doctor swings around on his daughter. "Why in the name of hell did you call them the same thing?" Back to the boy, he says, "Jonah. Sing me something."

Little Jonah starts out on a long, mournful canon. "By the waters, the waters of Babylon. We laid down and wept, and wept, for thee, Zion." God knows what he thinks the syllables mean. Little Joey, a year younger, hears the round and waits, nailing his entrance, as he does with his parents night after night. But tonight, neither parent chimes in, and the canon trickles off after only two entrances.

"Sing me another," Papap commands. And the boys, happy to oblige, start up another round: "Dona nobis pacem." William holds his finger up, cuts them off before the three words are out. "What about our music?" He looks at the boys. But it's their mother who answers.

"When was it ever ours, Daddy?" Ours: the black aristocracy, the Talented Tenth. The most despised people of the most despised people on earth.

He falls into oratory. "Before the Pilgrims," he says, still regarding his grandchildren. "We were here, making our sounds."

"I mean, when was it *yours*? Ours. Around the house. What music did we ever make our own? I had Mama's church tunes, everything that came out of the A.M.E. hymnal. And I had your set of Teach Yourself the Classics 78's. I used to sneak off with Charlie to listen to the wild sounds from New York and Chicago. All the stuff you never let us tune the radio to. 'Best way to have yourself treated like a savage is to sound like one.' I knew the music that scared you and the music that you felt you had to learn. But aside from a few turn-of-the-century rags you used to play when you thought nobody was listening—oh, I loved it when you played those!—I didn't even know what music you *liked*. I didn't even know you could . . ." She points toward the spinet, the smoking gun.

"You want these boys to sing? You want these boys to love . . . This boy." He points to the darker one. His hand chops the air, fighting off the creep of prophecy. He can't bear to look on his pronouncement. "This boy is going to be stopped, a quarter century from now. Going into some concert hall. Told there's some mistake. He wants the stage on the other side of town. Not his music, going on inside. Complex, cultivated stuff. He wouldn't understand."

"Dein, was du geliebt, was du gestritten." The words issue from nowhere, no person. "What you have loved, what you have fought for, that is yours."

Dr. Daley swings around to face the challenge. There was a time when he'd have asked where the words came from. Now he says, "Who let you think so?"

Delia rises, as on the day of Resurrection. She glides over the floor to her father. Before he can pull away from her, she's behind him, one hand draping onto the coiled mass of shoulder, one hand painting the patterned patch of baldness at the crest of his majestic skull. "What do you love, Daddy? What music do you love?"

"What music? Do I love?"

She nods, head jittering, teeth bared through her tears. Humming the first few bars of anything under her breath. Ready to be his little girl again at his first word.

"What music?" He thinks so long, he exhausts the catalog. "I sincerely wish that were the issue." He lets himself be stroked, though only in distraction. "You've dropped your babies right down in between, haven't you? Dead halfway. No-man's-land."

She stands bathed in unearthly calm. "We were already between, Daddy. We were always between."

"Not always."

And then her mistake: "Everybody's between something. Everybody's halfway." She fancies she speaks the words in something like her mother's voice.

But her father turns on her with a force that startles her fingers off him. He hisses at her, soft and civilized. "No, my little halfway opera singer. *Everyone* is not. Some people aren't even what they are. You think that just because their father is a white man, the world will—"

"A *white* man?" Jonah giggles. "A man can't be white! You mean like a ghost?"

William Daley stares at Delia, stopped in place. His face hangs broken, waiting for explanation. But frozen by that pianissimo, by what her words have done, she can say nothing.

The boy is enjoying himself. "How can a man be *white*? That's silly."

"Sing something for your Papap," their mother says. "Sing 'This Little Light of Mine.' "

"What are you teaching them?" The voice comes up at her out of the ground. A voice that puts an end to song. The voice of God rising up to ask Adam and Eve just what they thought they were hiding. Her mind snaps free to race ahead into its own answer. Adam and Eve, it hits her: Those two must have been a mixed-race couple. How else? What other scheme could have populated the whole world?

"We've thought about this, Daddy."

"You've thought about this. And what has your *thought* led you to think?"

David shakes himself from the undergrowth. He leans forward to give their reasons. But Delia holds out a palm to stop him. *Make yourself the equal, the owner of this explanation.* "We've decided to raise the children beyond race."

Her father turns, shakes his ears, deafened. Something pitiless infects his head. "Again?"

"One quarter of a century from now," David begins. Both Negroes ignore him.

"We've made a choice." Every word sounds, even to Delia, overmeasured. "We don't name them. They'll do that for themselves." Anything they want. "We're going to raise them for when everybody will be past color."

" 'Past color'?" The doctor sounds out the words, saying them out loud the way he repeats his patients' symptoms. "You mean you're going to raise them white."

The boys have lost interest, if they ever had any. They wander back to the piano to try another chorale. Delia hushes them. "Not right now, JoJo. Why don't you two go play in your room?"

She has never before told them to stop making music. Jonah starts plunking the keys at high speed, double, quadruple time, racing through the entire chorale before the prohibition can take effect. His brother looks on, horrified. Delia sweeps to the bench, lifts up the lawbreaker, swings him like the bob of a pendulum, then lowers him to the floor and starts him scampering toward the boys' room. She grazes his bottom for good measure, and the offender howls down the hallway, his little brother crying behind him in sympathy, limping in remembered pain.

Past color. My mother speaks these words to my grandfather in late September of 1945. I'm three years old. What can I hope to remember? My brother lies on his belly in our room's doorway, spying on adulthood down the hall. He's thinking about just one thing: how to get back to that piano and make some noise. How to recover the throne of sound that alone rights the world and sets him at the center of love.

My parents and grandfather crouch in a globe of light in the middle of edgeless shadow. They should know this, how small their circle, how big the surrounding dark. But something drives them on, something that isn't them but says it is. Something they need wants them so completely that they turn on one another to avoid losing it. I see them down the hall, a ball of burning sulfur in a borderless dark bowl.

Mama says, *We have to get there, somehow. Somebody has to jump.*

Papap says, *Beyond color? You know what beyond color means? We're already there. Beyond color means hide the black man. Wipe him out. Means everybody play the one annihilating game white's been playing since—*

The world is ending. Jonah and I know this already, and we know almost nothing. My brother will run out into the middle of them, seduce them back home with a song. But even Jonah has fallen under the spell of revenge. His wrong is private, and deeper than the world's. Scolded unfairly while playing.

Papap says, *What do you think they'll learn the minute they set foot out of your house?*

Mama says, *Everybody's going to be mixed. No one's going to be anything.*

Papap says, *There is no mixed.*

Da says, *Not yet.*

Papap says, *Never will be. It's one thing or the other. And they can't be the one, not in this world. It's the other, girl. You know that. What's your problem?*

Mama says, *People have to move. What world do you want to live in? Things have to break down, go someplace else.*

Papap says, *They've been breaking down black from day one. Sending it someplace else.*

Mama says, *White, too. White is going to change.*

Papap says, *White? Break down? Never, short of gunpoint.*

Mama says, *They will; they'll have to.*

And Papap answers her: *Never. Never. What happened this morning is all the future any of us is ever going to get.*

Then the real storm. I can't remember how it comes on, any more than I can remember myself. They've been talking a long time. Jonah falls asleep on the floor in the doorway to our room. I can't, of course, not with the grown-ups so badly wrong. Papap is pacing the dining room, a giant in a cage. He slams the walls with his palm. *Beyond color, beyond your own mother. Beyond your sisters and brothers, beyond me!*

Mama, dead still. *That's not what it means, Daddy. That's not what we're doing.*

What are you doing? What does it say on the birth certificate? You think you can override that?

More words I can't hear, can't get, can't remember. Something heated, between the two men. Worse than anger. Words sharpened to a point small enough to break the skin. And then my grandfather stands in the apartment's doorway. The door is open on September there in front of them, a gaping, heatless nothing. *Never,* he starts. And where can he go from there? *Your choice, not mine. Beyond me,* he says. And Mama says something, and Da says something, and Papap says, *How dare you?* And then he's gone.

I remember only my parents turning from the slammed door, both of them shaking. I see them seeing me, standing in the doorway with my ice bag. Holding it up for whoever might need it.

Mama is ill for a long time afterward. She's big with another baby. I watch her eat, hypnotized. She sees me see her, knows what I'm thinking, and tries to smile. She decides to have a baby, then starts eating for two. And the baby is down there in her stomach, grabbing half the food.

Something has left our lives and I don't know what. I think the baby will bring it back in. That's why they wanted to have it. To get Mama's happiness back, and fix what has broken.

I ask what the baby will be. *What do you mean?* they ask. *You mean a boy or a girl?* They say nobody can know what the baby is going to be yet. I ask, *Isn't it something already?*

It is. They laugh. *But we can't get to it. We have to wait. Wait and see what's coming.*

We wait until October, then November, strange territories with stranger names. I'm as miserable as I've ever been. *Isn't it here yet? Isn't it ever going to come?*

Perhaps tomorrow, they say. *We have to wait until tomorrow.*

And several times a day, I ask, *Is it tomorrow yet?*

For weeks, it's never tomorrow. Then overnight, it's yesterday. All yesterday, too far back to reach. And my father is dying on a bed in Mount Sinai Hospital. The only thing I need to know from him is what happened that night. But he's too sick, too medicated, too full of gravity—and then, too free—to remember.

SONGS OF A WAYFARER

Jonah left the United States at the end of 1968. No high-art gossip column reported the departure. At the moment when almost every other black singer, performer, artist, or writer cheered the birth of nationhood, my brother abandoned the country. He wrote from Magdeburg. "They love me here, Joey." He might have been Robeson, on his first visit to the Soviet Union. Everything there made a mockery of everything here. "The East Germans look at me and see a singer. I never understood that stare Americans always gave me, until I got away from it. Nice to know what it feels like, for a while, to be something other than hue-man."

The Magdeburg Festival sounded like high-art boot camp. "Living conditions are a bit Spartan. My room reminds me of our dorm at Boylston; only here, I don't have to pick up your shit." This from a man whose laundry I did every year we lived together. "Food consists of your more recalcitrant vegetables boiled within an inch of their lives. Making up for all hardships, however, is a steady stream of music-loving women. Now that's what I call a culture."

He marveled at the scope of the musical gathering, all the world-class singers the celebration brought together. Several clearly put the fear of God in him. But he seemed to come alive on the challenge of ensemble singing. He was a kid who'd shot backyard hoops his whole childhood, finally playing full-court ball. He reveled in the thrill of reading a dozen other musicians at once and fusing with these perfect strangers.

The European reporters demanded to know why they'd never heard of him before. He didn't dissuade them from publishing reports of American racism. He had offers to sing in a dozen cities, including Prague and Vienna. "Vienna, Mule. Think of the possibilities. More work than a short-order cook in Lauderdale during spring break. You simply have to come. That's my last word on the matter."

His letter took weeks catching up to me, because I'd moved. I couldn't afford to keep our Village apartment alone. I briefly put up with Da in Fort Lee, to his delight and daily surprise each evening when he came back to Jersey and found me still there. I heard him wandering the house in the middle of the night, chatting away with Mama, who seemed a better conversationalist than his son would ever be.

I couldn't stay in that house. I didn't mind my father's nightly chat with a dead woman. But the alarm I set off in my father's prim neighborhood was too much for me. The police gave me a week before they decided I couldn't be the man's gardener. The first time they detained and searched me, I had no ID and only the most implausible story: unemployed Juilliard dropout classical pianist, the black son of a white German physicist who taught at Columbia. Even after they finally agreed to call Da down to the station to check out my story, it took all night to free me. The second time, two weeks later, I was ready for them with a wallet full of documentation. But they wouldn't even let me make a phone call. They kept me overnight and let me go at nine the next morning, without explanation or apology.

I stopped leaving the house. For two months, I stayed home and practiced. I put the word out with everyone I knew that Jonah was gone. I was doing nothing, and would play with anyone for any kind of pay. I heard Jonah saying, *You undersell yourself. Make them hear you.*

Logically, I should have kept doing what I'd spent my life training to do. But that meant taking care of my brother. Jonah and I had lived for years in self-perfecting isolation. Now, as perfect as I had any hope of getting, I lacked the connections that any musician needed to survive.

I played a handful of exploratory tryouts. I'd arrange to meet some sterling mezzo or baritone in an uptown rehearsal space. When I showed up, the singer would recoil in reflex embarrassment: *Some mistake.* They'd fall all over themselves going over the score with me, practically trying to show me where middle C was.

It's hard to play well when you feel like a fish on stilts. And it's hard to sing when jarred out of your center. Most of the time, the trials ended in mutual praise and embarrassed handshakes. I played for a sumptuous soprano, a von Stade look-alike who liked what I did for her. She said no accompanist had ever given her such secured freedom. But I felt her struggling with all the overhead of traveling about the country with a black man, and frankly, I didn't much want the overhead of traveling around the country with her. We parted enthusiastically. She went on to a modest but rewarding career and I went home to cold noodles and more études.

I played for Brian Barlowe, three years before anyone ever heard of him. He sounded like the Roman soldier at the foot of the cross. He had that same confidence Jonah once had, the utter certainty that the world would love him for what he could do. Only Brian Barlowe's confidence was better placed than Jonah's. I'd take Jonah's voice over his in a heartbeat, at each man's prime. But Barlowe belonged already. His audiences needed to think about nothing but the confirming sounds pouring out of him. Listeners came away from a Barlowe recital surer than ever of their birthright to beauty.

We played together on three separate days over the course of a month. Brian was nothing if not careful, and he intended to choreograph his march into fame with absolute precision. I showed up each time, stupid with needing to show him that I could read his mind and make even him better than he was. But by the time Barlowe was convinced of my playing—and what's more, seeing that I could supply a transgressive frisson that would electrify his act—by the time he offered me a chance he was sure I'd leap at, my heart was no longer in it. The gratification of following Brian Barlowe around the world to the pinnacle of fame could not match the pleasure of handing the man back his scores and turning him down.

It dawned on me: I could accompany no one but my brother. When I played for others, for those who made music without the danger of having it taken away, the song never lifted off the page. With Jonah, a recital was always grand larceny. With the children of Europe, it was a revolving charge account. The joy of making noise was gone, even if the cold thrill of notes remained intact.

I sprouted two massive ganglions, one on each wrist: two cysts, like insect galls, as harsh as stigmata. Playing became unbearable. I tried every postural adjustment, even hunching over the keyboard on a low stool, but nothing helped. I thought I might never make music again. For weeks, I did nothing but eat, sleep, and nurse my wrists. I looked through the paper at the end of each week, scouting the want ads. I thought of becoming a night watchman in some high-rise business suite. I'd stroll around a graveyard of abandoned offices with a flashlight once an hour, and sit the rest of the time at a shabby wooden desk, pouring over a stack of Norton pocket scores.

I needed to get out of New York. By luck, I learned they were looking for barroom pianists for the season down in Atlantic City. Being dark would almost be an asset. I went down to a club that was advertising, a place called the Glimmer Room. The bar was something stuck in the La Brea tar pits—a complete sinkhole in time. Nothing had changed in the place since Eisenhower. The walls were full of signed black-and-white pub shots of comedians I'd never heard of.

I did a five-minute audition for a man named Saul Silber. My wrists still bothered me, and I hadn't improvised since my days in a Juilliard practice room with Wilson Hart. But Mr. Silber wasn't looking for Count Basie. The crowds had been ebbing in the Glimmer Room ever since the transistor. Woodstock was a wooden stake in its heart. The place was dying even faster than the city itself. Mr. Silber didn't understand why. He just wanted to staunch the bleeding any way possible.

He was a cauliflower of a man. "Play me what the kids are listening to these days." He might have been my father's more assimilated uncle. He had the accent—the ghostly highlights of Yiddish filtered through Brooklyn—that Da's kids might have preserved, had Da stuck with his people and had different kids. "Something out of sight, why don't you start me with."

I waited for him to name a tune, but he just waved me to go, his fisted cigar a conductor's baton. I sunk into a beefy "Sittin' on the Dock of the Bay," a tune I'd heard on the radio driving down. Since my brother had abandoned me for another country, I was safe in liking it. I savored the descending chromatic left hand, pumping it out in soulful octaves. Two strains in, Mr. Silber grimaced and waved his hands for a time-out.

"Naw, naw. Play me that pretty one. The one with the string quartet." He hummed the first three notes of "Yesterday," with a schmaltz three years too late or thirty too soon. I'd heard the tune thousands of times. But I'd never played it. I sat there in the Glimmer Room at the height of my musicianship. I could have reproduced any movement of any Mozart concerto on first hearing, had there been any I hadn't already heard. The problem with pop tunes was that, in those rare moments when I did re-create them at the piano, as a break from more études, I tended to embellish the chord sequences. "Yesterday" came out half Baroque figured bass and half ballpark organ. I covered my uncertainty in a flurry of passing tones. Mr. Silber must have thought it was jazz. He broke into a show biz smile as I hit the final cadence. "I can give you one hundred ten dollars a week, plus tips, and all the half-price ginger ale you can drink."

It felt like a lot of money, compared to washing dishes. I didn't even negotiate. I signed a contract without consulting anyone. I was too ashamed to run it past Milton Weisman, who, in a just world, should have had his cut.

I rented an efficiency a short walk from the Glimmer Room. I got my things from the Village apartment out of storage, sending the piano to my father's. He now had two keyboards and no one to play either of them. I set up our old radio next to my bed and tuned it to an AM countdown station. With my first two weeks' salary, I bought a trash can full of LPs—not a single track older than 1960. And with that, I commenced my education in real culture.

I played from eight at night until three in the morning, with a ten-minute break every hour. My sets for the first few weeks were shaky. Mr. Silber got on me for playing too much Tin Pan Alley. "Enough with the old people's music. Nix the Gershwin. Gershwin's for people dying of shuffleboard injuries up at the Nevele. We want the *new* stuff, the *mod* stuff." The man did a little dance step he mistook for the frug. Had I been able to do a deafening "Purple Haze," I would have, just to make Mr. Silber beg for a little Irving Berlin.

I learned more melodies in one month than I'd ever learn again. I could listen to an album of funk, folk, or fusion all afternoon and perform a reasonable facsimile that evening. My problem was never the notes. My problem was how to keep my performances as free and rangy as the originals. Up until midnight, I sounded pathetically trim. But I counted on late-night fatigue to kick in and help me find the groove. The tunes I played into the early-morning hours strained toward rules of harmony they didn't quite grasp. I let them yearn, rough, aching, and tone-deaf.

It took me months in the Glimmer Room to realize that what most people wanted from music was not transcendence but simple companionship, a tune just as bound by gravity as its listeners were, cheerful under its crushing leadenness. What we want, finally, from friends is that they have no more clue than we do. Of all tunes, only the happily amnesiac live forever in the hearts of their hearers.

Every hour I was off duty, I listened to the radio. I had two lifetimes to make up for. With my brother on the other side of the world, I moved through my days, humming all the hooks. Once I overcame my body's clock and learned the secret of the graveyard shift, I could play deep into the night, unafraid of ever being heard. Sometimes the keyboard felt like one of those cardboard foldouts that teachers in poor school districts use in group music lessons. Even on slow nights, the Glimmer Room was so choked with clinking glasses, catcalls, wolf whistles, hoarse laughter, cigarette-thickened coughs, waitresses calling drink orders out to the bar, air-conditioning kicking on and off, and the fused buzz of lubricated shaggy-dog stories that no one could hear me even if, out of some drunken nostalgia, they were actually trying to. I was just part of the general background radiation. That's what Mr. Silber was after. He didn't even want me using the short stick on the baby grand's lid. Hunched over the keys, I sometimes doubted that any sound came out of the instrument at all.

Even so, I felt guilty if I played a song the same way from one night to the next. You never knew what someone might hear by accident. I reinvented every fake-book trick of barroom pianists all the way back to slave days. A dry-ice version of "Misty." A slightly dyspeptic "I Feel Good." A "Love Child" agreeing to drop the paternity suit.

The Glimmer Room was white, as white as the dying resort town of Atlantic City pretended to be. But with the rest of dying whiteness, it wanted not to be. For the length of one dress-up evening anyway, the Glimmer Room's cash customers wanted out from under their long sickness, the rectitude that had kept their spines straight and their rights preserved for generations. They wanted a night out. They saw me and longed for the blues that had evacuated the jook joints fifteen years earlier. Unable to hear half the notes over the din, they thought they could make out the strains of real soul.

I played what I imagined they wanted. All I had to draw on was an out-of-tune baby grand and an incomplete Juilliard education. But the thing about music is that its tool kit is so small. Everything comes from everywhere. No two songs are further apart than half cousins by incest. A raised third or an augmented fifth, an added flat ninth, a little short-leg syncopation, an off-the-beat eighth note, and any tune could pass over the line. Music at night in a noisy bar didn't stop at two colors; it had more shades than would fit into the wildest paint box. If the Supremes could do the Anna Magdalena Bach notebook, even I could do the Supremes.

Tucked away in the corner of the Glimmer with a music-stand light, a tumbler of ginger ale, and a tip glass seeded with a few impudent dollar bills, I'd lose myself for weeks at a time. My wrists healed, and I filled with anonymous comfort. The great enemy was 2:00 A.M., when I'd hit a wall, my brain bleeding and my fingers numb. I'd be in the middle of a tune by some suburban quintet who thought they'd invented the submediant, when I'd completely lose my way. My fingers persisted after I forgot where the tune was going, and free association would lead me into half-remembered Czerny études. For lack of material, I'd put the strains of unrequited love through augmentation and diminution, stretti and inversions, as if they'd escaped from *The Well-Tempered Clavier.* I fished up old Schubert songs from my Jonah days and dressed them up like Top 40 hits, padding out the set until quitting time. Then I'd go home to my efficiency and sleep until afternoon.

When I got too strange in my tonal mixings, Saul Silber rode me back into the corral. "Play what the kids want to hear." "Kids" meant prosperous couples in their late thirties, looking for aura out in Pageant City. "Play the chocolate stuff. The mahogany stuff." Silber ordered music the way an interior designer bought books for nouveau riche libraries: by the size and color of the spines.

433

The mahogany stuff was richer than I could do justice to. But sometimes, as the place was closing up and the last few lushes downed one more round, I launched one of Mr. Silber's requests and lost myself altogether. I'd layer it with improbable counterpoint until I was back in the unburned apartment of my childhood, my mother and father making all tunes and times lie down with one another. I'd feel myself sitting on the bench alongside Wilson Hart, in a practice room at Juilliard, tracing hidden bloodlines. Then one night, as my fingers were about to secede from my hand and find their way back at last to that source of all improvisation, the escaping slave, I looked up and saw him, sitting by himself, the first black man to enter the Glimmer Room other than to wash dishes or play piano.

He was bigger than when I'd seen him last, almost a decade before. His face was fuller and sadder, but by the look of his clothes, he'd done all right for himself. He wore a slight, sad grin, all alone in this place in listening to every note I made. The sight of the man so stunned me, I stopped playing in midchord and let out a whoop, in key. I lifted off the piano bench. Wilson Hart, the man who'd taught me to improvise, had somehow tracked me down, even to this godforsaken place, had found me where I couldn't even find myself.

My fingers started up again, stuttering with shame. I'd made him a promise once, in a Juilliard practice room, to write down all the notes inside me. To compose something, music for the page. And here I was, a hack with a tip jar on my music rack, playing in a time-warp lounge, decomposing. But Wilson Hart had traced me here. He'd come by to listen, as if no time at all had passed since we'd last sat down to improvise together. All those notes were still in me somewhere, intact. Everything I'd ever lost would come back to me, starting with this man I'd never thanked for all he'd shown me. I wouldn't lose the second chance.

My hands, flushed off the keys, landed back on the suspended chord and bent it open. I'd been strolling through a kicked-back "When a Man Loves a Woman," mostly because I could make it last for fifteen minutes, the perfect antidote to the Nancy Sinatra navel lint a drunk had requested and then walked out on. When my hands landed back on the tune, they took possession, laying it out on a silver platter for my old friend. I was Bach at Potsdam, Parker at Birdland: there was nothing I couldn't do with this simple chord sequence. I wove in every countersubject from Wilson's and my shared past. I threw Rodrigo into the hopper, Wilson's beloved William Grant Still, even bits of Wilson's own compositions he had worked on so methodically in the years I knew him. I spun out references only he would place. For a few measures, keeping that ostinato figure as regular as a heartbeat—"when a man loves a woman, down deep in his soul"—I could have made any melody at all fit that one and complete it.

Across the dim room, the full figure of Wilson himself ate up my playing. His smile lost its sadness. His great arms clasped his table, and for a moment I thought he was going to lift it up in the air and twirl it in tempo. He recognized every message I threaded into the mix. I brought the thing into a hilarious homestretch, ending with a fat plagal cadence, a big old amen that left my old friend shaking his head in pleasure. In the Glimmer Room's darkness, his eyes asked, *Now how'd you learn to play like that?*

I bounded up from the bench and made for him. It wasn't time for my break, but Mr. Silber was free to replace me with the mod-chart crawler of his choice. Wilson's head shake swelled as I came near, and as I closed the distance, I felt how much I'd missed his deep charity toward the species—the only man I'd ever felt completely comfortable with. He smiled in more quizzical surprise as I approached, a smile that only broke when he saw mine crack and fall. In the light of his table's candle, Wilson Hart vanished and became someone from Lahore or Bombay—some land I'd never laid eyes on. I stopped ten feet from him, my past broken in front of me. "I—I'm sorry. I thought you were someone else."

"But I *am* someone else," the fellow protested with a bewildered, unplaceable accent. "And you play like no one else!"

"Forgive me." I retreated to the safety of my piano. Of course it wasn't Wilson Hart. Wilson Hart would never have entered a club like this, even by accident. He'd have been stopped before reaching the door. I fell back on the bench and launched into a brutal, humiliated "Something." When I dared to look up again at song's end, the stranger was gone.

Maybe because they'd never heard any quotations quite as crazed, or maybe under the mistaken impression that I was *inventing* something, a small circle of patrons actually started to listen. They'd sit at tables close to the piano and lean forward when I played. I thought at first that there was something wrong. I'd gotten used to sending my phrases off into the farthest reaches of space. Now, somehow, word had gone out. I wasn't sure I liked having an audience. All this avid *listening* reminded me too much of the world I'd come from. It disconcerted me.

Mr. Silber took me aside before I went on one night, toward the end of the summer. The season was ending, and I'd done nothing to prepare for winter. I felt incapable of moving out of Atlantic City. I was unable even to think of looking for work again. Returning to the music I'd betrayed was impossible. I suffered from a massive fatigue, many times bigger than my body. For the first time since birth, it felt simpler not to be alive at all. Mr. Silber held me by one shoulder and examined me. "Boy," he said, or maybe "My boy." He used them both. "You've got something." He tried for some tone of approval that wouldn't tip his hand. "I know we only contracted for the high season, but if you're not going anywhere, we could probably keep using you."

I wasn't going anywhere. This year or ever. All I wanted was to be used.

"With your playing, we can bring in listeners year-round."

"I'm running out of ideas," I warned him. "I'm out of touch."

"You know that stuff you've been playing? The crazy stuff? Your music? Just keep letting it flow. Wherever the spirit moves you! Make it up as you go along; then don't change a single note. Now, I'll have to cut you to one hundred, during the off-peak season, of course." But in a preemptive move, lest I head down the road to play at the Shimmer Room, he promised that the ginger ale would, forever onward, be complimentary.

The summer ended and the tourists disappeared. The town turned harder, inward. But Mr. Silber had guessed right: Enough people kept coming to the Glimmer Room to subsidize live music. I placed the faces of repeat offenders. Atlantic City *residents*: The concept seemed too sad to consider, though I now was one myself. Sometimes the regulars approached me during breaks. They'd speak in short, stressed words as if I couldn't quite follow their tongue. As if I were in and out of heroin-recovery programs. I'd do my best to accommodate, keeping my voice low and my answers peppered with mangled Brooklyn street slang. Mumbling always works wonders—an authenticity all its own.

One woman started showing up every weekend night. I noticed her the first time she came in, on the arm of a mallet-headed man four inches shorter than she was. I'd stopped noticing the striking women after a few months, but this one got me. She had that bruised hothouse flower look that always caught Jonah's eye. I wanted to run and find him, lure him back to America with a full report of this chess-piece creature. Her face was small and flawless, the color of spun sugar, trimmed by high cheeks and a magazine nose, with unnervingly straight glossy black hair that fell in a pert Prince Valiant helmet. She dressed against the times, in dated colors, with a taste for white blouses and hunter green skirts above dark stockings and granny boots.

She looked out of herself, as through a picture frame. Maybe she'd come to Atlantic City to take part in one of the beauty pageants and just stayed on. Maybe she was some third-generation clammer's daughter, or the scion of a ruined gambling family. I guessed something different every night. I felt myself grow happy when she walked in. Nothing more. Just a good warm sense of playing the way I liked to, as if the best set of the night could now begin. I was happy, too, when the mallet-headed man stopped showing. I didn't like how he steered her, using the small of her back as the wheel. Call it racism, but I didn't like someone who looked like him liking my music.

She'd sit at a tiny two-person table almost in the crook of the piano. The hostesses saved it for her. She'd sit and nurse an amaretto stone sour for hours. Men came by and mashed on her, sitting across the little table, their backs to me. But she always got them to leave within fifteen minutes. She wanted to sit by herself. Not alone, but with the tunes. I'd noticed it for weeks. Even when she stared into space, her straight black hair blocking her profile, I could still see it. She sang along. On almost every song I played, no matter how deep I buried the melody, she found and unearthed it. She even knew the second verses.

I tested her, taking her out for spins without her ever knowing. Her repertoire was huge, bigger than mine. I was learning the tunes, often as late as the afternoon I came in to work. This velvet-haired woman knew them all already. When I slipped in a jazzed-up, transmogrified Schubert or Schumann—imposters passing, for an evening, in that smoke-filled room—she'd sit and listen, cocking her head, puzzled that there could be a pretty tune she'd never heard. I studied her for the covers she liked, the ones that made that linen-colored face go Christmas. She whispered almost gravely to "Incense and Peppermints." But to "The Shoop Shoop Song," she positively squirmed in place. "Monday, Monday" left her subdued, while "Another Saturday Night" got her hopping. It took me a while to figure out the key. But once I did, the pattern rarely failed. Her musical passion obeyed the simplest rule in the world: She wanted to shim-sham-shimmy with the black and tan.

Once I figured out her songs of choice, I favored her with them.

Without our exchanging a glance—for she had a heart-stopping ability always to be staring at some distant place whenever I looked up—I made her know I was playing for her. I ran whole musical commentaries to her evening, playing "Respect" when guys tried to pick her up, "Shop Around" when I caught her checking out the men, "I Second That Emotion," early in the morning as she stifled a yawn. She loved when I dipped back into the thirties and forties—Horne, Holiday, all the contraband material Mr. Silber put on the forbidden list. She sat icy and statuesque, mouthing tunes from the year I was born. She herself couldn't have dated to a minute before the stroke of 1950. But the further back in time I reached, the more she delighted in the journey.

I stumbled onto her signature tune by trial and error. I'd played to her for about three months, maybe twenty visits all told. The two of us hadn't shared anything beyond one or two accidental, instantly impounded smiles. Yet I knew, if only because she'd rarely left mine, that I'd been in her thoughts for weeks. We had some destiny and were only sniffing around it, deciding how to draw near.

I'd been trying to put my left-hand strength to work by imitating Fats Waller, with limited success. Mr. Silber relaxed a little on the old stuff in the winter, when the clientele themselves turned nostalgic. I could get away with a few each night without reprimand. I lacked only Jonah to resuscitate those great lyrics by Andy Razaf, the prince of Malagasy, to turn my little fireside glow into barn burners. I sang them myself, under my breath, or watched them form on the lips of that white chess queen with the jet helmet hair. "Oh what did I do to be so black and blue?" Working through that glorious catalog, I came to "Honeysuckle Rose." My arrangement was so filled out with nectar, pistils, and stamens that Mr. Silber wouldn't have made out the tune, even if he'd been listening by mistake. But the effect on my private audience of one was electric. How she'd come to own the song, I couldn't imagine. But at the first chords, she turned into the sultriest of silent sirens. The tune went right into her, and she couldn't help herself. As I headed into the break, she chose that moment to smile right at me, cheeks tipped a little wickedly, lips announcing, *Don't need sugar; you just have to touch my cup.*

Yours? my eyebrows asked. She smiled, half coy and wholly terrified. *Yes, mine.*

I asked her, with a head flick, to get up and sing. I hit a right-hand riff that freed my left to crook an index finger at her. She pointed to herself, and I nodded gravely. She pointed to the floor, that odd reflex gesture: *Now?* I nodded again, graver still: *When else?* I kept the harmonies vamping, circling around the leading tone, filling for the two measures it took her to work up the courage and get to her feet. I'm not sure what she was worried about. She was wearing a long, straight burgundy slip dress that clung to her greedily, and she moved like a colt discovering her legs. She stepped into the piano curve and swung into a sweet, clear, sturdy alto. "Every honeybee fills with jealousy." Confection, goodness knows. My honeysuckle rose.

One or two cocktail loungers, surprised by the sound of a singing voice, spattered applause when she finished. She gave a quick flushed bow and looked about to free herself from the snare. I stood up and stuck my hand out at her before she could bolt. "I'm Joseph Strom."

"Oh! I know!"

"You do? Well, I don't."

"Excuse me?" Her speaking voice shocked me: a honking Jersey nasal that completely disappeared when she sang.

"I don't know. Who *you* are, I mean."

She smelled of something sweet I couldn't place. She blushed the color of hibiscus, twirling her hair's razor blackness around a shaking finger. And Teresa Wierzbicki told me her name.

Winter had set in meanly by then; the town was dead. But we began taking walks together along the ocean, as if it were the height of spring. She'd grown up near town and worked days at the saltwater taffy factory, the thing, after shellfish, that had birthed this place. Taffy was her twenty-four-hour perfume. She got out of work at five, we'd meet at six, walk until seven, and I'd go in to work at eight. Without any planning, it became our twice-weekly routine. I could lose myself in listening to her, or watching her walk. She walked sideways, staring at me as if I might disappear, moving with a clumsy fur-lined wonder.

I tried to take her to dinner a couple of times, but she seemed not to eat. She was shy when talking to me. "I hate my speaking voice," she apologized to the sand under her feet. "You talk. I love it when you talk." Mostly, Teresa wanted to breeze up and down the windy, deserted shore, scrawny and underdressed, leaning into the wind, humming constantly, and I, colder and more conspicuous than I can remember being in my entire life.

I was afraid to be seen with her. This town was not New York, and walking on the beach was asking for trouble. In season, I'd have been lynched, Teresa would have been thrown back on solo beachcombing, and Mr. Silber would have had to close up shop. Off season, there were fewer people around to care. And still, we drew enough venom-filled look-aways to stock the Garden State Snake Farm for years to come. This was what my parents had lived with every day of their lives. Nothing in me could have loved strongly enough to survive it.

The one time we were actually accosted, by a spreading middle-aged man who looked as if he had little more left to fear from the threat of mongrelization, Teresa let loose with such a torrent of invective—something about Christ on the cross, gonads, and a meat hook—that even I wanted to turn and run. At her yells, the man backed away, arms in the air. We walked away from the spot, mock-casual. I was stunned into silence, until Teresa giggled.

"Where on earth did you learn how to do that?"

"My mother used to be a nun," she explained.

But she was an innocent. She could have crawled up underneath the Pope's cassock and I still would have thought so. We didn't touch. She was frightened of me. I thought I knew why. But I didn't, and it took me weeks to realize. I was beyond her, a star in the inverted punch bowl of her firmament. My name appeared in Glimmer Room advertisements in the newspaper. Lots of people in town knew who I was and even heard me play. Most of all, I was a real musician, reading notes and everything, able to play, after one listen, songs just the way they appeared on the radio.

Terrie couldn't read music. But she was as musical a person as I've ever met. She listened to the lightest three-minute chart climber with an ache most people reserve for thoughts of their own death. One diminished chord in the right place could crack her ribs open and force her soul into the air. Music seeped up through the ground into her feet. Deprived for any length of time, she grew listless. Even the most insipid trip from tonic to dominant and back home could perk her up again.

She sucked every calorie out of a song. God knows, she had to get her nutrition somewhere. She lived off chord changes and the fumes from her candy factory. She cooked for me at her apartment on weekends, spending all Sunday with the kitchen radio on, whipping up heavy cream soups or seafood pastas. She made a linguini with white clam sauce like they served in Atlantis before it went under. Then she'd sit down at the shaky brown cardboard card table across from me, a candle between us, my plate heaped high, and hers with a sprig or two that she'd play air hockey with until it vaporized.

Each time I visited her, I had to get used to the smell all over again. The scent of saltwater taffy, all the confections she made on the assembly line, clung to her furniture and walls. When the concentrated sweetness choked me, I'd push for another walk along the freezing boardwalk. We took long rides in her Dodge, down to Cape May and up to Asbury Park. We used the car as a mobile radio platform. The Dodge had an AM with five plastic Chiclet stumps that, when shoved hard, forced the dial's red plastic needle to jump to the five main frequencies of her pleasure. She loved to hold the steering wheel with her right hand while reaching over—cross-handed, as in some tricky Scarlatti sonata—to find the perfect sound track for any given stretch of road: C and W, R and R, R & B, or, most frequently, decades-old smoky jazz. She could listen to anything soulful and find it good. And in her clear, if fragile, voice, she could make the most derivative tune please me.

Her record collection dwarfed the one Jonah and I had assembled since childhood. It was, like her driving, all over the road. She used some inscrutable organizational scheme I struggled for several visits to figure out. When I at last broke down and asked, she laughed, ashamed. "They're by happiness."

I looked again. "How happy the music is?"

She shook her head. "How happy they make me."

"Really?" She nodded, defensive. "Do they move up and down?" I looked again, and they became a giant *Billboard* chart tracking the inside of this woman's mind.

"Sure. Every time I take them out and play them, they go back in another slot."

I'd seen her do it but had never noticed. I laughed, then hated myself the instant I saw what my laugh did to her face. "But how can you ever find anything?"

She looked at me as if I were mad. "I know how much I like a thing, Joseph."

She did. I watched her. She never hesitated, either finding or replacing.

I scouted her spectrum of happiness one Sunday evening while Teresa busied herself glazing a ham in her kitchen. The rule I'd noticed in the Glimmer Room spread out before me. Petula Clark was consigned to the far left-hand purgatory, while Sarah Vaughan sat ascendant all the way to the right. This woman had little use for shiny, new, and light. The finish she wanted was smoky and deep, the longer cured the better.

I fell into dark thoughts. I was a fraud infiltrating that apartment while the misled woman labored over a ham for me. I hadn't considered what game we two were playing, how much she had assumed about me even before we brushed hands. I saw the person she must have mistaken me for all these weeks, the thinnest imposter, and I knew what would happen when she discovered who I really was.

I checked the records at the favored end of her collection, the peak of her pantheon: music being made just blocks from my home while I was growing up on Byrd and Brahms, heavy doses of the Strom Experiment. She loved all the music I'd only brushed up against in those few months when Jonah had gotten restless and we'd knocked around the Village jazz clubs, looking for easy transgression. Teresa thought the music was mine, by blood, down in my fingers, when all I did was steal it off records, as late as the afternoon I came into the club to play it. My sense of deception was so great and my sense of self so weightless that when she came into the front room with her arms full of Sunday dinner, I blurted out, "You like black music."

She set the hot dishes down on the makeshift dining table. "What do you mean?"

"Black music. You like it better . . . you prefer it to . . ." *To your own music,* was all I could think to say. *How came it* yours?

Teresa looked at me with a look I'd never seen on her face, the one I'd gotten from shopkeepers, ticket takers, and strangers since I'd turned thirteen, a look that knew, the moment the revolution came, that I would steal back from it all it had stolen from me over centuries. She walked over to where I stood and studied her collection in a way that she never had. She stood shaking her head, fixed by the right-hand side of her records, the tops of her privately owned pops. "But everybody loves those singers. It's not that they're black. It's that they're the best."

I was so agitated at dinner, I couldn't swallow. The two of us faced each other across that card table, each pushing our pink pork pucks around on our plates. I couldn't ask what I wanted to. But I couldn't bear silence. "How did you get onto the oldies? I mean, Cab Calloway? Alberta Hunter? Haven't you heard the word, girl? Don't you know you can't trust anyone over thirty?"

She brightened, grateful to be asked an easy one. "Oh! That's my *father*." She spoke the word with that chiding care we give those who've committed the gross error in judgment of becoming our parents. "Every Sunday morning of my life. The week wasn't finished until he spun his favorite records. I used to hate it. When I was twelve, I'd run from the house screaming. But I guess we finally love what we know best, huh?"

"What happened to him?"

"Who?"

"You said 'spun.'"

"Oh. My father?" She looked down at her food-spattered plate. "He's still spinning."

So was I. Teresa could feel how keyed up I was. I'll forever say that about her. She could hear me, even when I wasn't playing. "Would you like to go for a ride?" she asked.

"Sure. Why not? Unless you'd rather listen to something here?"

We were off a beat. "Listen to what?"

"Anything. You choose."

She went to the spread of records and wavered. I'd changed her rankings for her, forever. She went to the right and pulled out an Ella Fitzgerald covering Gershwin, Carmichael, and Berlin, pilfering back from the pilferers. Teresa dropped the scratching needle down upon a voice scatting away as if everyone in creation would get his own back on reckoning day. She swayed a little to the beat, lip-synching, as always. She closed her eyes and put her hands on her hips, her own dancing partner. Now and then, an involuntary pianissimo came out of her, trying to find a way back to its own scattered innocence.

She hummed to herself, drifting to her tattered brick-colored sofa. After a song, I went and sat with her. It surprised her. She held still. She'd never said a word about our not touching. I think she would have stayed with me forever, even at that unspoken arm's length, staying off at whatever distance she thought I needed and not one step farther. She let out a skyful of breath. "Ah, Sunday."

"Maybe Monday," I sang.

Teresa segued: "Maybe not." She turned toward me, pulling her feet up on the sofa underneath her. She looked down at her thighs, a little askew, the color of fine bone china. Her lips moved silently, as they had for so long in the darkness of the club, keeping me company each night. The warmth of the recording came from out of her soundless mouth.

Still, I'm sure to meet him one day, maybe Tuesday will be my good news day. My right hand lowered itself onto her leg and began accompanying. I closed my eyes and improvised. I moved from chords to free imitation, careful to keep to a decent range, between her knee and hiked-up hemline.

Teresa held her breath and became my instrument. I hit each note as squarely as if it were real. She heard my free flight in her skin. I could feel her feeling my fingers' tone clusters. Around *We'll build a little home for two*, I built an obbligato line so right, I was surprised it wasn't in the original. At *from which I'll never roam*, I roamed a little, beyond the deniable, up into the hemline octave. On the last two lines, Teresa joined in with a reedy harmony, one she'd sung a hundred times to herself, in this place, maybe even with someone else, before I came around.

When the song finished, I rested my hand on her leg, the silent keys. I couldn't feel my fingers to remove them. Her muscles twitched in cheerful terror. I could feel my own pulse pounding through my palm. Teresa stood. My fossil hand slid off her. "I have something for you." She walked across the room to her trinket-covered hutch. From behind a carved Indian elephant, she fished an envelope. It might have been sitting there for weeks. She brought it back to me and set it in my hands. On its white face, it bore the name Joseph, scribbled in childlike balloon letters. My hands shook as I opened it, the way they used to after crucial concerts with Jonah. I struggled to remove the contents without tearing. Teresa sat next to me, reached out, and ran the back of her hand against my neck. Like slipping on a new silk tie.

I worked at that envelope until I thought she'd take it from my hands and open it for me. I got the card out at last. Ter had made the thing herself, a cartoon of two tigers warily chasing each other around what looked like a palm tree. Inside, the same childlike scribble read "I will if you will."

It might have sat unopened on the hutch forever, waiting, for all time, for my hand to graze hers, even by accident. But it was ready the moment I did. The hidden patience of her hand-drawn prediction broke over me and I sat on her sofa, crying. She led me to her bed and put me in those sheets that smelled of saltwater taffy. She slipped from her clothes and stood open to me. I could not stop looking. I sat high up on a rock bluff, looking out on a surprise, twisting river valley. I'd thought she was cream, muslin, porcelain. But her body—her slender, sloping, undulating body—was all the colors there were. I moved over her, tracing with my fingers, my face up close to every inch of terrain, the light cerulean of her veins below her neck, the terra-cotta of her breasts' tips, the pea green smear of a bruise just above her hip. I gorged myself with looking at the spreading rainbow of her, until, shy again in the face of my pleasure, she leaned over and doused the light.

All that night, she brought me back to myself. I was in bed with a woman. I'd never before heard the whole tune, beginning to end. But I knew enough bars to fake it. I felt the muscles just under her thighs hunch up in surprise under my hand. Our skins pushed up against each other, shocked by the contrast, even in the dark. She hummed, her mouth to my belly; I couldn't make out the song. Her mouth opened in awe when I went into her. Her throat kept timeless time, and every one of her murmurs was pitched.

Afterward, she held on to me, her discovery. "The way you play. I knew it. Just by the way you play."

"You have to hear my brother," I told her, half-asleep. "He's the real once-in-a-lifetime musician."

I fell unconscious and slept the sleep of the dead, Teresa's hands still thawing out the crevasses of my back. When I woke, she hovered over me like Psyche, a glass of orange juice in her hands. The room was blazing. She was fully dressed, in her candy-factory clothes. My honeysuckle rose. I made space for her on the bed's edge. "I'm almost late. The key's in the music box on my dresser if you need it."

I took her hand as she stood. "I have to tell you something."

"Shh. I know."

"My father is white."

It wasn't what she expected. But her surprise vanished quickly enough to surprise me. She rolled her eyes. Solidarity of the oppressed. "Tell me about it. So's mine." She leaned back down and kissed me on the mouth. I could feel her lips, wondering how mine felt to her.

"Are you coming tonight?" I asked.

"That depends. You playing the good stuff?"

"If you're singing."

"Oh," she said, heading out the door. "I'll sing anything."

I dressed and made the bed, pulling the sheets over our still-fresh stains. I walked around her apartment, happily criminal, just looking at this new world. I stared at her collections, taking my own private tour of a distant ethnographic museum. Her life: ceramic frogs, a clock in the shape of the sun, purple bath soaps and sponges, slippers with crossed eyes stitched into their tops, a book on the picturesque barns of Ohio, inscribed "Happy Birthday from Aunt Gin and Uncle Dan. Don't forget you promised to visit soon!" Each of us is alien to every other. Race does nothing but make the fact visible.

I opened her closet and gazed at all her clothes. A line of slips hung on hooks against one wall, black and white sheathes whose edges I'd seen sticking out under her dresses, clinging to and imitating her. I went into the kitchen and sliced last night's ham for breakfast. I ate it cold, afraid to dirty her pans. I'd been here often, but never alone. I knew what the police would do if some law-abiding neighbor tipped them off to me. Just being here by myself in this alien woman's rooms was a life sentence. Safety meant leaving. But I had no place to go except back to my life.

I went to her record collection, the safest ground in this booby-trapped place. There wasn't a piece of classical music on her shelves except the hepped-up thefts of tunes long out of copyright. I started from the tops of her charts, looking for a song to play her at the club that night, something I might learn just for her. I slipped on a disk of Monk's and knew that everything on it was beyond my meager fake technique. Oscar Peterson: I laughed after four measures, exhilarated and demoralized. I played an Armstrong Hot Seven recording that Teresa had worn almost smooth. Everything I thought I knew about the man and his music vanished in a river of sound. I sampled people I knew only by reputation: Robert Johnson, Sidney Bechet, Charles Mingus. I stood surrounded in the wall-wide, rapturous choruses of Thomas A. Dorsey. I broke into Teresa's cache of blues: Howlin' Wolf, Ma Rainy. Junior Wells's harmonica cut me into thin strips and passed me through the reeds. Up at the very top of the collection were all her master women spell-casters. Carter, McRae, Vaughan, Fitzgerald: In each one, I heard Teresa twirling and wailing, losing herself in imitative ecstasy every night that she came home from the factory, singing her real image into being, alone in the dark.

I listened for hours. I switched tracks so fast, they piled up on top of one another. The whole claustrophobic classical catalog could not surpass this outpouring for breadth, depth, or heights. A massed hallelujah chorus poured out of Teresa's speakers, a torrent flowing over every river-bank the country could invent to hold it. This wasn't a music. It was millions. All these songs, talking to one another, all insinging and out-singing, back and forth at the party to end all celebration, into the wee hours of a suppressed national never. This was the house at the end of the long night, inviting, warm, resourceful, and subversive. And I was standing on the stoop, locked out, too late to bluff my way through the party's doors, listening to the sound roll through the windows and light the streets in all directions. I heard the play of voices through the shutters from the back alley. I eavesdropped shamelessly, not caring if I got arrested, caught in a sound that, even at this muffled distance, was more vital and urgent and jammed to therapeutic capacity with pleasure than any I'd ever make.

In that voyeur's elation, a single-word song on a 1930 Cab Calloway and His Orchestra recording stopped me cold. I read the title twice, fumbled the disk out of its jacket, put it on the player, and managed to bring the needle down on the cut without gouging the vinyl. There was Calloway, doing what sounded like a bad Al Jolson imitation, wailing away on a song called "Yaller":

> Black folk, white folk, I'm learning a lot,
> You know what I am, I know what I'm not,
> Ain't even black, I ain't even white,
> I ain't like the day and I ain't like the night.
> Feeling mean, so in-between, I'm just a High Yaller . . .

I listened through three times, learning the song as if I'd written it. I don't know what possessed me, but I played it that night at the Glimmer Club, after Teresa arrived. Hope is never more stupid than when it's within striking distance. She took her seat, up close to the piano, glowing with our new secret. She looked heart-stopping in a short brown tube dress I'd seen in her closet. I slipped the song late into the last set, when nobody was left to hear but her. I watched her face, knowing in advance what I'd get. Those lips that mouthed along with every other tune that evening, lips that had hummed wordlessly as we made love, held still and bloodless throughout my rendition.

She didn't wait for me at the end of that set. But she showed up the following night, so tentative and apologetic, I wanted to die. I went back with her to her apartment, although we had just a few hours before she needed to leave for work. We lay with each other again, but the song was stillborn between us. When I looked over the record collection after she left the next morning, the Calloway was gone.

We fell into a tradition. Every night she came to the bar, I'd get her up to sing for at least one song. At first, it made Mr. Silber crazy. "You don't think I have money to pay for two performers in the same evening?" I assured him he was getting the thing all my father's colleagues swore was impossible in our little neck of the universe: something for nothing. When Mr. Silber saw how much this thrill-nervous girl's clear old torch songs pleased the audience, he spun doughnuts. "Ladies and gentlemen," he took to announcing, "please welcome the Glimmer Room Musical Duet!"

We never rehearsed. She knew all her songs by heart, and I knew all her songs from her. I could anticipate what she was going to do, and on those rare occasions when her nervous enthusiasm tipped us over, our craft was easily righted. We weren't talking Scriabin, after all. But Teresa tapped into a musical ecstasy Scriabin only hinted at. Her whole body took up the pulse. With my chords solid beneath her, she let go—sexy, sultry, loose on a first-time spree. She had a lower register, a growl almost androgynous. The audience ate her up, and each night that she sang, at least a couple men in the darkened house would have given years for one taste more.

She was on the floor one night, singing Smokey Robinson's "You Really Got a Hold on Me" as if it were a controlled substance. We'd found the groove, sailing along in the full soul of the thing, when our hull scraped on some reef, forcing me to look up. Teresa was back on the beat almost instantly; no one had heard her bobble but her accompanist. She stiffened through the rest of the song. I traced her weird vibe to an older man who'd entered in midstanza and sat down in the back of the room, a man whose rifle-bore gaze Teresa studiously avoided.

He wasn't the mallet-headed escort I'd first seen her with. But he was another white man, one whose massive claim on her was obvious, even to the piano player. Teresa sang, "I don't like you, but I love you." I tagged along underneath, resolving stray dissonances, wondering whether her bridling was meant for me or this other fellow, a man I'd never seen before and felt no need to see again. "You really got a hold on me." Every demon music was supposed to banish, all the things that held her took hold in the melody. She limped through to the end, almost whispering the last phrase, afraid to look up. When she did, the man was standing. He seemed to lean over and spit, though nothing come out of his mouth. Then he made for the door.

Teresa turned to me and called out. I couldn't hear her, over her panic and the applause. She called again: " 'Ain't Misbehavin'.' " The only time she ever spoke to me in command. I started up the tune, my fingers in a forced march. But it was too late. The man was gone. Teresa, having ordered the melody, gagged it down. She sang her way through to the end. But the innocence in the song came out of her mouth twisted.

She waited for me afterward, as if nothing had happened. I suppose nothing had. But it ate at me, and when she asked in her shy, frightened way whether I wanted to go home with her, I answered, "I don't think you want me to."

She looked as if I'd just blackened her eye. "Why are you saying that?"

"I think you'd rather be by yourself."

She didn't ask for a reason, but went away in silence. That only enraged me. She came back to the club a few nights later, but I avoided her during breaks and never asked her up to sing. She stayed away for a week. I dug in and waited for her to call. When she didn't, I told myself that that was that. We never know. Nobody knows the first thing about anyone else.

She was waiting for me outside the club when I went to work the next week. She was in her candy-factory clothes. I saw her from a block away, time enough to prepare for the downbeat. "Aren't you supposed to be working?"

"Joseph. We have to talk."

"Do we?"

Suddenly, I was that thug who'd assaulted us on the freezing beach the winter before. She narrowed herself to the smallest slit and threw her words at me. "You smug little son of a bitch." She grabbed and pushed me. Then she buckled against the front wall of the club, sobbing.

I refused to touch her. It pretty much killed me, but I held to myself. I'd have given her anything, and still, she refused to tell me. Righteousness had me by the throat. I waited for her to catch her breath. "Is there something you want to say to me?"

This started her gasping again. "About what, Joseph? About *what*?"

"I've never asked anything from you, Teresa. You have unfinished business in your life? The least you can do is have the decency to tell me about it."

" 'Unfinished . . .' "

She wouldn't own up. I felt betrayed—by her, by the rules of decency, by her pretty singing, by that bending rainbow landscape of her body. "Want to tell me about the guy?"

"Guy?" Her confusion was complete. Then her face broke and rose. "Joseph! Oh, my Joe. I thought you knew. I thought . . ."

"What? Thought what? Why didn't you at least say something? Or is that part of the great unspeakable secret?"

"I thought . . . I didn't want to make it . . ." She hung her head in shame. For all of us, I suppose. "That was my father."

I looped back. "Your father came to hear you?"

"Us," she croaked. "Hear us." And he'd left in disgust before she could lure him back with his favorite song. I worked through the recap in silence. Her father, who made her listen every Sunday to a music he now hated her for falling in love with. Her lover, whom she mistook for a native speaker. My own Sunday music, which would only have thickened the man's invisible spit. Spit meant for me, but hitting his daughter.

I fell against the brick of the Glimmer Club, next to her. "Did you— have you talked to him since?"

She couldn't even shake her head. "Mom won't put him on when I call. She'll barely talk to me herself. I went by the house, and they—he came to the door and put on the burglar chain."

She broke down. I led her inside the empty club, where I could take her into a back room and put my arm around her without being arrested. Mr. Silber heard his prize nightingale crying, and he rushed about trying to make her a cup of weak tea.

"You can't let this happen." I stroked her hair, without conviction. "Family's bigger than . . . this. You have to patch things up. Nothing's worth a split this big."

She looked at me through the red, raw wet of her face. Horror spread there, spilled wine. She clamped a tourniquet around my upper arm and buried herself in my chest. I felt I'd just killed a child while driving and would spend the rest of my life with memory as my penance.

Teresa never used it against me, but I was all she had. Me and the saltwater taffy factory. My visits to her apartment now had a tinge of volunteer work. We ran out of things to say to each other, but Teresa never noticed. She could smile and say nothing for longer than I knew how to reply.

I grew obsessed with her father. I slipped little questions about him into our dinner conversations. It irritated her, but I couldn't keep from fishing. Where did he work? He was an appliance repairman in town. Where had he grown up? Saddle Brook and Newark. What did he vote?

Lifelong straight Democratic, just like my parents. I could never get to what I needed to know before she clammed up.

We ran out of things to do together, even in the few hours when we were both off work. I suggested we practice a little. I could give her some pointers. She leapt at the idea. She couldn't get enough. She wanted to hear everything I knew about breath support, open throat, covering—all the scraps I'd picked up from Jonah over the years. "Real singing. Famous singing." She had the same appetite for these professional secrets as her girlfriends at the factory had for Princes Charles and Rainier.

I told her what I knew. But everything I taught her made her worse. She'd sung just fine when she met me. Better than fine: beautifully. She turned every tune vulnerable. She knew what each song needed. She charmed without knowing—freshness, clarity, her inadvertent sexiness, that jumpy rhythm that took hold of her body and wouldn't let her go until the finish. But now, armed with the lessons I gave her, she began to make a stagy, polished, domed tone that sounded freakish. I'd cost her her father. I was costing her her voice. I'd probably cost her whatever friends she'd had before seeing me. We never spent time with anyone but ourselves. Teresa wasn't sleeping through the night anymore, and she only ate the barest minimum she could get away with. I was killing the woman. And I'd never asked her for a thing.

"I want to put more time into my singing," she said. "Maybe I should, you know, cut back on my work hours?"

My fault entirely. I should have known enough to stay away. Two months after her father had spit on the floor of the Glimmer Room, I found her sitting on her sofa in tears. "They've changed the locks. My parents."

Something clicked. The song she'd shouted for as the man was leaving: her daddy's favorite. The song she lip-synched to, the one I'd first fallen for: both written by the same duo. The songs of her Sunday-morning liturgy, preached by her old man. "What did he call you? Your father. What was his pet name for you?"

She wouldn't answer. She didn't have to, goodness knows.

We settled into a narrowed routine, simple enough for both of us. She surrendered her own place to our comfort. I grew careful of what I said. I told her her meat loaf with tomato sauce was the best thing I'd ever tasted, and paid the price for several weeks running. I happened to say robin's-egg blue was my favorite color, and found her the next Saturday, repainting the kitchen. We rarely went to my apartment. So far as I can remember, we never spent the night there. She abandoned, without asking, all the places I wouldn't take her to. I knew it was shame; I didn't know of what. I did love her.

I was alone in my apartment one afternoon in the summer of 1970. There was a knock at the door, rare enough in any season. I opened, off balance, and took a full three seconds to recognize my sister and Robert, her husband, my brother-in-law, with whom I'd spent all of forty minutes in this life, three years before. I stood staring, somewhere between fear and joy, until Ruth cleared her throat. "Joey, can you let us *in*?"

I fell over myself welcoming them. I squeezed her until Ruth begged for mercy. I kept saying, "I can't believe it." Ruth kept answering, "Believe it, brother."

Robert asked, "Believe what?" His voice's agitation could not keep out the amusement.

"How did you find me?" I thought she must have been in touch with Da. They were talking again. No one else could have told her where I was.

"Find you?" Ruth shot Robert a sad grin. She put her hand on my head, as if I had a fever. "Finding's the easy part, Joey. It's losing you that has been my lifelong problem."

I still didn't know what I'd done to her. I didn't care. She was back in my life. My sister was here. "When did you hit town? Where are you living these days?"

Their silence gave me an awful moment. Ruth gazed around my tiny cell of an apartment, terrified of something she was sure would pop out of the nearest cupboard. "Living? These days? Funny you should ask."

Robert sat on my rickety kitchen folding chair, one ankle on the other knee. "Would it be possible to put up here? With you. Just for a day or two."

They had no bags. "Of course. Anything. Always."

I didn't press them for information, and they didn't volunteer. Whatever was after them was only fifty yards behind, down the street, across the highway. I saw them look at each other and keep mum. They weren't about to make me accessory to anything. "Sit. Damn, it's good to see you. Here, sit. Can I get you a drink?"

My sister pinned my wrists like a loving nurse, grinning and stilling me. "Joey, it's just us."

452

Robert, the man my sister had tied her life to, a giant I didn't know from Adam, fixed me with his X-ray eyes. He seemed to me everything I wasn't: solid, substantial, centered, dedicated, dignified. His aura filled the room. "So how's the gig?"

I hung my head. "It's music. I'm taking requests. How about you?"

"Huh." He put his hands on his head, catching up to himself. "Us, too. We're taking requests, too."

"I read that Huey's free," I said.

From where she stood fiddling with the kitchen curtains, Ruth shouted. "Joey! Where did you find time to read that? I thought you were busy with your nightclub act."

She must have been near the club. Seen the posters. "Enlightened owners. They let me look at the papers on my breaks."

"Huey's free. True." Robert squinted at me, guessing my weight. "But everything the man has tried to do—the whole movement—is coming apart."

"Robert," Ruth warned.

"What's the difference? The shit's public knowledge."

I'd followed the stories, if only for their sake. The gun battle at UCLA. Hampton and Clark, the two Chicago Panther organizers, killed in their sleep in an illegal police raid. Connecticut trying Bobby Seale for killing a police informant. The FBI waging all-out war. Hundreds of members killed, jailed, or fleeing the country. Eldridge Cleaver in Cuba. I'd thought for a long time that Ruth and Robert, like Jonah, might have gone abroad. Seeing them cowering here, I wished they had.

"You know about the New York roundup?" The force of Robert's gaze terrified me.

"I read . . . The papers said . . ." I'd been unable to take the official reports in. Twenty-one Panthers arrested, charged with an elaborate plan to blow up a suite of civic buildings and kill scores of police. The group that my sister and her husband had helped to organize.

"The papers, man. You got to decide whether you're with the papers or with the people." He jutted his head, besieged, a rhetorical boy, a thousand years old, sick to death of the disaster this country had made of everything human. I wasn't with the papers. I wasn't with the people. I wasn't even with myself. I wanted to be with my sister.

"I'm starving," Ruth said.

It seemed a godsend, something I might help with. "There's an Italian place just down the street."

Robert and Ruth looked at me, embarrassed at my density. Robert reached into his pocket and drew out four crumpled dollar bills. "Could you bring us something back? Doesn't matter what, so long as it's hot."

I waved him off. "Back in a minute with the best bowl of steamers you ever tasted."

His gratitude ruined me. "Owe you one, brother."

I took the word all the way down to the ocean and back. When I returned, I caught them arguing. They stopped the instant my key hit the lock. "Now this is what you call shellfish," I said, sounding stupid even to myself. But Ruth was filled with thanks. She kissed, then bit, my hand. The two of them dug in. It had been some time. I waited until they'd gotten their fill. Then I tried to draw Robert out a little. Juilliard dropout, commencing his belated education.

Robert indulged me. We talked about all that had happened since I'd seen them last, the running battle of the last three years. I held out for the ghost of nonviolent resistance. Robert didn't laugh at me, but he refused to encourage the hope. "A small group has all the rest of us locked up down in the hold, and they're standing over the hatches with guns. The longer they do that, the harder they need to."

My sister waved her hands in the air. "It's not just the people with the power. It's the second-generation immigrants, locked down in the hold with us. First word they learn when they set foot in this country is *nigger*. People who have nothing, turning against one another. Pure *Kapo* system."

I listened, just listened, unable to add a word. When the clams were gone, we hit a lull.

"Joey," Ruth said. "You're sleeping with someone."

"How did you know?" I scanned the apartment for giveaways: pictures, notes, extra toothbrush. There were none.

"You seem good. Healthy." It seemed to relieve Ruth. I loved Teresa more in the moment my sister spoke those words than I had since she had first sung with me. "She white?"

Robert stood and flexed. "Okay, now. Time out. Give the man some peace."

"What? It's a legitimate question. Man's driving a shiny new vehicle. You ask him the make and model."

Robert caught my eye. "It's all right, brother. I'm sleeping with a German chick."

"If I find her, husband, I'll kill the both of you dead."

"Her father's disowned her," I said. "Teresa's father, I mean." It sounded like a bagatelle, next to whatever Robert and Ruth were facing.

Robert rubbed his globe of Afro. "Bad deal. We'll see about making her an honorary."

"Teresa." Ruth's smile tried to stay polite. "When do we get to meet her?" My sister wanted to meet me somewhere. Find a place alongside this world, big enough for both of us to move in.

"Anytime. Tonight."

"Maybe next visit," Robert said. "This one ain't exactly meet and greet."

His words yanked them out of my story world, and the two of them were fugitives again. We sat silently, listening to signals in the traffic outside. At last, Ruth said, "It's not that we don't trust you, Joey."

"I understand," I lied. I understood only their pacing, their animal panic.

Robert spoke into the tips of his folded hands. "The less we say, the easier for you." He might have been a university professor.

Ruth leaned back and sighed. My little sister, now decades older than I was, and pulling away at an accelerating pace. "So how's the Negro Caruso?" She clenched when she spoke.

"What can I say? He's singing. Somewhere in Europe. Germany, last I heard."

She nodded, wanting more, not wanting to ask. "Probably where he belongs."

Her husband stood and peeked through the kitchen curtains. "I'd go there myself, around about now."

"Oh would you?"

"In a heartbeat."

The idea amused Ruth. She cooed at him in German, every pet name Da ever used on Mama.

"I have to go work," I said. "Daily bread and all." I stuck my paws out and wiggled them, singing, without thinking, "Honeysuckle Rose."

"Wish I could hear you play that," Ruth said.

"I bet you do."

"Little Joey Strom, learning what side his bread is buttered on."

I studied her, the bruises of her two brown eyes. "Don't be ashamed of me, Ruth."

"Shame?" Her face crumpled. The house was on fire again, and she was standing out on the frozen sidewalk, biting the fireman. "Shame? Don't you be ashamed of me!"

"Of *you*! How could . . . You're out there working . . . giving yourself to things I wouldn't even have known about except for you."

My sister clamped tight on the muscles in her cheeks. I thought for a moment she might lose herself. But the spasm passed and she came back. This time, she didn't offer me a place in the movement or suggest that the desperate world might need even someone like me. But she did reach out one pink palm and place it on my chest. "So what do you play?"

"Name your tune, and I'll fake it."

Her smile bent her ears. "Joey's a Negro."

"Only in Atlantic City."

"Half Atlantic City's black," Robert said. "They just don't know it yet."

"You have to hear this man of mine. All America's African. Come on, sugar. Give him the spiel."

Robert smiled at her word choice. "Tomorrow. Tonight, I got to get some sleep. My brain's fried."

"Take my bed, you two. I'll stay with Teresa."

"Teresa." My sister laughed. "Teresa what?" I had to spell Wierzbicki for her. Ruth laughed again. "Does your father know you're balling a Catholic?"

I came home from Teresa's the next day. I stopped at the store and stocked up on beer, chicken, fresh-baked bread, news magazines—all the amenities I never kept around. But when I let myself into the apartment, it was empty. A half sheet of my torn music paper filled with my sister's handwriting sat on the kitchen table.

Joey,

We had to go. Believe me, it's safer this way. They're hounding us down, and you don't want in any deeper than you already are, just by being brother to this sister. You were a lifesaver to put us up. And it was good to see you haven't been completely broken. Yet! Robert says you're a good man, and I'm learning not to argue with my husband, because, honey, he never lets me win.

Take care of yourself and we'll do the same. Who knows? We all might live long enough to share more clams.

Blood's blood, huh, blood?

You'd better pitch this note when you're done with it.

She didn't sign it. But at the bottom, as an afterthought, she'd added, "Work on your brother for us, will you?"

As I held the note, it burned into me. I didn't throw it away when I was done. I left it out on the front table. Blood is blood. If any law-enforcement agents broke into my apartment, I wanted the words some-where easy to find. I refused to think about what those two had done, what would-be crime, what trouble they'd fallen into. We'd been born illegal. Just demanding that the law change was a crime. All I could do was wait to hear from them, whenever and wherever they surfaced. It wouldn't be soon.

I never told Teresa about the visit. I'd never have managed to intro-duce them. I'd have bounced between them, sheltering one from the other, the way Jonah once tried to deceive both his voice teachers. I'd never be whole. My parts didn't fit. I didn't want them to.

Right after the visit—soon enough for my knot-tying brain to imagine a link—Da forwarded a letter from Jonah, the first I'd heard from him since Magdeburg. The luster of communism had worn off. He'd made his way through East Germany—"Did the Leipzig pilgrimage without you, Mule"—performed concerted music in Berlin—"No lieder, though; who's loyal to you?"—then went back west to do *Das Lied von der Erde* in Cologne. He then crossed over into Holland and walked away with a plum prize at the 'sHertogenbosch competition.

> Not sure what happens next. The world seems to be my oyster at present, or at least my Zeeland mussel. Nobody has restricted my voice to any category short of *music*, although I confess I'm only understanding about 40 percent of anything anyone says, so they may be calling me the Prince of Darkness, as far as I know. I'm telling you, Mule, you're a prisoner in the States. Still a slave, a century after the fact. You can't even know what you're under un-til you're out from under it. You want to feel what it means to be without leg irons for the first time in your life? Come on over, be-fore the global spread of American culture turns us into darkies, even out here.

He gave the address of a management firm in Amsterdam where he could always be reached. "Always" had a rather narrow range for my brother.

Tucked into the note he forwarded from Jonah, Da included one from himself. He hadn't been down from the city to hear me play, and I'd discouraged him from thinking about coming. He had no sense of the stuff I played each night—the surfing anthems, the thinly veiled drug celebrations, the love songs to automobiles, hair dryers, and other motorized devices. In Da's mind, I was a concert pianist who made a living performing. His letter to me was short and fact-filled. He was advancing in his work, the problem he'd worried for three decades. "Where Mach meets the quantum, it must be timeless!" Crazy things were happening in physics again, the crazy things he'd predicted thirty years before. Multiple splintering universes. Wormholes. Nothing, of course, about the crazy things bringing *this* world down around his ears.

In the last paragraph of the note, almost an afterthought, to pad the letter out to respectable length, he added, "I am going to the hospital in two days for exploratory surgery. You aren't to worry. My symptoms are too unpleasant to describe on paper. The doctors just need to see what's going on inside, and for that, they need to crack me open!"

I got the packet the day after the surgery. I called home, but no one was there. He'd listed no other contact, not even the hospital where he was to be operated on. I called Mrs. Samuels, who gave me a hospital number. I knew from her voice that she was trying not to be the one to break the news. I went to Mr. Silber and asked for two days off.

"Who's supposed to play for my guests? You want me, maybe, to be the jazzman? You want me to pretend I can play like Satchmo Paige?"

I didn't tell Mr. Silber about my father. *My father's in the hospital* would mean *Big black buck dying of complications from type II diabetes.* If I told him pancreatic cancer, he'd want to know details. I couldn't go through that with Mr. Silber. *Your father, a Jew?* I couldn't force kinship on this man.

I did tell Teresa. She wanted to go with me, even on that first trip. "You don't need to," I told her. "But I might need you down the line." I didn't need to ask her to pace herself. She knew how long time was. She'd spent her own life waiting it out.

At the hospital, I suffered the usual farce. *His son?* The surgeon at Mount Sinai didn't bother disguising his shock. His disbelief had started long before, at the moment of incision. "This cancer has been working a long time. Years, perhaps." That sounded about right. "I can't see how anyone could have lived with this for so long and only now—"

"He's a scientist," I explained. "He's not from around here."

I found Da sitting up in bed, apologetic smile welcoming me. "You didn't need to come all this way!" He waved his palm at me, dismissing all diagnoses. "You have a life to lead! You have your job, out in Ocean City! Who's going to make music for your listeners?"

I spent two days with him. I returned the following week, this time with Teresa. She was a saint. She made half a dozen trips with me over the next four months. For that alone, I should have married her. Crisis brought out her art. She handled everything—all the routine realities I used to handle for Jonah when we toured and that I couldn't handle now. She didn't have to go with me. Didn't have to stand at my side and watch me watch my father disappear. I'd already cost her hers. It only crippled me worse, her insisting so gladly on helping me lose mine.

Da delighted in her. He loved the idea of my having found someone, this shining someone in particular. At first, our visits made him feel guilty. But he grew to depend on them. Da went home from the hospital, and Mrs. Samuels moved into the Fort Lee house, as she had in spirit many years before. Whenever Teresa and I showed up there, she made herself scarce. I never knew the woman. Perhaps my father and Mrs. Samuels might have gotten married, had any of his children given them the least encouragement. But I didn't want a white stepmother. And Da, too, could never have jumped off the world line that he'd drawn himself. How could he have explained to his second wife that he still held nightly conversations with his first?

Terrie and I sat with him as he went down. He must have felt the vigil as a sentence. I waited until I couldn't delay in good faith anymore. Then I wrote Jonah, care of the management agency in Amsterdam. I couldn't say "dying" in the letter, but I said as strongly as I could that Jonah might want to come home. With the letter chasing him around the stages of Europe, I figured it might be weeks before we'd hear. I had no way to contact Ruth, or any sense of how she might receive the news.

Da enjoyed our company, as far as it went. The fact is, we didn't spend much time together when Teresa and I visited. He grew furious with preoccupation, in the homestretch. He continued to work all the way to the end, more fiercely than I can remember him ever working. Science was his way of lengthening his shortened days. He worked until he was so drugged with palliative medication, he didn't even know he was working anymore. He tried to explain to me what was at stake. Some weeks, he seemed desperate. He needed to prove that the universe had a preferred rotation. I couldn't even wrap my head around what such a thing might mean.

He needed to show that more galaxies rotated in one direction than in the other. He sought a basic asymmetry, more counterclockwise galaxies than clockwise. He assembled vast catalogs of astronomical photos and was hard at work making measurements with a pencil and protractor, estimating rotational axes and compiling his data into huge tables. The work was a footrace he needed to win. Each day, he did a little more, on a little less strength.

I asked him why he was so desperate to know. "Oh. I think this to be the case, already. But to have the mathematical basis: That would be wonderful!"

I asked him as meekly as I could. "Why would that be so wonderful?" What need could anyone have for something so blindingly remote? I don't know if he heard my note—my resentment at his living and dying by another clock in another system's gravitational field, my anger at his listening for sounds that run on ahead of time, too far for human ears to hear. His obsession should have been harmless enough. It didn't enslave or exploit anyone's misery. But neither did it lift that misery or set a single soul free. Now that I had something to measure against, I knew my father to be the single whitest man in the world. How Mama could have thought to marry him and how the two of them imagined they could make a life together anywhere in this country would be secrets he'd take to the grave.

When Teresa and I went up to Da's, we'd end up playing cribbage in the front room while he sat in his study making desperate calculations. I apologized to my Polish saint in a thousand oblique ways, for hours at a shot.

"It doesn't matter, Joseph. It's so good for me, just to see where you grew up."

"How many times have I told you where I grew up? I'd rather have grown up in hell than here."

Too late, she rushed to fix her mistake. "Can we go over to the city? See your old . . ." And halfway in, she realized she'd made bad worse. We went back to cribbage, a game she taught me, one she used to play with her mother. The saddest, whitest, most inscrutable game the human mind ever invented.

One night, we sat together under the globe of a lamp, looking over the pictures that had survived the accident of my family. There were half a dozen from before the fire. They'd been pinned to a board in my father's office at the university for a quarter of a century. Now they'd come home, but to no home anyone in the pictures would have recognized.

One photo showed a couple holding a baby. A thickset man, his close-cropped hair already receding, stood next to a thin woman in a print dress, hair pulled back in a bun. The woman held a lump wrapped in a fuzzy blanket. Teresa hovered her nail above the infant packet. "You?"

I shrugged. "Jonah, probably."

A delicate pause. "Who are these two?"

I couldn't tell her. I had some memory of the man, but even that might have come mostly from this photograph. "My grandparents." Then, inspired stupidity: "My mother's parents."

In time, my father grew too sick to work. He still perched with his star charts and his tables of numbers, head bowed over the snaking Greek equations. But he could no longer force through the calculations. This puzzled more than hurt him. The medications had him in a place beyond pain. Or maybe he was confused by the facts' inability to keep pace with theory.

"Well?" I asked. "Does the universe have a preferred spin?"

"I don't know." His voice trailed the same wake of disbelief as if he'd discovered he'd never existed. "It seems to express no preference for rotation in any direction over the other."

Toward the end, he wanted to sing. We hadn't for years. I couldn't even say exactly when we'd stopped. Mama died. Jonah turned professional. Ruth quit her angelic voice in something like disgust. So family music ended. Then one day in the first midwinter of this new, alien decade, my dying father wanted to make up for lost time. He turned up a sheaf of madrigals, produced from the towering mounds of his office scribbles. "Come. We sing." He made us each take a part.

I looked at Teresa, who looked around for a place to kill herself. "Teresa doesn't read music, Da."

He smiled: We'd have our little joke. Then his smile died in comprehension. "How can this be? You have said she sings with you?"

"She does. She . . . learns everything by ear. By heart."

"Really?" He delighted in the idea, as if the possibility had only just occurred to him. One of those deathbed revelations over nothing. "Really? This is fine! We will learn this song for you, by heart."

I didn't want to sing trios with the terrified and the dying. I, too, had lost some basic faith in sound. The three of us could not possibly give Da what he needed—a glimpse of a world gone unreachable. Music had always been his celebration of the unlikelihood of escape, his Kaddish for those who'd suffered the fate meant for him. "How about T. and I sing something for you? Straight from the Glimmer Room, Atlantic City!"

"This would be even better." His voice fell away, almost inaudible.

I don't know how, but Saint Teresa rose to the awful moment. She, at least, still believed in music. I played on the piano that had sat for years in Fort Lee, untouched. And the white Catholic truck driver's daughter from the saltwater taffy factory sang like a siren. I came out of my fog to meet her. We started on "Satin Doll," as far from the Monteverdi that Da had picked out as distance allowed. And yet, as the satin doll maker himself once said, there were only two kinds of music. This was the good kind.

By then, Da's face was ashen and the laugh in his eyes was glaze. But when Teresa and I hit our groove, somewhere around the second verse, he lit up one last time. For my father, music had always been the joy of a made universe—composed, elaborate, complex: various arcs of a solar system spinning in space at once, each one traced by the voice of a near relation. But the pleasure that bound him to his wife had been spontaneous treasure hunting. They both went to their graves swearing that any two melodies could fit together, given the right twists of tempo and turns of key. And that insistence, it struck me, as Teresa and I careened down the tune Ellington put down, lay as close to jazz as it did to the thousand years of written-out melodies their game drew on.

As my pale taffy girl sailed over the melody, sounding more sweetly sustained than I'd ever heard her, I tapped into some underground stream and drew up broken shards, motives from Machaut to Bernstein, and slipped them into my accompaniment. Teresa must have heard the sounds turning strange beneath her. But she sailed right over them. Who knows how many of the quotes Da made out? The tunes were in there; they fit. That's all that mattered. And for the seven and a half minutes my woman and I made the song last, my family, too, was there inside our sound.

Baby, shall we go out skippin'? Take your freedom on the road once, before you die. The tune said yes, said name your ecstasy. Even a written-out melody had to be made up again, on the spot, each time you read it. The swinging little skip of a theme had been sung every imaginable way, a million times and more before this woman and I ever heard it. But Teresa sang it for my father in a way he'd never yet heard. There was only this onetime meeting between us and the pitches. These notes, at least, knew who *my people* were, all those lives lived out between the making up and the writing down. We are all native speakers. Sing where you are, even as it goes. Sing all the things that this life denied you. No one owns even one note. Nothing trumps time. Sing your own comfort, the song said, for no one else will sing it for you. Speaks Latin, that satin doll.

In the best world, Da would have been making music, rather than just taking it in. But in extremis, my father made a decent audience. He didn't move much, except at the core. His face opened up. When we hit the bridge, he seemed ready to rejoin all the spinning points of light in his galaxy catalog. We finished, Teresa and I grinning as we nailed the cadence. We'd gone outside ourselves, into the tune. Da rocked for two or three more measures, to a pulse we living aren't given to hear. "Your mother loved that song."

That seemed impossible to me. I couldn't get back there. I wasn't even sure my father had recognized the tune.

Da worsened, and still I heard nothing from Jonah. I had a hundred theories a day, each less generous than the last. Toward New Year's, Da asked if I knew where Jonah was. "I think he's singing Mahler in Cologne." The nearer death was, the more freely I lied. I made it sound as if the concert were taking place that week. My father once told us there was no now, now.

"In Köln, you say? Yes, of course."

"Da? Why 'of course'?"

He looked at me strangely. "This is where his family comes from."

"Really?" Teresa said. "You have family in Germany? We should go visit!"

I put my arm around her, killing all her dreams with gentleness. I never knew she wanted to travel. It had never come up between us.

Da himself was traveling, backward, faster than light. "My father's family. Centuries in the Rhineland. My mother's family were immigrants, you know."

I didn't. There was no end to what I didn't know.

"They came from the east. I don't even know what this region would be called now. The Ukraine, somewhere? Things . . . were not good for them there. So!" He squeezed a little laugh, as brittle as any that had ever come out of him. "So: *Sie bewegen sich nach Deutschland*."

And his three children were the end of the line. This, too, had been his choice: to preserve the past by merging it into some other path. The size of what I'd lost broke over me. "You should have taught us, Da. At least about our relatives."

His eyes flickered a little, at the chance that his every equation had been wrong. His glance crusted over with his own colossal betrayal. Then, in the nearness of death, he found himself again. He patted my arm. "I introduce you. You'll like them."

No doctor prepared me for his rate of fall. Da had asked me once, centuries ago, "What is the speed of time?" Now I knew: never a steady one second per second. My father's life popped the clutch. Within a few days, he went from hobbling around home to one last tubular metal bed at Mount Sinai Hospital. I dashed off another note to Amsterdam: "If you're going to come, come now." I sent Teresa back to Atlantic City, over her objections. She had to keep her job; I'd already cost her everything else. There were things I still needed from Da, things that could happen only inside the circle of that smallest race: one father and son.

I put it to him one afternoon, when the morphine drip held him still in the middle ground between composed and improvised, between evasion and vanishing. By then, he must have realized I would be the only one of his children to be with him here on this last stop.

"Da?" I sat by his bed in a molded-plastic chair, both of us inspecting the lime green cinder-block wall six feet away. "That night? The one when you and . . . my grandfather . . ."

He nodded—not to cut me off, but to spare me saying it out loud. His face screwed up into something worse than cancer. A lifetime of refusing to talk about it, and now his mouth pulled open and closed, like a trout in the well of a boat, gasping under this sudden sea of atmosphere. He worked so hard to find the first syllable, I almost told him to rest and forget. But the need was on us both now. Worse than the need to seal a last closeness. My father had lost me my mother's family, and never said why. The effort he went through then, in his last bed, was worse than any salvage could justify. I sat there, an impassive jury, waiting to see how he'd hang himself.

"I . . . loved your grandfather. He was such an enormous man. No? *Grosszügig*. Noble. His mind wanted to take in everything. He would have been a perfect physicist." For a beat, my father's ravaged face found pleasure. "He cared for me, I think. More than just for the husband of his daughter. We spoke often, of many things, in New York, in Philadelphia. He was so fierce, always ready to fight for your mother's right to be happy, anywhere in the world. When we first told him your brother was on the way, he groaned. 'You are making me a grandfather before my time!' We took you babies to Philadelphia, for holidays. Everything was welcome. Yes, of course, there were problems with—what?—*Übersetzung.*"

"Translation."

"Yes. Of course. My English is going. Problems with translation. But he knew me. He recognized me."

"And you recognized him?"

"What he didn't know about me, I didn't know, either! Maybe he was right. Yes. Maybe." My father fell into a reverie. I thought he wanted to sleep. I should have made him, but I kept still. "He challenged my war work. You know, I solved problems during the war. I helped with those weapons."

I nodded. We'd never talked about it. But I knew.

"He challenged. He said those bombings were as racial as Hitler. I said I didn't work on the bombings. I did not have anything to do with those decisions. I said such use wasn't about white and dark. He said everything—the whole world—was about white against dark. Only, the white didn't know this. I said I wasn't white; I was a Jew. He couldn't understand this. I tried to tell him the hatred I got in this country, that I never talked about to anyone. We told him that you children would not be white against dark. Your grandfather was a huge mind. A powerful man. But he said we were doing wrong, raising you children. He said we were performing a . . . *Sünde.*"

"Sin. You were sinning."

"Sin. *Ein Zeitwort?*"

"Well, it's a noun, too."

"That we were sinning, bringing you boys up as if there would be no white versus dark. As if we were already there, present in our own future."

I closed my eyes. My father's was not a future the human race would ever stumble into. If my grandfather, if my own father . . . The words tore out of me before I thought them. "It didn't have to be all or nothing, Da. You could have at least told us . . . We could at least have been . . ."

"You see. In this country, in this place? Everything is already all or nothing. One or the other. Nothing may be both. Of this, your mother and I, too, are guilty."

"We could at least have talked about this. As a family. Our whole lives."

"Yes, of course. But whose words? This is what your grandfather . . .

what William wanted to know. We tried to talk about it, as a family, that night. But once those things were said, once we went to that place . . ."

He went to that place all over again. Pain that cancer had not succeeded in putting in his face, memory now did. I was a boy again, cowering in my open bedroom doorway, hearing my world, my father's, my mother's all cave in.

"He said there was a struggle. A struggle we were—what? 'Turning our backs on.' Your mother and I said no; we were that struggle. This: making you children free, free to define. Free of everything."

"Your mother and I" no longer sounded like a whole. And *"Free of everything,"* a kind of death sentence.

My father lay propped in his bed, the kind of motorized bed that can be set to every position except comfortable. He spoke through narrowed mouth, his eyes closed, from a place I'd banished him to. "Horrible things, we said, that night. Terrible things. We played 'Who owns pain?' 'Who has suffered the greater wrong?' I told him the Negro had never been killed in the numbers of the Jews. He said they *had*. This I didn't understand. He said no killing could be worse than slavery. Centuries of it. The Jews had never been enslaved, he said. In one heartbeat, I was a Zionist. They were, I said; they were enslaved. Too long ago to count, he said. How long ago counts? I asked. Yes, how long ago? When is the past over? Maybe never. But what did this have to do with the two of us—this man and me? Nothing. We were to live now, in the present. But we just couldn't reach there."

I touched his ravaged shoulder through his flimsy hospital gown. My palm said, *You can stop. You don't need to do this.* Da felt the touch prodding him on.

"Your mother was silent. Watching everything break open. Her father and I were talking enough for all humanity. He . . . called me a member of the killer race. I . . . used my family. My parents and sister, in the ovens. I used them as proof. Of something. The hatred I took in, for being something I never was."

"I understand, Da." I would have said anything to close that box back up.

"When William left that night, he said we forced him. He said we didn't want you two to know your Philadelphia family. 'If they're not going to be black, these boys, they can't have their black family.' This made your mother furious. She said unfortunate things. Everything her father had ever taught her, everything he believed . . . But this, we never said. We never said you would not be black. Only that you would be who you were: a process, first. More important than a thing. He called this idea 'the lie of whiteness.'"

"A quarter of a century? You don't cut off all contact because of a single night. Angry words. Every family has anger. Every family says things it wishes it hadn't."

"Your mother and I, the two of us, we knew what would come. Your future had already talked to us. Your future made us! And made us choose. We thought we knew what things would come to you. But your Papap . . ." He darkened. Messages missing, disappearing, unopened, unsent. "Your Papap did not see these."

There was a thing stronger than family, wilder than love, worse than reason. Big enough to shred them all and leave them for dead. All my life, that thing had pinned me. Its nurses wouldn't let me into this hospital room, couldn't accept I was this dying man's son. And still I didn't know what this thing wanted from us, or how it had grown so real. "So that's it, Da? One night's craziness caused a permanent break? For this one night, we—Mama never saw her own family again?"

"Well, you know, it's a funny thing. I didn't see that night would be a break. Neither did William. For a long time, I thought he would come to us, that we were right and he would come to agree, in time. But he must have been waiting for us, too. Then, in that waiting, righteousness took us over." He closed his eyes and thought. "And shame. It was ourselves we didn't know how to find. Ourselves we didn't have the heart to go meet again. This is the force of belonging. After that, after your mother died . . ." I put my hand on him again. But he'd already been convicted. "After your mother died, I couldn't any longer. The last chance had closed up. I was too ashamed even to ask that big man's forgiveness. I sent them the news, of course. But I thought . . . I was afraid she died because of me."

I would have cried out, *Impossible,* except his own daughter had said as much. He looked at me, pleading. I could not exonerate or condemn. But there was something I might do. "Da? I could . . . find them. Now. Tell them."

"Tell them what?" Then he heard what I was asking. His head went back into his pillow. Everything he knew about time made him believe that only perception divided the future from the past. His eyes flickered,

4 6 7

as if our family were already here, in this green cinder-block room, all false world lines redrawn. Then his lips spasmed, his brows and cheeks collapsed on each other, and his face blanched, condemning itself. He shook his head. And with that shake, he slipped the last dragline with which life held him.

He went fast after that. He passed in and out of consciousness. We didn't say much more to each other, beyond logistics. He called out two mornings later, in blinding pain: "Something is wrong. We have made a terrible mistake. We have chopped up our house for firewood." His eyes still looked at me, but they sat so deep with animal incomprehension, they no longer knew me. Disease and the morphine drip split him between them. The maze of muscles around his eyes showed him hearing all sorts of sounds, the most glorious music. But he couldn't get over the wall, where the sound came from. The eyes pleaded without focus, asking if I remembered. In his face was the horrified suspicion that he'd made it all up.

I remembered the day he took us to Washington Heights for the magic substance, *Mandelbrot*. The day he told us that every moving object in the universe had its own clock. One look at his face showed how uncoupled our clocks had become. In the five seconds I spent taking that glance, decades sheared off into his silent bay. In my few breaths, he had time to audition the entire available repertoire. Or maybe, as I raced, my clock buzzing around in front of him, his own had already stopped, stranding him on the upbeat of some permanent open-air concert on the mind's Mall.

And then, one last time, time started up again. I was sitting by his bed flipping through a six-month-old copy of *Health and Fitness* that the hospital scattered around its rooms like warrants. I thought today might be the day. But I had thought that for the last three mornings running. It had been forever since Da had said anything. I talked to him as if he were still there, knowing my words had to sound like spinning galaxies. I sat with the magazine spread on the rolling meal table, reading about living with rosacea. I had one ear on him, waiting for any change in his breathing. It felt exactly like the years I'd spent accompanying Jonah, bent over my score, listening for the silent indicator that the piece was about to head off into uncharted waters.

Then it did. Da leaned forward off his canted bed and opened his eyes. He coughed up something that took me some seconds to identify. "Where's my darling?" I waited, paralyzed. The shudder would wear him out, break him again. But then, harsher, more terrified, he burst out, "*Wo ist sie?* Where is my treasure?"

I stood to calm him, lower him back to the pillow. "It's okay, Da. Everything's all right. I'm here. It's Joseph."

He flashed in anger. My father, who was never angry at me in his entire life. "Is she safe?" His voice belonged to someone else. "You must tell me."

I stood at the crash of two lives, not knowing which to answer. "Da. She's not here anymore. She . . . died." Even now, I couldn't say *burned*.

"Died?" His voice suggested some misunderstanding, probably simple, he couldn't puzzle out.

"Yes. It's okay."

"Died?" And then his whole body bucked in electroshock. "Died? My God, no! My God! It can't be. Everything——" He flailed at the IV tubes and made to swing his feet out of bed. I was around the bed faster than he could move, pinning him. He shouted, "She can't be. *Das ist unmöglich.* When? How?"

I held his wasted one hundred pounds back against the bed. "In a fire. When our house burned. Fifteen years ago."

"Oh!" He grabbed my arm. His whole body relaxed in gratitude. "Oh! God be thanked." He settled back, satisfied.

"Jesus Christ. Da? What are you saying?"

He closed his eyes and a smile played on his lips. He clawed the air until his hand found mine. "I mean my Ruth." He slipped back against the bed. "How is she?" The words exhausted him.

"She's good, Da. I saw her not long ago."

"Really?" Pleasure battled with irritation. "Why didn't you tell me this?"

"She's married. Her husband's name is Robert. Robert Rider. He's . . ." A big man. An enormous man. "*Grosszügig.*"

Da nodded. "This much, I have already thought. Where is she now?"

"Da. I'm not sure."

"She's not in trouble?"

"Nothing serious." My concert days were over, but I'd learned to improvise.

The morphine washed back over him. He drifted, and I thought he fell asleep. But after a moment, he said, "California. Maybe she is in California."

"Maybe, Da. Maybe California."

He nodded, calmed. "I've thought so." When he opened his eyes again, they were salt. "She disowned me. She said her struggle is not mine." Acid filled his face, as if what was coming might still destroy everything that had already been. He worked to breathe. I sat calming him, as I used to calm Jonah when his attacks were on him. "When you see her, you must tell her. Tell her . . ." He fought for clarity, waiting for that message from the past to catch up with him. Then he closed his eyes and smiled. "Tell her there is another wavelength everyplace you point your telescope."

Three times, he made me promise to tell her. That night, without talking again, my father died. It was something like a hemiola, a change in meter. A sudden, unprepared cross into a new key. In every piece of music worth playing, some moment gathers, moving its chords forward, casting ahead for one quick tightening of the air around it to the endless organizing silence beyond the double bar.

Da died. There was no death rattle, no relaxing of the bowels. I told him he could go. Instead of taking that next small step into his local future, he doubled back and forever rejoined where he'd already been. I called the nurses. And then my own line bent on, away from his, into an unknown place.

I thought death would be different this time, knowing in advance. It was. It was steeper. Mama never had a chance to disappear, she was gone so instantly. But she didn't really die for me until the man who chatted with her in the kitchen in the middle of the night fifteen years after her death joined her. Da was gone, taking with him all my connection to her, to us. When he stopped, so did my past. Everything was fixed now, beyond growing. The bird and the fish can fall in love, but their only working nest will be the grave.

I turned helpless in the face of the hundreds of tasks death requires. The hospital helped; they'd seen this before, apparently. Da had told me nothing of what he wanted. He'd made no preparations for the inevitable. Jonah and Ruth were nowhere. Cremation seemed simplest. It had done for Mama. That was the easiest of the choices. At the moment when I most needed to be out of this world, up in the star map, among the rotating galaxies, I was dragged back to make countless decisions about things I couldn't care about. Everyone needed signatures: the university, the state, the federal government, the bank, the neighborhood—all those anxious poolings that Da had gotten through his life largely by ignoring.

Teresa held me together, phoning from Atlantic City. She came up for one long weekend. She seemed to grow surer and more capable as I fell apart. Everything she did was one more thing I didn't have to. "You're doing fine, Joseph. All the right things." She supplied a steady source of practical advice to the heir of a family that had always been practicality's sworn enemy. She stayed alongside me for the million deaths by decision that surviving requires.

After I'd made all the most irreversible choices my father's death demanded, Jonah called. His voice was full of buzz and echoing delay. "Joey. I just got your message. I've been away. I'm . . . not with that old management anymore."

"Jesus, Jonah. Where the fuck have you been?"

"Don't swear at me, Joey. I'm down in Italy. I've been singing at La Scala."

The only news that could redeem Da's death: My brother had followed through on the thing our parents raised us for. "La Scala. Serious? Singing what?"

"It . . . it doesn't matter, Joey. Nothing. Tell me about Da."

It hit me only then. Jonah didn't know. I thought the news would be *in* him, like migration in a bird. He should have known the instant it happened. "He died. A week ago last Wednesday."

For a long time, there was only breathing and transatlantic static. In silence as long as a funeral song, Jonah replayed the life. "Joey. Oh God. Forgive me." As if his being away had made this happen.

I heard him over the line, his breath shortening, on the edge of a full-fledged choking attack. He was trying to figure out how to stop what had already happened. When he could talk again, he wanted details, all the nonevents of Da's last days. He demanded to know everything our father had said. Anything Da might have left behind, something to send him. I had nothing. "He did . . . he made me promise to give Ruth a message."

"What?"

"He said, 'There's another wavelength everyplace you point your telescope.'"

"What the hell does that mean, Joey?"

"He . . . something he was working on, I think. He stayed busy. It helped a little."

"Why Ruth? What possible interest . . ." She'd betrayed him again, by stealing Da's last message from him.

"Jonah. I have no clue. Between the medications and the disease, he was gone a long while before he left."

"Is Ruth there?"

I told him that I'd heard nothing from her since her surprise visit. He listened, saying nothing.

"What did you do with the body?" As if it were evidence I had to dispose of.

I told him all the decisions I'd made. Jonah said nothing. His silence rebuked me. "What did you want me to do? You turn your back on us. You leave me to go through this alone while you—"

"Joey. Joey. You did just fine. You did perfect." Grief came out of him in staccato sobs. Almost laughs, really. Something had gotten away from him, an absence he'd regret forever. "You want me to come back?" His words slurred together. "You want me to?"

"No, Jonah." I wanted him to, more than anything. But not because I asked.

"I could be there by next week."

"No point. Everything's done. Over."

"You don't need help with things? What will you do with the house?" The Jersey home Da thought we might, in some other universe, share.

"The will says that's up to a majority of his children."

He struggled with something. "What do you want to do?"

"Sell."

"Of course. At any price."

Da was huge between us. Our father wanted me to ask. Somewhere, he wanted to know. "What were you singing at La Scala?"

Silence flooded the line. He thought it too soon to come back to this life. But I was Jonah's only link now. Me and Ruth, whom neither of us could reach.

"Joey? You'll never believe this. I sang under Monera."

The name came from so far away, I was sure it, too, had to be dead. "Jesus Christ. Did he know who you were?"

"Some dusky American tenor."

"Did you ask him about . . ."

"I didn't have to. I saw her. She came backstage opening night." He paused, racing himself. "She's . . . old. Adult. And married. To a Tunisian businessman working out of Naples. He looks just like me. Only darker."

I was his accompanist again, waiting out the caesura, holding on to its nothingness until his inhale started us up again.

"She apologized. In English, which her husband doesn't speak. 'You deserved a note.' How old were we, Joey? Fourteen? The year Mama . . . The day Da . . ." Only a lifetime's training kept his voice his. "Real blacks die of gunshot wounds, right? Overdoses. Malnutrition. Lead poisoning. What do halfies die of, Joey? Nobody dies of numbness, do they?"

"What happens now? You going to do more opera?" Something in me had to keep track. Some part of me still had to tell Da.

"Mule?" He was traveling out beyond my reach, at a speed that collapsed all measure. "Opera is nothing to do with what we thought. Absolutely nothing. I had to see it down in Italy, the place it came from. With the native speakers, the owners. Opera's somebody else's childhood. Somebody else's nightmare. I think I'll head to Paris for a while."

"France?" French was his worst singing language. He'd always mocked the place. "To do what? Go back to lieder?" I worked to keep my voice neutral. Like an ex-wife encouraging her husband to go out dating again.

"I'm tired of it, Joey. Tired of singing alone. Unless you . . . Where am I going to find another accompanist with telepathy?"

I couldn't tell if he was asking or rejecting me. "What are you going to do, then?" I saw him singing Maurice Chevalier songs in the Metro, a felt hat catching the centimes.

"There has to be life beyond opera and lieder. Didn't your mother ever tell you? Let every boy serve God in his own fashion."

"What's yours?" Each answer seemed more murderous than the last.

"Wish I knew. It has to be out there." He fell silent again, ashamed of surviving. I felt him working up again to ask me to come out and join him. But I never got the chance to turn him down. When he spoke again, it was to more than me. "Joey? Have him a little memorial service. Just us? Play something good for him. Something from the old days."

"We already did."

I felt it go through him, the stab of freedom he'd gone after. "You sure you don't want me to come back?"

"You don't need to." I gave him that much.

"Joey, forgive me."

I gave him that, too.

It took me several days to grasp that I didn't have to go in to the hospital anymore. There was nothing to do but close up Da's house. I came up for air, browsed the papers, caught up on what had happened while I was away in death's waiting room. The National Guard had killed some college students. The FBI was arresting priests for helping people burn their draft cards. Hoover issued a nationwide warning against "extremist all-Negro hate-type organizations." He meant my sister and her husband, all the criminal elements that undermined my country.

I wanted out of Fort Lee as fast as possible. First, I had to go through the house and its contents. The few family keepsakes of value I put into rented storage. The man's wardrobe, unchanged since 1955, I packed off to the Salvation Army. I sold the piano Da had bought for me, along with the few valuable pieces of furniture, and put the cash in a certificate of deposit for Ruth and Robert Rider.

I looked in my father's jumbled files for an address for my mother's family. I found one in his lists of contacts, that wad of three-by-five cards he kept bound with a thick rubber band. The card, in my father's handwriting, was younger than it looked. It was thumbed-up, dog-eared, and smudged enough to be a faked antique. At the top, on the double red line, in caps, ran the name DALEY. Below it was a Philadelphia street address. There was no telephone number.

I pulled the card out of the rubber-banded pack and left it out on the kitchen counter. I looked at it a hundred times a day for three days. One call to directory assistance, and within two minutes, I could be talking to my unknown relatives. *Hello, this is your grandson. This is your nephew. Your cousin.* They'd ask me, *And where do you live? What do you do? How come you sound like you do?* Where could I go from there? I couldn't use Da's death as an excuse for making contact. Their own daughter had died, and that hadn't brought us back together. Every time I looked at the address, I felt the distance compound down all the years of my life. The gap had widened so far, I couldn't even find my side of it. The rift was too big to do anything but preserve.

My father's contact file had no card with the name STROM on the top. It had shocked me, while he was dying, to hear him even speak of his family. There was no one on his side to give this news. You can jump into the future, he often told us, all the while we were growing up. But you can't send a message back into your own past. All I could do with Da's death was file it away, a message to some later self who'd know what to do with it.

Toward the rest of the house's goods, I was merciless. Nothing even made me flinch until I hit my father's professional papers. I knew nothing about my father's last work, aside from his needing to prove that the universe favored a direction of spin. After several days of poring over the toppling paper towers in his study, I knew I'd never be able to cope on my own. Unlike music, his physics had some real-world meaning, however abstract that meaning had become. He'd published nothing of consequence for years. But I was terrified that the handwritten scrawl and the tables of figures scattered around his study might hide some scrap of worth.

I called Jens Erichson, Da's closest friend at Columbia, a high-energy physicist who happened to be an amateur singer. He was Da's rough contemporary, the colleague in the best position to appraise all my father's piles of Greek scribbling from his final months. He greeted me warmly over the phone. "Mr. Joseph! Yes, of course I remember you, from years ago, before your mother . . . I sometimes came up to your house, for musical evenings." He was delighted to learn I'd become a musician. I spared him the messy details.

I couldn't stop apologizing. "I shouldn't saddle you with this. You have your own work."

"Nonsense. If the will made no provisions for professional executor, it's because David assumed I'd be there. This is nothing. Heaven knows, he solved enough problems for the rest of us over the years."

We set up a time for him to come by. I took him into the study. An involuntary sigh escaped his lips when he saw what was waiting. He hadn't imagined what he'd signed on for. We spent two days, like archaeologists, boxing up and labeling the papers. The work required gloves, a whisk broom, a field camera. Dr. Erichson took the boxes with him back to the university, over my conscience-stricken stream of gratitude. I put the house on the market and returned to Atlantic City.

I checked in with the Glimmer Room. I wasn't surprised to learn that Mr. Silber no longer needed my services. He'd hired another piano player, a sandy blond guy from White Plains named Billy Land, who learned to play on a Hammond B3 and who could play all of Jim Morrison and the Doors in at least three different keys, sometimes all three at once. Everyone had what they needed. I was free at last. I thought about asking Teresa to see about getting me a job at the saltwater taffy plant.

Dr. Erichson called me after three weeks. "There are some portions of interest in the papers. With your permission, I'll pass those along to the interested parties. The other ninety percent . . ." He struggled with how to lay it out for me. "Did your father ever mention to you the concept of preferred galactic rotation?"

"Many times."

"He got this concept from Kurt Gödel, down in Princeton." The fellow refugee my father had called the greatest logician since Aristotle. "The work goes back a quarter century. Gödel found equations compatible with Einstein's General-Field Theory. I don't know quite how to say this. They allow time to coil up upon itself."

Something from my childhood pushed up above water. Old dinner-table conversations, from a prior life. "Closed timelike loops."

Dr. Erichson sounded both surprised and embarrassed. "He told you about them?"

"Years ago."

"Well he came back to them, at the end. The mathematics is in place. It's peculiar, but simple. Once the conditions are identified, the extraction of the looping solutions is straightforward. At the limits of gravitation, General Relativity permits at least the mathematical possibility of a violation in causality."

"I don't understand."

"Your father was exploring curves in time. On such a curve, events can move continuously into their own local future while turning back onto their own past."

"Time travel."

Dr. Erichson chuckled. "All travel is time travel. But yes. That seems to be what he was after."

"Is this idea real? Or is it just numbers?"

"Your father believed that any equations permitted by physics are, in some sense of the word, real."

All things that are possible must exist. He'd said so all his life. That was his creed, his freedom. It was the thing, alongside music, that most moved him. Perhaps it *was* music to him. Whatever the numbers permitted must happen, somewhere. I didn't know how to ask. "These loops are real? Physics really allows them?"

"If any physics allows the violation of causality, that physics is wrong. Every scientist I know believes this. It's the law on which all others are based. Yet as far as General Relativity is concerned, these equations would indeed apply, given a universe where the galaxies had a favored rotation. If this is the case, General Relativity needs repairing."

The star charts. The endless tables. "What did he find out? What did he . . . conclude?"

"Well. I can't afford to put real time into this. At a glance, it seems he hadn't yet detected any preference."

Another direction of rotation everyplace you looked. "But if he had?"

"Well, the equations exist. Time would close back upon itself. We could live our lives always. Folding onto ourselves, forever."

"If he didn't find a preferred rotation, does it mean there is none?"

"That, I can't answer. I haven't the time for this problem that your father did. Forgive me."

"But if you were a betting man?"

He thought slowly, about something we weren't designed to wrap our thoughts around, at any speed. "Even with a closed timelike loop . . ." He belonged to my father's people: the people who needed to get things right. "Even then, you could travel back into a given past only if you'd been there *already*."

I formed an image for his words, but it became something else even as I fondled it. My father had needed some way to get back to my mother, to send her a message, to deflect and correct all that had happened to us. But in Dr. Erichson's universe, the future was as unfixable as the past was fixed.

"No time travel?"

"Not in any way that might help you."

"What happens is forever?"

"This seems to be the case."

"But it's possible to change what hasn't happened yet?"

He thought for a long time. Then: "I'm not even sure what such a question means."

AUTUMN 1945

She turns to see her JoJo, the little one, standing in his doorway, holding his ice bag up to the incurable sprain. The slammed front door still shudders with her father. Delia Strom turns from it, reeling, and there is her little boy, crippled already by selflessness, watching the thing that will grind him underfoot. He just stands there, offering, terrified, ready to give away everything. Sacrificed to something bigger than family. Something that trumps even blood.

She sweeps the boy into her arms, sobbing. It scares the child more than what has just happened. Now his brother's up, too, tugging her leg and telling her everything will be okay. David, the equation solver, stands behind her, looking through the door's glass for any moving shadow out on the street. She turns to him. He holds one hand on the knob, ready to chase down the street after her father. But he doesn't move.

Neither boy asks where their Papap is. It could be tomorrow for them already. It could be next week. Papap here; Papap gone. They are still trapped in the eternal now. But they see her crying. They've heard the hostility, even without understanding. Already she's losing them to this larger thing, the invention that will take them. Already they've been identified. Already the split, the separate entrance, the splintering calculus.

"Nothing," David says, looking through the pane. She doesn't know what he means. Her father has left her with this man, this bleached man with the accent, who helped to build that final blinding-white weapon. "There is nothing. Come. We all go to bed. Troubles will wait for tomorrow. *Darüber können wir uns morgen noch Sorgen machen.*"

Hitler's language. She never once thought that thought, all during the war. She stayed alongside him, singing lieder—German tunes, German words—for four long years, afraid of being heard and turned in by the neighbors. But still, she kept their part-song vigil, safeguarding that sound against its many mobilized uses. They both cheered this war: war against pedigreed supremacy, against the final nightmare of purity. Whatever the Allies killed in Berlin was to have died here, too. But nothing has died back home. Nothing but her willful ignorance. Her father has walked out on her. Walked out on her for forgetting a war one hundred times longer and more destructive, the piecemeal annihilation of a people. Walked out on her for walking out. *You've thrown in your lot. Chosen your side.* But she has chosen nothing, nothing but a desire to be through with war and to live the peace she and hers have already paid for so many times over.

There is no peace. Troubles will wait for tomorrow. Tomorrow—*tomorrow, already*—they're too ashamed even to look each other in the eye. David goes to work, and what exactly that work is, she can only guess. He leaves her alone with the boys, as her father has left her alone with the family she has made. Alone with two children, from whom she must hide all the doubt in creation. She reads to them from someone else's books. She plays with them—die-metal trucks and dowel houses that come from someone else's construction dreams. In the afternoon, they sing together, the boys outdoing each other in naming and making the notes. If her father is right, then all the wrongness of the world is right. If her father is right, she must begin to tell her children: *This* is not yours, nor *this*, nor *this*, nor *this* . . . She can't sacrifice her boys to that preemptive lynching, not today or ever. But if her father is right, she must ready them. If he's right, then all of history is right, permanent, inescapable.

But her father's resolution only stiffens hers. She won't surrender anything. Yes, of course: She'll give them warmth, welcome, riffing, the congregating joy of call and response, a dip in that river, deep enough to sport in all their lives. She must give them the riches that are theirs by birth. *Negro. American.* Of course they must know the long, deadly way those terms have come. But she refuses to give them self by negation. Not the old defeating message that they've already been decided. All she can give them is choice. Free as anyone, free to own, to attach themselves to any tune that catches their inner ear.

But maybe her father *is* right. Maybe it's only their lightness that gives them even the slightest leeway. Maybe choice is just another lie. There is a freedom she wouldn't wish on anyone. She takes her boys outside, west, toward the river, down to the nearest strip of green in all this stone, the three of them out in the open air for all to appraise. She sees their triad of tones through the parkgoers' gazes. Her body flinches, as always, under the assault. She hears what her neighbors call this freedom she would give. *Striving. Passing. Turning.* But what of her boys' other family, that lineage she knows nothing about, cleaned out, solved, finally, by this world that stands no complications? Isn't that family every bit as much theirs?

In the park, her boys climb on a set of concrete stairs as if it's the greatest playground ever built. Each step is a pitch they cry out as they pounce on. They turn the staircase into a pedal organ, chasing up the scale, hopping in thirds, stepping out simple tunes. Two other children, white, see their ecstasy and join, hurtling up and down the flights, screaming their own wild pitches until their parents come shepherd them away, their averted glances apologizing to Delia for the universal mistake of childhood.

The incident does nothing to lessen her JoJo's joy. Their manic pitch-climbing continues unabated. She can tell them now or wait for simplifying whiteness to inform them later. This is the choice that leaves her no choice. She knows what's safest, the best defense against the power that will otherwise lynch them. The first attack, the first hate-whispered syllable will name them. They'll suffer worse than their mother ever suffered, pay most for being unidentifiable. But something in Delia needs to believe: A boy learns by heart the first song he hears. And the first song—the *first*—belongs to no one. She can give them a tune stronger than belonging. Thicker than identity. A singular song, a self better than any available armor. Teach them to sing the way they breathe, the songs of all their ancestries.

When David comes home, she recognizes him again. The two of them: theirs. Her whole body shakes with relief, as if she's stepped out of neck-high burial in a snowbank. She lurches down the front hall to grab him. Surely, if two people love the same thing, they must love each other a little. He takes her in his arms at the door, even before he takes off his hat. "This is not forever," he says. "We will all be back, once more in the same place." But they can't be *back*, because they never have been. Not in the same place. Never even once.

After dinner and singing, radio and reading to the boys, they lie in bed. They talk into the night, softly to each other, after the boys fall asleep. Her JoJo can hear anyway. The words of this conversation go straight into dreams that will vex them for the rest of their lives.

"He's angry with me," David says. "Yet I feel I've done nothing wrong. Only what my country has asked of me. What everyone would have done."

This angers *her*. It makes her Daddy wrong. Some man should apologize, even if he's the injured party. *Because* he has been injured. For a moment, she hates them both, for neither saving her. "He's angry with *me*," she whispers back. But she doesn't say why. That, too, is a loss of faith. Thinking David would never understand.

"We can call him tomorrow. Explain that it has all been a confusion. A *Missverständnis*."

"It isn't," she hisses. "That isn't what it was." She feels her husband's body tense in the first edge of anger against her, her opposition. Is no one above this need to be redeemed?

"What is it, then?"

"I don't know. I don't care. All I know is that I'm sick of it. I want it to be over."

His hand slides sideways across the sheet and finds hers. He thinks she means last night's argument. This private war. "It will be over. It must be. How can something so angry last forever?"

He thinks she means *Rassenhass*. "It already *has*."

He listens to her. If nothing else, this. "You want it to be over. But how should it end? How should the world best be? I mean, one thousand years from now? Ten thousand? What is the right place? The place we must try to reach?"

She's never really had to say, not to herself, let alone anyone other. Every perfect place she starts to name already has a piece of evil slithering through it. She wants to stop talking, to roll over and sleep. She has no answer. But he asks her. This is the conversation, the terms of the contract they must improvise.

"The right place . . . the place I want . . . Nobody owns anybody. Nobody has claim on anything. Nobody's anybody. Nobody's anything but their own."

She squeezes shut her eyes. The only place that calms her a little. The only place she can live. The only sane landing place. If it's the right place for a thousand years from now, why not for her boys? For patience means submission, and waiting is never.

"This is where we go live, then. We call your father tomorrow."

"He won't . . . get it."

"We call. We talk to him."

What ignorance. Her father's right: right about all things. She's the one trying to get away, trying to trick the truth. She has no right to call and talk to him. All she has a right to is lasting reprimand.

"Remember what we saw," David says. "Remember what's coming."

She can't decide now whether what they saw even belonged to this world. No: It's too soon for this life, too far out ahead of anything their children can reach. Something in this place needs race. Some ground-floor tribalism, something in a soul that won't be safe or sound in anything smaller or larger. The day violence gets them, the day her boys meet those centuries of murder, on that day, they will hate her for not giving them the caste this caste-crazed country finally demands. But until that day, she'll give them—however illusory or doomed—self. And let the image stand in for the thing.

She will not cut them off from their own. "We call tomorrow," she says. But tomorrow comes and goes without a call. Shame blocks them, guilty memories. She can't bear those words again, those accusations cutting her to the quick. She has no answer but this deliberate theft, this criminal leap ahead, this shortcut across one thousand years.

The baby's coming. *"The baby's coming"*: This is her Joseph's universal cure, his answer to all things. The child has taken ownership of the mystery, this new life from nowhere. He wants Delia to eat more, to make the baby come faster. He wants to know what day the baby will arrive, and when *this* day will become that one.

Three weeks go by, with no contact from Philadelphia. Then a month. The same fire-forged pride that allowed her father to survive this country now turns to the task of surviving her. She can't bear it, not with the new baby on the way. Something horrible is happening, fueled by love, something she can't put right in herself, in her father, a fear as wild as the fear of losing oneself, going under.

She crumples and gives in. She writes a letter to her mother. It's the child's first trick, playing on her weaker parent. The letter smacks of cowardice. She types it without a return address, so her daddy won't throw it out unopened. She mails it from New Jersey, laundering the postmark. She lies from the very first sentence: says she doesn't know what happened, doesn't understand. She tells her mama she needs to talk, to work out a way to patch things up. "Anywhere. I'll come to Philadelphia. It doesn't have to be the house. Anyplace we can talk."

She gets a note back. It's little more than an address—Haggern's, a sandwich shop on the edge of the old neighborhood, a short-order grill where her mother used to take her when they went shopping—along with a date and time. "You're right. The house is not a good idea just now."

The sentence destroys Delia. She's a wreck until she steps on the train to Philly. She's showing now, huge with her new one. She needs to get right with her folks before she delivers. Though she's not due for weeks, this heaviness feels like she could give birth any second. She takes the boys with her on the train—too long to leave them with Mrs. Washington. Her mother will want to see them. They'll make the meeting easier.

She's sitting at Haggern's a quarter hour before she needs to be. It surprises her when her mother walks in with the twins. They've just been shopping. It presses on Delia's chest harder than she can understand. Her mother looks furtive, conspiratorial. But the thrill of seeing her grandsons smoothes out her crumpled face.

Lucille and Lorene: Can it have been that long? Just months, but there's something new to them, suddenly adult, an earnest show of long skirts and pleated blouses, a new weight in their step. "How'd you girls get grown up so fast? Turn around. Turn round; let me look at you! Where'd you find those shapes overnight?"

Her sisters look at Delia as if she has declared against them. *Daddy has said something.* But they eye her swollen belly as well, their envy, fear, and hope all rolled into one. Nettie Ellen slings into the booth across from Delia and the boys. She reaches across, taking their pale heads into her searching hands. But even as she fondles them, she murmurs to her daughter, "What in heaven's name you say to that man?"

"Mama, it's not like that."

"What's it like, then?"

Delia feels weary and older than the earth. Silted, slow, and winding like a switchback river. But wronged, too. Betrayed by her bedrock trust. Hurt by ones who know her hurt. That horrific night: David and her father trading accusations: an Olympics of suffering. The moral leverage of pain. Two men who couldn't hear their nearness. They're the ones who ought to be sitting in this booth, across from each other. Not this old fallback alliance, mothers against men. Delia tries for her mother's eye, just a little flicker to show that the alliance still holds. "He doesn't like the way I'm rearing up my young."

"He don't like you scrubbing these leopards spotless."

"Mama," she pleads. Her eyes dart downward.

"Girls? Take your nephews over to that gum-ball game at Lowie's." She fishes in her pocketbook for two nickels for her grandsons to feed the mechanical gum-ball claw. The same prehistoric Saturday ritual she and Delia shared.

Delia scurries in her purse to beat her mother. "Here. Here, now. Take these."

The twins don't want anyone's coins. "We're not children," Lucille says.

Lorene echoes her. "Come on, Mama. We know what's happening."

Nettie Ellen touches the teen conspiratorially. "Don't I know that, child! It's your nephews, need a little expert tending."

The secret appeal overwhelms them. They sweep the boys up the way they used to during the war, when they'd push the infants around the block in strollers. They show their sister up, proving how fierce love ought to be. Then Delia and her mother are alone. Alone as on that day, up in her attic practice room, when Delia first spoke about the man she'd fallen for. How fine her mother had been, after the first shock. How solid and broad, this woman, whom time gives no reason to feel anything but eternal distrust. How good they've all been, her family. A blackness big enough to absorb all strains.

"I'm so tired, Mama."

"Tired? What you tired of?" The warning audible: *I was tired before you were born. I didn't raise you to give in to tired.*

"I'm tired of racial thinking, Mama." The bird and the fish can fall in love. But there's no possible nest but *no nest*.

A deep bronze waitress comes by to take their order. Nettie Ellen orders what she always orders at Haggern's, since time began. Coffee, no cream, and a piece of blueberry pie. Delia orders a chocolate doughnut and a small milk. She doesn't want it and can't eat it. But she has to order it. Every time they've ever come here, she has. The waitress slides off, and Nettie Ellen's eyes follow. "You tired of being colored. That's what you're tired of."

Delia tries on the accusation like a gown. A prison uniform. Something in stripes. "I'm tired of everybody thinking they know what colored means."

Her mother looks around the shop. A teenage boy in white slacks, shirt, and a little dress-infantry paper hat mans the grill. Two old waitresses with stovepipe legs carry fries from the counter to the wooden tables. A young couple slumps over a shared soda in the booth across the way. "Who's telling you that? Nobody here's going to tell you what colored means. Only the o-fay do that."

Her mother speaks that forbidden word. Once, at twelve, Delia had her mouth washed out with soap for using it. Something has broken down: the rules, or her mother. "My boys are . . . different."

"Look around you, girl. Everybody here's different. Different's the commonest thing going."

"I've got to give them the freedom to be—"

Her mother pinches up her face. "Don't you dare talk to me about freedom. Your brother died in the war—for that word. A black man, fighting to give folks in other countries a freedom he wouldn't ever've had in his own, even if he came back here alive."

"Lots of people died in the war, Mama. White people. Black people. Yellow people." Her boys' other family.

"Your husband didn't. Your husband—" She stops, unable to slander the father of her grandchildren.

"Mama. It's not what you think."

Her mother searches her. "Oh, don't I know that. Nothin's ever what *I* think."

"It's not one thing against the other. We're not taking anything away. Just giving. Giving them space, choice, the right to make a life anywhere along—"

"This why you married a white man? So you could make babies light enough to do what they wouldn't let you do?"

Delia knows why she married a white man. Knows the exact moment she was bound to him. But never in a million years could she explain to her mother what happened that day on the Mall, the future she saw.

Her mother stares out Haggern's window at the passersby. "You could have stayed with us, sung every week for God and the people who need to hear Him. Why you need a fancy concert hall, where nobody gets to move or join in? There are more places to sing with us than you could have sung in a lifetime. More places to sing down here than there are in heaven."

The kind of praise . . . the music I've studied . . . Every answer Delia thinks of breaks under its own weight. She's saved by the waitress, who arrives with their orders. Steam still rises from Nettie Ellen's slice of pie. The waitress slides it over. "Look here! This pie was hiding deep in the oven. Thinking itself too grand to come out and get eaten."

"You try it yet?" Nettie Ellen asks.

"Ha! This place look like they treat me that good?"

"You go on have yourself a slice; tell them to put it on my bill. Go on!"

"Bless you, ma'am, but I gotta watch my figure. My man likes me all skinnied down. 'Like a bar of soap at the end of the washing month.' "

"My man always trying to get me to fill out."

"Gimme some of that. He got a son?"

"One." Two, once. "But you're going to have to wait another couple years before that particular pie comes out of the oven."

"You come get me." The waitress waves them both away, along with all the world's foolishness. "I'll be here."

Delia will die of exile. She lived here once. Her boys never will. Never the leveling sass of a nation that sees through every pretension. One with more places to sing than even heaven. "Colored's got to get bigger, Mama." Something her daddy told her all her life.

"Colored, bigger? Colored's got no room to get bigger. Colored's been smashed down to the biggest little thing that can be, without disappearing. *White's* got to get bigger. White's never had room for nobody but itself."

They pick at their snacks in silence. If only the children would come back. Prove to them both that nothing has changed. *Still your boys. Still your grandchildren.*

"White's just one color. Black's everything else. You gonna raise them to have a choice? That choice don't belong to you. It don't even belong to them. Everybody else is gonna make it for them!" Nettie Ellen puts down her fork. She's in her daughter's eye. "My own mother. My own mother. Had a father was white."

The words rock Delia. Not the fact, which she long ago gathered, in the cracks of the family history. But her mother's saying so, here, out loud. She shuts her eyes. In such pain, they could travel anywhere. "What . . . what was he like, Mama?"

"Like? We never laid eyes on that man. Never showed his face a day to any one of us. Never even helped pay part of her child's way. Could have been anyone. Could have been your own man's grandfather."

Delia coughs a low, horrible gurgle. "No, Mama. David's grandfather . . . was never anywhere near Carolina."

"Don't you mouth me. Don't you backtalk."

"No, Mama."

"Here's the thing I never understood. If white is so God-awful almighty, how come fifteen of their great-great-grandparents can't even equal one of ours?"

Delia can't help test a smile. "That's just what I'm saying, Mama. Jonah and Joey, half their world . . . Don't they come just as much from—"

"You hear anything from the man's parents?"

David has written a hundred letters, probed scores of vaults: Rotterdam, Westerbork, Essen, Cologne, Sofia, all the systematic German records of the abyss. "Nothing yet, Mama. We're still searching."

Both women bow their heads. "White folks killed their grandparents. You can't lie to them about that. You get them ready. That's all your father's saying, child."

"It won't always be this way. Things are changing, even now. We have to start making the future. It's not going to come any other way."

"Future! We got to make the here and now. We don't even have that to live in, yet."

The daughter looks away, at this room of people without a present. She doesn't know how, but when she hears her boys sing, when they set out on their tiny adventures of canon and imitation, she finds her here and now, large enough to live in.

In that awful blood right, exercised so often as she was growing up, her mother reads her mind. "I never cared what music you sang. I never understood it myself. But anything you sang was fine by me, so long as you sang with everything you owned. And never called yourself anything you weren't. What you going to tell them to call themselves?"

"Mama. That's the point. We're not calling them anything. That way, they'll never have to call another person——"

"White? You raising them white?"

"Don't be silly. We're trying to raise them . . . beyond race." The only stable and survivable world.

"'Beyond' means white. Only people who can afford 'beyond.'"

"Mama, no. We're raising them . . ." She looks for the word, and can only find *nothing*. "We're raising them what they are. Themselves first."

"Ain't nobody so fine they deserve to put themselves first."

"Mama, that's not what I mean."

"Nobody's so good as that." Four big beats of silence. Then: "What you going to give them, for everything you take away?"

Suppose it's theft. Murder. The children return, saving Delia from answering. All four are rolling in hilarity. The girls pretend to be giant mechanical claws, their shrieking nephews the helpless gum balls. Nettie Ellen brings them into line with one sharp eyebrow.

"Grandmop," Jonah says. "Aunties are crazy!"

She wraps her arms around the boy, petting his halfway hair. "How're they crazy, child?"

"They say a lizard's just a snake with legs. They say singing's just talking, only speeded up."

Their waitress comes to see if the children want to eat. The boys draw her up short. Delia sees the woman eye her boys' skin tones, telling God knows what explanatory story. The waitress points at Jonah. "This ain't the one I'm supposed to wait for, is it?"

Nettie shakes her head. Delia looks down, full of tears.

The children have their pie. For another fifteen minutes, she, her mother, her sisters, and her children are all there, talking, needing no name for anything but one another. She and her mother fight over the bill. She lets her mother win. They stand on the sidewalk, outside Haggern's. Delia leans into her sisters, waiting for the invitation—*Of course, child!*—to come back to the great house just blocks away. Her home. There on the moving street, she waits her awkward eternity.

"Mama," Delia begins, her voice as tight as the day of her first professional lesson. "Mama. I need your help with this. Get me back with the man."

Nettie Ellen takes her by the elbows, fierce with knowing. "You can get back. You're not even apart. You two just having a bad hour. 'This too shall pass,' the Book says. You just call him up on the telephone and tell him you're sorry. Tell him you know you're wrong."

Delia stiffens. The condition of belonging: She and her husband, the thing they've thought about and chosen, must be surrendered as wrong. She may be wrong, wrong in all she's decided, wrong in each thing she chooses, but she is right in her right to be. In the only world worth reaching, everyone owns all song. This much her father long ago preached to her, and this much he forces on her now.

They go their separate ways, Nettie and the twins to the doctor's house, Delia and the boys to the train. Delia squeezes her sisters before they part. "Stop growing up so fast, now. I want to be able to recognize you, next time I see you."

She tries—tries to call her father. She waits another week, hoping seven more days might blunt all conditions. But the phone call gets off to a catastrophic start and goes south from there. Then she, too, is saying horrible things into the phone, things she's not capable of saying, things whose sole point is to leave her with things worth regretting forever.

Her time comes. She wants to turn to stone. She wants to lie in bed and never stand again. Only the boys get her through. Only that glance ahead, at company coming. She writes Nettie Ellen another note. Still her mother's daughter.

Mama,

The baby's coming. It'll have to be this week or next. I can't make it past that. This one's strong. Takes after its grandfather, I guess, and it's wearing me out. I'd so love if you could help again, like you did with Jonah and Joey. It'd be so good to have a woman to mind the boys. You know how helpless men are, when it counts. David would love it, too. You tell me what we can do to make this possible. It wouldn't be right, having your new grandchild without you around! All love ever, Dee.

Every manipulation available. She's not above anything that redemption might call for. But she's not ready for the note she gets back.

Child,

It was not easy for me to marry your father or have his children. Maybe you never thought that. He and I came from different worlds, different as anything you think you've gotten into. But I loved the man and I made him the promise like the Book talks about: "Intreat me not to leave thee, or to return from following after thee, for whither thou goest, I will go. And where thou lodgest, I will lodge. Thy people shall be my people, and thy God my God. Where thou diest will I die, and there will I be buried." There's nothing I put above this, and don't ask me to. I understand you have to make the same promise to you and yours. I'm not casting you out, and you know we're ever waiting to take you back in, when you want and when you need.

It's signed "With love, Mrs. William Daley." By letter's end, Delia's whole body convulses. When her husband finds her, the baby has already breached. He needs to call an ambulance, to rush mother and daughter to the hospital. She never tells him about the note, the only truth she ever conceals from him. When they tell her the child's a girl, she says, "I know." And when her husband asks, "What should we name her?" she says, "Her name is Ruth."

DON GIOVANNI

Half a dozen places in Atlantic City might have hired me. This was the early 1970s, still the waning heyday of live music, and the music I played offended no one but me. There was a war going on. Not capitalism versus socialism, the United States versus Vietnam, students against their parents, North America versus the rest of the known continents. I mean the war of consonance against dissonance, electric against acoustic, written against improvised, rhythm against melody, shock against decency, long hair against longhair, past against future, rock against folk against jazz against metal against funk against blues against pop against gospel against country, black against white. Everybody had to choose, and music was your flag. Who you were depended on your radio presets. "Whose side," the song wanted to know. "Whose side are you on?"

The secret to the music I'd played at the Glimmer Room was that it never committed. My professional survival consisted of playing a music that belonged to no one. Maybe every tune I played could be blood-typed, aligned with some warring faction. But I played with a strange, nonnative accent no one could quite place. By the time I'd put a song through the wringer of my self-taught riffing and seasoned it with the scraps of three hundred years of forgotten keyboard works, nobody could quite name it to claim or blame.

I couldn't bear to return to playing. The house in Fort Lee sold. I paid the taxes on it and put the balance of Da's assets in three accounts, one for each of us. My share meant that, for some finite but considerable number of months, I didn't have to make a living by faking musical pleasure. Teresa encouraged me to languish for as long as I needed. She thought I was in mourning. She thought I only needed time to get my feet on the ground, and for that, she made me the most solid base imaginable. Saint T. cooked and took me outside for walks and warded off with a glance the gatekeepers of pedigree who might otherwise have beaten me to a pasty pulp.

Those weeks were much like real life, except for my constant flinching. "Sweet?" I said to her in the dark, on my half of her borrowed pillow. We got to the point where she could name that tune in one note. "You have to make up with your father. I can't take it anymore. It's on my conscience. You have to. There's nothing more important."

She lay on the bed next to me, silent, hearing what I was afraid to say. We both knew the only way that reconciliation could happen. She'd already written her father off, had already given up her family for a higher ideal. I could almost live with a choice that good. Except that her higher ideal was me.

She bought me a little Wurlitzer electric piano. It must have cost two years of saltwater taffy savings, and it was only a tenth of the instrument that I had sold for a few hundred dollars after my father died. She showed up at my place the day of delivery, hiding her face in excitement and fear. "I thought you might want something to practice on. And to work with. While you're . . . while you aren't . . ."

She couldn't have hurt me more with a knife to the chest. I stared at the piano in its shipping container, the open casket of a lynching victim. I couldn't tell her. The little thing was a double amputee. It had only forty-four keys, half what I needed to believe in it. Even the simplest arrangement would scrape its head on the ceiling. The thing's action was like a screen door that wouldn't close. I felt I was playing in winter gloves. It resembled a piano less than the Glimmer Room resembled those concert halls Jonah and I had once played. As I looked at her gift, Teresa sat hunched, a hand to her mouth, afraid to breathe, estranged from her family, her savings account wiped out. We'd all die of unreturnable kindness. Misplaced love supreme.

"It's wonderful. I can't believe it. You shouldn't have. I don't deserve this. We have to send it back." A look came over her like I'd killed her dog. "Of course we'll keep it. Come on. Let's sing." Leaden-fingered, I spun out a few arpeggios and launched into "Honeysuckle Rose." All she'd hoped for. I could do that much.

The short, black, crippled handbag of a keyboard became my penance. I came to prefer playing on it over playing a real keyboard, the way a person with a sprained back might come to prefer sleeping on the floor over sleeping on a mattress. I liked playing it without turning the power on. The keys made a muffled, thumping pitch, their sound buried under a bushel. I wanted to shrink down, into a miniature shoe-box performance. If I had to play, the smaller the better.

Teresa wanted nothing from the gift except to please. That's what destroyed me. She thought I missed playing, that I needed some lifeline to keep me afloat. A woman with her work history should have thrown me out on my ear. But so long as she could help me keep my music alive, she didn't care if I ever went back to work. We had our piano. For a while, we sang almost every evening, now that my performing didn't get in the way. For the first time since childhood, I played for no reason but playing. When Jonah and I had toured, we were never alone. We were always answerable, first to the notes on the page and then to the bodies in the auditorium. Even when we rehearsed, twisting around the tune in lockstep, other ears were already listening between us. Teresa and I were all alone. We collided into each other, faltering and finessing our way across a finish line, each deferring to the other. We had no printed notes to prop us or impede us, no listening ear, no living audience to interfere. Nobody to hear but each other.

She'd get sullen and apologetic when we didn't swing. She had this little stutter-step thing she'd picked up from Sarah Vaughan, who'd picked it up from Ella Fitzgerald, who'd picked it up from Louis Armstrong, who'd picked it up from the deep recesses of his orphanage's singing school. I'd follow out the phrases, thinking, *She's never going to make it*. It made her nuts every time I'd try to hook up with her hiccups. She was all rhythm and line, the syncopated flight from the rest of her life. I was all harmony and chord, packing each vertical moment with sixths, flatted ninths, more simultaneous notes than the texture would bear. But somehow, we made music together. Our tunes turned their back on the wide outside, willfully ignorant and almost too beautiful, some nights, in pleasing no one but their makers.

While Teresa was at the factory packing taffy, I read the news or watched daytime television. I no longer practiced, aside from picking up a song or two in the late afternoon, before Teresa came home. I took the time to learn what had happened in the world since the death of Richard Strauss. The television jumbled my viewing days, until I didn't know how many months had passed. I watched the My Lai trial and the crumbling of peace with honor. I watched Wallace get shot and Nixon get reelected and go to China. I watched the Arabs and Israelis recommence their eternal war, pushing the world to the unthinkable brink. I watched Biafra die and Bangladesh, Gambia, the Bahamas, and Sri Lanka get born. I sat still while a handful of pre-Americans declared their own breakaway, recovered country, which lasted for seventy days. And I felt nothing but anesthetized shame.

For one brief moment, it was *nation time*, crowds of people chanting, their voices shaking with the belief that their hour had finally come. Then, just as quickly: no nation. Systematically, the U.S. government buried Black Power. Newton and Seale, Cleaver and Carmichael: The movement's leaders were jailed or driven from the country. Scenes from Attica leaked out, an inferno deep enough to match any nation's. George Jackson was killed by prison guards in San Quentin. He was exactly Emmett Till's age, my brother's age. The official report said he was leading an armed revolt. Fellow inmates said he was set up and murdered. SNCC was broken up for parts and the Panthers destroyed by COINTELPRO. Somewhere out there, my fugitive sister and Robert were hiding, among the other twice-defeated, all those who worked to steal their country back and were destroyed in the process.

When I could not dose myself with current events, I flipped through sitcoms, game shows, and soaps. Nothing Jonah and I were guilty of in all our performing years could match, in sheer flight from the present's nightmare, the best of contemporary culture. Armstrong died, and then Ellington. The heartbeat of what should have been my country's music changed. The thing that replaced it, the official sound track for all seasons that overgrew every cultural niche like kudzu claiming an abandoned vehicle, declared that rhythm consisted of slamming down hard on beats two and four and harmony meant adding a daring seventh now and then to one of two combating chords. There was no place in earshot I wanted to live. It was impossible even to think about performing in front of other people, ever again.

"Have you ever thought about composing?" Teresa asked one night as we were drying dinner dishes.

"I'm okay," I said. "I can get a job."

"Joseph, that's not what I'm asking. I just thought that maybe, with all this time, you might have something . . ."

Something inside me, worth writing down. It hit me—why I was afraid to get another nightclub job. I was afraid that Wilson Hart might really show up someday, wherever I was noodling, and ask to see the portfolio of pieces I'd promised him to write. *You and me, Mix. They're gonna hear our sounds, before we're done with this place.* I was destined to disappoint everyone I loved, everyone who thought there might be something in me worth composing.

Terrie's patience with me was more deadly than any racial assault. I went out the next day and bought a box of pencils and a sheaf of twenty-inch cream-stock music paper. I bought paper with grand staff systems, paper with treble staffs and piano systems, paper with unmarked, unjoined staffs—anything that looked remotely serious. I had no idea what I was doing. I stacked up the blank scores on the electric piano and lined up the pencils in neat rows, each one sharpened to a lethal weapon. Teresa's barely suppressed excitement at my fortress of composition supplies hurt me more than my father's death.

All day long while I waited, jittery, for Teresa to come home, I pretended to write music. Fragments of phrases crawled in clumps here and there across the cream stock, like spiders making nests in the corners of abandoned summer homes. I'd jot down a strain, motif by motif. Sometimes the strains would collide together into near melodies, every articulation literally spelled out. Sometimes they stayed nothing more than a series of tetrachords without rhythmic values or bar lines. I was writing for no ensemble, no instrument at all, not even piano and voice. My imagined audience was spread all over the map, and I could not tell if I was writing pop songs or thorny, academic abstraction. I never erased a note. If a phrase hit a wall, I'd simply start over again somewhere else, on an unused staff. When a page filled up, I'd flip it over and fill the back. Then I'd start another.

These were the longest days of my life, longer by far than my days in a Juilliard practice room, longer, even, than the days I'd spent at the side of my father's hospital bed. I worked it out at one point: I was writing down about 140 notes an hour—two and a third triads every three minutes. Sometimes the act of filling in a single note head could absorb me for half an afternoon.

My bits of graphite scratching remained stubbornly wooden. The puppet refused to sit up and speak. But now and again, at enormous intervals, always when I'd lost track of myself and forgotten what I was after, the edge of something truly musical would shake loose. I'd feel myself racing ahead of myself, out beyond the phrase, into the next arc of a line whose accidentals were there even before my pencil could fix them. My whole body would rally, drawn up into the forward motion, throwing off the leadenness I'd felt for years, without feeling. I'd flood with more ideas than I could hold, and I had to force my pencil into a panicky shorthand just to keep up. For the length of this rush of notes, I owned music's twelve tones and could make them say what life had only ever hinted at.

But then I'd make the mistake of going back and playing these self-propelling themes out loud. After a few chords, I'd begin to hear. Everything that I wrote down came from somewhere else. With a rhythm slightly bobbed or taken out, a pitch swapped or altered here and there, my melodies simply stole from ones that had used and discarded me sometime in the past. All I did was dress them up and hide them in progressive dissonance. A Schütz chorus we sang at home, pieces from Mama's funeral, the first Schumann *Dichterliebe*, the one that Jonah loved, split ambiguously between major and relative minor, never to resolve: There wasn't an original idea in me. All I could do—and that, only without knowing—was revive the motives that had hijacked my life.

When Teresa finally did come home after work, she'd try clumsily to mask her thrill at my growing stack of penciled-up pages. She still couldn't read music very well, and there wasn't much music there for her to read. Sometimes, even before she'd changed out of her briny factory clothes, she'd stand at the piano and ask, "Play a little for me, Joseph." I'd play a bit, knowing she'd never hear the rip-offs hidden in it. My scribbles made Teresa so happy. Her $120 weekly wage was barely enough to support her on her own. But she gladly floated me, and would go on doing so forever, all in the belief that I was making new music for the world.

Our shared fantasy of two-part harmony would start up again each night, tiding us over until the next morning. Sometimes the two of us could find nothing better to do together than watch television. Dramas about white people suffering the hardships of rural life, miles from civilization, years ago. Comedies about working-class bigots and the lovably hateful things they said. Epic sporting conflicts whose outcomes I can't remember. The national fare of the 1970s.

Teresa didn't like watching the news, but I pushed. Eventually, she caved in and let us watch David Brinkley over dinner. My sense that the world was ending slowly died out, leaving me with the sense that it already had. I fell into the most powerful of addictions: the need to witness huge things happening at a distance. I had the zeal of a late-day convert, my whole sheltered life to make up for. Here were storm and stress, all the violent, focused disclosures of art, on a scale that left the music I was fiddling with flat and pointless.

We were watching one night when I found myself staring down Massachusetts Avenue, past the drugstore where I'd once bought an ID bracelet for Malalai Gilani and failed to get it inscribed. My path up to that very evening seemed, for a moment, to be the piece I was so desperate to write, the one I'd set down in memory during all those hours in the practice rooms at Boylston. Teresa was the woman Malalai had grown into, or Malalai the girl I'd thought Teresa had been. Of course the bracelet wasn't inscribed; it had been waiting for my adulthood to inscribe it.

The camera panned down Mass. Ave., the tunnel of my life unfolding on Teresa's eleven-inch television screen. Then by some nonsensical cut meant to deceive those who'd never lived there, the camera jumped impossibly from the Fens to Southie, the other side of Roxbury. Children were getting off a bus. The voice of invisible network television authority declared, "Children bussed to their first day of school were met with . . ." But the sound track meant nothing. We had only to look: rocks and flying sticks, a fury-twisted mob. Teresa clamped down on my arm as children outside the arriving busses gave a delighted, drunken first-day welcome: *"Hey, nigger! Hey, nigger!"*

It read like some primordial, inbred scene that was supposed to have died out in the swampy South, back before my childhood's end. I forgot what year we were in. This year. This one. Teresa's eyes stared straight ahead, afraid to look at me, afraid to look away. "Joseph," she said, more to herself than me. "Joe?" As if I could be her explanation. A white girl from Atlantic City, watching this scene. A girl whose father had for years told her where all the trouble came from. And in her look, I saw what I looked like to her. She wanted the news story to end and knew it couldn't. She wanted me to say something. Wanted to pass over, as if nothing needed saying.

I pointed at the screen, still excited by the sight of my old neighborhood. "That's where I went to school. The Boylston Academy of Music. Six blocks up that street and make a left."

I'd known for a long time, but it took me years to admit. War. Total, continuous, unsolvable. Everything you did or said or loved took sides. The Southie busses were only news for a quarter of a minute. Four measures of andante. Then Mr. Brinkley went on to the next story—the crisis in the space program. It seemed humankind had walked on the moon half a dozen times and brought back several hundred pounds of rock, and now it didn't know what else to do with itself or where else in the universe it wanted to go.

I lay next to Teresa that night, feeling the length of her tense with me. She needed to say something, but she couldn't even locate the fact inside herself. In that silence, we belonged to different races. I didn't know what race I belonged to. Only that it wasn't Ter's.

"God should have made more continents," I said. "And made them a lot smaller. The whole world, like the South Pacific."

Teresa had no idea what I was talking about. She didn't sleep that night. I know—I was awake to hear her. But when we asked each other the next morning, we both said we'd slept fine. I stopped watching the news with her. We went back to singing and playing cribbage, working at the factory and plagiarizing the world's great tunes.

Another year collapsed, and I heard nothing from my sister. Wherever she and Robert were hiding, it was nowhere near my America. If they'd risen again in the already-amnesiac seventies under assumed names, they did not risk notifying me. Somewhere during those missing months while I'd watched TV, I'd turned thirty. I'd celebrated Jonah's the year before that, sending him a little cassette of Teresa and me performing a Wesley

Wilson song, "Old Age Is Creeping Up on You," with Teresa doing a scary Pigmeat Pete and me supplying a little Catjuice Charlie in the response. If Jonah ever got the tape, I never heard. Maybe he thought it was in bad taste.

He did write. Not often, and never satisfactorily, but he did let me know what was happening. I got the story in bits and pieces, in clippings, reviews, letters, and bootleg recordings. I even heard accounts from envious old school friends who'd stayed in the classical ghetto. My brother was making his way, stepping into the world he knew would eventually belong to him. He was one of the new wave's newer voices, a breath of fresh revision from an unexpected quarter, a rising star in five different countries.

He lived in Paris now, where no one questioned his right to interpret any piece of vocal music that fell within his copious range. No one challenged his cultural rights except, of course, on national grounds. The reputation that had plagued him in the States—that his voice was too clean, too *light*—melted away in Europe. There, they heard only his limber soar. They handed him a beautifully furnished future to move into. They called him "effortless," Europe's highest compliment. They said he was the concert tenor the 1970s had been waiting for. They meant that as a compliment, too.

Now that he had no bad rap of lightness to overcome, Jonah often soloed with orchestras. The reviews adored how he could make even the most complex, thickly layered twentieth-century textures feel airy and audible. He soloed under the same conductors whose recordings we'd grown up on. He performed Hindemith's *Das Unaufhörliche* with Haitink and the Concertgebouw. He did the tenor solo in Szymanowski's Third Symphony—*The Song of the Night*—with Warsaw, standing in for the ailing Józef Meissner, who let the understudy do the role only twice before racing back to reclaim it. The French critics, suckers for discovery, praised the still-little-known piece as "voluptuous" and the increasingly visible singer as "floating, ethereal, and almost unbearably beautiful."

But Jonah's new signature piece was *A Child of Our Time*, Michael Tippett's haunted wartime oratorio, the present's answer to Bach's *Saint Matthew Passion*. Only Tippett's protagonist was not the Son of God, but a boy abandoned by all divinity. A Jewish boy, hiding in Paris, enraged by the Nazi persecution of his mother, kills a German officer and touches off a pogrom. In place of Bach's Protestant chorales, Tippett sought something more universal, more able to cross all musical borders. His material reached him by chance, on a wartime radio broadcast: the Hall Johnson Choir performing Negro spirituals.

Here was the hybrid piece Jonah was born to sing. How the Europeans connected him to the music—what they heard or saw—I can't imagine. But over the course of a few years, my brother sang the massive work with four conductors and three orchestras—two British and one Belgian. He recorded the piece in 1975 with Birmingham. It made his name, everywhere except in his own country. In the wads of newspaper clippings he sent me, often with not even a note, he was depicted as a still-young voice pushing outward, threatening to become a secular angel.

He'd called me from Paris, back in 1972, in tears at the news of Jackie Robinson's death. "Dead, Mule. Rickey threw the poor bastard into the cauldron and wouldn't let him do anything but hit the ball. 'I want a man who's brave enough not to fight back.' What shit is that, Joey? A lose-lose situation, and the man *won*." I couldn't tell why he was calling. My brother knew nothing about baseball. My brother hated America. "Who's hot now, Mule?"

"You mean singers?"

"Ballplayers, you bastard."

I hadn't a clue. The Yankee broadcasts were hardly on my daily diet.

Jonah sighed, his breath echoing down the transatlantic delay. "Mule? *It's a funny thing.* I had to move here to learn how hopeless I am. This whole City of Light crap? Total fabrication. One of the most smugly racist towns I've ever lived in. New York makes this place look like Selma. They want to see a birth certificate before they'll sell me cheese. I got beaten up by this guy down in the Thirteenth. Really beaten. Don't worry, bro. I'm talking six months ago. Went at me with fists. Broke a molar. I'm sitting there slapping him like some gonad-clipped castrato, thinking, *But they don't have a Negro problem here!* I'm thinking Josephine Baker, Richard Wright, Jimmy Baldwin. I'm telling this guy, 'Your people *love* my people.' Turns out—the accent, the heavy tan—he thought I was Algerian. Punishing me for the revolution. Jesus, Mule. By the time we're dead, we'll have paid for every sin on earth except our own."

Riffing for me. But who else would buy this performance? Paris was no better or worse than any capital. What crushed him was the loss of his would-be hideout. He'd dreamed of total self-reinvention, a home that would grant him a permanent reentry visa. No place on any implicated continent would ever give him that.

"I don't know how much longer I can live here, Joey."

"Where would you go?"

"I'm thinking maybe Denmark? They love me in Scandinavia."

"Jonah. They love you in France. I've never *seen* such notices."

"I'm only sending the good ones."

"Are you sure that leaving Paris is smart, professionally? How will I reach you?"

"Easy, fella. I'll be in touch."

"Do you need cash? Your share . . . your account with the money from the house . . ."

"I'm flush. Let it ride. Play the market or something."

"It's in your name."

"Great. So long as I don't change my name, I'm in business." He made a quick accelerando—"Miss you, man"—and hung up before I could miss him back.

The longer I composed, the more fraudulent I became. My notes were going nowhere but backward. Even I couldn't abuse Teresa's arts grant forever. Unfit for any honest work, I advertised for piano students. I worked forever on the ad: "Juilliard-trained"—I never claimed to have *graduated*—"concert pianist, good with beginners . . ." It amazed me to think how the words *concert pianist* still conjured something in this country, long after concerts ceased to draw.

Sometimes parents jerked when they met the man behind the ad. They let their child take a token lesson. Then they apologized, explaining that their child really wanted to study the cornet. It never bothered me. I wouldn't have studied piano with me, either. I couldn't see why anyone wanted to study piano anymore anyway. In another few years, we'd all be replaced with Moog synthesizers. To the electronic future, the best musicians already proclaimed, *Those of us already dead salute you.*

But somehow, I managed to draw students. Some of them even seemed to enjoy playing. I got eight-year-old working-class kids who hummed over the keys. I got middle-aged recidivists who simply wanted to play the "Minute Waltz" again in something under a hundred seconds, before they died. I taught natural talents who got by on an hour of practice a week and earnest acolytes who'd go to their graves trying to play those lines that taunted them in their sleep, floating just out of reach of their fingers. Not one of my students would end up onstage except at their school's talent show. They or their parents were still victims of that discredited belief that equated playing a little piano with being a little more free. I tried to fit the student to the path, to have each one pick his or her own way through the centuries of overflowing repertoire. One little middle-class *Mayflower* descendant caught fire with his father's old John Thompson method, striving to play every poky folk tune at flat-out prestissimo. The daughter of two Hungarian escapees who came over in the wake of '56 giggled her way through Bartók's *Mikrokosmos*, screwing up her face at the gentle dissonances in the contrary motion, hearing some dim echo that wasn't, any longer, even racial memory. I had no blacks. The black students of Atlantic City studied in some other classroom.

I worked to make the dying notes come alive. I had my students play at glacial speeds, doubling the tempo every four bars. I sat next to them on the piano bench, playing the left hand while they played the right. Then we switched and started over again. I told them this was an exercise in developing two brains, the clean split of thought needed for independent equal-handedness. I tried to make them see that every piece of music was an infant uprising that stumbled onto democracy or died on the page.

I taught one girl, a high school junior, named Cindy Hang. She wouldn't tell me her real first name, her birth name, although I asked her several times. She said she was Chinese—the answer of easiest resort. Her father, a loan officer from Trenton who'd adopted her, along with a younger Cambodian boy, said Hmong. Her English was a soft-pedaled mezzo piano, although her grammar already ran rings around her native-born classmates. She spoke as little as possible, and when she could get away with it, not at all. She'd come to the piano late, starting only four years before, at thirteen. But she played like a crippled cherub.

Something in her technique startled me. Out of pure greed, I gave her ridiculous pieces—Busoni, Rubenstein—show pieces and schmaltz I had no stomach for. I knew they'd come back in a few weeks, pulsing as I'd never heard them. Like the Bible translated into the clicks and hums of whales: incomprehensible, alien, but still recognizable. Her fingers invented from scratch the idea of harmonic structure. She listened with them, a safecracker feeling the tumblers through gloves. She stroked the keys as if apologizing to them in advance. But even her lightest touch had the force of a refugee displaced by organized violence.

Every lesson with Cindy Hang left me feeling criminal. "I've got nothing to teach her," I told Teresa. Saying even that much was a mistake.

"Oh, I bet there's all sorts of things you can teach her."

Her voice fell into a note it never sounded. But I refused to be baited. "Anything I teach her will destroy what she does. She has the most amazing touch."

"Touch?" Like I'd hit her.

"Ter. Sweetie. The girl is only seventeen."

"Exactly." Her voice clutched tight to nothing.

Things got worse. After Cindy's lessons, I felt Teresa straining for the ordinary. She'd ask, "How'd it go?" And I'd answer just as casually, "Not bad." I had a lengthy mental list of pieces I couldn't assign the girl—*Liebesträume*, the *Moonlight*, "Prelude to a Kiss," any *Fantasie*. All the while, Cindy Hang worked harder and played more dazedly, no doubt wondering why the better she performed, the more remote her teacher became.

I had felt no desire for the child until Teresa suggested it. Then, in the smallest, deniable increments, she grew to consume me. I'd meet her nightly in my dreams, the two of us thrown together in some mass wartime deportation, reading each other's needs without the weight of earthbound speech. I dressed her in navy blue, a midcalf dress with wide shoulders, now four decades out of date. Everything was right, except the hair, which curled in my dreams. I'd put my ear to that brown ravine beneath her clavicle, the one saw in waking, while she sat upright on the bench, playing for me. When I touched my ear to her skin, the blood coursing underneath it sounded like chant.

Cindy Hang's skin was perfect—that nonaligned brown belonging to half the human race. I loved the girl for her vulnerability, her total bewilderment at where she'd landed, the tentative attempts at recovery in her fingers' every probe. I loved how she sounded, as if she'd come from another planet—something this planet would never house. I told myself for weeks there was no problem. But I wanted something from Cindy Hang, something I didn't even know I wanted until Teresa's jealousy pointed it out to me.

We played together, Mozart's D Major Sonata for piano four hands, Köchel 381. I assigned the piece just to allow me to sit by her on the piano bench. There are only four profound measures in the piece; the rest is mostly note spinning. But I looked forward to it as to nothing else in my life. It brought me back da capo, to where I'd started. We played the middle movement together, a little slower than it should go. She took the upper part and I supported her. My lines were full and broad. Hers were the lightest exploration, like a bird foraging. I felt I was striding through a crowded fairgrounds with a happy child on my shoulders.

One lesson, we played it perfectly. Under our fingers, the modest little piece completed what it was meant to do in this life. We finished playing, my pupil and I both aware of what we'd just done. Cindy kept still on the bench next to me, head down, looking at the keys, waiting for me to touch her. When I didn't, she looked up, her mouth a crooked smile, desperate to please. "We can try it again? From the beginning?"

I called her father. I told him that Cindy was extremely talented, "a real musician," but that she'd outgrown everything I was able to teach her. I could help him find someone who'd move her forward. In fact, I felt secretly sure any other teacher would kill all that was strangest and most luminous in her playing. That scumbled virtuosity of the nonnative speaker wouldn't survive her first real lesson. But whatever another teacher might do to her was better than what I would, if she studied with me another week.

Cindy's father was too confused to object. "Would you like to talk to her? Explain this to her yourself?"

I must have said something absurd, because I can't remember it. I got off the line without talking to her. For months afterward, I said nothing to Teresa. My telling her would only confirm her fears. When I told her at last, she was truly miserable, all the misery that only truth can bring. She dragged around for two weeks, trying to fix things. "Maybe you should give up teaching, Joseph. You haven't worked on your own music since you started."

I stopped dreaming of Cindy Hang, except for that strange, surgical otherworldliness of her playing. In her hands, the long lines of Europe became something they'd never recognized in themselves. I never heard the likes of her sound again. Alone of all my students, the girl might have learned to make music at will. But the way she played would have had to die, on the way to any real stage.

Banishing Cindy brought Terrie and me closer for a while, if only in shared guilt. Teresa had given up more to live with me than I could ever repay. I carried that fact around with me like a prison record. I grew daily more certain that she couldn't afford to be with me. She wanted to devote herself to someone who'd devoted himself to the thing she loved most in all the world. She wanted to marry a musician. It was that simple. She wanted me to marry her. She thought that signing the papers, making it official, would destroy our perpetual anxiety and bring down all walls. *He's my husband,* she could explain to the venomous cashiers, to the men who followed us down the street, threatening, to the police cars tracking our public movements. *He's my husband,* she'd say, and they'd have no comeback.

Sometimes at night, stirred by our closeness in the dark, she brought it up in whispers. She painted a fantasy for me, a house, a sovereign state of our own with its own flag and national anthem, perhaps a growing populace. I never objected, and in the dark, she took my willing listening as assent.

With the future in limbo between us, my ability to make music do anything fell almost to zero. The world away from the keyboard was even worse. Running the vacuum for half an hour exhausted me. A trip to the grocery store swelled into an expedition to scale Everest. *Maybe we ought to marry,* I thought. *Marry and move to someplace survivable.* But I didn't know how. If Teresa just took care of everything, handled all the mechanics, told me when it was over . . .

Inert, I figured that the odds of my dying before having to act on anything like an implied promise would eventually grow overwhelming. I was over thirty, the age beyond which no one was to be trusted. Teresa closed in on the same landmark, the age beyond which an unmarried woman probably never would be. It should have seemed natural to me. It was what I'd grown up knowing: a spouse of each color. But a quarter of a century had beaten the natural out of me. All my family's lessons had reduced to one: No one marries outside their race and lives.

Teresa thought of me as half white. We sang together, and never had a problem. She thought she recognized me. She saw me working away, trying to write white music. Everything I kept from her allowed her to go on thinking as much. Once she asked about my father's family. She wanted something to attach to. "Where are they from?"

"Germany."

"I know that, goof. Where in Germany?"

I didn't have a good answer. "They lived in Essen, until the war. My . . . father was from Strasbourg, originally."

"Originally?"

I laughed. "Well, originally, I guess they all came from Canaan."

"Where?" All I could do was touch her hair. "Well, where are they all now?" Not a hesitation. She was that pure.

"Gone."

She worked on this. Her own people had cut her off, but she knew where everyone was. She still sent cards on every cousin's birthday, even if the rate of return had dropped near zero. "Gone?" Then it hit her, and she needed no more clarifying.

She asked about Mama's people. I told what I knew. Doctor grandfather and his wife and children in Philadelphia "When can I meet them, Joe?" No one called me Joe. "I'd be happy to go with you, anytime." I couldn't even tell her. We weren't even close enough to be different species.

I saw what I was doing to her only by accident. Once a week, I still went through her collection and learned a track for her. After dinner, I sat down at the Wurlitzer, fiddled around on arpeggios, then launched into an introduction. Her game was to figure out the tune and be ready to sing on the first verse's downbeat. She always was, her face alight, as if I'd just handed her a wrapped gift. One night in April of 1975, we ripped through a try at "There's a Rainbow Round My Shoulder," a song I'd never come across until that afternoon. Terrie got as far as

> Hallelujah, how the folks will stare,
> When they see the diamond solitaire,
> That my little sugar baby is gonna wear!
> Yes, sir!

She broke off, a mangle of laughing and crying. She came and threw her arms around my shoulders, and for another few measures, I goofed around on five straitjacketed notes. "Oh, my Joe-bird. We've got to do it. Got to make it legal!"

I looked at her and said, like some 1930s hepcat, "Whatever my little sugar baby wants. Who am I to break the law?" She seemed as happy at these words as if we'd gone and done the deed already. Just the intent seemed enough.

Two weeks later, rooting through her records in search of another captive, I glimpsed a sheet of fancy rag paper sticking out from a stack of books on her writing desk. The color caught my eye, and I excavated it, a handmade wedding invitation. Across its middle, there bent a great rainbow arc. Along the top ran the hand-lettered message: "There's a rainbow round my shoulder." Inside the arc, she'd penned, "And it fits me like a glove." Below, in a file of straight lines, Teresa had written, "TIME," "DATE," and "PLACE," all of which she'd left trustingly blank, pending happy consultation with me. Under these, she'd written, "Come help us celebrate the union of Teresa Maria Elisabeth Clara Wierzbicki and Joseph Strom." At the very bottom, in a jaunty hand, she'd added, "Hallelujah, we're in love!"

The thing sunk into my chest up to the hilt. She wanted people there, a public declaration. I might somehow have managed to slip off to a justice of the peace, provided we never actually told anyone. But a wedding, with invitations: impossible. To whom could she have thought we'd send invitations? My family was dead and hers had disowned her. We shared no friends in common, none who would come to such a party. I pictured her scenario: walking down the aisle of some religious structure, part Catholic, part A.M.E., part synagogue, her Polish factory workers and my Black Panther connections eyeing one another across the median. The two of us, in front of a room of people, cutting into a three-tiered wedding cake. Hallelujah, how the folks would stare.

I buried the unfinished project back under her books, just as I'd found it. I never said anything. But she knew. Something in the way I behaved toward her, too brightly affectionate. I kept bracing for the presentation, the finished invitation. *Here: I made this for you.* But the moment never came. Teresa's handmade celebration disappeared from the stack on her desk into some solitary hope chest she never opened for anyone.

That's when I gave up all pretense of composition. I boxed up my sheaf of pencil-scratched music stock and consigned it to storage.

I heard from Jonah again, not long after. He never made it to Scandinavia. "Dear Bro," his letter started. "Big doings here. I've found my calling." As if singing with the London Symphony Orchestra and l'Orchestre philharmonique de Radio-France had been a wrong number.

I was in Strasbourg, doing the bounding tenor bit to the millionth rendition of the almighty NINTH this season, a truly gimmicky performance in the new "Capital of Europe," with soloists, conductor, and musicians from two dozen countries. Not sure who I was supposed to represent. We were thundering around the back stretch when, all of a sudden, the grotesqueness of the situation finally dawned on me. All my life, I've been this dutiful trooper for late-day cultural imperialism. *Alle Menschen werden Brüder*: Christ on a bloody crutch. Gimme a break. What planet does that guy live on? Not ours; not the Planet of the Apes.

I got through the piece all right, but afterward, I developed this profound allergic reaction to everything past 1750. I canceled three engagements, all big, blowsy nineteenth-century puff pieces. I managed to stumble through a large-forces staging of *The Creation* down in Lyon without tossing my cookies, but it was nip and tuck . . . When I got back to Paris, I happened by chance to catch this group from Flanders, a dozen singers, performing at the Cluny. I've never heard anything like it. Like landing after a long, rough flight and having your ears pop. In all those big-hall, 150-performer things, I'd forgotten what singing was supposed to be about . . . A thousand years of written-out scores, Joey. And we've only ever bothered with the last century and a half. We're living in this one little wing of a rambling mansion . . . A thousand years! You have any idea how big a place that is?

Big enough for my brother to disappear into at last.

It's taken me a while to purge my voice of all the tacky tricks and show-time shit I've been stroked for these last few years. But I'm finally clean. I've followed this group, the Kampen Ensemble, up to Ghent, and at last I have a worthy teacher again, after a long, lonely spell in the desert: Geert Kampen—a real master, and one of the most musical souls I've ever met. I'm just another reed in his little collegium, and we're hardly the only group plunging into this stuff. Suddenly, the past is the coming thing. There's a whole school up in the Netherlands, and one's even starting back in Paris. Something's happening. A whole wave of people reinventing early music. I mean the earliest. Just wait, Mule. This movement will hit the States in a few years. You guys are always behind the times, even when it comes to being behind the times! And once it hits, you'll see: Nostalgia will never be the same again . . .

I've learned not to speak French in the Flanders shops, though German doesn't go over a whole lot better. Even English doesn't entirely convince people I'm not a Turkish "guest" laborer here to take coal-mining jobs away from the natives. I am, however, never safer than when the words are sung. I did manage to salvage the best of Paris and carry her up to civilization with me. Her name is Celeste Marin. She knows all about you, and we're both waiting for you to get your ass out here so you can meet my new woman and hear my new voice. Better hurry. Not even the past can last forever.

I read the letter with mounting panic. Halfway through, I wanted to send him a telegram. My brother had achieved a level of success that almost justified the botched experiment our parents made of us. And on the verge of real recognition, he'd taken it into his head to walk away again, into some cult. My own disaster of a life lost its last shot at redemption. So long as I'd sacrificed myself to launch Jonah, I hadn't entirely wasted myself. But if he bagged everything, then I was truly lost. I started to write him, but I couldn't. I had nothing to say except *Don't do it. Don't throw away your chance. Don't trash your calling. Don't mock Beethoven. For God's sake, don't move to Belgium. Above all, don't marry a Frenchwoman.*

I bought some recordings by the Kampen Ensemble, which I had to special-order. I listened to them in secret when Teresa wasn't home, hiding them, like porno, where she'd never come across them, even by accident. The crumhorn-infested disks had an alien charm, like coming across an elaborate piece of wrought iron in a dusty store, something that meant life or death to some farmer once but which now had no function in the whole known world. Nothing in the thickets of complex counterpoint remotely resembled a hummable tune. The singers pared their voices back to dry points and reined in their phrases until nothing wavered or swelled. Everything we'd most loved in music was only hinted at, waiting to be born. I couldn't hear what electrified Jonah. He was a master chef who'd perfected the secret of nuanced sauces renouncing the kitchen and taking to nuts and berries. It seemed a cheap escape. But then, I was a second-rate, fifteen-hour-a-week piano teacher and abortive composer, living off a factory worker's good graces. In Atlantic City.

Alone during the day, I took the contraband records out and listened. The third time through the earliest Kampen Ensemble disk, an old Orlando Lassus song separated itself from the other chansons. "Bonjour mon coeur." I'd known the tune from before it had been written. "Hello my heart, hello my sweet life, my eye, my dear friend." And in the piece, I heard myself, at my first hearing. I backed down that narrow air shaft the wrong way, before our years of touring, before Juilliard's prison practice rooms, before Boylston's chamber choir, down below our earliest family evenings, each of us on an independent part. "Hello my completely beautiful, my sweet spring, my new flower." In the song's first four notes, I stood outside that stone room where I'd heard that tune for the first time. I'm seven; my brother is eight. My father has just taken us to the northern tip of the island, a medieval cloister, where singers unravel their amazing instant. "My sparrow, my turtle dove. Good morning, my gentle rebel." And afterward, my brother declares, "When I grow up? When I'm an adult? I want to do what those people do."

I didn't know then who "those people" were. I didn't know now. I knew only that we weren't them. Hearing the song, I was filled with an urge to return to the Cloisters, a place I hadn't been for decades. Standing in that place might spring some memory, take me back to where we were headed, help me find what was happening to Jonah. I asked Ter if she'd like to go to the city. Her eyes shone like hard candy.

"You kidding me? Manhattan? Just you and me?"

"And six and a half million potential mass murderers."

"New York, New York. My man and me, loose in the city!" It had been some time, it seemed, since we'd taken a holiday. I'd dragged her underground, into the inner keep of my isolation, and she had followed, for music's sake. But there was no safety, it had turned out, even in solitude. Especially there. "NYC! We're going to start at Bloomie's and head south. And we're not going to stop until we find you a suit."

"I have a suit."

"A modern suit. A nice concert suit, with a nice flare and without any safety pins holding it together."

"Why in the world would I need a suit?" Teresa shrank from my words, and the light went out. "I need to get shoes first," I said, and she returned a little.

I suggested that after we'd shopped, we might head up to see the Cloisters. Teresa thought the place was a sporting arena. Her eyebrows bounced when I told her. "I didn't know you were Catholic!"

"I didn't, either."

We spent the morning shopping in public, a compendium of my largest private hells. Teresa dealt with all slights as she always did, pretending that everything shy of direct aggression wasn't happening. "What are pianists wearing onstage these days? What's in style for concert attire this year?"

"Not this," was all I could say.

Her frustration mounted. Anxious about making it to Washington Heights, I agreed to a hopeless, brown, double-breasted thing of no use except to further drain savings. "You sure? This is good, you think? You'll be a babe slayer in it, anywhere you play. I'll tell you that much, buster."

We left the suit for alterations, giving me another week to bail out of the purchase and lose no more than the deposit. We took the Uptown A. All the while, hanging on her strap, Teresa sang Ellington and Strayhorn in my ear, like the most shameless out-of-town tourist. Feeling the bored smirks of every passenger in the car, I harmonized sotto voce.

They'd rearranged the Cloisters in the years since I'd been—moved the stones, shrunk them down, simplified the vaults and capitals. Teresa couldn't figure out the ersatz medieval grab bag. "You mean this guy just went around buying up monasteries all over the place?"

"The ways of white folk are beyond understanding."

"Joseph. Don't do that."

"Do what?"

"You know what. How do you *buy* a monastery anyway?"

"Huh. How do you *sell* one?"

"I mean, buy a Spanish, get a Portuguese half price?" I squeezed her until she glinted. "And then they just put them all back together like some big jigsaw? Buy me one of these, Joseph. Nice row of columns. Wouldn't these look great in the backyard?"

"We'd need a backyard first."

"You're on. I'd settle for one of those. Can I get that in writing?"

She loved the Unicorn Tapestries, and she cried for the beast in captivity. *"Einhorn,"* I said out loud.

"Say what?"

"Nothing."

This was my outing; Teresa couldn't understand why I wasn't enjoying these extraterrestrial artifacts. I ran through the rooms, blasting past the exhibits with less attention than Jonah and I had given them a quarter century earlier. I stepped into the cold stone room where we had heard our singers that day, and I saw my brother leap up from the chair to touch the pretty lady who had come to sing for us. Beyond that, no messenger. We abandoned the time hole after an hour. Teresa was elated; I felt more listless than I had since hearing from Jonah. He'd moved on to a world whose key I couldn't find.

"Let's walk." Teresa nodded, happy with any idea I put to her. We cut through Fort Tryon Park. I looked for two boys, seven and eight, amid the crowds lining the paths, but I couldn't find us among so many like-colored decoys, all speaking Spanish. The wave of Dominicans had begun, one that would, in another decade, recolonize the island's tip as a million Puerto Ricans had once colonized Brooklyn and East Harlem throughout my childhood. The aging Jews were still there, those who'd refused to move south to a city of Cuban escapees. Strangers who'd have greeted my father on sight pulled back from me in fear. Written already, in their faces: The lease had expired on this, their neighborhood.

"There's a bakery around here," I said to my Polish Catholic honky shiksa. "Right around here someplace."

But I was turned around. We dragged up and down streets, stumbled upon the concrete steps—completely changed—doubled back along our path until Ter had had enough. "Why don't you just ask somebody?"

Approach a stranger: The idea would never have occurred to me. We asked a deliveryman. "Frisch's Bakery?" I might as well have been speaking Provençal. "In your dreams, maybe." Finally, one promenading woman wearing a silver suit dress and a turquoise and smoky quartz bracelet stopped, more out of alarm than pity. She was out for a stroll in her finest attire, as if the city hadn't gone to hell in a hackney all around her since the war. It surprised her that I spoke intelligible English. She could have been my aunt. The fact would have killed her on the spot.

"Frisch's? Frisch's up on Overlook?"

"Yes, that's it! That's the one." Edging away, palms up, harmless.

My *Tante* snorted. "You're going to need more than good directions. It closed down ages ago. Ten years, if you're lucky. What are you looking for, dear?" Her voice bent down with burden, her penance for coming to this mixed land.

Teresa, too, turned to me. Yes, what *are* you looking for?

I spoke my humiliation. *"Mandelbrot."*

"Mandelbrot!" She examined me to see how I could have discovered this secret password. "Why didn't you say so, dear? Frisch's, you don't need. Down to the next street, make a left. Halfway up the block on your left."

I thanked her again, in zeal proportional to how worthless her information was to me. I cupped Teresa by the shoulder and dragged her off toward the street *Tante* had indicated.

"What's *Mandelbrot*, Joseph?" In her mouth, the word turned to enriched flour.

"Almond bread." Lost in translation.

"Almond bread! You like almond bread? You never told me. I could have made you . . ." Teresa, her face contorted, struggled with the indictment. *If you'd only told me, brought the affair home and put her into bed with us.*

We found the bakery. Nothing resembling Frisch's. The thing they sold as *Mandelbrot* might as well have been cinnamon toast. We sat on a bench and picked at it, our day in the city ending. I looked up the street at a man combing through a wire-mesh trash can. Tomorrow was just that light on the horizon, rushing to catch up with yesterday. This was the street Da had brought us along, telling us how all the universe's clocks kept different times. The same bench, though *same* seemed meaningless.

We'd eaten nothing all day. But Teresa picked at her almond bread as at some stale Communion wafer. She tore off hunks and tossed them to the pigeons, then cursed the birds for swarming her. I sat next to her, waylaid in my own life. The boys and their father passed us while we sat on this bench, but they didn't yet know how to see us. There was no place I could get to from this where and when. I rose to go, but I couldn't walk. Teresa was clamped onto me, holding me in place. "Joseph. My Joe. We have to make it legal."

"It?" Trying to smash all clocks.

"Us."

I sat back down. I studied the man working the trash can, who was unfolding a shiny packet of aluminum foil. "Ter, we're good. Aren't you happy?" She looked down. "Why do you always say 'make it legal'? You afraid of being arrested? You want some contract in case you need to sue me?"

"Fuck the law. I don't give a shit about the law." She was crying, forcing her words through closed teeth. "You keep saying okay, but nothing happens. It's like your music. You say you want to, but you don't. I keep waiting for you. It's like you're just killing time with me. You think you're going to find somebody better who you'll really want to marry, really want to make—"

"No. Absolutely not. I will never, never find anyone else who . . . is better to me than you."

"Really, Joseph? Really? Then why not prove it?"

"What do we have to prove? Is love about proving?" *Yes,* I thought, even as I asked. *That's exactly what love is.* Teresa leaned her head over her knees and began to sob. I stroked her back in big sweeping ovals, like a child practicing his cursive *O*'s. I learned to write from Mama, but I couldn't remember her ever teaching me. I rubbed Ter's back as she heaved, feeling my hand from some distant, insulated place.

A man in a black suit and crushed porkpie hat, older than the century, shuffled by. At the sound of danger, his shuffle accelerated to a crawl. Then, seeing that our tragedy wouldn't hurt him, he stopped. "Is she sick, the girl?"

"She's fine. It's just . . . *Leid*." He nodded, squinting, and said something in Da's language I didn't catch. All I heard was the brutal reprimand. His shuffle ramped up again, but he stopped and looked back every twenty paces. Checking whether to call the *Polizei*.

I knew Teresa's need for marriage, the one she couldn't speak. If she married, her family might relent and retrieve her. If we stayed as we were, we'd confirm their worst slander. She'd be forever living in sin with a freeloading black who didn't even care enough to give her a ring.

But marriage was impossible. It was wrong in a way I couldn't begin to say. My brother and sister made it impossible. My father and mother. Marriage meant belonging, recognizing, finding zero, coming home. The bird and the fish could fall in love, but the here and now would scatter every thieved twig they might assemble. I don't know what race Teresa thought I belonged to, but it wasn't hers. Race trumped love as surely as it colonized the loving mind. There was no middle place to stand. My parents had tried, and the results were my life. Nothing I felt the need to reproduce.

I was back in a cold December in Kenmore Square in Boston. My brother, slapped down for kissing a girl of another caste, the first wrong turn of his life, was telling me that we were the only race that couldn't reproduce ourselves. I'd thought him crazy. Now it seemed obvious. Of all the music Teresa and I might raise our children on, there wasn't a single tune that could be theirs, unquestioning, unquestioned, sung the way they breathed. Teresa thought she'd gone beyond race. She thought that she'd paid already. She had no idea. I had no way of telling her. "Teresa. Ter. How can we?"

I wasn't sure what I was trying to say. But Teresa was. She flung her head up. " 'How can we?' *How can we?*" Her words were terrible, drugged. I thought she might be cracking up. I looked around, scouting for the nearest public phone. "How can we *sit* here?" Her enraged red face swung back and forth, a refusal so violent, it begged for restraint. Her words slurred crazily. "How can we *live* together? *Talk* to each other?" She half-stood, then slammed down again. She turned away from me, suffocating, her lips twisting without sound. Her arms were in front of her, tearing in disgust at the air. I wrote big, cursive, reassuring *O*'s into her back until, in a fury, she wheeled around and flung my hand at me. I didn't dare move. Toward or away—equal disasters. My head was blank, pitchless, colorless. If she'd had a knife, the woman would have used it. Then Teresa calmed. That's what time is. Da explained it to me once. Time is how we know which way the world runs: ever downward, from crazed to numb.

We went back to Atlantic City together, obeying some force one notch down from choice. We resumed living together in a kind of suspended motion of dead people. The battered wedding plans never arose again, except in our thoughts, every minute we were in each other's presence. Time did its randomizing run. Two more months down the further slope, my brother called. Teresa picked it up. By that electric pause after she said hello, I knew it was him. Her receiver hand started to shake, excited: Yes, it was Teresa, yes, *that* Teresa, and yes, she knew who he was—all about him, where he was—and yes, his brother was there, and yes, no, yes, and she giggled, completely seduced by whatever little half-hearted sweet talk he worked on her. She handed the phone to me, soft as she hadn't been since we took our death holiday in the city.

"She's got a pretty voice, Mule. You sing with her?"

"Something like that."

"What's the top of her range?"

"How you doing, Jonah?"

"You sure she's Polish? She doesn't sound Polish. What's she look like?"

"What do you think? How's Celeste?"

"Not taking to Belgium too well, I'm afraid. She thinks they're all savages here."

"Are they?"

"Well, they do eat fries with their mussels. But they sight-read like nobody's business. I want you to come see for yourself."

"Whenever. You got a ticket for me?"

"Yep. When can you leave?" We hit one of those big rallentando measures, the kind we used to take so effortlessly together, in late Romantic lieder. Mutual mind reading, under the gun, two moving targets. We still had it. "Need you, Mule."

"Have you any idea what you're asking? You haven't a clue. It's been years since I've played anything real." I glanced up, too late, at Teresa, who was fussing with the coffeemaker. Her face was broken. "Anything classical, I mean."

"No, bro. *You* don't know what I'm asking. There're pianists on every street corner here, selling little ivory-coated pencils to make ends meet. That, or they're on the National Arts Register dole. I wouldn't be calling if all I needed was a damn piano player."

"Jonah. Just tell me. Make it fast and painless."

"I'm forming an a cappella group. I have two high voices that'll make you want to take your own life. Gothic and Renaissance polyphony. Nothing later than 1610."

I couldn't stop laughing. "And you want me to—what? Keep your books for you?"

"Oh, no. We'll hire a *real* crook to do that. You, we need for the bass."

"You've got to be kidding me. You know the last time I sang seriously? The last voice lesson I had was sophomore year in college."

"Exactly. Everyone else I've listened to has been ruined by training. You, at least, won't have anything to unlearn. I'll give you lessons."

"Jonah. You know I can't sing."

"Not asking you to *sing*, Mule. Just asking you to be the bass."

He went through the arguments. He was after an entirely new style, so old that it had passed out of collective memory. Nobody knew how to sing this stuff yet; they were all improvising. Power was dead—vibrato, size, fire, lacquered glow, all the arsenal of tricks for filling a big concert hall or soaring above an orchestra had to be killed off. And in their evac-uated place, he needed lightness, clarity, pitch, angels on pins.

"Imperialism's over, Mule. We're going back to a world *before* domina-tion. We're learning to sing like ancient instruments. Organs of God's thoughts."

"You're not going spiritual on me, are you?"

He laughed and sang, "Gimme that old-time religion." But he sang in a high, clear *conductus* style, something from the Notre Dame school, eight hundred years ago. "It's good enough for me."

"You're mad," I said.

"Joey, this is about blending. Merging. Giving up the self. Breathing as a group. All the things we used to think music was, when we were kids. Making five voices sound as if they're a single vibrating soul. So I'm out here thinking: Of everyone I know in the world, who reads me the best? Who do I share the most genetic material with? Whose throat is closest to mine? Who has more musical feeling in his little finger than anyone else has in their whole—"

"Don't patronize me, Jonah."

"Don't argue with your elders and wisers. Trust me on this, Mule. Have I ever not known what I'm doing?" I had to laugh. "I mean, recently."

He talked logistics. What he wanted to sing; how to best lift this new, unborn group into orbit. "Is it viable?" I asked.

"Viable? You mean can we make a living?"

"Yes. That's what I mean."

"How much money did you say we ended up with, from Da?"

I might have known: funded, our whole lives, by our parents' deaths. "Jonah. How can I?"

"Joey. How can't you? I need you. Need you in on this. If this thing happens without you, it's meaningless."

When I hung up, I saw Teresa cowering in the corner, an old white lady whose home had just been broken into by a dark young man. She waited for me to explain what was happening. I couldn't. Even if I'd known.

"You're going to him, aren't you? You're going over there." I tried to say something. It started as an objection and ended up a shrug. "Fuck you," Saint Teresa said. My honeysuckle rose. "Go on. Get out. You never wanted me. You never wanted to make any of this happen." She leaned forward, her head darting, looking for a weapon. Teresa shrieked at me, full voice, for all the world to hear. If our neighbors called the police, I'd spend the rest of my thirties in jail. "From the beginning, I've made myself over for you, for anything that might . . ." She broke down. I couldn't take one step toward her. When her head came up, her words were brittle and dead. "And all along, you were just waiting for him to call with some better offer."

Conviction entered her, the true fire of performance. She ran to the shelf that carried her hundreds of LPs, and with the kind of strength mothers tap into when they lift automobiles off their pinned children, she tore the shelf out of the wall and filled the room that had been ours with a trash heap of song.

Rootie comes. "It's a miracle," Da says. That much is obvious, even to me. First she's pale and milky, like a potato without the skin. In a few weeks, she's brown, like a potato with the skin back on. Nothing is one color for very long. First, Root is smaller than the smallest violin, but soon she's too big for me to lift easily. Just like Mama was big before Ruth came, and now she's back to small again.

I ask Mama if Root will be in our school. Mama says she already is. Mama says everybody's in school, always. "You?" I giggle at the idea, embarrassed. "Are *you* still in school?" She smiles and shakes her head, like she's saying no. But she's not. She's saying the saddest yes I've ever heard.

Jonah's faster than I am in lessons, but Mama says when we're alone that that's because he had a head start. I try harder, but that only makes my brother try harder, too, just enough to stay ahead and beat me. Every day, we do something we've never seen before. Sometimes even Mama's new to it. Little Rootie just lies there and laughs at us. Da's away teaching physics to grown-ups because everyone's always in school. When Da comes home, we play at more school, right through dinner and into the evening, when, to close each day, we sing together.

But even before the singing at day's end, we have songs. Songs about animals and plants, the presidents, states and capitals. Rhythm and meter games about fractions; chords and intervals for our times tables. Experiments with vibrating strings teach us science. We learn birds by their calls, and countries by their national anthems. For every year that we study in history, Mama has the music. We learn a little German, French, and Italian through snippets of aria. A tune for everything, and everything a tune.

We go to the museums or the park, collecting leaves and insects. We take tests—sheets of questions on smudgy newsprint that Mama says the state needs in order to see if we're learning as much as other boys. Jonah and I race through, trying to get the most questions done the fastest. Mama sings to us—"The race is not to the swift"—and makes us go back over.

Life would be practice for paradise if it were only this. But it isn't. When the other boys on our street come home from their schools, Mama sends us out—"at least one hour"—to play. The boys always find something wrong with us, and our punishments are always new. They blindfolded us and hit us with sticks. They use us as home plate. Jonah's not big enough to try to refuse. We hide in secret alley spots, inventing stories to tell Mama on our return, spending the hour singing funny, dissonant rounds, rounds so soft that our torturers can't hear.

Mama has an answer for the world. When we're out together, at the dentist's office, in the grocery store, or on the subway train, and someone says something or shoots us the evil eye, she tells us, "They don't know who we are. They think we're somebody else. People are floating in a leaky boat," Mama says. "Afraid they're going under." Our mother has an answer for that fear. "Sing better," she says. "Sing more."

"People hate us," I tell her.

"Not you, JoJo. They hate themselves."

"We're different," I explain.

"Maybe they're not scared of different. Maybe they're scared of same. If we turn out to be too much like them, who can they be?" I think about this, but she doesn't really expect an answer. She cups us both by the crowns of our heads. "People who attack you with *can't* are afraid you already can."

"Why? How can that hurt them?"

"They think all good things are like property. If you have more, they must have less. But you know, JoJo? Everybody can make more beauty, anytime they need."

Months later: "What do we do if they attack?"

"You've got a weapon stronger than anyone's." She doesn't even have to say it anymore, she's said it so often. *The power of your own song.* I don't correct her. I no longer tell her that I don't know what that means.

I come home one day, my upper-right canine knocked out by a boy three years older. I don't tell my mother. It would only hurt her. When she sees my new gap, she shouts. "You're getting so big, JoJo. So big so fast." But the new tooth is weeks coming in. I smile at her, every chance I get. Once, she looks away, crying in what I think is shame at her gap-mouthed boy, grinning his obliging toothlessness. I'll take fifty years learning to read her.

Why do we need to go out at all? This is what we boys want to know.

Why can't we stay in and read, listen to the radio, pitch pennies or skip rope in the cellar for exercise, like Joe Louis does? My parents can read each other's minds. They always give the same answer to these questions. They practice in advance. They know when the other has already built up a boy's will or countered a boy's won't.

"This family's not fair," Jonah says. "Not a real democracy!"

"Yes, it is," Da tells him. Or maybe Mama. "Only, big people get two votes."

They complete each other's sentences and finish each other's half-sung phrases. Sometimes, humming out loud over breakfast or housecleaning, they land on the same downbeat of the same tune, a piece neither has sung for weeks. Spontaneous unison. At the same tempo, in the same key.

I ask Da, "Where do we really come from, Germany or Philadelphia? What language did we speak before we learned English?"

He studies me to see what I'm really asking. "We come from Africa," he says. "We come from Europe. We come from Asia, where Russia really is. We come from the Middle East, where the earliest people came from."

That's when Mama chides him. "Maybe that was their *summer* home, sugar."

I know ten names: Max, William, Rebecca, Nettie, Hannah, Charles, Michael, Vihar, Lucille, Lorene. I see family pictures, but not many. On bad nights, when Ruth is ill or something has broken between Mama and Da, I send these names messages.

Jonah asks, "What color was Adam?" He smirks, knowing he's breaking the law.

Mama looks at him sideways. But Da brightens. "This is a very good question! On how many issues do science and religion give exactly the same answer? All of the peoples on earth must have the same ancestors. If only memory were a little stronger."

"Or a little weaker," Mama says.

"Think of it! Arising once, in one place."

"Except for those Neanderthal stallions jumping the fence."

Da blushes, and we boys laugh, too, no clue except the general silliness. "Before that, I mean. The first seed."

Mama shrugs. "Maybe that one blew in the window. From outdoors."

"Yes," Da says, a little startled. "Probably you are right!" Mama laughs, nudging him in scandal. "No, truly! This is more likely than native-grown. Given the earth's youth, the size of all outdoors!"

Mama shakes her head, her mouth bunched up on one side. "Well, children. Your father and I have decided. Adam and Eve were little and green."

We boys laugh. Our parents have gone mad. Speaking total nonsense. We can't understand a word. But Jonah understands something I don't. He's faster, with a long head start. "Martians?"

My mother nods gravely, our great secret: "All of us, Martians."

All the world's people: We get them in geography, history. Tens of thousands of tribes, and not one of them ours. "We have no people," I tell my parents one night before bed. I want them to know. Protect them, after the fact.

"We *are* our people," Da says. Every month he writes letters to Europe. Searching. He's been doing that for years.

Mama adds, "You're out front of everyone. You three just wait long enough, everybody's going to be your people." We cobble up a national anthem out of stolen parts.

"Do we believe in God?" I ask.

And they say, "Let each boy believe in his own fashion." Or something like that, just as unhelpful, just as impossible.

My mother sings at churches. Sometimes she takes us with her, but Da, never. The music is something she knows and we don't. "Where does it come from?" Jonah asks.

"Same place all music does."

Already, Jonah isn't buying. "Where's it going?"

"Ah!" she says. "Back toward *do*."

We stand next to her in the pews, hands to the flat of her hips, feeling the vibrations coming through her dress, the deep fundamentals that surface from her with such clear power that people can't help but turn around and stare at the source. We go to churches where everyone pretends not to look. We go to churches where the sound is ecstatic, cheered and clapped every which way, picked up and rolled into a dozen unplanned codas. We go to a place where the thundering, swaying, bliss-swelling choir sends a heavy woman in front of us into convulsions. She leans over, and I think she's pretending to be sick. I laugh, and then I stop. Her body switchbacks side to side, first in time to the music, then cut time, then triple double. Her arms work like a sprinter's, and her breasts fly out like counterweights to her heaving. A girl, maybe her daughter, holds her and sways with her, still singing to the music that mounts up from the choir. "Day is coming. Day is coming. When the walls will all come down." The woman next to her, a perfect stranger, fans her with a handkerchief, saying, "That's right; that's all right now," not even looking. Just following the mountain of music.

Maybe she's dying. My mother sees my first-time terror. "She's all right, JoJo. Just coming through."

"Through to where?"

My mother shrugs. "To where she was before she came here."

Every church we visit has its own sound. My mother sings them all, running beyond the roll of the notes. Shining like that far horizon, where all notes go. What you love more than your own life must finally belong to you. What you come to know, better than you know your own way home, is yours.

At night, we sing. Then music envelops us. It offers us its limited safety, here on our street, however long a way it has come. It never occurs to me that the sound isn't ours, that it's the last twitch of someone else's old, abandoned dream. Each piece we do springs into being right here, the night we make it. Its country is this spinet; its government, my mother's fingers; its people, our throats.

Mama and Da can sing right off the page, songs they've never seen before, and still sound like they've known them from birth. We sing a song from England: "Come Again, Sweet Love Doth Now Invite." Soon we all climb up that scale together—"to see, to hear, to touch, to kiss, to die"—building step by step until we pull back at the peak, the "die" at the top of the phrase just a plaything sound we fondle, tuning to one another. Five phrases, sparkling, innocent, replaying the courtiers' party game from the day of this tune's making, that festive beauty, financed by the slave trade.

Jonah loves the song. He wants more by the same maker. We sing another: "Time Stands Still." It takes me until this moment, *this one*, setting these words down half a century on, to find my way back, to come through to this song. To see the day and place we were signaling all those times we took the song on the road. To hear the forecast in that read-through. For prophecy just remembers in advance what the past has long been saying. All we ever do is fulfill the beginning.

"Time stands still with gazing on her face." I gaze and time stands. My

mother's face, soft in the light of this song. We sing a five-part arrangement, which Jonah makes us take so slowly that each note hangs in the
air, a broken pillar with vines growing over it. That's all he wants: to stop
the melody's forward motion and collapse it into a single chord.

He doesn't want us to finish. But when we do, for one last little specious now, he's in bliss, the bliss underneath the chord. "You like the old
ones?" Da asks. Jonah nods, although he hasn't once thought that any of
these tunes might be older than another. They're all the same age as our
parents: one day younger than creation.

"How old is that song?" I ask.

Our father's eyes sweep upward. "Seventy-seven and three-quarters
Rooties."

My sister howls with pleasure. She waves her hands in the air. "No,
no!" She puts her palm on her chin, her index on her cheek, her elbow in
her other hand, mocking the posture of thought. Already she's eerie,
copying postures and poses, donning their worldliness as if she understands them. "I think it's . . . yes!" Her finger shoots into the air, her head
bobbing *eureka*. "Seventy-six and three-quarters Rooties! Not counting
the first Rootie."

"How many Mamas?"

Da doesn't even have to think. "Just over eleven."

Mama's offended. She pushes away his attempt to hug her. "Almost
twelve."

I don't understand. "How old is Mama?"

"Eight and a half hundredths of this song."

"How many yous?"

"Ah! This is a different question. I've never told you how old is your
old man?" He has, a million times. He's zero, no years old at all. Born in
1911, in Strasbourg, then Germany, now France, on what was then
March 10, but during the hours that were lost forever when Alsace capit-
ulated and at last adjusted its clocks to Greenwich. This is the fable of his
birth, the mystery of his existence. This is how a young boy's life was
snared by time.

"Not even nine of him," Mama taunts. "Your old man is an *old* man.
Only nine of your father's great long lives, and you're back to Dowland!"

My parents are different ages.

"Nay," my father says. "One may not divide by zero!"

I don't ask how many Jonahs, how many Joes.

"Enough foolishness." Mama is the queen supreme of all American Stroms, now and forever. "Who let all this math in the house? Let's get on with the counting."

Stand still and gaze for minutes, hours, and years to her give place. Our father discovers how time is not a string, but a series of knots. This is how we sing. Not straight through, but turning back on ourselves, harmonizing with bits we've already sung through, accompanying those nights we haven't yet sung. This is the night, or might as well be, when Jonah cracks the secret language of harmony and breaks into our parents' game of improvised quotations. Mama starts with Haydn; Da layers on a crazed glaze of Verdi. The bird and the fish, out house hunting, lacing the nest with everything that fits. Then Jonah, out of nowhere, adding his pitch-perfect rendition of Josquin's *Absalon, fili mi*. And for that feat, at so tender an age, he wins from my parents a look more frightened than any look that strangers have ever painted us with.

And later, when Einstein comes by the house for music night, playing his violin with the other physicist musicians, he needs give only the slightest push to shame my parents into sending their boy away. "This child has a gift. You don't hear how big. You are too close. It's unforgivable that you do nothing for him."

The nothing my mother has given him is her own life. The unforgivable thing she's guilty of: the steady rhythm of love. "The child has a gift." And who does the great white-maned man think has given it to him? Every day, a school for that gift, costing no less than everything. She gives up her own gift, her own growth, her own vindication. But this is blackness, too: a world of white, declaring your efforts never enough, your sounds insufficient. Telling you to send the boy off, sell him into safety, let him fly away, give him over to mastery, lift him over that river any way you can. Never telling you what land you send him to, there on the far side.

Maybe she dies never questioning. Thinking the size of her boy's skill has forced her hand. Believing in the obligation of beauty, a willing victim of high culture. Maybe she dies not knowing how there is no better school than hers. For here's her boy, her eldest, stealing the keys of music, that music denied her. I see the look my parents trade then, pricing the experiment they've been running. Calculating the cost of their union.

What of Ruthie's gift, had Mama lived? My sister, at four, is the fastest of all of us, latching onto the most elaborate melody, holding it high and clear, whatever the changing intervals around her. Soon, she is a genius mimic, doing Da, doing Mama, destroying in pitch-perfect parody her brothers' walk and talk. Wheezing like the postman. Stuttering sententiously like our parents' favorite radio sage. Doddering like the aged corner grocer until Mama, gasping through tears, begs her for mercy. This is not parroting, but something more uncanny. Root seems to know things about human invention that her handful of years can't have taught her. She lives in the skin of the people she replicates.

But my sister is a lifetime younger than we are. Three years between us: time enough to split us beyond recognition. Each of us is a fluke of our one thin moment. Four and a half years from this night, Mama will be where no years can touch her.

Her death cuts us all loose in time. Now I'm almost twice my mother's age. I've come through some warping wormhole, twisting back to see what she looked like, reflected in the light of her family. Her face stands still with gazing on all that it won't live to see. Now it is as old, as young, as all other things that have stopped.

With nothing to check my memory, I can trust nothing. Memory is like vocal preparation. The note must center in the mind before the voice can land on it. The sound from the mouth has been sent out long beforehand. Already she opens to me in that look, one that takes years to reach me: her terror at hearing her prodigy son. This is the memory I send on ahead, my clue to the woman, when all other clues are long gone. She trades the look with my father, seeing what they've made, a secret, terrible acknowledgment: *Our child is a different race from either of us.*

I get my own look from her, to set alongside that one. Just once, and so fleeting that it's over before she launches it. But unmistakable: It comes three days before I leave to join my brother in Boston. I'm taking what both of us know is our last private lesson together. We've been working through the Anna Magdalena notebook. Most of the pieces are already too easy for me, although I never say so. Even great players still play these, we tell each other. It's a family notebook, Mama says, something Bach made to build his wife a home in music. It's a family album, like the Polaroids my parents keep of the years we've been through. Postcards savored and kept safe.

Da is at the university. Ruth is on the floor, ten feet from the piano, working on her clothespin-family dollhouse. Mama and I flip pages in the album. We're supposed to be doing social studies—the developing nations—but we're playing hooky, with time so short. There's no one to scold us. We play through a pack of easy dances, stretching them, jazzing them, as light as rain in the desert, turning to dust before it hits the roofs.

We turn to the arias, the part of the notebook we love best. With them, one of us can sing and the other play. We do number 37, "Willst du dein Herz mir schenken." Mama sings, already a creature from another world. But I can't hear that from here, the only world where I've ever lived. I start in on number 25, but before we can get three measures into it, Mama stops. I do, too, to see what's wrong, but she waves frantically for me to keep playing. Rootie the mimic is towering above her clothes-pin family, standing as she's seen Mama do a thousand times, posed in front of a room full of listening people, Mama herself, at one-third size. Little Root's voice enacts an adulthood already in her. She takes over from my mother "Bist du bei mir," singing it for her, to her, *as* her.

My seven-year-old sister has learned the stream of German words phonetically, just from hearing Mama sing it two or three times. Ruth can't understand a word she sings in her father's language. But she sings knowing where every word heads toward. She sings the song Mama and Da played in my grandparents' parlor on his first visit there. *Ach, wie vergnügt wär' so mein Ende.* Ah, how pleasant would my end be.

I play it through, and Rootie sails smoothly into harbor. Mama holds herself, her hands knotted in front of her, motionless, conducting. At the end of the song, my mother stares at me, dumbstruck. She begs me, the only other soul within earshot, for an explanation. Then she moves to Ruth, stroking and marveling, cooing and combing in thrilled disbelief. "Oh, my girl, my girl. Can you do *everything?*"

But for an instant, she sounds me. Da isn't here; I'm her only available man. Maybe it's me—the *me* who sees her now, half a century on—whom she seeks out. Her eyes strike down with prophecy. She searches me for explanations of what's to come. She hears it in Ruth's song: what's waiting for her. In her panicked advance look, she makes me promise her things I can't deliver. Her look swears me to a vow: I must take care of everyone, all her song-blasted family, when I'm the only one who re-members this glimpse of how things must go. *Watch over this girl. Watch over your brother. Watch over that hopeless foreign man who can't watch over any-thing smaller than a galaxy.* She looks right at me, forward across the years, at my later self, grown, broken, the only person who stands between her and final knowing. She hears effect before cause, response before call: her own daughter singing to her, the one tune that will do for her funeral.

She packs me off to Boston to join my brother. On the day of my real departure, she's all pained smiles. She never mentions the moment again, even in her eyes. I'm left to think I must have invented it.

But I was there for the rehearsal. And there again, with Ruth, in concert. And still here, brought back to do the encore, although my every performance was able to save exactly no one. Half a century past my mother's death, I hear that cadence she caught that day. She doesn't anticipate what will happen to her so much as she *remembers* it. For if prophecy is just the sound of memory rejoining the fixed record, memory must already hold all prophecies yet to come home.

MEISTERSINGER

He met me at Zaventem Airport, Brussels, like a limo driver looking for his fare, holding up a hand-lettered sign reading PAUL ROBESON. The grand tour of Europe's capitals had done little for his sense of humor.

In fact, I was glad for the cue. I might have missed him in the crowd without his waving the stupid sign for all countries to see. He had a beard, a little goatee midway between Du Bois and Malcolm. He'd grown his hair almost to his shoulders, and it was straighter than I could have imagined. He'd gotten *bigger*, for want of a better word, although his weight hadn't changed from his days at Juilliard. The sea green shiny jacket and steel gray trousers added to the performance. He seemed more pallid. But then, he'd been living in a country where the sun canceled appearances more often than a hypochondriac diva. He looked like Christ should have been depicted these last two thousand years: not a Scandinavian in a toga, but a scruffy Semite clinging to the edge of northeast Africa, the oldest contested border between colliding continents.

He was more excited to see me than I expected. He waved the placard in the air, doing a little allemande. I dropped my bags at his feet and snatched the sign out of his hand. "Mule, Mule." He hugged me, rugburning my scalp with the butt of his hand. "We're back, brother." I was giving him something. I didn't know what. He grabbed the larger of my suitcases, groaning as he deadlifted.

"It's your fault," I said. "They almost didn't let me through customs, with all the peanut butter."

He sniffed the bag. "Ah! My country's supreme contribution to world culture. This stuff's going to kill us—on a good baguette."

525

"I had to throw away half my wardrobe to make room for it."

"We have to rethread you here, anyway." He picked at my clothes. I noticed the males around us, each with an urbane, shiny variant of Jonah's own seasick tones. We pushed through the gauntlet waiting at the arrival door. "You get away okay?"

I lifted my shoulders and let them fall. I'd left Teresa, feeling as if I'd swung my legs out of bed and stepped on the collie that watched dutifully over me at bedside. Everything from my collarbone to my knees felt scrubbed hollow with steel wool. Teresa had nursed me through the anesthesia of my father's death just so I could feel this: a jittery water-slide ride out over nothingness, into total autonomy. Everything I looked on felt like death. Even this airport wore the lurid colors of a Gothic Crucifixion.

Above the Atlantic coming over, trapped inside a bank of gauzy cumulus, I thought my skin was scaling off me. The seat tray, the paperback book I clutched, the seat underneath me all atomized. The choice to go to Europe closed back up around me, like the Red Sea in reverse. I'd abandoned a woman devoted to me, to devote myself again to my brother. I'd finally given up waiting for my sister to contact me, and I had left her no forwarding address. After such leaving, nothing could be wholly good again. I felt as miserable as I ever have in this life. And as free.

Jonah saw how shaky I was. I opened my mouth to answer his question, but no word cleared. Around us, heavy cigarette smoke, the scent of salty black anisette candy, posters for products priced in imaginary currencies whose uses I couldn't guess, fragments of opaque language over the airport PA, leather suits and pastel dresses in outlandish and jagged cuts all eddied, illegible to me. I lived nowhere. I'd left my mate. I'd put everything decent and certain to the match. There was no one to save me from the aloneness that had always wanted me but my even more uncoupled brother. I opened my mouth. My lips threatened to keep on opening until they peeled off. Nothing would snag into sound.

"She'll live," Jonah said. He put his arm around me, humming some pulsing organum I couldn't make out. "Don't change your money here. It's theft. Celeste's waiting at the car. We're parked illegally. All of Europe's parked illegally. Come on. I can't wait for you to meet her."

We walked through the universal carbolic of airports, here mentholated. Conversations broke over us like newscasters covering the fall of Babel. A party of fey windmill faces fringed in straw made me think

Dutch, until Portuguese invective poured out of them. A knot of swarthy smugglers—ridges of black bushy eyebrow cresting their foreheads—had to be Albanian, yet they swore at one another in singsong Danish. Turks, Slavs, Hellenes, Tartars, Hibernian tribesmen: all past tagging. I felt I was back in New York. Only the Americans were dead giveaways. Even if they babbled in Lithuanian, I knew my countrymen. They were the ones in white shoes and the J'AIME LA FRANCE stickers on their carry-ons.

Jonah dragged me through the arrival area as through a New Wave film. *Europa*. I should have felt something, some shock of recognition, having dedicated my life to re-creating this place in the colonial wilds. But I didn't; not a spark. I might as well have been air-dropped deep into Antarctica. A hospital chill crept up my legs as we descended the escalator. We came out in front of the terminal. The first spring breezes of Flanders blew over me, and I thought I might suffocate. I needed Teresa like I needed air. And I'd deliberately come to a place where I'd never be able to reach her.

We crossed to the parking lot. Jonah stopped traffic with one hand, the way von Karajan pulled the full stampede of the Berlin Philharmonic into a brusque ritard. Ranks of Peugeots and Fiats seemed parked sideways, each no longer than a real car was wide. In front of us, a cigarette-dangling father and elegant, scenery-chewing mother herded their pastel children into a car smaller than the ones Shriners used for Independence Day parades. Five toy cars beyond, a mahogany woman in a shock white blouse and red wraparound skirt leaned against a green Volvo. I couldn't help staring. The ensemble—sin red, snow white, forest green, and deep russet skin—was like some newly liberated country's flag. She was breathtaking, and three shades blacker than anything I'd expected to see in Belgium. I imagined I'd be the most conspicuous entity this side of the Urals. I smiled at the worn provincial maps I carried in my head. However this woman had come, her route was at least as unlikely as mine.

We schlepped my bags toward the woman, until I got the sickening sense Jonah was going to try to pick her up, even with his own French mate waiting within earshot. I nudged his shoulder to change course, and he nudged back. I thought, *Not on my first day.* The woman turned when we were ten paces away, too close to duck. Before I could plead innocence, she broke into a dizzying smile. *"Enfin! Enfin!"*

Jonah was all over her, without setting down my bag. *"Désolé du retard, Cele. Il a eu du mal à passer la douane."*

She answered in a stream so rapid, I couldn't make out a word. She seemed happy with me but cross with him. Jonah was amused at the entire world. I was somewhere between the Azores and Bermuda. My chestnut-haired Celeste, with her striped chemise and soft felt hat, slipped her pretty neck into the notch of a custom-made guillotine and waved good-bye. I reached forward to shake the hand of Celeste Marin, the only Celeste there was. She said something welcoming, but all I heard were her lips. I mumbled, *"Enchanté,"* worse than the worst Berlitz flunky. She giggled, grabbed me to her, and kissed my cheeks four times in alternation.

"Seulement trois fois en Belgique!" My brother's scold was pitch-perfect, some hectoring song by Massenet. With all those years of vocal coaching, his overdeveloped ear left him passing for native. Celeste swore floridly. That much I understood. But when she turned and asked me an extended question that couldn't be answered by a coin-flipped *oui* or *non*, I could only tilt my head in what I hoped seemed sophistication and say, *"Comment?"*

Celeste erupted in distress. Jonah laughed. "She's speaking English, Mule, you sharecropping woolhead." Celeste lobbed a few more incendiary profanities in my brother's direction. He cooed her out of her unhappiness. *"Encore une fois."*

Now cued, I made her out. "How does it feel to be out of your country for this first time?"

"I've never felt anything like it," I assured her.

We smashed the bags into the trunk and were off. Celeste rode shotgun and I hid in the backseat. For fifty kilometers along a highway that might have been I-95, except for the road signs in three languages and the tile-roofed towns with their Gothic spires, my brother pestered me with questions about the latest Stateside developments. I couldn't answer most of them. Now and then, Celeste turned around to offer cheese or oranges. When she faced front again, I lost myself in her astonishing fall of hair. It took me thirty kilometers to remember enough French to ask where she came from. She said the name of a town—mere pretty syllables. I asked again: Fort-de-France.

"Est-ce que cela est près de Paris?"

My brother almost drove into the median. "Close, Mule. Martinique."

We got to Ghent mercifully quickly. Friends of Mijnheer Kampen had rented them a row house last renovated in the late seventeenth century. "Fifty smackers a month. They just want to keep it free of squatters. It's on Brandstraat," Jonah announced. "Fire Street." He seemed to enjoy speaking the name. The lot was just big enough to back a two-manual harpsichord into. But the roost went straight up, four stories in all. I was to live in the top, the highest aerie, outfitted with bed, basin, dresser, and two shelves of books I couldn't read. Jonah led me up the stairs and sat a moment.

"She's stunning," I said.

"I've noticed."

"What does she think of your line of work?"

"*My* work? I didn't tell you? She's our high soprano."

I holed up in that attic and slept for two days. When I came back to life, we sang. Jonah took me to a converted packing warehouse two hundred meters from Brandstraat that Kampen's circle leased for rehearsal space. There my brother showed me what had happened to him. He threw his cardigan on the bare floor and dropped his shoulders as if he were a corpse preparing for ocean burial. He rolled his head through three complete circles. And then, like the silver swan, he unlocked his silent throat.

I'd forgotten. Maybe I'd never known. He sang in that empty packinghouse as I hadn't heard him sing since childhood. Every nub in his sound had been burned away, all impurity purged. He'd found a way at last to transmute baseness back into first essence. Some part of him had already left this earth. My brother, the prizewinner, the lieder recorder, the soloist with symphonies, had found his resounding no. He sang Perotin, something we'd had in school only as history, the still-misshapen homunculus of things to come. But in Jonah, all stood inverted: more good in the bud than in the full flowering. He'd found the freshness of *always*, of *almost*. He made that vast backward step sound like a leap ahead. The whole invention of the diatonic, everything after music's gush of adolescence had been a terrible mistake. He hewed as closely to a tube of wood or brass as the human voice allowed. His Perotin turned the abandoned warehouse into a Romanesque crypt, the sound of a continent still turned in upon itself for another sleeping century before its expansion and outward contact. His long, modal, slowly turning lines clashed and resolved against no harmony but themselves, pointing the way down a reachable infinity.

His voice sounded the original prime. He'd gotten past any emblem that others had made of him. In the United States, he'd looked too dark and sounded too light. Here, in the stronghold of medieval Ghent, all light and dark were lost in longer shadows. His voice laid claim to a thing that the world had discarded. Whatever this sound had once meant, he changed it. Our parents had tried to raise us beyond race. Jonah decided to sing his way back *before* it, into that moment before conquest, before the slave trade, before genocide. This is what happens when a boy learns history only from music schools.

His voice was the child's I once sang with, back at our lives' downbeat. But onto the boy's free-ranging soar, he grafted a heavier-than-air flight all the more exhilarating, filled with fallen adulthood. What had once been instinct was now acquired. The range had pushed upward by urgent relaxation. Time was already grinding his sound down, pulling it back in to earth and amnesia. The dullness that all voices suffer simply by sticking around long enough already announced itself in his tone's zenith. But his turns felt even surer, more wire-guided, as precise as radar, like a monk's surprise levitation in his isolated cell.

He showed me his new voice, exposing a tender wound. He was like someone who'd walked away from an accident, transfigured. He sang for only thirty seconds. His sound had pulled in so it might fit anywhere and never be denied. It defined itself, like a split in the side of the air. Everything that had happened to us, and everything that never would, returned to me, and I began to cry in recalling. This once, he didn't mock me, but just stood, shoulders dropped, tilting his head toward where that sound had gone. "You're next, Joey."

"Never. Never."

"Right. It's *never* that we're after."

He broke me down, all that day and the next. We worked for hours before he let me even make a peep. He stripped me back to the root, reminding me. "Drop everything. You won't know how much you're carrying until you set it down. Let your skeleton hang from the base of your head. You knew how to do this, years ago. A baby holds himself with more grace than any adult. Don't try," he whispered from above the battlefield. "You're *being* too much. Be nothing. Let it go. Lower yourself into your own frame." He opened me from the core until I stood, a hollow tube. How much work it took to find the effortless. We went for days, until I couldn't hear him, but only a voice inside me, repeating, *Make me an instrument of your peace.*

On the third day, he said, "Breathe a pitch." I knew by then not to ask him which. He brought me up from a trance of repose into simple resonance. "God's tuning fork!" He aimed only for solidity, sustain. He turned me into a solitary menhir, out in a green field, his fundament, his bass, the rock on which he could build perfect castles of air.

Everything I knew about singing was wrong. Fortunately, I knew nothing. Jonah didn't insist that I forget everything I'd ever learned about music. Only everything I'd learned since leaving our home school.

He bid me open my mouth, and, to my amazement, the sound was there. I held the pitch for four andante beats, then eight, then sixteen. We sustained long, whole tones for one whole week, and then another, until I couldn't say how long we'd been at it. We cycled out each other's notes, blending. My job was to match my shaky color to his exact shade. He tracked me through my whole range. I felt each frequency coming out of me, focused and shaped, a force of nature. We held unison pitches all the way out to tomorrow. I'd forgotten what bliss was.

"Why are you surprised?" he said. "Of course you can do this. You used to do it every night, in another life."

He banned me from the group's rehearsals. He didn't want me thinking about anything but pure held tones. When Celeste or the other Kampen disciples—a Flemish soprano named Marjoleine deGroot, Peter Chance, an astonishing Brit countertenor, or Hans Lauscher, from Aachen—gathered in the warehouse, trying out their sounds in various ensembles, I was sent back to my upper room to meditate on C below middle C.

Now and then, Jonah let me out for breaks. With a fold-up tourist map, I explored my new city. Jonah gave me a sheet of data he'd written out longhand, to hand to strangers if I got lost. "Careful. Don't jog anywhere. Don't say anything in Turkish. They'll still beat you bloody, just like back home."

A hundred steps from our front door, I could be in any year at all. I determined to take Flanders in, and Flemish, too, the way Jonah taught me to take in my own voice. I absorbed the streets at random, wandering through a place that had been going downhill since 1540. Shards of Ghent stuck out from the past's sooty mass, gems that history forgot to spend before it died. I loitered along the guild houses on the Koornlei or roamed the torture museum of Castle 'Gravensteen. I wandered into St. Baafs Cathedral by accident and found myself standing in front of the greatest artwork ever painted. In the unfolded *Mystic Lamb*, three times longer than me, I saw the mythic silence that my brother wanted to sing.

Nothing about this place was my home. But neither was America anymore. I'd simply traded the discomfort of citizenship for the ease of a resident alien. I mimicked the native dress, ditched my tennis shoes, and never spoke an unsolicited word aloud. From the distance of four thousand miles and eight hundred years, I saw what I had looked like to my native land.

After two months, we tried a song. We did Abbess Hildegard: *"O ignis spiritus paracliti, vita vite omnis creature"*: "O fire of the comforting spirit, life of the life of all creation." Jonah intoned the words, and I joined him in unison. We zeroed out the motionless chant. Then we set out on thousand-year-old canons. Jonah wanted to relive the birth of written music, to reach out for the extreme of what we weren't, a thing we ought never, in a thousand years, have been able to identify. But we identified, *idem et idem*. He needed me to match his sound, to fuse our voices into a single source, to revive, in this foreign place, our old real-time telepathy. From years of touring, our minds could still meld without a word. We still turned as tightly as schooling fish, not me with him or him with me, but the two of us, fused.

At the keyboard, my fingers could generally do what my head wanted. My voice, so much closer to my brain, could rarely seize the prize. At times, Jonah sloughed me off like a kid flung from the end of a playground chain of Crack the Whip. But our calisthenics brought me up to speed, the speed of stillness, of Abbess Hildegard's extraplanetary flight: *vita vite omnis creature*.

In this way, one day, years before any justice should have allowed it, I recovered a voice. The singer I'd begun life as came back from the dead. Jonah fished me out of myself, all but intact. "How did you know? How could you be sure I was still in there?"

"You used to sing. All the time. Under your breath. At the keyboard."

"Me? Never. You lie."

"I'm telling you, Joseph. I don't lie anymore. I used to hear you."

It didn't matter how he knew, or what he thought he'd heard. I could sing. I'd do: a darker take on his genetic material, solid enough to carry the bass. When I was ready at last—the outward confirmation of his inner ear—Jonah added Celeste. For the first time since our school days, my brother and I made music with someone who wasn't us.

I'd grown no closer to Celeste in Ghent than we'd been in the airport parking lot the day they picked me up. She and my brother had the rapport that exists only between two people incomprehensible to each other. They chattered all the time, but never about the same thing at once. When the three of us were together, the French blazed past my ability to split the elided syllables. Then Celeste would address me in an English so joyously makeshift, all I could do was nod and pray. At nights, in our ancient row house, I heard them doing each other, three stories below. They hummed to each other, like Penderecki's threnody, like Reich, Glass, the new minimalists, the latest rage in stylish circles. Their voices ascended in slurred quarter tones, crested in held dissonant intervals, then cooled off by appoggiaturas. They were busy turning themselves into a new species, and for that, they needed a new courtship song.

So I'd heard Celeste Marin's singing voice already, before we sang together. This daughter of Caribbean business elites—generations of mixed-race rum magnates—sang with *antillais* abandon. But I wasn't prepared for our French fourteenth-century trios. When we three made our first attempt to harmonize, I stopped after eight notes. Her voice *was* Jonah's, pitched up into soprano again, before his voice broke forever. Whatever her voice had sounded like in her days at the Paris Conservatory, before she met Jonah, it now sounded more like a female Jonah than Ruth or Mama ever had.

We tried out a piece—a Solage chanson: "Deceit Holds the World in Its Domain." We surged to the end on rising delight. The last note died away, dust motes suspended in the light of light. I was beside myself. It had been lifetimes since I'd felt so lifted, so afraid. I couldn't sleep that night, knowing what we had. Neither, it turned out, could Jonah. I heard him climbing the wooden stairs to my crow's nest. He came into my room without knocking and sat on the foot of my bed in the dark. "Jesus, Joey. This is it. We're home free." I saw him in silhouette punch the air like some teenager finding himself alone with the ball in the end zone. "All my life. All my life, I've been waiting for this." But he couldn't say what "this" was.

"What about the others?" Some hunger had caught hold of me. I was ready to cast the others aside, rather than let them slow us down even a beat.

Jonah laughed in darkness. "You'll see."

I saw, the next week, when all six of Jonah's hand-selected voices met to sight-read. The others had been singing together in assorted groups for two years, honing their precision sacraments. They'd sprung their combined sounds on audiences in Gothic ghost towns around the Low Countries, France, and Germany. They knew what they might do together, and were having trouble keeping their secret. But five-sixths is as shy of perfection as any fraction. Every new voice starts a group out again, from zero.

I went into that first rehearsal wrecked by stage fright. These people owned the world that I only glimpsed now from a distance. They'd spent their life singing; I was a recovering pianist. The languages we sang were theirs by birth; I got through them by phonetics and prayer. My brother staked his reputation on me. Everything set up for me to fall neatly on my ambiguous face. All I had was a scrap of prophecy, the days through which I came.

We read through a chanson by Dufay—"Se la face ay pale"—and then that oldest of parody masses, based on the same tune. It felt like breaking into a tomb that had been sealed for half a millennium. Ten years later, the rage for authenticity would prohibit using women's voices at all. But for a brief moment, we thought we had the future pegged and the past cleanly identified.

When the body breaks free of its boundary skin, it rises. How many people, trapped in time's stream, get to feel, even for an instant, that they've climbed up out of the current and onto the banks? Jonah grabbed the tenor and the women lifted, three steps and a leap into weightlessness, scraping the keystone of the highest vault. Their certainty powered me, and the notes rolled off the page into the air without my doing much but spotting them.

The blend was so tight that each new imitative line sounded like the same voice curling back on itself. I'd stepped in front of a dressing room mirror and splintered into whole societies. Now and then, the released lines collapsed back into the unity that birthed them. The universe, Da once proved to his own satisfaction, could be described by a single electron, traveling back and forth in time along an infinitely knotted path whose resulting connect-the-dots shapes formed all the matter in existence.

When we finished, the silence we'd opened rang like a bell. Peter Chance, who sang like a van Eyck angel but who spoke like an unsexed Anthony Eden, took out a pencil and began making tiny reprimands in his part. "Anyone care to place a modest wager on our prospects?"

Celeste asked Jonah for a translation. A grinning Marjoleine deGroot supplied it, for Jonah was staring up at the roof beams, exultant. We looked at one another the way musicians do, slant but seeing all, every one of us terrified to try it again. We wanted to put the sheet music down, walk away, and forever protect that moment. Jonah returned to earth and pulled another mass out of his binder. "Shall we have a go at the Victoria?"

The Victoria sailed up past the Dufay, dropped notes and all. The shower of sound from our initial try gave way to the first feel for how to group-drive this thing. Heaven's signal bled in and out, like an FM station in a storm. But the message was firm in us. We sprang loose, cut capers, wheeled about. I was their man. My brother had known. When the notes stopped, Hans Lauscher looked down the bridge of his nose and said, "You are hired. How much do you want an hour?" His accent shocked me: the ghost of my father's.

Celeste blessed me in profuse island slang. Marjoleine, with the closest thing to glee her native climate permitted, threw her Flemish arm over my shoulder and thumped me as if I'd just put a header in the back of the net in a qualifying match against the Netherlands. "You don't know how many basses we have already tried! Good voices, too, but just not right with us. Why didn't you come to us sooner? How much time we would have saved." I looked at Jonah. He grinned without embarrassment, as pleased with his duplicity as he was with his brilliant hindsight.

The fusing of six jagged personalities didn't happen at once. The delicate dance of negotiated tensions obeyed its own musical shorthand. We had our daily doses of nervous outbursts and repaired hysterics. We practiced in a ring of black music stands, everyone but the fastidious Hans in stocking feet. Sometimes we taped ourselves on an old reel-to-reel, and then the six of us lay flat on our backs against the wood floors of our warehouse stage, conducting our prior lives, singing unison encouragements to the fixed fossil record.

We were a synchronized underwater ballet. Ten hands worked the air, shaping the wayward notes, waving like a Flanders wheat field in the wind. Celeste and Marjoleine especially needed to dance, the arc of the music and the line of their muscles weaving and meeting. Peter Chance, who'd spent his choirboyhood in the chancel of King's and had stayed on in Cambridge when his voice broke, delighted in the newfound freedom of movement the group allowed him. Hans Lauscher did at least wag his shoulders, which, for a Rhinelander, was almost *Swan Lake*. Even Jonah, who'd once shamed Mama into keeping still when she sang, and who, during his lieder years, had made unholy drama by standing dead stationary in the crook of the piano, now turned fluid. He crooked his knees and curled forward into the top of his phrase, ready to mount up into empty space and keep on climbing. The use of music is to remind us how short a time we have a body.

When we were hitting on all cylinders, Jonah blessed us. Tied to his omnipotent tenor, we might travel anywhere, run any theft. But when we were off, falling back to earth in a fiery ball like Icarus, his patience grew as thin as a snake's skin. Then six bruised egos spent hours trying to coax the damn carcass back to life again.

We were like a commune or an infant church: from each according to her abilities. Hans was our font of Teutonic scholarship, a walking manuscript library on a par with Vienna or Brussels. Peter Chance, who'd read Renaissance history at King's, was our source on performance practice. Celeste served as articulation coach, softening, closing, and relaxing our vowels while tightening our intonation and polyphonic textures. Marjoleine was the verbal interpreter, glossing sense and phrasing stress points in any language we sang in. I did the structural analyses, finding how best to juxtapose long note values and rapid passages or bring out the subtle undulations of pulse.

But Jonah ruled over us all. His face, our focal point, filled with driven will. Our years apart weren't enough to account for everything he now knew. All I could figure was that he hadn't *learned* it. He remembered, resurrecting that dead world as if it had always been his. Through Kampen, he'd acquired a grasp for early idiom. He knew, within a week of reading a piece, how best to find its otherworldly hum. He could get at the universe hidden in any work, find the meter of a line, play the text, harmony, and rhythm off one another, revealing the message that existed only in the tension among them. He led us through a thicket of counterpoint to those moments of convergence that life denied him.

He shaped the group like a Kyrie. He delayed our first appearance. We were ready to sing for months before we actually did. Each singer went on working outside the group. Marjoleine ran three church choirs. Celeste blasted out background vocals in Europop radio anthems. Hans and Peter both sang and taught. Jonah took on assorted gigs, performing early music, especially with Geert Kampen, whose Kampen Ensemble, now veterans, were our North Star. But the six of us, together, held back for a last bar, reluctant to lose this moment when we were the only ones who knew the ring of possibility.

We sang for Kampen, in the chancel of St. Baafs. The church was deserted except for a few startled tourists. It felt like singing for Josquin himself. When we were done, Mr. Kampen sat in his choir stall, his shock of white hair falling over his forehead. I thought he'd taken offense at some turn in our interpretation. He just sat there, for five whole lento measures, until, behind his tiny granny glasses, the man's eyes dampened. "Where did you learn this?" he asked Jonah. "Surely not from me." And over my brother's horrified objections, he proclaimed, "You must teach me now."

Voces Antiquae debuted at the Flanders Festival in Brugge and followed up at the Holland Festival in Utrecht. We made our initial beachhead in the fifteenth century—Ockeghem, Agricola, Mouton, Binchois, a motley mix of regional styles. But our great signature piece was Palestrina's Mass, *Nigra sum sed formosa*, a private joke between Jonah and me. It's a Daley-Strom thing; you wouldn't understand. Jonah insisted we perform everything from memory. He wanted the danger. Soloists play without music all the time. But if they lose themselves, they can swim up alongside their own fingers, and no one but the fellow in row four with the pocket score is the wiser. With ensembles, each mind's memory map must be identical. Lose yourself and there's no return.

Written music is like nothing in the world—an index of time. The idea is so bizarre, it's almost miraculous: fixed instructions on how to re-create the simultaneous. How to be a flow, both motion and instant, both stream and cross section. While *you* do this, *you*, *you*, and *you* do otherwise. The score does not really set down the lines themselves; it writes out the spaces between their moving points. And there's no way to say just what a particular whole sums to, short of reenacting it. And so our performances rejoined all those countless marriage parties, births, and funerals where this map of moving nows was ever unrolled.

In the world lines traced out in these scores, Jonah at last came into his own at-one-ment. His six voices cartwheeled around one another in unleashed synchrony, each creating the others by supplying their missing spaces. We sang the Palestrina, a piece that, by the kind of rough estimate Da loved, had been performed on the order of a hundred thousand times. Or we brought to life the Mouton manuscript Hans Lauscher discovered, which hadn't sounded a peep since its first performance five hundred years ago. In both cases, we slipped alongside every performance that had happened or was still to come.

That's why Jonah insisted that we surrender the safety of the page. We lived, ate, and breathed the printed instructions until they vanished, until we composed the written-out invention afresh, in the moment of our repeat performance. He wanted us to stand onstage, open our mouths, and have the notes just there, like a medium possessed by the soul she channels. He had us walk out from as many entrances as possible, in our daily clothes, as if we'd just bumped into one another on the street. This was still the era of black-tie concert dress. Jonah had donned monkey suits for years. The biggest shock available to him was the ordinary. We just appeared, as impromptu as the gift of tongues. We stood, scattered across the floorboards, as far from one another as we could get, like some multiple-body physics problem. That gave us maximum voice separation, the fullest possible depth. It made blending, precision attacks, and releases that much harder to pull off, and it left us, each night, courting disaster. But that space turned us into six soloists who just happened to align into a single crystal.

The sound we made glinted like the best hedge against all debased currencies. Jonah wanted every interval redeemed. Every resolved suspension shone out like tragedy averted; every false relation was the drift of a soul in agony; every *tierce de Picardie* delivered a life beyond this one. A reviewer in *De Morgen*, still reeling from the effect, expressed the strongest reservation leveled against us: "If anything, the sonority suffers from relentless divinity. Too many peaks; not enough valleys."

Even that barb was laced with gratitude. Everywhere, for an instant, people wanted to be saved. Our sudden popularity surprised everyone except Jonah. Within a year, every festival in Europe with an arts subsidy wanted us. In that most select of dying worlds, we were the flavor of the hour. Our recording of the Palestrina Masses on EMI—a label that could have bought and sold a hundred Harmondials—won a pair of awards and sold enough copies to pay the rent on Brandstraat through the next century.

A thousand years of neglected music came of age everywhere at once in a dozen countries. Not just our group: Kampen, Deller, Harnoncourt, Herreweghe, Hillier: an avalanche intent on remaking the past. Curators had championed dead music for decades, each with their own new versions of annihilated history to promote. And all that time, audiences had never treated these revivals as anything more than exotic wallpaper. Our new generation of performers was more razor-fine and aura-wrapped, more underwritten by scholarship. But that alone couldn't explain why, for a few years, the *Creator Spiritus* had the nearest thing to a resuscitation it would ever get.

"I have a theory," Hans Lauscher said in a hotel in Zurich.

"Careful," Marjoleine warned. "A German with a theory."

Jonah waved like a referee. "Easy, folks. Switzerland. We're on neutral territory."

Hans flashed the theory of a smile. "Why this rage for a deceased musical style that can mean nothing to anyone? I am blaming the recording industry. Capitalist exhaustion through the flooding of consumer markets. How many more Mozart *Requiem*s can you make? How many Schubert *Unfinished*s? The more we feed our appetites, the more appetite we have. We must give the buyers something new."

"Even if it's ancient," Peter Chance said.

"All music is contemporary," Jonah said. And that's how he wanted us to sing: as if the world would never abandon this instant.

I remember the six of us, after a concert at the Castello di San Giorgio in Mantua, well after midnight in a warm May. The lights of the city threw the castle and Ducal Palace into enchanted outline. We stepped into a town square unchanged since the Gonzaga court stumbled upon the madrigal. We moved through the intact fantasy as through a stage set. "It's a vein!" Celeste exclaimed. "We have a total vein!"

"Indeed," Peter Chance echoed. "We're supremely jammy." As always, I was the only one struggling with English.

"How did we get here?" Marjoleine asked. "I trained for opera. Until a few years ago, I knew nothing before Lully." She looked at Hans, our manuscript scholar.

He held up both hands. "I am a Lutheran. My parents would die all over again if they knew I was singing Latin Masses. You!" he said, fencing my brother with a finger. "You are the one who has corrupted us."

Jonah gazed around the square, by the light of the Gonzaga moon, whose inconstancy he'd just that evening invoked in song. "Not my fault. I'm just a poor black Harlem boy."

Peter Chance let slip a sound, half titter, half censor's whistle. He gave his head a circumspect shake toward Celeste in the moonlight, decodable to everyone. Jonah returned the Cambridge chorister's incredulity with his own, in American dialect. And there in the moon-muted Piazza Sordello, the penny dropped, in five different currencies.

"Are you having us on?" Chance sounded more Oxbridge than I'd ever heard him. "You can't be *serious!*"

"You didn't know? You didn't know!" Some hybrid of amused and crestfallen.

"Well, I knew there was some . . . some ancestry, of course. But . . . you're not *black*, for heaven's sake."

"No?"

"Well, not like, say . . ."

"We have counted up the numbers," Celeste bragged. "We believe I may have as many—*Comment dit-on?*—*arrière-grands-parents blancs* as these men here."

Peter inspected me: I, too, was turning on him. "And how many white great-grandparents, exactly?"

Jonah snickered. "Well, that's being black, you see. Hard to say, exactly. But more white than black."

"That's just my point. How can you call yourself . . . looking the way you . . . ?"

"Welcome to the United States."

"But we're not *in* the damn United . . ." Peter Chance tumbled headlong down the hill we'd made him. At the bottom, he sat in a dazed heap. "Are you *sure*?"

"Are we sure, Joseph?" Jonah's smile was a calm Sargasso.

I turned toward a lost night, the last night I saw my grandfather. "That's what it says on our birth certificates."

"But I thought . . . I was under the impression you were . . . *Jews*?"

"Germans," Hans said. He leaned against the rusticated walls, studying a thread in his shirtsleeve. I couldn't tell how many categories were on the table.

Jonah nodded. "Think Gesualdo. Ives. It's a progressive idiom. Totally archaic. *C'est la mode de l'avenir.*"

Celeste grabbed him under the arm. She clucked her tongue, bored. "*C'est pratiquement banal.*"

"*C'est la même chose,*" I offered. I'd die doing my own brand of Tomming. My very own.

The six of us stood under the Ducal Palace arcade. Peter Chance already looked at us differently. Jonah wanted to say something to break this group apart and lay waste to everything he'd made. But he'd already set alight every other place he might live. I figured the others would slink off in embarrassment, each to their own *gens*. But they hung tight. Jonah stood in the Piazza, a duke about to bid his courtiers good night. "I say we blame this whole early music boom on the English and their damn choirboys."

"Why not?" Hans Lauscher grabbed the chance. "They've had the ownership papers for everything else, at one time or another."

"A British plot," Marjoleine agreed. "They never could sing with any vibrato."

The evening's exchange changed nothing, nothing visible anyway. Voces Antiquae went on singing together, more eerily synchronized than ever. From Ireland to Austria, we fell into what passed for fame, in early music circles. We were doomed to it. What Jonah really needed from that ringing, translucent sound was to be cut loose, unbranded, anonymous, as far away from notice as notice could get. But one last time, music let him down.

Since moving to Europe, I hadn't kept up with the United States. I no longer followed current events, much less current music. I didn't have time, given how hard I had to work to keep from dragging the others down. What little I did hear confirmed me; the place had gone stranger than I could imagine. Its appetite for law and order grew as insatiable as its taste for drugs and crime. I read in a Walloon magazine that an adult American man was more likely to go to prison than attend a chamber music concert.

In a hotel in Oslo, I chanced across an English newspaper headline: FOURTEEN DEAD IN MIAMI RACE RIOTS AFTER POLICE ACQUITTED. I knew what the officers had been acquitted of, even before I read the lead. The paper was a month old, which only added to the horror of knowing. Worse could have happened since, and I'd never hear until too late. Jonah found me in the lobby. I handed the page to him. Giving him a newspaper was like giving Gandhi a stack of soft-core porn. He read the story, nodding and moving his lips. I'd forgotten that: My brother moved his lips when he read.

"We haven't been away as long as it feels." He folded the paper into neat vertical thirds and handed it back to me. "Home's waiting for us anyway, anytime we need it."

Two nights later, in Copenhagen, I realized why he'd dragged me across the world to be with him. We were in the middle of the Agnus Dei from Byrd's five-part Mass, scattered across the stage, singing as hot as stars spun out somewhere in the gas clouds of the Crab Nebula. He was sending a message out to other creatures who'd never understand the expanse between us. For this, he needed me. I was supposed to give his monastic ensemble some street cred. Jonah had enlisted us all in a war to outshame shame, to see which noise—this shining past or the present's shrill siren—would outlast the other.

We made some money, but Jonah wouldn't move out of the Brandstraat. Instead, he sank a fortune into renovating the dive, filling it with woodcuts and period instruments that none of us played. Those panic spells and shortness of breath that had bothered him for years more or less disappeared. Whatever youthful terror they were recalling had been put to bed, outlived.

Voces Antiquae used two publicity photos, both black-and-white. In the first, some trick of the light made us all fall into a narrow tonal register. The second spread us over the latitudes, from equatorial Celeste Marin to sun-starved Peter Chance at the polar circle. Most magazines ran the second, playing up the group's United Nations nature. A Bavarian feature called our sound "Holy Un-Roman Imperial." Some overworked British journalist came up with "polychromal polytonality." Flacks and hacks waxed on about how our multiethnic makeup proved the universal, transcendent appeal of Western classical music. They never mentioned how the earliest of our music was as much Near Eastern and North African as it was European. Jonah didn't care. He had his sound, one that, with each passing month, grew clearer, finer, and less categorizable.

He and Celeste came home one day in the winter of 1981, giggling like schoolchildren who'd stumbled onto a dictionary of taboo words. She wore a garland around her temples, prim white daisies that her hair turned into tropical hothouse blooms. "Joseph Strom the First." Jonah saluted me. "We've got a secret."

"That you're just dying to broadcast over the World Service."

"Perhaps. But can you guess, or do we have to cue you?"

I looked, yet couldn't believe. "This secret of yours. Does it sound like Mendelssohn?"

"In some countries."

Celeste stepped forward flirtatiously and kissed me. "My brother!" I'd sung with her for four years, in ten nations, and she still seemed farther away than Martinique.

They went to Senegal for a honeymoon: vacationing in an imagined common origin. "It's amazing," his postcard from Dakar said. "Better than Harlem. Everywhere you look, faces darker than yours. I've never been so comfortable in my life." But they came back shaken. Something happened on that trip they never spoke about. They'd toured some moss-covered coastal prison where the deeds had been transacted, the commodities stored. Whatever Jonah was looking for in Africa, he found it. He wouldn't be going back anytime soon.

We made two more recordings. We won prizes, grants, and competitions. We gave master classes, did live radio, and even made occasional television appearances on the BRT, NOS, and RAI. Nothing was real. I lived in the sound alone, making sure only to catch all the trains and planes. My bass got better, simpler, more effortless, with month after month of work.

I reached that age where every six weeks, I had another birthday. I turned forty, and didn't even feel it. It hit me that I'd given most of my thirties to my brother, as I'd once given him my twenties. Jonah had gambled on returning me to singing, and we made the gamble pay. I'd never be a transcendent bass; I'd started lifetimes too late. But I had become the foundation for Voces Antiquae, and our sound came from all six of us. Yet even as I reached my singing peak, I heard my tone wearing away, concert by concert, chord by chord. As doomed lives go, singers are not quite basketball players. But the eternity we make for fifty minutes every night lasts, if the wind is with us, for only a score of years.

It stunned me to discover I'd been in Europe for over half a decade. In the first year, I'd learned what it meant to be forever American. In the next two, I learned how to hide that fact. Then somewhere, I crossed an invisible line where I couldn't tell how far I'd drifted from my inalienable birthright. All that time, we didn't step foot on our home continent. There weren't enough bookings to make a tour worthwhile, and we had no other reason to return. The country had named an actor to the helm, one who proclaimed it morning again in America and who napped most afternoons. We couldn't go back there, ever.

I could follow conversation now in five languages and acquit myself in three, not counting English and Latin. I went sight-seeing when we toured, now that I no longer had to spend every waking hour vocalizing.

Visiting dead landmarks became my hobby. Sometimes I saw women. In moments of unbearable loneliness, I thought of the years I'd lived with Teresa. Then being alone seemed more than complex enough. I was a forty-year-old man living in an adopted country that took me for a guest laborer, with my forty-one-year-old brother and his thirty-two-year-old wife, who treated me as if I were their adopted child.

Everything I had belonged to him. My pleasures, my anxieties, my accomplishments and failings: These were all my brother's piece. So it had always been. Years would go by, and I'd still be working for him. There came a month when I needed a secret project or I would disappear forever into his accompaniment. The nature of the work made no difference. All that mattered was that it remain unsponsored, unaccountable, and invisible to my brother.

This time, my supplies were more modest. I carried around Europe a single A4 notebook, clothbound at the side, with eight blank staffs per page. On long train rides to distant concerts, in hotels and dressing rooms, in the dull, wasted stretches of fifteen minutes and half hours that ravage a performer's life, I fished for tunes in me that were worth writing down. I did not compose. I was more of a psychic, a medium taking dictation from the other side. I'd hover with my pencil over the blank ledger lines and just wait, not so much for the prediction of an idea as for the revision of a memory.

Just as when I'd tried to compose in the States, everything I wrote down was some tune from my earlier days, changed just enough to be unrecognizable. If I studied what I wrote long enough, I could always find a source hiding in it, evading and yet craving detection. Only now, instead of the misery that this discovery caused me in Atlantic City, I felt an excruciating release in watching these hostages escape. Over the course of three slack afternoons, I labored over an extended passage that took me until I was free of it to recognize as a reworking of Wilson Hart's chamber fantasy, the one that years ago had struck me as a reworking of "Motherless Child." I'd sworn to him to write what was in me, and managed only to rewrite what had once been in him.

But the scribbling was mine, and had to be enough. My notebook filled up with floating, disconnected fragments, each of them pointing toward some urgent revision they couldn't get to. The tunes spelled out the story of my life, half as it had happened to me, and half as I'd failed to make it happen. I knew that none would ever become the mystery it was after. All I could hope to do was stumble about, belatedly throwing open their cages.

Jonah often saw me struggling away. He even asked me once. "So what's with the hush-hush hobby, Joseph? Business or pleasure?"

"Business," I told him. "Unfinished."

"You writing a good thousand-year-old Mass for us to do?"

"We're not good enough," I said. That was enough to guarantee he'd never ask again.

In the world we occupied, our future was fixed and we could do nothing about it. But the past was infinitely pliable. We were in the thick of a movement that made sure history would never be what it used to be. Every month brought a new musical revolution, constantly updating where music had come from. Supporting evidence for half the revolutions was scant, and the experts lashed into one another with the fury of the antiballistic missile treaty debate. Voces Antiquae was ahead of the curve on the newest developments in oldest performance practice. We sang one voice per line three hundred years after and five years before it was the hot thing. Jonah applied the ethereal sound to anything that stood still long enough for the treatment. He fully subscribed to Rifkin's bombshell theory that Bach intended his sacred music to be sung one singer to a part. Jonah was convinced on sonority alone; no amount of documentary proof either way could alter his conviction.

He wanted to perform Bach's six motets—just us and a couple of ringers to pad out the eight-part extravaganza, *Singet dem Herrn ein neues Lied*. The others—Hans in particular—opposed the idea. The music was a full century younger than the latest piece we'd ever sung. It lay way outside the idiom we'd perfected. Our caution maddened Jonah. "Come on, you bastards. A world masterpiece that hasn't been sung properly in all its two hundred and fifty years. I want to hear these things once before I die, when they're not a Sherman tank with one tread falling off."

"It's Bach," Hans objected. "Other people already own this. People know these pieces, forward and retrograde."

"They only *think* they know them. Like they thought they knew Rembrandt, until the grime came off. Come on. 'Sing unto the Lord a *new* song.' Johnny Bach, heard for the first time."

That became the project's slogan, the one EMI promoted our recording with. Whatever the legitimacy of the performances, our agility justified them. The thing about Bach is, he never wrote for the human voice.

He had some less plodding medium in mind to carry his memo into space. His lines are completely independent. His part-writing combs out some extra dimension between its harmonies. Most performances go for majesty and end up mud. Voces Antiquae went for lightness and wound up in orbit. The group's turning radius, even at highway speeds, was uncanny. We brought out counterpoint in the works that even Hans had never heard. Every note was audible, even the ones buried alive in that thicket of invention. We goosed the giddiness and laid into the passing dissonances. We brought those motets back to their medieval roots and pushed them forward to their radical Romantic children. By the time we finished, no one could say what century they came from.

Our disc was notorious from its day of release. It started a pitched battle, venomous in proportion to how little was at stake and how few people cared. I don't mean *Le sacre du printemps* or anything. But there was flack. The new had lost its capacity to shock; only the old could still rattle people. We were derided for emasculating Bach and praised for sandblasting a monument that hadn't been hosed down in a long time. Jonah never read a single review. He felt we'd acquitted ourselves well, maybe even superlatively. Yet he wasn't satisfied. He'd wanted to make that music give up its secrets. But that was something it wasn't going to do until long after we were all dead.

We toured with the motets but returned, after a while, to our roots. We revived the Renaissance in every burg in Germany. We sang in Cologne, Essen, Göttingen, Vienna—every city Da had ever mentioned to us. But no relatives ever came out of the audience after any of our concerts to claim us. We sang in King's College Chapel, a homecoming for Peter Chance and a stunned first for the Strom brothers. Jonah craned up at the fan vault, which no photo can even be wrong about. His eyes dampened and his lips curled bitterly. "Birthplace of the Anglican hoot." He was coming home to a place that would never be his.

We spent five days in Israel. I imagined that our Counter-Reformation Masses and courtier chansons would have to sound absurd in this permanently embattled world. But the halls wouldn't release us without several encores. Memory was resourceful. It could reclaim any windblown trinket and weave it into the nest. In Jerusalem, on the tour's last concert, we sang in a futuristic wood-lined auditorium that might have been in Rome, Tokyo, or New York. The audience was unreadable: two sexes, three faiths, four races, a dozen nationalities, and as many motives for listening to the chant of death as there were seats in the house.

From my spot on the stage lip, I keyed on a woman in the second row, her body stenciled with sixty-year-old state messages, her face an inventory of collective efficiencies. Four chords into our opening Machaut Kyrie, it hit me: my aunt. My father's sister, Hannah, the only one of his family whose wartime death had never been certain. She and Vihar, her Bulgarian husband, had gone underground before my birth, and there the trail ended. My father, the empiricist, could never bring himself to declare her dead. Hannah was, compared to the size of history, a particle so small, her path could not be measured. The Holocaust had annihilated all addresses. Yet here Aunt Hannah was, returned by our performance. She must have seen the posters announcing our tour. She'd seen the name, *her* name, two men the right age and origin . . . She'd come to the concert, purchased a seat up close so she could study our faces for any trace of bloodline. Her resemblance to Da was uncanny. Time, place, even the nightmare gap between their paths: Nothing could erase the kinship. She looked so much like Da, I knew Jonah had to see it, as well. But his face throughout our concert's first half showed no sign of any audience at all. Between this familiar stranger scrutinizing me and my brother refusing to catch my eye, it took a lifetime's practice to go on singing.

I cornered Jonah at intermission. "You didn't notice anything?"

"I noticed your focus flying around like some high-wire—"

"You didn't see her? The gray-haired, heavy woman in the second row?"

"Joseph. They're *all* gray-haired, heavy women in the second row."

"Your aunt." If I'd lost my mind, I wanted my brother to know.

"*My* aunt?" He put his fingers to his chest, running the calculations. "Impossible. You are aware, aren't you?"

"Jonah. Everything's impossible. Look at us."

He laughed. "There is that."

We went back on. At our first shared tacet measure, I caught him looking. He flashed me a quick peripheral glance. *If anyone in the world is our aunt, it's her.* She, for her part, gazed into us like surgery. She took her eyes off me only to look at Jonah. During the curtain call, she fixed me with a look that scorned all forgetting: *Strom, boychik. Did you think I would never find you?*

The reception lines that night were endless. Scores of people, still savoring the frozen hour they'd just inhabited, tried, by standing next to us and shaking our hands, to postpone, a little longer, their relapse into motion. I couldn't focus on the compliments. I darted through the crowd, about to find a family, however small and distant. Excitement was just terror that hadn't yet imagined its own end.

The crowd thinned out, and I saw her. She was holding back, waiting for a lull. I grabbed Jonah and pulled him with me toward our flesh and blood, using him like a shield. She smiled as we closed on her, a thrill that looked around for a place to bolt.

"*Tante Hannah? Ist es möglich?*"

She answered in Russian. In a broken pidgin of languages, we three worked it out. She knew the name Strom only from our recordings. She closed her eyes when we told our half of the story, said who we thought she was. Hers were my father's closed eyes.

"This aunt of yours. I knew thousands of your aunts. I was with them." She breathed in and opened her eyes again. "But now I am here. Here to tell you so."

Every muscle in her face was ours. We couldn't stop pushing for some proof of kinship: town names, what we knew of our grandmother's Russian roots, anything to find the connection. She smiled and shook her head. The shake was Da's. And in that one tremor, I knew him. Jewish grief. Grief so great, he never had an answer for kinship but to keep it from us.

Her English was weak, and she shuddered at German. What little Russian we had came from Rachmaninoff and Prokofiev. But her words were clear as silence: *You are one of us, always. Not by law, but the law is a technicality. You could convert. Rejoin. Relearn, even for the first time.* "You know," she told us, by way of good-bye, "if you want family? You are sharing family with half this audience."

We were singing in late July of 1984, in the Palais des Papes at the Avignon Festival, when my family found me. Word came from our arts management in Brussels, who'd gotten it in a telegram from Milton Weisman, our old agent. Mr. Weisman would die the next year, never having owned a fax machine or heard of E-mail. Milton Weisman: the last man in the developed world to send telegrams.

The telegram was stuffed inside an envelope and sent by overnight courier to our hotel in Provence. I picked it up at the front desk with my room key, figuring it was some contract I'd forgotten to sign. I didn't read it until I was in my room.

Bad news from home. Your brother has been killed. Call your wife as soon as this reaches you. My regrets. Forgive this messenger. Ever. Milton.

I read it again, and wound up even further from sense. For the sickest interval, it was really Jonah, dead in some freak alternate world just now collapsing into mine, replacing the one I'd foolishly held faith with. Then it wasn't Jonah, but some brother I'd never known. Then it wasn't even me, my brother, my wife, but a split-off Strom family trapped behind soundproof glass, rapping on it in silent horror.

I went down the hall to Jonah and Celeste's room. My hands were shaking so badly, I had to knock twice. Jonah opened the door and read my face at once. All I could do was shove the words into his hands. I followed him into his room. Jonah put the telegram on his bed, still looking at it. He raised his palms. "The man is a lot older than when we worked with him. That must be it."

" 'Forgive this messenger'?"

Jonah nodded, conceding a point I didn't even know I'd made. "So call."

"Call who? My *wife*?" But I knew who Milton Weisman meant. He was from another time, a moral man whose names for things were as dated as the music he represented. He'd neglected to give any phone number. He figured I'd remember.

I sat on Jonah's hotel bed for minutes, eyes closed, a receiver in hand, a parody of prayer, trying to remember the number in Atlantic City I once knew as automatically as I knew the changes to "Honeysuckle Rose." Memory required forgetting everything, especially the hope of recall. At last my fingers dialed, the numbers still in my muscles, the way pieces of piano music still lived in my fingers long after I'd forgotten all about them. A pitched jangle at the other end announced *the States*. Colors that were submerged in me surfaced at that sound. I sat savoring them—Coltrane, high-fat ice cream, the *Times* on a Sunday, the sound of a Middle Atlantic drawl. I was like a wino window-shopping outside a package store.

The number had been disconnected. An operator with a Spanish accent gave me another. I dialed the new number, my courage beginning to falter. Then she picked up. For a moment, I'd called to tell her I'd be late for breakfast. Muscle memory, too, the thing that doesn't stop until our muscles do. I heard myself ask, "Teresa?" A second later, before she could say anything, I heard myself ask again. My voice bounced back in maddening delay, the time it took for the word to make the loop from Europe to outer space to America back up to the communications satellite and down to Europe's surface again. Canon at unison.

She needed no other sound. She struggled to say the syllables of my name, not quite managing. At last she got out a comic, choked "Jo-ey!" The nickname she rarely called me, out of too much love. She laughed, and that sound, too, quickly broke up and weeded over.

"Teresa. Ter. I got the strangest message. From Milton Weisman . . ." I could barely talk, distracted by the echo of my own voice bouncing back like crazed, imitative counterpoint against my own words.

"Joseph, I know. I told him to write you. I'm so sorry. It's so horrible."

Her words were pure dissonance. I couldn't find the key. I had to force myself to wait, so our words wouldn't collide in the satellite echo. "What is? His cable made no . . ."

She drew up short. I heard her turn like a massive freighter, doubling back to fish me out of the water. "It's your sister. She called me. She called *me*. She must have remembered my name from . . ." From when I had never introduced them. The idea of hearing at last from a woman Teresa had wanted to love broke her down into time-lapse crying.

"Ruth?" At that syllable, Jonah jerked up in the chair where he listened. He stood and leaned toward me. I held him off with a palm. "What's happened? Is she . . . ?"

"Her husband," Teresa cried. "It's so awful. They say he was . . . He didn't make it, Joseph. He isn't . . . He never . . ."

Robert. My wave of relief—*Ruth alive*—snapped back in horror: *Robert dead*. The whiplash shut me down, and I couldn't breathe. Teresa started talking again before I started hearing. She laid out a thing I'd need explained to me over and over again. Even now. She went on in detail, details impossible for her to know and useless to my understanding.

I must have cut her off. "Is there a way I can reach her?"

"Yes." Excited, ashamed. Part of the family at last. "She gave me a number, in case . . . Just a minute." And in the seconds it took Teresa to find her address book, I lived all the lives that mine had beaten out of me. I sat holding the line, stopped. Robert Rider was dead. My sister's husband—killed. Ruth, from nowhere, wanted me to know. She had tracked me back to the woman who would always know how to find me, the woman who faithful Joseph was sure to stay with forever. But I'd sentenced that woman to oblivion years ago.

In the seconds while I waited for Teresa to come back, she became infinitely vulnerable to me, infinitely good. I'd hurt her beyond imagining, and here she was, glad for the chance to help me in my hour. All good things were scattering. Death fed faster, the more it took. We get nothing; a handful of weeks. The best we have is broken up or thrown stupidly away. Teresa came back on the line and read me a number. I wrote it down, blindly. I'd forgotten how many digits an American phone number had. Teresa corrected my mistakes in dictation, and we were done.

"I love you," I told her. And got back silence. Of all the things I thought she might say, this wasn't one. "Teresa?"

"I . . . I'm so sorry, Joseph. I never met them. I wish I had. But I'm as sorry as if he'd been . . ." When she started again, it was forced natural. "Did you know I got married?" I couldn't even exclaim. "Yep, married! To Jim Miesner. I'm not sure you two ever met." The bullet-headed man she used to come to my bar with, before me. "And I've got the most beautiful little girl! Her name is Danuta. I wish you could meet her."

"How? How old is she?"

She paused. Not the pause of satellites. "Five. Well, closer to six." Her silence was defensive. But we all have the right to make what we need. "I . . . I'm back with my family. With my father. You were right about all of that."

I got off the phone, polite to the point of numb. I wobbled to my feet. Jonah was looking at me, waiting. "It's Robert."

"Robert."

"Robert Rider. Your brother-in-law. He was shot by a policeman over a month ago. There was an arrest. Some struggle. I . . . didn't get all the details."

Jonah's shoulders tensed. What details? Death settled all the details. In his face, I read the extent of his banishment. Ruth had tried to contact me. The calls, the messages, all for me alone. She'd never once tried to reach him. "How is she?"

"Teresa didn't know."

"I meant Teresa." He flicked his fingers toward his chest: *Give it here.* I didn't know what he wanted until I looked down and saw the telephone number crumpled in my palm. I handed it over. "Area code two-one-five. Where is that?"

Nowhere I'd ever lived. He gestured toward the phone. I shook my head. I needed time. Time to put together all the time that had just come apart.

We sang that night. With what concentration I had, I braced for catastrophe. But somehow we survived, dragged along by overpractice. We took the slowest Josquin in history. Those in the audience who weren't scandalized or bored to death fell through the auditorium floor and descended into the cracks between space. Whatever the final verdict, no one would ever hear its like again.

I lay in bed that night thinking of Ruth. Our sister had been way out ahead of us. She'd jumped into the future long before Jonah or I had admitted to the present. She'd seen what was coming down. She was riding the nightmare before her older brothers had awakened from the dream. I'd always imagined that Ruth's suffering came from being too light to merit race's worst injuries. That night, in a crowded hotel in Avignon where most guests assumed I was from Morocco, I finally saw. Race's worst injuries are color-blind.

Something kept Jonah up, too. It wasn't the Josquin. At 3:00 A.M., I heard him pacing in the hall outside my door, wondering whether to knock. I called to him, and he walked in as if keeping an appointment. "Pennsylvania," he said. I just blinked in the dark. "Area code two-one-five. Eastern Pennsylvania." I tried to fit the information to my sister. Da's last hallucination had her moving to California. That's where I'd always imagined her. Jonah didn't sit. He stood at the window and pulled back the drape. On the horizon, the Palais des Papes glowed like a monstrous Gothic illuminated manuscript. "I've been thinking." He made the words stretch from last afternoon all the way back several years. "She must be right. Ruth must be right. I mean, about . . . the fire. No other way."

He looked out the window, on all the violence he'd so long and beautifully denied. Jonah had met Robert only through me. The details of Robert's death were to us still as obscure as God. But this death confirmed the central fact of our lives, the one we'd forever kept as abstract as the art we gave ourselves to. We'd lived as if murder weren't constant in the place we came from. We hid in the concert hall, sanctuary from the world's real sound. But thirty years ago—a lifetime—long before we knew how to read the story, stray hatred scattered us. As Jonah said the words, the fact turned obvious. And just as obvious: Some part of me had always believed.

He stood for a long time, saying nothing. Nor could I say anything to him. But Jonah was my brother. We had, at one time or another, played everything together. Alone of all things, we knew each other. He'd taught me, and I him: All music lived and died inside the rests. Sometime around four o'clock, he said, "Call her." He'd been keeping his eye on the clock, on the time differences, for the very last moment it would be decent to call.

I jacked myself out of bed, threw on a robe, and sat again with a phone in my hands. I tried to pass the receiver to him, but he refused. He wasn't the one she'd called. I dialed the number, methodical as scales. Again, the jangle of an American ring, followed by its transatlantic echo. Between each ring, I rejected a thousand opening words. *Rootie. Root. Ms. Strom. Mrs. Rider.* Laughing, grieving, begging her forgiveness. Nothing felt real. *Ruth. It's Joseph. Your brother.*

Then the click of the receiver lifting on that other continent, the sound of a voice that killed all preparation. Instead of my sister, an old man. "Hello?" he challenged. A man who sounded a hundred years old. I froze in his voice, worse than stage fright. "Hello? Who's there? Who is this?" On the line, in the room behind him, younger voices asked if there was something wrong.

Paths collapsed upon themselves. "Dr. Daley?" I asked. When he grunted, I said, "This is your grandson."

THE VISITATION

During the call to Philadelphia, Jonah hovered at my elbow. But he wouldn't take the phone when I handed it to him. Speech without pitches terrified him. He wanted me between him and where we came from. My grandfather put Ruth on the line. She tried to tell me what had happened to Robert, but she couldn't begin. Her voice was past anger, past warmth, past memory. Past everything but shock. The month since her husband's death had done nothing to help her back. Nor would years.

She got out two numb sentences. Then she gave me back to our grandfather. William Daley couldn't quite grasp which of Ruth's brothers I was. I said I'd very much like to meet him. "Young man, I turned ninety six weeks ago. If you want to meet me, you'd best catch the next flight out."

I told Jonah I wanted to go. The idea of returning twisted Jonah's face, half temptation, half disgust. "You can't fix anything, Joey. You know that? You can't fix what's already happened." But he pushed me away with his free hand while he pulled with the other. "No, of course. Go. One of us has to. It's Ruth. She's back." He seemed to think I might at least fix the things that hadn't happened yet.

I bought an open ticket. Ruth was back. But she'd never really left. We were the ones who'd gone away.

My uncle Michael met me at Philadelphia International. He wasn't hard to pick out of the crowd. All I had to do was look. He picked me out, too, as soon as I came through the passenger chute. What could be easier? Bewildered, middle-aged, mixed-race boy gazing all over the place in excitement and shame. I moved toward him, holding my two carry-ons in front of me as if they were delinquent children. My uncle came up to me, as shaky as I was, but empty-handed. After a second's hesitation, he took my shoulders with the strangest, most wonderful grace. *Don't know you. Don't know why. But I will.*

It amused him, how awkward two total strangers could be. We were total foreigners, connected by blood in another life. "You remember me?" Dazed, I did. I'd last seen him for all of four minutes, when I was thirteen, a third of a century ago, at my mother's funeral. Even more remarkable: He remembered me. "You've changed. You've gotten . . ." He snapped his fingers, jogging his memory.

"Older?" I suggested. He clapped his hands and pointed at me: *Bingo.*

He took one of the bags and we walked the long concourse to the parking lot. He asked about the flight, Europe, and my brother. I asked about Ruth—alive; Dr. Daley—also, remarkably. Michael told me of his wife and children, his lot in life. He was a personnel officer at Penn. "Only do this chauffeur job in my after hours, when vanished relations come back from the dead." He looked me up and down, in the wonder of genetic recognition. We looked more like each other than either of us could accept. He seemed to be deciding whether his own nephew could really be white.

His car was the *Hindenburg*. Years in a small foreign country will do that to a person's sense of scale. Michael started the engine, and a burst of exuberance blared out of the dashboard. It was only two beats, but at a volume I'd forgotten, from a rhythm section wider than oppression is long. It had been forever since I'd heard anything like it. In something short of embarrassment, Michael leaned forward and snapped off the stream.

"Please. Don't shut it off for me."

"Just old R & B. My feel-good. My church. What I listen to when I'm alone."

"It sounded like a dream."

"You'd think a man well into his fifties would have outgrown that."

"Not until we die."

"Amen. And not even then."

"I used to play that stuff." He looked at me in disbelief. "In Atlantic City. Only, you know, solo piano. Tip glass on the music rack. Liberace Covers Motown. The old Eastern European émigrés who came down for holidays couldn't get enough."

Michael coughed so hard, I thought I'd have to take the wheel.

"People are strange."

He whistled. "You got that. Stranger than anyone." He flipped the radio back on, although he doused the volume. We listened together, each according to his needs. By the time we hit the heart of town, we were harmonizing. Michael did this outrageous full-pipe falsetto, and I hit the changes in the bass. He smiled at my passing tones. Theory can help get you through a shortfall of soul—at least in the easy keys.

We turned off the highway onto local streets. The size of the most modest apartment block amazed me after years in hunchbacked Ghent. We neared his boyhood house. Michael grew morose. "Rough times. Trickle down shakes the last few golden drops on inner Philly. Every cheap scrap of manufacture has headed offshore. Then it's our fault for doing crack."

I was at sea. I couldn't even ask for definitions.

Michael looked out the window, seeing his old neighborhood through my eyes. His face was racked with betrayal. "You would have loved this street. So fine once. No way you can even recognize it now. We've been trying to get the doctor out of here for the last five years. He's not moving. Insists on dying inside that monstrosity. Riding out the decline and fall until the house collapses around him or his body gives up, whichever comes first. 'What would happen to Mama if we sold the house to strangers?' "

"Mama?" My grandmother. Nettie Ellen Daley. "Isn't she . . ."

"Oh, yeah. Completely. Two years ago. The doctor hasn't quite come into possession of the fact yet. A real ass-buster, I have to tell you. My sisters and me, coming all the way in here, five times a week. We go through caretakers like chocolate through a dog."

His street indeed reeled from the present. Even the most stately old houses had died intestate. We slowed and turned into the driveway of an ample house bucking the tide around it. Michael flipped off the radio as we hit the driveway mouth. He caught me smiling at the gesture. "Old habit."

"Not his music of choice?"

"Don't get him started on it."

We were still yards from the house. "His hearing's really that good?"

"My Jesus, yes. You got it from somewhere, didn't you?"

The shock of that thought was still banging around in me when a figure drifted out onto the lawn to meet us. A full, fluid, statuesque woman, one shade paler than I remembered her. I was out of the car without feeling myself leave. Michael stayed behind the wheel, giving us our minute. She had her head down as I closed the distance. She wouldn't look at me. Then I put my arms around my sister.

Ruth wouldn't hold still for the embrace. But she gave me more than I'd hoped, and I held her longer than I had all my life. Three full seconds: It was enough. She pulled free to look at me. She wore red robes and a green-and-black headdress that even I knew was supposed to invoke Africa. "Ruth. Let me look at you. Where've you been?"

"In hell. Here. This country. How about you, Joseph?" Her eyes were deep and broken. Something was wrong with her arms. She hadn't seen me for even longer than I hadn't seen her.

"I've missed you." Almost chant.

"Why come back now, Joey? Black men are killed every week. Why did you wait until it was . . . ?"

For you, Ruth. I came back for you. Nothing else big enough to bring me.

A young boy, maybe a fifth grader, materialized on the lawn beside us. I didn't see him come up, and the sudden apparition scared me. He was dark, closer to Michael than to Ruth or me. Michael got out of the car and I turned to him. Happy for the deflection, I waved toward the boy. "Yours?"

Michael laughed. "You're stuck on the escalator, man. You're in a time hole. My oldest daughter has one of her own almost this old!"

"Mine," Ruth said.

"Not yours," the boy told her.

My sister sighed. "Kwame. This is Joseph. Your uncle." The boy looked as if we were collaborating to cheat him out of his inheritance. He didn't say, *Not my uncle*. He didn't have to. Ruth sighed again. "Oakland. That's where we've been. Oakland." The word went up my spine like prophecy. "Community organizing. Working."

"Then the cops killed my dad," Kwame said.

I put my hand on his shoulder. He shrugged it off. Ruth put her hand where mine had been, and he suffered it, but believing nothing. Ruth steered her child toward the house, and we men followed.

My mother's father waited just inside the door. His close-cropped hair was Niagara white. The air around him, like the high-tide mark on a beach, still registered how large a man he'd been. He wore a steel gray suit. Everyone had dressed for this occasion except me. He tilted his head back to get me in the bottom pane of his bifocals. "Jonah Strom."

"Joseph," I said, holding out my hand.

My objection angered him. "I still don't see why she had to give you boys the same name. Never mind. *Es freut mich, Herr Strom.*" He took my hand, even as I shrank. *"Heißen Sie willkommen zu unserem Haus."*

I stood there gaping. Uncle Michael chuckled as he dragged my bags upstairs. "Don't let him fool you. He's been practicing for the last three days."

"He can make hotel reservations and change your currency for you, too," Ruth said.

Dr. Daley threatened to break forth in Sturm und Drang. *"Sie nehmen keine Rücksicht auf andere."* Something more than three days' practice.

Ruth put her arm around him. "It's okay, Papap. He's not an other. He's one of us."

From the hall to my right came crying. A startling sound: the wail of a creature wholly dependent on the unknown. Ruth moved toward the cry almost before I heard it. She slipped into the distant room, murmuring as if to herself. When she came back, she held a dozen-pound squirming infant trying to fling itself free to safety or death.

"Also mine," Ruth said. "This is little Robert. Five months. Robert, this is your uncle Joey. Haven't told you about him yet."

Michael set me up in an upstairs room. "This was my brother's. We're moving Kwame into the twins' old room." I was violating a sanctuary. But there was no place else to go. "Sleep," my uncle told me. "You probably need it." And then he left for his own home.

Ruth came by to check on me. She held little Robert, who every so often stabbed out with his arm to prove my existence. My sister talked to him steadily, sometimes words, sometimes just pitched phonemes. She stopped only to ask, "You good?"

"I am now."

She shook her head, looking at her baby but talking to me. "Can I get you anything?"

"You call him Papap."

Little Robert stared at me. His mother wouldn't. "I do. Kwame, too. We've called him that for years." Then she turned: *You have a problem with that?* "That's what he said you used to call him."

"Ruth?"

"Not now, Joey. Maybe tomorrow. Okay?"

Then she went slack, some tendon cut. She hunched over, as if the baby had swelled to tremendous weight. She lowered herself to the foot of the bed. I sat next to her and put my arm on her back. I couldn't tell if she wanted it there or not. She began to heave, her muscles lifting and falling in rhythm. Her shaking was tight and small, softer than winter branches scraping a roof. Only when little Robert began to cry, too, did she pull herself up into words.

"It's so old, Joey. So old." Her calm was forced. She might have meant anything. Every human nausea was older than she could say.

"The license plate was hanging down. He was driving back on Camp-bell on a Thursday night. Not even that late—nine-thirty-five. Not even in an especially bad neighborhood. Coming home from a council meeting. He was trying to get a shelter built. The man worked all the time. I was home with Kwame and . . ." She lifted little Robert, her face twisted. I pressed her shoulders: tomorrow would be fine. Or never.

"Two policemen pulled him over. One white, one Hispanic. Because the rear license plate was hanging down a little. Robert told me the day before that he was going to fix it. He got out of the car. He always got out when the police stopped him. He always wanted to take the issue back to them. He got out of the car to tell them he knew all about the license plate. But they knew all about the license plate, too. It came out at the hearing. They ran the number through their system while they were pulling him over. So what those two cops saw was a big, belligerent former Panther with a record coming out of the car at them. Robert always carried his wallet in his front coat pocket. Said he didn't like to sit on his fortune. He reached into his coat pocket to get his wallet, and these two cops swung into covered positions behind their doors, guns drawn, yelling at him to freeze. He whipped his hand out of the coat to get it up in the air. I know it. He knew exactly . . ."

Ruth handed me the baby. She jerked her hands in the air in the oddest way. No place to put them. She wrapped them around her head and pressed, forcing back what was left of her brain.

"Why do I even have to say this? You know before I tell you. So old. Oldest song in the whole sick hymnal." Her words were stale paste. I strained to hear her. "Nothing you can do with your life, but this country's going to make you a cliché. The shining emblem of your kind."

Little Robert began to shriek. I had no clue what to do. I hadn't held a baby for twenty years. I bounced him, a dotted rhythm, and it helped a little. I hummed, long and low, a ground bass. My nephew put his hand to my chest in wonder. He felt the note there, and his wails turned into startled laughter. The sound brought Ruth back. She stood and traced small circles around the bed. Little Robert squealed, hand to my chest, demanding more.

"The thing was, Joey, they didn't kill him. If they'd killed him, we might have had an uprising, even in Oakland. They did exactly what years of training primed them to do. They aimed for the legs with rubber riot-control bullets, and managed to shatter his right kneecap. Knocked him to the pavement, where he lay screaming. When he got through the pain, he started cursing them out with American history. They probably wanted to put a metal bullet through his skull just for naming them. The paramedics came. Twenty-two and a half minutes after they were called. They got him on the operating table and cut open his knee. According to the autopsy, he died of complications due to anesthesia."

She stopped and took little Robert back from me. He started wailing again, reaching for my chest. He was ready to nose-dive out of her arms for a chance to feel those vibrations again. Only when Ruth hummed would he calm down. I listened to her notes. Untrained, a little hoarse. But full as the ocean when the moon pulled.

"The man didn't die from complications, Joey. He died from simplifications. Simplified to death." The last word fell off, near silence. "There was a hearing but no trial. Two-week suspension from the force for one,

and three weeks for the other. No criminal charges. Justifiable precau-
tionary measure in a high-risk situation. Meaning a war zone. Everybody
knows. Every nigger coming at the law, reaching into his coat pocket . . ."

Her voice bottomed out. Had anyone put a gun in her hands, she
could have gone into the street and used it without aim or emotion. Ruth
toted her child in automatic circles around our dead uncle's room, humming as the boy needed her.

"Everybody knows. Oldest song and dance there is. We can't even
hear it anymore, it's so in us. Not a lynching, see? Just self-defense. Not
murder; an accident. Not racism; just an unfortunate reaction that his
profile created in . . . Tell me another one, Joey. One that doesn't turn
everyone in it into a . . . One of the cops sent me a grief-stricken apology
by registered mail."

"Which one?"

"Does it matter? The white. Does it matter? None of it . . . none of
this would have happened if . . ." If this wasn't this world. "What else you
want to know, Joey? What else you want to me to tell you?" She stopped
pacing and faced me, a reference librarian handling a nuisance client.
What else? About Robert's death, about Robert, about the police, about
the hearing, about Oakland, about the law, about the oldest song there is,
the song of songs that trumps all others? *How can you sing? How can you
sing the things you sing?* "Ask me. I know every detail. All the events I
wasn't there to live through. I'm trapped in it, Joey. Again and again.
What am I supposed to do with this? What am I supposed to tell you?"

I thought she was breaking down. Then I realized that she wasn't talking to me at all. These last two questions were for her son, who only
smiled at me from the curl of her arm and tried to vocalize.

Ruth turned to me, numb. "You sleep." The words branded me, an accusation. It was too late for me to change my ways now, this late at night.

Sleep was beyond imagining. I lay in bed at 2:00 A.M., turning over
a hundred times before the clock's minute wheel turned over once. I
couldn't locate myself: upstairs, turning in bed, in the middle of a house
whose banned image had run my life without my once being able to form
it. When I did sleep, my dreams filled with sirens and gunfire.

I went downstairs at 5:30, unable to stay in that padded coffin another
minute. I needed to sit, there at the hour before anyone else was alive,
and steal my way back into this house I'd long ago lost. Going downstairs,
I saw Jonah tearing up the steps behind our uncle Michael, with a boy not
yet four struggling to keep up with them. A force of nature stood at the

stair bottom, shouting, *No running in this house!* The house had shrunk, like a fetus in formaldehyde. Only the contour of these stairs remained, and the sound of our running.

I wasn't the first awake. Dr. Daley sat at the kitchen table, hunched over last night's newspaper. He had on a shirt and tie, changed from yesterday's. He looked up at my footfall. He'd been waiting for me, whatever the hour. He studied me from his chair, his face demanding to know what we were to make of a waste so large. Who taught people to throw away the thing they most feared losing?

"Cup of coffee?"

"Please."

"How do you take it?"

"I . . ."

The smallest hint of amusement staked out his mouth. *"Milchkaffee? Halb und halb?"*

"Something like that."

He sat me down and brought me coffee, just right, as if he'd seen me make it. The color of my sister's hand. Dr. Daley sat across from me and folded the paper in neat quarters. "Do you want to hear my definition of life? Of course you do. Harassment and coffee, day after day. All right. First. You talked to your sister?"

"Briefly."

"So you know what you've come home to." I nodded, but I knew nothing. All I could hear was that one-syllable locale. He held silent for the barest moment, giving a eulogy he'd had to give too often in his life. He tightened his lips and returned to the unlivable. Public again. "Now then. Your father."

It took me a long sip before I realized he was asking a question. Then I couldn't figure out what the question was. "I . . . My father?"

"Yes. David. How is the man?" He wouldn't look at me. No one knew the first thing about anyone else.

"There's no saying," I said. And I couldn't manage any more.

My grandfather looked up, diagnosing my answer. His chin made a tiny lift and fall. "I see. How long ago?"

"Ten years. I'm sorry—twelve. Almost thirteen. Nineteen seventy-one."

"I see." He pressed his hands against his face. Nothing more to outlive. "Your sister will want to know. You know that?"

"I'm not sure. Given everything."

He stared at me, livid. "Of course she'll want to know! Do you think a week has passed when she hasn't thought about him?"

I felt what it must have meant to be this man's child. We sat for a long time. I sipped; he glowered. At last, he snorted. " 'No saying.' " He nodded his head, smirking at my formulation. "Your brother?"

My brother. How much of a lifetime I'd spent answering that question. "He's well. He's happy living in Belgium. Singing early music."

My grandfather didn't bother to move his head. *I've no time for your foolishness. The question's a simple one. Do you mean to answer or not?* "Am I going to see my oldest grandson again before I die?"

I felt my blood rising. "There's . . . there's never any saying with Jonah, either."

Papap grinned grimly. "Still after his kind of freedom. I remember that from when he was six months old. Is he finding it, do you suppose?"

His tone held something of judgment, without the sentence. I had my private guess. "You have to hear him sing." The only answer that answered him.

Dr. Daley rose and took my emptied coffee cup and saucer. I stood to help him and he waved me down. "It doesn't seem as if I'm going to be granted that experience in this lifetime." He washed my dirty dishes and, hands trembling, placed them in the strainer, next to his own. "I've tried more than once to tell your sister what came between us. Yes, the innate insanity governing all races. But don't be misled. We put our personal stamp on it. Your father and I. Your parents . . ."

He came back to the breakfast table and lowered himself into his chair, where he'd taken breakfast for the last half a century. Same table, with everything else in existence around it changed.

"Your parents thought they saw some way out of the rule. The rule of the past." He stared out onto the spring lawn, trying to picture what they saw. "They wanted a place with as many categories as there were cases. But they still had to bring you up *here*." His voice was desperate, racing the clock. "They wanted a place where everyone was his own tone." He shook his head. "But that's blackness. There is no shade it doesn't already contain. You weren't any more double than any of us. Your mother should have known that."

Footsteps came down the stairs, and my sister wandered in. She toted little Robert, and something heavier. She wore the same red robes and green-and-black West African headdress as she'd worn the day before. My sister the widow. Her face was bleary with the hour. "This child had me up all night." On cue, the baby gurgled with pleasure. How could either of them live?

"That's their job description." Our grandfather, lifelong family practitioner, stood to make coffee for Ruth. It seemed an old ritual. To me, he said, "I made things worse."

Ruth needed no program. She'd been listening on the stairs. She shook her head. "You did nothing, Papap. They were living a dream. Mama's the one who married a white man. She chose her path."

"I was too proud. Your mother always said so." He froze in place. "I mean, your grandmother." He brought Ruth her coffee—black, with a teaspoon of sugar. "I was afraid. Afraid of losing myself in their idea. The orienting righteousness. Afraid of—"

"Of whiteness's whole sick trip," Ruth interrupted. "Fucked-up. To a man."

"Don't swear."

"Yes, Papap." She bowed her head to this ninety-year-old, like a child of nine.

"I made your grandmother pay for my principles. I lost her her daughter, her grandchildren. I never got to see you come into . . ."

Ruth stood and traded him a cup of coffee for the baby. She took the cup and sipped. Then she started hot cereal and fruit mash for little Robert. "You didn't make her, Papap." The old man raised his hand to his head to deflect the words. "Grandma was with you all the way."

"And who was I with?" Dr. Daley asked no one. No one who could hear him. "Hypodescent. You're familiar with the word?" I nodded. I was the word's boy. "It means a half-caste child must belong to the caste with the lower status."

Ruth spooned food into little Robert's mouth with one hand and stirred the air with her other. "It means white can't protect its stolen property, can't tell the owners from the owned, except by playing purebred. They're pure all right. Pure invention. One drop? One drop, as far back as you can go? Every white person in America is passing."

He thought a moment. "Hypodescent means we're supposed to take everybody else in. All the rest."

"Amen," Ruth said. "Everyone who's not insane with inbreeding is black."

"Everyone. All the half-castes and quarter-castes and one-thirty-second-castes. We should have made room for you."

"Don't you blame yourself for what other folks went off and did."

He didn't hear her. "All of us! You think you three were alone?" His eyes begged me, as if only my nod might set the long wrong right. "You think you were the first in the world to live this line? Your grandmother, half white. My family. Right out of the slave owner's loins. My family's name. The whole race. One look at us. We've had the Europeans living in us for three hundred years. I've always wondered what America might have been had the one-drop rule worked the other way."

Ruth shushed him. "Papap, you're going senile at last."

"A mighty nation. As good as its best myth about itself."

"Wouldn't be the U.S. That's for damn sure."

Dr. Daley watched his granddaughter feed his great-grandson, a soul too grabbing and exploratory to survive the world. "I let that madness break my family."

"They broke mine anyway," Ruth said.

We sat silent. Only the baby had heart enough to make even the simplest sounds. Soon, even he would know. Everything was laid down for him, before he even spoke his own name: his father, his grandmother, his broken line all the way back to the start of time. I couldn't stay here. I couldn't go back to the pretty sleep of Europe. I'd been raised to believe in self-invention. But any self I might invent would be a lie.

Ruth had beaten me to this future. She knew long ago that one day I'd have to catch up with her. "Funny thing about one drop? If white plus black makes black, and if the mixed-marriage rate is anything above zero per year . . ." Ruth's eyes rallied on the kind of thought experiment her father had loved. The old slaveholder's property protection was now its victims' only weapon. Blackness was the arrow of time, the churning tribe that gathered itself while purity chose its privileged suicide. "Follow out the curve. Just a matter of time, and everybody in America will be black."

"I thought . . ." My voice sickened me. "I thought you were against black marrying white."

"Honey, I'm against *anyone* marrying white. Mixed marriage mixes you up something permanent. But so long as people are fool enough to try it, I'm fool enough to be the beneficiary." She looked at our grandfather. He was shaking his head in great arcs of fatal resignation. "What? You got a problem with that math?"

"Ain't gonna work." The only time the man ever slandered the rules of grammar. "As soon as they see it coming, they'll repeal the rule."

A sound like thunder broke loose, confirming him. My nephew Kwame appeared on the stairs, a silver box in his hands and two wired foam-lined cups strapped to his ears. Vibrations pulsed out of him, staggered syncopations I couldn't follow or score. Under the beats was a cadence of rhythmic berating. The pulse pounded the air around him. I gasped at what it was doing to the insides of his head.

Papap gestured his great-grandson to remove the phones and kill the tape. The boy did, in a cloud of venomous grumbles that no adult could hear or interpret. The doctor rose up, an Old Testament prophet. "If you want to scramble your brains, go bang your head against a wall."

"Don't dis my tracks," Kwame answered. "My music's def."

"If you want deaf, just poke sticks in your ears. You call that music? It doesn't even have pitches. It's not even savage." Our grandfather turned to Ruth for backup.

"Oh, Papap! We've been over this. That's our sound. Comes right out of all the salvation we've ever made for ourselves. Right down from the old dirty Dozens."

"How do you know about the Dozens?" Ruth blanched, and the old man patted her arm. "Don't mind me. I know. Same place I learned it. Some cultural prophet, desperate to preserve our heritage."

Ruth howled. "Don't you worry about preserving our heritage! Every white boy on five continents wants a piece of this."

"They biting our lines," Kwame said. "Totin' their own Alpines. Wiggas can't cope, our sound so dope!"

He swiveled his head, jutting it right and left with fluid pride. His little brother giggled and reached. Kwame went back under the headphones, lost to us. Ruth, baby mash all over her, put her arm around our immaculate grandfather. He suffered its stains. "You're worse than my own father. He used to get on me all the time about my music. I swore I'd never do that to any child of my own."

"He did?" I asked, incredulous. "He used to ride you about *music?*"

She groaned as if whipped. "All the time. James Brown. Aretha. Anything that had the least power. Anything of any use to me. He wanted me to go your route, his route. Why do you suppose the street hates your tunes, Joey?"

For the same reason that those tunes had been the street's salvation once—because they're useless. Our grandfather groaned, too, a soft old gospel subito, remembering old judgments, shattered trusts, allegiances killed in the honoring. He stared on his own headstone and read the things he'd said to his daughter, written there in granite. He held Ruth by the wrist, flashing a look of desperation. "What's music, that anyone should wreck their life over it?"

"When did he die?" Ruth asked, late that day.

I thought, for one mad beat, we'd switched lives. "He? Not long after I saw you last. I tried reaching you every way I could think."

"You didn't think of this way." She simply stated the fact, helping me catch up to her past. Her tears were quiet and cast away, no comfort for anyone. She cried to herself, not caring that I overheard. All her mournings gathered together. It was a long time before she spoke again. "Such an oblivious bastard. You think he ever knew what he did to us?"

I felt no need to fight over the man's identity. I couldn't even do that for my own, anymore.

"What did he die of?" I must have stayed silent longer than I realized. "I have a right to know. It might have some bearing on my sons."

"Cancer."

She winced. "What kind?"

"Pancreatic."

She nodded. "We get that, too."

"There's some money. I set it up in an account in your name. It's worth something by now."

She struggled. Repugnance versus need: I'd never have imagined the size of either. Her face went hunted. She couldn't decide what was hers by right and what she'd disowned. "Later, Joseph. Give it time."

"He left you a message." I hadn't considered it for a decade. "Something I was supposed to tell you."

Ruth cowered, as if I were battering her. I held out my palms. I felt no investment in the matter one way or the other. I only wanted to tell her and be done.

She pressed her palms to her temples, hating me for allowing this to get to her. Her fists balled up in the last counterattack of capitulation. "Let me guess. 'I know you're really a good girl. All is forgiven.'"

"He said to tell you there's another wavelength everyplace you point your telescope."

"What the fuck's that supposed to mean? You tell me what in hell I'm supposed to do with that." She'd wanted another message, one she didn't know she wanted. This one only left her more brutally orphaned.

"He wasn't well, Ruth. He was saying all sorts of things by the end. But he made me swear to tell you, if I ever got the chance."

Da's last words were too muddled to sustain resentment. She couldn't war with something so hopeless. "The man never knew how to talk to me." She let herself cry. "Never on this planet."

"Ruth. I can't stop thinking . . . about Robert." She coughed up a dead little pellet of irony. *You can't?* "Forgive me. Do you mind my asking?"

She shrugged: *You can't ask me anything I haven't asked myself.*

"What did the two of you do, in New York?"

She looked at me, confused. "What did we *do?*"

"When you came to my place that day in Atlantic City. You were in trouble. Something really wrong. The law was after you."

Her look fell away, too weary even for disgust. "You'll never, never get it, will you?" her voice filled with pity. "My brother."

"You said the police ran Robert's plates through the police computer. That he . . ."

My sister breathed in, trying to make room for me. "We ran a shelter program for neighborhood kids. That's what we *did*. Made them sing 'Black Is Beautiful' over their cornflakes. Everything else was Hoover. He turned us into the number-one threat to American security. Government agents calling us in the middle of the night, threatening to spread our brains across the pavement. Saying they'd send us to prison for the rest of our lives. We were already in prison, Joey. That's our crime. It was eating their conscience, what they've done to us. That's what we did in New York. And that's what we kept on doing in Oakland. Until they got Robert and he died in their hospital."

That was the last white question I ever asked her.

My grandfather's house was an open territory, untroubled by schedule. There was a purpose to life on Catherine Street, but no fixed pace. The family gathered my second night. My uncle Michael showed up with most of his family: his wife, his two daughters, and my cousins' children. I met my twin aunts, Lucille and Lorene, their husbands, and several of their children and grandchildren. I was a curiosity: the prodigal, the chameleon. For a moment, everyone needed a peek. But in a family that size, no novelty holds the stage for long. They fussed over me, heard what little I had to say for myself, then went back to fussing over Dr. William, the patriarch, or little Robert, the clan's latest Benjamin.

Ruth and Robert had been coming here for years, since just after they'd stopped in Atlantic City, looking for a place to hide. "It was the easiest thing in the world to look them up, Joey. You could have done it anytime you wanted."

The Daleys had a rolling ease, the high spirits of folks in a bomb shelter, holding out on makeshift joy. When three or more of them were in the same room, there was music. When they reached a critical mass, everyone started singing. After a period of negotiated chaos—*Get off of my line and get one of your own. What you mean* your *line? I've been singing that line since before you were born*—the Daley tabernacle choir settled into its singular five-and-a-half-part harmony.

I sang along where I could latch on, scatting or faking some pig Latin melisma when I didn't know the words. My early music bass sat well enough amid the full-throated riches that no one noticed it. No one stood out, and nobody sat out, either. The family made even Dr. Daley take a chorus or two in his nonagenarian growl. They allowed no exempted audience: each to a part, the praise of his choice.

Michael played Charles's old tenor sax, his brother's ghost still there in every keypad click. Lucille's eldest son, William, played bass guitar as if it were as limber as a lute. Almost everyone could lay into the parlor piano, four, six, sometimes eight hands at a time. *What did you think? Where did you suppose you got it from?* I was lucky to grab some buried interior line, needing all ten fingers to keep up. No one asked me to solo, or to solo any more than anyone else.

The instrument was a minefield. Half a dozen keys, including middle C, buzzed or bleated or no longer rose. "That's part of the game," Michael explained. "You got to make a noise while staying out of the potholes." In the middle of a huge ad hoc chorus, I stopped and saw the keys I was pressing for what they were. The ones my mother had learned on.

So long as the house was full of singing relatives, Ruth seemed as close to peaceful as I'd seen her look since Mama died. During that first barnburner night, she stretched out on a sofa, a truculent son under one arm, a happy baby sleeping on a cushion, and her slain husband seated next to her. Safe, she let loose with a descant that made me want to stop singing for good. I came and stood by her. She opened her eyes and smiled. "This is why we came back here."

"Maybe why *you* came," Kwame corrected, hearing every word from under his headphones.

"How long have you been here?"

"This visit? Since just after Robert . . ." She looked around, then cradled her forehead in her palm, rubbing out the nightmare again. "How long has that been anyway?"

My aunts Lucille and Lorene ran the choir at Bethel Covenant, the church where they, their parents, and their children had all gotten married, the church where my mother was baptized and where they'd all learned to sing. To their father's despair and their mother's delight, they chose the church over the law, for which they'd trained. Lucille played the organ and piano while Lorene conducted the choir, a good slice of which consisted of their own children. The second Sunday after my arrival, Ruth decided we'd go hear them. "All of us," she warned her son, grandfather, and brother as one.

Dr. Daley made the most noise. "Let me die in peace, a godless heathen."

"The man's right," Kwame said. "We gonna fight. Heathen of the world, unite."

"I never went for your mother. I never went for your grandmother."

"You'll go for me," Ruth said.

"Well, I'm going to sit with this young man here, and we're going to talk about Nietzsche and Jean-Paul Sartre."

I didn't have the heart to tell him this atheist Jew had sung more Catholic settings in the last five years than most of the pious attend in a lifetime.

I wasn't the lightest person in church. Not even in our half of the pews. Bethel Covenant proclaimed the gospel: Color's in the equation, but it's not the only variable. Ruth caught me staring at one redheaded choir girl, pale as a Pre-Raphaelite model. "Oh, she's black, brother."

"How do you know?"

"Black people always know."

"Hell with you, too, baby."

My sister fought back her smirk. "Don't swear in church, Joey. Wait until we're back out in the parking lot. In fact, not only is she black; she's kin of yours. Don't ask me exactly how. Some third cousin once removed."

Not surprisingly, the choir sounded much like jubilee night with the

Daleys. But not until the anthem did I learn why I was there. The tune was that old nineteenth-century warhorse, "He Leadeth Me," the solo line sung by a fresh-faced woman with a tight Afro who was several years my junior. The first verse came off pretty straight, the way it's written down in the old Methodist hymnal. Yet the soloist was so brilliant, even Kwame, busy practicing his graffiti signature on every inch of a mangled church bulletin in advance of spraying it all over Oakland, looked up to see who made such glory.

By the second verse, I was just about standing. The girl had pipes that could drain Alaska. Her pitch was something NASA used to guide satellites. She lifted up the hobbled tune and spun it about on her outstretched fingers, passed it between her legs and behind her back, and floated it over her head. Every tone in the waterfall spray was its own cut lapidary. I swung around to Ruth for explanation, but she stared straight ahead, smirking, pretending not to notice.

The voice swept outward, peeling off cloak after cloak until its light began to sear. All the while the full choir, steady as a heartbeat, swelled the refrain: "He leadeth me. He leadeth me." And on into new keys: "He leadeth me." Their gospel wall made, for the soloing girl, a rock-hard foundation from which to launch any praise at all. She rose up into the ear's ionosphere, eyes alight, lifting in the humility of absolute delight, as close as the soul comes to knowing its own amplitude. I couldn't believe she was improvising those huge aerial profusions with such certainty. Yet neither did I think for a moment that such fresh bursts could have been written out in advance.

The hymn built up in ever-breaking waves. Hands sprouted in the air around us. I was beside myself, unable to hold the beauty as it passed. I looked at Dr. Daley, shaken out of everything but the question: *Who?* He nodded gravely. "That's Lorene's baby." I couldn't marry the woman; she was my first cousin. "That's Dee."

I turned back to my sister at the sound of the name. Her smile was broken into scrap by the long way here.

"My God. What a voice. She needs the best training possible."

My sister hissed, loud enough for those in the pew ahead of us to hear. "Asshole. You think *that* is some spontaneous jungle talent? She *has* had the best training possible. Can't you hear?"

"Who? Where?"

"They're falling all over her. At Curtis."

After the service, we waited in the receiving line to meet the phe-nomenon. My cousin Delia recognized me as we approached. I guess I wasn't too hard to pick out. Before Ruth could do introductions, the girl waved her off. She stared at me. "You've got a hell of a lot of nerve." A knot of Sunday celebrants turned to study the commotion. "Coming in here, the picture of innocence. You got to answer for what you've done."

The list formed in my mind. I was ready to sign it all and serve any penance. I felt the heat emanating from this woman. Ruth and Dr. Daley stood at my elbow, silent bailiffs. I knew what I'd done. My family had known, long before I did. There was no choice but to stand still and re-ceive the awful sentence.

"Whose idea was it to do that Bach like that?"

It took me half the length of a chorale before I could even feel relief. And another half a phrase before I could answer, "Ah! Everyone has their own Bach." She was still scowling, shaking her angry head. "Was it too small for you?" This had been our most faulted transgression: one voice per line. Thinking heaven might answer to the private call.

My cousin glared at me, smoldering like Carmen. "You owe me a car."

"I . . . a car?" My checkbook ready already.

"I had your little motets on the tape player while trying to drive. Right through the red light at Sixteenth and Arch. Glorious! Didn't even know I was in the intersection until this Ford Escort came through at nine o'clock and clipped my wings. Escorted me right back to this world, thank you. *Sing Unto the Lord a New Song?*"

"That's the one."

"Well, you did that all right. Umm-*hmm*. That one was righteous!"

I took forever to figure out the simplest things. "You like it? It suited you?"

"You owe me a car. Nice reliable Dodge Dart in a pretty red."

Anyone but a musician might tell you that all silences sound the same. But Ruth's silence, on the way home, modulated into a new song.

I heard Delia's Bach not long after that. She soloed across town in a pan-Philadelphia performance of the B Minor Mass. Jonah might not have favored such high-powered magnificence. But even he, hearing this, would have been delivered. Delia's *Laudamus Te* carried all the rapture that that Latin-writing Lutheran posted forward in it. Every note was faultless, as written. And yet it swung, kicking back and dancing like there was no tomorrow. Which there isn't. Ever. That eerie, unearthbound work had found its celebrant. *Praise is praise,* my cousin's voice said. *Music's music. Don't let anyone tell you otherwise.*

Two nights later, I heard her sing Villa-Lobos's *Bachianas brasileiras* no. 5. The piece had long ago become a theme-park poster for itself, as over-played and unhearable a monument as Wilson Hart's adored Rodrigo, done in by too much love. But in Delia Banks's sinuous, ethereal turns, it went desperate for me again, mystic, possessed, sexy, a single endless se-quence spun out of one breath. It wasn't even that I'd never heard it properly. I'd simply never heard it. Her version sighed past any of the scores of recordings I knew. And hers would never be recorded.

I had lunch with her, just the two of us, almost clandestine, in the same diner where my mother and grandmother had once secretly met. "Ghosts everywhere," Delia said. "We're lucky they're so big on sharing."

I didn't know how to speak my pleasure. "You could have . . . Name the life you want." Times had changed. Or would have to, for this woman. "You can have the international concert career of your choice." I knew the odds, yet knew, too, how little I was exaggerating. A person could live his whole life chasing music and be lucky to hear one time-sent voice. I was near kin to two of them.

My cousin favored me with a high-watt version of her stage smile, the one that made her audiences love her before she opened her throat. "Thank you, sir. You say the sweetest things, for a lost soul."

"I'm serious."

"I know you are." The waitress came and Delia traded barbs with her. When the woman left, my cousin shook her head at me. "You ever sing at Salzburg?"

"Several times. A beautiful place. You'd love it."

"I know. I've seen the movie. The one with that spinning nun? You ever sing at the Festival d'Art lyrique d'Aix-en-Provence?"

"We once won a prize there." As I answered, it dawned on me: Delia already knew.

"You happy?" She knew the answer to that one, too. "Ask me if I'm happy. Ask me what kind of career I want. I got everything in the world already, cuz. Got my church. Who'd need a bigger stage than that? I've got people I love singing with me, building the sound, taking me higher. Every piece we do, we make our own, whatever post office it came on through. I got a repertoire long enough to last me two lifetimes. One short and the other long."

I went wily and virtuous all at once. "You owe it . . . to the source of your gift not to hide that light under a bushel. To bring that sound to as many people as possible."

Delia thought about my words. They troubled her, a slip of evil moving about in the Garden. "No. This isn't about bigger numbers. Are you happy? You can't make anyone happy if you're not happy yourself."

She had my X-rays clipped up on the light box just to the side of our booth, and she didn't at all like what she saw. I had to take the offensive, before she finished me off. "Are you afraid?"

The idea amused her. "Of who?"

I might have drawn her up a list: all the people who'd want you dead just for traveling on the only passport you get. She knew the costs, hidden and obvious, even just for singing across town. Avoidance might not be fear. It might be more like fear's opposite. "Simple preference, then?"

"Oh, I'll sing whatever glory's sitting on the music stand."

"But only religious music."

Delia played with the salt and pepper shakers. "All music's religious music. All the good parts anyway." It was true: Even her languorous, sultry Portuguese siren song had seduced for a brighter flame.

"Well, I've heard what you did to that backwoods German cracker. So I know this isn't about cultural ownership."

"Oh, but it is." As soon as she spoke the words, everything was. No culture without owners, without owned.

"You're anti-Europe?" Sick, imperial, supremacist, and striving to please the eternal angels.

" 'Anti-Europe'?" Delia rolled her eyes. "Can't very well be that. Though Europe has cost me more cars than we're going to talk about today, honey. No, can't be anti-Europe without doing more amputation than is good for a body. Every song we sing's got white notes running through it. But that's the beauty of the situation, cuz. We're making a little country here, out of mutual theft. They come over into our neck of the woods, take all we got. We sneak over into their neighborhood, middle of the night, grab a little something back, something they didn't even know they had, something they can't even recognize no more! More for everybody that way, and more kinds of everybody." She shook her head. A low mezzo growl of despite came out of her chest. "No. Can't be anti-Europe when everyone's part Europe. But got to be pro-Africa, for the same reason."

Surely her church loved her too much to keep her to themselves. "Thousands could hear you. Hundreds of thousands."

"As many as hear your brother?" She regretted the words as soon as they were out.

"You could change the way people think."

"Change! You still waiting for music to cure us? Bach? Mozart? Nazis love them, too. Music never cured anyone. Look at your poor sister. Look at her man. Figure that out with music. Do you have a single song you can sing her to take care of her now? One single song that can do anything for her, that won't shrivel up and die of helpless shame?"

It wasn't too late for me to learn a trade. Some honest living. I could still type. Typing and filing for a pro bono law firm. I took a breath, went down into my bass days with Voces Antiquae, already ancient history. "The song is only as good as its listener."

"Your sister. *For* her. For *her*."

I looked for what I believed. "Maybe we sing for ourselves."

"At least that. Nothing without that. But nothing if only that. We need a music that sings to anyone. That makes them sing. No audience!"

"AM radio."

"Can't hurt me with that."

"Gospel sings to anyone?" I had another list for her, if she wanted it.

"Anyone with ears to hear."

"That's just it. Our ears only hear what sounds people get a chance to know."

"Oh, people know. Listen. Every beautiful sound comes from saying what's happened to us. Well, name someone who's had more happen to them than us."

"Us?"

"Yes, cuz."

Her words blunted the ones that were loaded in my throat. I had no comeback but the one that shamed me most. "I'm greedy. I want to hear . . ." All those implicated, complicit, compromised old warhorses. She could work their salvation. Only a black voice could do that now. "I want to hear that music . . . redeemed." Hear it be, at last, what it had always pretended to be.

Delia glowed a moment with the thought. But I was the devil, tempting her to turn stones into bread. "Cuz, cuz. You're not getting this. I've got my church. My Jesus."

"Doesn't he come from Europe?"

She grinned. "Ours comes from a little south of there. Listen to me. I've got my work. I've got *ours*. You hear how glorious that word sounds? I don't blame you for living your life. You were raised when we still thought the only way to get what they got is to copy their stuff. We're us and ain't never gonna be them, and where's the pain in that? Just as big— bigger, given the whole story. Why you working so hard over something you can't save and doesn't want to be?"

For the same reason that makes us sing anything. I glanced around the restaurant. All shades imaginable. Nobody much cared that I was there or had any stake in my desperation. I looked at my cousin. The national color averaged out somewhere between us. "You're saying separate but equal?"

"That's right. Where's the problem? Different cultures, equal status."

"Equal status with the dominant culture?"

"They only dominate those they can."

"I thought the whole point was that separate could never be—"

"There's a big difference now. Now, it's our choice."

But if it were impossible—impossible to search for chords outside of us, impossible to find that scale, that tune that sang beyond this time and place . . . I wanted more than this invented moment and this enforced difference, more than this wary truce pretending to be the peace we'd always been seeking. I tried with everything in me. I turned her words around more ways than there were ways to turn. "You're saying that you can only sing what you are?"

The coffee came. By the time the waitress left, they'd exchanged recipes, boyfriend grievances, and phone numbers. Then it was just the two of us. Delia wrapped her hands around her hot mug, drawing heat and horizon-wide pleasure. "Where were we again? No, no. I think it's more like: You can only be what you sing."

"My sister could have been a singer. She had a voice to convert anyone."

"Joseph Strom!" I jerked my head up. For a moment, she was my mother, reprimanding a boy of nine. My cousin's eyes were wet. She shook her head, horrified. "Listen to her, for once. Just listen."

I did. It would have come to me, sooner or later. I joined Ruth one evening for her routine walk around the neighborhood. Our aunts and uncle told her she was crazy, taking her life in her hands. They didn't even like to ride down the street with their windows rolled up. Her evening walks sent Papap into fits. She waved them all away. "I'm safer out here than I am standing in front of Independence Hall. I'd sooner trust my life to the worst crackhead than to any police officer in this country."

Much of the neighborhood was out on their front porches, living in public, the way people lived in Ghent, the way few Americans above the poverty line lived. My sister greeted everyone we passed, sometimes by name. "I like to think about Grandma and Papap walking out here when they were young."

"Do you ever think about Da's parents, Ruth? I'm not fighting with you. I'm not . . . I'm just . . ."

She held up her palm sideways and nodded. "I've tried. I can't even . . . You know, I'm addicted to the survivor accounts. I've seen every Holocaust documentary ever made. You'd have to be dead to have a memory big enough. The way I think about . . . our other grandparents? The supremacists got them, too."

"Even though they were white."

"They weren't white. They weren't even the same species. Not to the people running the ovens. We were sent along with them, what few of us were there."

" 'We'?"

She heard, and nodded. "I mean the other us."

One would have to be dead already to survive such inheritance. We passed a row of century-old houses, now carved up into rented rooms. Ruth hummed under her breath. I couldn't make out the tune. When the tune changed to words, she seemed to speak to someone across the street. "Look, Joey. It's easy. The easiest question in the world. If they come and start rounding us up, which line are you going to get into?"

"No question. Not even a choice."

"But they've *been* rounding us up, Joey." She spread her hands around the neighborhood. "They're rounding us up now. They'll keep rounding us up, for as long as there's a calendar."

I tried to follow her. When she spoke next, it reeled me back from Da's deep-space catalog.

"You should have married that white girl, Joey. I'm sure she was nice."

"Is. Is nice. But I'm not."

"Incompatible?" I looked at her. Her mouth twisted into a crook of empathy.

"Incompatible."

"Take two people."

I waited. Then I realized this was the entire recipe. "Two people. Exactly."

"Mama and Da would have had to divorce. If she'd lived."

"You think?" The stories we told about their story no longer mattered to them.

"Of course. Look at the statistics."

"Numbers never lie," I said, in our old German accent.

She winced and grinned at the same time. Hybrid vigor. "Robert and I were incompatible. But it worked."

"What about his parents?"

Ruth looked at me, seeing ghosts. "You never knew? Your own brother-in-law?" Blaming, taking the blame. "I never told you? Of course not; when could I have? Robert was raised in a foster home. White folks. Only in it for the aid checks."

We covered two blocks. We were hit up twice for cash, once to help get a car out of hock to drive a wife to the hospital and once to tide a man over until an accident at his bank could be ironed out in court. Both times, my sister made me give them five dollars.

"They're just going to buy booze or dope with it," I said.

"Yeah? And what world-fixing were you getting up to with it?"

Every third yard was a pachyderm's graveyard of shopping carts, washing machines, and stripped Impalas whose last highway would be four cinder blocks. A cluster of kids Kwame's age worked a basketball in an empty lot, dribbling between the larger shards of glass, using oil drums for their picks and rolls, and chucking the ball at a rim that seemed made from an old TV antenna. Every square foot of concrete was garlanded in tendrils of graffiti, the elaborate signatures of those who were prevented from putting their names on anything else. The block housed more poverty per yard than even my sister could identify with. The furnaces of progress were busy burning all the fuel they could find.

Whatever dream my brother and I had been raised on was dead. Incredible to me: the *1980s*. Uplift had fallen deeper than the place where it had started, back before hopes were raised.

My years in Europe opened my eyes to the place stamped on my passport. Three months before, with Voces, I'd toured the Adriatic, singing an old Latin monastic text: "Teach me to love what I cannot hope to know; teach me to know what I cannot hope to be." Here I was, walking through a ruined Philadelphia with my sister, begging to be what I couldn't know, trying to know what I couldn't love. All song that didn't hear this massacre was a lie.

My sister saw her own landscape. "We need control of our own neighborhoods. It wouldn't solve things, of course. But it would be a start."

Always another start. And a start after that. "Ruth?" I was willing to look at any misery around me, except my sister. "How long are you planning to stay around here?"

"You still on white people's time, aren't you?" I spun around, stiffening. Then I felt her arm slipping through mine. "Funny thing? My Oakland? It looks a lot like this."

"You could move."

She shook her head at me. "No, I couldn't, Joey. It's where all his work went. It's where . . . he died." We walked in silence, turning the last corner to Papap's house again. Ruth stopped and blurted, "How am I supposed to do this, Joey? A ten-year-old on his way to hell and another little half-year-old with a murdered father."

"What are you saying? Kwame's in trouble?"

She shook her head. "You'll go to your grave a classical musician, won't you? A black boy in trouble. Imagine." I pulled away from her, and she exploded, throwing her hands in the air. She brought them back down over her face, like falling ash. "I can't. I can't. I'll never make it."

My first thought, God help me, was, *Make it where?* I closed the distance and put my hands on her shoulders. She threw them off. As quickly as her tears came, they stopped. "Okay. Okay. No crisis. Just another husbandless single sister mother. Millions of us."

"How many of you got brothers?"

Ruth squeezed my arm, a frantic tourniquet. "You don't know, Joey. You can't begin." She felt me flinch, and grabbed on tighter. "I don't mean that. I mean what's happened to us, since you took off. The bottom's dropped out of the whole country. Like living through a lifelong air raid. For a boy, a little boy?" Her shudder passed through me. I'd never feel safe again. "You haven't noticed it, in him? You really haven't noticed?"

"Kwame? No. Well, he dresses . . . a little like a criminal."

She barked in pained amusement and smacked the air. "All the kids do now. And half the adults, too."

"And I've noticed he hates policemen."

"That's just common sense. Survival benefit."

We stood still outside our grandfather's house. I looked in and saw him at the window, pulling back a white curtain to look at us. Dr. Daley: the family practitioner under siege in the neighborhood he'd once served. He motioned violently for us to come in. Ruth nodded and held up a finger, bargaining for thirty seconds. Seeing no immediate emergency, he let the curtain fall and retreated.

Ruth leaned toward me. "Kwame's not like Robert. He has Robert's healthy resentment. But Robert always had a counterplan. He was always working on an answer. One more public education drive, one more demonstration. Kwame's got the rage, but not a single answer for it. Robert used to keep him in line by challenging him. Used to say, 'Best thing to do when you're feeling mad is make something of yourself that's not them.' When Kwame explodes, I do what Robert used to do. I sit him down with a sheet of paper and colored pencils. Or park him in front of a box of paint. Kwame can make—oh! The wildest things. But since . . . The last few times I tried to sit him down . . ."

Then the boy appeared at the window, watching us. Through the glass, even with his headphones and their pounding pulse, he heard us talking about him. Fury and apathy fought for a controlling interest in his eyes. My sister looked back at her son, smiling at him through her panic. But what can you hide from a child who has already seen death? She turned and grabbed me just below the collar. "How much are we talking about, Joey? My portion of . . . the savings?"

Ruth's third of the inheritance had been sitting in balanced investments, compounding for more years than her son had lived. It couldn't match that boy's compounded experience, but it was a usable sum. I gave her an estimate. Her face did its own skeptical calculation. "We have some, too, Robert and I. And Papap keeps offering—the piece Mama never got. We could get matching funds. There are sources—not many, but they're there. It's all Robert wanted. His last sustained plan before . . . He worked so hard on it, I can see the blueprints."

I was afraid to ask her to make sense. She started up again, steering me toward the door. "Joseph Strom. How would you like to give your nephew music lessons?"

I pressed back, feeling her hand's resistance. "Ruth. Don't even joke. What could I possibly . . . He'd eat me alive."

She laughed and shook her head, dragging me on toward the door. "Oh, Kwame's nothing, baby. Wait until you get a classroom full of ten-year-olds! Wait until little Robert comes up through the ranks."

That's how I returned to Oakland with my sister and her sons. It was as easy as falling. As soon as Ruth described Robert's school to me, I knew I'd been looking for a reason to keep me from returning to Europe. Something big enough to put up against the salvage of the past. Nothing else had claim over my life. My single problem lay in breaking the news to Jonah.

We called him from Philadelphia just before we left. I had trouble finding him at home, in Ghent. When he heard my voice, Jonah made it sound as if he'd been waiting for weeks at the side of the phone. "Damn it, Mule. I've been dying by inches here. What's happening?"

"Why didn't you just call if you wanted to hear from us?"

"That wouldn't exactly be hearing from you, would it?"

"I'm going to California. Ruth's building a school."

"And you are going to . . ."

"Fucker. I'm going to teach for her."

He thought a moment before saying anything. Or maybe it was the transatlantic lag. "I see. You're quitting the group. You're going to kill Voces Antiquae?" With the bull market in early music not even starting to peak, superlative, vibrato-free voices were springing up all over. I'd always been the ensemble's weak link, the amateur latecomer. This was my brother's chance to replace me with a real bass, a trained one, someone who could do justice to the others and lift them to that last level of international renown that had vaguely eluded us. He didn't have to mourn the loss of my voice. He needed only to let me know how completely I'd betrayed him.

"Well, we had our run, didn't we?" His was the voice of the future past. He sounded light-years away, anxious to get off the phone and start auditioning my replacements. "So how is your sister?"

"You want to talk to her?"

From the kitchen counter, where she'd been pretending not to listen, Ruth shook her head. Jonah said, "I don't know, Joey. Does she want to talk with me?"

Ruth cursed me under her breath as I handed her the phone. She took the receiver as if it were a bone club. Her sound was small and flat. "JoJo." After a while: "Long time. You old yet?" She listened, dead. Then she sat up, defending. "Don't start this. Just . . . don't." After another pause, she said, "No, Jonah. That's what *you* should do. That's what you should fucking do."

She lapsed into another listening silence, then handed the phone to Papap. He shouted into it. *"Hallo. Hallo? Dieses ist mein Enkel?"*

The words ripped me. They did worse to Ruth. She came over to me and whispered, so Europe couldn't hear. "You sure about this? You had work. Maybe you belong over there."

She just wanted noise from me. She couldn't bear the sounds of that other conversation. We talked in a drone, drowning out Papap and listening in by helpless turns. He and Jonah talked for three or four minutes, nothing, everything—collapsing decades into a few hundred words. Papap grilled Jonah about Europe, Solidarity, Gorbachev. God only knows what answers Jonah invented. "When are you coming home?" Papap asked. Ruth tried to talk over the words, as if that would erase them. But that's the thing about sounds: Even when they all happen at once, none of them cancels out the others. They just keep stacking up, beyond any chord's ability to hold.

There was a silence, out of which Papap suddenly charged, enraged. "You don't know what you're talking about. Behind the times. Come back and listen. Every song and dance in this country has gone brown." Ruth and I quit our deaf show. She stared at me, but before I could even shrug, our grandfather was sailing. "You think you're a traitor out there? You're nothing but an advance scout. A double agent . . . Well, call it that, too, if you like. Name an immortal piece that wouldn't sound better sung by the hired help. That little world you've been scouting is going to be overrun with black, once we show the least little bit of interest. *Sie werden noch besser sein als im Basketball.*"

Ruth quizzed me with a look. I felt myself giggling bitterly. "Just like basketball," I translated. "Only better."

They improvised their good-byes and my grandfather hung up. "Interesting man, your brother. He didn't know that the Soviet Union had a new leader." He chuckled, his shoulders jarring loose from his body. "I'm not entirely sure he'd heard of basketball, either."

"What did he say to you?" I asked Ruth.

"He said I should travel. Get my mind off the past."

The whole family showed for our departure. My uncle Michael, my aunts Lucille and Lorene, most of their kids and grandkids—I still didn't know all their names. They gathered the night before we left, to send us out. We sang. What else was there? Delia Banks was there, her sound as wide as a flowering chestnut and as delicate as sweet williams. She didn't solo, except for an aerial twelve bars. Tunes fell in line, jumbling up and overlapping, talking to one another, taking themselves as their only topic. The Daley game, too, was Crazed Quotations, drawn from another well, the water colder and more bracing. *Where do you think your mother got it from?* The send-off had no sadness. We'd meet back here next year and the year after, we and all our dead, as our dead had been meeting here without us every prior year. And if not here, then that flatted-seventh somewhere else.

Late that night, after the last cousin left, Papap came into his dead son's room, the room that for weeks I'd inhabited. He held a stiff, shiny square of paper. He sat in his boy's ancient chair, next to where I stretched out. I scrambled to my feet, and he waved me back down.

"Your sister got most of the keepsakes. I gave what I had to her years ago. I didn't know you'd be showing up. But I found these for you." A Polaroid of my brother and me opening Christmas presents, a photo Da had taken and given to the Daleys. And an older Brownie photo of a woman who could only be my mother. I couldn't stop looking. I took it in in long gasps, a suffocating man needing air. It was the first fresh look I'd had of her since the fire. In the tiny black-and-white print, a young woman—far younger than I was now—of uncertain tone but clearly African features looked back through the lens, smiling weakly, seeing on the exposing film everything that would happen to her. She wore a dress of midcalf length with wide, pointed shoulders, the height of fashion in the years before my birth.

"What color is this dress?" I heard myself ask from a long while off.

He studied me. He saw my hunger, and it threatened to kill him. He tried to talk but couldn't.

"Navy blue," I told him.

He held still for a time, then nodded. "That's right. Navy blue."

We said good-bye to Papap. He wouldn't let us pretend we'd ever see him again in this life. Ruth took her leave of our grandfather as if he contained all those people she had never gotten to say good-bye to. And he did. He came out onto the lawn as we got in the car, suddenly frailer than ninety. He took my hand. "I'm glad to have met you. Next life, in Jerusalem."

My grandfather was right: Every music in America had gone brown. Our drive across the continent proved it. The car took me back to those days, Jonah and I crisscrossing the United States and Canada. The place had gotten infinitely bigger in the intervening years. The only way to get across a place so huge was still by radio. Every signal our receiver found—even the C and W stations drifting across the Great Plains—had at least one drop of black sloshing around in it. Africa had done to the American song what the old plantation massas had done to Africa. Only this time, the parent was keeping custody.

Ruth and I took turns driving and looking after little Robert. "You make this almost easy," she said. "The trip out was hell."

"I helped, Mama," Kwame shouted. "I did the best I could."

" 'Course you did, honey."

The driver got to choose the station, although Kwame's need for a shattering bass beat usually dictated. He liked the ones whose rhythms were like Chinese water torture, the ones that forced the chords into your auditory canal with a syringe.

"What's this called?"

"Hip-hop," Kwame said, giving even those two syllables a rhythm I'd have to work at.

"I'm too old. Too old even to listen from a distance."

My sister just laughed at me. "You were born too old."

The country had strayed into musics beyond my ability to make out. I could only take them in contained doses. Now and then, during the three-day marathon of my belated education, I backslid and trolled for my own old addictions. The flood of now—the music that people really used and needed—had risen so high that only a few scattered islands of by-passed memory remained above water. When I managed to find classical stations at all, they beamed out a continuous stream of Vivaldi's *Four Seasons* and Barber's *Adagio for Strings*. Soon there would be only a dozen pieces left from the last thousand years of written music, pressed into anthologies suitable for seduction, gag gifts, and raising your baby's IQ.

"Does this make my people an oppressed minority?" I asked Ruth.

"We'll talk when they start shooting at you."

Culture was whatever survived its own bonfire. Whatever you held on to when nothing else worked. And then, it didn't, either.

Somewhere past Denver, driving, I chanced upon a clear signal of a chorus that, within three notes, I pegged as Bach. Cantata 78. I peeked at the backseat, where my nephew twisted and fidgeted. A look passed across his face, not even engaged enough for contempt. The music might have come from Mars, or farther. This was the boy, and hundreds like him, who I was now supposed to teach about music.

The opening chorus died away. I knew what was coming, though I hadn't heard the piece for ages. Two beats of silence, and then that duet. "Wir eilen mit schwachen, doch emsigen Schritten." My brother at ten, Kwame's age, had bounded along that upper line with eager steps, lost in the euphoria of his own voice. The soprano this time was another boy lost in time, as good as my brother had been, as drunk on the notes. The lower voice, now a countertenor, came alive in the game of harmonic tag, rejuvenated by trying to keep up with the boy he, too, must once have been. The two of them were high, clear, and fast as light. I looked at Ruth to see if she remembered. Of course, she couldn't have. The boys flew, the music was good, and my life bent back on itself. I flew alongside these notes, racing myself toward what they wanted me to remember, until the flashing red lights in my rearview mirror stopped me. I looked down at the speedometer: eighty-nine miles an hour.

By the time I pulled over and the squad car nosed up behind us, Ruth was in pieces. She shrieked, "Don't get out of the car. Don't get out." Kwame crouched on the backseat, pressed up against the door, ready to leap out and grab the cop's gun. Little Robert started to wail, as if that terror really did start in race's womb. My sister struggled to comfort him, calming and wrestling him down.

"This is it," Kwame said. "We dead."

The police car sat behind us, running our plates, toying with its food. When the officer got out of the car, all three of us let out our breath. "Thank God," Ruth said, not believing. "Oh God, thank you." The man was black.

I rolled down the window and fed him my license before he could ask. "You know why I pulled you over?" I nodded. "Is this car yours?"

"My sister's." I waved toward Ruth. She had one hand on the baby and the other stretched across the seat, restraining Kwame.

The officer pointed. "Who's that?"

I looked down to where he pointed: the radio, Cantata 78 still pouring out of it. In the panic of the moment, I'd forgotten it was even on. I looked back at the policeman and smiled apologetically. "Bach."

"No points for the obvious. I mean, who's singing?"

He took my license and retreated to his car. Two lifetime prison sentences later, he returned and handed it back to me. "You have better things to do with your hundred and twenty bucks?"

Kwame understood the question before I did. "Build a school."

The policeman nodded. "Keep it below allegro next time."

Twenty miles down the interstate, Ruth burst out cackling. Nerves. She couldn't stop. I thought I'd have to pull over. "You damn honkies." She sucked air between her hysterical sobs. "They let you walk, every single time."

DEEP RIVER

This is how time runs: like some stoked-up, stage-sick kid in his first talent show. One glance at that audience out there past the footlights and all those months of metronome practice vanish in a blast of presto. Time has no sense of tempo. It's worse than Horowitz. The marks on the page mean nothing. I hit Oakland, and my life's whole beat doubled.

I moved into the second story of a chewed-up gingerbread house ten blocks from my sister's, near the interstate. I could walk to Preservation Park in twenty minutes. But then, I could also see the North Star on clear nights with my naked eye. De Fremery was a lot closer. The park's old Panther Self-Defense outreaches were history, but the rallies went on, as timeless as the crimes they countered.

I passed through the East Bay like a masked figure through some Act Four costume party. For the first weeks, walking home through my new neighborhood at night, I felt every conscience-stricken terror my country had trained me to feel. I saw how I looked, dressed, sounded, and moved. I'd never been more conspicuous, even in Europe. Even I would have singled myself out to hit.

But no one sees anyone else, in the end. This is our tragedy, and the thing that may finally save us. We steer only by the grossest landmarks. Turn left at bewilderment. Keep going till you hit despair. Pull up at complete oblivion, turn around, and you're there. After six months, I knew all my neighbors' names. After eight, I knew what they needed from the world. After ten, what I needed from them. It might have taken longer, but I'd been born into an outsiders' club. The only surprise about Oakland was how huge and shared outsideness could be.

From the beginning, Jonah's and my performance had been whiteness, the hardest piece to make both believable and worth listening to. Now I entered another concert, the block party of the ticketless, where they had to let you in if you only so much as showed.

We heard from Uncle Michael before that first year was out. Dr. Daley had died in his sleep, just shy of his ninety-first birthday. "The first thing he ever did that didn't take work," Michael wrote.

As for me, nothing I do will ever be effortless again. I feel like I'm twelve and helpless. His age ends with him. We're all drifting now . . . Lorene said he'd waited until he got a chance to make the acquaintance of his missing grandchildren . . . We'll spare you all the surprises we found while going through his belongings. Nobody dies without telling everything. But one thing we found, you'll want to hear about. You remember that mahogany desk he worked at in his study, Ruth? We wanted to save it, with the other pieces in the house worth saving. When we pulled the thing away from the corner, we found a yellowed folder, tucked between a piece of panel and the wall. It was all your clippings, Joseph, all the reviews of you and your brother. He'd been keeping them for years, hiding them from Mama. He kept them back there so long, he forgot they were there . . .

If that much hasn't made you hang yourself yet, here's the awful part. I helped the girls clean out Mama's dresser two years ago, when she died. She kept a hidden clippings file, too. Secret keepsakes. We never told the man. You see how blood feuds go. Do white people do this to themselves, too?

The letter felt like lung surgery. A man and a woman joined together for decades, their own nation, and my parents' experiment had split them. No one was left to beg forgiveness from. I had no one to atone to but myself. I lay in bed much of the weekend after reading the letter, unable to get up. When I did, I was filled with the need for real work.

For that, Ruth provided. She'd raided the Unified School District for a dozen of the most urgent teachers in the Bay Area, all old acquaintances. They were waiting for her, as much victims of contemporary education as the most hardened dropout. Her board had so much combined experience that theory could find no hiding place among them. They turned up sums of money hidden under rocks and tucked away in widowers' mattresses. They were not above crackpot grant applications, community begging, rummage sales, and the common shakedown. One large anonymous no-strings gift helped seed a permanent endowment. We set up camp in an abandoned food store leased to us for little more than the insurance and taxes. New Day Elementary School—K through 3—opened in 1986 and was fully accredited within three years. "The first four years are everything," Ruth said. Tuition depended upon means. Many of our parents paid in volunteer work.

She took me on probation, until I got certified like everyone else. I taught days and went back to school nights. I got my master's in musical education just as Ruth completed her Ed.D. In every working week, my sister astonished me. I never imagined I could help make something happen in the actual world. It had never occurred to Ruth to bother doing anything else. "It's a little thing. Flower coming up through the concrete. Doesn't break the rock. But it makes a little soil."

I learned more in my first four years teaching for New Day than I'd learned in the forty years before that. More about what happened to a tune on its way back to *do*. It seemed I had some time left after all to sample the sounds that weren't mine, to study their scales and rhythms, the national anthems of all the states I couldn't get to from my place of origin. At New Day, we came into an idea that was simplicity itself. There was no separate audience. There were no separate musics.

We had words and phonics and sentence cadences. Numbers and patterns and rhythmic shapes. Speaking and shouting. Birdsong and vibration; tunes for planting and protection; prayers of remembering and forgetting, sounds for every living creature, every invention under the sky and each of that sky's spinning objects. All topics talked to all others, through pitches in time. We rapped the times tables. We chanted the irregular verbs. We had science, history, geography, and every other organized shout of hurt or joy that's ever been put on a report card. But we taught no separate cry called music. Just song everywhere, each time any child turned his or her head. The occult mathematics of a soul that doesn't know it's counting.

"I'm not looking for miracles," Ruth told me. "I just want more kids reading at grade level than we have families living at the median."

We didn't have much money for instruments. What we lacked, we made. We had steel drums and glass harmonicas, cigar-box guitars and tubular bells. We wrote out our own arrangements, which each new wave of children learned afresh. Every year had its composers, its choruses, its prima donnas, its solid, no-nonsense sidemen. My kids howled for me almost as they might have, had I not been there. I did nothing but give them room.

Ruth challenged me once. "Joey, let me take you to a record store. It's like the year you went to Europe, you stopped listening to—"

"No more room, Ruth. My scores are all full."

"Nonsense. You'll love what's going on. And your kids will be much—"

"Hold up. Here's the deal." She could see me shaking, and she took my arm. I dropped several decibels. "Here's what I can do for you. I am giving these kids something that no one else in the world is ever going to give them. No one. But me."

She stroked me, as scared as I was. "You're right, Joey. I'm sorry. You're the music teacher. And I'm not the cops." It was the only time we struggled over curriculum.

I might have married, now. The picture of Mama that Papap had given me sat framed atop my bookshelf full of music-education texts: The woman I'd spend my life with, the ghost that had kept me from marrying Teresa was returned home. I lived surrounded now by women who'd been everywhere my mother had, who'd passed auditions beyond the one Mama had been turned away from, women who might wake me from nightmares I didn't even know I was having, women whose split lives might dovetail perfectly with mine. But I had no time to meet and court a wife. All I had time for was my children and their songs.

I was putting in more hours working for Ruth than I had working for Jonah. The job took all I had, and for the first time in my life, I did work that wouldn't have been done if I wasn't doing it. It should have been enough, everything that was lacking in my life in Europe. But it wasn't. Something in me still needed out. The place I had come from was dying, for lack of a way of getting to where I was.

I wasn't alone, stranded in the standing present. My nephew Kwame never went to New Day School. He was too old by the time our alternative was under way. I saw him only once or twice a month, when I went to Ruth's for Sunday dinner. Truth was, Ruth gave so much of herself to her concrete-defeating flower that her own boy ended up taking private lessons in latchkey school. He doubled in size from eleven to thirteen. His voice dropped through the floor and thickened so much, I had trouble understanding him. He started to scare me, just the way he hung and talked. Oakland came and found him out and solved his father's death. Rhythm freed him: the trick it always promises. He dressed in rage, an apprentice criminal, yards of baggy black sailcloth for a shirt, sagging jeans, the bill of his Dodgers baseball cap tipped back onto his thickening neck, or, later, a stocking pulled over his head. He held his fingers splayed like chopsticks, rapper-style, slicing the air. All he needed was a snub-nosed gun.

I tried giving him piano lessons. They weren't even a disaster. I was his uncle, whatever that meant. He felt his father's ghost too strongly to dis me outright. But my chords were worthless to him. He couldn't even slander me, so clueless did I come. My nephew's hands could span a tenth on the keyboard with ease, magnificent. But ten minutes a week of practice was beyond him. Like asking someone to carry a stone around with him, just for the good it might do his soul.

Each lesson forced us more into the open. "This thing play 'Dope-man'? This thing play 'Fuck tha Police'?"

He couldn't get to me; I'd been gotten to already, too long ago. "It plays anything you want. You just have to get good enough to tell it how."

What owns us? What can we own? Kwame tried to plunk out his untranscribable rap. It was like doing sculpture with a trowel. The results only made him furious. He brought in a disk for us to work with. To spite me, really. "You'll like this. Wreckin' Cru. Old-time shit. Still uses keyboards."

I looked at the date. Eighteen months old. He played me a track with a wild, irregular synthesizer riff. I ran it back for him, note for note. Took everything I had left in me.

"Damn," Kwame said in a low, affectless monotone.

More out of curiosity than to impress him, I tried the line again, this time juked up, hammered out, fitted with a good Baroque figured bass. Then I tried to fugue it. Sampling the sampler. The whole system runs on theft. *Tell me what hasn't already been stolen?*

When I finished, my nephew just stared at me, shaking his head. "You the illest, you know that?"

"I am aware."

His was an act, but not an act—this gangsta son of a doctor of education. He went with the tune that best served him. Kwame's at least had some angry fire that my dress-up had lacked. We go through our lives playing ourselves. Black is and black ain't. Ten years on and he'd lose this music, too. Every affluent white kid from Vancouver to Naples would be playing him.

His two uncles had sung about that theft once, a wasted old tune and even older words. We'd performed it in a converted shipping house in The Hague that had amassed fortunes on the triangle trade: *What we love is left us.* Kwame rapped for me, songs about killing police or Koreans, about putting women in their place. He giggled over the words when I asked him. I wasn't sure he knew what they meant. I didn't. But his body knew, in every twitch of those sinuous slingshot rhythms: Here was all the room he had to live.

He came to lessons with his eyes red, his body heavy, the muscles in his face sluggishly amused at the entire white-owned world. His clothes held that sweet, acrid smell of burning rope I remembered from my brother's forays in the Village a quarter of a century ago. Jonah had run his experiments for a while, then graduated. Kwame, I thought, would, too. I considered mentioning things to Ruth. But that would have killed what little trust her son and I had won.

Ruth came to my apartment late on a winter night in 1988, Robert in tow. The child was only four, but already smart enough to guess everything that adults really meant when they cooed at him. Now he stood tugging at his mother's knees, trying to make her laugh. She didn't even feel him there.

"Joey, the child wrecked my car. Wrapped the bumper around a telephone pole two blocks down my street. That thug friend of his, Darryl, was sitting next to him in the passenger seat with an open bottle of malt liquor. God knows where they stole it."

"Is he okay?"

"Was until I got my hands on him. He's lucky we got to them before the police did." She paced around my tiny living room. I knew enough not to offer any comfort. All she wanted was a living ear. "I'm losing him. I'm losing my firstborn."

"You're not losing him. You know children, Ruth."

"I've been losing him since Robert was killed."

"It's just kid's stuff. Wildness of the times. He'll grow out of it." She shook her head, struggling with some holdout fact. "Tell me," I said.

She twisted in place. "Tell you what?"

"Whatever it is you're not telling me."

She deflated. She sat down between me and her younger son. "He's taken to calling me . . . names." She fought to keep her voice. She looked at little Robert, who, on cue, walked off into my bedroom to play. Ruth leaned in toward me. "We argued. He called me 'white.' White! 'You so white, woman. Little car wreck. Nigga don't care 'bout no old hooptie.' Where does that come from? The boy's fourteen years old, and he's holding his genes against me! Hating me for infecting him."

Her body shook as if she were freezing. I had nothing for her. No consolation, even remote. "Wait," I said. "Just wait a couple of years. Sixteen, seventeen. When it really starts."

"Oh Jesus, Joey. No. If he comes up with worse than that, I'll die."

She survived. But not from Kwame's lack of enterprise. Even as her school took off—winning awards, securing grants, appearing in a regional television feature—Ruth's teenage son ran his own race. I never heard half the stories; Ruth was ashamed to tell me. I never saw Kwame anymore. He stopped coming by for the lessons that infuriated both of us. Six weeks after he quit showing up, Ruth asked how the lessons were going.

Kwame had the words BY ANY MEANS tattooed across his belly. He sculpted geometrical shapes into his cropped hair and wore a shirt reading SICK IS on its back and MY MUSE on its front. He came home with failing grades, strings of unexcused absences. The harder Ruth tried to get through to him, the deeper he tunneled.

Then Kwame and four friends—including his copilot Darryl—were caught in the school bathroom, next to a toilet with enough methamphetamine floating in it to kill a racehorse. It wasn't clear which boys were the leads and which only sang in the chorus. Ruth argued at the school hearing that what her son needed most was meaningful discipline, something both he and his school could turn to real use. But after Kwame quoted an Ice Cube lyric in his own defense, the principal opted for expulsion.

Ruth found him a private school that took probationary cases. It was a boarding school, like his uncles had gone to centuries ago, but with a somewhat different curriculum. This one was strictly votech. Ruth couldn't afford to send Kwame there, even with contributions from me. But keeping him out would have bankrupted her.

"Every night," she told me, "it's always the same. I dream someone in uniform is holding his head down to the concrete with a gun."

It seemed to me his school was working. When I saw Kwame now, he felt lighter, less brittle, with less of that junked-up edginess. He still chopped the air with his crooked forearms and folded his fingers into his armpits defensively. But his humor flashed faster and his diatribes were more likely to include himself as a fair target. He and two friends formed a band called N Dig Nation. Kwame rapped and played the record player. "I do the ones and twos." His rhythms were so dense and irregular, I couldn't write them down, let alone clap them. The band played for pulsing gatherings of high school kids, each crowd larger and more hypnotically satisfied than the last.

I sent Jonah and Celeste cards every Christmas and birthday. I wrote a couple of real letters, telling him about our venture: Ruth's endless energy, Kwame's struggles, my teaching games, the current crop of genius first graders, the set of pitched percussion instruments we had managed to buy for my classroom. I didn't mention my lingering emptiness. I sent everything off to the Brandstraat. For a year, I heard nothing back. I wasn't even sure the man still lived in Europe.

He called me in March of 1989. Just after midnight. I picked up the phone and heard the great horn blare from the third movement of Beethoven's Fifth. After four notes, I was supposed to come in on the third below. I didn't. I just listened to him sing another two measures before he crumbled away in scolding. "Shame, shame! We'll have to give you a measure of pickup next time."

"Or try another piece," I said, only half-awake. "What's up, brother?"

"You're a cool cat, Joey. So I owe you some letters. I'm calling, okay? That's what's up."

"Who's dead?"

"Everyone I know or care for. We're coming to the States. The group."

"No joke? You? Here?"

"I'm calling before I come, so you won't rag me."

"Voces Antiquae does their first North American tour."

"We could have done it years ago. All in the timing. Did you like the

Gesualdo?" I paused so long, we both figured things out. "You never bought it. You never even looked it over in a music store? How about the stuff before that? The Lassus? The hocket song collection?"

I took a breath. "Jonah. Lassus? Hockets? Not where I live. Not in my neighborhood."

"What do you mean? You live in the Bay, right? They don't have music stores in Berkeley?"

"I've been busy. This teaching gig is two full-time careers. I can't tell you the last time I've been anywhere but the school, the grocery store, or the Laundromat. In fact, I can't tell you the last time I was at the Laundromat. Berkeley might as well be Zanzibar."

"What the hell? You teach music, don't you?"

"You'd be amazed how big the field is. So what's this tour about? I can't believe you're finally going to give your countrymen another shot at you."

"Twelve cities, eight weeks." He was really wounded, and fighting not to sound it. "I guess I'm lucky there are still twelve cities left in the States that book oldies acts, huh?"

"That's counting Dallas and Fort Worth separately, right?"

"We're playing your little backwater at the beginning of June."

"My little . . . Not possible."

"What do you mean, 'Not possible'? You telling me I don't know where we're booked?"

"I'm telling you there's no way you're singing in Oakland."

"Oakland, San Francisco. Same place, right?"

My laugh was like hot tea going down my windpipe. "You come out, I'll show you around. So how's everyone in the group? How's Celeste?" Now his rest told everything. Too late, I asked, "How long ago?"

"Let's see. Within the last year. It's fine. Mutual consent. What do they call it? Amicable."

"What happened?"

"You know these mixed marriages. They never work out."

"Was there . . . someone else involved?"

"That depends on what you mean by 'involved.' " He spelled it out for me. Kimberly Monera, the blond, bloodless, anemic ghost, had tried to come back to him. Brown child in tow, Tunisian marriage smashed, famous father disowning her, she showed up in northern Europe. She hunted Jonah down and told him that he'd been lodged in the dead center of her imagination, with no one else even close, her whole music-ruined life. "I did nothing, Joey. Didn't even touch her, except to turn her back around to face Italy and pat her shoulders good-bye."

"I don't understand."

"You think I do?" His voice sounded as it had at fourteen. "As soon as I sent her away . . . nothing."

"What do you mean, 'nothing'?"

"I mean, I felt *nothing*. Zero. Total anesthesia. I didn't even want to look at Celeste. I didn't even want to sit in the same room with her. Don't blame her for splitting. And it wasn't just her. Sleeping, eating, drinking, playing, singing: everything that used to be pleasure. Gone."

"How long did that last?"

"How long? What time is it now?"

I panicked, as if it were still my job to keep the show rolling. "But you're still recording. Still performing. You're about to do the debut American tour."

"Funny thing. Get the discs. Have a listen. Somehow, it's done wonders for my voice."

I felt myself slipping back into his orbit. I had to lash out. "Send me one. You have my damn address. Send me one, and I'll listen."

He asked about Ruth, and then about his nephews. I gave him the short version. By the time he hung up, I was deep in all the numbness that had swallowed him. Our worlds had fallen off each other's radar. His performance in San Francisco would have come and gone, and I'd never have heard about it, even in passing.

Three weeks later, a stack of discs arrived. Inside was a short note. "I'm having tickets sent out. For the four of you, or whoever you can scalp them to. See you in June."

The picture on the Gesualdo CD shocked me. The whole of the newly reconstituted Voces Antiquae stood in a midrange shot in the portal of a Gothic church. They were all white. From that distance: every one of them. I got as far as getting the disc out of the shrink wrap and putting it in the player. But I couldn't bring myself to listen.

"Go with me," I begged Ruth. "Not for him. For me. When was the last time I asked you for anything?"

"You ask me for something every week, Joseph. You ask for more gear than my science teachers."

"I mean for me."

She picked up the cover of the Gesualdo. Her hands were shaking, as if he could reject her even through that object. Her eyes strayed across the group's photo. Her mouth twisted a little. "Which one's Jonah? Just kidding." She pulled out the liner notes and read the first paragraph. The cadence of the words angered her, and she handed the disc back to me.

"What do you think? Just to hear."

Her voice was ragged. "Go ask the boys."

The real CD in a real CD jewel box did intrigue Kwame. This was before worldwide make-your-own. "I got an uncle in a crew? That's dope. Put it on, brother. Let the brother do his shit." My nephew didn't last through the first hemiola. "You fuckin' with my *bean*, 'Tween."

Little Robert, next to him, squealed with delight. "Yeah! Don't be fuckin' our beam!" I stared at him. He smirked and clapped a hand over his mouth.

I went back to Ruth. "So what did they say?" she asked. For a moment, she seemed to be hoping for a yes.

"They're going to wait for the video."

She lifted her palms. "What do you expect, Joe? Not our world."

"Our world's anywhere we go."

"They don't want us there. So we don't have time for it."

"Can't be both, Ruth. Can't both them and us decide." She said nothing. "He wants you to go, Ruth. He wants us all to be there."

I held out the tickets Jonah had sent. She gazed at them without touching. "Forty-five dollars? Can we just take the cash instead? Think of all the subsidized lunches . . ."

"Ruth? For me? It's eating me up inside."

She considered it. She really did. But the last sadness in my life was minuscule compared to what still had hold of her. She smiled a little, but not at me. "Can you imagine Robert and me dressing up to go to a show like this? Not without a purse full of smoke bombs, honey." Then, not looking at me, forgiving me my trespass: "You go if you want. I think you ought to." I turned to go. "He can always come by here, if he wants."

The Friday of the concert, I went alone across the bay to Grace Cathedral. I knew the drill well enough not to contact Jonah beforehand. Of course, he didn't contact me. I sat unrecognized in the fake Île-de-France nave, amazed by how many people turned out for the event. All my life in classical music, the audience had consisted of the disaffected and the dying. Mostly the dying. Either the art truly belonged to another lost time or certain human beings woke one day, crippled with age and desperate to learn a repertoire that was heavier than the rest of existence, before death came and stripped us of all our tribes. Sounds almost as old as death itself, sounds that had never belonged to them, sounds that no longer belonged to anyone. For what could belonging mean to the dead?

But this crowd was young, vital, manicured—crisp with the next new thing. I listened to two couples behind me as the preconcert excitement gathered, comparing the virtues of the Tallis Scholars and the Hilliard Ensemble the way one might compare two subtle Burgundies. I couldn't follow the discography. I'd been away too long. I twisted around to check the swelling crowd. No more than twelve black faces were in attendance. But of course that was a count no one could make just by looking.

The house went hushed and the group sauntered on. The applause bewildered me. The church was full of fans, people who'd been waiting years to hear this blending. A blast of panic: I wasn't dressed. I didn't know the program. There was no way I could get up onstage without humiliating myself. A second later, I was again blissfully no one.

The six voices—two of them unknown to me—wandered at random to their marks on the stage. They dressed more silkily than we had back when. Otherwise, they sought that same casual, choreographed shock. My brother stopped and turned, staring out over the heads of the audience. The others seemed ambushed by calm. They stood for an awful moment, as we must have stood, building the intake, looking inward. Then the first fifths crystallized out of them.

All six were past words. But Jonah floated above the stage. He sang like someone from beyond the grave who'd managed to return for one remembering moment to don again the surprise of flesh. Everyone in the cathedral fell back against their pews. My brother had confessed to me the source of that perfection when we'd spoken over the phone. He'd tapped into the pure, voluptuous power of indifference, the sound of how good all sounds will sound to us once we're past them.

After the second burst of applause, he seemed to see me, ten pews back. But the smile was too small for even professional recognition. He gave no sign for the rest of the performance that he felt anything but disembodied grace. He'd gotten beyond not only race. He'd gone beyond being anything at all.

My impatience blotted out the second half of that rapturous program. The lovelier the sound, the more criminal I felt sitting and listening. By the second encore, John Sheppard's *In manus tuas*, I replayed in my mind every petty betrayal I'd ever committed. The fiercely applauding audience made the group sing two more encores.

I was a wreck by the time I found my way into the receiving line. Jonah sprang forward when he saw me near the head of the queue. But the light in his face dulled a little as he approached me. "You're by your-self? Sorry, Joey. That's not what I meant."

"Of course I'm by myself." When were we ever anything else?

"They didn't want to come?" It seemed to confirm his worst suspi-cions.

Every lie we'd ever told ourselves occurred to me. I spared him all of them.

We were surrounded by packs of envious people who just wanted to stand close to these singers who'd thrown off all chains and could make sounds others only dreamed of. All nearby heads appraised us with that look that listens while pretending not to. Jonah stared at me. "Why not? Why wouldn't she? How long . . ." I lifted my palms, pleading. He pursed his lips. "Fine." He put his hand around my shoulders and led me back to where the other antique voices stood. "So what did you think of that Tav-erner? Was that the closest thing you've ever heard to God?"

Then there were the others. Hans Lauscher greeted me with awkward affection. Marjoleine deGroot swore I looked younger than when I'd left. Peter Chance patted my back. "How long has it been?"

I smiled as well as I could. "Since at least 1610."

Everyone wanted the reunion to end as quickly as possible. Jonah had to return to attending to his fans. He was grace itself. He signed programs and smiled for pictures with the heavy donors. Total strang-ers wanted to invite him to fancy dinners, introduce him to celebrities, throw parties in his honor. Although this was ensemble work of the most selfless order, even the tone-deaf could hear where the magic came from. The gentry of the silicon age wanted my brother to love them as they al-ready loved him. I stood by and watched Jonah charm his admirers like some high-art faith healer. It was after midnight by the time we were alone.

"You promised me a tour of your backwater," Jonah said.

"Not this late. They'll shoot us. Come say hello to Ruth. Tomorrow morning."

He shook his head. "She doesn't want that."

"She doesn't? Or you don't? Somebody has to go first, Jonah."

He put his hands on my chest. "You've got some new forte hints in there, brother." His smile died at my silence. He withdrew his hand. "I can't. I can't force myself on them."

"Come to school on Monday. Meet the kids. She'll be there. It'll be easy."

"I wish I could. We leave tomorrow." It seemed almost to save him.

"Come over in the morning at least. No ambushes. I'll buy you breakfast."

"You're on. Draw me a map."

He came to the apartment. By the time I opened the door, he'd had a chance to compose his face. "We've lived in worse," I reminded him.

"Beats where I'm living now, actually. Celeste kept the Brandstraat place." He pored over every American commodity in my kitchen— peanut butter, corn on the cob, cold cereal. "Look at this!" He held a cardboard box of oat squares with a picture of two little mixed-race kids, their smiling faces labeled TWIN PACK.

"Multiracialism's hot," I told him.

"That was our problem, Mule, a million years ago. We didn't have the right marketing!"

I took him to my habitual breakfast place, second-guessing the choice a hundred times. We walked. Jonah took in the blocks, crumbling or gentrifying, rising up or succumbing to a war fought house to house, a war he'd spent his life evading. He walked alongside me, nodding. I gave him running color commentary—who'd been evicted, who'd been bilked out, who'd gotten arrested. My neighbors waved or called out Saturday breakfast greetings. I called back, making no introductions.

"It reminds me of the old neighborhood," Jonah said.

"What old neighborhood?"

"You know. The Heights. Our childhood?"

I stopped and gaped. "It's nothing like New York. It couldn't be further from our childhood if you——"

"I know that, Joseph. That doesn't mean it can't remind me."

Milky's was its usual Saturday-morning carnival. Parents of my students, my colleagues, my neighbors, the staff and regulars: Everyone asked about Ruth and the boys, how the latest school expansion plans were going, how I'd been, who the hell this foreigner was. Milky himself came to greet us in full green silk Chinese pajamas with a navy pea coat over them. "Your brother, you say? Never shit a shitter, Joe Strom."

Only after we slipped into a booth did I get a chance to breathe. Jonah grinned from across the linoleum table. "You sly mother. You're more famous than I am." He insisted on ordering everything I did. "It's Denver tonight. The Alps. I'm screwed for air supply already, the way it is."

All breakfast long, he asked about his nephews. I gave him the facts: Kwame's cage-rattling, word-battling rap. Little Robert's lightning speed with reading, writing, and, most of all, numbers. Jonah kept nodding and pressing for details.

We passed through the greetings gauntlet again on the way out. By now, the funky foreigner with the ironed T-shirt and creased khakis was a regular, and all my friends urged him to come back next week.

"I'll be here," Jonah lied. Bald-faced. "Have my usual ready." Milky and company laughed, and I hated my brother. Two weeks and he, too, might have belonged.

"Come to Ruth's," I said outside the diner.

"Can't. I have to meet the group at the airport in fifty minutes."

"You'll never make it."

"I'll set my watch back." We turned down my street, Jonah in thought. "So you're good, then? This is it? This is all that you need?"

I nodded, ready to lie to him. Ruth, the school, my students: They were considerable. But they were not, in truth, all I needed. I was missing something I could not even name. Something in my past was waiting to be permitted. Some piece inside me needed scoring out, the one I'd once promised Will Hart I'd write down. But I could no longer hear where my notes were pointing. The chance to compose them had passed me by.

We stopped on the sidewalk in front of my building. I looked at my brother, his clothes flapping in that clement breeze. I was not good, not altogether. Not even close, in fact. I was still working for someone else. Some other blood-relation claim on me. But I wasn't about to give Jonah the satisfaction of hearing as much. "Yep," I said. "This is it. All anyone could ask for."

"What are you teaching them? Your fourth graders. What kind of music?"

"K through three. And I'm teaching them everything."

"Everything, you say?"

"You know. The good stuff. Pitches in time."

"What kind of everything?" He eyed me. Too much to duck. He looked at his watch, already dashing.

"I give them what's theirs. Their music. Their identity."

"What's theirs, Joey? If you have to give it . . . You give them *their* music? Their *identity*? Identical to what? Only thing you're identical to is yourself, and that only on good days. Stereotyping. That's what you're giving them. Nobody's anybody else. Their music is whatever nobody can give them. Good luck finding that."

He wasn't entirely dead yet. His soul's handover deal had been signed and sealed but not yet delivered. I grabbed his elbow and slowed him. "Maestro. Chill, huh? I get them to teach me the songs they know. I trade them for a few old tunes. Stuff nobody else knows. I give them all kinds of noise—a little gospel swell, a little twelve-bar, even a little Pilgrim and Founding Fathers crap now and then. Theirs? Not theirs? Who the hell am I to say? It's only music, for God's sake."

We'd gotten as far as my apartment. I motioned for him to come up for a moment. Jonah wagged his head. He looked around my neighborhood. "Unbelievable, Joey. You're passing. You're really passing. Remember how they used to call Jonah Strom the black Fischer-Dieskau?"

"Nobody ever called you that, Jonah. That was you."

"Well, you've become the black Joseph Strom." He cuffed my shoulder and turned to get back into his rental. There was pride; there was envy. Not dead yet. He had at least two out of the big seven covered. "Don't worry, brother. Your secret's safe with me."

I couldn't help watching for the reviews in New York, where the Voces Antiquae tour wound up. It was their hour onstage, or at least their fifteen minutes. The New York critics fell over one another declaring how long they'd been waiting for such a sound. Jonah sent me the clip from the *Times*—"All Ars Antiqua Is Nova Again"—afraid I might miss it. The piece singled him out as perhaps the clearest-voiced male singing early music in any country. No mention of color, outside the vocal. He'd clipped his business card to the corner of the rave and scribbled, "Warmest regards, your leading Negro recitalist."

At last he had the vindication he'd so long sought. He had the listening world's adulation, and he made a sound that stood for nothing other than what it was. But he and I both knew that the heat from that "nova" was thrown off from a core already burned through.

Yet his act had one more twist. Now that he stood for himself alone, he belonged to everyone but himself. His brilliance caught the moment's buzz; his sound became anyone's to interpret. Fame is the weapon of last resort that culture uses to neutralize runaways. A few months after his group made its North American tour, their Gesualdo recording won a Grammy. In December of 1990, they were named the oxymoronic "Early Music Performers of the Year." I actually saw a poster of them, like a police lineup, on the wall of a music shop in downtown Oakland where I'd gone to buy mallets.

The kicker came half a year later, three months after Rodney King began being beaten nightly on ghostly videotape. Ruth showed up one morning in my broom-cupboard office at the school, waving the latest issue of *Ebony*. "I can't believe it. I can't *take* it." She threw the magazine down on my desk, shaking all over. She pressed her lips to her teeth to keep from crying. I opened to the cover story: "50 Leaders for Tomorrow's America." I flipped through the list of scientists, engineers, physicians, athletes, and artists, testing each entry for its power to offend. I waded through the entire roster before I saw him. I raised my eyes to my sister's. Hers were running in tears. "How, Joey? Tell me how." She stamped the ground. "It's worse than minstrelsy."

I had to look down, back at the incredible page. "I don't know how. Bastard's not even *in* America. At least he's buried down there in slot number forty-two, where he can't hurt nobody."

An awful sound escaped her. It took me two seconds to decide: *Laughter.* Maniacal. She reached out toward me. "Give it back. I have to show my sons."

I was there at dinner that night, when she did. "Your blood relation," she told them. "I knew this boy when he was no bigger than you. You see where you can go with a little effort? Look at all those stars he's up there with. All the good they've gotten up to."

"Half of them really white," Kwame declared.

Ruth stared him down. "Which half? You tell me."

"All those technocrackers. Look at this motherfucker: He don't even know he's nathan. CEO? That's Casper the Ethnic Oreo."

"This one?" little Robert said, pointing and smirking. "This one's really white?"

"What makes them white?" Ruth challenged.

"This," Kwame said, dismissing the whole magazine. "This caveboy noise. Whole white devil power shit."

"What if I told you half the white race was walking around black and didn't even know it?"

"I'd say you be bugging. Illin' on your children."

His mother shot me a silent appeal. "She's right," I said. "White's got to prove white, all the way back. Who can do that?"

My nephew appraised me: hopelessly insane. "Wack. Don't even know what I'm saying."

Little Robert held up both arms. "The whole human race started in Ethiopia."

Kwame took his little brother in a headlock and Indian-burned his scalp until the seven-year-old screamed with pleasure. "That's right, bean boy. You all that. You my whole Top Fifty for Tomorrow, all rolled in one."

Robert was the kind of child for whom his mother's school was invented. He blazed through the day's subjects, alarming his muzzy schoolmates. Every bit of learning that caught his eye, he set up in the sky like a glittering star. Stories left him dizzy with pleasure. "Is this real?" he'd want to know about every Reading Hour book. "Did this ever happen yet?"

He was his mother all over again, doing voices, tilting his head and squinting like the latest ridiculous adult. He built a walking robot out of Lego blocks that brought the whole first grade to a thirty-minute standstill. Math was his sandbox. He solved logic puzzles two grades above him. With nothing but poker chips and a world map, he designed games of complex trade. He loved to draw. History kept him sick with attention; he didn't yet know that the stories were already over. He wept when he learned about the boats, the sealed holds, the auction blocks, the destroyed families. For Robert, everything that happened was still happening, somewhere.

But he could fly only so long as no one paid him any mind. The minute anyone fussed over him, he watched himself, and fell. The world's praise of any black child carries an annihilating surprise. I'd grown up on it. Robert had only to hear that he might be doing something remarkable for him to stumble in apologies. He only wanted to be liked. Special meant wrong. In my class, he shone like the aurora. His voice anchored the whole alto section. But every time his marveling classmates mocked his skill, he hid his light back under a bushel for another several weeks.

For show-and-tell on the musician of his choice, he brought in the *Ebony*. It was months old, but he was still thinking about it. The room tittered as he spoke, and I hushed them, making things worse. All these black men making the future—fifty of them. And one of them was supposed to be Robert's uncle, who'd changed the future of music a thousand years old. A brother, his mother had told him, might do anything. Robert spoke with that blast of pride already shot through with embarrassment and doubt.

Two weeks after the oral report, he came into my class with a sheaf of pages, each marked in a rash of colored-pen hieroglyphics. "This is mine. I wrote this." He raced to explain the elaborate musical notation he'd devised, a system describing subtle changes in pitches and duration, notation that preserved many things lost in the standard staff. He'd written independent *parts*, thinking not only in running lines but also in a series of vertical moments. His chords made sense—delaying, repeating, turning back on themselves before coming home. His brother had sold for pocket change the little electric keyboard I'd given them. Ruth had no other instrument in the house. Robert had not only invented a system of notation from scratch; he'd written this whole work of harmony in his mind's ear.

"How did you do this? Where did this *come from?*" I couldn't stop asking him.

He shrugged and cowered, crumbling under my awe. "Came from me. I just . . . heard it. You think it sounds like anything?"

"We have to find out. We'll perform it." The idea made him pleasantly ill. "What's it for?" He stood there, bewildered by the question. "I mean, what instruments?"

He shrugged. "I wasn't thinking about . . . instruments."

"You mean you want it sung?" He nodded. First he'd thought of it. "Do you have words?"

He shook his head and axed the air. "No words. Just music." Words out loud would poison it.

He taught the class to read his notation, and we performed the piece in school assembly. Robert conducted. So long as his music lasted, his soul climbed up into an ice blue sky on a bolt of mustard yellow. Five groups of voices chanted back and forth to one another, just as his notes said, clashing and cohabiting. His rowdy counterpoint came from another orbit, until then invisible. The sounds in his head kept him from hearing the din of the assembled gym. But the moment the piece was over, the noise broke over him.

The applause threatened to stop Robert from breathing. His eyes went wide, searching the room for a fire exit. Kids whistled and catcalled, teasing him. He bowed and knocked over the conductor's stand. It brought down the house. I thought he might suffocate on the spot. Every muscle in his face worked to declare, *Nothing special. Nothing out of the ordinary.* He flinched and fended off every admiration while jumping up to look out over the heads of his peers, trying to scout down the only opinion that mattered to him: his adored brother's.

Kwame lumbered up afterward in his low-riding jeans. He'd skipped a day of his own school to be there. His arms made those little cartwheel jerks I couldn't decode, half praise, half ridicule. His face screwed up to one side. "What you call that?"

Robert died by inches. "I call it 'Legend.'"

"What legend? You think you're a legend? No pump, no bump. Who you down with anyway?" Neither boy looked at me. They couldn't afford to.

I thought the child would break apart, right there in front of the entire assembled New Day School. Kwame saw it, too. He puppy-cuffed his listless brother. "Hey. I said, *Hey.* It's fresh. It's slamming. You come marinate with me and my homies next time Dig's in the house. See how you make some real G-funk."

In his final year of votech school, Kwame's band had grown to fill his entire horizon. They'd achieved a kind of mastery, one whose words entirely eluded me but whose pulse even I couldn't deny. He had nothing else. Ruth tried to stay with his every evasion, keeping him accountable while propping him up without his knowing. "You thinking beyond school?"

"Don't ride me, Mama."

"Not riding. Helping you scout."

"Me and the Nation. We can make it work. I don't mean bank. Just making it."

"You want to rap, then you need a battle. Just find something to hold yourself together while you make yourself the best."

She unloaded on me privately. "God, I wish I weren't an educator. I'd whack that child up side of the head until he got his life in order."

In August, a car in a Brooklyn Hasidic rebbe's motorcade ran a red light, hit another car, swerved onto the sidewalk, and killed a Guyanese boy Robert's age. For three days, Crown Heights hammered itself. Kwame and N Dig Nation wrote a long rap that replayed the madness from every available angle. The song was called "Black Vee Jew." Maybe it participated; maybe it revealed. You never know with art.

"Your grandfather was a Jew," I told him. "You're a quarter Jewish."

"I hear you. That's def. What you think of that noise, Uncle bro?"

Whatever the words, the song got the group its first airtime—real radio, all over the Bay. It intoxicated Kwame. "Beats the best method that bank can buy." The band made five hundred dollars each. Kwame spent his on new audio equipment.

Late in September, Ruth called me up, out of control. All three members of N Dig Nation had been arrested for breaking into a music store in West Oakland and leaving with two dozen CDs. "They're gonna finish him. He's nothing but meat. They'll kill him, and no one will know." It took me a quarter of an hour to talk her down enough to get her to meet me at the station where Kwame was being held. Ruth came apart again when we got there and she saw her son in handcuffs.

"We weren't biting nothing," Kwame told the two of us. He sat behind a metal gun rail, a bruise covering the side of his face where the cops had held him to the wall. He was swaggering with the fear of death. "Just a little who ride."

I thought Ruth might kill the boy herself. "You speak the language I taught you."

"We buy stuff from the man all the time. His door was wide open. We were just gonna take a listen and bring all that noise back to him when we got done."

"Records? You stole *records*? What kind of suicidal—"

"CDs, Mama. And we didn't steal any."

"What in the name of Jesus did you think you were doing, *stealing records*?"

He looked at her with an incomprehension so great, it was almost pity. "We're on the way up. We have to drop science. Bust the bustas. Know what I'm sayin'?"

Ruth was brilliant at the sentencing. She asked for a punishment that might save a life, rather than waste it. But the judge pored over what he called Kwame's "history," and he decided that society was best served by putting this juvenile menace away for two years. He stressed the seriousness of breaking and entering, while Kwame kept saying, "We didn't break." Property was the heart of society, the judge said. The crime of theft tore out that heart. As his sentence was being read, Kwame muttered just loud enough for me to hear, "The man's nathan. He's not even dead."

Two days later, my sister saw her son off to prison. "Your father was in jail once. You remember why. So what are you going to do with this? That's what the world wants to know." She was crying as she spoke, crying for everything that had ever happened to this boy, all the way back for generations before his birth. Kwame couldn't hold his head up long enough to meet her eye. She lifted it for him. "Look at me. *Look at me.* You are not just yourself."

Kwame nodded. "I hear you." And then he was waving good-bye.

Once Ruth was alone with me, she fell apart. "White teen goes to jail, it's a pencil entry on the C.V. Youthful foolishness. Something to laugh at down the line. Black teen goes to jail, it's another fatality. Judgment on the entire race. A hole he'll never climb out of. It's my fault, Joseph. I put them here. I didn't have to drag them back into the cauldron. I could have set them up in some sleepwalking suburb."

"Not your fault, Ruth. Don't crucify yourself for half a millennium—"

"You see what he's done to Robert. Big brother's going to be the hero of a lifetime. Prerolled role model. That child sits in his room inventing whole new schools of arithmetic on his interlocking knuckles. He's taught himself plane geometry. But he won't count to twenty without mistakes if his brother's looking at him the wrong way. Doesn't want to be anything he's not supposed to be. And he could be anything. *Anything he wants . . .*"

We both heard at the same time, as soon as the words came out of her mouth. Ruth looked at me, her nostrils flared. "Her son's quit the country and her grandson's in prison." Then her throat caved in and she howled. "What have we done to her, Joey?"

Robert made his way through the third grade, toward his graduation from New Day School. He butted up against that age when it was murder for Ruth to encourage him in anything. Whatever she praised in him, he abandoned. With half his attention, he'd fill a sheet of blank newsprint with astonishing geometries. But if she hung it on the wall, he'd tear it down and burn it.

"I'm going to lose him, Joseph. Lose him faster than I lost Kwame."

"You haven't lost Kwame." Kwame had, in fact, started a course in mechanical drawing at the prison.

We'd been to see him almost every weekend. "This place is for marks," he told me. There was something incredulous about his insight. "Know what? They built this prison to fit us. Then they build us to fit it. Not me, Uncle. Once I stroll, this place can rot with my history in it." He and his mother started a little ritual each time we said good-bye. *How long? Not long. Meet you back in the new old world.*

In early 1992, Jonah wrote to say he was coming through town in late April to sing at the Berkeley Festival. That's how pointless separate continents had become. I wrote him back on a school fund-raising postcard: "*I heard you* last time." And below the school's address, I wrote out the date of his concert, the time 1:30 P.M., and my class's room number.

My class didn't need any special audience. There was no audience now, where I came from. There was only choir, and we'd have gone on preparing our score whoever showed up or didn't on any given day. I was a grade school teacher of music. I lived for it, and that's exactly how my kids sang. And yet I had given Jonah the time and room number of my best lot—real air walkers, his unmet nephew Robert among them. I told them we might have a special visitor. Even that much felt wrong.

I worked hard to make that day the most ordinary that had ever been. No chance he could make it: I'd guaranteed that when choosing the date. He never did anything the afternoon before a concert. But if, in some parallel universe, he did, we were ready with a sound that would unmake him.

By the time I set up for that afternoon class, I was gripped by a stage fright more violent than the bout that had once almost cost us Jonah's first major competition. Children sense everything, and mine broke out with bursts of teasing, all of them sung, per the class rule. I settled them down and started them in on scalar swells, our usual warm-up. "I'm still standing," up to the top of their giggling ranges and gently down again. My brother didn't show. He couldn't. There was nothing left of him, outside the concert hall. He'd disappeared into consummation. My body began to feel the relief of not having to meet him this time around.

We rolled out our stuff. Not *despite*. Not even *anyway*. With no one to impress, we delighted ourselves: all we have, really, when everything's figured. We followed the usual steps to daily ecstasy. First, we laid down the elementary pulse, what my father years ago called "the laws of time." Two kids on toms gave us a groove good enough to stay in for as long as we could move. Then we layered on the beat, Burundi drumming, a long, relaxed twenty-four-pulse cycle, with another half dozen players on pitched percussion doing what they'd have done gladly for a living all life long, plus some.

When all the plates were in the air and spinning, we cracked open some tunes. My kids knew the drill. They had been through it often enough to bring it to elementary school perfection. I conducted from the piano, waving my finger in the air, landing on a girl in a mint jumper, her hair in cornrows, grinning, already picked before I even knew I was picking her.

"What are you thinking about when you wake up?" I tossed the question above the trance of cycling pulses. This girl, my beacon Nicole, was ready for it.

> Breakfast is on, and
> I'm gonna eat like a Queen!

Mayhem reigned, but the rhythm held. She soloed, then settled into a cycle of her own. We took her pitch as home and set up camp. I pointed to another favorite in the front row, lanky, eager Judson, his tapping cross-trainers the size of his chest. "What did you think about last night, falling asleep?" Judson already knew.

> Man, I was running,
> through a long silver tunnel,
> faster than anyone.

The two of them spun around each other, finding their entrances, nudging their pitches and syncopations to fit. I took a few more in that pitch center. "Where's your safest place in the world?"

> There's a spot on a hill
> at the end of my street
> where I can look out
> over everything.

"What did you see on the way to school? When are you best? Who you going to be this time next year?" I brought them in, clipping a phrase, drawing another out, speeding or slowing them as needed to get the roux to set. Half a dozen singers hung on to one another in midair, constantly changing, unchanged. I hushed them into a diminuendo, then started up five more. I played out the new starting pitch, then built a group at the dominant. *Your five favorite words. The dream Saturday afternoon. Your name if your name wasn't yours.* I waved them into an alternation: one-five, five-one.

Then came the leap into changes. I thumped a key and pointed, and three singers transposed their phrase to that new place in the scale. They still knew, at age eight: a pitch for every place we have to go.

My choir started smirking, but not on account of my conducting. The singers' mouths gaped, huge as fish in an aquarium, at something over my shoulder. Keeping time, I turned, to see Jonah standing in the classroom door, his own mouth open, a lesson in how to make a throat wide enough for rapture. I couldn't stop to greet him; my hands were full of notes. He gestured me to turn back around and keep afloat that feather on the breath of God.

I hushed the first two groups and took them both aside, readying a third to travel into the relative minor. *The most scared you've ever been. Five words you'd rather die than hear.* I traced my finger in the air, searching for someone to sing *The heaviest weight pressing on you*, and landed on Robert. He took only two beats. He, too, was waiting for me.

My Daddy is dead
and my brother's in prison.

When is the zero of change, the spot in time when time begins? Not the big bang, or even the little one. Not when you learn to count your first tune. Not that first now that twists back on itself. All moments start from the one when you see how they all must end.

Robert drew his thread, looping it over and over, into the elementary pulse. A cloud passed over the choir, but our song already anticipated that change in the light. I now had all the chords I needed to get anywhere pitches could go. I brought the lines in and out, swelled and hushed, slowed, then sped, chopped and extended, plucking out a solo and pasting together quartets, moving the whole freely from one key to another.

My Daddy is dead.
And I was running.
To that spot on a hill.
Where breakfast is on and I can look out,
but my brother's in prison.

They knew already how to make it go. They ceased to care about the strange adult or even notice him. We stayed in the swell, working our favorite rondo form, coming back, whenever we strayed too far, to a full choral shout of "I'm still standing." I pulled out every stop, everything every student of mine had ever taught me about how music runs. It shamed me that I needed so badly to impress him. As if joy ever needed justifying, or could justify anything. And my shame stoked me to lift all my voices higher.

We rose as far as we ever had. We flowed back into ourselves, and I stirred the waters for one more full flood before returning to sea level. But as we crested one last time, I heard a ringing like a bell. Its attack was something only weather made. I hadn't conducted it; it came from outside my students' ranges, but nestled into their outlined harmonies, notes so sustained they were almost stopped. It took me an instant, forever, to place: my brother singing Dowland. The tune came from a life ago. The words from yesterday:

Bird and fish can fall in love.

I turned around to see, but Jonah waved me back again. He came alongside the end of the choir's back row. The resonance he released rang like a gong. But my kids knew a good thing when they made one. I kept conducting, and they kept coming back in. I stole a look at Jonah. He lifted an eyebrow at me like he used to do, back in the day. And we were off.

Everywhere I brought my class, he found a way to follow. This time, I made him read *my* mind. Accompany me. Scraps of will-o'-the-wisp, poet love, songs of the death of children, the Dies Irae, old broken have-mercies: He fit them into the running chorus, changed by everything they harmonized. He gave them game. He sang in that high, clear, inevitable blade of light his whole lifetime had gone into perfecting. Even the children felt the power. Always the same seven words, scatting where he needed, as if born to it.

We circled on a giant updraft, drifting through the keys. His voice, joined to the voices of my children, was like a lamp in the night. We could have stayed up there for years, except for one accident. When he slipped into the classroom, Jonah failed to close the door. So every chant of "I'm still standing"—*a little bit louder now; a little bit softer now*—washed down the hall, the free property of anyone who heard. I didn't realize we were disturbing the peace until the chorus joined in behind me.

A sober instructor of social studies came by to hush us up but then stayed on to sing. The woman who taught first grade math got everyone clapping. Kids pressed into the room until it was strictly SRO. Not one of them audience. The bigger the chorus grew, the faster it drew. Then our mountain of sound fell away for a measure, and not on my cue. I knew by the next upbeat what it had to be. I saw her in the doorway, even before I turned around: the school's director.

I can't tell what Ruth heard. Her face showed nothing. But there were her singing kids, small for the last time, and there was her brother, singing for her for the first time since we were small. Every stacked sound stayed whole in the changing chord. Then there was one more ob-bligato line. Who knew where the tune came from? She made it up. Im-provised. The words, though, were given her:

But where will they build their nest?

Ruth's voice went through me like death. Refusal, lament: the only answer to his holdout hope. I felt as I had when I'd heard her sing back in Philadelphia. Infinitely bereft. Her voice was lovely enough, even in ruin, to prove how the dream of music was never more than that.

One by one, I brought the lines back home. The cycles of rhythm came to rest, the pulse unwove, and the room erupted, applauding itself. Kids broke loose in all directions, a spontaneous uprising that declared the rest of the hour a national holiday. A ring formed around Jonah. "How'd you do that?" Judson grilled him. By way of answer, Jonah let loose with a bolt of Monteverdi.

My family cowered in the celebrating room. Robert drifted to his mother's side, guilty, caught in the act. She slunk toward me, as if I, of all people, offered safety. "Robert," Ruth told the boy, in that same weary fear with which she sent the bird and the fish, homeless, away, "that's your uncle."

611

"I know," the boy scolded. He tried, in his excitement, to avoid the eyes of all adults. He pointed at me. "Your brother."

Then Jonah stood beside us. "You hear that? Did you *hear*?" He reached to hug his sister.

Ruth stepped back. "Don't! Too long. You can't just . . ." She lost control of her voice. But she refused to cry.

Robert clenched, ready to protect her. Jonah grazed Ruth's arm, deniable free comfort. Then he turned to clap my shoulder. "You're a genius. The van Karajan of music. Now that's using the stick." He looked down at the half-sized figure at his waist. Recognition knocked him back. "Neph," he said, exploring his own awe.

"What's that?" Robert asked, a sucker for a puzzle. "Something like a nephew?"

Jonah nodded soberly. "A lot like a nephew." He looked up at Ruth. "Amazing. He's beautiful."

"Why should that be amazing?" Cold as memory.

"That's not. My luck is."

Robert screwed his face up. "Your voice does funny things."

"My standing here at all. My seeing you."

Ruth snapped her head away. "You're heavier," she said. She looked back. Jonah held out his arms and looked down the length of his body. "I mean . . ." She traced her own throat.

"Don't say heavier. Say richer."

"Why are you here? Why did you come back?"

The child chorus drifted reluctantly from the room to their next assignments. My students. Jonah raced to the door to slap their hands. It bought him time. He came back, talking to Robert, gazing around the room. "Look at this! I had no idea. So this is your school!"

"My mama's," Robert said.

"Yours," Ruth told her child. Tears now. But the voice was hers.

"Fantastic," Jonah said. "I haven't had so much fun with singing since . . ." He looked at Robert. "Since I was you. You heard what that sounded like? This is it. This is the next thing. People have never heard anything like this."

Ruth's laugh was incredulous. "Maybe not your people."

"I'm serious. That was a *sound*. We could get there. Make this go. Play anywhere. I'm telling you. People need this."

Ruth was shaking her head, her mouth pulling at her ears. "People have had this forever."

"Not me."

"Exactly."

"Ruth. I'm here. I'm asking. You can't leave me hanging."

"You left us."

"You have your work," I said.

He dismissed me. "We've been on autopilot for almost two years. It's pretty much over, antiquity. Heaven has played. I need something closer."

"You?" I searched for irony, but he was grave. "You can't quit. It's a dying art. Who's going to keep it alive if you quit?"

"Never fear. Western concert music is in the able hands of millions of Koreans and Japanese."

Ruth felt it then, too. The bottomless well he'd fallen into. My sister held her son by the shoulders, armor in front of her. She reached out over Robert and cupped the back of Jonah's neck. "Some folks die the way they were born."

"All folks," I said.

A smile ripped through Jonah. His sister was talking to him. Touching him. Didn't matter what she was saying, how many barbs.

"Neph?" Jonah looked down at Robert. The future's court of appeals. "Sing with me?"

"My mama says you're a land unto yourself. You always make your own rules."

"Where did you hear that?" Ruth said. "I never in my life . . ."

"You ever break the law?"

Jonah regarded his flesh's half-sized image. "All the time. Me and your uncle JoJo here? We trashed them all. Major-league transgressors. We broke laws you never even heard of."

Robert shot me a doubtful look. But his doubt floundered when he saw me remembering. "You ever go to jail?"

Jonah shook his head. "They never caught us. We were in the papers a few times, leading suspects. But they never caught up with us." And he made a sign, swearing the boy to secrecy.

"You ever kill anyone?"

Jonah thought. No more hiding. "A couple times. Pushed a woman in an oven once. I wasn't much older than you."

The boy looked to his mother for help. Ruth pressed her hand to her shaking lip. Robert looked at me, sense's last resort. I motioned toward the deserted room. "I need to straighten up here."

Ruth wrestled free of herself. "And I've got a school to run. And you, young man. Don't you need to be somewhere? Mrs. Williams, for math? Hmm?"

"Know what else you need?" I could hear it in Jonah's voice. Desperate fishing. "An African name. Like your brother."

It stopped them both, mother and son. Ruth stared. "How do you know about African names?" *How do you know about his brother?*

"Oh, please. I've been to Africa many times. On tour. Senegal, Nigeria, Zaire. They love us there. We're more popular in Lagos than we are in Atlanta." He took his nephew by the shoulders. "I'm going to call you Ode. Good Bini name. It means 'Born along the road.'"

The child checked his mother. Ruth cast up her hands. "If the man says so."

"What does Kwame mean?"

"Haven't a clue. Ode is the only one I know. That's what they named me, last time I was there."

"Ode?" Robert asked, doubtful.

His uncle said, "Roger."

"Ode," Robert said, pointing at me. Got it?

I showed him my palms. "Fine with me. From now on. Until you tell me to stop."

He dashed off to his last class, criminally late. The abandoned adults fell silent. Ruth and Jonah traded a few hostages, both trying hard to leap twenty years. She and I walked him out to the parking lot, where he grew eager all over again.

"Come on. Bird and Fish, Incorporated. Why not? Make a new species? Old wine in new bottles. Sing unto the Lord a new song. Be great for the kids. Talk about education. This thing could be the best thing ever for your school."

"How would it do anything for this school?" Even Ruth's suspicion sounded administrative. I looked at her through Jonah's widening eyes.

He stared at her across confusion too wide to bridge. "Come on. Classics meets the streets. Make your baby hipper *and* smarter. There's a ready market. The country's been waiting for it."

She hung her head and let it shake, awed by the distance. She couldn't help snickering. " 'Waiting'? You really mean it, don't you?" She tipped her face skyward. "Oh God. Where do I start?"

He smiled back, desperate. "Start by picking your top kids and letting me find us a promoter."

"Where have you been living? Have you no eyes?"

"The eyes are only mediocre. But the ears are extraordinary."

"Then listen, damn you. *Listen*, for once."

"I did. It's good, Ruth. Better than either. Better than identity. Hybrid vigor."

She slumped in the face of his hopelessness. He wanted it to be capitulation. But he saw what it was. In an instant, he knew: This chorus was the thing he'd trained for his whole life. And somehow his life's devotion —his uncompromising will, his wriggling free, always toward this unseen goal, untyped, note by note, perfecting his own line—was exactly what would keep this all-keys choir from ever being his.

When he spoke, he was a child, broken and bare. "You think about it. No rush. I'll put some ideas together. I'll call you before we head to L.A."

Ruth might have killed him with the smallest-caliber monosyllable. But she didn't. Jonah stood in front of her. "Twenty years. Why?" She bit her lip and shook her head—not at his question, but at him. He nodded. "Won't be so long, next time." She let him embrace her, and she held on, even as he pulled away. He didn't embrace me; for us, it had been only three. Instead, he shoved into my hands an article he'd clipped from the previous day's *New York Times*. April 24: "Scientists Report Profound Insight on How Time Began."

"You have to read this, Joey. Message from Da, from beyond the grave."

Jonah drove off. Ruth waved a little, after he was too far to see. She felt no need even to mention his scheme to me. We were our brother's future. But he wasn't ours.

He didn't call us before he went to L.A. The press of performing tied him up. The Berkeley Festival was a resplendent conquest, by all paid accounts. He and Voces Antiquae flew down to Los Angeles on the second-to-the-last day of April. Their plane was one of the last to land at LAX before the outbreak shut down all incoming flights.

Ruth called first, that Wednesday night. She spoke so softly into the phone, I thought there was something wrong with the line. She kept saying, "Joey, Joey." I was sure one of the boys was dead. "They let them all go. All four of them. Not guilty on every count. Beaten fifty-six times, on videotape, for the whole world to see, and it's like nothing happened. It's not possible. Not even here."

Jonah's article from the *Times* had been the first piece of news I'd read for months. I'd given up on current events. News was nothing to me, a cruel tease. It was nothing but the delusion that things were still happening. I'd dismissed it. All my news came down to New Day School. I'd forgotten the King verdict was even due. As Ruth told me of the blanket acquittal, I'd already heard the outcome, word for word, a long time before.

Now news took me in again. I flipped on my set while Ruth was still on the line. Aerial-reconnaissance video showed what I thought at first was King. But this was another man, the other color, pulled from his truck and stoned live for the cameras. "Are you seeing this?" I asked her. Something in me wanted her to hurt. To kill her self-possession as dead as mine. "You see where belonging gets us?"

"It's never ending," my sister kept saying into the receiver. And it was. The staff of New Day kept a broadcast going in the teachers' room all Thursday. Nobody was really teaching. We all kept slipping in to watch. Not even horrified. Just dulled, in that place that would forever return to claim us all. Plumes of fire streaked the skyline of the dying city, burning out of control. The police retreated, leaving the streets to looters of every persuasion. The National Guard assembled on their beachheads but couldn't move out for want of ammunition. Shops went up in flames like shavings in a kiln. The body count climbed. One of the third-grade teachers turned on a set in a classroom, thinking it might be instructive. She turned it off again five minutes later, instruction outgrowing itself. The rout was total, and as darkness fell again the second day, hell spread so fast, it felt positively willed.

Ruth wouldn't go home alone. She demanded I have dinner with her. While we ate, all hope burned. "What are they doing?" my nephew asked. "What's happening there? Are they having a war?" My sister stared at the news feed throughout dinner, biting her lip. I'd never before seen her refuse to answer Robert's questions.

"Where's your brother?" she asked. "Why the hell doesn't he call us?" I didn't say he was lying on the pavement in South Central, sight-singing the sky. I let Ruth's question, too, go unanswered.

He called, with answers, at 2:40 A.M. Friday. I must have been dreaming, because I was talking to him before I heard the phone ring. He sounded thrilled, on the verge of some huge insight. "Joey? Mule? I'm here. Again." I had to wake up enough to hear he was in shock. "You see what this means? Right back dead in the middle of it. I heard the whole thing, at least until they got my ear. Every line. Tell her that. You have to tell her."

I pulled my head from out of sleep and tried to talk him down. "Jonah. Thank God you're safe. It's okay, now. They said on the news tonight. Things are returning to normal."

"Normal? This is normal, Joey." Shrieking: *"This."*

"Jonah. Listen to me. It's okay. Are you at the hotel? Just stay inside. The army—"

"Inside? *Inside?* You never had a clue, did you? Fool!" I heard the nakedness. He'd thought me a fool all our shared life. And he was right. But he blasted forward, unable to wait for either of us. He was struggling to breathe. "I've been out in the middle of this since yesterday afternoon. I went in, Mule. Looking for what I was supposed to do. Did everything I know. I stood on a burning corner and tried to form a pickup chorus of 'Got the whole world in his hands.' You have to tell her that. She's wrong. Wrong about me. Don't let her think what she thinks." His voice was huge with the performance of a lifetime. He was drawing on that ancient lesson his lover-teacher once gave him: *If you can't be someone more than yourself, don't even think about walking out on stage.*

"I'll tell her, Jonah." I had to repeat it before he calmed down enough to make sense.

He tittered as he spoke. "They canceled the concert. I guess the early music crowd was afraid to come out for a Last Judgment. The Europeans were freaking. Trapped in the country of their worst nightmares. They barricaded themselves in the hotel. I had to go back, Joey. It was you and me, the night of our first recording." The curve of his life was calling for him to come trace it, somewhere out there in the burning streets.

He headed into the violence, toward the pitch of maximum distress, with nothing but his overtrained ears to lead him on. "What did you look like?" I asked.

"Look? Like me!" It took him a moment; he was still reeling. "Chino pants and a teal Vroom and Dreesmann dress shirt. I know: total suicide pact. Oh. A solid black T-shirt underneath that says FEAR NO ART. The limo wouldn't take me past the I-Ten. I must have gone the last two miles on foot. Can't remember everything. Out of my gourd, Joey. That crowd. You remember. I no longer meant myself. I was walking back into the sea. Taking my first voice lesson. *Dum, dum, dum.* There was nothing.

Nothing but fires. Götterdämmerung on a two-billion-dollar budget. Mule. I thought opera was someone else's nightmare. I never knew that someone else was me.

"I just followed the smoke. Kept looking around for you. I wound up in some flaming retail strip. Every sheet of glass for blocks around was lying on the pavement, sparkling like rosin. Palm-sized hunks of concrete, whipping through the intersection. Couldn't count the sides. Latinos, Koreans, blacks, white guys in uniform. I might have been singing. Standing in the middle of the cross fire. This piece of paving stone size of my shoe heel hits me in the side of the head. Ripped into my temple. I just stood there snapping my fingers, first on one side of my head, then the other. Deaf in my left ear. *Me*, Joey. Can't hear a damn thing! Listen!" He fumbled to switch the phone to his other ear. "Hear that? Nothing!

"That's when I find myself. I start running. Blood is streaming out of my ruined ear. They can't hit me twice. I figure I'm safe, right? They can't come after me. Who knows what color I am? I'm nobody. Safer than I've been since . . . Something's pulling me, like Brahms. Like this is going on again, for eternity. I'm back here for a reason. Across the street, at the end of the next block, these kids are pouring out of a hardware store, arms full. You remember? Power drills. A workbench. An electric saw. They see me just standing there. *Score something, you choosy mother-fucker.* One of them stops, and I think he's going to dust me. Shoot me. He stops and hands me this can of paint and a handful of brushes. Like he's God, and this is just for me. I'm trying to pay him. To pay the sacked store. He's just screaming and laughing at me.

"Like it was my calling, Joey. Out of my mind! I started walking around, marking people. Started with myself. I thought I was the angel of the Lord, putting a safe marker on everyone I could find. Passover. Everybody was going to be medium brown. That was the plan anyway. Somebody didn't want to be painted. Smashed me into a wall and spilled what was left all over me. Next thing I know, policeman's got my neck pinned to the concrete with a riot stick. They throw me into an armored van and haul me off to a station, where they take my statement. I should have lied to them. Told them I was someone else. They wouldn't even fucking book me. I couldn't even get myself arrested. They're holding thousands of people for curfew violation, and they toss me back. Too many real criminals. You sing *what*? You live *where*? And they believed me. Figure nobody could make up that scale of madness. They send me to the fucking hospital! Damn them to hell. I didn't stay. I came right back here and called you."

He made me promise again to tell Ruth, first thing in the morning. I told him to go to the hospital and have his ear looked at as soon as we hung up. And to call me when he'd spoken with a doctor.

"Doctor, Joey? They're all tied up. Real things. Death and such. Not some foreigner's hurt ear." He gasped for air. From the far end of a bad connection, he went into a suffocation fit. The one that all his youthful panic attacks had been all along remembering.

I talked him down, as I had done so many earlier times. I walked him around his hotel room. And then he was calm again, wanting to talk on into the night. I kept telling him to call for help, but he didn't want to hang up on me. "Tell her, Joey. Tell her I've been there. Tell her nobody's done. Everyone's going somewhere else. Next time. Next time."

I got him off the phone at last. "A doctor, Jonah. Your ear." I tried to sleep but couldn't. In my waking dreams, the shells that held us encased cracked open like chrysalises, and the fluid that was us flowed out, like reverse rain, back up into the air.

Hans Lauscher found him the next morning, a little after ten o'clock, when Jonah failed to show up for breakfast. He was stretched along the bed, still dressed, on top of the bedspread. The stream of dried blood down one side of his pillow made Hans think he'd hemorrhaged. But my brother had simply stopped breathing. The television in his hotel room was on, tuned to the local news.

REQUIEM

We buried Jonah in Philadelphia, in the family cemetery. A month later, Ruth and I flew out to perform at his European memorial. The service was held in Brussels, in half a dozen languages, all of them sung. There was no eulogy, no remembrance but music. Dozens of people sang, people Jonah had performed with throughout the last years of his life. Our piece was the most recent, and surely the rockiest. Ruth sang "Bist du bei mir," that little song of Bach's that Bach never wrote:

> If you are with me, I'll go gladly
> to my death and to my rest.

Ah, how pleasant would my end be,
with your dear hands pressing
shut my faithful eyes!

We sounded as if we hadn't made music since our mother's funeral.
Like we were music's shaky discoverers, the first to have stumbled across
the form. Like we might never make it back to tonic. Like tonic was going someplace else, always a moving *do*. Like everyone would have to own
every song, before the end. Ruth sang as she remembered him, no part of
us barred. And he was in her voice.

It was the first time my sister had ever been abroad. She stood at the
top of the Kunstberg, the Mont des Arts, crying over how every curbside
banality struck her with wonder. For a long time, she couldn't place the
feeling that gripped her. Then, in the middle of the Grande Place, we
overheard a light-skinned, angular-featured black couple marveling over
the guildhalls in Portuguese.

"Nobody here has the slightest idea where I come from. Nobody cares
how I got here. They're not even trying to guess. I could be anyone." The
utter freedom terrified her. "We have to get back to America, Joey." Our
hellish utopia, that dream of time. The thing the future was invented for,
to break and remake.

"How far is Germany?" I told her, and she shook her head, unsteady.
"Next time."

Little Robert identified himself to every stranger by his African name.
It thrilled him to be asked if he came from the Congo. By the time we
flew back to the Bay, he was chattering at the flight attendants in both
French and Flemish.

If our father was right, time doesn't flow, but is. In such a world, all the
things that we ever will be or were, we are. But then, in such a world,
who we are must be all things.

So I stand on the edge of the reflecting pool with my two nephews.
We've left their mother, over her vocal objections, back at the Smithso-
nian. "I don't see why I can't just hang out there in the crowd, next to
you. I won't say a word."

"We been over this a million times," her eldest says again. "You promised me, before we started."

"How much unity can this thing proclaim if the women have to stay
home?"

"The women don't have to stay home. The women get to go anyplace in our nation's capital they want. Why don't you go visit Howard? Didn't your Papap . . ."

"Maya Angelou's going to be there. She's a woman. She's going to give a speech."

"Mama. You promised. Just . . . give us this?"

So it's just we three men, there on the Mall. I'm going to be discovered and sent home. At any moment, my nephews will make me go wait for them, back in the hotel room.

Kwame stands in this runaway crowd, scared by its magnificence. A mild October, but he's shaking. He's wobbly on his pins, like a bamboo beach house in a heavy tide. This is his doing, his atonement, his escape plan, and he stakes himself on it working. Still, he's staggered by how many other stakeholders have turned out for the day.

He has managed to stay in the free world for a full two years. One speeding ticket, one apartment eviction, but no more slavery. "It's over," he tells me. "That me is dead." He's been out for two years, and in that time he has worked four jobs and played with three different new bands. The jobs have gotten harder and the music a shade more melodic. Two months ago, he became a welder. When he landed it, he told me, "I'm staying with this one for a while, Uncle JoJo." I told him I was sure he would.

He stands in the milling crowd, talking to a perfect stranger, a bronze man almost my age in a University of Arizona sweatshirt, with a son years younger than Robert. "Not sure I'm crazy about the man," the stranger says, apologetic.

"Nobody's crazy about the man," Kwame reassures him. "The man's a hatemonger. But this whole thing's bigger than the man."

"Did you know Farrakhan is a trained concert violinist?" I contribute this, even at the risk of irritating Kwame. A put-down and tribute. Remembering all passing things.

"Get out of here. No shit?" Both men are amused—the crediting and discrediting.

"How do you play a violin through a bow tie that size?" It's the last thing our unknown friend says before the crowd swallows him.

Kwame watches the man disappear, holding his son's hand. Delinquent, remembering, my nephew calls out a panicked "Robert!"

"Ode," comes the angry voice from two yards behind him.

"Whatever, brother. You stay close, you hear me?"

"Hear you," the sullen eleven-year-old answers. But only because his brother rules.

Kwame is the boy's god, and the older boy can do nothing about it. When Kwame went to prison, little Robert was inventing complex number games, whole systems of calculation. When he returned, his little brother wanted nothing more than to follow him down to damnation. "School's for fools," the child told him. Resolute, proud, and as shrewd as the god he modeled on. "Fools and house niggers."

"Who told you that? You give this field nigger the man's address. I'm a have a little parlay with him."

But the boy read his brother's every word as an initiation rite, a test of his downness. "You playing me. You like school so much, how come you're not still in it?" *You like caveboys so much, how come you got a record?*

"Don't you close that book, bean boy. Stop being so cat. Your father. Your father studied math, Beanie. Don't you know that?" *And your grand-father. Where do you think you got it from?*

To this, his little brother only shrugged. The whole ascendant, world hip-hop culture exposed all the million futilities of such Tomming. That was then. This is now.

"Beanie. You're my ticket onward. Don't you think big no more?"

Ode only smiled, seeing through the psych-out. There was nothing bigger, in his eyes. Nothing bigger than his ex-con brother.

This is my oldest nephew's penance, the reason we're here. He wouldn't have made us fly out to Washington, wouldn't even have crossed the street for something so slight as self-affirmation, if not for his brother. Kwame knows what self is his. We're here only for Robert, who every two minutes threatens to disappear into the crowd in search of the real action.

I turn around and stare down the length of the reflecting pond to the steps of the memorial. The woman who sang on those steps because she could not sing inside has died, two years ago, in April, just as Kwame left prison. An alto singing scraps of Donizetti and Schubert changed my nephews' lives. No, that makes no sense. Her impromptu concert did not change them. It made them.

Kwame follows my glance back along the length of the Mall. But he can't see the ghost. The sight of the Lincoln Memorial twists my nephew's features. "Man's a bald-faced nigger-hater. Why we still worship him? Freed the slaves? Mother didn't free nothing."

"We'll see," I say. Kwame just stares at me, as if I've finally gone over. I shake his shoulder. "Caught between a racist cracker and an anti-Semite minister of God. Between a piece of marble and one very hard place. What's a brother to do?"

The brothers to our right throw us a look. Those in front of us turn around, smiling.

The podium comes to life and the signifying begins. At any moment, Kwame and Robert will ask to move up front, just a little, without me. Some tacit understanding: *Nothing personal, Uncle bro, but this whole healing thing isn't really about you.* But in this life, even as I stiffen for it, the request never comes.

The papers will count a grudging couple of hundred thousand. But this is a million if it's a man. Tens of millions; whole lifetimes of lives. I've never stood in a gathering so large. I expected claustrophobia, agoraphobia, the choke of old stage fright. I feel only an ocean of time. Things reaching themselves. The feeling grows, strange and magnificent and tainted as anything human, only many times bigger.

I can't say what my nephews see. Their faces show only thrill. A million is nothing to them. Nothing alongside the size of their transmitted world, the giant screens, the monster concerts in international surround sound, the global transports that their world daily broadcasts. But maybe they're right where I am, every bit as awed by this millionfold makeshift fix, this pressing to redeem. Maybe they feel it, too, how likeness has it all over difference, for sheer terror. If there's no mix, there's no move. This is what the million-man minister means, despite what he thinks he's saying. Who is enough, in being like himself? Until we come from everyplace we've been, we won't get everywhere we're going.

Kwame cranes to see the podium and make out the speakers. Robert—Ode—wasted by all the talk, finds a friend his age. They size each other up and move into the aisle to teach each other moves. The celebrities, songwriters, and poets take their turns, then give way to the minister. He plays the crowd. He brings out Moses, Jesus, Mohammed. He takes a shot at Lincoln, at the Founding Fathers, and Kwame has to cheer him. He says how all prophets are flawed. He says how we are more divided now than the last time we all stood here. He starts to ramble, to invoke weird numerologies. But all the numbers come down to two. A long division.

"So, we stand here today at this historic moment." The sound fans out, tiny and metallic, lost in the endless space it must fill. "We are standing in the place of those who couldn't make it here today. We are standing on the blood of our ancestors."

People on all sides of us call out names. Some massive church. My nephews know the drill anyway, by another path. "Robert Rider," Kwame calls. His voice breaks, not because he remembers, but because he can't. "Delia Daley," he adds. He might go further back.

"We are standing on the blood of those who died in the Middle Passage . . . in the fratricidal conflict . . ."

Those around us name their dead, and because he feels me standing there, my nephew adds, "Jonah Strom."

The notion's so crazy I have to laugh. Transformed by death: my brother's operatic debut at last. Then I hear little Robert bragging to his newfound friend, "My uncle died in the Los Angeles riot." And I suppose, in some world, he did. His last performance on that long, self-singing vita.

"Toward a more perfect union." The minister does not know whereof he speaks. Union will undo his every call to allegiance, if allegiance doesn't do us all in first. I'm standing in this million-man mass, a billion miles away, grinning like the idiot my brother knew I was. An old German Jew proved it to me, lifetimes ago: Mixing shows us which way time runs. I have seen the future, and it is mongrel.

Kwame chooses that moment to whisper to me. "The man's a chicken-head. Thing's fuckin' obvious to anyone who's clocking. Only one place we can go. Everybody's going to be a few drops everything. What the fuck? I say let's just go do it and get it done with."

I shake my head and ask him. "Where do you think you got that from?"

The minister is going for a record-breaker. But he has the crowd to help him. We wave our hands in the air. We give fistfuls of money. We embrace total strangers. We sing. Then the classically trained violinist tells us, "Go home. Go back home to work out this a-tone-ment . . . Go back home transformed." We end like every other thwarted, glorious transformation in the past, and all the pasts to come. Home: the one place we have to go back to, when there's no place left to go.

But our boy has other destinations, farther afield. The speeches break up and the crowd folds into itself, embracing. Kwame hugs me to him, an awkward promise. We part from the clinch embarrassed, and look around for Robert. But he's vanished. We see the friend he was hanging with, but the boy has no idea where Robert has gone. Kwame shakes him, almost yelling, and the frightened child starts to cry.

My nephew descends into his worst recurrent nightmare. And mine. This is his doing. He's brought his brother here, keeper-style, thinking to undo his own influence. He waved off all Ruth's warnings. He promised her a thousand times: "Nothing can go wrong." He's kept the boy on the shortest of leashes, all through this mammoth crowd. And now, in the first dropped glance, we've lost the child, as if he were just waiting for the chance to break free.

Kwame is frantic. He runs in all directions at once, toward any half-sized figure, shoving men aside to get past. I try at first to keep up with him. But then I stop short, a sense of peace coming over me, so great that I think it will be fatal. I know where Robert has gone. I could tell Kwame. I have the whole piece, the whole song cycle there, intact, in front of my sight-singing eyes. The piece I've been writing, the one that's been writing me since before my own beginning. The anthem for this country in me, fighting to be born.

I try to tell my nephew, but I can't. "Don't panic," I say. "Let's stay close by. He's around here somewhere." In fact, I know exactly how close the lost boy is. As close as a promise to a long-forgotten friend. As close as the trace of tune turning up in me at last, begging me to compose it.

"Shut the fuck up," Kwame shouts. "I got to think." My nephew can't even hear himself. He runs through all the options that cloud his desperate brain. He plays out every scenario, sure that only the worst can ever happen, finally, to the likes of us. He's lost his brother in a million dispersing men. This is his final punishment, for all he's done and left undone.

And then his brother emerges from the underworld, there in front of us. He's jogging toward us from up on the steps of the Lincoln Memorial. He waves smartly, as if he's only been away on a prearranged outing, no more than five minutes, max. In truth, it can't have been much longer. For Kwame, it's been another jail sentence. Life.

Relief spills over into rage. "Where the fuck have you been, Bean? What are you trying to do to me?" Strung out, fatherless. At the mercy of every past. He'd slap the boy if I weren't there.

The look of bewildered adventure falls from Robert's face. He stares out on the place he's come back to. He shrugs and folds up his arms like shields in front of his chest. "Nowhere. Just out talking. Meeting people."

The question that was bursting in him dies unasked. Kwame, too, his head sunk down, hears all the promises he has just made mocking him, as vain as any music.

"Well?" Ruth greets us, ready for all the stories. "How do you feel? Was it amazing?"

All three of us keep silent, each boy for his own reasons.

"Come on. Tell me. What did they say? Was it everything you . . . ?"

"Ruth," I warn.

Her eldest puts his chin on the crown of his mother's head and cries.

Not until that long flight back across the continent does Ode ask. And then, not us, but his mother. It's dusk when we get to the airport, and night for the length of the flight. We rise up over the layer of cloud, nothing above us but darkness. Kwame, across the aisle from me, is writing a song about the march. He needs to redeem it. The song is all in his head, committed to memory. He hands me the phones for his disc player. "Ay yo trip. New L.A. crew. Check out the bomb bass line."

I place it in two notes. "Gregorian cantus firmus." A Credo already a millennium old by the time Bach used it.

"No shit?" His eyes glint, fishing for me. "Motherfucker makes a def sample." He takes the phones back, slaps his thighs in a haunted, broken rhythm. The day's panic is already just a memory. All notes are changing again. "Me and my crew, we got to get jumpin'."

This, too, is forever true. "Mine, too," I tell him. My piece is inside me, ready for writing down—the same piece that has long ago written me. My crew is inside me, jumping at last. And the first jump they make will be, as ever, *back*.

Little Robert sits in the window seat, his mother next to him. He fidgets from Ohio to Iowa, craning to see something out of the square of window. But the pane refuses to reveal anything but an opaque black wall.

"What you looking at, honey?"

He stops, ashamed at being caught.

"What is it? You see something up there?"

"Mama, how high are we?"

She can't say.

"How far are we from Mars?"

She's never thought to wonder.

"How long would it take . . . ? Mama?"

More questions than he's asked her since he was seven. She sees his old sandbox love of math trying to reenter him. A signal, beckoning. She braces for the next question, praying for her sake that she won't miss them all.

"Mama, wavelength's like color, right?"

She's almost sure. She nods slowly, ready to improvise if need be.

"But pitch is wavelength, too?"

She nods more slowly now. But still yes.

"What wavelength do you think they are—on other planets?"

Her face contorts. The answer struggles up from where she's held it so long. Words pour into my sister, words I've forgotten years ago. Words waiting for the past to reach them. She jerks upright, as if she'll stop the plane, turn around, parachute out over the Mall. No time to lose. "Where on earth . . . ? Who did you hear that . . . ?"

She feels her son coil back into his armor, and she breaks. An injured laugh, an uncompleted tune. Someone walking toward her who she thought was buried. Of course. The message was for *him*, her child. Not beyond color; *into* it. Not or; *and*. And new ands all the time. Continuous new frequencies. Where else could such a boy live?

She bends over him and tries to say it. "More wavelengths than there are planets." Her voice is everywhere but on pitch. "A different one everywhere you point your telescope."

THEE

The boy is lost, cutting back and forth in the indifferent crowd, on the verge of howling. A colored boy, one of hers. He runs in one direction, stops, hopeless, then cuts back. The crowd is not hostile. Only elsewhere.

Her German man, this helpless foreigner she has just said good-bye to forever, calls out. "Something is wrong?" And the boy almost bolts from them, lost for good.

"That's all right, now." Something old in her speaks. "We ain't gonna hurt you."

And he comes to them. As if his mother never once warned him about the danger of strangers. He comes to them, struck by a thing so strange, he can't help himself. She can't imagine what puts such astonishment in his face. And then, of course, she can.

He asks where she comes from. "Not far," she tells him, knowing what he really wants to ask.

"My brother's lost."

"I know he is, honey. But we're gonna help you find him."

He tells her his name. One she has never heard of. She tries to get the child to show them where he lost his brother. But the long, receding lines of Washington, the drift of the dispersing crowd, and the boy's growing fear dislocate him. He drags them to a spot, refuses it, and drags them off again.

It saves her from her own displacement. She walks uncertainly, still under the spell of Miss Anderson's otherworldly power. The threads of that sound still coat her, like a cobweb she sweeps at but can't comb free. Something anxious between her and this man, some tie they shared a moment ago that she doesn't even want to think of straying near. No link but a common love of the repertoire. No force but the voice they've just lived through. But something more: the way he heard her singing along, aloud to herself, and felt it as a gift, a given. The shock of it, to be taken just this once, not as another species, nor as the identical same. To be heard simply as someone who knows and can hit the notes. Who has the right and the reason to produce them.

She's glad they have this boy. His closer crisis holds them together a little longer. They have already said good-bye. The continent of this German's ignorance, the sweet land of liberty that denies him the slightest toehold of comprehension, spreads out, uncrossable, in front of them. She can't be the one to explain it to him. To tell him what wars he has fled into, replacing the ones he just escaped. The list of what they can never know of each other is longer than infinite. Curiosity must die, as always, in the cradle. But for just these few moments, they share this lost boy.

The German fascinates this Ode. Something he can't make out, that stops all figuring. "Where *you* from?" he asks, and the man answers, deadpan, "New York."

"My mama's from New York. You know my mama?"

"I haven't been there very long."

The boy walks between them, a hand in each of theirs. Fear takes years off the child. Frightened, he seems no more than seven. He speaks with a mania that makes him impossible to understand.

"I would like very much to see you again," David Strom says over the boy's head.

What she has dreaded and known. Hoped against and held still for. "Forgive me," she says, unable to do the same. "It's impossible." She wants to say, *This is a law of matter, like the ones you study. Nothing to do with you or me. The physics of the world we belong to. The simplest is.*

But the physicist makes no response. He points to the Memorial, where Miss Anderson's words still ring. "That is where we need to go. Where we can see everyone, and they us. Underneath the statue of that man."

Ode is shocked he doesn't know Lincoln. Delia is shocked when the boy calls the Emancipator a racist. David Strom is too baffled to be shocked by anything.

They make camp on the steps. Her job is to scout for a frantic Negro searching for his lost kin. His job is to comfort the boy. This he does with an ease that stuns her. For the boy's entertainment is every bit the man's. Within a minute, they're talking about the stars and planets, frequencies and wavelengths, distances so great, no message can cross them and be read, matter so dense that space collapses into it, places where the rules of length and depth get bent double and flipped about in the Creator's trick mirror. She hears the man tell the boy, "Every moving thing has its own clock." Then she hears him go back on himself, say there is no time, that time is simply unchanging change, no less and no more.

This so hooks the boy that for a minute, he forgets he's lost. He fills with the million questions of boyhood—the rule-break of rocket ships, the speed of light, the curve of space, the unfolding flow, frozen messages skipping free. How? Where? Who? She watches the two of them hatch travels to any dimension. She flashes on her own prejudice: *What's a black boy want, wasting time with this?* But then: *Do whites own the heavens, too, like they own "O mio Fernando"?*

The boy grows wild with ideas. She hears the man answer, not with impossibles, but with the same suspended maybe with which he listened to the impossible contralto. The same way he listened to Delia herself: notes first, tune after. She frowns: *Of course there is no time. Of course there's nothing but standing change. Music knows that, every time out. Every time you lift your voice to sing.*

He sits on the steps in his rumpled suit, just talking to the boy. The simplest thing in the world. The most natural. And the boy lights up, leveling challenge after challenge in wondrous attack. She sees him like this for years to come, boys at a table, questions and answers. And then she sees him never. Her heart tightens round itself, closing up with a death so practical, she cannot counter it.

The boy jerks up from his pleasure, alarmed. "How come you two together? Don't you know about black and white?"

She knows. Over the Potomac, a few hundred yards from where they sit, love between a white man and black woman is a crime worse than theft, worse than assault, punishable as harshly as involuntary murder. David Strom glances at Delia for explanation, the official adult line. She has none.

The boy shakes his head at her. She should know. "The bird and the fish can fall in love. But where they gonna build their nest?"

Now the German jerks up, a shock beyond reflex. "Where have you heard this?" The boy cups his hands into his armpits, scared. "This is a Jewish saying. How have you learned this saying?"

The boy shrugs. "My mama sang it. My uncle."

"Are you Jewish?"

The laugh rips out of Delia, before horror can stop it. This man's eyes beg her for an explanation. She could end her own life now, easily.

The scientist can't fathom it. "This is a Jewish saying. My grandmother used to say this. My mother. They meant people must never . . . They thought that time . . ."

But she knows what they thought. She knows this man's people, without a word. All in his face: the end they have tried to stave off with this ban, and the ban that has come to end them anyway.

He's undone by wonder. "How can you know this, unless . . . This is remarkable. You have this, too?"

All in his face, and hers: that danger so great that it forces this ban. There is no threat greater than extinction in closeness. The threat that drove the voice of a century out of doors. The threat of all singing. We do not fear difference. We fear most being lost in likeness. The thing no race can abide.

She remembers everything, all that must come to them. The sound is everywhere in her. Now it's right in her range: *my country*, *thee*, *thee*. She knows this boy. He's fighting to bring himself into being, willing them the way on.

"The bird and the fish can make a bish. The fish and the bird can make a fird." He chants the words, raps them, a cantering, desperate rhythm. A continent rising. Syncopated pitches in time. All he wants is to go on playing. All available combinations. Go on singing himself into existence, starting up my piece, my song.

That fierce, haunted beat shakes the white man loose. He, too, places the boy. Who else? What else? The inevitable enters him with the full force of discovery. "The bird can make a nest on the water."

My mother looks out on the long space spreading in front of them. "The fish can fly." She drops her eyes and colors deeply.

"You are blushing," my father exclaims. Already learning.

"Yes." My mother nods. Agreeing, and worse. "Yes. We have this, too."